PRAISE FOR
HEATHER
GRAHAM

"Graham paints a vivid and detailed picture...
she is an incredible storyteller, a weaver of words."
—*Los Angeles Times*

"...knows what her readers want,
and delivers with panache!"
—*Publishers Weekly*

"A writer of incredible talent..."
—*Affaire de Coeur*

Heather Graham describes her life as "busy, wild and full of fun." A master storyteller with over ten million copies of her books in print around the world, Heather says her first career choice was not writing but acting on the Shakespearean stage. Happily for her fans, fate intervened, and now she is a *New York Times* bestselling author. Married to her high school sweetheart, this mother of five spends her days picking up the kids from school, attending Little League games and taking care of two cats. Although Heather and her family enjoy traveling, southern Florida—where she loves the sun and water—is home.

HEATHER GRAHAM

Summer fires

HARLEQUIN®

TORONTO • NEW YORK • LONDON
AMSTERDAM • PARIS • SYDNEY • HAMBURG
STOCKHOLM • ATHENS • TOKYO • MILAN • MADRID
PRAGUE • WARSAW • BUDAPEST • AUCKLAND

HARLEQUIN BOOKS
225 Duncan Mill Road, Don Mills,
Ontario, Canada M3B 3K9

ISBN 0-373-83478-0

SUMMER FIRES

Printed in U.S.A.

CONTENTS

DARK STRANGER

PART 1

The Stranger

Chapter One

Summer, 1862
The Kansas/Missouri border

The hoofbeats were the warning. The relentless, pounding hoofbeats. The sound of them sparked a sense of primal fear deep inside Kristin. Strangely, before she'd first felt the staccato rhythm through the ground, she hadn't contemplated such a danger. The day had been too ordinary, and perhaps she had been too naive. She had expected a storm, but not of the magnitude that was to come.

It began with the stillness in the air. As she came along the path through the orchards from the river, Kristin paused. The breeze had dropped. The day had gone dead still. The sudden calm gave her a strange feeling, and she searched the sky. Overhead, she saw blue, a beautiful blue. No clouds marred that endless blue.

It was the calm before the storm, she thought. Here, on the Missouri side of the Kansas-Missouri border, storms were frequent and vicious. Blue skies turned to smoke, and vicious twisters whirled out of nowhere.

Then she heard the hoofbeats.

She looked out across the plain that stretched away from the house. A tumbleweed caught by a sudden gust of wind blew across a patch of parched earth.

Bushwhackers.

The word came unbidden to her mind, and raw fear swept through her, fear and denial. Please, God, no...

Pa! Matthew, Shannon...

Kristin began to run. Her heart began to race, thundering along with the sound of the hoofbeats.

Pa was already dead, she reminded herself. They'd already come to kill him. They'd come, on a cloudless day, and they'd dragged him out in front of the house. He had drowned in a pool of his own blood while she had stood there screaming. There had been nothing, *nothing* she could do.

Matthew was safe. He'd gone off to join up with the Union Army near the Mississippi. He had said she would be safe. After all, they'd already killed Pa in his own front yard, killed him and left him bleeding.

Bleeding. They called it "bleeding Kansas," and though they were on the Missouri side of the border here, the blood ran thick and deep. The War Between the States had boiled down to a barbarian savagery here. Men did not just fall in battle here, they were cruelly, viciously executed—seized, judged and murdered. Kristin had few illusions; one side was almost as bad as the other. The dream of freedom, the dream of endless land and a life of dignity and bounty had drowned in rivers of blood. The dream was dead, and yet it seemed that was all she had left to fight for. Her father had died for it, and they thought she would flee, but she wouldn't. She couldn't. She had to fight. There was nothing else to do.

Shannon.

Cold dread caught in her throat. Shannon was up at the house. Young, frightened, vulnerable.

Her feet slapped against the dry earth as the hoofbeats came closer. How many of them were there? Maybe twenty, like the day they had come to kill Pa? Maybe not so many. Maybe they knew that Matthew had gone off to fight in the war and that no one remained behind but the girls, the foreman, a maid and a few young hands. She almost felt like laughing. They'd tried to take Samson and Delilah the last time they had come. They didn't understand that the two were free, able to make their decisions. Pa wasn't a fanatical abolitionist; he had just liked Samson, plain and simple, so he had freed them on the occasion of their marriage. Little Daniel had been born free, and they'd all come here together in search of the dream...

Kristin stumbled and fell, gasping for breath. The riders were just behind the trees to her left. She heard screams and shouts, and she knew they were slaughtering whatever cattle they could lay their hands on. This wasn't war.

This was carnage.

She staggered to her feet, smoothing back stray tendrils of hair still damp from her early-morning swim in the river.

They could hold the attackers off. She would be prepared this time. She wouldn't assume that some of these men would be old friends and acquaintances. She wouldn't assume that they were human, that they knew anything about morals or ethics or simple decency. She didn't think she would ever trust in such things again.

Suddenly, while Kristin was still several hundred yards from the house, the horsemen burst through the trees.

"Samson!" she screamed. "Samson! Get me Pa's six-shooter. Samson!"

Samson, a tall, dignified black man, burst through the front door. He glanced at Kristin, then at the horsemen racing through the corn, trampling the tender green stalks.

"Run, Miss Kristin, run!"

She could hardly breathe, could hardly speak. "Pa's Colt, get me the Colt! Tell Shannon to get to the cellar!"

"Samson, what is it?"

Samson turned to see Shannon standing behind him in the hallway.

"Bushwhackers," he said grimly. "Where's Delilah?"

"Out back, feeding the chickens."

She was in the barn. His wife was in the barn. God, he prayed silently, give her the good sense to stay there!

"Shannon," he told her, "you get yourself in the cellar."

She turned away, and Samson hurried back to the hallway, then paused. He thought he'd heard something around back. When the sound wasn't repeated, he looked out the front door again. He could see the riders, and he could see Kristin running.

There were about twenty men, Samson reckoned. Just an offshoot of a bigger raiding party, probably. Some of Quantrill's raiders.

Quantrill himself was a damned butcher. He sanctioned the horror, and the death. Once upon a time he'd been friends with Gabriel McCahy, Kristin and Shannon's father, but one of his henchmen, a man named Zeke Moreau, had wanted Kristin. She hadn't wanted anything to do with him though. She was in love with Adam Smith. But Adam was dead now, too. Dead like her pa, dead like hundreds of men.

Now Zeke Moreau was coming back. He was coming for Kristin. Samson was sure of it.

"Samson!"

Her eyes met his, desperate, pleading.

Those might be God-fearing gentlemen out there, but if they captured a black man after he had leveled a Colt at them, even in his own defense, they would skin him alive.

It didn't matter. Gabriel McCahy had been the most decent man Samson had ever met. He would lose his skin over old Gabe's daughter if he had to.

He swung around, ready to rush into the house and get the guns. Then he paused, his eyes going wide and his throat closing up, hot and dry.

Zeke Moreau was already in the house. He was standing in the hallway, on the polished oak floor, and he had a double-barrelled shotgun leveled right at Samson.

A slight sound caught Samson's attention. He turned swiftly to see that another man was holding Delilah, one arm around her waist, a hand tight against her mouth.

"Watch it, Samson," Zeke said. "Be quiet now, or I'll hang you, boy. Hang you 'til you're dead. Then I'll see that your woman and your kid wind up on the auction block down Savannah way."

Zeke Moreau smiled slowly. He was dark-haired, with a dark, curling moustache, and Samson thought he would look more at home on a riverboat with a deck of cards than he did now, standing there in chaps and a vest, holding a shotgun. He was a good-looking man, except for his eyes. Cold, pale eyes, just like Kristin had always said.

Samson smiled back. "You murdered Gabriel, didn't you?"

Zeke rested his shotgun against his thigh. Samson was a big man, a good six-foot-six, and he was all muscle. But Zeke knew Samson wasn't going to move. Not while Delilah was being held.

"Now, Zeke, Gabe was my friend. He had some bad acquaintances, and he shot off his mouth too much, but I was mighty sorry to hear what happened to him. And it hurt me, hurt me bad, to hear about young Matthew running off to join up with them Yanks.''

''Samson!''

He spun around at the sound of Kristin's voice. Just as she reached the steps, her voice rose in a sudden scream.

The horsemen had reached the steps, too and Kristin was trapped. She was choking in a cloud of dust as they circled her, chasing her back into the center of their trap every time she tried to elude them.

As Samson watched, she cried out and ran again. An Appaloosa ridden by a yellow-toothed scavenger in a railroad man's frock coat cut her off completely. She turned again, and the man rode closer, reaching down to sweep her up. She clawed at him, and Samson saw the blood run down the man's cheek. Kristin cursed and swore, fighting like a tigress. The Appaloosa reared and shrieked as its rider wrenched hard on the reins. The man struck out with a whip, and Kristin fell. As Samson watched, the Appaloosa reared again and again, its hooves just missing Kristin's face.

She didn't move, didn't flinch. She just stared up at the man, hatred in her eyes.

Samson charged toward the door, but Zeke stepped up behind him, slamming his head hard with the butt of his shotgun.

Kristin cried out as she saw him fall through the doorway, blood trickling down his forehead.

Then she saw Zeke. He stepped over Samson's body and onto the porch. A man came from behind, holding Delilah. She screamed, and the man laughed, then threw her down on top of Samson. Sobbing, she held her husband.

The horses around Kristin went still, and the men fell silent.

Kristin got to her feet and stared at the man. She even managed a semblance of a smile.

''Why, Mr. Moreau, what a pleasure.'' Her voice dripped with sarcasm.

Zeke Moreau let out a long sigh. ''Dear, dear Kristin. It just never seems to cross that little mind of yours that you're in deep trouble, girl.''

''Trouble, Zeke? I'm not in any trouble. Trouble is something that's hard to handle. You're just a fly to be swatted away, nothing more.''

"Look around, Kristin. You know, you've always been a real sassy piece of baggage. The boys and me, we think it's about time you paid for that. You *are* in trouble, honey. Deep trouble.'' He started walking toward her.

Kristin held her ground. She'd never known what it was like to hate before. Not the way she hated Zeke. Her hatred for him was fierce and intense and desperate. She stared at him and suddenly she knew why he had come, knew why he was moving slowly, why he was smiling. This was vengeance, and he meant to savor it.

She didn't give a damn. She wasn't even really frightened. She knew that she would scratch and claw and fight just as long as she was still breathing, as long as her heart was still beating. He couldn't understand that she had already won. She had won because she hated him so much that he *couldn't* really touch her.

Zeke kept walking toward her, his smile still in place. "Fight me, Kristin,'' he said softly. "I like it that way.''

"You disgust me,'' she hissed. She didn't tell him that he would pay, didn't threaten revenge. There was no law to make him pay, and whatever revenge she dealt out would have to be now.

"You know, once upon a time, I wanted to marry you. Yeah, I wanted to head out to the wild, wild west and make you my wife. I wanted to hit the gold fields out in California, and then I wanted to build you a fine house on a hill and make you into a real lady.''

"I am a real lady, Zeke. But you're just dirt—and no amount of gold could make you anything but.''

She raised her chin slightly. There was a hard core of fear inside her, she realized. This man didn't want her to die. He wanted her to pay. He wanted her to cry out in fear, wanted her to beg for mercy, and she was afraid that he could make her do it.

Zeke would never, never be prosecuted. No matter what he did to her.

He smiled and lunged toward her, and his men hooted and called from the backs of their mounts.

Kristin screamed. Then she grabbed a handful of the loose Missouri dirt, cast it into Zeke's eyes and turned to run.

The Appaloosa came at her again, with its dead-eyed rider. She tried to escape, but the animal reared, and she had to fall and roll to avoid its hoofs.

She heard Zeke swearing and turned to see that he was almost upon her again. The dirt clung to his face, clumps of it caught in his mustache.

She leaped up and spun toward him. The catcalls and whistles from the mounted men were growing louder and more raucous.

Escape was impossible. Zeke caught hold of her arms. She slammed her fists against his chest and managed to free herself. In a frenzy, she brought up her knee with a vengeance. Zeke let out a shrill cry of pain; his hold on her eased, and she broke free.

Someone laughed and before Kristin could gain her breath the back of Zeke's hand caught her. Her head swam, and she felt his hands on her again. Wildly, she scratched and kicked and screamed. Sounds rose all around her, laughter and catcalls and cheers. Her nails connected with flesh, and she clawed deeply. Zeke swore and slapped her again, so hard that she lost her balance and she fell.

He was quick. He straddled her while her head was still spinning. The hoots and encouraging cheers were growing louder and louder.

She gathered her strength and twisted and fought anew. Zeke used his weight against her while he tried to pin her wrists to the ground. Gasping for breath, she saw that while she might be losing, Zeke's handsome face was white, except for the scratches she had left on his cheek. He was in a cold, lethal rage, and he deliberately released his hold on her to slap her again with a strength that sent her mind reeling.

She couldn't respond at first. She was only dimly aware that he had begun to tear at her clothing, that her bodice was ripped and that he was shoving up her skirt. Her mind cleared, and she screamed, then began to fight again.

Zeke looked at her grimly. Then he smiled again. "Bitch," he told her softly. He leaned against her, trying to pin her mouth in a savage kiss while his hands roamed over her.

Kristin twisted her head, tears stinging her eyes. She could probably live through the rape. What she couldn't bear was the thought that he was trying to kiss her.

She managed to bite his lower lip.

He exploded into a sound of pure rage and jerked away, a thin line of blood trickling down his chin.

"You want it violent, honey?" he snarled. "That's the way you're going to get it then. Got that, Miss High-and-Mighty?"

He hitched up her skirt and touched her bare thigh, and she braced herself for the brutality of his attack, her eyes shut tight.

Just then the world seemed to explode. Dirt spewed all around her; she tasted it on her tongue.

Her eyes flew open, and she saw that though Zeke was still posed above her he seemed as disoriented as she was.

Even the men on horseback were silent.

A hundred yards away, stood a single horseman.

He wore a railroad man's frock coat, and his hat sat low over his forehead, a plumed feather extending from it.

He carried a pair of six-shooters, holding them with seeming nonchalance. Yet one had apparently just been fired. It had caused the noise that had sounded like an explosion in the earth. Along with the six-shooters, there was a rifle shoved into his saddle pack.

His horse, a huge sleek black animal, began to move closer in a smooth walk. Finally he paused, only a few feet away. Stunned, Kristin stared at him. Beneath the railroad coat he wore jeans and a cotton shirt and he had a scarf around his throat. He wasn't wearing the uniform of either army; he looked like a cattleman, a rancher, nothing more.

Or a gunfighter, Kristin thought, bewildered.

His face was chiseled, strong. His hair was dark, lightly dusted with gray. His mustache and beard were also silvered, and his eyes, beneath jet-black brows, were silver-gray, the color of steel.

"Get away from her, boy," the stranger commanded Zeke. His voice was deep, rich. He spoke softly, but the sound carried. It was the voice of a man accustomed to being obeyed.

"Who's gonna make me?" Zeke snarled.

It was a valid question. After all, he was surrounded by his men, and the stranger was alone.

The man tipped his hat back from his forehead. "I'm telling you one more time, boy. Get off the lady. She doesn't seem to want the attention.''

The sun slipped behind a cloud. The stranger suddenly seemed no more than a silhouette, an illusion of a man, atop a giant stallion.

Zeke made a sound like a growl, and Kristin realized that he was reaching for his Colt. She inhaled to scream.

She heard a sound of agony rend the air, but it wasn't hers. Blood suddenly streamed onto her chest. In amazement, she realized Zeke had cried out, and it was Zeke whose blood was dripping down on her. The stranger's bullet had struck him in the wrist.

''Fools!'' Zeke shouted to his men. ''Shoot the bastard.''

Kristin did scream then. Twenty men reached for their weapons, but not one of them got off a shot.

The stranger moved quickly. Like double flashes of lightning, his six-shooters spat fire, and men fell.

When the shooting stopped, the stranger dismounted. His guns were back in his gun belt, but he carried a revolver as he walked slowly toward her.

He tipped his hat to Zeke. ''I don't like killing, and I do my damnedest not to shoot a man in cold blood. Now, I'm telling you again. Get away from the lady. She doesn't want the attention.''

Zeke swore and got to his feet. The two men stared at one another.

''I know you from somewhere,'' Zeke said.

The stranger reached down and tossed Zeke his discarded Colt. ''Maybe you do.'' He paused for just a moment, arching one dark brow. ''I think you've outworn your welcome here, don't you agree?''

Zeke reached down for his hat and dusted it furiously against his thigh, staring at the stranger. ''You'll get yours, friend,'' he promised softly.

The stranger shrugged in silence, but his eyes were eloquent.

Zeke smiled cruelly at Kristin. ''You'll get yours, too, sweetheart.''

''If I were you,'' the stranger said softly, ''I'd ride out of here now, while I still could.''

Furiously, Zeke slammed his hat back on his head, then headed for one of the now riderless horses. He mounted the animal and started to turn away.

"Take your refuse with you." The stranger indicated the dead and wounded bodies on the ground.

Zeke nodded to his men. A number of them tossed the dead, wounded and dying onto the skittish horses.

"You'll pay," Zeke warned the stranger again. Then his mount leaped forward and he was gone. The stranger watched as the horses galloped away. Then he turned to Kristin and she felt color flood her face as she swallowed and clutched her torn clothing. She stumbled to her feet.

"Thank you," she said simply.

He smiled, and she found herself trembling. He didn't look away gallantly. He stared at her, not disguising his bold assessment.

She moistened her lips, willing her heart to cease its erratic beating. She tried to meet his eyes.

But she couldn't, and she flushed again.

The day was still again. The sun was bright, the sky blue.

Was this the calm before the storm?

Or had some strange new storm begun? Kristin could sense something in the air, an elusive crackling, as if lightning were sizzling between them. Something tense and potent, searing into her senses.

And then he touched her, slipping his knuckles beneath her chin.

"Think you might offer a drifter a meal, Miss—"

"McCahy. Kristin McCahy," she offered softly.

"Kristin," he murmured. Then he smiled again. "I could use something to eat."

"Of course."

She couldn't stop staring at him now, searching out his eyes. She hoped fervently that he couldn't feel the way she was trembling.

He smiled again and brushed her fingers with a kiss. Kristin flushed furiously, suddenly aware that her breast was almost bare beneath her torn chemise and gown. She swallowed fiercely and covered herself.

He lowered his eyes, hiding a crooked smile. Then he indicated Samson, who was just coming to in the doorway. "I think we should see to your friend first, Kristin," he said.

Delilah stood up, trying to help Samson. "You come in, mister," she said. "I'll make you the best meal this side of the Mississippi. Miss Kristin, you get in here quick now, too. We'll get you some hot water and wash off the filth of that man."

Kristin nodded, coloring again. "Shannon?" She whispered softly to Delilah.

"Your sister's in the cellar. Things seem to be all right. Oh, yes, bless the heavens, things seem to be all right."

The stranger started toward the steps, and Kristin followed, watching his broad shoulders. But then she paused and shivered suddenly.

He had come out of nowhere, out of the dirt and dust of the plain, and he had saved her from disaster and despair.

But Zeke Moreau had ridden away alive.

And Zeke Moreau would surely ride back, once the stranger had ridden on and she was alone again.

It wasn't over. Zeke had come for her once, and he would come again. He wasn't fighting for Missouri, for the South, for the code of chivalry. He was in this to loot, to murder, to rob—and to rape. He would come back for her. He sought out his enemies when they were weak, and he would know when she was weak again.

They would have to leave, she thought. This was her home, the only home she could remember. This land was a dream, a dream realized by a poor Irish immigrant.

But that immigrant lay dead. Gabriel McCahy lay with his Kathleen in the little cemetery out back. He lay there with young Joe Jenley, who had tried to defend him. The dream was as dead as Pa.

She couldn't just give it up. She had to fight the Zeke Moreaus of the world. She just couldn't let Pa's death be in vain.

But she had fought, and she had lost.

She hadn't lost, not this time. The stranger had come.

Kristin straightened, squared her shoulders and looked after the tall, dark man who was moving up her steps with grace and ease. The man with the set of six-shooters and the shotgun. The man who had aimed with startling, uncanny precision and speed.

Who was he?

And then she knew it didn't matter, she just didn't care. Her eyes narrowed pensively.

And she followed the curious dark stranger into her house.

Chapter Two

A fire burned warmly against the midmorning chill in the enormous kitchen. Even with her head back and her eyes closed, she could imagine everything Delilah was cooking from the aromas that surrounded her over the rose scent of her bath. Slab bacon sizzled in a frying pan along with hearty scrapple. There would be flapjacks, too, with melted butter and corn syrup. Delilah was also going to cook eggs in her special way, with chunks of ham and aged cheese. They were usually careful about food these days. If Quantrill's raiders didn't come looking to steal horses and cattle—or worse—the Union side would come around needing supplies. Kristin had long ago been stripped of all her illusions about the ethics of either side. There were men on both sides who claimed to be soldiers but were nothing but thieves and murderers. This wasn't a war; it was a melee, a bloody, desperate free-for-all.

It was amazing that the family still had enough to eat. There was the secret cellar, of course. That had saved them many a time. And today it didn't matter. Today, well, today they all deserved a feast.

The stranger deserved a feast.

The kitchen door was pushed open, and Kristin sank deeper into the bubbles that flourished in the elegant brass bathtub, an inheritance from Kristin's mother, who had dragged it all the way over from Bristol, in England.

She needn't have feared. It was only Delilah. "How you doin' there, child?" she demanded. She reached into the cabinet above the water pump and pulled out a bottle of Kristin's father's best Madeira. She set the bottle and a little tray of glasses on the counter and pulled the kettle off the kitchen fire to add more steaming water to Kristin's bath.

Kristin looked into Delilah's dark eyes. "I feel like I'm never going to get clean, Delilah. Never. Not if I wash from here to doomsday."

Delilah poured out the last of the water, warming Kristin's toes. Then she straightened and set the kettle down on the hearth. She walked over to the stove to check the bacon and the scrapple. "It could have been a lot worse," she said softly, staring out the window at the now deceptively peaceful day. "Thank the Lord for small miracles." She looked back at Kristin. "You hurry up there, huh, honey?"

Kristin nodded and even managed a small smile. "Do we have a name on him yet?"

The kitchen door burst open again. Kristin shrank back and Delilah swung around. It was Shannon, looking flushed, pretty and very excited.

"Kristin! You aren't out of there yet?"

Kristin looked at her sister, and she didn't know whether to be exasperated or relieved. She was still shaken by the events of the morning, but Shannon had put them all behind her. Of course, Shannon had been down in the cellar. And that was what Kristin had wanted. It seemed that everyone here had lost their innocence. The war didn't let you just stay neutral. Man or woman, a body had to choose a side, and you survived by becoming jaded and hardened. She didn't want that for Shannon. She wanted her sister to retain a certain belief in magic, in fantasy. Shannon had turned seventeen not long ago, and she deserved to be able to believe in innocence. She was so young, so soft, so pretty. Blue-eyed and golden blond, a vision of beauty and purity. Kristin didn't think she'd ever looked like that. When she looked at herself in the mirror she knew that the lines and planes and angles of her face were hard, and that her eyes had taken on an icy edge. She knew she looked much older than eighteen.

She had aged ten years in the last two. Desperation had taught her many lessons, and she knew they showed in her face.

"I'm coming out in just a minute, Shannon," Kristin assured her sister.

"Slater," Delilah said.

"Pardon?" Kristin asked her.

"Slater." Shannon came over to the bathtub, kneeling beside it and resting her elbows on the edge. "His name is Cole Slater."

"Oh," Kristin murmured. Cole Slater. She rolled the name around in her mind. Well, that had been easy enough. Why had she thought it would be so difficult to drag the man's name out of him?

Shannon jumped to her feet. "Kristin's never coming out of this old tub. Shall I get the Madeira, Delilah?"

"Sounds like someone's got an admirer," Kristin murmured.

"I'm trying to be polite," Shannon said indignantly. She arranged the little glasses on a silver serving tray. "Honest, Kristin, he's a right courteous fellow, and he told me I shouldn't rush you, says he understands you might feel you need a long, long wash. But I think you're just plain old rude and mean. And you know what else I think? I think you're afraid of him."

Kristin narrowed her eyes at her sister, tempted to jump from the tub and throttle her. But it was far more serious than that. "I'm not afraid of Zeke Moreau, or even Bill Quantrill and all his raiders, Shannon. I just have a healthy respect for their total lack of justice and morality. I'm not afraid of this drifter, either."

"But you *are* beholden to him," Delilah reminded her softly.

"I'm sorry," Shannon murmured.

When Kristin looked at her sister, she saw the pain that welled up in her eyes, and she was sorry herself. Shannon had lived through the same horrors she had. She just wasn't the eldest. She wasn't the one with the responsibility.

She smiled at Shannon. "Bring the Madeira on in, will you please? I'll be right out."

Shannon smiled, picked up the tray and went out of the kitchen. Kristin grinned at Delilah. "Pa's Madeira, huh? You must think highly of this drifter."

Delilah sniffed as she fluffed out the clean petticoat she'd brought down from Kristin's room. She sent Kristin a quick glare. "He ain't no ordinary drifter. We both know that. And you bet I think highly of him. Moreau might—just might—have left you alive, but he'd have hanged Samson. Slater kept my husband alive and he kept me from the block at the slave market. You bet I think highly of him.''

Kristin grinned. From what she remembered of her lovely and aristocratic mother, she knew Kathleen McCahy would have been shocked by such blunt language. Not Pa, though. Pa had made himself a rancher and a farmer; he'd learned all the rough edges of the frontier. He'd have laughed at the plain truth of her statement. Then he'd have been grateful to have Delilah safe and sound, because she and Samson were part of the family, too.

''Want to hand me a towel, Delilah?'' Kristin said, thinking again about the stranger who had arrived among them just in the nick of time. No, he wasn't any ordinary drifter, not judging by the way he handled a weapon. What was he, then? A gunslinger from down Texas way, maybe? Perhaps he'd come from farther west—from California, maybe. Somewhere he'd learned to make an art of the use of his Colts.

He made an art of the simple act of walking, too, she thought. She shivered suddenly, remembering the silence that had followed the sudden burst of gunfire. She remembered the way his eyes had looked as he'd ordered Zeke away from her. Slate-gray eyes, steel eyes, hard and merciless. She remembered the way his frock coat had fallen along the length of his tall body, remembered his broad shoulders, remembered the way he'd looked at her. A heat that didn't come from the water seemed to flutter to life deep inside her.

It hadn't been a romantic look, she reminded herself. She knew about romantic looks. She knew about falling in love. It was easy and gentle. It was slow and beautiful. It was the way she had felt about Adam, and it was the way he had felt about her. When he had looked at her, he had looked into her eyes. He had held her hand, awkwardly at first. He had stuttered sometimes when he had spoken to her, and he had whispered tenderly to her. That was romance. That was love. She had never felt this shameful burning inside when she had been with Adam. She had been content to hold his hand. They had been content to sit and dream. She had never once imagined him…naked.

Appalled by her thoughts, she swallowed hard. She hadn't imagined any man naked, and certainly not this stranger. No, he had not given her any romantic looks. What he had given her was an assessment. It had been just as if he were studying a horse and liked what he saw, good bones and decent teeth. And then he had smiled, if not tenderly, at least with a certain gentility.

Still, the way he had looked at her…

And he had seen her nearly naked.

Color seemed to wash over her body. She rose to reach for her towel, then fell back into the water again, shamed by the way her breasts swelled and her nipples hardened. She prayed that Delilah hadn't noticed.

"You cold?" Delilah asked her.

Delilah had noticed.

Kristin quickly wrapped the big towel around herself. "A little," she lied.

"Get over by the fire. Dry off good and I'll help you get your clothes on."

Kristin nodded, rubbing her pink flesh dry. The fire warmed her, the flames nearly touching her. At least she would have an excuse for being red.

When she was finished she sank into the old rocker by the fire and Delilah brought over her corset, pantalets and stockings. Kristin quickly slid into the knit stockings and pantalets, and Delilah ordered her to hold her breath while she tied up the corset.

Kristin arched a tawny brow when she saw the dress Delilah had brought down for her. It wasn't one of her usual cotton day dresses. It was muslin, with soft blue flowers and double rows of black-and-white lace edging along the puff sleeves, the bodice and the hem. It was one of her best dresses.

"Delilah—"

"Put it on, child, put it on. We are celebrating here, remember?"

"Oh, yes." Kristin grinned, but then she started to shiver again. She was afraid she was going to burst into tears. They were never going to be done with it. They couldn't ignore it, and they couldn't accept it. Pa had been murdered, and the same—or worse—could have happened today. Today could have been the end of everything.

They had been saved today, but it was only temporary. Zeke would be back.

"Lordy, Lordy," Delilah said. She and Kristin hugged one another, holding tight.

"What are we going to do?" Delilah said.

"We—we have to convince him to stay around a while," Kristin said softly.

"Think he needs a job, maybe?" Delilah said hopefully.

"Does he look like he needs a job?" Kristin said, smiling shakily as she pulled away. She turned her back to Delilah. "Hook me up, please."

Delilah started with the hooks, sweeping Kristin's bountiful hair out of the way. When she was done she stepped back, swirling Kristin around. She surveyed her broadly, then gave her a big smile. "Miss Kristin, you're the prettiest little thing I ever did see!"

Kristin flushed. She didn't feel pretty these days. She felt tired and old and worn most of the time.

"Brush your hair now. Your little Chinese slippers are by the door. Slip them on. And go out there and see what else you can find out about that man beyond his name."

"Yes, yes," Kristin murmured. Delilah searched her pockets for a brush. Kristin stood on tiptoes to stare into the small mirror on the kitchen door. She combed out her hair, leaving it thick and free and a little wild. She looked too pale, she thought. She pinched her cheeks and bit her lip. Then she thought about the man beyond the door again and all the color she could have wanted flooded into her face.

"Thanks," she said, handing the brush back to Delilah. Then she pushed the door open and hurried out.

She went through the family dining room first. Ma had always wanted a dining room, not just a table in the middle of everything else, as in so many ranch homes. Dining rooms were very proper, Ma had thought. And it was nice, Kristin decided now. The Chippendale table was covered with a lace cloth and with Ma's best silver, crystal and Royal Doulton plates. The table was set for three. The four young ranch hands they had remaining ate in the bunkhouse and she couldn't let a stranger know that she and Shannon usually just sat down with Samson and Delilah. Of course, they didn't use the silver or the crystal or the Royal Doulton every day, either.

After the dining room she came to the parlor. There was another big fireplace here, and a braided rug before it, over the hardwood floor. Large windows looked out on the sunshine. Ma had liked things bright, even though there were heavy velvet-and-lace curtains in crimson softened by white that could be closed at sunset to hold in the warmth. The furniture here was elegant, a small settee, a day-bed and fine wood chairs, and a spinet that both girls had learned to play. It was a beautiful room, meant more for a lady than for a man. Kristin knew she would find the stranger and her sister in the next room, Pa's office and library. That was a far more comfortable room, with rows of books, a huge oak desk and a pair of deacon's benches that drew up to the double-sided fireplace.

Kristin was right. When she came through the parlor doorway, she saw that the stranger—no, Cole, his name was Cole Slater, and she had to stop thinking of him as the stranger—was indeed in this room. It was a great room. It smelled of pipe tobacco and fine leather, and it would always remind her of her father.

Cole Slater looked good here, as if he fit the place. He'd removed his plumed hat, his spurs and his railroad coat. Kristin paused, annoyed that she was trembling again just at the sight of him. He was a handsome man, she thought, though not in any usual way. He was far from pretty, but his steel-gray eyes were arresting, and what his face lacked in actual beauty it made up in strength. It was fine-boned yet powerful, sensual yet hard. And Kristin thought that she saw still more in his face. Cole Slater was another one who had lost all his illusions. She saw it when their eyes met. She studied him, and it was several long moments before she realized that he was studying her, too.

His knee was up, and his booted foot was resting against one of the footstools that seemed to have been cast haphazardly alongside the rows of books in the study. His boots were high, like cavalry-issue boots. His trousers hugged his long legs, betraying the lean muscles there, the trim line of his hips and the contours of his strong thighs and buttocks. His shoulders were broad, and he was tightly sinewed, and yet, he gave the appearance of being lean. A tuft of dark hair showed where his shirt lay open below his throat, and Kristin thought that his chest must be heavily matted with it.

Then she saw that his gaze was resting on her chest, too, and that just the hint of a smile was playing at the corners of his mouth. She almost lowered her lashes. Almost. She kept her eyes level with his and raised her chin a fraction. Then she inclined her head toward the glass of Pa's that he held—the little pony glass seemed ridiculously small contrasted with the size of his bronzed hand and the length of his fingers—and smiled graciously. "I see that Shannon has been taking good care of you."

He grinned at Shannon, who sat on one of the deacon's benches with a happy smile glued to her features. "Your sister is a most courteous and charming hostess."

Shannon colored with pleasure at the compliment. Then she laughed and jumped to her feet with the curious combination of grace and clumsiness that always reminded Kristin of a young colt. "I'm trying, anyway," she said. "And you two haven't been properly introduced. Miss Kristin McCahy, I give you Mr. Cole Slater. Mr. Slater, my sister, Miss Kristin McCahy."

Cole Slater stepped forward. He took Kristin's hand, and his eyes met hers just before his head lowered and his lips touched her hand. "I'm charmed, Miss McCahy. Quite charmed."

"Mr. Slater," she returned. She tried to place his accent, but she couldn't. He didn't sound as if he came from the deep South, and he didn't sound as if he came from any of the New England states. He wasn't a foreigner, but he didn't speak with the twang of the midwesterner, either.

He was still holding her hand. There was a feeling of warmth where his lips had touched her flesh, and the sensation seemed to seep into her, to enter into her bloodstream and head straight for the coil of liquid heat that churned indecently near the very apex of her thighs.

She pulled her hand away.

"We really don't know how to thank you, you know," she said, remaining still and seeking out his eyes again.

"I don't want to be thanked. I stumbled along at the right moment, that's all. And I'm damned hungry, and everything cooking smells damned good. A meal will make us even.''

Kristin raised a brow. ''You'll forgive me if I find my life, my friends, my sister, my sanity, my—''

''Chastity?'' he offered bluntly.

''My person,'' she returned quietly, ''are worth far more than a meal.''

''Well, now...'' He set his empty glass down, watching her thoughtfully. ''I reckon that you are worth much, much more, Miss McCahy. Still, life isn't like a trip to the dry-goods store. I don't sell my services for any price. I was glad to be here when I was needed. If I helped you—''

''You know that you helped me. You saved all of us.''

''All right. I helped you. It was my pleasure.''

His voice matched his eyes. It wasn't quite a baritone, but it was still deep and full of the same hard, steely confidence. A drifter, a man who knew his guns. He had faced death out there today almost callously. Where did such a man come from?

Kristin stepped back. He was a tall man, more than six feet, and she was no more than five foot two. She felt more comfortable when there was a little distance between them.

And distance helped keep her heart from pounding, helped keep her blood from racing. Dismayed, she wondered what it was about him that made her feel this way. She never had before, not even with Adam.

Of course, not even Shannon could be completely innocent here. This was a working ranch, after all. Her father's prize bulls were the most valuable possessions he had left behind, and no matter how many of their cattle were stolen, Kristin knew they could start over with the bulls. But because of them and the other animals on the ranch, none of them could escape the details of the act of procreation.

Of course, watching the bulls made it all seem horribly crude. And nearly falling prey to the likes of Zeke Moreau made the bulls look like gentlemen of quality. She had never—never—imagined that a woman could actually wonder about what it would be like with a man, think about his hands touching her, think of his lips touching places other than her mouth.

She wanted to scream. She wondered suddenly if Cole could read her mind, for he was smiling again, and his smile seemed to reach into the heart and soul and heat of her. He knew.

She scowled and spun around, forgetting that he had saved her from a fate worse than death.

"I believe the meal that is worth so much to you is just about on the table, Mr. Slater. Shannon...let's all come along, shall we?"

Cole Slater followed his hostess through the parlor and into the formal dining room, suddenly and keenly aware of the soft scent of roses wafting from her flesh.

Then he noted that the fragrant flesh was as soft and smooth and tempting as cream silk. Her hair, loose around her shoulders, was like spun gold. And her eyes were level and filled with a surprising wisdom.

She was a very beautiful woman.

Outside, not so long ago, he had seen her differently. He had seen the Missouri dirt that had clung to her, and he had seen her spirit, but he had seen someone very young then. A girl, over-powered but fighting madly. Memory had clouded his vision, and he had seen the world through a brilliant red explosion.

He should have killed the bastard. No matter what his own past, no matter his codes when it came to dealing out death, that was one bastard he should have killed. Zeke Moreau. He had recognized Cole. Well, Cole had recognized Zeke, too. Zeke was one of the creatures that had been bred here in this den of blood, creatures that could shoot an unarmed man right between the eyes without blinking.

Zeke wanted this girl bad. No, this woman, he thought, correcting himself. She really wasn't a child. What was she? Twenty, perhaps? Older? Her eyes spoke of age, and so did the grace of her movements, and the confidence with which she spoke.

She was built like a woman.

Longing, hard and desperate, like a lightning bolt out of a clear blue sky, suddenly twisted and seared into him, straight into his groin, with a red-hot heat that was even painful.

He was glad he was walking behind her and Shannon. And he was glad his button-fly trousers were tight.

He clenched his teeth as another pain sizzled and burned in the area around his heart. This was a decent woman, this girl who had fought a strong man so desperately. Decent and still innocent, he imagined—thanks to his timely arrival.

This was the kind of girl men married.

Exhaling through clenched teeth, Cole wondered if there was a bordello anywhere nearby. He doubted it. There was probably a cold river somewhere, though. He would eat and then head out and hit that river.

Damn her, he thought suddenly, savagely. So she was innocent—maybe. The way she had looked at him had been too naked. He had seen too many things in her eyes. Too much that was sensual and tempting. He could have sworn she had been wondering about things that she shouldn't have been wondering about.

He would eat and then get out. And he would bear in mind that his range of experience far surpassed hers. Did she think she could play cat and mouse with him? She might not know it, but she was the mouse.

Still, when she seated herself at the head of the table, he felt the lightning again. It filled the air when she spoke. It raced through him when she lightly brushed her fingers over his hand as she reached for the butter. It filled him when their knees brushed beneath the table.

"So..." She handed him a plate of flapjacks. "Where do you hail from, Mr. Slater?"

Kristin watched as the stranger helped himself to the flapjacks. He buttered them lavishly, then poured what seemed like a gallon of syrup over them. He shoveled a forkful into his mouth, chewed and swallowed, then answered her.

"Oh, here and there."

Here and there. Kristin sat back, dissatisfied.

Delilah came into the room, bringing more coffee. "Mr. Slater," she said, filling his cup again, "can I get you anything else?"

"Thank you, Delilah, no. This is one of the finest meals I've ever had."

Delilah smiled as if someone had just given her the crown jewels.

Kristin sent her a glare over Cole's bowed head as he sipped his coffee.

Delilah nudged her firmly. Kristin sighed inwardly, and her eyes answered Delilah's unspoken question. She knew as well as Delilah that they needed Cole Slater.

"Where are you heading, Mr. Slater?" she asked.

He shrugged. "Just drifting at the moment, Miss McCahy."

"Well," Kristin toyed idly with her fork. "You certainly did drift into the right place for us this morning, sir."

He sat back, studying her in a leisurely fashion. "Well, ma'am, like I said, I'm right glad to be of service." She thought that was all he was going to say, but then he leaned forward, his elbows on the table, his steel-gray eyes on hers.

"How did you get on the wrong side of this Moreau man?" He paused again, just for a split second. "Isn't he one of Quantrill's boys?"

Kristin nodded.

Shannon explained, "She turned him down, that's what happened. Pa used to know Quantrill. The bastard—"

"Shannon!" Kristin protested.

Shannon ignored her. "They act like he's Jesus Christ come back to life, some places in the South—"

"Shannon! What would Pa say! You're supposed to be a lady!"

Shannon grimaced in exasperation and submitted reluctantly to Kristin's chastisement. "Oh, all right! But Mr. Slater, Quantrill is a bloody traitor, that's all!" She insisted. "He used to be a jayhawker out of Kansas, preying on the Southerners! Then he led a band of abolitionists down here, pretended he was spying out the terrain and turned on his own people! He got out of it by passing out a lie about his older brother being killed by jayhawkers. He didn't have an older brother, but those stupid fools fell for it!"

Kristin looked at her plate. "Quantrill is a murderer," she said softly. "But he usually leaves women alone. He won't let them be murdered."

"But Zeke would," Shannon said. "Zeke would kill anybody. He wants to kill Kristin now, just because she turned him down. She was in love with Adam, you see."

"Adam?"

"Shannon!"

"Adam, Adam Smith. Adam was like Pa. He had no stake in this war. He just wanted to be a rancher. But when the bushwhackers came and killed Pa, Adam went out with a group of jayhawkers to find Zeke's boys. Kristin didn't know about it, not until they sent her back his horse. They killed him down southwest somewhere, and we don't even know where they left his bones. At least Pa is buried out back."

Kristin felt his eyes on her again. She looked up, but that steel-hard gaze was unreadable.

"So this was no random raid here today," he said. It was a statement, not a question.

"No," Kristin admitted. She felt as if she were holding her breath. He must realize that once he left they were all at the mercy of Zeke's bushwhackers again.

"You should get out," he told her.

"What?"

"You should get out. Pack your bags, get some kind of an escort and get the hell out."

It was a cold, callous statement. But what could she say in reply? He had stumbled upon them and he had saved her, but it had happened almost by accident. He didn't owe her a thing. She already owed him.

"I can't get out. My father died for this land. I owe it to him to keep it for him."

"To keep it for what? Your father is dead, and if you stay you'll probably wind up that way, too."

"That's all you can say?"

"What do you want me to say? I can't change this war, and I can't change the truth. Trust me. I would if I could."

For the first time she heard the bitterness in his voice. She wondered briefly about his past, but then she saw that he was rising, and panic filled her. He couldn't be about to ride away.

She stood. "You're not leaving?"

He shook his head. "I saw a few cigars in your father's study. Mind if I take one out back?"

Kristin shook her head, speechless. He wasn't leaving. Not yet.

She heard his footsteps as he walked through the dining room, heard them soften as he walked over the braided rug by the stairs. A moment later she heard the back door open and close.

"Kristin, are you all right?"

Kristin saw that Shannon was watching her, grave concern in her eyes.

"You're all pale," she said.

Kristin smiled, biting her lower lip and shaking her head. She squeezed Shannon's hand. "Help Delilah with the chores, won't you?"

Shannon nodded. Kristin turned around and followed the path the stranger had taken out of the house.

He was out back, puffing on one of her father's fine Havana cigars, leaning against the corral and watching as a yearling raced along beside its mother.

He heard Kristin and turned his fathomless gray gaze on her as she approached. He waited, his eyes hooded and curious.

Kristin wasn't at all sure how to say what she had to say. She folded her hands behind her back and walked over to him with what she hoped was an easy smile. Once she had thought she had the power to charm the male of the species. Once. She had been able to laugh and tease and flirt, and at any dance she had been breathless and busy, in unending demand.

Those days seemed so long ago now. Now she felt very young, and totally unsure of herself.

She had charmed boys, she realized. This was a man.

Still, she came over to him, leaning against the wooden gate of the corral.

"It's a good ranch," she told him.

He stared at her relentlessly, she thought. He didn't let a woman use her wiles. He didn't let her smile or flirt or tease.

"It's a good ranch," he agreed.

"Did I tell you just how much we appreciate your timely arrival here?"

"Yes, you did." He hiked himself up suddenly and sat on the

gate, staring down at her. "Spit it out, Miss McCahy," he demanded, his eyes hard. "You've got something to say. Say it."

"My, my, you are a discerning man," she murmured.

"Cut the simpering belle act, Kristin. It isn't your style."

She flashed him an angry glance and started to turn away.

"Stop, turn around and tell me what you want!" he ordered her. He was a man accustomed to giving commands, she realized. And he was a man accustomed to his commands being obeyed.

Well, she wasn't going to obey him. She had paused, but she straightened her shoulders now and started to walk away.

She heard his boots strike the dirt softly, but she didn't realize he had pursued her until she felt his strong hands on her shoulders, whirling her around to face him. "What do you want, Miss Mc-Cahy?" he demanded.

She felt his hands, felt his presence. It was masculine and powerful. He smelled of leather and fine Madeira and her father's fine Havana cigar. He towered over her, and she wanted to turn away, and she wanted to touch the hard planes of his face and open his shirt and see the dark mat of hair that she knew must cover his chest.

"I want you to stay."

He stared at her, his eyes wary, guarded. "I'll stay until you can get some kind of an escort out of here."

"No." Her mouth had gone very dry. She couldn't speak. She wet her lips. She felt his eyes on her mouth. "I—I want you to stay on until—until I can do something about Zeke."

"Someone needs to kill Zeke."

"Exactly."

There was a long, long pause. He released her shoulders, looking her up and down. "I see," he said. "You want me to go after Zeke and kill him for you."

Kristin didn't say anything.

"I don't kill in cold blood," he told her.

She wanted to lower her eyes. She had to force herself to keep meeting his demanding gaze.

"I—I can't leave this ranch. I can give you a job—"

"I don't want a job."

"I—" She paused, then plunged on desperately. "I can make it worth your while."

He arched a brow. Something brought a smile to his lips, and suddenly his face was arrestingly handsome. He was younger than she had thought at first, too. But then he was talking again.

"You—you're going to make it worth my while."

She nodded, wishing she could hit him, wishing he would quit staring at her so, as if she were an unproved racehorse.

"Come here," he said.

"What?"

"Come here."

"I—I am here."

"Closer."

He touched her. His hands on her shoulders, he dragged her to him. She felt the steely hardness of his body, felt its heat and vibrancy. Through his pants and through all her clothing she felt the male part of him, vital and pulsing, against the juncture of her thighs. She still stared at him, wide-eyed, speechless, her breasts crushed hard against his chest as he held her.

He smiled crudely. Then his lips touched hers.

Curiously, the touch was very, very light. She thought she might pass out from the feel of it, so startling, so appealing. His lips were molded to hers....

Then hunger soared, and his tongue pressed between her teeth, delving deep, filling her mouth. She was engulfed as his mouth moved over hers, his lips taking hers, his tongue an instrument that explored her body boldly and intimately. Her breasts seemed to swell and she felt her nipples harden and peak almost painfully against his chest. He savaged her mouth, moving his tongue as indecently as he might have moved another part of his hard body...

Something inside her exploded deliciously. Heat coursed through her, filling her. She could not meet the power of his kiss, but she had no desire to fight it. It was shameful, maybe more shameful than what had happened to her this morning.

Because she wanted it.

She savored the stream of liquid sensations that thrilled throughout her body. Her knees shook, and the coil deep inside her abdomen that was so much a part of her womanhood seemed to spiral to a peak, higher and higher. She wanted to touch him. To bring her fingers against him, exploring. To touch him as his tongue so insinuatingly invaded all the wet crevices of her mouth...

Then he released her. He released her so suddenly that she nearly fell, and he had to hold her again to steady her.

He stared down at her. Her lips were wet and swollen, and her eyes were glazed. He was furiously angry with himself.

"Worthwhile?" he asked.

Kristin's mind was reeling. What did he mean?

"You don't even know how to kiss," he told her.

"What?" she whispered, too stunned to recognize the anger rising inside her.

"I'm sorry," he said. His voice was softer now.

"Damn you!" Kristin said. "I'll make a bargain with you! If you'll just stay—"

"Stop it!" he said harshly. "I'm sorry. I just don't have the time or the patience for a silly little virgin."

"What?" She stepped back, her hands on her hips, and stared at him. The insolence of him! She wanted to scream and she wanted to cry.

"I don't want a love affair, Miss McCahy. When I do want something, it's a woman, and it seldom matters who she is, just so long as she's experienced and good at what she does. Understand?"

"Oh yes, I understand. But I need help. I need you. Doesn't that mean anything?"

"I told you, I don't want a virgin—"

"Well then, excuse me for an hour, will you?" Kristin snapped, her eyes blazing. "I'll just run on out and screw the first cowhand—oh!"

She broke off in shock as he wrenched her hard against him. "Shut up! Where the hell did you come up with language like that?" he demanded heatedly.

"Let me go! It's none of your business! It's a rough world here, Slater!" she flailed desperately against him. He didn't feel her fists, and he didn't even realize that she was kicking him.

"Don't ever let me hear you say anything like that again!"

"Who do you think you are, my father?" Kristin demanded. She was very close to bursting into tears, and she was determined not to, not here, not now—not anywhere near this drifter. He had made her feel as young and naive and foolish and lost as Shannon. "Let me go!"

"No, I'm not your father. I'm a total stranger you're trying to drag into bed," he said.

"Forget it. Just release me and—"

"You just stop, Miss McCahy!" He gave her a firm, hard shake, then another. At last Kristin stopped fighting. Her head fell back, her hair trailing like soft gold over his fingers, her eyes twin pools of blue fire as she stared into the iron-gray hardness of his.

"Give me some time," he said to her very softly, in a tone that caused her to tremble all over again. "I'll think about your proposition."

"What?" she whispered warily.

He released her carefully. "I said, Miss McCahy, that I would think about your proposition. I'll stay tonight. I'll take my blanket out to the bunkhouse, and I'll give you an answer in the morning." He inclined his head toward her, turned on his heel and started off toward the house.

Chapter Three

When she walked back into the house, Kristin was in a cold fury. She didn't see Cole Slater anywhere, and for the moment she was heartily glad.

He had humiliated her, plain and simple. She'd been willing to sell honor, her pride, her dignity—and he hadn't even been interested in what she'd had to sell. She wished fervently that she wasn't so desperate. She'd have given her eyeteeth to tell the man that he was a filthy gunslinger, no better than all the others.

Yet even as she thought of what she'd like to be able to say to him, she realized it would be a lie. He'd saved her from Zeke, from the man who had murdered her father. She owed him.

And she'd paid, she thought drily. With humiliation.

Shannon wasn't around when Kristin reached the dining room. Delilah was there, though, humming a spiritual as she carefully picked up the fine crystal and china on the table. She glanced Kristin's way curiously and kept humming.

"Where's Shannon?" Kristin asked.

"Out feeding the chickens," Delilah said.

Kristin decided to help clear away the remains of the meal, but when her fingers clenched too tightly around a plate, Delilah rescued it from her grip. "Sorry," Kristin muttered.

"Kristin, for the sake of your mama's fine things, you go do something else here this morning, hm?"

Kristin stepped away from the table, folding her hands behind her back.

"You didn't ask where Mr. Slater had gotten himself off to," Delilah said.

"I don't care where Mr. Slater has gotten himself off to," Kristin replied sweetly.

Delilah shot her a quick glance. "The man saved our lives," she said sharply.

Kristin strode furiously across the room to look out the window. "He saved our lives...and he really doesn't give a damn."

"He's riding out?"

Kristin exhaled slowly. She could see Shannon by the barn, tossing feed to the chickens. If she had any sense she would leave. Shannon was precious to her, just as Delilah and Samson were. She should do whatever was necessary to protect them.

But the dream was precious, too. The dream and the land. And where would she go if she did leave? She could never embrace the Southern cause—she had been treated too cruelly by the bushwhackers here for that—nor could she turn against Missouri and move into Yankee territory. She wanted desperately to fight, but she was helpless.

It didn't matter where she went, Richmond, Virginia or Washington, D.C. Nowhere was life as cruel and violent as it was here on the border of "bleeding Kansas." Nowhere else did men murder each other so callously.

"Kristin?" Delilah said.

"Slater..." Kristin murmured. Her pride was wounded, she realized. She had offered up her finest prize—herself—and he had informed her crudely that he wasn't interested.

"Kristin, if you're mad at that man for something, you remember the rest of us here. You understand me, missy?" Delilah came toward her, waving a fork. Kristin tried not to smile, because Delilah was deadly serious. "Quantrill's men get ahold of us and they'll think nothing of a hanging. You saw what they did to your pa. I got a baby boy, Kristin, and—"

"Oh, Delilah, stop! I'm doing my best!" Kristin protested. She tried to smile encouragingly. She couldn't quite admit to Delilah yet that she had offered her all and that it hadn't been enough. She hadn't even tempted the man.

She clenched her teeth together. She'd like to see him desperate, his tongue hanging out. She'd like to see him pining for her and be in the position to put her nose in the air, cast him a disdainful glance and sweep right on by. Better yet, she'd like to laugh in his face. If it hadn't been for this war, she could have done just that. She could have had any rich young rancher in the territory. She could have had—

Adam. She could have had Adam. A numbing chill took hold of her. Adam had loved her so much, and so gently. Tall and blond and beautiful, with green eyes that had followed her everywhere, and an easy, tender smile.

Adam was dead. The war had come, and Adam was dead, and she had few choices. Yes, Slater had humiliated her. But part of it was the fire. Part of it was the feeling that he had embedded in her, the hot, shameful longing for something she didn't know and didn't understand. She had loved Adam, but she had never felt this way when she had been near him. Never. Cole Slater *did* frighten her. She didn't like the feelings he evoked in her. They shattered her belief in her own strength.

"Cole Slater is staying tonight," she told Delilah.

"Well, glory be!"

"No, no," Kristin said. "He's bunking with the hands for the night. He'll, uh, he'll probably be gone by morning."

"By morning?" Delilah repeated blankly. "Kristin, I don't want to suggest anything that ain't proper, but chil', I'm just sure that if you tried being friendly to the man..."

"Delilah," Kristin murmured, her sense of humor returning at last, "I'm sure I don't remember what proper is anymore. I tried. Honest to God, I tried." She shrugged. "I'm not going to do you any good around here. I'll see you in a bit, huh?"

She hurried toward the stairs, giving Delilah a quick kiss on the cheek as she passed. She felt the older woman's worried gaze follow her, but by the time she reached the landing, she had forgotten about her.

The house felt so empty now.

Delilah and Samson and their baby had the rooms on the third floor. Kristin's and Shannon's were here on the second floor. But

Matthew's room was empty now, as was the big master bedroom where her father and mothers had slept. The two guest rooms were empty, too. They hadn't entertained guests in a long, long time.

Kristin walked down the hallway, not toward her own room but toward the room that had been her parents'. She opened the door, stood there and smiled slowly. Her mother had been dead for years, but her father had been unable to part with the big Bavarian sleigh bed that his wife had so cherished. After her death he'd slept in it alone. And it was beautiful still. Delilah kept the mahogany polished and the bedding clean, as if she expected Pa to come back anytime.

Kristin walked into the room. There were giant armoires on either side of the window. One still held Pa's clothes, and the other still held her mother's.

We don't take to change easily here, Kristin thought. She smiled. It was the Irish blood, Pa had always told her. They were too sentimental. But that was good. It was good to hold on to the past. It helped keep the dream alive. Someday Pa's grandchildren would have this room. Matthew's children, probably.

If Matthew survived the war. It couldn't be easy for him, a Southern boy fighting in the Yankee army.

Kristin turned away. If Zeke Moreau had his way, none of them would survive the war. And when he was done torturing and killing, he would burn the house to the ground.

She started to close the door. Then she hesitated and turned back. She could suddenly see Cole Slater stretched out on that sleigh bed. It was a big bed, plenty big enough for his height and for the breadth of his shoulders. She could imagine him there, smiling lazily, negligently. Then suddenly, a whirlwind, a tempest of heat and fire…

She gritted her teeth, closed her eyes tightly and swore. She was sick of thinking about Cole Slater, and she was sick of remembering how grateful she had to be to a man who made her feel this way.

She slammed the door to her parents' room and hurried to her own. She threw her good dress on her bed and did likewise with her silk slippers and her corset. She slipped on a chemise, a cotton shirt, a pair of breeches and her high leather boots, and headed straight for the stables. She didn't bother with a saddle, but grabbed a bridle from a hook off the wall for Debutante and slipped into the stall to find her horse.

Debutante was an Arabian mare, a gift to Pa from one of the men he'd done business with in Chicago. She was a chestnut with white stockings, a deep dish in her nose and a tail that rode as high as the sun. Kristin loved her. She was amazed that the horse hadn't been stolen yet, but so far she had managed to have the horse out in the far pasture when the various raiding parties had swept through.

"Hello, you beautiful thing," Kristin whispered as she slipped the bit into the mare's mouth. Debutante nudged her. Kristin stroked the horse's velevety nose, then leaped on her back. Debutante nudged the stall door open, and Kristin gave her free rein as they left the stables behind.

It felt good to ride. It was good to feel the wind strike her cheeks, to feel the coolness of the air as it rushed by her. She was glad she had come bareback. She could feel the power of the animal beneath her, the rhythm of her smooth gallop, the great constriction and release of superbly toned muscle. Kristin leaned close to Debutante's neck. The horse's mane whipped back, stinging her cheeks, but she laughed with delight, glad simply to be alive.

Then Kristin realize she was being followed.

She wasn't sure how she knew she was being followed, except that there was an extra beat to the rhythm churning the earth, something that moved in discord.

She tried to look behind her. Her hair swept into her face, nearly blinding her.

There was a rider behind her. A lone figure, riding hard.

Panic seized her. She was already riding like the wind. How much harder could she drive the mare?

"Debutante! Please! We must become the wind!" She locked her knees more tightly against the animal's flanks. They were moving still faster now. The Arabian mare was swift and graceful, but the horse behind them seemed to be swifter. Either that, or Debutante's stamina was fading.

"Please!"

Kristin leaned closer to the mare's neck. She conjured up a mental image of the terrain. Adam had once owned this land. Ahead, just to the right, was a forest of tall oaks. She could elude her pursuer there.

The trees loomed before her. She raced the mare into the forest, then reined in when the trees became too dense for a gallop. She moved to the right and to the left, pushing deeper and deeper into the maze of foliage. Then she slid from the mare's back and led her onward.

Kristin's heart was pounding as she sought shelter.

If Zeke had come back, if he found her now...

She would pray for death.

But he was alone this time, she thought, praying for courage. She could fight him.

A twig snapped behind her. She spun around. She couldn't see anything, but she knew that her pursuer had dismounted, too, that he was still following her.

The branches closed above her like an arbor. The day was not bright and blue here, it was green and secretive, and the air was cold. She began to shiver.

She wasn't even armed, she realized ruefully. She was a fool. After all that had happened this morning she had ridden away from home without even a pocketknife with which to defend herself.

Kristin searched the ground and found a good solid branch.

Another twig snapped behind her. She dropped the mare's reins and crouched down against an oak. Someone was moving toward her.

Someone was behind her.

She spun around, the branch raised, determined to get in the first blow.

"Son of a bitch!" he swore.

She had gotten in the first blow—just barely. The man had raised his arm, and the branch struck it hard.

The impact sent her flying, her hair in her eyes. She landed in the dirt, and he was on top of her in an instant. She slammed her fist into his face, and heard a violent oath.

"Stop it! Kristin!"

He caught her wrists and straddled her.

She blinked and went still. It was Cole Slater.

"You!"

He rubbed his jaw. "You pack a hell of a punch."

"A hell of a punch?" she repeated. "You—you—" She was trembling with fear and with fury. She didn't mean to strike him again but she was nearly hysterical with relief, and she moved without thinking, slapping him across the face.

She knew instantly it was a mistake. His eyes narrowed, and everything about him hardened. Kristin gasped and looked around her for another weapon. Her fingers curled around a branch, and she raised it threateningly.

Cole wrenched the branch from her grasp and broke it over his knee, then pulled her roughly against his chest.

"What do you think you're doing?" he asked.

She had never seen him so furious, not even when he had gone up against Zeke and his gang of bushwhackers. Then he had seemed as cool as a spring stream. Now his eyes were the dark gray of a winter's sky, and his mouth was a white line of rage.

Kristin clenched her teeth hard, struggling to free herself from his grip. "What am I doing? You scared me to death."

He pulled her closer, and when he spoke again, his words were a mere whisper. "You're a fool, girl. After a morning like this you take off into the woods, without a word, without a care."

"I'm not a fool, and I'm not a girl, Mr. Slater, and I'd appreciate it, sir, if you would take your hands off of me."

"Oh, great. We have the grand Southern belle again."

Kristin gritted her teeth, wishing she could stem the rising tide of rage within her, rage and other emotions. He was too close. He was touching her, and she could feel the power of his anger, the strength of his body, and she was afraid of her own reactions.

"Let go of me. Just who the hell do you think you are?"

"The man who saved your life."

"I'm getting tired of eternal gratitude."

"Gratitude? A crack with a stick?"

"I didn't know it was you! Why didn't you say something? Why didn't you let me know—"

"You were running that mare a little fast for casual conversation."

"Why were you chasing me?"

"Because I was afraid you were going to get yourself in trouble."

"What were you afraid of? I thought you'd decided I wasn't worth the effort."

"I hadn't made any decisions yet. You are a girl, and you are a fool. You didn't give Moreau's men a chance to get far enough away. I didn't save you this morning for a gang rape this afternoon."

"Well, Mr. Slater, I wouldn't have been an annoying little virgin then, would I?"

Kristin was stunned when his palm connected with her cheek. Tears stung her eyes, though she wasn't really hurt. She hadn't expected his anger, and she hadn't imagined that she could humiliate herself this way again.

"Get off me!" she demanded.

"I don't want to hear it again, Kristin. Do you understand me?" He stood and reached down to help her up. She ignored his outstretched hand, determined to rise unaided, but he wouldn't even allow her to do that. He caught her arms and pulled her up. She hated him at that moment. She hated him because she needed him. And she hated him because this heat filled her at his touch, and this curious longing grew within her. She was fascinated by the scent of him, amazed by her desire to touch his face, to feel the softness of his beard....

To experience the sweeping wonder of his kiss once again.

She jerked free, and the leaves crackled under her feet as she whistled for Debutante. He followed behind her, dusting his hat off on the skirt of his coat.

"Kristin..."

She spun around. "You know, I've been wondering where you come from. You certainly aren't any Southern gentleman."

"No?" he queried. They stared at one another for a moment. Then his lips began to curl into a rueful smile. "I'm sincerely beginning to doubt that you're a Southern lady—or any kind of a lady, for that matter."

She smiled icily. She could manage it when he wasn't touching her. Then she turned away from him, squared her shoulders and walked toward her waiting mare.

"Sorry. I haven't had much time lately for the little niceties of life."

When she reached Debutante, he was there beside her. She didn't want his help, but he was determined to give it anyway. He lifted her onto the mare's back and grinned up at her.

"I may have to accept your generous offer."

"My generous offer?"

"Yes." His eyes suddenly seemed dazzling. Smoke and silver. His smile lent youth and humor to his features. He laughed. "I may have to bed you yet. To save you from yourself."

She wanted to say something. She wanted to say that her offer was no longer valid, that she would rather go to bed with Zeke and every single one of his raiders, than spend a single night with him, but the words wouldn't come. They weren't true. And it didn't matter, anyway, because he had already turned away. He picked up the reins of his big black horse and leaped upon the animal's back with the agility of long practice.

Kristin started out of the forest, heading for the house. She didn't look back. She rode ahead all the way. He rode behind her, in silence.

By the time they reached the house she was trembling again. She didn't want to see him, she didn't want to talk to him. The whole thing had been a deadly mistake. He needed to get his night's sleep and head out in the morning.

She didn't even know who the man was! she reminded herself in dismay.

When they had dismounted she spoke at last, but without looking at him. "The hands eat out in the bunkhouse at about six. Sleep well, and again, thank you for rescuing us all. I really am eternally grateful."

"Kristin—"

She ignored him and walked Debutante toward the stables. Her heart began to pound, because she imagined that he would follow her. He did not.

She didn't rub Debutante down as she should have. She led the mare into the stall and removed her bit. In a worse turmoil than she had been in when she had left, she walked to the house.

Cole Slater was no longer in the yard. Kristin walked into the house. It was silent, and the drapes were drawn against the afternoon sun. Kristin bit her lip, wondering what to do. Depression suddenly weighed heavily upon her. It was all lost. She would have to leave, and she would have to be grateful that they were alive and accept the fact that nothing else of their life here could be salvaged.

She wasn't sure it mattered. They had already lost so much. Pa. Adam. Her world had been turned upside down. She would have done anything to save it. Anything. But anything just wouldn't be enough.

With a soft sigh, she started up the stairway. At the top of the stairs, she paused, her heart beating hard once again.

There was someone there, on the second floor with her.

There was someone in her parents' bedroom.

She tried to tell herself it was Delilah, or Shannon, but then she heard Delilah calling to Shannon below and heard Shannon's cheerful answer.

"Oh, God," she murmured, her hand traveling to her throat.

Something inside of her went a little berserk. She couldn't bear it if Zeke or one of his cronies had managed to enter that room. Her father's room, a place he had cherished, a place where all his dreams remained alive.

She ran toward the doorway. If Zeke had been in the room, she might have managed to kill him with her bare hands.

But it wasn't Zeke. It was Cole Slater. He had his blanket laid out on the comforter, and he was taking things from it. He looked up at her in surprise as she stared at him from the doorway. He frowned when he noticed the way her breasts heaved and noticed the pulse beating hard at the base of her throat. He strode to her quickly.

"Kristin, what happened?"

She shook her head, unable to speak at first.

"I—I didn't expect you. I mean, I didn't expect you to be here," she said.

He shrugged and walked back into the room, taking a shirt from the blanket and striding toward her father's armoire. "I didn't intend to be here. Delilah insisted there was plenty of room inside the house.'' He paused and turned back to her. ''Is there something wrong with that? Do you want me out of here?''

She shook her head and had to swallow before she could speak again. ''No...uh, no. It's fine.'' He was going to come toward her again. Quickly, before he could come close enough to touch her, Kristin turned and fled to the sanctuary of her own room.

She didn't know what seized her that afternoon. She didn't dare sit and think, and she certainly couldn't allow herself to analyze.

She went out in the early evening to speak with the hands. There was Jacob, who was nearly seventy, and his grandsons, Josh and Trin, who were even younger than she was. Their father had been killed at Manassas at the beginning of the war. And there was Pete, who was older than Jacob, though he wouldn't admit it. That was all she had left—two old men and two young boys. Yet they had survived so far. Somehow they had survived so far.

Cattle were missing again. Kristin just shrugged at the news. Zeke's boys had been through. They had simply taken what they wanted.

Pete wagged a finger at her. ''We heard what happened, missy. I think it's time you got out of here.''

She ruffled his thin gray hair. ''And what about you, Pete?''

''I've gotten along this far. I'll get along the rest of my days.''

She smiled at him. ''We'll see.''

''Hear tell you've got a man named Slater up at the house.''

Kristin frowned. ''Yes. Why? You know him, Pete?''

Pete looked down at the wood he was whittling, shaking his head. ''Can't say that I do.''

She thought the old man was lying to her, and she couldn't understand it. He was as loyal as the day was long.

''You just said his name. Slater.''

''Yeah, I heard it. From someone. Just like I heard tell that he managed to get rid of the whole lot of the thieving gutter rats.'' He looked up, wagging his knife at her. ''You can't beat the likes of Zeke Moreau, Kristin. He doesn't have a breath of mercy or justice in him.'' He spat on the floor. ''None of them do, not the jayhawkers, not the bushwhackers. It's time to get out.''

"Well, maybe," Kristin said distractedly. She stood from the pile of hay she'd been sitting on. "Maybe."

"Your Pa's dead, Kristin. You're smart and you're tough. But not tough enough to take on Zeke on your own."

He looked at her expectantly. She felt like laughing. Everyone thought she could help. Everyone thought that all she had to do was bat her eyelashes at Cole Slater and he'd come straight to their rescue. If they only knew.

"We'll talk about it in the morning," she told him.

When she returned to the house, it was dinnertime.

Delilah had set out the good china and fine crystal again. She'd made a honeyed ham, candied yams, turnip greens and a blueberry pie.

Shannon and Cole Slater talked all through the meal. There might not have been a war on. There might not have been anything wrong with the world at all, the way the two of them talked. Shannon was beautiful and charming, and Cole was the perfect gentleman.

Kristin tried to smile, and she tried to answer direct questions. But all she could remember was that he had rejected her—and that she needed him desperately. She hated him, yet trembled if their hands so much as brushed when they reached for something at the same time.

She drank far too much Madeira with dinner.

When he went out back to smoke a cigar afterward, Kristin decided to take another bath. She hoped Delilah would think she hadn't been able to wash away the miserable stench of the morning.

Shannon was a sweetheart, tender and caring. Kristin realized when Shannon kissed her good-night that her sister was suffering more then she had realized. She was just taking it all stoically, trying to ease Kristin's pain with smiles and laughter.

Shannon went to bed.

Kristin dressed in her best nightgown. It had been part of her mother's trousseau. It was soft, sheer silk that hugged her breasts in a pattern of lace, then fell in gentle swirls around her legs.

She sat at the foot of her bed in the gown, and she waited. She was still, but fires raged inside her.

She had to make him stay, no matter what it took.

This was something that she had to do.

She heard his footsteps on the stairs at last. She heard him walk down the hallway, and then she heard the door to her parents' room open and close.

She waited, waited as long as she could, as long as she dared. Then she stood and drifted barefoot across the hardwood floor. She opened her door and started across the hall. She nearly panicked and fled, but something drew her onward. She wondered if she had gone mad, wondered if the world really had been turned upside down. Nothing could ever be the same again.

She hated him, she told herself. And he had already turned her down once.

One day she would best him.

She placed her hand on the doorknob and turned it slowly. Then she pushed open the door.

The room was dark. Only a streak of moonlight relieved the blackness. Kristin stood there for several seconds, blinking, trying to orient herself. It was foolish. She had waited too long. He was probably fast asleep.

He wasn't asleep. He was wide awake. He was sitting up in bed, his chest bare. He was watching her. Despite the darkness, she knew that he was watching her, that he had been waiting for her and that he was amused.

"Come on, Kristin," he said softly. He wasn't whispering like a man afraid of being caught at some dishonorable deed. He was speaking softly out of consideration for the others in the house, not out of fear. He wouldn't give a damn about convention, she thought. And yet he seemed to expect her to respect it.

Men.

"I, uh...just wanted to see if you needed anything."

"Sure." He smiled knowingly. "Well, I don't need anything. Thank you."

The bastard. He really meant to make it hard for her.

"That's a nice outfit to wear to check on your male guests, ma'am." He said the last word with a slow, calculated Southern drawl, and she felt her temper flare. Where the hell was he from?

"Glad you like it," she retorted.

"Oh, I do like it. Very much."

This was getting them nowhere. No, it was getting *her* nowhere. "Well..."

"Come here, Kristin."

"You come here."

He grinned. "If you insist."

She should have known he would be lying there nude beneath the sheets.

Well, she had come to seduce him, after all.

She just hadn't imagined his body. The length of it. She couldn't remember what she had imagined. Darkness, and tangle of sheets... She had known it involved a naked man, but she hadn't known just how a naked man could be.

She tried to keep her eyes on his, aware that a crimson tide was rushing to her face. She wished she had the nerve to shout, to run, to scream, but she didn't seem to be able to do anything at all.

Her eyes slipped despite her best efforts, slipped and then widened. She knew that he saw it, and she knew that he was amused. But she didn't move and she didn't speak, and when he stood before her at last, his hands on his hips, she managed to toss her head back and meet his gaze with a certain bravado.

He placed his hands against the wall on either side of her head. "Like what you see?" he inquired politely.

"Someone should really slap the living daylights out of you," she told him sweetly.

"You didn't do badly."

"Good." She was beginning to shake. Right now it was a mere tremor, but it was growing. He was so close that...that part of his body was nearly touching the swirling silk of her gown. She felt his breath against her cheek. She felt the heat radiating from him. She bit her lip, trying to keep it from quivering.

He pushed away from the wall. He touched her cheek with his palm, then stroked it softly with his knuckles. She stared at him, unable to move. She knew then that he could see that she was trembling. His eyes remained locked with hers. He moved his hand downward and cupped her breast.

The touch was so intimate, so bold, that she nearly cried out. He grazed her nipple with his thumb, and sensations shot through her with an almost painful intensity. She caught her breath, trying desperately to keep from crying out. And then she realized that he was watching her eyes carefully, gauging her reactions.

She knocked his hand away and tried to push by him, but he caught her shoulders and threw her against the wall.

"I hurt your feelings before. But then, I don't think that you were lacking in self-confidence. You must know that you're beautiful. Your hair is so golden and you have the bearing of a young Venus. Kristin, it isn't you. It's me. I haven't got any emotion left. I haven't got what you need, what you want. Damn it, don't you understand? I want you. I'm made out of flesh and blood and whatever else it is that God puts into men. I want you. Now. Hell, I could have wanted you right after I ripped another man away from you. I'm no better than he is, not really. Don't you understand?"

She drew herself up against the wall. She hated him, and she hated herself. She had lost again.

"I only know that I need you. Emotion! I saw my father murdered, and Adam..."

"Yes, and Adam."

"And Adam is dead, too. So if you're worried about some kind of emotional commitment, you're a fool. I want help against Zeke Moreau."

"You want me to kill him."

"It's worth any price."

"I told you...I don't murder men in cold blood."

"Then I just want protection."

"How badly?"

"Desperately. You know that."

"Show me."

She stepped toward him and placed her hands around his neck. Suddenly she realized that she hadn't the least idea of what to do. Instinct guided her, instinct and nothing more.

She stepped closer, pressing against him so that she could feel the length of his naked body through the thin silk of her gown. She wound her arms around his neck and came up on tiptoe to press her lips against his, summoning up the memory of the kiss he had given her. She felt him, felt the instrument of his desire pulsing against her. She felt the muscles of his chest and belly and thighs. Then she felt his arms, powerful around her.

Then she plunged her tongue into his mouth and the world began to spin. She had come to seduce him, and she was ready to fall against him, longing for him to sweep her away.

To help her...

She felt the passion in him as he held her, and for a moment, victory was hers. She burned, she longed, with an astonishing hunger, and she could not know where it would lead. His lips held hers, his mouth devoured hers, and with each second that passed she entered deeper into a world that was pure sensation. Her pulse soared, and there was a pounding in her ears that was like the rush of the sea. His kiss was her life, his body was her support. She was afraid, and she was ecstatic.

And then he suddenly pushed her away.

His breathing was coming rough and ragged.

He watched her for a long, long moment. She felt his eyes on her, felt them as she would have felt an approaching storm. Then he shook his head.

"Go to bed, Kristin."

She inhaled sharply, furiously. "You let me make a complete fool of myself and then you— Damn you!"

Kristin slammed her fists against his shoulders, catching him off guard. He staggered, and she found the doorknob. Throwing the door open, she tore across the hall. She threw herself onto her own bed, tears hovering behind her lashes, fury rising in her throat.

The door crashed open behind her, and she spun around. He had followed her across the hall without even bothering to dress.

"Get out of here!" she snapped, enraged.

He ignored her and strode calmly toward the bed. Kristin shot up, determined to fight. It was all to no avail. His long stride quickly brought him to her. She came to her knees hastily, but he joined her on the bed, grabbing her hands and pressing her down.

"I should scream!" she told him. "Samson would come and—"

"Then scream."

She held her breath. He pressed her down on the bed and straddled her.

"Why won't you leave me alone?"

"You wanted to make a deal," he said harshly.

"What?"

"You said you wanted to make a deal. All right. Let's talk. I'm willing to negotiate."

PART 2

The Lover

Chapter Four

Kristin was glad the room was steeped in darkness. His features were shadowed, his body was shadowed, and she prayed that her own emotions were hidden by the night. She wanted to hate him. She could not. She wanted to think, to reason, and she could think of nothing but the hard male body so hot and intimate against her own.

He had come here, naked, to accept her proposition, it seemed. And yet he was angry again, angrier even than before. Hard and bitter and angry.

Moonlight cast a sudden soft glow over the room. She saw his features, and they were harsh, taut, almost cruel, as if he were fighting some inner pain.

"Negotiate?" she whispered.

"First, Miss Kristin, if you're going to play a game of chance, make sure you're playing with a full deck."

"I don't know what—"

"Exactly. That's why I'm going to explain things to you. I'll meet any man in a fair fight, but I won't go out and commit murder, not for you, not for myself, not for anyone. Do you understand?"

She nodded. She didn't understand him at all, but she was suddenly too afraid to do anything else. She had lost her mind. The war and the bloodshed had made her insane. She, Kristin McCahy, raised to live up to the highest standards of Southern womanhood, was lying on her bed with a naked stranger.

And she wasn't screaming.

"No involvement, Miss Kristin." The mock drawl was back in

his voice, making her wonder again where he hailed from. She was filled with awareness of him. His muscled chest was plastered with crisp dark hair. She thought of how quickly he had drawn his Colts and his rifle, and she shivered. He carried with him an aura of danger that drew her to him despite her best intentions.

His sex pulsed against her belly, and she fought wildly to keep her eyes glued to his. It was all she could do to remember that she had intended to seduce him, to leave him gasping and longing and aching, his tongue hanging out for her.

He would never long for her that way, she realized now. Nor would he be denied. He had mocked her, but now he was determined to have her, and she felt sure he must despise her more with each passing second.

She steeled herself and whispered harshly, "No involvement. You needn't worry. I need a gunslinger. I could never love one."

A slight smile curved his lip. "This deal is made on my terms, lady. No involvement, no questions. And I won't murder Zeke. I'll go after him when I can. I'll do my damnedest to keep you and Shannon safe and your place together. But I've got other commitments, too, Kristin. And I can't forget them."

She didn't say anything. She didn't know what to say or do, didn't know where to go from here. This was so easy for him. He was so casual. He didn't even seem to know he was naked.

He touched her cheek, brushing it with his fingertips. "Why?" he said suddenly.

She shook her head, uncomprehending. "Why what?"

"This is all Zeke wanted."

"I hate Zeke. I hate him more than you could ever imagine. He killed my father. I'd rather bed a bison than that bastard."

"I see. And I'm a step above a bison?"

"A step below."

"I can still leave."

Panic filled her. She wanted to reach out and keep him from disappearing, but her pride wouldn't let her. Then she realized that he was smiling again, that he was amused. He leaned down low and spoke to her softly. His breath caressed her flesh, and the soft hair of his beard teased her chin. "There's one more point to this bargain, Miss McCahy."

Her heart was suddenly pounding mercilessly, her body aching, her nerves screaming.

"What's that, Slater?"

"I like my women hungry. No, ma'am, maybe that's not enough. I like them starving."

Words and whispers could do so much. As much as his slow, lazy, taunting smile. Fever ran through her, rife and rampant. She wanted to strike him because she felt so lost, and in spite of herself, she was afraid. She wasn't afraid he would hurt her. She might have gone insane, but she believed with all her heart that he would never hurt her. And she wondered, too, if this madness hadn't been spawned by the very way he made her feel, alive as she had never been before, haunted and shaken and...hungry, hungry for some sweet sensation that teased her mind and heart when he was near.

And yet she lay stiff and unyielding, numbed by the fear that swept through her, the fear that she would be unable to please him, the fear that she didn't have what it would take to hold him. Women... He had used the plural of the word. He liked his women hungry....

No, starving.

She didn't know him, and she didn't want involvement any more than he did, and yet this very intimacy was involvement. Even as she lay there, unable to move, she felt a painful stirring of jealousy. She had sacrificed so very much pride and dignity and morality for this man, and he was herding her together with every other female he had ever known.

He touched her chin. Then he brushed her lips with his, with the soft sweep of his mustache.

"Hungry, sweetheart." She sensed his smile, hovering above her in the dark. "This is as exciting as bedding a large chunk of ice."

She struck out at him blindly, but he caught her arms and lowered his weight onto her. She clenched her teeth as his laughing eyes drew near.

"Excuse me, Mr. Slater. My experience is limited. You wouldn't let me run out and screw a ranch hand, remember?"

"Kristin, damn you—"

"No, damn you!" she retorted, painfully close to tears. This couldn't be it. This couldn't be the night, the magic night she had wondered about in her dreams. No, it couldn't be, she thought bitterly. In her dreams this night had come after she had been married. And Adam had been in her dreams. And there had been nothing ugly or awkward about it. There hadn't even been any nude bodies, except beneath the sheets, and even then she had been cloaked all in white and he had whispered about how much he loved her and how beautiful she was and it had been wondrously pure and innocent....

She hadn't known these feelings then. And she hadn't known she could sell herself to a man who didn't even really want her.

"Please!" she cried suddenly, trying to escape his touch. Tears were beginning to sting her eyes, and she didn't want him to see them. She couldn't bear any more humiliation. "Just leave me alone. I—I can't be what you want, I can't—"

"Kristin!"

She went still when she heard the pained tenderness in his voice. He touched her cheek gently. Then he lay beside her and swept her into his arms.

She was stunned to realize that he was trembling, too, that his body was racked by heat and fever. He murmured her name again and again, and his lips brushed over her brow, as light as air. "Don't you see? I don't want to need you like this. I don't want to want you!"

There was passion in his voice, dark and disturbing. There was bitterness in it, too, pained and fervent, and as he continued to touch her, his emotions seemed to burn and sear her along with his touch. His hands were tender, then demanding, then gentle again.

"I don't want to want you," he murmured, "but God help me, I do."

Then he kissed her, and there was nothing left to worry about, for she was suddenly riding swiftly across the dark heavens and there was no time to think, no time for reason. She could only hold tight.

It all seemed to come together, everything she had felt since she had first set eyes on the man. Hungry...his mouth was hungry, and he was devouring her. His lips molded and shaped hers, and his tongue seemed to plunge to the very depths of her being, licking her deep, deep inside, taunting her, arousing her still more.

His hands roamed her body with abandon, abandon and a kind of recklessness. He caressed her tenderly, even delicately, then touched her with a force that told her that he wanted to brand her, wanted to leave his mark on her.

She never knew where the awe and the trembling and fear ceased and something entirely different began. She didn't even know when she lost the elegant nightgown brought west in her mother's trousseau, for his touch was so sweeping, so swift, so heady. She knew only that her breast was suddenly bare and his mouth was upon it. He cupped the soft mound of flesh with his hand, his lips hard around the nipple, drawing, suckling, raking the peak with his teeth as he demanded more and more.

She nearly screamed. She had never imagined such intimacy, and she never dreamed that there could be anything like the sensation that gripped her now with burning fingers, drawing a line of raw excitement down her spine and into her loins. She clutched his shoulders, barely aware that her nails were digging into him, that she was clutching him as if he were a lifeline in a storm-swept sea.

And still the tempest raged. His lips found her throat, and he raked his palm down the length of her, kneading her thigh and her buttocks. He moved swiftly, and she tried to follow, but she could not, for she was breathless, gasping in shock and amazement at each new sensation. He began anew. He touched her, held her, all over again. His lips trailed a line down the valley between her breasts to her navel, and the soft, bristling hair of his mustache and beard taunted her naked flesh mercilessly. She felt his knee force her thighs apart, and she knew that she was close to the point of no return, to being changed forever, and even then she could not keep pace with the winds that buffeted her.

And then he stopped. His palms on either side of her head, he caressed her with that curious tenderness he possessed and lowered his head to hers, whispering into her mouth.

"Hungry?"

She didn't want to face it. It was too new, too startling. She lowered her head and nodded, but it wasn't enough, not for him.

"Kristin?"

"Please..."

"Tell me."

"Oh, God!" she cried, trying to twist away from him. His palms held her fast, and her eyes were forced to meet his. Her lips were moist and her hair was a mass of gold between them, startlingly pale against the darkness of his chest.

He smiled at her, watching her as he drew his hand down to the pulse at her throat, then over her breast, down, down, to draw a circle on her abdomen and then plunge lower. He kept his eyes on her as he stroked her upper thigh. Then, suddenly, he swept his touch intimately inside her, moving with a sure, languorous rhythm.

She cried out again and tried to burrow against him, but he held her away from him. He watched her eyes, watched the rise and fall of her breasts, watched her gasp for air.

He caught her lips with his own, caught them and kissed them, and then he whispered against them again.

"Yes. You are...hungry."

Was this it? Was this the hunger he demanded, this burning sensation that filled her and engulfed her? She was grateful for the darkness, for the night, for with the moon behind a cloud, she could believe that all her sins were hidden, all that she had bartered, all that she had given so freely. She couldn't believe how she lay there with him, and yet she would not have changed it for the world. A soft cry escaped her, and she threw her arms around his neck, hiding against his chest at last. Something surged within her, and she gasped and murmured against his chest, barely aware that her hips were pulsing to his rhythm, that he hadn't ceased taunting her, that his strokes were growing more enticing.

Cole knew vaguely that he shouldn't be there. He should have told her that morning that nothing could make him stay, nothing could make him help her. She was the last thing in the world he needed. He had commitments of his own, and come heaven or hell or death itself, he meant to see them through.

And this innocence...

This, too, was the last thing he needed. She was hardened, and there were jagged edges to her. War did that. War and death and pain and blood. But the innocence was still there, too. He had thought he could make her run, and he had thought he could be strong enough himself not to touch her. He was used up. He knew that. He was used up, and she deserved more than that. He was still alive, though, still breathing, and she touched every raw cord of desire within him. Maybe he had known what was to come, and maybe he hadn't expected it at all, but now that it was happening, he couldn't even try to deny it. She spun a golden web of arousal and passion as soft and silky and luxuriant as the long strands of hair that tangled around them both, dampened by the glistening sheen of their bodies. She had beautiful features, exquisite features, fine, high cheekbones, a small, slim nose and eyes like an endless blue sky, darkly fringed with rich lashes and glazed now with blossoming passion. And her mouth...it was full and giving, sensual in laughter, sensual when her lips parted beneath his own. She was soft, she was velvet and she was created for desire, with high, firm breasts, a slim waist and flaring hips, and smooth, fascinating buttocks. He hadn't meant to stay. He hadn't meant to come here, and he hadn't meant to stay. He hadn't meant to touch her....

But he had.

And she moved. She moved with exquisite grace. She made sweet, soft sounds that entered his loins and caused the blood to pound in his head so that he could think no more. Only one thought guided him, and that was that he had to have her, had to have her or go mad. Her nipples pressed against his chest, and she arched against his hand. Despite his best efforts, the agony of the past was erased, the vengeance of the future forgotten. Even the present meant nothing at all. All that mattered was this woman, and she was hot and wet and begging for release.

He pulled her to him almost roughly. Her eyes widened, and he commanded her to hold tight. He caught her lips in a heady kiss and swept his hands beneath her. He fought hard to remember her innocence. He kissed her with sweeping ardor, and then he entered her.

He was slow, achingly slow, and she was sleek and damp, a hot sheath ready to encase him, and still he felt her shudder, heard the sudden agonized cry that she muffled against his chest.

He'd heard it before. On his wedding day.

The irony, the bitter, bitter irony touched him for a moment, and for a moment he hated her and himself. For a moment he was still. Then he felt her shudder again and thought she might be crying, and then he was whispering things without thinking.

Yes...he'd been here before. Making love tenderly to a woman for the very first time. Her very first time.

He held her, caressed her, promised to help her. And then he moved again, slowly at first, carefully, tenderly.

And then she was moving beneath him, subtly at first. She was taking him in, and the tears were gone, and the shock was gone, and the desperate tension was growing again.

Care and consideration left him. A thirst that he was frantic to slake ripped through him and into his loins. He couldn't remember ever being so fevered, and still the sensations grew. He touched her breasts, struck anew by their beauty. He inhaled the clean, sweet scent of her tangled hair and the fever soared higher and higher. He wrapped her legs tightly around him and cupped her buttocks, and rocking hard, filled her with himself again and again. He threw back his head and rough sound tore from him as the relief began to shake and convulse through his body. Again and again he spilled into her. She cried out, her voice ragged. He was aware that she had reached some sweet satisfaction, and he was pleased. She fell still, and the last of the fever raked through him. He thrust deep, deep inside her one last time. It was shattering, and he couldn't remember when he had known such a deeply satisfying climax.

He fell to her side, covered with sweat, breathing heavily.

She was silent. He touched her cheek and found tears there.

Suddenly he was furious with himself and with her. This should never have happened. She should have married some young buck and worn white, and she should have been loved, not just desired.

She twisted away from his touch, and he let her go. She turned her back on him, and he wondered if she was crying again. Maybe she had a right to, but it was damned insulting. He'd taken even greater care with her than he had with—Elizabeth. With Elizabeth.

There. He dared to think her name.

Though he gritted his teeth and wished it away, agony gripped him from head to toe. He wondered if the pain would ever leave him.

"You can...you can go back now," Kristin said suddenly.

"What?" His voice was sharp.

"Our deal." She spoke softly, her voice a mere whisper, as if tears hovered behind her words, tears and just a touch of anxiety. "It's—it's made now, isn't it?"

He hesitated before he answered her. "Yes, your bloody bargain is made, Miss McCahy."

"Then you could...you could go back. Across the hall."

He didn't know what demon seized him. He didn't care if he was heard by the others in the house, didn't care about anything at all. He sat up in a sudden fury and wrenched her around to face him. He spoke bitingly, trying to make every word sting like the stroke of a lash.

"Not on your life, my little prima donna. You invited me in here. Now you've got me. That was the game, Kristin. You knew it was going to go by my rules—"

"My God!" she cried, jerking away from his touch. "Have you no consideration, no—"

"Compassion? Not a whit. This is what you wanted, and now you've got it."

She was beautiful still, he thought. The moonlight was playing over her breasts, and they were damp and shimmering and very, very fine, the nipples still enlarged and hard. He felt a quickening inside him all over again, and with it felt the return of the pain. The pain of betrayal. It was all right with whores, with tavern girls. It was something else with this innocent young beauty.

He scowled fiercely and turned his back on her. "Go to sleep, Kristin."

She didn't move. She didn't answer him. Not for endless seconds.

"Go to sleep?" she repeated incredulously.

"Damn it, yes, go to sleep." He swung around again and pressed her down on the bed. She started to fight him, and he wasn't in the mood to take it. Dark anger was in him, dark, brooding anger, and though he didn't mean to be cruel to her, he didn't seem to be able to help himself. He caught her shoulders and shook them. "Good night, Kristin. Go to sleep."

"Leave," she said stubbornly.

"I'll be damned if I will."

"Then I'll leave."

"And I'll be damned if you'll leave, either. Now go to sleep!"

He turned around, offering her his back once again. He didn't know why he had started this bout, but now that he had begun it, he wasn't about to lose.

He felt it when she started to rise, and he turned with frightening speed, sweeping his arm around her waist and holding her still. He felt her heart beating like that of a doe.

"Go to sleep!"

He heard her teeth grating, but she didn't move, not again. He knew she was planning to wait until he fell asleep, then slip away.

He smiled. She had another think coming. He would feel her slightest movement. He would awaken.

When she did try to move, he kept his eyes closed and held her fast. He heard her swearing softly, and he heard the threat of sobs coming to her whispering voice.

But then it was she who fell into an exhausted sleep. And it was he who awoke first with the morning. He stood and stretched and padded naked to the window and looked out on a beautiful summer's day. It was a fine ranch, he thought. Then he sighed, and he knew that she would think she had sold herself dearly in the night.

He had sold himself dearly, too. He had sold his honor, and he would have to stay, and he would have to protect her.

He walked over to the bed. The evidence of their night together was painfully obvious in the twisted bedding.

Her face was covered by long, soft tendrils of hair that picked up gold from the sun. A hand seemed to tighten around his heart and squeeze. Cole stepped closer to the bed and covered Kristin with the top sheet and the comforter. Then he stepped to the door, glanced out and returned to the room across the hall to wash and dress.

Kristin knew it was late when she awoke. She opened her eyes and saw that the sun had risen high, then closed her eyes again and discovered that she was shaking.

She had almost believed that she had dreamed the entire episode.

But she hadn't. Cole Slater was gone, but he had definitely been there, and just thinking about everything that had happened made her shake again and burn crimson to the roots of her hair.

A knock sounded at her door. "Kristin?"

It was Shannon. Kristin sat bolt upright and looked at the bed. The comforter seemed to hide the sins of the night.

"Shannon, just a minute!" she cried out. Her gown was on the floor beside the bed. She made a dive for it, wincing at the soreness that plagued her thighs. Then she realized that the gown was torn and ragged, and she knew why it had seemed to melt away the night before. Bitterly she wound it into a ball, stuffed it into her dresser and dragged out an old flannel gown. Breathless, she told Shannon to come in.

Shannon came in with a pot of coffee and a cup and breakfast on a silver tray. Kristin stared at it blankly and arched a brow at her younger sister.

"Good morning, sleepyhead," Shannon told her.

"Breakfast? In bed?" The ranch was a place where they barely eked out their existence. Breakfast in bed was a luxury they never afforded themselves. "After I've slept all morning?"

"Delilah was going to wake you. Cole said that maybe things had been hard on you lately and that maybe you needed to sleep."

"Oh, Cole said that, did he?"

Shannon ignored the question. "I rode out to the north pasture with Cole and Pete, and everything's going fine for the day."

Kristin kissed her sister's cheek and plopped on the bed, wincing again. It even hurt a little to sit.

She felt her face flood with color again, and she lowered her head, trying to hide her blush behind her hair. She still didn't know if she hated him, or if her feeling had become something different, something softer.

A little flush of fever seemed to touch her. She was breathing too fast, and her heart was hammering. She couldn't forget the night. She couldn't forget how she had felt, and she didn't know whether to be amazed or grateful or awed—or ashamed. The future loomed before them. They had a deal. He had said he would stay. And he hadn't left her room, and she—

She couldn't help wondering what he intended for their personal future together. Did he mean to do it...again?

"My Lord, Kristin, but you're flushed!" Shannon said with alarm.

"I'm all right," Kristin said hastily. She sipped the coffee too quickly and burned her lip. She set the cup down. "This was really sweet. The breakfast."

"Oh," Shannon said nonchalantly, "this was Cole's idea, too. He seemed to think you might have a little trouble getting up this morning."

"Oh, he did, did he?" She bit so hard into a piece of bacon that her teeth snapped together. He was laughing at her again, it seemed, and he didn't even have the decency to do it to her face. She longed for the chance to give him a good hard slap just once.

She caught herself. He had warned her. They were playing by his rules. And there was only one thing she was gaining from it all. Safety. She had agreed to the rules. She had meant to seduce him, she had meant for it all to happen, she had wanted the deal. It was just that she wasn't at all sure who had seduced whom.

"Where is Cole now?" she asked Shannon. She was surprised to find that she had a ravenous appetite.

Shannon shrugged. "I'm not sure. But do you know what?" she asked excitedly.

"No. What?"

"He says he's going to stay around for a while. Isn't that wonderful, Kristin?"

Kristin swallowed and nodded. "Yes. It's wonderful."

"Samson says it's a miracle. He says God has looked down on us with mercy at long last."

"The Lord certainly does work in mysterious ways," Kristin murmured dryly.

Shannon, who had seated herself at the foot of the bed, leaped up and hugged Kristin. "We're going to make it," she whispered. "We're really going to make it."

She had underestimated Shannon, Kristin realized. She had felt their father's death every bit as keenly as Kristin had.

And because she felt it so strongly, she had learned to hate, just as Kristin had.

"I've got to get back downstairs. Delilah is baking bread and making preserves and I promised to help."

Kristin nodded. "I'll be right down, too."

When her sister had left, Kristin washed hastily. She couldn't help remembering every place he had touched her, everything he had done to her. And then, naturally, she started trembling again, thinking about the feeling that had come over her. In the midst of carnage, a brief, stolen moment of ecstasy.

Shameful ecstasy.

Ecstasy.

She wondered if it had ever really been, if it could ever come again.

She dressed, trying desperately to quit thinking. If she didn't, she would walk around all day as red as a beet.

She dressed for work. There was some fencing down on the north side, and she had told Pete she'd come out and look at it. The stash of gold hidden in the hayloft was dwindling, but they could afford to repair the fencing. And if she could just hang on to her stock a while longer, she could command fair prices from any number of buyers in the spring. She had to remember that she was fighting for the land. Nothing else mattered.

In breeches and boots, Kristin started for the doorway. Then she remembered her bedding, and the telltale sheets.

Delilah usually did the beds. She kept the house with Shannon's help. Samson kept it from falling apart. Pete and Kristin ran the ranch. That was just the way things had worked out.

But she didn't want Delilah doing her bed. Not today.

He liked his women hungry. *Women.* Plural.

Kristin let loose with a furious oath and ripped the sheets from the bed. She jumped up and down on them a few times for good measure, then realized how ridiculous she was being and scooped them up. She carried them down with her to the stables, stuffing them into the huge trash bin. She would burn them later, with some of the empty feed bags.

She headed for the stable, determined to saddle Debutante and ride out. She paused in the doorway, aware that Cole was there, brushing down his black thoroughbred stallion. It was a beautiful animal, Kristin thought.

Very like the man who owned him.

She wasn't ready to see Cole Slater yet. She almost turned around, ready to change her plans for the day to avoid facing him. But he had sensed her there, and he turned, and there seemed to be nothing for her to do but stand there and meet his stare.

It was long, and it was pensive, and it gave no quarter. She would never accuse the man of being overly sensitive or overly polite. His gray eyes were sharp and curious, and she still thought he must be amused by her, because he was smiling slightly. There were times when she thought he hated her, but then he would stare at her in a way that warmed her and offered her a fleeting tenderness.

Very much like the way he made love...

She shouldn't have thought it. The color that had so alarmed her rose to fill her face, and she had to lower her eyes to still the blush. She prayed fervently that she could appear sophisticated for just this one encounter. But it was impossible to stand here now, fully clothed, and not remember what had gone on the night before. Things could never be the same again. She could never see life the same way again. She could never see him the same way again, for she knew the power of the form beneath the shirt and jeans, and he knew all that made up the woman she was.

"Sleep well?" he asked her after a moment.

There was something grating in the question, something mocking, and that helped. She squared her shoulders and tried to walk by him, heading for Debutante's stall. He caught her arm and swung her around. His eyes were serious now.

"Where do you think you're going?"

"Out to the north pasture. I have to see the fencing. I should have gone yesterday, but..." She paused, her voice fading away.

He shook his head impatiently. "I'll meet Pete."

"But it's my ranch!"

"And it's my life, Miss McCahy." He dropped her arm and put his hands, the currycomb in one, on his hips. "You're taking up my time. We made some ridiculous deal—"

"Ridiculous deal!" She was choked with rage. She was going to slap him this time. Right across the face.

She didn't make it. He caught her wrist. "I'm sorry, Kristin. I didn't mean it that way."

"I'm so terribly sorry if I disappointed you."

She'd thought his eyes would drop with shame. They didn't. Hers did. He was still smiling.

"You didn't disappoint me. You surpassed my wildest expectations. I'm sorry. I didn't mean to insult you. I meant that you really should be the hell out of here."

"You're not reneging?" she asked crisply.

He smiled slowly, tilted back his plumed hat and shook his head. "No, Kristin," he said softly. His low, grating voice sent tremors up her spine. "I never renege on a deal. But I'll be damned if I'm going to stick around so you can run off and be swept away beneath my very nose."

"But I—"

"Forget it, Kristin. I warned you. We play by my rules. And you're not riding out anywhere."

"But—"

"You ride out, I ride out."

"But...but you've already been...paid!" Kristin exploded.

His brows shot up, and his lips curled mockingly. "Paid?"

"You know what I mean."

He shook his head. "I sure as hell don't! That was it? One night in your arms and I'm supposed to gladly lay down my life and die?"

"You are no Southern gentleman."

"Did I say I was?"

"You are no gentleman at all!"

"I never claimed to be one, Kristin. In fact, I haven't made any claims to you at all. Remember that."

"I find it difficult to forget."

"Are you trying to renege?" he queried softly.

She drew herself up stiffly, determined to counter-attack. "So you're not from the South?"

"Does it matter where I'm from?"

"Maybe it does!"

He caught her hand and held it. They stared at one another. Behind them, the massive black stallion snorted. Cole stared at her seriously for a long moment and then said, "No, it doesn't, Kristin. Nothing about me matters at all. No questions. No involvement. Remember that."

She jerked her hand away. "I'll remember, Mr. Slater."

She started toward Debutante's stall. Maybe she couldn't go riding, but she had to get away. She would take a moment to stroke the mare's velvet nose, and then she would escape. She didn't know how she would be able to bear it, though. She would be like a caged animal with all the emotions that were playing havoc in her heart.

She patted Debutante's nose and promised the horse in a low whisper that she would come out and give her a good grooming as soon as *he* was out of the stable.

Then she turned around, determined to walk out of the stables with her head held high, determined to hang on to her few remaining shreds of dignity.

"By the way, Kristin..." he began.

She paused, her back to him. She straightened, stiffening her shoulders, and turned in a swift circle. He wasn't watching her. He was combing the stallion's shining flanks.

"Why don't you move your things into the larger bedroom? We'll have more space there."

"What?"

"You heard me."

"But—but everyone will know! And just how many times do you intend to...to..."

"Get paid?" he suggested politely. He didn't even seem to be paying attention to her. He stroked the stallion's ears, then stared directly at her. "You want blood, Kristin. That's an expensive commodity. And as far as everyone knowing is concerned, that's exactly what I want."

"But—"

"I make the rules, remember?"

"I can't! I can't go by this one—"

"Delilah will understand. So will Shannon and Sam and Pete and everyone else. And if Zeke Moreau hears anything about it, he'll get the message, too."

"But—"

"Do it, Kristin."

She spun around in a dead fury again. She didn't look back. She stormed into the house, wishing desperately that *she* were a man. She would run away and join the army in two seconds.

She wouldn't even give a damn whose army she joined. Just as long as it was someone who hated Quantrill and his animals.

"Kristin, that you?" Delilah came into the hallway, smiling. "Want to give us a hand with the wax? I could surely use some help stirring. I've got Shannon jarring and sealing while I've been kneading the bread."

"Er...of course," Kristin said. She'd much, much rather run away and join the army.

Shannon gave her a bright smile when she came into the kitchen. "Did you find Cole?"

"Yes. I found him."

Shannon nodded. It was obvious that she approved of it all. They were all mad, Kristin decided.

"He wants me to move into Pa's bedroom with him," she blurted out.

Shannon had been holding a jar of jam, sealing it with wax. The jar slipped from her fingers and shattered loudly on the floor.

Delilah sent the bread she was kneading into the air. It fell back on the block table.

Both of them stared at her. Then they glanced at one another. Neither of them said a word.

"Say something!" Kristin demanded. "Help me make some kind of a decision!"

"You can't!" Shannon gasped.

"Seems to me like you've already made your decision," Delilah said softly. "But it ain't right. It just ain't right. Still..."

"He's much, much better than Zeke Moreau," Shannon said. She stooped to pick up the broken glass and the jam that was seeping into the floorboards. "Yes, maybe you have to. And he *is* much better than Zeke."

"So that's why I'm sleeping with a stranger." Kristin sank into a chair before the fire. "I cannot believe I'm doing this," she murmured.

"These are different times," Shannon murmured, staring at the floor. She looked up at her sister. "Kristin, we can't be blind to the facts! We need him. We need him, or else we just have to give up and pull out."

"Shannon!" Kristin exploded. "You're shocked, and you know it. Pa must be turning in his grave. We don't even know where Cole Slater comes from!"

Shannon's beautiful blue eyes widened. "But of course we do, Kristin."

"What?"

Shannon smiled broadly. "He's from Missouri. He was originally from Virginia, but his family bought a big spread out here. I think he comes from tobacco money, a lot of it. He went to West Point. He was in the same class as Jeb Stuart!"

Kristin stared at her sister, who appeared about to swoon. Shannon thought that the Confederate general Jeb Stuart was the handsomest, most gallant gentleman in the whole world. Shannon's reaction to Stuart's name didn't surprise her, but the fact that she seemed to know so much about Cole stunned her.

"What?" she repeated numbly.

Shannon sighed with supreme patience, as if she were the elder, explaining things to a sullen child.

"He's a Virginian, Kristin, moved to Missouri. He went to West Point. Once upon a time he was in the army in Kansas. He and Stuart served together."

"Wonderful," Kristin murmured.

So he *was* a Southerner. And he wasn't in uniform. He was one of them, one of the breed that ran with Quantrill....

She was a Southerner herself, she thought dully. Not all Southerners were like Zeke Moreau.

But Cole...

Cole had talked freely to Shannon. But the questions hadn't all been answered yet.

He had gone to West Point. He had served in the Union Army before the war with the gallant Southern calvary officer, Jeb Stuart.

But he wasn't wearing a uniform now. Not the Union's, and not the Confederacy's. Why not?

Delilah stirred something over the fire. She wiped her hands on her apron. "Well, Kristin? What do we do? If you want, I'll go move your things."

Kristin swallowed. She wanted to protest. She wanted to refuse Cole Slater.

She looked at Delilah. Delilah wasn't making any judgments.

Kristin nodded. She could give up the place or she could hold tight to Cole Slater. She really had no choice. But she vowed to herself that she'd find out everything there was to know about the man.

Chapter Five

Kristin spent the day worrying about the night ahead. She prowled around upstairs, trying to keep busy. Though she hated it, she did what Cole had told her to, taking a few of her dresses and nightshirts and putting them in the armoire in her parents' bedroom.

Shannon came upstairs while she was at it. There was something about her knowing glance that made Kristin feel terribly ashamed. "Cole—Mr. Slater—thinks that Zeke ought to think there's something…um, that he and I, that…"

"I understand," Shannon said softly. Even her innocence was dead, Kristin thought. There was an awkward silence, but then Shannon came into the room and hugged her. "I like him," she told Kristin. "I like him a whole lot."

"Only because he knows Jeb Stuart."

Shannon made a face. "That helps." She sat down on the bed. "What happened here?" she queried softly.

"What do you mean?" Kristin asked her.

"So many men are so fine. General Lee is such a gentleman, by all accounts. And Jeb Stuart is so dashing! And then out here…"

"We get the bushwhackers and the jayhawkers," Kristin finished for her. She sat down beside Shannon and hugged her. "And don't forget," she reminded her, "we have a brother fighting in Mr. Lincoln's army."

"I never forget!" Shannon said.

They sat there in silence for a long time. Then suddenly, there was a volley of shots from outside. Kristin leaped to her feet and raced to the window.

Cole was out back with Samson. He'd set a few rows of old liquor and tonic bottles on the back fence to serve as makeshift targets. He'd already shot up the first set.

Kristin watched as he reloaded, then twirled his six-shooter in his hand and shoved it back in its holster. He paused. Then, in the wink of an eye, he cleared away another row. Then he spoke to Samson, and Kristin realized that it was a lesson.

Then it was Samson's turn with the guns. Kristin strained to hear Cole's words.

"Quantrill's boys usually carry four or five Colts, a shotgun or a rifle or maybe both. That's why they keep licking the pants off the Union troops. They're well armed, and the boys in blue are still trying to fire off muzzle-loading carbines. Zeke will always be well armed. So we've always got to be prepared to outshoot him in return. You understand, Sam?"

"Yes, Mr. Slater, that I do."

"Let's try it again. Hold your hand steady, and squeeze the trigger, don't jerk it."

Cole took off his plumed hat, ran his fingers through his hair and set the hat back on his head, low over his eyes. Then he said, "Go!" and Samson drew. He shattered a fair number of the bottles, then laughed. Cole slapped him on the back, congratulating him. Then the men's voices grew low, and Kristin couldn't hear any more.

Suddenly Cole looked up at the window. It was too late. She couldn't draw away.

He smiled and waved. She almost waved back, but then she realized that Shannon had come up beside her and that it was her sister he was waving to, because she was waving down to him.

"We're moving Kristin in!" Shannon called down.

Kristin was mortified. She felt his eyes on her, she saw his slow, lazy smile. She wanted to hit Shannon over the head. She backed away from the window instead.

"You coming up?" Shannon called.

"Shannon!" Kristin hissed.

But Cole shook his head. He looked handsome then, as tall as Samson, and hard and lean in his long coat and his plumed hat. "Tell your sister I'm on my way out to find Pete. Might be gone awhile. If I can take care of some things today, I will.''

Shannon turned to Kristin. "Cole said—"

"I heard what Cole said."

"Shannon!" Cole said.

"Yes, Cole?"

"Tell your sister I may be back late. Tell her she doesn't have to wait up."

Shannon turned to Kristin. "Cole said—"

"I heard what Cole said!"

Kristin spun around and stormed out of the room. She returned to her own room and slammed the door. She sat down on her own bed and pressed her hands against her temples. She had a staggering headache, and her nerves were as shattered as the bottles Cole had shot up.

Well, he had shattered her world, too.

She needed to get this over with quickly. She needed him to be around. She wanted him. She hated him.

She wished to God she knew him. She wished to God she could get to know him. But she didn't think he would let anyone get close to him. Anyone at all.

No involvement...

She didn't want any involvement. And he couldn't possibly make her as nervous as Zeke Moreau made her hateful.

Or could he?

If he came back at all that night, Kristin never knew it. She lay on her parents' bed until the wee hours of the morning, and then exhaustion claimed her. When she awoke, it was almost noon. No one came for her. When she dressed and went downstairs, Delilah was busy with a big pot of lye and Shannon was putting their last two-year-old colt through his paces. Kristin longed to do something, to ride somewhere, but Samson found her in the stable and warned her that Cole had said she should stay close to home. She bit her lip but did as she was told, and Samson proudly showed her something of what he had learned.

Kristin was impressed with his newfound skill with a gun, and she told him so, but then she rested her chin on the fence and sighed. "Is it enough, Samson? Is it enough against Zeke?"

"Maybe not me alone, Miss Kristin, but Mr. Slater had all the boys out here this morning, and he can teach a whole lot about gun play, as well as practice it."

"You sound like you like him a lot, Samson."

"Yep. Yes, miss, I do. He complimented me on my language this morning, and when I told him how big your pa was on learning he said that he thought fine men came in both black and white, and that he was mighty proud to know me."

Kristin smiled. "That's nice, Samson. That's mighty nice."

They were both silent for a moment. Then Kristin began to grow uncomfortable, wondering what he really thought of what was going on with Cole Slater.

"The world just ain't the same anymore, Miss Kristin," Samson said at last. "The world just ain't the same." He chewed on a long blade of grass and stared out at the pastureland. "No, the world just ain't the same, and we can only pray that it'll right itself when this awful war is over."

Kristin nodded. Then she turned to him and gave him a big hug. She didn't know what she'd do without him and Delilah.

She didn't see Cole again all that day and night. He was still out with Pete and the boys at dinnertime, and later, much later, she heard laughter and the strains of Pete's fiddle coming from the bunkhouse. That night she slept alone again in the big sleigh bed in her parents' room.

In the morning she didn't know if he had ever come to bed or not. For some reason, she didn't think he had, and she wondered why he was taunting her this way when he seemed to have so little real interest in her. Her temper rose, but then she remembered that she should be grateful to have him here. And then she was afraid he would leave.

And then she hated him. He was supposed to want her. They were supposed to have a deal. She was supposed to loathe him for taking advantage of her weakness. But she was the one left wondering and wanting. No, not wanting. Merely curious, she assured herself. But she couldn't deny that she had been in a fever ever since he had come. She simply couldn't deny her emotions.

Then he was there. He was there all day. He passed her in the hallway and tipped his hat to her, a smile of amusement tugging at his lips.

"Wait!" she cried. "Where are you going?"

"Rounding up strays."

"Let me come."

His smile faded. "No."

"But—"

"My rules, Kristin."

"But—"

"My rules."

She gritted her teeth and stiffened, watching him for a moment in simmering silence. He smiled again. "But I will be back for supper this evening. Steak and sweet potatoes and Delilah's black-eyed peas, and blueberry pie for dessert. And then..." He let his voice trail off. Then he lifted his hat again and turned and left.

And she didn't even know where he had spent the night.

It was another wretched day. She fed the chickens. She groomed her horse. She played with little Daniel, marveling in spite of herself at the way the child grew daily. She wandered around upstairs. Then she found herself sitting at the foot of the big sleigh bed.

His blanket lay on the floor next to the dresser. Kristin hesitated, staring at it for a long while. Then she got up and went over to it.

And then she unrolled it and went through his personal belongings.

There wasn't much. If he had a wallet, he had it with him. There was a shaving mug and a tin plate, a leather sack of tobacco, another sack of coffee and a roll of hard tack.

And there was a small silver Daguerreotype frame.

Kristin stared at it for a moment then found the little silver clasp and flicked it open.

There were two pictures in the double frame. The first was of a woman alone, a very beautiful woman, with enormous eyes and dark hair and a dazzling smile.

In the second picture the woman was with a man. Cole.

He was in a U.S. Cavalry uniform, so the picture must have been made before the war. The woman wore a beautiful, voluminous gown with majestic hoops, and a fine bonnet with a slew of feathers. They weren't looking at the camera. They were looking at one another.

There was such tenderness, such love in their eyes, that Kristin felt she was intruding on something sacred. She closed the frame with a firm snap and put it back inside the blanket, trying to put everything back together as if she hadn't touched it at all. It didn't make any difference, she told herself dully. He should expect people who didn't know a thing about him to check up on him. No, that didn't wash, not at all, not even with her.

The woman was dead, she thought.

She didn't know how she knew, but she knew. Cole Slater had loved her, and Kristin was certain that he wouldn't be here with her now if the woman in the picture were still alive.

There seemed to be an ominous silence all over the house as dinnertime approached. Delilah had been out to feed the hands, and the table was set for the family.

Set for three.

They weren't using the fine service that evening. Shannon had set out the pewter plates, and the atmosphere in the dining room seemed as muted and subdued as the dull color of the dishes.

Cole had stayed out all day. Kristin had done her best to be useful, but the day had been a waste. There was no way out of it. She couldn't forget Cole's promise that he would be there that night, and she couldn't forget the woman in the picture, and she couldn't forget the startling array of emotions that it had all raised within her.

Kristin had dressed for dinner.

She was a rancher, and this ranch on the border between Kansas and Missouri was a far cry from the fine parlors and plantations back east, but she was still a woman and she loved clothes.

It was a weakness with her, Pa had told her once, but he'd had a twinkle in his eyes when he'd said it. He'd always been determined that his daughters should be ladies. Capable women, but ladies for all that. He had always been pleased to indulge her whims, letting her study fabrics, and to pick up her *Lady Godoy's* the minute the fashion magazine reached the local mercantile. Her armoire was still filled with gowns, and her trunks and dressers held an endless assortment of petticoats and hoops, chemises and corsets, stockings and pantalets. They had all lent a certain grace to life once upon a time. Before the carnage had begun. By day they had worked for their dream, and the dust and the tumbleweed of the prairie had settled on them. At night they had washed away the dust and the dirt, and after dinner Pa had settled back in his chair with a cigar and she and Shannon had taken turns at the spinet. Her own voice was passable. Shannon's was like that of a nightingale.

And there had been nights when Adam had been there, too. Sometimes winter had raged beyond the windows, but they had been warm inside, warmed by the fire and by the love and laughter that had surrounded them.

That was what Zeke had hated so much, she thought. He had never understood that laughter and love could not be bought or stolen. He had called her a traitor to the Southern cause, but she had never betrayed the South. She had merely learned to despise him, and so she had lost her father, and then Adam, too.

Today she could remember Adam all too clearly. He had loved books. He had always looked so handsome, leaning against the fireplace, his features animated as he spoke about the works of Hawthorne and Sir Walter Scott.

No one had told her that Adam was riding out after Zeke. She'd never had the chance to try to stop him.

And now she wondered painfully if she had ever really loved him. Oh, she had cared for him dearly. He had been a fine man, good and decent and caring, and he had often made her laugh.

But she had never, never thought of Adam in the way that she had Cole Slater, had never even imagined doing with Adam the things she had actually done with Cole Slater.

And she didn't love Cole Slater. She couldn't love him. No, she couldn't love him, not even now. How could a woman love a man who had treated her the way he had?

But how could she forget him? How could she forget all she had felt since she'd first seen the man? How could she forget all that had passed between them? Kristin realized that it was difficult just to be in the same room with him now. Her breath shortened instantly, and she couldn't keep her gaze steady, and she wanted to run away every time he looked her way. She couldn't look at him without remembering their night together, and when she did she wanted to crawl into a hole in the ground and hide. She was ashamed, not so much because of what she had done but because she had been so fascinated by it. Because she still felt the little trickles of excitement stir within her whenever he entered the room, whenever she felt his presence.

She knew instinctively when he came into the house for dinner.

Fall was coming on, and the evening was cool. She had dressed in a soft white velvet gown with black cord trim. The bodice was low, and the half sleeves were trimmed in black cord, too. The skirt was sweeping, and she had chosen to wear a hoop and three petticoats.

She'd made Delilah tie her corset so tightly that she wasn't sure she'd be able to breathe all evening.

Her appearance had suddenly become very, very important to her. He hadn't been cruel to her, but he had been mocking, and he'd warned her again and again that this terribly intimate thing between them had nothing to do with involvement. Her pride was badly bruised, and all she had to cling to was her dream of leaving him panting in the dust. Someday. When she didn't need him anymore.

She'd braided her hair and curled it high atop her head, except for one long lock that swept around the column of her neck and the curve of her shoulder to rest on the mound of her cleavage.

She never used rouge—Pa hadn't allowed it in the house—but she pinched her cheeks and bit her lips, to bring some color to her features. Still, when she gazed at her reflection in the mirror over the dresser—she had refused to dress in the other room—she was terribly pale, and she looked more like a nervous girl than a sophisticated woman in charge of her life, owner of her property, mistress of her own destiny.

She tried to sweep elegantly down the stairs, but her knees were weak, so she gave up and came down as quickly as she could. Shannon was setting cups on the table. She stared at Kristin with wide blue eyes, but she didn't say anything. Nor did Kristin have to question her about Cole.

"He's in Pa's office," Shannon mouthed. Kristin nodded. Nervously, she started through the house. She passed through the parlor and came around, pausing in the doorway.

He was sitting at her father's desk, reading the newspaper, and his brows were drawn into such a dark and brooding frown that she nearly turned away. Then he looked up. She was certain that he started for a moment, but he hid it quickly and stood politely. His gaze never left her.

"Bad news?" she asked him, looking at the paper.

He shrugged. "Not much of anything today," he said.

"No great Southern victory? No wonderful Union rout?"

"You sound bitter."

"I am."

"You got kin in the army?"

"My brother."

"North or South?"

"North. He's with an Illinois troop." Kristin hesitated. She didn't want him to feel that they were traitors to the Southern cause. "Matthew was here when Pa was killed. He learned a whole lot about hatred."

"I understand."

She nodded. Then curiously she asked him. "And have you got kin in the army, Mr. Slater?"

"Yes."

"North or South?"

He hesitated. "Both."

"You were in the Union Army."

"Yes." Again he paused. Then he spoke softly. "Yes. And every time I see a list of the dead—either side—it hurts like hell. You've seen the worst of it, Kristin. There are men on both sides of this thing who are fine and gallant, the very best we've ever bred, no matter what state they've hailed from."

It was a curious moment. Kristin felt warm, almost felt cherished. She sensed depths to him that went very far beyond her understanding, and she was glad that he was here for her.

However briefly.

But then he turned, and she saw his profile. She saw its strengths, and she saw the marks that time had left upon it, and she remembered the woman in the picture, and that he didn't really love her at all. And she felt awkward, her nerves on edge again.

"Supper's about on the table," she said.

He nodded.

"Can I...can I get you a drink? Or something?"

Or something. She saw the slow smile seep into his lips at her words, and she blushed, feeling like a fool despite herself. He nodded again.

"Madeira?"

"A shot of whiskey would be fine."

Kristin nodded, wondering what had prompted her to say such a thing. He was closer to the whiskey than she was, and he knew it, but he didn't make a move to get it. He kept staring at her, his smile mocking again.

She swept into the room and took the whiskey from the drawer. They were very close to one another. He hadn't changed. He was still wearing tight breeches and a cotton shirt and his riding boots. She knew he had ridden out to meet with Pete, and she knew, too, that he seemed to know something about ranching. Well, he was from somewhere around here, according to Shannon.

She poured him out a double shot of the amber liquid, feeling him watching her every second. She started to hand him the glass, but he didn't seem to notice. His eyes were on hers, grown dark, like the sky before a tornado.

He reached out and touched the golden lock of hair that curled over the rise of her breasts. He curled it around his finger, his thumb grazing her bare flesh. She couldn't move. A soft sound came from her throat, and suddenly it was as if all the fires of hell had risen up to sweep through her, robbing her of all strength. She stared up at him, but his eyes were on her hair, and on her flesh where he touched her. She felt heat radiating from the length and breadth of his body, and yet she shivered, remembering the strength of his shoulders, the hardness of his belly, the power of his thighs.

And she remembered the speed of his draw. He was a gunslinger, she thought, bred to violence.

No. He had been to West Point. He had served as a captain in the U.S. cavalry. That was what he had told Shannon, at least.

Did any of it matter? He was here, and as long as he was here she felt safe from the Zeke Moreaus of the world. And yet, she thought, their's must surely be a bargain made in hell, for when he looked at her, when he touched her even as lightly as he did now, she felt the slow fires of sure damnation seize her.

"Do you always dress so for dinner?" he asked her, and the timbre of his voice sent new shivers skating down her spine.

"Always," she managed to murmur.

His knuckles hovered over her breasts. Then his eyes met hers, and he slowly relinquished the golden curl he held. Expectation swirled around them, and Kristin was afraid that her knees would give, that she would fall against him. The whiskey in the glass she held threatened to spill over. He took the glass from her and set it on the desk. She felt heat where his fingers had brushed hers, and it seemed that the air, the very space between them, hummed with a palpable tension.

"You are a very beautiful woman, Miss McCahy," he told her softly, and she felt his male voice, male and sensual, wash over her.

"Then, you're not...you're not too disappointed in our deal?"

He smiled again, and his silver-gray eyes brightened wickedly. "Did we need a deal?"

"I don't know what you mean," she told him, though she knew exactly what he meant.

The light went out of his eyes. He picked up the whiskey and swallowed it quickly. "I'm still damned if I know what the hell I'm doing here," he muttered.

"I thought—" she began, and her face flamed.

He touched her cheek. "You thought the payoff went well, is that it?"

She shoved his hand away. She didn't want him to touch her, not then. "You do have a talent for making a woman feel just like river slime," she said, as sweetly as she could. He arched a brow, and she saw fleeting amusement light his features. She could hold her own in any fight, she thought, but only for so long. She needed to escape him now.

"I didn't mean to make you feel like...river slime."

"Don't worry. You already did so. Last night." With a sweetly mocking smile, Kristin turned to leave.

Then she paused and turned toward him again, biting her lip. She kept forgetting how much she needed him. Her eyes must have widened with the realization, for he was smiling cynically again and pouring himself another shot of whiskey.

"Don't worry," he told her smoothly. "I'm not walking out on you. Not yet."

Kristin moistened her lips. "Not yet?" she whispered.

"Why, Miss McCahy! I really couldn't leave a lady in such distress, could I?"

"What do you mean by that?"

He raised the glass. "Take it as you will, ma'am."

Kristin swore under her breath and strode over to him again. She snatched the glass from his hand and thought seriously of pouring the contents over his head. His eyes narrowed, and she quickly reconsidered.

She swallowed the whiskey down so quickly that her head spun in an instant and her throat burned with the fury of a brush fire. A double shot, straight. But she steeled herself, and she still managed to smile sweetly. "You don't owe me anything."

"No, darlin'. You owe me." He smiled, took the glass from her and poured another double. "And I'm real anxious for the next installment."

Kristin snatched the glass again and swallowed the liquid down. She didn't know if she was alive with anger or with desire.

She slammed the glass down and tried to spin around. He caught her arm, pulling her back. She tossed her head back, staring into his eyes.

"Isn't it what you want?" he asked her.

"I want revenge, nothing more," she told him.

"Nothing more?"

"I want you to—I want you to stay. I want to hold on to the ranch. I just want to hold on to what is mine."

"The precious ranch," he muttered darkly.

Fear fluttered briefly in her heart. "Cole...Mr. Slater, you really wouldn't...you wouldn't go back on your word, would you?"

"Not so long as you follow the rules."

Her head was really spinning now. He had poured so much whiskey, and she'd swallowed it down so fast. He was so warm, and so damn vibrant, and so shockingly male. And she'd already been in bed with him.

Her mother would be spinning in her grave, Kristin thought.

He was using her. He was using her because he had loved another woman and now he just didn't give a damn.

"Your rules! Just don't forget that the place belongs to me!"

She wrenched free of him, and this time she walked out. She wasn't afraid of him leaving. He was having too fine a time torturing her to leave now.

When she reached the dining room, she was startled to discover that he was behind her. He had followed her, as silent as a wraith. It was disconcerting.

"Stop it!" she demanded.

Shannon came out of the kitchen. Delilah was behind her. Both women stopped, startled.

Cole ignored them both. "Stop what?" he demanded irritably.

"Sneaking up on me!"

"I wasn't sneaking up on you. You told me it was time for supper, so I followed you."

"Whoa!" Shannon murmured, looking at her sister. "Kristin, you've been drinking!"

"Yes!" she snapped, glaring at Cole. "And I'll probably do a whole lot more drinking before...before..."

"Oh, hell, will you just sit the hell down!" Cole growled. He caught her hand, pulled out a chair and directed her into it with little grace. Her wide skirts flew. He pressed them down and shoved her chair in.

Kristin wanted to be dignified. She wanted to be sophisticated and elegant, and most of all she wanted to be in control. "You arrogant scallywag!" she said quietly, her voice husky with emotion.

"Kristin, shut up."

That was it. She started to push herself away from the table, but his hand slammed down on hers, holding her fast. "Kristin, shut up."

"Bas—"

"Now, Kristin." He came closer to her, much closer, and spoke in a whisper. This was between the two of them. "Or else we can get up and settle this outside."

The whiskey seemed to hit her anew right then, hit her hard. She thought she was going to scream. She burst into laughter instead. "Outside? With pistols?"

"Hardly, but you can call it what you want, darlin'."

The buzz of the liquor was nice. If he stayed around too long, Kristin thought, she'd find herself turning into a regular old drunk.

"Shall we eat?" Cole asked politely.

There was silence in the room. Shannon was staring at him.

"Sit!" he told her.

Shannon sat hastily, then lowered her head before looking surreptitiously over at Kristin, who hiccuped loudly.

Cole groaned, then he looked up at Delilah. "Don't you and Samson usually eat?"

"Oh, no, sir!" Delilah protested. "Why, you know it just wouldn't be right for black folks—"

"Delilah, cut the...er—" He broke off, looking from Samson to Kristin. Shannon was about to laugh.

"Manure," Kristin supplied.

Shannon did burst into laughter. Even Delilah grinned. Cole said, "Get your husband, woman, and sit down and eat. I once had the opportunity to discover that a black man could save my hide as good as a white one. Let's just have supper and get it over with, shall we?"

"Yessir, yessir," Delilah said, chuckling. "My, my, my," she muttered, moving off toward the kitchen.

Kristin sat primly, her hands folded in her lap. Her dress felt ridiculously heavy, now that she was sitting. She felt as if she was about to fall over. She realized that Cole was looking at her, but it didn't matter very much, and that was a nice feeling.

Delilah walked back in from the kitchen.

Cole gazed at her expectantly. "You've never washed her mouth out with soap, huh?" He indicated Kristin.

Kristin decided that she could sit straight. She told Cole that he reminded her of the stuff that people needed to wipe off their boots before they came in from the barn.

Shannon gasped, and then she began to giggle. Delilah stood stock-still. Samson, coming in behind his wife, turned an ashen color.

Cole was dead still. Explosively still. And then explosively in motion.

He was up, and Kristin sobered enough to know a moment's panic as he came around behind her and purposely pulled her chair away from the table. He lifted her, and her petticoats and hoops and shirt went flying. Kristin swore at him and pounded on his back.

"Cole!" Kristin gasped.

What manner of man had she let loose in her home, she wondered.

He started for the stairs.

"What are you doing?" she shrieked.

"Putting you to bed."

"I don't want to go!"

"My rules, Miss McCahy."

They were all watching her, Shannon and Delilah and Samson, and they weren't doing a thing to save her. They were just staring. She raised her head and saw that Delilah was openly grinning and Samson was hiding a smile.

"You son of a bitch!" she yelled.

"We are going to have to do something about that mouth of yours," Cole vowed grimly.

"This is my house!"

"My rules!"

She told him what he could do with his rules, but it was too late. They were already up the stairs. He booted open the door to the room he had decreed they would share, and before she knew it she had landed on the bed. She wanted to get back up, but she groaned instead and clutched her temples.

His leering face was above her.

"Why, what's the matter, Miss McCahy? Why, I would have thought you could drink any man west of the Mississippi under the table."

"Madeira," she whispered. "Not whiskey."

He showed her no mercy. Suddenly his hand was on her leg and he was pulling off her shoe. She managed to pull herself up to a sitting position and pummel his back. "What are you doing?"

"Taking your shoes off." But her shoes were off, and his hands were still on her, slipping along her calf, then her thigh. When his fingers touched her thigh, she gasped and tried to stop him. "Damn you Cole Slater—"

Her words ended in a gasp, for he turned quickly, pulling hard on her ankle so that she was lying flat on her back again. Her silk stockings came free in his hands, and he tossed them carelessly on the floor. She tried to rise, and he came down beside her on the bed, his weight on her.

"Where the hell are the damn ties to these things?" he muttered, working on her hoop.

Kristin struggled to stop him, but he found the ties. She reached for his hands, but they had already moved, freeing her from her hoop and petticoats, and he pulled her up, working on the hooks of her gown. In seconds he had it free and she was down to her pantalets, chemise and corset.

"Come here!" he demanded roughly. Kristin cried out, trying to elude him, but he pulled her back by the corset ties. He lossened the ties, and she gasped, amazed by the air that rushed into her lungs. But then she was naked except for her sheer chemise and pantalets, and his presence was overwhelming.

She began to protest. He caught her shoulders and slammed her down on the bed.

"Calm down and sleep it off!" he commanded.

He was straddling her, and his eyes were like steel. She wanted to slap his superior face. She tried. She missed by a mile, and he caught her hand.

"My rules."

She told him again what he could do with his rules.

"Stay here alone, or I'll stay here with you."

She went still, trying to grasp the meaning of his words. The room was spinning madly.

Then she understood. He stared at her. Then he lowered his head toward her and kissed her, and somewhere, within her hazy mind and her bruised heart she knew that he did desire her. And she knew, too, that he didn't love her, not at all.

His kiss was hard and demanding and, in its way, punishing. But then it deepened, and it was rich, and it betrayed a growing passion and hunger. She felt her body respond. She felt his hands move over her, felt him grow warm and hard. She began to tremble and suddenly she wanted him, but she wanted him loving her, loving her tenderly, not just wanting her with the raw desire that had finally brought him to her.

His mouth opened and closed hungrily upon her flesh. His teeth grazed her throat, and the tip of his tongue teased the valley between her breasts. He was a flame setting on her, seeping into her, and she was stunned that he could so easily elicit this willingness...

This eagerness...

Within her. She stiffened, fighting the whiskey haze in her heart and in her mind. She had to stop him. He hadn't meant to do this, not now. He had stayed away from her on purpose, she was certain of it. He wanted no involvements.

And she could too easily fall in love with him.

She forced herself to feel nothing, to allow the bitterness of the last years to invade her, so that his searing warmth could not touch her. When he rose above her, she met his steely gaze and spoke to him in a quiet, toneless voice.

"Who was she? Your wife?"

She might have struck him. All the heat left him. It was as if he turned to ice. He stared at her, his jaw constricted, his features as harsh as a desert. He rolled away from her and sat on the side of the bed. His fingers threaded through his hair, and he pressed his hand against his temple as if he were trying to soothe some awful pain.

"Go to sleep," he told her. "And stay off the hard stuff from now on."

Kristin cast her arm over her eyes. "Your rules," she murmured.

"I don't like this kind of a fight, Kristin," he said dully, "but..."

"But?"

"You start it, and I'll end it. Every time."

She felt his weight lift from the bed, and she started to shiver.

Suddenly she was warmed. He had laid a blanket over her, and he was close by her again.

"Go to sleep," he said softly, his voice almost tender again.

Almost.

He got up and walked away. She heard the door close quietly, and to her great dismay she closed her eyes and started to cry as she hadn't done since they had come to tell her that Adam was dead.

Chapter Six

It was the liquor, Kristin thought. Lying in the darkness, feeling miserable, she put her arm over her eyes and felt her head spin, and she wondered what had made her drink so much so fast. She was humiliated, but it was her own fault, and she was in no mood to do anything about it, except to suffer in silence.

And, in a way, she wasn't sorry. She could dimly hear the sounds of dinner, and she wondered if Samson and Delilah had sat down to eat. Cole Slater was an unusual man. A very unusual man.

The darkness closed in and whirled around her. She knew she ought to be sorry she had let the liquor ignite her temper, but instead she was glad of it. She didn't feel the awful pain for once. She didn't remember what it had been like to see Pa die, to see Matthew turn his back on his own people and ride away with the Union forces.

She didn't even quite remember what it was like to be with Cole Slater. To be so nervous that she lost all the wisdom her harsh life had taught her. To be afraid in a way, and yet to want something, some intangible thing, so badly.

Curiously—bless the liquor—she felt at peace.

She closed her eyes, and she must have dozed. Then she must have awakened, or else she was dreaming, because when she opened her eyes, the room was bathed in moonlight. Her mind was still spinning, and she still felt at peace.

He was in the room with her.

He had come in quietly, and the door had closed softly behind him. He stood just inside of it, his hands on his hips, and watched her where she lay upon the bed. The moonlight fell on his features, and they were both harsh and curiously beautiful. For the longest time he stood there. The wind seemed to rise, not to a moan, but to a whisper. She imagined that outside tumbleweeds were being caught and tossed in the strange, sweet dance of the West, buffeted as she was being buffeted. Her heart rose and fell like that tumbleweed, tossed around heedlessly.

No...

He was a marvelous creature, sleek as a cougar, sharp as an eagle. He was still standing there, his hands on his hips, his head at an angle, as if he were waiting, as if he were listening to the curiously tender whispering of the wind.

Then he moved. He unbuttoned his cuffs. He took off his boots and stripped off his socks. He came to her in silence, barefoot, and he dropped his gun belt beside the bed. Then he looked down at her, and saw that her eyes were open. "You're still awake."

She nodded gravely, and then she smiled. "I'm sorry. I was out of line this evening. And I...I don't want to fight."

Unbuttoning his shirt, he sat beside her on the bed. His eyes remained on hers. He reached over and touched her cheek. "I don't want to fight, either, Kristin. You've had a hard time of it, and you've done well. Someone else might have shattered a long, long time ago."

The gentle whisper of the wind was in his voice, and there was an evocative tenderness in his fingertips as they brushed her cheek. She didn't reply, but kept her eyes on his, and then the whisper of the wind seemed to sweep into her, to permeate her flesh and fill her veins. She was warm, and achingly aware of herself, and of the man. Surely, she was still asleep. Surely it was all a dream. It was a spell cast by the moonlight. It lived in the clouds of imagination.

But it was real. Very real. He leaned over then and caught her lips in a curious kiss. It was light at first. He tasted her lips, teasing them with the tip of his tongue. Then he plunged his tongue deep into her mouth, and she wrapped her arms around his neck and felt the rugged, steel-muscled frame of his chest against her. She felt his hands on her, rough and tender. Then his hands were in her hair, threading through the tendrils, and he was stroking her arm as he moved his lips over her throat and down to the place where her breasts spilled provocatively from her lace chemise. His mouth fastened over her nipple through the sheer fabric, and she cried out softly. He shifted swiftly, taking her mouth again, taking her cry into him.

He stood, dropping his shirt and stripping away his pants. The moonlight fell on him. He was tall and rugged, lean and sinewed, his skin shining almost copper in that light, his shoulders shimmering with it. She stared at him. If this was a dream, she was grateful for it. She wanted him. She wanted him with her heart and with her mind, she wanted him with every fiber of her being. She wanted him desperately.

She was not to be denied.

He came down beside her and took her in his arms, and she strained to meet his kiss again. He unlaced her chemise, and her breast spilled from it. He lowered his head again, touching her nipple with his tongue, fondling the weight of her breast with a touch so achingly soft.... She was barely aware that she arched to him, that she dug her fingers into his hair and cried incoherently for him to come to her. But it was not to be. His hands brushed her flesh, and where they had been she yearned for them again. His kisses ranged over the length of her, a mere breath, a mere whisper, and then were gone. She writhed. She tried to hold him, to pin him down. And she felt something move in her, like lava rising to the surface of the earth. She felt the earth teeming and bubbling with heat and steam, and still he pressed her. She moved her hands against him, felt the tension in his taut muscles, and touching him inflamed her, bringing her to still greater heights. She no longer knew herself. She had become some strange wanton. She felt his hands on her hips, and on her belly and she moved toward the feel of them, the promise of them. He made her touch him, and the pulsing heat and size of him gave her pause. Then a curious elation filled her, and for a moment she was afraid she might faint.

Her remaining clothes were gone now. Like him, she lay naked in the moonlight, her skin shimmering like copper beneath its glow.

Time had lost all meaning. She lay upon clouds of moonlight, and all that was real was the hardness of this man, the demand in his eyes. The wind had become the ragged cry of his breath, and the storm was the near-savage urgency that drove him. He did not tease. He sucked hard on her breast until she thought she would explode. He did not shyly caress her thighs, but stroked within, to the heart of her, and as he touched her, he caught her cries again with his lips. He knelt before her, caught her eyes again, then watched her, before he caught the supple length of her legs and brought them around him. He stared at her as he lowered his head, and she opened her mouth to stop him, but she could not.

He touched her intimately, with a searing demand, and she tossed her head, savagely biting her own lip so as not to scream. She could not bear it, and despite her efforts she did cry out. She lunged forward, she convulsed and she heard the soft tenor of his laughter. She longed to strike him, to hide from him. But he was above her, and he had her hands, and suddenly he was within her, igniting a fierce burning, and it was all happening again, all beginning again. His hands roughly cupped her buttocks, and again he led her into a shattering rhythm.

The clouds danced around them. She closed her eyes and buried her face against his chest, and she tasted the salt on his body. There was nothing gentle in him then. He moved in a frenzy, violent, urgent, and though she feared she would lose herself in him, she clung to him and fought to meet his every move. Ecstasy burst through again, even stronger than before, and she dug her fingers into his flesh, convulsing against him. He shuddered strongly against her, and she was filled with their mutual heat. Then he fell from her, smoothing the wild tangle of her hair.

They didn't say anything. Not anything at all.

The wind had died down again. It was a mere whisper. It caught the tumbleweeds down below and tossed them around.

Her heart was still beating savagely,. He must have felt it when he put his arm around her and pulled her against him. It was a wonderful way to sleep, her back to his chest, his fingers just below the full curve of her breast. She didn't think about the wind, or the night. The moonlight was still shining down on them. Perhaps it had all been a dream. She didn't want to know. She closed her eyes, and at long last the spinning in her head stopped. She slept.

* * *

He slept, too, and it was his turn to dream. The nightmare of the past, the nightmare that haunted him whether he was awake or asleep, came back to him now.

The dream unfolded slowly, so slowly. It always came to him first with sound...a soft, continual thunder, like the beating of drums. It was the sound of hooves driving across the earth, driving hard. Then he heard the shouts. They made no sense at first, they meant nothing, nothing at all. Then he realized that the hooves were churning beneath him. He was the rider. He was riding hard, riding desperately, and all he wanted to do was get home before...

Smoke. He inhaled sharply and it filled his nostrils and mouth with an acrid taste. There was something about that smell... He could feel a trail of ice streak along his spine. He recognized the awful odor of burning flesh.

Then he saw the horror up ahead. The house was burning; the barn was burning.

And he saw Elizabeth.

She was running, trying to reach him. He screamed her name, his voice ragged and harsh, and still he felt the movement beneath him, the endless thunder of the horse's hooves. He rode across the plain, across the scrub brush. And she kept coming. She was calling to him, but the sound of her voice could not reach him. She could not reach him.

She fell and disappeared from sight. He rode harder, and then he leaped from the horse, still shouting her name, over and over. He searched through the grass until he found her. Her hair, long and lustrous and ebony black, was spread over the earth in soft, silken waves.

''Elizabeth...''

He took her into his arms, and he looked down, and all that he saw was red. Red, spilling over him, filling his hands. Red, flowing in rivers, red...the color of blood.

He cast back his head, and he screamed, and the scream echoed and echoed across the plain....

He awoke with a start.

He was covered in sweat, and he was trembling. He shook his

head, trying to clear it, and gazed at the woman beside him. He saw her golden hair, and the easy rise and fall of her chest with her breath.

She hadn't awakened.

He rose and went to the window, where he stared out at the moon. He hadn't woken her; it was going to be all right. Maybe he was getting better; at least he wasn't screaming out loud anymore.

He walked over to the bed and stared down at her; and she seemed incredibly young and pure, and very lovely. His fingers itched, and he wanted to shake her, to tell her that she didn't understand how deadly the game she was playing could be.

His fingers eased. Maybe she knew.

He went back to the window and stared at the moon again. Slowly, the tension left him, and he sighed. He went back to bed, but he couldn't bear to touch her, even though he knew that someday soon he would. He needed to touch her, just as he needed air to breathe.

He didn't sleep. In time, dawn came. He rose and dressed, then went outside. He gazed out over the plain, and in his mind he saw Elizabeth again, running toward him. He closed his eyes, and she was gone, but the pain was still with him, filling him, gnawing at his insides. He straightened his shoulders, and the pain slowly began to ebb, but it never fully left him. It clutched his heart with icy fingers, and he wondered what the hell he was doing here, then reminded himself that he had agreed to a "deal," and he might as well get on with it. He turned around and stared at her window. She was sleeping just beyond it. He marched back to the house.

She'd never expected to be awakened so rudely. One second she was so deep in blissful sleep, and the next she felt his hand against her rump. Her *bare* rump. He'd pulled the covers away from her.

Protesting, she grabbed the covers and sat with them pulled up to her chin, her eyes blazing with fury and indignation. He was up and dressed, standing at the foot of the bed and surveying her with cold eyes.

"I want you in the office. Now. If you want my help, you'd better show me the books."

"I'll come down to the office when I'm ready," she snapped. She couldn't understand the man. She couldn't understand his strange, distant behavior after the things they had shared in the night. It hurt.

"Get up."

She narrowed her eyes at this new battle.

"You get out and then I'll get up. When I'm ready."

He grabbed the sheets again. She lunged for them but she was too late, and he stripped them away. He eyed her dispassionately, his steely gaze sweeping over her form. She jumped out of bed, swearing once again, and leaped toward him, her temper soaring. He caught her arms, and his smile was curiously grim and somehow self-satisfied. It was as if he had been trying to pick a fight. She tried to wrench free of his touch. She didn't like the daylight on her naked flesh, and she didn't like the disadvantage of being undressed while he was clad from his scarf to his boots. He pulled her close against him. She felt the bite of his belt buckle and the texture of his shirt, but most of all she felt a hot tempest of emotions within him, no matter how calm, cold and in control he looked.

"I told you," he said sharply, "I call the shots. And you can't laze in bed all morning. You're a rancher. You should know that. Or do you just play at this thing? When you feel like riding with the boys, you do. And when you feel like playing the Southern belle, then you do that, too."

She was furious, but she smiled to hide it. Tense and still against him and staring up into his eyes, she smiled. "I don't play at anything, Mr. Slater. I am a rancher, and probably better at it than you ever were or could be. I just don't have to be as ugly as a mule's rump to do it. You call the shots? Well, that's just fine. When you want me up from now on, you knock. One knock, Mr. Slater, and I promise I'll be right out in less than five minutes. But don't you ever, ever touch me like that again!"

His brow arched slowly, and she saw his smile deepen. He released her and put his hands on his hips. She felt his gaze sweep over her again like fire. For a moment she thought he was going to sweep her up in his arms, right there, right then, in broad daylight. For a moment she was certain he was going to carry her over to the bed and take her there and then, with the morning sun shining on them.

She'd have to protest, she'd have to scream....

For the life of her she didn't know if she was afraid or if she wished he'd take a step forward and sweep her up in his arms....

He tipped his hat to her.

"I call all the shots, Kristin. All of them."

He turned around then and left her. The door closed sharply behind him.

She washed and dressed, wondering again what kind of a monster she had brought into her home. She touched her cheeks, and it was as if they were on fire.

When she came down the stairs, he was just finishing his breakfast. He tossed his checkered napkin on the table and rose at the sight of her. Kristin went to her chair.

"Flapjacks, honey?" Delilah asked her.

Cole was around the table before she had a chance to sit. He took her arm.

"Give her a cup of coffee, Delilah. Nothing else for the moment. We've got work to do."

She could make a scene, as she had at dinner. Delilah was staring at her, and Samson was staring at her, and so was Shannon. Her sister's eyes were very wide. They were all waiting.

Bastard! she thought. He was at fault! But she had been at fault the night before, and she knew she would look like a spoiled fool again if she created a problem.

"That's right. This is a busy, busy day, isn't it?" she said sweetly. "Coffee, Delilah." She accepted a cup and smiled her gratitude, gritting her teeth. She freed her arm from Cole's grasp. "Do come, Mr. Slater. The day is wearing on."

He followed her into the office, then swept past her, taking a seat behind her father's desk. He'd already been in there that morning, she was certain. He had the ledgers out, and before she could even seat herself he was firing out a barrage of questions. Where did she buy her feed, how much, how often? Had she considered moving any of the herd to avoid soldiers, Union and Confederate? Had she thought of leaving more pasture time, had she thought of introducing new strains? And on and on.

She didn't falter once. She was a rancher. She was bright, determined and well schooled, and she wanted him to know it. It occurred to her that he was just some drifter, that he had no rights here at all. But then she remembered that she had asked him to stay, that she had been desperate for him to stay.

That she had been willing to do anything at all to make him stay. And he had stayed, and she wasn't the same person anymore, not in any way. But whoever she was now, he wasn't going to treat her this way.

Suddenly he slammed the ledger he was examining shut and stood up. He stared across the desk at her, and for a moment she thought he must hate her.

He had saved her from Zeke, she reminded herself. He had ridden in, all honor and chivalry, and he had saved her from Zeke. Now he looked as if he wanted to flay her alive himself.

He looked as if he were about to say something. He shook his head impatiently. "I'm going out," he said. He jammed his hat low on his head, and came around the desk.

Kristin rose quickly and, she hoped, with dignity. "If you'd let me come with you—"

"No. I don't want you with me."

"I could show you—"

"God damn you, can't you hear? Or are you just incapable of listening? I'll see things myself. I'll see what I want to see. And you'll stay here by the house. Roam too far and come across Zeke and you'll wind up on your own this time. I swear it."

It might be better! she longed to shout. But she didn't do it, because it wasn't true. Zeke had killed her father. No matter how outrageously bad Cole's manners were turning out to be, he didn't compare with Zeke.

She crossed her arms over her chest and leaned back. "Don't let me keep you," she said sarcastically.

He walked past her.

She didn't know where he went. She was pretty sure he was never far away, but he didn't come by the house.

He had left a newspaper on the table, and she sat down and stared at the articles. War. It was all about war. About the Union troops holding Kansas, about the measures they intended to take against Quantrill and his raiders.

War and more war. The Union held New Orleans, and Grant was swearing he'd have Vicksburg soon. But whether the Union held sway or not, there was something that couldn't be changed. In the East, Lee was leading them all a merry chase. He had fewer men, he had less ammunition, he had less food. But he was brilliant, and not even the fact that the paper had been published in a town filled with Yankees could change the tenor of the articles. The South was strong. They could beat her and beat her, but she had the genius of Lee and Stonewall Jackson, and she had the daring of Jeb Stuart and Morgan Hunt and others like them.

Kristin laid her face against the cool wood of her father's desk. The news didn't make her happy or proud. It filled her heart with dread. It meant the war was going to go on and on. Nobody was going to go out and whomp the pants off anybody else. It was just going to keep going.

And Quantrill's outlaws would keep raiding and raiding....

After a while, Kristin lifted her head. There was a knock at the door. Delilah was there. She stuck her head in hesitantly.

"How about something to eat? Flapjacks and bacon?"

Her stomach was rumbling. She was starving. She hadn't had any supper, and she hadn't had any breakfast. She stood up and slid her hands into her back pockets.

"Flapjacks sound great."

"Fine. Come along."

"Delilah, wait."

Delilah hesitated there in the doorway. She met Kristin's eyes.

"Delilah, am I doing the right thing?"

"Honey, you're doing the only thing."

Kristin shook her head. "He made a fool out of me last night, Delilah."

"You let that happen."

"Yes, I did. But—"

"We need him," Delilah said bluntly. Then she smiled and gazed at Kristin, and Kristin was sure she was blushing beneath the gold and mahogany of her coloring. "We need him, and I like him. I like him just fine. You did well."

Kristin blushed herself. "I didn't marry him, Delilah. I'm...I'm his...mistress, Delilah."

"You did well," Delilah repeated. "I like him. I don't care what he seems to be, he's a right honorable fellow." She was silent for a moment. "You come along now and have something to eat."

Kristin did.

Then she set to the housework with a vengeance, cleaning and sweeping. Later she went out to the barn and spent some time grooming the horses that weren't out with the hands. She came back in and bathed, and while she sat in the tub she decided that although her feelings about him were entirely different from her feelings about Zeke, she still hated Cole Slater. She couldn't even take a bath in peace anymore. She kept thinking about him the entire time. She wanted to be clean, and she wanted to smell sweet, because she could just imagine him...

She promised herself she would be cool and aloof and dignified through dinner and all through the evening.

She promised herself she would be cool and aloof and wouldn't allow him to touch her.

But he didn't come back for dinner. He didn't come back at all. At midnight she gave up and went upstairs. She managed to stay awake for an hour, but then she fell asleep. She had taken care to dress in a high-necked nightgown, one with a multitude of delicate little buttons at the throat.

Cole stayed out for a long time that night, waiting for her to fall asleep. He smoked a cigar and sipped a brandy and wondered where Quantrill's boys might be.

Quantrill was no bargain, Cole thought, but he wasn't the worst of the lot. He rode with some frightening company. Bill Anderson was a blood-thirsty soul. Zeke was a horror. Cole had heard that some of the men liked to fight the way the Indians did, taking scalps from their victims.

Quantrill for the South...

And the likes of Lane and Jennison for the North. Killing anyone and anything that stood in their way. Making a jest out of a war that was being fought desperately on both sides for different sets of ideals.

Smoke rose high above him, and he shivered suddenly. He hadn't been able to get Elizabeth's face out of his mind all day. But now, curiously, when he closed his eyes, he saw Kristin. Saw her fighting for all she was worth. Saw her fallen in the dirt.

He stood up and dusted off his hands on his pants.

Kristin was alive, and Elizabeth wasn't. Elizabeth had died because of Doc Jennison and his jayhawkers; Kristin had been attacked by the bushwhackers.

He was angry with her for being alive, he realized. She was alive and Elizabeth wasn't. And he knew he couldn't explain that to her.

He threw his cigar down in the dirt and snuffed it out with the heel of his boot. Then he turned around. He couldn't back down on any of the demands he had made of her. Not ever. It was just part of his nature, he supposed. And it was important that Quantrill know that he was living with her—intimately.

He looked up at the house and swore, then entered it quietly. For a moment he paused in the darkness of the entry. It was a good house. It had been built sturdy and strong, and it had been made into a home. It had grace.

He paused and inhaled deeply. Then he started for the stairway and climbed the steps silently. He reached his room and opened the door, thinking that she must have returned to her own room.

She hadn't. She was curled up on the bed. Her hair spilled over on his pillow.

He cast aside his clothes impatiently and approached the bed, but before he could pull back the covers, his hand brushed a tendril of hair that lay on his pillow, and its soft scent rose up to greet him. Heat immediately snaked through him. He didn't want it this way. But all he had to do was touch her hair and see her innocent form and he was tied into harsh knots of desire.

He didn't have to give in to it, he reminded himself.

He stretched out and stared at the ceiling, drumming his fingers on his chest. She was sound asleep, and even if she were not she would surely not be particularly fond of him at the moment.

A minute later he was on his side, just watching her. He throbbed, he ached, his desire thundering, clamoring for release.

He touched her hair again and reminded himself that it should be black. He didn't love this girl.

He slipped his hand beneath her gown and slowly, lightly stroked her flesh, following the line of her calf, the length of her thigh, the curve of her hip. He rounded her buttocks with a feathery touch, then gently tugged her around and pressed his lips against hers.

She responded, warmly and sweetly and instinctively, to his touch. Her arms swept around him and her body pressed against his. Her lips parted and he plundered the honey-warm depths of her mouth with his tongue. His body pressed against hers intimately. He pulled her gown up farther and wedged his hips between her bare thighs. Her eyes remained closed. She was barely awake.

Then she awoke fully. Her eyes widened, and she pressed furiously against his shoulders. He thought he saw tears sting her eyes as she pronounced him a son of a bitch.

"I know," he told her.

"If you know—"

"I'm sorry."

He tried to kiss her again, but she twisted her head, and his lips fell against her throat.

"You behave like a tyrant."

"I know. I'm sorry."

"You treat people like servants—"

"I know. I'm sorry."

"You behave—"

Her mouth was open, and he caught her lower lip between his teeth and bathed it with his tongue. Then he began to move against her. He caught her cheeks between his palms and stroked her hair, and when she stared up at him again, gasping for breath, he kissed her again quickly, speaking against her lips.

"I am sorry. So damned sorry, for so damned much."

She was silent then, staring at him in the darkness. She was very still, very aware of his sex throbbing against her, so close. If she fought him he would leave.

She didn't fight him. She continued to stare at him, and he met her eyes. Then he moved, thrusting deep inside her. She let out a garbled little sound, and her arms came around him and she buried her face against the hard dampness of his shoulder. Her long limbs came around him, and he sank deeper into her and then deeper still.

She was instinctively sensual, and she offered him greater solace than he could ever have imagined. When it was over he lay with her hair tangling over his naked chest and reminded himself again that it was blond and not ebony black. They were strangers who had stumbled together. They had answered one another's needs, and that was all.

If he closed his eyes he would see her, Elizabeth, racing toward him. Running, running, running...

But it was not Elizabeth's face he saw in his dreams. Sweet blond hair flowed behind the woman who ran to him in his dreams. Kristin raced to him in the night, and he wanted to reach for her, but he was afraid to. He was afraid he might fail.

He was afraid he would take her in his arms and find her blood on his hands. He was afraid he would see Kristin's exquisite blue eyes on his and see her blood running red onto his hands.

Chapter Seven

When Kristin awoke, she could hear gunfire. Looking out the window, she saw that Samson and Delilah were practicing with Cole's six-shooters. She dressed quickly in a cotton shirt and pants and boots and hurried downstairs and out to the pasture. Delilah stumbled from the recoil every time she fired, but she had a set and determined expression on her face. Samson laughed at her, and she gave him a good hard shove. Cole actually grinned. Then he looked at Kristin and saw that she wasn't happy at all. Perched on a fence, he nodded to her and arched a brow, and she flushed. The nights they shared were real, she thought. But the nights were one thing, and the harsh light of day was another. She wasn't going to act like a child again, and she wasn't going to try to pretend that he hadn't touched her in a way she would never forget, that he hadn't awakened her to something incredible. What if it was wrong according to all moral and social standards? Murder was wrong, too. The world wasn't run according to moral standards anymore. She didn't mind getting close to Cole. He knew how to treat a woman, knew when to be tender, knew when to let the wild winds rage. Even now, as his eyes flickered over her, she felt the warmth of their intimacy, and it wasn't an unpleasant feeling, despite her current impatience. Cole just didn't seem to understand what he was doing to her. He didn't speak. He watched her. Waiting.

"Miz Kristin, I am going to get this down pat!" Delilah swore.

Kristin tried to smile. "Delilah, you can master anything you set your mind to. I've see you." She set her thumbs in the pockets of her pants and said to Cole, "May I speak with you a moment?"

"Speak," Cole said flatly. He had said he was sorry about lots of things, but his manner toward her didn't seem to be much better today than it had been before. And he didn't come down from the fence.

"Alone," she said.

He shrugged, and started to climb down.

"Don't you bother, Mr. Slater," Samson said behind her. Kristin whirled around in surprise. Samson looked at her, his expression almost sorrowful, and gave her a rueful grin. "Meaning no disrespect, Miz Kristin, and you know it. But you're gonna tell him that you don't want him teaching us any more about gunfire. 'Cause of us being free blacks. She thinks that if we don't shoot they'll just put us on a block and not think to shoot us or string us up. Delilah and me talked about it a long, long time. We're in this together. If there's more trouble, we got to stick together. Delilah's got to shoot just like everybody else. You see, Miz Kristin, I been a free man now a long time. And it's mighty sweet."

"Samson..." Kristin swallowed and closed her eyes. "Samson, if you're alive, you can get free again. If you're dead—"

"I believe in the good Lord, Miz Kristin. And one day there's going to be a meetin' 'cross that river. And I ain't going to that meetin' being no coward, or a man who didn't live up to what I believe in. We're in this together, Mis Kristin."

She stared furiously at Cole. He shrugged.

"You fool!" she snapped at him. "Samson is a black man."

"Samson is a man," he replied. "A free man. Your daddy made him so. The way I see it, he's made his choice."

They were all staring at her. No one said anything, and no one moved. The sun streamed down on them all. Cole kept watching her. She couldn't begin to read the emotions in his eyes. *I don't know this man, I don't know him at all,* she thought in sudden panic. But did it matter? she asked herself. It couldn't matter. The die had been cast.

"I've got to get back to the house now," Delilah said. "I've got to get Daniel and let Shannon come on down here."

"Shannon?" Kristin whispered.

Cole hopped down from the fence at last. He took his gun from

Delilah, and he slowly and deliberately reloaded it. His hat shaded his eyes from her when he spoke. "You want your little sister to be defenseless?" He looked straight at her.

Kristin smiled sweetly and took the gun from him. He had a row of bottles set up on the back fence. She took her time, aiming as slowly and deliberately as he had loaded. She remembered everything her father and Adam had ever taught her. Remember the recoil, and remember that it can be a hell of a lot for a small woman to handle. Squeeze the trigger gently. Don't jerk back on it....

She didn't miss once. Six shots, six bottles blown to bits, the glass tinkling and reflecting the sunlight as it scattered. With a very pleasant smile, she turned to Cole, daintily handing him the Colt.

He wasn't amazed; he didn't even seem surprised. He studied her. He slipped a second Colt from his gunbelt and handed it to her.

"What happens when the target moves?" he demanded.

"Try me."

Cole nodded to Samson. Samson grinned approvingly. He picked up a bottle and sent it flying high and fast into the air. Kristin caught the missile at its peak, just before it curved back downward to earth. Once again the sun shimmered on the exploding pieces, and they fell in a rainbow of color.

"Not bad," Cole murmured. He nudged back his hat and looked at her sharply. "And Shannon?"

Shannon was already on her way to the yard from the house. Delilah had gone inside. Shannon was dressed like a ranch hand today, too. She seemed all the more feminine for the way her budding curves filled out her shirt and breeches. She glanced slyly at Kristin, and Kristin knew that she was thinking of the fiasco at dinner the night before. She was tempted to give her a sharp slap, but that would be wrong, and she knew it. She decided to ignore her sister's amusement. "Shannon, Cole wants to see you shoot."

"I know." She smiled at Cole. Shannon liked him. A lot. Kristin wanted to spin her around and shake her. He'll be gone in a blink one day! she wanted to tell her sister. Don't care too much!

Then she wondered if Shannon needed the warning, or if Kristin did.

"Show him," Kristin suggested.

Shannon proceeded to do so. She was an even better shot than Kristin, and Cole told her so. He didn't seem to give anyone lavish praise, but he was always gentler with Shannon than with anyone else.

"Good. Damned good," Cole told her.

Shannon flushed, delighted by the compliment.

Kristin turned on her heel and headed for the house. He didn't want her riding away from the house, and he would insist that she stay. If she didn't, he would leave her to the mercy of the bush-whackers. She was going to be mature today, mature and dignified, and she wasn't going to get into any fights over the ranch.

"Kristin!" he called to her.

She turned to look at him.

"What are you doing?" His plumed hat was set at a cocky angle, his hands were on his hips, and his frock coat hung down the length of his back. There was something implacable about him as he stood there, implacable, unfathomable and hard. But that was why she had wanted him. He couldn't be beaten. Not by Quantrill's gang. Not by her.

That last thought made her tremble slightly. She clamped down hard on her jaw and wondered just how long the war could last, and wondered if maybe she shouldn't run after all.

"Paperwork," she told him calmly. "I wouldn't dream of going against your rules, Mr. Slater," she said, and walked away.

He rode out later. She knew when he rode out; she heard the sound of his horse's hooves as she sat in the office, trying hard to concentrate on numbers. She walked out front and watched him, and she was restless. This was hard. She had always been such an important part of things.

But they were playing for high stakes. Damned high stakes. She forced herself to sit down again. She weighed the prices she could receive for her beef against the distances she would have to take the herd to collect the money. Then her pencil stopped moving, and she paused and chewed the eraser, and she wondered what it would be like when he came home for dinner that night.

If he came home for dinner that night.

It didn't matter, she told herself. She was forgetting that this whole thing was business. She was certain Cole never forgot for a moment that it was a deal they had made and nothing more.

She had to learn to be aloof. Polite and courteous and mature, but aloof. She had to keep her distance from him. If she didn't, she would get hurt.

Maybe it was too late already. Maybe she had already come too close to the fire. Maybe no matter what happened she was doomed to be hurt. She wasn't so naive that she didn't know she pleased him, but neither was she so foolish as to imagine that it meant anything to him. There was a coldness about him that was like a deep winter frost. It wasn't that he didn't care at all—he did care. But not enough. And he never could care enough, she was certain.

She gave herself a mental shake and decided that she would have to remember herself that it was business—all business. But still she wondered what he would be like if he returned for dinner, and she swore to herself that her own behavior would be the very best the South had ever had to offer.

Cole did return.

And Kristin was charming. She dressed for dinner again, elegantly, in a soft blue brocade with underpanels and a massive, stylish skirt. She remembered her mother, and she was every bit as gracious as she had been. She was careful to refer to him as "Mr. Slater" all the way through the meal. He watched her and he replied in kind, perfectly courteous, as if he'd been trained for society in the finest drawing rooms back East.

When the meal was over, he disappeared outside. Kristin tried to stay up, but at last everyone else had gone to bed, and she walked up the stairs and to the window. She could see him out on the porch, smoking one of her father's fine cigars and drinking brandy from a snifter. He was leaning against one of the pillars and looking up at the night sky.

She wondered what he was thinking, where his heart really lay.

He turned and stared up at her, there in the window. Her face flamed, but he smiled at her.

"Evening," he said softly.

She couldn't reply to him. He watched her curiously for another moment, and his smile deepened, striking against his well-trimmed beard and mustache.

"I'll be right up."

Her heart hammered and slammed against her chest, and she nearly struck her head trying to bring it back in beneath the window frame. She clutched her heart and reminded herself that she had decided to be mature and dignified and not get as flustered as a schoolgirl.

But she was still trembling when he came up the steps. She heard his footsteps in the hallway, and then he opened the door and came into the room. She was still dressed in her blue brocade. He stared at her for a moment, watching the way her breasts rose and fell above the deep décolletage of her gown. He saw the pulse that vibrated against the long, smooth line of her throat. He smiled, and she sensed the curious tenderness that could come to his eyes. "Come here," he told her softly. He held out a hand to her, and she took it and found herself in this arms. And there was nothing awkward about it at all. He kissed her and touched her face, and then he turned her around, and the touch of his fingers against her bare back as he released her gown set her skin to glowing. Like her heart, her flesh seemed to pulse. It occurred to her that he disrobed her so expertly because he had done the same for many women, but it didn't really matter. All that mattered was that her clothing was strewn on the floor and that he was lifting her in his arms and that the soft glow of the moon was with them again. He carried her to the sleigh bed and set her down, and she saw the passion rise in his eyes and come into his touch. She wrapped her arms around him and sighed, savoring the exquisite feel of him against her, the masculine hardness of muscle and limb, the starkly demanding feel of his shaft against her. Somewhere the tumbleweeds tossed, and somewhere the wind blew harsh and wicked and cruel, but here a tempest rose sweet and exciting, wild and exhilarating.

Somewhere battles raged. Somewhere Northerner fought Southerner, and the nation ran with the blood shed by her youth. Blood washed over Kansas and Missouri as if some shared artery had been slashed, but for tonight, Kristin didn't care.

She was alive in his arms, feline and sensual. She was learning where to touch him, how to move with him and against him and how to leave the world behind when she was with him. No drug and no liquor could be so powerful as this elation, so sweet, so all-encompassing.

That night he slept. She stared at his features, and she longed to reach out and touch them, but she did not. She decided that even his nose was strong, long and straight, like a beak against his features. His cheekbones were high, his forehead was wide and his jaw was fine and square beneath the hair of his beard. She wondered at the fine scars that criss-crossed his shoulders and his chest, and then she remembered that he had been with the Union cavalry before the war, and she wondered what battles had done this to him. She longed to touch him so badly....

She reached out, then withdrew her hand. He was an enigma, and he was fascinating. He drew her like the warmth of a fire, and she was afraid. There was so much she didn't know about him. But her fear went deeper than that, for she sensed that though he cared he would never stay. He liked her well enough. He could even be patient with her temper and her uncertainties. He could be careful, and he could be tender, and he seemed as immersed in this startling passion as she was.

But she sensed that he would not stay, could not stay. Not for long. Worse, she sensed that he could never love her, and that she could fall in love with him all too easily. Already, she thought, other men seemed to pale beside him.

Other men...if any remained when the carnage was over.

She walked to the window and looked out at the night. The moon was high, and the paddocks and the outbuildings looked so peaceful there, rising against the flatland. She sighed. For the rest of the country the war had begun when the first shots had been fired at Ford Sumter back in April of '61, but Kansas seemed to have been bleeding forever, and Missouri along with it. The Army of Northern Virginia had defeated the Army of the Potomac at Manassas twice, while along the Mississippi the Union troops were faring a bit better. The North had won the Battle of Shiloh, and just last April New Orleans had fallen to Union troops under Farragut.

It should matter, she thought. It should matter to her who lost and who won. She should care. At Sharpsburg, Maryland, by Antietam Creek, both sides had suffered horribly. She had been in town when the list of the dead had arrived, and it had been devastating. The papers had all cried that the single bloodiest battle of the war had been fought there, and that men had slipped in the blood, and that bodies had fallen on top of other bodies. All she had seen was the tears of the mothers, the sweethearts, the lovers—the families of boys who had left to join the Union Army and the families who had sons fighting with the Confederacy. She had looked for Matthew's name, and she had not seen it, and she had thanked God. But then she had felt the tears around her, felt the agony of the parents, the sisters, the brothers. And yet sometimes it felt as if the real war were remote here. Here the war had been reduced to sheer terrorism. Men did not battle men; they set out to commit murder.

Here it had become a question of survival. All she wanted to do was survive.

She shivered suddenly and realized that she had come naked from the bed and that the night air was cold. She turned and saw that Cole was awake. His eyes were caught by the moonlight as he watched her. They glimmered curiously, and again she wondered at his secret thoughts. Then his gaze fell slowly over the length of her and she realized again that she was naked, and that his very eyes could touch her like a caress.

"Are you all right?" he asked her.

She felt as if she were going to cry, and she didn't know why.

"I was just thinking about the war," she said quietly.

Something covered his eyes, some careful shield. "It seems far away right now, doesn't it? Then again, I don't think we're even fighting the same war as the rest of the country here." There was a harsh bitterness in his tone, and she suddenly felt cold, as if she had turned him against her, or as if she had even made him forget she was there. But then his eyes focused on her again, and they were rueful and surprisingly tender. "Don't think about it," he told her. "Don't think about the war. You can't change it."

She wanted to say something, but she couldn't find her voice, and so she nodded.

"Come back to bed. It's late," he said. Even when he whispered, his voice was so deep. It entered into her and became the wind again.

She forgot about the war. She forgot about the rest of the world. His voice, his beckoning, had that power over her. Her stomach fluttered and her nipples hardened, and she felt she had to cover herself quickly. She had become so bold, so brash. She was standing here naked as a jaybird, and they were talking, and she should have the decency to reach out for something and cover her nudity.

But she did not. She straightened and tossed back her head, and her hair, golden fire in the moonlight, tumbled down the length of her back. She walked toward him. If nothing else, perhaps they could have honesty between them. She honestly wanted him. She wanted these nights. She wanted the way she felt in his arms, wanted this ecstasy that seemed sweeter than life itself.

She came, he thought, very slowly, very sinuously. She allowed a natural sway to come into her walk, and she moved with a feline grace and purpose that set his blood aflame. He was glad that covers lay over his body, for his response to her was instant and instinctive. He clenched his fists at his sides and waited for her. Waited until she stood above him. Then he reached out, pulled her down to him and held her in his arms. He savaged her lips, groaning with the sweet, aching pleasure of it.

He had never thought it could happen, but he had found an oasis with her. He had known she was beautiful, like a sunrise, like the corn that had grown endlessly in the fields before they had run with blood. He had known that he wanted her.

He had not known how badly, how completely, he would come to need her.

Her eyes were a distant sea that claimed him, and the golden skeins of her hair were webs that entrapped him and brought him softly into a dream of paradise. He could not love her, but he could want her, and he did. He hungered for her, as if he could not be filled. She sated him completely, but then she touched him again, or she moved, or she whispered, and he wanted her again. He had taken her from innocence and he had set the woman within her free, and though she came to him with sensual grace, she held on to something of innocence too, and he wondered at that gift. He had to touch her, had to run his fingers over the fine, delicate beauty of her face, had to press his palms against the lush curve of her breast. He had to breathe in her scent.

It had to end, he knew. But he groaned aloud as her nails stroked against his back, as her hips thrust forward. It had to end, he reminded himself....

But then he ceased to think and gave way to urgent need and fevered desire. He looked into her eyes, blue eyes that were soft, radiant and glazed with passion. He swept her beneath him, and he sank into her as he sank into the dream. She eased the pain. She gave him moments of ecstasy. He could not remember ever having needed a woman so badly. He could not remember so insistent a beat, so desperate, so thunderous a rhythm.

This was like nothing he had ever known. Beautiful, sleek, sensual, she moved beneath him. He became as taut as wire, then shook and shuddered, and spasms continued to rack him.

Later she slept. He cast an elbow behind his head and stared bleakly at the ceiling, shadowed in the moonlight.

It was wrong, he thought. When vengeance lay upon his soul and his heart was barren, it was wrong.

But he could not, would not, make himself cease. She had come to him with the deal. He had not wrung it from her.

That didn't excuse him.

But he needed her....

That didn't excuse him, either. But it mattered. Somehow they had interwoven their lives, and that—as with so many other things—was simply the way it was.

That was simply the way it was.

But still he turned to her. He saw the beautiful curves of her body as she slept, and the tangle of her hair over her shoulders, falling to her flanks, wild and yet somehow virginal. He saw her features, her parted lips and the soft way she breathed. He saw her brow, and he touched it gently, trying to ease the frown line from it. She seemed so very young to have suffered so very much. But she was a fighter. No matter what they had done to her, she had come back up, kicking, fighting. Maybe that was why he couldn't leave her.

He had to leave her, he reminded himself. Soon.

This time it was he who rose. He walked to the window and looked out at the moon. He would have to leave soon, for a time, at least.

He watched the moon, and at last he shrugged. He'd get to the telegraph office tomorrow and hope he could get a message through. He didn't know how long he would have to be gone, but he didn't want her alone. Not now.

Just how long could he guard her?

And would he keep dreaming? He closed his eyes. Dreaming again and again, of one death, of another…

The question washed over his heart, cold as ice. He didn't know. No, he did know. Come hell or high water—or Yankees or Quantrill's raiders—he would find a way to guard her. He wasn't sure why. Maybe it was because this was a matter of honor, and there wasn't much honor left in his world.

And maybe it was because he wanted her so badly. Because she was the only antidote to pain. Because when he was with her he could almost forget…

He didn't want to forget.

Yes, he did. For those few moments.

Whatever the reason, he thought impatiently, he had struck a bargain. He would protect her. He would protect her if she grew hair all over her body and sprouted a full mustache, he swore to himself.

Then he smiled slowly. He was one hell of a liar, he thought, even to himself. She needed him, and he wanted her. That was the bargain.

No. He would protect her, damn it and he would do it so that he never had to hold her bleeding in his arms. He clenched his jaw to keep from crying out. He would protect her because he could not let it happen again.

He breathed slowly and tried to relax.

He would protect her. He had the power. They would help each other, and then he would ride away. The war had to end some day.

Please, God, he thought bleakly. It had to.

The days passed and things were very much the same. After a few days Cole let Kristin ride with him. It was necessary, because the men were busy with the cattle. Kristin showed Cole the length and breadth of her land. She showed him the water holes, and where the land was apt to flood when the rains came too heavily. They went out together searching for a calf that had strayed, and they went into town to buy a length of fencing for the north pasture.

But things felt strange even though they were together. They were polite workmates, cool, courteous acquaintances. Kristin and Shannon always dressed for dinner, because Kristin was determined to cling to what was left of civilization in her life, and the evening meal was her chance to do that. But the conversation there was stilted, too. Cole seldom had much to say to her that wasn't directly concerned with the ranch, with guns, with warnings about the future. She was never to wander around unarmed, and neither was Shannon. He didn't seem to need to warn Delilah or Samson.

He was always polite to Shannon. It seemed to Kristin that her little sister was growing up before her very eyes. Shannon would be eighteen soon, and she was beginning to look every inch the woman. Cole treated her like a child, not condescendingly but with a gentle patience that irritated Kristin. She would have liked some of that patience for herself. Sometimes she asked him very blunt questions, but he invariably ignored her or turned the tables on her. When she demanded to know why he insisted on being such a mystery to her, he merely replied that she had no right to know anything about his past or his future and that she shouldn't be asking.

It didn't matter if she walked away from him, and it didn't matter if she made a sharp reply. He just let her go, or he let her say whatever she wanted and then walked away himself.

But the nights were always the same.

There were times when she couldn't believe she was the same girl who had first met him, innocent, frightened, naive. Even when she felt her temper soar she longed for the night. And even if she turned away from him he stroked her back slowly, moving his fingers down her spine to her buttocks, so lightly that she thought she had imagined it. But his touch was lightning, and it always instilled the same seeds of desire within her. If she really tried to ignore him and he let her be, she sometimes resorted to a soft sigh, feigning sleep, and rolled against him...until he touched her again. Then she sensed his smile, and knew that he knew that she wasn't asleep at all, and that he didn't mind pretending that he needed her more than she needed him.

It went on....

It went on until she woke up one morning, cold and alone. That wasn't so unusual. He was able to get by on much less sleep than she. But somehow she didn't think he had awakened and gone downstairs. She felt a growing sense of dread.

He was gone.

She heard sounds. A rider. Wrenching a sheet from the bed, she raced to the window and stared down at the paddock area. A man had just come riding in on a big bay horse.

She put her hand to her mouth, biting down hard to keep from crying out. He was dressed in gray. She studied the uniform and gold trim.

Cavalry. The man was a Southern cavalry officer.

She turned around and dressed quickly, finding pants and a shirt and her boots. She told herself that she was a Southerner, that she had been born a Southerner and that only Quantrill had made her fear and hate her own people. She tried to smile, reminding herself that Shannon's great hero was Jeb Stuart, a Southern cavalry officer.

It didn't help. Fear raced through her, and she wondered if the officer had been sent by Zeke or his men.

Cole had told her never to walk around unarmed. She had proven she could use a Colt six-shooter and use it well. She slid her narrow gun belt over her hips and nervously checked to see that her weapons were loaded. Then she started down the stairs.

The house was silent. Where was Shannon? she wondered. She couldn't help it. She had awful visions of her beautiful sister caught in the stables with the men all out on the ranch, caught and thrown down in the hay and viciously raped.

She swallowed and tried to tell herself that she was panicking for nothing. But the house was silent, and she still sensed that Cole was gone. Not just off on the ranch somewhere—gone. She couldn't have explained how she knew. It was an emptiness. It festered inside her, and it held her in an awful anguish.

But this...

This was more urgent. "Delilah?"

No one answered her. Delilah was not in the kitchen, and neither was Samson. She didn't hear the baby crying, and she had no idea where Shannon was.

And the cavalry officer hadn't come to knock at her door.

She crept out the back door, careful to keep it from slamming behind her. Walking as quickly and silently as she could, she came around the corner of the house. The man was gone, and the horse was gone.

Her heart was beating much too quickly. She dropped low and raced over the dry sand to the barn. She followed the line of the buildings, coming closer and closer to the corner.

She paused and inhaled sharply. Her blood raced, and she tried desperately to still her erratic breathing.

She rounded the corner and she came face-to-face with an Enfield rifle.

Behind it stood the man in the Confederate cavalry officer's uniform. It was worn and faded, the gold epaulets frayed.

"Drop it!" he warned her. His eyes were teal, a beautiful color. They were also sharp as razors.

She realized that she was aiming the Colt at him.

"You drop it!" she barked.

He smiled. She realized that he was young and very, very good-looking. And familiar in some way she couldn't quite put her finger on.

"This Enfield can blow a hole right through you."

"It's not a totally dependable weapon."

"At this range? Impossible to miss."

"A Colt will scalp you faster than an Indian would dare dream."

He was tall, masculine and elegant in the worn uniform. He didn't intend to harm her, she was certain. But she didn't lower the barrel of the gun. She had learned not to take any chances.

"Kristin McCahy?"

"Yes."

He laughed and lowered the rifle. "Why in God's name were you sneaking up on me like that?"

She jammed the Colt into her holster, instinct assuring her that she was in no danger. She shook her head ruefully.

"I'm sorry. This is my property. And you are a total stranger, you know. Slinking around on it. My property, that is. I mean…who the hell are you?"

"Slinking?" he inquired indignantly, but there was a twinkle in his eyes. He swept his hat from his head and bowed deeply, an elegant and manly cavalier. "Miss McCahy, I assure you that Slaters do not slink."

"Slater?" she demanded with a quick frown.

"Captain Malachi Slater, ma'am. Cole's brother. On leave—and on new duty, or so it seems. You mean to tell me that Cole didn't say anything?"

She felt as if her knees were going to crumble. Cole was gone. And he hadn't even said goodbye.

"Cole—"

"He had a few things to attend to. I'll be with you for a while. If you don't mind."

She did mind. She minded terribly. Not that Malachi was here, but that Cole was gone. She forced herself to smile and to extend her hand. "Why, Mr. Slater, I'm thrilled and grateful for your appearance. Completely thrilled and entirely grateful."

"Thank you, Miss McCahy." He took her hand and raised it to his lips. Then his blue eyes met hers again and she was certain that he knew everything. And there was something in his gaze that suggested that he understood her feelings.

She withdrew her hand suddenly. "Oh, my God!"

"What?"

"You're a Confederate officer."

He stiffened, and his jaw took on a stubborn set that reminded her of his brother. "Miss, last I heard, Missourians were still considering themselves Southerners—for the most part, that is."

Kristin nodded vaguely. "Well, yes, Mr. Slater. But this is a border country. Half the land around here is occupied by Federal forces."

"Don't worry about me. I'll change into civilian clothing quickly, and I'll avoid the Federals."

She shook her head again. "It's just that, well, I have a brother who is a—"

"A Yankee?"

"Ah...yes, a Yankee."

He looked a lot like Cole. A whole lot. He was very tall and very broad-shouldered in his dress shirt and cape, and at the moment he looked very severe, as if he were about to explode.

But he didn't explode. He suddenly started laughing. "Well, it's one hell of a war, isn't it, Miss McCahy? One hell of a war."

Suddenly the wall behind them exploded. Wood chips went flying from the solid impact of a bullet.

"What the hell?" Malachi shouted. He dragged her to the ground, shielding her with his body. Once again there was the sound of gunfire, and another bullet tore into the walls, sending more wood chips cascading down on them.

"Damn it, what the hell!" Malachi repeated.

What the hell indeed? Kristin had no idea who was firing at them.

Chapter Eight

Kristin lay facedown on the ground, dirt in her mouth, with Malachi on top of her, protecting her. Finally the firing stopped and she heard soft footsteps.

"Get off her, Reb!" Kristin almost laughed out loud with relief. It was Shannon.

"Watch it with that thing, little girl," Malachi said slowly, easing himself away from Kristin. He had angry narrowed eyes leveled on her sister. Kristin sprang to her feet and stepped between them. Shannon's temper was flaring, and her eyes were sparkling dangerously.

"I'm not a little girl, Reb, and I swear I'm damned accurate with this Colt," Shannon replied.

"Why, you little—" Malachi began.

"Stop, stop!" Kristin begged, reaching for the gun. She couldn't imagine trying to explain to Cole Slater why they had murdered his brother. "Shannon—"

"He's a Reb, Kristin. He's probably one of Quantrill's—"

"Don't you know a regular cavalry uniform when you see one, girl?"

Kristin lost patience and swung around. "Mr. Slater, please, just for a minute, shut up. Shannon, this is Cole's brother."

"Brother?"

Her eyes wide, she looked at Malachi, then at Kristin again. "Are you sure? They don't look much alike!"

"We have identical big toes," Malachi snapped sarcastically. Shannon stiffened.

Then, suddenly, there was the sound of another explosion. The three of them stared at one another blankly. Wood chips flew as a second bullet struck the barn wall above their heads.

"Get down—" Malachi began.

"Drop that gun!" The order was spoken in a commanding, masculine tone.

Shannon wasn't about to obey. She spun around, aiming. Malachi swore and slammed his fist down on her wrists. The Colt fell to the ground, and Shannon turned on Malachi, swearing and flailing at him with her fists. Malachi swore in return, and Kristin wondered how the two of them could be going at one another this way when someone else was firing at all three of them. They were warning shots, she realized. She stared blankly across the yard and saw that another man had come out of the shadows of the porch. He was younger than Cole and Malachi and dressed like a rancher in high boots, a long railway frock coat and a slouch hat that sat low on his forehead. Malachi paid no attention to him. As he came forward, the stranger tipped his hat to Kristin.

"They've got a set of rotten tempers between them, huh?"

"Do they?" Kristin crossed her arms over her chest and stared at the young man who had been doing the shooting. Shannon was still shrieking, fighting the hold Malachi had on her. Kristin ignored them both and kept staring at the newcomer. "Why were you shooting at us?"

"I thought she meant to poke a hole right through old Malachi there," he said solemnly. He had cloudlike blue-gray eyes and tawny hair. He smiled again. It was an engaging smile, and Kristin almost smiled, too, in spite of herself.

"I take it you're another Slater? Or are you a friend of the family?"

He stuck out his hand. "Jamie, ma'am."

Malachi let out something that sounded like a growl. "Damned brat bit me!" he thundered.

"Shannon!" Kristin implored.

She might have bitten Malachi, but the bite didn't keep him from maintaining his hold upon her, his arms around her waist. Her toes were barely touching the ground.

"Ah, Malachi." Jamie shook his head sorrowfully and said to

Kristin, "He met Grant at Shiloh but he can't handle a little wisp of a girl."

"I'm not—" Shannon began.

"You are a foolish little brat!" Malachi said, releasing her at last and shoving her towards Kristin. She would have swung at him again, but Kristin caught her sister's arms. "Shannon, please!"

But Shannon was still staring at Malachi, seething. "I am not a brat, Reb. You attacked my sister—"

"And you attacked my brother," Jamie said pleasantly. "We're all even. And if Cole were here he'd say the entire lot of us were a pack of fools playing around with firearms. But then, Cole isn't here, and that's why Malachi and I are. Maybe we ought to try and start over."

"Cole sent you, too?" Kristin asked Jamie.

"Yes, ma'am, he did."

"I see," Kristin said stiffly.

Jamie grinned broadly. "No, ma'am, I doubt if you see at all. He had some business to attend to."

"I told her," Malachi said.

"My brother is a cavalry officer," Shannon snapped at Malachi, ignoring everything else. "And if he knew you were on his property he'd skewer you right through!"

He shook his head, looking as if he were about to explode. Then he exhaled in an exaggerated display of patience. "I thought I was supposed to be looking out for Quantrill, not a two-bit piece of baggage!" He shoved his hat down hard over his forehead and started walking toward the house. Kristin, amused, stared after him. Shannon, amazed, placed her hands on her hips.

"Where do you think you're going?" she called.

Malachi stopped and swung around. "In. For coffee and breakfast. And if you don't like it, little girl, that's just too damned bad. You take it up with Cole the next time you see him. He asked me to be here, and I'm here, and I won't be leaving, not until he gets back. Until that time, you do us both a favor. You stay clear of me. Way clear." He paused, then swore softly again. "Hell, I could still be out there with the Yankees. It'd be a hell of a lot less nerve-racking than a morning here!'' Once again he turned. Kristin saw that Delilah was on the steps, watching them. She was grinning broadly.

"You must be Mr. Malachi."

Delilah's voice floated down to Kristin, and Kristin arched a brow at her. She and Shannon hadn't known that Cole's brothers were coming, but Delilah had. Cole had told Delilah what he was up to, and he hadn't said a word to them.

She gritted her teeth, damning Cole a thousand times over. What was this business he had to attend to? They had made a deal. Zeke was still out there somewhere. She didn't need a pair of baby-sitters. She needed to have Zeke taken care of.

And she needed to have Cole talk to her, to tell her about his life, not just walk away from her when the sun came up.

"You come on in," Delilah was saying to Malachi. "Breakfast's on the table, boys. Breakfast's on the table."

Kristin felt Jamie watching her. She turned to him, and she flushed, surprised by the knowing assessment she saw in his eyes. He had been reading her mind, or else he had been wondering about her relationship with his brother. No, he seemed to know what their relationship was already. She could read that in the look he was giving her.

Then he smiled, as if he had already decided that he liked her, and so she smiled, too. She liked Jamie. And she liked Malachi. She even liked the war he was waging with Shannon. She had felt like laughing as she'd watched them and she hadn't felt like laughing in a long time.

"I'm awful hungry, too," Jamie said. He offered her his arm. "Shall we go in for breakfast?"

Kristin hesitated, then took his arm, and they started toward the house. She paused, turning back to her sister. "Shannon?"

"I'll skip breakfast," Shannon said heatedly, her bright blue eyes still on Malachi's retreating back. "I don't rightly feel like sitting down with—" She paused when she saw that Jamie was studying her intently. "I'm not hungry." She spun around and stomped off to the barn. Kristin looked at Jamie again.

"Just where is Cole? I don't need looking after like this, you know. Cole and I had a—an agreement."

She studied his eyes, trying hard not to flush.

"You talk to Cole about his whereabouts later," Jamie said flatly. Neither of the Slaters was going to say a thing about Cole's absence, she realized. "And we're here 'cause of your agreement. We know Quantrill and his boys. We're just here to see that you're safe. Do you really mind? Terribly?"

"No, I, uh...of course not. You're both very welcome," she said, forcing herself to smile. They were welcome, they really were. It was just that...

It was just that she wondered where the hell Cole had gone. She wondered if it had to do with another woman, and she wondered if she could bear it if it did.

Don't fall in love with him! she warned herself again. But he was gone, and she was aching, and it was too late. He wasn't involved and she was, and it was gnawing away at her. She forced her smile to remain in place. "Jamie, you are very welcome. Come on. Delilah makes an incredible breakfast."

He rode southeast the first day. The farther east he went in Missouri, the more closemouthed and careful people were about Quantrill and his gang.

It was natural, he supposed. It had all turned into such a hideous, ugly thing. The ugliness had taken hold way back in the 1850s when John Brown had come into Missouri with his followers and killed slaveholders. Cole didn't really know what to think of John Brown. He had seen the man at his trial, and he had thought then that old John Brown spoke like a fanatic. But he had also thought that he spoke from conviction, too, when he said that only a bloodbath could cleanse the country of the sin of slavery.

John Brown and his followers had gone on to raid the arsenal at Harper's Ferry. Robert E. Lee—then an officer of the United States Army—had been sent in to capture John Brown. Jeb Stuart had been with the forces sent to Harper's Ferry, too.

Cole had been with them himself, riding right alongside Jeb. They had captured John Brown and taken him to Charlestown to stand trial. There hadn't been any Confederacy then. And Cole hadn't known what was to come.

In the North they had quickly begun to sing, "John Brown's body lies a-molderin' in the grave," conveniently forgetting that even if the man had been a God-fearing murderer, he had still been a murderer.

And in Missouri men had learned to retaliate.

Quantrill and his raiders were worshipped by the people here, people who had known nothing but death and destruction from the Kansas jayhawkers. Cole had to be careful. When he stopped at a farmhouse, he quickly made his presence known. He asked for a sip of water from a well, then asked if anyone knew where he might find Quantrill or any of his boys. He was polite, and he smiled, and he used his best country accent, and he kept it filled with respect.

In return he was pointed more and more toward the south. Finally, in a small town almost fifty miles south of Osceola, he heard that Quantrill was at the local saloon.

No one was afraid there. Quantrill's boys were in charge. The South had a good grip on its own here. At a farmhouse outside the town, Cole was invited in for a meal, and the farmer assured him that he could find Quantrill at the saloon at about six that evening.

Cole rode in carefully. If he saw Quantrill first, or Anderson, he'd be all right, but he didn't want to run into Zeke, not now. In case he did, though, he rode in with his six-shooters and two shotguns loaded and ready.

Things were quiet enough as he rode into town. It was almost as if there were no war. Nicely dressed women with stylish hats stood outside the mercantile. As he rode slowly along the dusty main street, they stared at him, and he tipped his hat. They blushed and whispered to one another.

That was when Cole realized that the quiet little town was pulsing with an inner excitement and that things weren't really quiet at all. He could hear the sound of laughter and piano music up ahead and saw a sign that read Red Door Saloon. There were at least eight horses tethered out front.

Quantrill and company do reign here, he thought. He reined in his horse and dismounted, dropping the reins over the post in front of the saloon and dusting off his hands. Then he headed for the red door that had given the saloon its name.

He opened the door and stood there, blinking in the dim light. Then he swiftly cast his gaze over the Red Door's patrons.

Zeke wasn't there.

But William Clarke Quantrill was, playing cards at a round table, leaning back with a thin cigar in his mouth. He was a pale, ashen man with dark hair and a neat brown mustache. He saw Cole just as Cole saw him, and he smiled. He tossed his cards down and stood. He was of average height, about five foot nine. There was nothing about the man to label him the scourge of the West. Nothing except his eyes. They were pale blue and as cold as death.

"Cole. Cole Slater. Well, I'll be damned. To what do I owe this honor?"

Cole didn't answer him. He'd already looked around the room, and looked hard. Zeke wasn't there, but Cole was certain that Quantrill wasn't alone. He wasn't. Cole recognized the other four around the table as young recruits. The two James boys, Jesse and Frank, were there, along with Bill Anderson and little Archie Clements. Cole was sure, too, that Quantrill had more men in the saloon. It wasn't that he had anything to fear here. He was a hero in these parts. It didn't matter that he made out lists of men to be executed. It didn't matter that his men were rapists, murderers and thieves. All that mattered was that what had been done to the Missourians by the jayhawkers was being returned to the Kansans twice over by the bushwhackers.

Cole hadn't come here to do battle, anyway. He strode into the saloon, toward the poker table. The piano player had stopped playing. Everyone in the room was watching him.

He reached Quantrill. Quantrill had his hand extended. Cole took it. "Quantrill," he acknowledged quietly, nodding to the other men at the table. "Jesse. Frank. Archie. Bill. You all look fit. War seems to agree with you."

"Bushwhacking agrees with me," Archie Clements admitted freely. He was dark and had a mean streak a yard wide. "Hell, Cole, I couldn't make it in no ordinary unit. Besides, I'm fighting Yanks for Missouri, and that's it. 'Course, now, you aren't so much regular army, either, are you, Cole? What do they call you? A spy? A scout? Or are you still just a raider?"

"I'm a major, Archie, and that's what they call me," Cole said flatly.

Quantrill was watching the two of them. He turned to the piano player and said, "Hey, what's the problem there, Judah? Let's have something light and fancy here, shall we? Archie, you and Bill take the James boys over to the bar for a whiskey. Seems to me that Cole must have made this trip 'cause he's got something to say. I want to hear it."

Archie stood, but he looked at Cole suspiciously.

"You alone, Cole?"

"That's right, Archie. I'm alone."

Archie nodded at last. Young Jesse James kept staring at Cole. "It was good to see you again, Major Slater. We miss you when we ride. You were damned good."

Damned good with his guns, that was what the boy meant. What the hell was going to be in store for these men when the war was over? If they survived the war.

"You take care, Jesse. You, too, Frank," Cole said. He drew up a chair next to Quantrill. Quantrill started to deal out the cards. "You still a gambling man, Cole?"

"Always," Cole told him, picking up his cards. A buxom brunette with a headful of rich curls, black fishnet stockings and a blood-red dress came over. She nudged up against Quantrill's back but flashed Cole a deep, welcoming smile.

"Want some whiskey for your friend there, Willy?"

"Sure. Bring over the best. We've got a genuine Confederate scout in our midst. But he used to be one of mine, Jennifer. Yep, for a while there he was one of my best."

"He'd be one of anybody's best, I'm sure," Jennifer drawled, fluttering her dark lashes.

Cole flashed her an easy smile, surprised to discover that he felt nothing when he looked at her. She was a pretty thing, very sexual, but she didn't arouse him in the least. You're too satisfied, he warned himself. He found himself frowning and wondering if he shouldn't be interested. At least then he'd know he could be. He shrugged. He was committed—for the moment. And he'd be taking a long ride away soon enough. There'd be plenty of time to prove things to himself then if he had to. That bothered him, too. He shouldn't have to feel the need to prove things to himself.

He shouldn't feel any of these things. Not when his wife lay dead.

"Get the man a whiskey," Quantrill said sharply. Jennifer pouted, then spun around. "What's this all about?" he demanded of Cole.

"The McCahy girls," Cole said flatly.

Quantrill frowned. He didn't seem to recognize the name, and Cole felt sure he wasn't acting. "I don't know them."

Jennifer returned with a new bottle of good Irish whiskey and a pair of shot glasses. She was going to pour out the amber liquid, but Quantrill shooed her away and poured out the shots himself.

"Your man Zeke has been after them."

Quantrill met his frown. "Zeke? Zeke Moreau? I didn't even know the two of you had met. Zeke came in after you were gone."

"Not quite. We met. But I don't think he remembered me when we met again."

Comprehension dawned in Quantrill's cold eyes. "The farmhouse? Near the border? That was you, Cole?"

"Yeah, that was me." Cole leaned forward. He picked up his glass and swallowed down its contents. It was good. Smooth. The kind of stuff that was becoming rare in the South as the war went on and on. He poured himself another shot. He could feel Quantrill's eyes on him. He sensed that Quantrill wasn't angry. He seemed amused more than anything else.

"So you came back to beat my boys up, huh?"

Quantrill poured himself another glass of whiskey, then sat back, swirling the liquid, studying its amber color. Cole looked at him. "No, I just happened by your boys at work, and I'll admit I was kind of sick to my stomach at the war they were waging. They dragged out an old man and killed him. Then they came back after his daughter. Seems the lady had the bad luck to dislike Zeke."

Quantrill shrugged. His amusement was fading. "You don't like my methods?"

"You've become a cold-blooded killer, Quantrill."

"I didn't know anything about the McCahy place."

"I believe you," Cole said.

Quantrill watched him for a moment, a sly smile creeping onto his lips again. "Hell, Cole, you're starting to sound like some damned Yankee."

"I'm not a Yankee."

"Yankee lover, then."

"I don't want the girl touched, Quantrill."

"My, my..." Quantrill leaned back, idly running a finger around the rim of his glass. "Seems to me that you weren't so finicky back in February of '61, Mr. Slater. Who was heading up the jayhawkers back then? Was it Jim Lane, or was Doc Jennison calling the shots by then? Don't make no real matter, does it? They came riding down into Missouri like a twister." He came forward, resting his elbows on the table. "Yessir, just like a twister. They burned down your place, but that wasn't enough. They had to have their fun with Mrs. Slater. Course, she was a beauty, wasn't she, Cole?"

Cole felt his face constrict. He felt his pulse hammering against his throat. He longed to jump forward and throttle the life out of Quantrill, to close those pale, calculating eyes forever.

"Nope, you weren't so finicky about methods when I met you first, Cole Slater. You had revenge on your mind, and nothing more."

Cole forced his lips to curl into a humorless smile. "You're wrong, Quantrill. Yeah, I wanted vengeance. But I could never see murder done in cold blood. I could never draw up a list of men to be gunned down. I could never see dragging terrified, innocent women out of their beds to be raped and abused. Or shooting down children."

"Hell, Cole. Children fight in this war."

"And that's the hell of it, Quantrill. That's the whole bloody hell of it. The war is hell enough. The savagery is too much."

"We fight like we've been attacked, and that's the plain truth of it. You go see the likes of Lane or Jennison. Tell them about innocents. You can't change the war, Cole. Not you, and not anybody else. Not anybody."

"I didn't come here today to end the war, Quantrill," Cole said calmly.

"You just want me to rein in on Zeke, is that it?"

"Well," Cole told him casually, "you can rein in on him or I can kill him."

Quantrill grinned and shrugged. "You're overestimating my power, Slater. You want me to call Zeke in when this girl isn't anything to you. Not anything at all. She's not your sister and she's not your wife. Hell, from what I understand, Zeke saw her first. So what do you think I can do?"

"You can stop him."

Quantrill sat back again, perplexed. He lifted a hand idly, then let it fall to his lap. "What are you so worried about? You can outdraw Zeke. You can outdraw any ten men I know."

"I don't perform executions, Quantrill."

"Ah...and you're not going to be around for the winter, huh? Well, neither are we. We'll be moving south soon enough—"

"I want a guarantee, Quantrill."

Quantrill was silent. He lifted his glass, tossed back his head and swallowed the whiskey down in a gulp, then wiped his mouth with his sleeve. His eyes remained on Cole. He set the glass down.

"Marry her."

"What?" Cole said sharply.

"You want me to give the girl a guarantee of safety. A girl Zeke saw first. A girl he wants—badly, I'd say. So you give me something. Give me a reason to keep him away from her. Let me be able to tell the men that she's your wife. That's why they have to stay clear. She'll be the wife of a good loyal Confederate. They'll understand that."

Cole shook his head. "I'm not marrying again, Quantrill. Not ever."

"Then what is this McCahy girl to you?"

What indeed, he wondered. "I just don't want her hurt anymore, that's all."

Quantrill shook his head slowly, and there was a flash of something that might have been compassion in his pale eyes. "There's nothing that I can do, Slater. Nothing. Not unless you can give me something to go on."

The damnedest thing about it, Cole thought, was that Quantrill seemed to want to help him. He wasn't trying to be difficult and he wasn't looking for a fight. He was just telling it the way it was.

"We will be gone pretty soon," Quantrill said. "Another month of raids, maybe. Then the winter will come crashing down. I intend to be farther south by then. Kansas winter ain't no time to be foraging and fighting. Maybe she'll be safe. From us, at least. The jayhawkers might come down on the ranch, but Quantrill and company will be seeking some warmth."

"Another month," Cole muttered.

Quantrill shrugged.

The two men sat staring at one another for several moments. Then Quantrill poured more whiskey.

He couldn't marry her. She couldn't be his wife. He'd had a wife. His wife was dead.

He picked up the whiskey and drank it down in one swallow. It burned. It tore a path of fire straight down his throat and into his gut.

"You going east?" Quantrill asked.

Cole nodded. Maybe he shouldn't have, but Quantrill knew he would have to get to Richmond sooner or later, and probably sooner.

Cole let out a snarl and slammed his glass down on the table. The piano player stopped playing again. Silence filled the saloon, like something living and breathing. All eyes turned toward Cole and Quantrill.

Cole stood. "I'm going to marry her," he told Quantrill. Then he looked around at the sea of faces. "I'm going to marry Kristin McCahy, and I don't want her touched. Not her, and not her sister. The McCahy ranch is going to be my ranch, and I'm promising a slow, painful death to any man who thinks about molesting any of my property."

Quantrill stood slowly and looked around at his men. "Hell, Cole, we're all on the same side here, aren't we, boys?"

There was silence, and then a murmur of assent. Quantrill lifted the whiskey bottle. "Let's drink! Let's drink to Cole Slater's bride, Miss McCahy! Why, Slater, not a man jack here would think to molest your property, or your woman. She's under our protection. You've got my word on it."

Quantrill spoke loudly, in a clear voice. He meant what he said. Kristin would be safe.

Quantrill offered Cole his hand, and Cole took it. They held fast for a moment, their eyes locked. Quantrill smiled. Cole stepped back, looked around the room and turned to leave. He had his back to the room, but he had probably never been safer in his life. Quantrill had guaranteed his safety.

He walked through the red door, his shoulders squared. Outside, he felt the sun on his face, but the breeze was cool. Fall was fading, and winter was on its way.

He had just said he would marry her.

Hell.

The sun was bright, the air was cool, and the sky was cloudless and blue. He stared at the sun, and he felt cold. He felt a coldness that seeped right into him, that swept right around his heart. It was a bitter cold, so deep that it hurt.

He found his horse's reins and pushed the huge animal back from the others almost savagely so that he could mount. Then he turned and started at a trot down the street.

It couldn't be helped. He had said he would do it, and he had to carry it through.

He had to marry her.

It wouldn't be real, though. It wouldn't mean anything at all. It would just be the way it had to be, and that would be that.

The cold seeped into him again. It encompassed and encircled his heart, and he felt the numbness there again, and then the pain.

He couldn't do it. He couldn't marry another woman. He couldn't call her his wife.

He would marry her. But he never would call her his wife.

Malachi was the more serious of Cole's two brothers, Kristin quickly discovered. Like Cole, he had gone to West Point. He had studied warfare, from the campaigns of Alexander the Great to the American Revolution to Napoléon's grand attempts to take over Europe and Russia. He understood the South's situation in the present struggle for independence, and perhaps that understanding was the cause of gravity. He was on leave for no more than three weeks, so he would have to be returning soon to his unit. Kristin wondered if that meant Cole would return soon. Malachi was courteous to her. He seemed to be the last of the great Southern gentleman, perhaps the last cavalier. Shannon retained her hostility toward him, though. Since Malachi's arrival, she had become a Unionist. She loved to warn both Malachi and Jamie that her brother would come back and make them into nothing more than dust in the wind. Jamie was amused by Shannon. Malachi considered her a dangerous annoyance. Since Kristin had her own problems with Cole, she decided that Shannon was on her own.

Kristin didn't think Matthew would make it home. The last letter she had received from him had stated that his company had been sent East and that he was fighting with the Army of the Potomac.

Malachi didn't wear his cavalry butternut and gray while he was with them at the ranch. He fit into Matthew's breeches fine, and since Federal patrols had been known to wander over the border, it seemed best for him to dress in civilian clothing. Two weeks after his arrival, Kristin heard hoofbeats outside and hurried to the porch. To her vast astonishment, Jamie sat whittling on the steps while Malachi held Shannon in a deep engrossing embrace, kissing her as hotly as a newlywed. Stunned, Kristin stared at Jamie. Jamie pointed to two men in Union blue who were riding away.

"She started to mention that things might not be all they seemed," Jamie drawled. "Malachi didn't take kindly to the notion of spending the rest of the war in a Yankee prison camp."

There was a sharp crack. Kristin spun around to see that Shannon had just slapped Malachi.

Her sister's language was colorful, to say the least. She compared Malachi Slater to a milk rat, a rattlesnake and a Texas scorpion. Malachi, her fingerprints staining his face, didn't appreciate her words. Kristin gasped when he dragged her onto his lap and prepared to bruise her derriere.

Shannon screamed. Jamie shrugged. Kristin decided she had to step in at last. Kristin pleaded with him, but he ignored her at first. She hadn't the strength to come to physical blows with him, so all she could do was appeal to his valor. "Malachi, I'm sure she didn't mean—"

"She damned well did mean!" Malachi shouted. "And I may fall to a Yankee bullet, but I'll be damned if I'll rot in a hellhole because this little piece of baggage has a vicious heart!"

His palm cracked just once against Shannon's flesh.

"Rodent!" Shannon screeched.

"Please—" Kristin began.

Malachi shifted Shannon into his arms, ready to lecture here.

Then Jamie suddenly stood up, dropped his knife and the wood he'd been whittling and reached for his Colt.

"Horses!" he hissed.

A sudden silence settled over them. Malachi didn't release Shannon, but she froze, too, neither sniffling in indignation nor screaming out her hatred.

Kristin glanced at Jamie. She could tell he was afraid that the Union patrol was on its way back. That Malachi's act just hadn't been good enough. That Shannon had exposed them all to danger.

They all saw the riders. Two of them.

Kristin saw Jamie's tension ease, and then Malachi, too, seemed to relax. Even his desire for vengeance against Shannon seemed to have ebbed. He suddenly set her down on the wooden step, not brutally but absently. Still, Shannon gasped out, startled. Malachi ignored her. Even Kristin ignored her. Kristin still couldn't see the riders clearly, but apparently Malachi and Jamie knew something.

Then she realized it was Cole's horse. It was Cole, returning.

Instantly she felt hot and then cold. Her heart seemed to flutter in her breast. Then butterfly wings seemed to soar within her, and she was hot and then cold all over again.

Cole...

No matter what she wanted to think or believe, she had thought of nothing but him since he had gone away. Waking or sleeping, he had filled her heart and her mind. She had touched the bedding where he had lain and remembered how he had stood, naked, by the window. She had remembered him with the length of her, remembered the feel of his fingers on her flesh, the staggering heat of his body against hers, the tempest of his movement. She had burned with the thoughts and she had railed against herself for them, but they had remained. And in her dreams she had seen him naked and agile and silent and sleek and coming to her again. And he would take her so tenderly into his arms...

And in her dreams it would be more than the fire. He would smile, and he would smile with an encompassing tenderness that meant everything. He would whisper to her, and the whispers would never be clear, but she would know what they meant.

He loved her....

He did not love her.

He rode closer, a plump, middle-aged man at his side. She barely noticed the other man. Her eyes were for Cole, and his rested upon her.

And her heart ran cold then, for he was staring at her with a startling dark hatred.

Her fingers went to her throat, and she backed away slightly, wondering what had happened, why he should look at her so.

"Cole's back," Jamie said unnecessarily.

"Cole!"

It was Shannon who called out his name, Shannon who went running out to him as if he were a long-lost hero. Kristin couldn't move.

Cole's horse came to a prancing halt, and Shannon stood there, staring up at him in adoration, reaching for him. To his credit, Kristin admitted bitterly, he was good to Shannon. His eyes gentled when they fell upon her, and if there was a certain impatience about him, he hid it from her well. He dismounted from his horse in front of the house. Both Jamie and Malachi stood there watching him in silence, waiting for him to speak. He stepped forward and greeted both of his brothers.

"Malachi, Jamie."

He grasped both their hands, and Jamie smiled crookedly while Malachi continued to observe him gravely. Then Cole's eyes came to her again, and she would have backed up again if she hadn't already been flush against the door. His gaze came over her, as cold as the wind of a twister, and perhaps, for just a second, with the same blinding torment. Then the emotion was gone, and all that remained was the staggering chill.

Her mouth was dry, her throat was dry, and she couldn't speak.

She was grateful then for Shannon, who told Cole how glad she was to see him, how grateful she was that he was back.

Then she was suddenly still, and Kristin realized that the pudgy middle-aged man was still sitting atop his horse, looking at them all. She was the hostess here. She should be asking him in and offering him something cool to his throat from the dust and dirt of his ride. She should be doing something for Cole, too. If she could only move. Cole should be doing something, too, she thought, not leaving the little man just sitting there.

She forced her eyes away from Cole's to meet those of the man. She even made her lips curl into a semblance of a welcoming smile. "Hello, sir. Won't you come in?"

Jamie smiled. "Welcome, stranger. Cole, you're forgetting your manners. Who is this man?"

Cole turned to the man on the horse. "Sorry, Reverend. Please, come down."

"Much obliged," the man said, dismounting from his horse. Jamie stepped forward to tether the horses. The wind picked up and blew a handful of dirt around.

"This is the Reverend Samuel Cotter," Cole said. "Reverend, my brothers, Malachi and Jamie. And Miss Kristin McCahy in the doorway there, and Miss Shannon McCahy here by my side."

The reverend tipped his hat. "A pleasure, ladies. Gentlemen."

Then they were all just standing there again. The reverend turned his hat awkwardly in his hands. He had a nice face, Kristin thought. Heavy-jowled, with a nice, full smile and bright little eyes. She wished she could be more neighborly, but she was still having difficulty moving.

"Maybe we should all move into the house," Jamie suggested.

"Perhaps the reverend would like a sherry," Shannon murmured.

"The reverend would just love a whiskey!" the little man said, his eyes lighting up.

Malachi laughed. Cole came forward, his hands on his hips. He stood right in front of Kristin, and his eyes were just like the steel of Malachi's cavalry sword. His hands fell on her shoulders, and she almost screamed.

"You're blocking the door, Kristin," he said.

"Oh!" She moved quickly, jumping away from his touch. Her face flushed with color. She looked at the little man. "Forgive me my lack of manners, sir. Please, please, do come in." She paused, looking at Cole's hard, dispassionate features, then back at the reverend. "Um...just what are you doing here, sir?"

The little man's brows shot up. "Why, I've come to marry you, miss."

"Marry me?"

"Why, not myself!" He laughed hard, enjoying his own joke. "I've come to marry you to Mr. Slater here."

"What!" Kristin gasped. She turned to stare at Cole again. She saw the ice, and the hatred in his eyes, and she thought it must be some horrible joke.

"Oh, no! I can't marry Mr. Slater." She said it flatly and with grim determination.

His hands were on her shoulders once again. His eyes bored into hers, ruthless, demanding. His fingers bit into her flesh, brutal and challenging.

"You will marry me, Kristin. Now. While we have the nice reverend here. It took me four days to find him, and I don't intend to have trouble now."

She gritted her teeth against the pain of his touch, against the force of his will. She wanted to cry, but she couldn't do that, and she couldn't explain that she couldn't possibly marry him, not when the mere idea made him look at her with such hatred.

"I will not—"

"You will!"

He turned around and shoved her through the door to the house. His touch stayed upon her, the warmth and strength of his body radiated along her spine, and his whisper touched her ear like the wind.

"Damn it, Kristin, stop it! You will do this!"

Suddenly tears glistened in her eyes. She'd dreamed about just such an occasion, but it hadn't been like this. He hadn't looked at her this way.

"Why?" she managed to whisper.

"We have to."

"But..." She had to salvage some pride. "I don't love you."

"I don't love you."

"Then—"

"Kristin, you've got your choices."

"I see. This is another threat. If I don't go through with this, you'll ride away."

"I have to ride away, Kristin. No matter what. And this is the only safeguard I could find for you."

"I can't do it—"

"Then plan on entertaining Zeke Moreau, Kristin. And if you can't think about yourself, think about Shannon."

"This is a travesty!"

His eyes burned with silver emotion for a moment. He was a stranger again as he stood there, touching her yet somehow distant from her.

"War is a travesty, Kristin. Cheer up. If it ever ends, you can divorce me. I'm sure you'll have plenty of cause. But for the moment, Miss McCahy, get into the parlor, stand sweetly and smile for the nice reverend, please."

PART 3

Her Husband

Chapter Nine

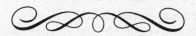

It was not what she had expected her wedding day to be like, and it was certainly not what she had dreamed it would be like.

Cole and the reverend were still covered with dust from their ride. She wore a simple cotton day dress with a single petticoat, since Cole had sworn impatiently when she had murmured something about changing. Shannon was wearing a shirt and trousers. The only concession to the fact that it was a wedding was the little bouquet she held, hurriedly put together by Delilah from ferns and late-blooming daisies.

They stood stiffly in the parlor. Cole was brusque, and the reverend tried to be kind. Malachi stood up for Cole, and Shannon acted as bridesmaid. Jamie, Delilah and Samson looked on. The reverend kept clearing his throat. He wanted to say more, wanted to speak about the sanctity of marriage and the commitment made thereby between a man and a woman. Cole kept shifting his weight from foot to foot. Then he snapped at the man, "Get on with it!"

Hastily the reverend went on.

Kristin listened to the droning voice and found herself looking around her mother's beautiful parlor and wondering what it had been like for her parents. Not like this. They had loved one another, she knew. She could remember her father's eyes, and the way they had misted over when her mother's name had been spoken. They had built their lives on a dream, and the dream had been a good one.

But they weren't living in a world of dreams, and Cole didn't love her. He didn't even pretend to love her.

"Kristin?"

"What?"

Startled, she looked up at him. She realized that they were standing side by side, she in simple cotton, he in denim and Missouri dust. His hand was around hers, and his flesh felt dry and hot. He squeezed her hand, and she gasped at the pressure, her eyes widening.

"Kristin!" His eyes were sizzling silver and dangerous. "The reverend just asked you a question."

She looked at the reverend. He was flushed and obviously uncomfortable, but he tried to smile again.

"Kristin...do you take this man for your lawful wedded husband, to have and to hold, from this day forward, to love, to cherish and to obey in all the things of this earth?"

She stared at him blankly. It wasn't right. He didn't love her. And she was falling in love with him.

"I, er..."

"Kristin!" The pressure of his fingers around hers was becoming painful.

"Cole..." She turned to him, trying to free her hand from his grasp. "Cole, this is marvelously noble of you, honestly. But I'm sorry, I don't think—"

"Kristin!" Shannon gasped.

"Kristin..." Cole began, and there was a definite threat in his tone, like a low rumble of thunder. What could he do to her, here, with all these people, she wondered recklessly.

He caught her shoulders and jerked her against him. The revered was sucking air in and out out of his cheeks very quickly. "Mr. Slater, if the young lady isn't prepared to take this step, if she isn't completely enamored of you—"

"She's enamored, she's enamored!" Cole snapped. He wound his fingers into Kristin's hair and kissed her hotly. He kissed her with such conviction and passion that she felt herself color from the roots of her hair to her toes. His lips molded around hers, and his tongue plunged deep into her mouth. She couldn't breathe, and she could barely stand, and her knees were beginning to shake.

"Really, now—" the reverend protested.

"They really *are* in love!" Jamie assured him cheerfully.

"Cole—" Malachi tapped his brother on the shoulder, "I—er...think you've made your point."

Cole lifted his lips from Kristin's by just a whisper. His eyes burned into hers. "Say 'I do,' Kristin. Say it."

She inhaled. Her ribs felt as if they had been crushed. She tried to shake her head, but it wouldn't move. "Say 'I do,'" he insisted.

She felt as if the trembling in her heart were an earthquake beneath her feet. She parted her lips, and they felt damp and swollen.

"For God's sake, do it!" Shannon whispered. "We need him. Don't be so naive!"

She nodded, but she couldn't speak. Cole caught her fingers and brought their hands together and squeezed. "'I do,' Kristin! Say it!"

She formed the words at last. I do.

"Go on!" Cole roared at the reverend.

The reverend asked Cole the same question he'd asked Kristin.

He almost spat out the answer. "I do!" His lips twisted bitterly, as if, having forced her to do what he wanted, he had found a new contempt for her. She tried to wrench her hand away from him, but he held her firm and slipped a ring on her finger. It was a wide gold band, and it was too big for her.

She heard Delilah saying that if they twined some string around it it would fit fine.

Then the reverend announced that they were man and wife, and Cole released her. No one said anything, not a single word. The silence went on and on, but Delilah finally broke it.

"This calls for some of that fine white wine in the cellar, I think. Samson, you go fetch it up here, please."

"Yessir, a wedding sure calls for wine," Samson agreed.

The room seemed very still, and Kristin was still unable to move. She was hot and cold by turns. She had never felt more alone in her life. Cole had moved away from her, far away, as if he couldn't bear to touch her now that the words had been spoken. He thanked the reverend and paid him. Then he seemed to notice Kristin again. She had to sign the marriage certificate.

She balked again. He grabbed her hand and guided it to the paper, and she managed to scratch our her name. Nothing seemed real. Delilah said she would set out a cold supper, and Shannon promised to help. Somehow Kristin wound up in one of the big plush wing chairs in the parlor. Jamie stood beside her, resting a hand on her shoulder.

"He's really not as bad as he seems, you know," he whispered.

She clenched her teeth together to keep them from chattering. "No, he's worse." Jamie laughed, but there was an edge to his laughter. He sat down on the sofa across from her and took her hands in his. His eyes were serious. "Kristin, you have to try to understand Cole."

"He doesn't want to be understood," she replied softly.

"You're not afraid of him, are you?" he asked.

She thought for a moment, then shook her head, smiling ruefully. "Afraid of Cole? Never. He saved my life. No, Jamie, I'm not afraid of him. I just wish that—"

"That what?" Jamie murmured.

They could both see Cole. He was rubbing the back of his neck as he talked to Malachi. He looked tired, Kristin thought. She bit her lower lip, and wished for a moment that the marriage was real. She wanted to tiptoe up behind him and touch his shoulders with soothing fingers. She wanted to press her face against the coolness of his back and pretend there was no war, no Zeke, no chaos.

"I wish I understood him," she said at last, staring straight at Jamie. "Want to help?"

He straightened and released her hands. "I'm sorry, Kristin. I can't." He stood and smiled down at her. "Look at that, will you? Delilah is a gem. A cold supper, indeed. She's got biscuits and gravy, turnip greens and a shank of ham over there. Come on!" He took her hands in his again and pulled her to her feet. Suddenly, impulsively, he gave her a kiss on the cheek. "Hey, welcome, sister," he whispered.

Some instinct caused her to look behind him. Cole was watching them. He scowled darkly and turned his attention to Malachi again.

"I'm not very hungry, Jamie," Kristin said. It was true. She wasn't hungry at all. She smiled at him, though and whispered, "Thank you, Jamie!" She felt like crying again, and she shook herself impatiently. It was absurd. She had stood tall in the face of tragedy. Now there was only confusion, but it was tearing her apart.

Cole didn't seem to be very hungry, either. He waited with barely concealed impatience for his brothers to finish their meal. When they had, he started toward the door with long strides, and they followed. He paused in the doorway and said to Kristin, "We're going to ride out and take a look at things. I want to tell the ranch hands."

He was going to announce their wedding the way he might have spread the news of a battle. She nodded, wondering again at the fever that touched his eyes. He couldn't wait to be away from her, she thought. Then why, she thought angrily, had he done it at all? Surely his obligation to her wasn't as great as that.

She didn't say anything. He looked at the reverend, thanking him again for making the trip and urging him to make himself at home. Then he paused again. Malachi and Jamie shifted uncomfortably, exchanging worried glances.

"Write to your brother," Cole told Kristin. "Write to him immediately. There's a good possibility I may stop a Yankee bullet before this is all over, but I don't intend it to be because of a stupid mistake."

Then the three of them were gone. Kristin stood up, watching as the door closed, listening as their booted feet fell against the floorboards of the front porch.

Then, ridiculously, she felt her knees wobbling. She heard a humming in the air, and it was as if wind were rising again, bringing with it a dark mist.

"Kristin!"

She heard Shannon calling her name, and then she heard nothing. She sank to the floor in a dead faint.

Several hours later the Slater brothers rode back from their inspection of the ranch. They'd told all the ranch hands about the marriage. Old Pete had spit on the ground and told Cole he was damned glad. He seemed to understand that with Cole and Kristin married, they were all safer from Zeke Moreau. He didn't seem to care much whether the marriage was real. He seemed to think it was none of his business.

The brothers had gone on to ride around the perimeters of the McCahy ranch. It was a quiet day. By the time they headed back for the house, night was coming and coming fast. Still, when they were within sight of the place, Cole suddenly decided he wanted to stop and set up camp.

Jamie built a fire, and Malachi unsaddled the horses. Cole produced a bottle of whiskey and the dried beef and hard tack. By then the stars had risen, bright against the endless black velvet of the night sky.

Malachi watched Cole, and he noticed the nervous tension that refused to ease from his features. There was a hardness about him today. Malachi understood it. He just didn't know how to ease it.

Let it rest! Malachi thought. Let it go. Kristin McCahy—no, Slater now—was young, beautiful and intelligent, and if he wasn't mistaken, she was in love with Cole. Cole was too caught up in his memories of tragedy to see it. Even if he did see it, it might not change anything. Malachi knew his brother had acted out of a sense of chivalry. He also knew Kristin would have preferred he hadn't. Malachi sighed. Their personal lives were none of his business. He had to leave. He was a regular soldier in a regular army, and his leave was about up.

"This is kind of dumb, ain't it?" Jamie demanded, swallowing some of the whiskey.

"Dumb?" Cole asked.

"Hell, yes. You've got yourself a gorgeous bride, young and shapely—"

"And what the hell do you know about her shape?" Cole demanded heatedly.

"Come on, you can't miss it," Malachi protested dryly. He was determined to have a peaceful evening. He sent Jamie a warning scowl. They both knew what was bothering Cole. "Jamie...stop it."

"Why? Does Cole think he's the only one who's been hurt by this war?"

"Damned brat—" Cole began angrily.

"But the damned brat came running when you asked, Cole, so sit back. Hell, come on, both of you stop it."

"I just think he should appreciate the woman, that's all. And if he didn't mean to, damn it, he shouldn't have tied her up in chains like that."

Cole, exasperated, stared at Malachi. "Will you shut him up, or should I?"

"There's a war on, boys!" Malachi reminded them both.

"He should be decent to her—" Jamie began.

"Damn it, I am decent to her!" Cole roared.

"Leaving her alone on her wedding night—"

"Leaving her alone was the most decent damned thing I could do!" Cole said. He wrenched the whiskey bottle from his brother's hands. "You're too young for this stuff."

"Hell, I'm too old," Jamie said softly. He grinned ruefully at his brother, and all the tension between them seemed to dissipate. "I'm twenty, Cole. By some standards, that's real old. Seventeen-year-old boys are dying all over the place."

"Quantrill is running a bunch of boys," Cole said. He lifted his hand in a vague gesture. "The James boys. The Youngers. And that butcher Bill Anderson. He's just a kid."

He swallowed the liquor, then swallowed again. He felt like being drunk. Really drunk.

Malachi reached for the bottle. The firelight played over his hair, and he arched his golden brows at Cole. "You think that Quantrill can really control his men? That marrying Kristin can keep her safe?"

Cole looked out at the Missouri plain before him, gnawing on a blade of grass. He spit out the grass and looked over at his brothers, who were both looking at him anxiously. If he hadn't been knotted up inside he might have smiled. They were both concerned. There was something about the McCahy place that got to a man. He could understand how even the great struggle between North and South had ceased to matter here, had ceased to matter to Kristin. The brutality here was too much. It left the mind numbed.

"I know Quantrill is about to head south for the winter. He doesn't like the cold. He'll make one more raid, I'm certain. Then he'll head on somewhere south—maybe Arkansas, maybe Texas. I'll stick around until he moves on. Then I'll go on over to Richmond. If I can just find some train tracks that are still holding together, I should make it in time."

"If Jefferson Davis is still in the Cabinet," Jamie said glumly.

Cole looked at him sharply. "Why? What have you heard?"

"Nothing. It's just that the battle of Sharpsburg left a lot of dead men. A whole lot of dead men."

"Watch your step around here," Malachi warned Cole. "There's Federal patrols wandering all around the McCahy place."

"Yeah, I know."

"That little witch just about got me hauled in today."

"Witch?" Cole asked.

"Shannon," Jamie supplied.

Malachi grunted. "I envy you your wife, Cole, but not your in-laws."

"And he doesn't mean the Yankee brother." Jamie laughed. "It's a good thing Malachi has to ride out soon. I don't think she's too fond of him, either."

Malachi looked as if he wanted to kill somebody, Jamie thought, but at least Cole laughed, and Cole needed it the most. "What have I missed?" Cole asked.

"The antics of a child," Malachi replied, waving a dismissing hand in the air. He reached for the liquor bottle. It was going down quickly.

"Some child!" Jamie said. "Why, she's coming along just as nicely as that wife of yours, Cole."

Malachi and Cole looked at one another. "We could end this war if we just sent this boy to Washington to heckle the Union commanders," Malachi said.

Cole grunted his agreement. Jamie grinned and lay back against his saddle, staring up at the stars. "You know, Cole," he said suddenly, "I am sorry about the past. I sure am."

There was a long silence. The fire snapped and crackled. Malachi held his breath and held his peace.

"But if I were you," Jamie went on, "I wouldn't be out here with my brothers. Not when I had a woman like that waiting. A woman with beautiful blond hair and eyes like sapphires. And the way she walks, her hips swinging and all... Why, I can just imagine what it'd be like—"

"Son of a bitch!" Cole roared suddenly. He stood up, slamming the nearly empty whiskey bottle into the fire. The liquor hissed and sizzled. Jamie leaped to his feet, startled by the deadly dark danger in his brother's eyes. Malachi, too, leaped to his feet. He couldn't believe that Cole would really go for Jamie, but then he had never seen Cole in a torment like this. Nor had he ever seen Jamie so determined to irk him.

"Cole—" Malachi reached for his brother's arm, and they stared at one another in the golden firelight.

"No!" Jamie told Malachi, his eyes on Cole. "If he wants to beat me up, let him. If he thinks he can strike out at me and feel better, fine. Let him hurt me instead of that poor girl waiting for him at the house. At least I understand why he strikes out. Hell, she doesn't even know why he's so damned hateful."

"What the hell difference does it make?" Cole thundered. "All she wanted from me was protection!"

"She deserves some damned decency from you!"

"I told you—"

"Yeah, yeah, you came up with some puny excuse. You are a bastard."

"You don't know—"

"I know that it wasn't my wife killed by the jayhawkers, but we loved her, too, Cole. And she loved you, and she wouldn't want you making your whole life nothing but ugly vengeance."

"Why, I ought to—"

"Cole!" Malachi shouted. Between the three of them, they'd consumed almost an entire bottle of liquor. This wasn't a good time for Jamie to be goading Cole, but Jamie didn't seem to care. And now Cole was losing control. He shook off Malachi's arm and lunged at Jamie with a sudden fury. Then the two of them were rolling in the dust.

"Jesus in heaven!" Malachi breathed. "Will the two of you—"

"You don't know! You don't know anything!" Cole raged at Jamie. "You didn't find her, you didn't feel the blood pouring out all over you! You didn't see her eyes close, you didn't see the love as it died. You didn't watch her eyes close and feel her flesh grow cold!"

"Cole!"

His hands were around Jamie's neck, and Jamie wasn't doing anything at all. He was letting Cole throttle him. Malachi tried to pull him off, and Cole suddenly realized what he was doing. Horrified, he released his brother. Then he stood and walked away, his back to his brothers.

"I need to stay away from Kristin," he said softly.

Jamie looked at Malachi and rubbed his throat. Malachi spoke to Cole.

"No. You don't need to stay away from her. You need to go to her."

Cole turned around. He came over to Jamie and planted his hands on his brother's shoulders. "You all right?"

Jamie nodded and grinned. "I'm all right."

Cole walked over to his horse. He untied the reins which were tethered to a tree, and walked the horse into the open. Then he leaped up on the animal's back without bothering to saddle it.

"You going back?" Malachi asked.

"Just for another bottle of whiskey."

Malachi and Jamie nodded. They watched as Cole started back toward the house, the horse's hooves suddenly taking flight in the darkness.

"He's just going back for another whiskey bottle," Jamie said.

Malachi laughed. "We betting on when he's going to make it back?"

Jamie grinned. "You get to bring his saddle in the morning." He lay down again and stretched out, feeling his throat. "Too bad I wasn't blessed with sisters!" He groaned.

Malachi grunted, pulled his hat low over his face and closed his eyes. The fire crackled and burned low, and at last the two of them slept.

Cole heard one of Pete's hounds barking as he approached the house. Then Pete himself, shirtless, the top of his long johns showing above his hastily donned trousers, came out to challenge him.

"Just me, Pete," Cole assured him.

"Evening, boss," Pete said agreeably, and headed back to the bunkhouse.

Cole dismounted from his horse, sliding from the animal's back without his accustomed grace. He gave his head a shake to clear it. The whiskey had gotten to him more than he would have cared to admit, but not enough to really knock him out the way he wanted, not enough to take away the last of his pain. He was determined to be quiet, but it seemed to him that his boots made an ungodly noise on the floorboards of the porch.

The house was dark. He stumbled through the hall and the parlor and into what had been Gabriel McCahy's office. He fumbled around for a match and lit the oil lamp on the desk, then came around and sat in the chair, putting his feet up on the desk and digging in the lower right hand drawer for a bottle of liquor—any kind of liquor.

Then he heard a click, and the hair on the back of his neck stood straight up. His whiskey-dulled reflexes came to life, and he slammed his feet to the floor, reaching for his revolver.

He pointed it at the doorway—and right at Kristin, who stood there with a double-barreled shotgun aimed at his head. He swore irritably, returning his gun to his holster and sinking back into his chair.

"What the hell are you doing?" he growled.

"What am I doing? You son of a bitch—" She lowered the shotgun and moved into the room. She stopped in front of the desk, caught in the soft glow of the lamplight. Her hair was loose, a soft storm of sunshine falling over her shoulders. She was dressed chastely enough, in a nightgown that buttoned to her throat, but the lamplight went through the fabric and caressed her body. He could see all too clearly the sway of her hips, which Jamie had so admired. He could see the curve of her breasts, the flow and shape of her limbs, and suddenly the sight of her hurt him. It was as if some mighty hand reached down and took hold of him, squeezing the life from him. He felt his heart pounding, felt his shuddering pulse enter his groin and take root there. His fingers itched to reach out to her, to touch her. She was staring at him, her blue eyes a raging sea of fury, and not even that deterred him. It only made the pulse within him beat all the harder.

He didn't love her. To love her would be disloyal. But he had married her. What the hell else could she want?

"What are you doing in here?" she snapped.

"Kristin, put the gun down. Go to bed."

"You scared me to death! And *you* taught *me* not to go wandering around unarmed!"

"Kristin, put the gun down." He hesitated. Then he smiled suddenly. "Come on. We'll go to bed. Together."

Her eyes widened. "You're out of your mind, Cole Slater."

"Am I?" He came around the desk, slowly, lazily, yet purposefully. Kristin raised the shotgun again.

"Yes! You are out of your mind."

"You're my wife."

"And you walked out of here this afternoon and didn't come back until three in the morning—after treating me with the manners of a rabid squirrel. I promise you, Mr. Slater, if you think you're going to touch me, you're out of your mind."

He *was* out of his mind, and he knew it. He swallowed raggedly. He had forgotten so much. He had tried to forget. He had forgotten that she could hold her head with such incredible pride. He had forgotten her eyes could snap this way, and he had forgotten that her mouth was wide and generous and beautifully shaped. He had forgotten that she was beautiful and sensuous, and that her touch was more potent than whiskey or wine or the finest brandy. He had forgotten so much....

But now he remembered. The revealing lamplight glowed on the lush curves of her body, and the thunder inside him became almost unbearable. He took a step forward, and she cocked the shotgun. His smile deepened.

"Fire it, Kristin."

"I will, damn you!"

He laughed triumphantly, stepped toward her again and took the shotgun from her hands. He pulled her hard against him, and he lowered his head and seized her lips in a kiss. It was not at all brutal, but it was filled with a shocking need and a shocking thirst. For an instant she thought to twist from him, but his kiss filled her with a searing, liquid heat, and she felt as if she were bursting with the desire to touch him, to be touched by him.

He broke away from her, and his eyes sought hers. "No!" she told him angrily, but he smiled and swept her up into his arms. Her eyes were still angry but she locked her arms around his neck. He carried her effortlessly through the darkened parlor, up the stairs and into the bedroom. He closed the door with his foot and set her down by the window. The moonlight found her there, dancing over her fine, delicate features and her rich, feminine curves.

"You're horrid," she told him.

He smiled tenderly. "You're beautiful."

"You're filthy."

He kissed her forehead, and he kissed her cheeks, and he rimmed her lips with the tip of his tongue, teasing them, dampening them. His fingers went to the tiny buttons of her gown, and he tried to undo them but they wouldn't give, and he finally ripped the gown open impatiently. The moonlight fell on her naked flesh. He groaned and kissed her shoulder and her throat, feeling the urgent quickening of her heart.

"Does it matter so terribly much?" he whispered.

She didn't answer. He stroked her breast. Then he lowered his head and touched his lips to the nipple. He teased it with his teeth, then sucked it hard into his mouth and finally gentled it with his tongue. Rivers of pleasure streaked through her, and she threaded her fingers roughly into his hair, and he savored the little tug of pain. He lowered himself slowly to his knees, holding her hips, then her buttocks.

"Does it matter so terribly much?" he repeated, looking up into her dazed eyes. He teased her navel with the tip of his tongue.

"Yes!" she whispered. He started to move away from her, but she wouldn't let him. He bathed her belly with kisses, cupping her buttocks hard and pressing close to her, sliding his tongue along the apex of her thighs and into the golden triangle there. She shuddered and cried out, but he held her firmly, and when it seemed she was about to fall he lowered her carefully to the floor. He touched her gently and tenderly, and then he brought his mouth over hers again. "Does it really matter so terribly much?" he demanded.

She closed her eyes and wrapped her arms around his neck. "No," she whispered, and she released him to tug at his buttons and then at his belt buckle. She groaned in frustration, and he helped her, stripping quickly. She was so very beautiful, there in the full flood of the moonlight. All of him quickened, and desire spread through him like a raging wind, and he cried out in a ragged voice. She was there, there to take him, there to close around him, a sweet and secret haven. Nothing on earth was like this.

He sank into her, swept into her, again and again. She rose to meet his every thrust, and the pulse raged between them. She was liquid fire when she moved. She was made to have him, made to love him, made to take him. The culmination burst upon them swiftly. She gasped and shuddered, and he thrust heatedly, again and felt his climax spew from him. He held her tight. He felt the sweat, slick between them. He felt the rise and fall of her breath and the clamor of her heart, slowing at last.

He stroked her hair, and he marveled at the ecstasy of it.

Then he remembered that he had made her his wife, and suddenly he hated himself again.

He should have said something. He should have whispered something to her. Anything. Anything that was tender, anything that was kind.

He couldn't bring himself to do it.

Instead, he rose, his skin glistening in the moonlight. Then he bent down and took her naked form in his arms. She was silent, her eyes lowered, her hair a tangle around them.

He laid her down upon the bed. Her eyes met his at last, and he saw in them a torment that seemed to match that within his heart. She was so very beautiful. Naked, she was a goddess, her breasts firm and full and perfect, her limbs shapely and slim, her belly a fascinating plane between her hips. He pulled the covers over her. Her sapphire eyes still studied him.

"I'm...I'm sorry," he muttered at last.

She let out a strangled oath and turned away from him.

He hesitated, then slipped in beside her. He crossed his arms behind his head and stared up at the ceiling, wishing he were drunker, wishing fervently he could go to sleep.

But he lay awake a long, long time. And he knew she didn't sleep, either.

At dawn he rose and left.

And at dawn Kristin finally slept. She had the right to stay in bed all day, she told herself bitterly. She was a bride, and this was the morning after her wedding day.

Cole wasn't in the house when she finally did get up. Shannon told her he had gone out with Malachi.

Jamie was there, though. He told her that they were low on salt and that they needed a couple of blocks for the cattle to lick through the winter. Cole had said that she and Pete were to go into town and buy them.

The Union had control of most of the border area—despite Quantrill's sporadic raids—and the town had managed to remain quieter than the McCahy ranch. Kristin was glad to take the buckboard and ride into town with Pete. She was glad to be away from the house.

It was a three-hour ride. The town of Little Ford was small, but it did have two saloons, one reputable hotel, two doctors old enough to be exempted from military service and three mercantile stores. In Jaffe's Mercantile she saw Tommy Norley, a newspaperman and and old friend of Adam's from over the Kansas border.

"Kristin!"

He was limping when he came over to her. He tipped his hat quickly, then took both her hands in his. "Kristin, how are you doing out there? Is everything all right? You and Shannon should have moved on, I think. Or maybe into town. Or maybe out to California!"

She smiled. He was a slim man, pale-faced, with a pencil-thin mustache and dark, soulful eyes.

"I'm doing well, Tommy, thank you." She searched his eyes. She had last seen him when they had buried her father. He had written a scathing article about guerrilla attacks.

"You should move, Kristin."

She chose to ignore his words. "Tommy, you're limping."

He smiled grimly. "I just got caught by Quantrill."

Her heart skipped a beat. "What do you mean? What happened?"

"The bastard attacked Shawneetown last week. I was with the Federal supply train he and his maniacs caught up with on their way in." He paused and looked at her, wondering how much he should say to a lady.

"Tommy, tell me! What happened?"

He took a deep breath. "Kristin, it was awful. Quantrill and his men came after us like a pack of Indians, howling, shouting. They gunned down fifteen men, drivers and escorts. I rolled off the side of the road, into the foliage. I took a bullet in the calf, but I lived to tell the tale. Kristin, they went on into town and murdered ten more men there. Then they burned the village to the ground."

"Oh, God! How horrible!" Kristin gasped.

"Kristin, come to Kansas. I'm opening an office in Lawrence, and I'm sure you'll be safe."

She smiled. "Tommy, my home is in Missouri."

"But you're in danger."

"I can't leave the ranch, Tommy." She wondered if she should tell him that she had married to save her ranch and that she would probably be in real danger from her new husband if she deserted him and ran off to Kansas.

"You should have seen them," Tommy murmured. "Kristin, they were savages. You should have seen them."

She held on to the counter in the mercantile, suddenly feeling ill. He kept talking, and she answered him as politely as she could. She cared about Tommy. He had been a good friend to Adam. It was just that Adam had begun to fade from her life. It was not that she hadn't loved him. She had. But Cole was a stronger force in her life.

Kristin hesitated, then asked him if he thought he could get a message to Matthew for her. He promised to try, and she bought some stationery from Mr. Jaffe and quickly wrote a letter to Matthew. It wasn't easy to explain her marriage. She did it as carefully and as cheerfully as she could, then turned the letter over to Tommy, hoping she had done well.

She kissed Tommy and left him. Pete had gotten the salt licks, and he had stacked the remaining space in the buckboard with alfalfa to help get them through the coming winter.

She told him about Shawneetown, then fell silent. The news bothered her all the way home.

When they arrived at the ranch, she still felt ill. She went out back and stood over her parents' graves. Cold and chilled, she tried to pray, but no thoughts came to her mind.

A while later she felt a presence behind her, and she knew that it was Cole. She was angry, and she didn't know why, unless it was because she knew he didn't love her, and because she knew she was falling in love with him. He was attracted to her, certainly. Maybe he even needed her. But he didn't love her.

She spun around, ready to do battle.

"Quantrill and his animals attacked Shawneetown last week. They killed the men escorting a supply train, and then they went into the village and killed some more, and then they burned the whole place down."

His eyes narrowed, and he stared at her warily, but he didn't say anything. She walked up to him and slammed her fists against his chest. "He's a captain! The Confederates made him a captain!"

He grabbed her wrists hard. "I don't condone Quantrill, and you know it. The Missouri governor considers him and his raiders like an elephant won at a raffle."

"Let go of me!" she hissed furiously.

"No. You listen to me for a minute, lady. Quantrill has no monopoly on brutality! Quantrill came *after* the likes of Lane and Jennison. Unionists, Kristin! Jayhawkers! You want to know some of the things they've done? They've ridden up to farmhouses and dragged men out and killed them—men *and* women! They've murdered and they've raped and they've tortured, exactly the same way Quantrill has! You remember that, Kristin! You bear that in mind real well!"

He pushed her away from him and turned, his long, angry strides taking him toward the house. The rear door opened and then slammed shut, and he disappeared inside.

She waited a moment, and then she followed him. She didn't know if she wanted to continue the fight or try to make up with him somehow.

It didn't matter. He wasn't in the house anymore.

And that night he didn't come back at all.

Chapter Ten

Cole might have slept somewhere else during the night, but he appeared at the breakfast table in the morning. Kristin was angry and wondered what everyone must think. He came and went like the breeze, with no regard for her feelings. Kristin was sharp when he spoke to her. When he asked her to pass him the milk, she seriously considered splashing it in his face or pouring it in his lap. He caught her hand and the pitcher before she could do either. He stared at her hard, and she looked away.

She didn't like Cole's ability to stay away from her. She wanted to fight with him. She wanted to do anything just to bring him close to her again. It was an effort to turn away from him, to find some trivial thing to discuss with Jamie and Shannon.

Cole remained in a foul temper all day. With winter coming on, there was a lot to do. Cole was anxious to have it all done before he left for the East and before Malachi and Jamie had to leave to rejoin their units. They spent the day gathering up as much of the herd as they could for Pete to drive to market. Kristin had been surprised that Cole was willing to let her sell the beef on the Union side of the line, but he had reminded her that the ranch belonged to her brother, Matthew, and that Matthew was fighting for the Union. Cole couldn't go north himself, but Pete could handle the cattle drive, and Malachi and Jamie would be around until he got back at the end of the week.

By dinnertime, Cole seemed to be in a somewhat better mood, and Kristin maintained a polite distance from him. Cole, Jamie and Malachi all sat down to dinner with Kristin and Shannon that night.

Delilah refused to sit and made a big fuss over everyone. Jamie made the meal a pleasant affair. He told the two girls about a pair of hammers his mother had bought for Cole and Malachi when they were boys and about how the two of them had used their hammers on one another. Even Shannon laughed and refrained from engaging in verbal warfare with Malachi. Cole listened to the story with a smile on his face, and at one point his eyes met Kristin's and he gave her an entrancing grin and a sheepish shrug.

After dinner, Kristin played the spinet and Shannon sang. She sang a few light tunes, then gave a haunting rendition of "Lorena", a ballad about a soldier who returns from the wars to find that his love is gone. When it was over, they were all silent. Then Cole stood up and told Shannon in a strangled voice that her singing was very beautiful. He excused himself and left them.

Kristin bit her lip as she watched him leave the room. Jamie gave her an encouraging pat on the knee, and Malachi practically shoved Shannon out of the way and began a rousing chorus of "Dixie."

When he had finished, Shannon regained her place and sang "John Brown's Body."

"Shannon McCahy, you are a brat," Malachi told her.

"And you're a rodent," Shannon replied sweetly.

"Children, children!" Jamie protested with a sigh.

But Shannon said something, and though Kristin could see that Malachi was striving for patience, he replied sharply, and the battle was on once again.

Kristin rose and left them bickering. She went upstairs and was surprised to find that Cole was already in bed. She thought he was asleep, but when she crawled in beside him, trying not to disturb him, he turned over and took her in his arms. She tried to study his eyes in the darkness, but she could see only their silver glow. She tried to speak, but he silenced her with a kiss. Tenderly at first, and then with a growing passion, he made love to her. When it was over, he held her close, his bearded chin resting against the top of her head. He didn't speak, and neither did she. She knew he lay there awake for a long time, and she wished she could reach out to him, wished she knew what to say to him. She could not apologize, for she had done nothing wrong. She kept silent.

Eventually Kristin fell asleep.

Sometime later, something woke her. She didn't know what it was at first. She heard something, some hoarse, whispered words that she didn't understand. Struggling to free herself from the web of sleep, she opened her eyes, just as Cole's arm came flying out and slammed against her shoulder.

She sat up in bed, calling out his name. He didn't answer her, and she fumbled for a match to light the oil lamp on the bedside table. The glow filled the room and fell on Cole.

The bare flesh of his shoulders and chest was gleaming with sweat. The muscles there were tense and rigid and knotted. His fingers plucked at the sheet that lay over him.

His features contorted, his head tossing from side to side, he screamed, "No!" His entire body was stiff and hard.

"Cole!" Kristin pleaded, shaking him. "Cole—"

"No!" he screamed again.

She straddled him, took him by the shoulders and shook him hard, determined to wake him.

His eyes flew open, but he didn't see her. He called out again, and then he struck out at her, and the force sent her flying to the floor. He jerked upright as she fell. Stunned, Kristin sat on the hard floor, rubbing her bruised behind.

"Kristin?"

He whispered her name slowly, fearfully. There was something in his voice that she had never heard before, a frightened tone, and it touched her deeply.

"I'm here," she whispered ruefully.

He looked over the side of the bed and swore. He leaped swiftly from the bed, and took her in his arms. She felt the pounding of his heart, felt the tremors that still racked him as he laid her down on the bed again.

"I hurt you. I'm so sorry."

His voice was deep, husky. She felt her own throat constrict, and she shook her head, burrowing more deeply against his naked chest. "No. You didn't hurt me. I'm all right, really."

He didn't say anything. He didn't even move. He just held her.

She wanted to stay there, where she was, forever. She had never felt so cherished before. Desired, admired, even needed. But never so cherished.

"You had a nightmare," she told him tentatively.

"Yes," he said.

"I wish you would tell me—"

"No."

It wasn't that he spoke so harshly, but that he spoke with absolute finality. Kristin stiffened, and she knew he felt it. He set her from him and rose. She watched as he walked over to the window, and as he stood there in the moonlight a dark web of pain seemed to encircle her heart. He walked with a pride that was uniquely his. He stood there for a long time, naked and sinewed and gleaming in the moonlight, and stared out at the night. Kristin watched as his muscles slowly, slowly eased, losing some of their awful rigor.

"Cole—" she whispered.

He turned back to her at last. He walked across the room, and she was glad when he lifted the covers and lay beside her again, drawing his arm around her and bringing her head to his chest. He stroked her hair.

"Cole, please—"

"Kristin, please. Don't."

She fell silent. His touch remained gentle.

"I have to leave tomorrow," he said at last.

"Where are you going?"

"East."

"Why?"

He hesitated for a long time. "Kristin, there are things that you probably don't want to hear, and there's no good reason for me to tell you."

"No questions, no involvement," she murmured. He didn't answer her, but she felt him tighten beneath her.

"It's late," he said at last. "You should—"

She rose up and touched his lips with her own, cutting off his words. She wondered if she should be angry, or at least cool and distant. Nothing had changed. He had married her, but he still didn't want any involvement.

That didn't matter to her. Not at that moment. She only knew that he was leaving, and that in these times any man's future was uncertain at best. She ceased the flow of his words with the soft play of her tongue and leaned the length of her body over his, undulating her hips against his groin and the hardened peaks of her breasts against his chest. She savored the sharp intake of his breath and the quick, heady pressure of his hands upon her back and her buttocks.

Now it was her turn to inflame him. She nuzzled her face against his beard, and she teased his throat and the hard contours of his shoulders and chest. She tempted him with her tongue and with her fingertips and with the entire length of her body. She moved against him, crying out again and again at the sweet feel of their flesh touching. She teased him with her teeth, moving lower and lower against him. He tore his fingers into her hair and hoarsely gasped out her name. She barely knew herself. She was at once serene and excited, and she was certain of her power. She took all of him without hesitation. She loved him until he dragged her back to him and kissed her feverishly on the lips, then drew her beneath him. There was a new tension etched into his features, and a new blaze in his eyes. Taut as wire, he hovered above her. Then he came to her, fierce and savage and yet uniquely tender.

She thought she died just a little when it was over. The world was radiant, painted with shocking strips of sunlight and starlight, and then it was black and she was drifting again.

He held her still. He didn't speak, but his fingers stroked her hair, and for the moment it was enough. His hand lay over her abdomen. Tentatively she placed her fingers over his. He laced them through his own, and they slept.

But in the morning when she awoke, he was gone.

Three days later, Kristin was pumping water into the trough when she looked up to see a lone rider on the horizon, coming toward the house. For a moment her heart fluttered and she wondered if it might be Cole returning. Then she realized it couldn't be him. It wasn't his horse, and the rider wasn't sitting the horse the way he did.

"Malachi!" she called. He and Jamie would be with her for another few days. She frowned and bit her lip as she watched the approaching rider. It wasn't Zeke, she knew. Zeke never rode alone.

Besides, there was no reason for her to be afraid of Quantrill's boys. Cole had gone through with the wedding to protect her, and anyway, Quantrill was supposed to be moving south for the winter. There was no reason to be afraid.

She was afraid anyway.

"Malachi—" she began again.

"Kristin?" He appeared at the door to the barn, his thumbs hooked in his belt, his golden brows knit into a furrow. He hurried over to her and watched the rider come. His eyes narrowed.

"Anderson," he murmured.

"Who?"

"It's a boy named Bill Anderson. He's...he's one of Quantrill's. One of his young recruits."

"What does he want? He is alone, isn't he?" Kristin asked anxiously.

"Yes, he's alone," Malachi assured her.

Jamie appeared then, coming out of the barn, his sleeves rolled up, his jacket off. He looked at Malachi. "I thought Quantrill was already on his way south. That's Bill Anderson."

Malachi nodded. "He seems to be alone."

The rider came closer and closer. He was young, very young, with a broad smile. He had dark, curly hair and a dark mustache and beard, but he still had an absurdly innocent face. Kristin shivered, thinking that he was far too young to be going around committing murder.

He drew his horse up in front of them. He was well armed, Kristin saw, with Colts at his waist and a rifle on either side of his saddle.

"Howdy, Malachi, Jamie."

"Bill," Malachi said amiably enough. Jamie nodded an acknowledgment.

"Cole's headed east, huh?" Anderson asked. He smiled at Kristin, waiting for an introduction. "You his new wife, ma'am? It's a pleasure to meet you."

He stuck out his hand. Kristin thought about all the blood that was probably on that hand, but she took it anyway and forced herself to smile.

"I'm his new wife," Kristin said. She couldn't bring herself to say that it was a pleasure to meet him, too. She could barely stand there.

"Kristin Slater, this is Bill Anderson. Bill, what the hell are you doing here? There's a lot of Union soldiers around these parts, you know," Malachi said.

"Yep," Jamie agreed cheerfully. "Lots and lots of Federals in these parts. And you know what they've been saying about you boys? No mercy. If they get their hands on you they intend to hang you high and dry."

"Yeah. I've heard what the Union has to say. But you've been safe enough here, huh, Malachi? And you, too, Jamie."

"Hell, we're regular army," Jamie said.

Anderson shrugged. "They have to catch us before they can hang us. And I'm not staying. I just had...well, I had some business here-abouts. I've got to join Quantrill in Arkansas. I just thought maybe I could come by here for a nice home-cooked meal."

Malachi answered before Kristin could. "Sure, Bill. Jamie, why don't you go on in and ask Delilah to cook up something special. Tell her we've got one of Quantrill's boys here."

Jamie turned around and hurried to the house. Delilah was already standing in the doorway. As Kristin watched, Shannon's blond head appeared. There was a squeal of outrage, and then the door slammed. Jamie came hurrying back to them.

"Malachi, Delilah says she needs you. There's a bit of a problem to be dealt with."

Malachi lifted an eyebrow, then hurried to the house. Kristin stood there staring foolishly at Bill Anderson with a grin plastered to her face. She wanted to shriek, and rip his baby face to shreds. Didn't he understand? Didn't he know she didn't want him here?

Men using Quantrill's name had come here and murdered her father. Men just like this one. She wanted to spit in his face.

But he had evidently come for a reason, and Malachi seemed to think it was necessary that he be convinced that Kristin was Cole's wife and that this was Cole's place now.

Kristin heard an outraged scream from the house. She bit her lip. Shannon obviously realized that one of Quantrill's men was here, and she didn't intend to keep quiet. She certainly didn't intend to sit down to a meal with him.

Anderson looked toward the house, hiking a brow.

"My sister," Kristin said sweetly.

"Her baby sister," Jamie said. He smiled at Kristin, but there was a warning in his eyes. They had to make Bill Anderson think Shannon was just a little girl.

And they had to keep her away from him.

Apparently that was what Malachi was doing, because the screams became muffled, and then they were silenced.

Malachi—the marks of Shannon's fingernails on his cheek—reappeared on the front porch. "Come on in, Bill. We'll have a brandy, and then Delilah will have lunch all set."

Bill looked from Malachi to Kristin and grinned. "That came from your, uh...baby sister, Mrs. Slater?"

"She can be wild when she wants," Kristin said sweetly. She stared hard at Malachi. He touched his cheek and shrugged. Kristin walked by him. "Too bad they can't send her up to take on the Army of the Potomac. We'd win this war in a matter of hours. Old Abe Lincoln himself would think that secession was a fine thing just as long as Shannon McCahy went with the Confederacy."

"Malachi!" Kristin whispered harshly. "You're talking about my sister!"

"I ought to turn her over to Bill Anderson!" he muttered.

"Malachi!"

Anderson turned around, looking at them curiously. "Where is your sister?" he asked.

"The baby is tucked in for her nap," Malachi said with a grin. "We don't let her dine with adults when we have company in the house. She spits her peas out sometimes. You know how young 'uns are."

Kristin gazed at him, and he looked innocently back at her. She swept by him. "Mr. Anderson, can we get you a drink? A shot of whiskey?"

"Yes, ma'am, you can."

Kristin took him into her father's study and poured him a drink.

As he looked around the room, admiring the furnishings, Malachi came in and whispered in her ear.

"Shannon's in the cellar."

"And she's just staying there?" Kristin asked, her eyes wide.

"Sure she's just staying there," Malachi said.

Soon they sat down to eat. Sizzling steaks from the ranch's own fresh beef, fried potatoes, fall squash and apple pie. Bill Anderson did have one big appetite. Kristin reminded herself dryly that he was a growing boy.

He was polite, every inch the Southern cavalier, all through the meal. Only when coffee was served with the pie did he sit back and give them an indication of why he had come.

"Saw your husband the other day, ma'am."

Kristin paused just a second in scooping him out a second slice of pie. "Did you?" she said sweetly.

"Sure, when he came to see Quantrill. He was mighty worried about you. It was a touching scene."

She set the pie down. "Was it?" She glanced at Malachi. His eyes were narrowed, and he was very still.

"He used to be one of us, you know."

"What?"

Despite herself, Kristin sat. She sank right into her chair. "What?" she repeated.

Jamie cleared his throat. Malachi still hadn't moved.

Bill Anderson wiped his face with his napkin and smiled pleasantly. "Cole is one of the finest marksmen I ever did see. Hell, he's a one-man army, he's so damned good. It was nice when he was riding with us."

Kristin didn't say anything. She knew all the blood had fled from her face.

Bill Anderson forked up a piece of pie. "Yep, Cole Slater was just the same as Zeke Moreau. Just the same."

Malachi was on his feet in a second, his knife at Anderson's throat. "My brother was never anything like Zeke Moreau!"

Jamie jumped up behind him. He was so tense that Jamie couldn't pull him away. Kristin rushed around and tugged at his arm. "Malachi!"

He backed away. Bill Anderson stood and straightened his jacket. He gazed at Malachi, murder in his eyes. "You'll die for that, Slater."

"Maybe I'll die, but not for that, Anderson!" Malachi said.

"Gentlemen, gentlemen!" Kristin breathed, using her softest voice. "Please, aren't we forgetting ourselves here?"

It worked. Like most young men in the South, they had both been taught to be courteous to females, that a lack of manners was a horrible fault. They stepped away from each other, but their tempers were still hot.

"You came here just to do that, didn't you?" Malachi said quietly. "Just to upset my sister-in-law. I'm willing to bet Zeke Moreau asked you to do it."

"Maybe, and maybe not," Anderson said. He reached over to the sideboard for his hat. "Maybe she's just got the right to know that Cole Slater was a bushwhacker. You want to deny that, Malachi?"

Kristin looked at Malachi. His face was white, but he said nothing.

Anderson slammed his hat on his head. He turned to Kristin. "Mighty obliged for the meal, ma'am. Mighty obliged. Cap'n Quantrill wants you to know that you should feel safe, and he's sorry about any harm that's been done to you or yours. If he had understood that your loyalties lay with the Confederacy, none of it would have come about."

It was a lie, a bald-faced lie, but Kristin didn't say anything. Anderson turned around, and she heard the door slam shut as he left the house.

Delilah came in from the kitchen. The old grandfather clock in the parlor struck the hour. They all stood there, just stood there, dead still, until they heard Bill Anderson mount his horse, until they heard the hoofbeats disappear across the Missouri dust.

Then Kristin spun around, gripping the back of a chair and staring hard at Malachi. "Is it true?"

"Kristin—" he began unhappily.

"Is it true?" she screeched. "Is Cole one of them?"

"No!" Jamie protested, stepping forward. "He isn't one of them, not now."

She whirled around again, looking at Jamie. "But he was! That's the truth, isn't it?"

"Yes, damn it, all right, he was. But there was a damned good reason for it."

"Jamie!" Malachi snapped.

"Oh, God!" Kristin breathed. She came around and fell into the chair. Malachi tried to take her hand. She wrenched it away and jumped to her feet. "Don't, please don't! Can't you understand? They are murderers! They dragged my father out and they killed him!"

"There are a lot of murderers in this war, Kristin," Malachi said. "Quantrill isn't the only one."

"It was Quantrill's men who killed my father," she said dully. "It was Quantrill's men who came after me."

Malachi didn't come near her again. He stood at the end of the table, his face pinched. "Kristin, Cole's business is Cole's business, and when he chooses, maybe he'll explain things to you. He's asked us to mind our own concerns. Maybe he knew you'd react just like this if you heard something. I don't know. But you remember this while you're busy hating him. He stumbled into this situation. He didn't come here to hurt you." He turned and walked to the door.

"He rode with Quantrill!" she whispered desperately.

"He's done the best he knows how for you," Malachi said quietly. He paused and looked back at her. "You might want to let your sister go when you get the chance. I tied her up downstairs so she wouldn't take a trip up here to meet Bill Anderson. He might not have liked what she had to say very much…and he might have liked the way that she looked too much."

He went out. The clock suddenly seemed to be ticking very loudly. Kristin looked miserably at Jamie.

He tried to smile, but the attempt fell flat. "I guess I can't tell you too much of anything, Kristin. But I love my brother, and I think he's a fine man. There are things that maybe you can't understand just yet, and they are his business to discuss." He paused, watching her awkwardly. Then he shrugged and he, too, left her.

It wasn't a good day. She sat there for a long time. She even forgot about Shannon, and it was almost an hour before she went downstairs to release her. When she did, it was as if she had let loose a wounded tigress. Shannon cursed and ranted and raved and swore that someday, somehow if the war didn't kill Malachi, she would see to it that he was laid out herself.

She would probably have gone out and torn Malachi to shreds right then and there, but fortunately he had ridden out to take a look at some fencing.

Shannon was even furious with Kristin. "How could you? How could you? You let that man into our house, into Pa's house! After everything that has been done—"

"I did it so that Quantrill would leave us alone from now on! Maybe you've forgotten Zeke. I haven't!"

"Wait until Matthew comes back!" Shannon cried. "He'll take care of the Quantrill murderers and Malachi and—"

"Shannon," Kristin said wearily, "I thought you were going to take care of Malachi yourself?" She was hurt, and she was tired, and she couldn't keep the anger from her voice. "If you want to kill one of the Slater brothers, why don't you go after the right one?"

"What do you mean?" Shannon demanded.

"Cole," Kristin said softly. She stared ruefully at her sister. "Cole Slater. The man I married. He rode with Quantrill, Shannon. He was one of them."

"Cole?" Shannon's beautiful eyes were fierce. "I don't believe you!"

"It's the truth. That's why Bill Anderson came here. He wanted me to know that I had married a man every bit as bad as Zeke Moreau."

"He's lying."

"He wasn't lying. Malachi admitted it."

"Then Malachi was lying."

"No, Shannon. You two have your differences, but Malachi wouldn't lie to me."

Shannon was silent for several seconds. Then she turned on Kristin. "They are Missourians, Kristin. They can't help being Confederates. We were Confederates, I guess, until...until they came for Pa. Until Matthew joined up with the Union. And if Cole did ride with Quantrill, well, I'm sure he had his reasons. Cole is nothing like Zeke. You know that, and I know that.''

Kristin smiled. Shannon was right, and so was Malachi. Cole was nothing like Zeke, and she knew it. But she was still hurt, and she was still angry. She was angry because she was frightened.

And because she loved him.

''Maybe you're right, Shannon,'' she said softly.

''Cole would never do anything dishonorable! He wouldn't!'' Shannon said savagely. ''And—''

''And what?''

''He's your husband, Kristin. You have to remember that. You married him. He's your husband now.''

''I'll give him a chance to explain,'' was all that Kristin said. She would give him a chance. But when? He was gone, and winter was coming, and she didn't know when she would see him again.

Two days later Pete and the hands returned from the cattle drive, and Jamie and Malachi prepared to ride back to the war. Kristin was sorry she had argued with Malachi, and she hugged him tightly, promising to pray for him. She kissed Jamie, and he assured her that since his unit was stationed not far away he would be back now and then to see how she and Shannon were doing.

Shannon kissed Jamie—and then Malachi, too. He held her for a moment, smiling ruefully.

Then the two of them rode away.

Kristin stood with Shannon at her side, and they watched until they could no longer see the horses. A cool breeze came up, lifting Kristin's hair from her shoulders and swirling around her skirts. Winter was on its way. She was very cold, she realized. She was very cold, and she was very much alone.

Chapter Eleven

Winter was long, hard and bitterly cold. In December Shannon turned eighteen and in January Kristin quietly celebrated her nineteenth birthday. They awaited news from the front, but there was none. The winter was not only cold, it was also quiet, ominously quiet.

Late in February, a Union company came by and took Kristin's plow mules. The young captain leading the company compensated her in Yankee dollars which, she reflected, would help her little when she went out to buy seed for the spring planting. The captain did, however, bring her a letter from Matthew, a letter that had passed from soldier to soldier until it had come to her.

Matthew had apparently not received the letter she had written him. He made no mention of her marriage in his letter to her. Nor did he seem to know anything about Zeke Moreau's attack on the ranch after their father's murder.

It was a sad letter to read. Matthew first wrote that he prayed she and Shannon were well. Then he went into a long missive on the rigors of war—up at five in the morning, sleeping in tents, drilling endlessly, in the rain and even in the snow. Then there was an account of the first major battle in which he had been involved—the dread of waiting, the roar of the cannons, the blast of the guns, the screams of the dying. Nightfall was often the worst of all, when the pickets were close enough to call out to one another. He wrote:

We warn them, Kristin. "Reb! You're in the moonlight!" we call out, lest our sharpshooters take an unwary lad. We were camped on the river last month; fought by day, traded by night. We were low on tobacco, well supplied with coffee, and the Mississippi boys were heavy on tobacco, low on coffee, so we remedied that situation. By the end of it all we skirmished. I came face-to-face with Henry, with whom I had been trading. I could not pull the trigger of my rifle, nor lift my cavalry sword. Henry was shot from behind, and he toppled over my horse, and he looked up at me before he died and said please, would I get rid of his tobacco, his ma didn't know that he was smoking. But what if you fall? he asks me next, and I try to laugh, and I tell him that my Ma is dead, and my Pa is dead, and that my sisters are very understanding, so it is all right if I die with tobacco and cards and all. He tried to smile. He closed his eyes then, and he died, and my dear sisters, I tell you that I was shaken. Sometimes they egg me on both sides—what is a Missouri boy doing in blue? I can only tell them that they do not understand. The worst of it is this—war is pure horror, but it is better than being at home. It is better than Quantrill and Jim lane and Doc Jennison. We kill people here, but we do not murder in cold blood. We do not rob, and we do not steal, nor engage in any raping or slaughter. Sometimes it is hard to remember that I was once a border rancher and that I did not want war at all, nor did I have sympathy for either side. Only Jake Armstrong from Kansas understands. If the jayhawkers robbed and stole and murdered against you, then you find yourself a Confederate. If the bushwhackers burnt down your place, then you ride for the Union, and the place of your birth doesn't mean a whit.

Well, sisters, I do not mean to depress you. Again, I pray that my letter finds you well. Kristin, again I urge you to take Shannon and leave if you should feel the slightest threat of danger again. They have murdered Pa, and that is what they wanted, but I still worry for you both, and I pray that I will get leave to come and see you soon. I assure you that I am well, as of this writing, which nears Christmas, 1862. I send you all my love. Your brother, Matthew.

He had also sent her his Union pay. Kristin fingered the money, then went out to the barn and dug up the strongbox where she kept the gold from the cattle sales and the Yankee dollars from the captain. She added the money from Matthew. She had been feeling dark and depressed and worried, but now, despite the contents of Matthew's letter, she felt her strength renewed. She had to keep fighting. One day Matthew would come home. One day the war would be over and her brother would return. Until then she would maintain his ranch.

By April she still hadn't been able to buy any mules, so she and Samson and Shannon went out to till the fields. It was hard, back-breaking labor, but she knew that food was growing scarcer and scarcer, and that it was imperative that they grow their own vegetables. Shannon and she took turns behind the plow while Samson used his great bulk to pull it forward. The herd was small, though there would be new calves soon enough. By morning Kristin planned the day with Pete, by day she worked near the house, and supper did not come until the last of the daylight was gone. Kristin went to bed each night so exhausted that she thought very little about the war.

She didn't let herself think about Cole, though sometimes he stole into her dreams uninvited. Sometimes, no matter how exhausted she was when she went to bed, she imagined that he was with her. She forgot then that he had been one of Quantrill's raiders. She remembered only that he was the man who had touched her, the man who had awakened her. She lay in the moonlight and remembered him, remembered his sleek-muscled form walking silent and naked to her by night, remembered the way the moonlight had played over them both...

Sometimes she would awaken and she would be shaking, and she would remind herself that he had ridden with Quantrill, just like Zeke Moreau. She might be married to him now, but she could never, never lie with him again as she had before. He was another of Quantrill's killers, just like Zeke. Riding, burning, pillaging, murdering—raping, perhaps. She didn't know. He had come to her like a savior, but Quantrill's men had never obeyed laws of morality or decency.

She wanted him to come back to her because she could not imagine him dead. She wanted him to come back to her and deny it all.

But he could not deny it, because it was the truth. Malachi had said so. Malachi had known how the truth would hurt, but hadn't been able to lie. There was no way for Cole to come and deny it. There was just no way at all.

Spring wore on. In May, while she was out in the south field with Samson, Pete suddenly came riding in from the north pasture. He ignored the newly sown field, riding over it to stop in front of Kristin.

"He's back, Miz Slater, he's back. They say that Quantrill is back, and that Quantrill and company do reign here again!"

The house was still a long way off when Cole reined in his horse and looked across the plain at it. Things looked peaceful, mighty peaceful. Daisies were growing by the porch, and someone—Kristin? Shannon?—had hung little flowerpots from the handsome gingerbread on the front of the house.

It looked peaceful, mighty peaceful.

His heart hammered uncomfortably, and Cole realized that it had taken him a long time to come back. He didn't know quite why, but it had taken him longer than necessary. He hadn't been worried at all, at least not until he had heard that Quantrill was back. He didn't understand it. All through the winter, all through the early spring, he'd had dreams about her. He had wanted her. Wanted her with a longing that burned and ached and kept him staring at the ceiling or the night sky. Sometimes it had been as if he could reach out and touch her. And then everything had come back to him. The silky feel of her flesh and the velvety feel of her hair falling over his shoulders. The startling blue of her eyes, the sun gold of her hair, the fullness of her breasts in his hands...

Then, if he was sound asleep, he would remember the smell of smoke, and he would hear the sound of the shot, and he would see his wife, his first wife, his real wife.... Running, running... And the smoke would be acrid on the air, and the hair that spilled over him would be a sable brown, and it would be blood that filled his hands.

It hurt to stay away. He needed her. He wanted her, wanted her with a raw, blinding, burning hunger. But the nightmares would never stay away. Never. Not while his wife's killer lived. Not while the war raged on.

He picked up the reins again and nudged his mount and started the slow trek toward the house. His breath had quickened. His blood had quickened. It coursed through him, raced through him, and it made him hot, and it made him nervous. Suddenly it seemed a long, long time since he had seen her last. It had been a long time. Almost half a year.

But she was his wife.

He swallowed harshly and wondered what his homecoming would be like. He remembered the night before he had left, and his groin went tight as wire and the excitement seemed to sweep like fire into his limbs, into his fingertips, into his heart and into his lungs.

They hadn't done so badly, he thought. Folks had surely done worse under the best of circumstances.

When the war ended...

Cole paused again, wondering if the war would ever end. Those in Kansas and Missouri had been living with the skirmishing since 1855, and hell, the first shots at Fort Sumter had only been fired in April of '61. Back then, Cole thought grimly, the rebels had thought they could whomp the Yankees in two weeks, and the Yankees had thought, before the first battle at Manassas, it would be easy to whip the Confederacy. But the North had been more determined than the South had ever imagined, and the South had been more resolute than the North had ever believed possible. And the war had dragged on and on. It had been more than two years now, and there was no end in sight.

So many battles. An Eastern front, a Western front. A Union navy, a Confederate navy, a battle of ironclads. New Orleans fallen, and now Vicksburg under seige. And men were still talking about the battle at Antietam Creek, where the bodies had piled high and the corn had been mown down by bullets and the stream had run red with blood.

He lifted his hands and looked at his threadbare gloves. He was wearing his full dress uniform, but his gold gloves were threadbare. His gray wool tunic and coat carried the gold epaulets of the cavalry, for though he was officially classified a scout he'd been assigned to the cavalry and was therefore no longer considered a spy. It was a fine distinction, Cole thought. And it was damned peculiar that as a scout he should spend so much of his time spying on both sides of the Missouri-Kansas border. He wondered bleakly what it was all worth. In January he'd appeared before the Confederate Cabinet, and he'd reported honestly, as honestly as he could, on the jayhawkers' activities. Jim Lane and Doc Jennison, who had led the jayhawkers— the red-legs as they were sometimes known because of their uniforms—were animals. Jim Lane might be a U.S. senator, but he was still a fanatic and a murderer, every bit as bad as Quantrill. But the Union had gotten control of most of the jayhawkers. Most of them had been conscripted into the Union army and sent far away from the border. As the Seventh Kansas, a number of jayhawkers had still been able to carry out raids on the Missouri side of the border, plundering and burning town after town, but then Major General Henry Halleck had ordered the company so far into the center of Kansas that it had been virtually impossible for the boys to jayhawk.

As long as he lived, Cole would hate the jayhawkers. As long as he lived, he would seek revenge. But his hatred had cooled enough that he could see that there was a real war being fought, a war in which men in blue and men in gray fought with a certain decency, a certain humanity. There were powerful Union politicians and military men who knew their own jayhawkers for the savages they were, and there were men like Halleck who were learning to control them.

No one had control of Quantrill.

By that spring, General Robert E. Lee had been given command of the entire Confederate Army. When he had met with that tall, dignified, soft-spoken man, Cole had felt as if the place he.had left behind could not be real. War was ugly, blood and death were ugly, and screaming soldiers maimed and dying on torn-up earth were ugly, too. But nothing was so ugly as the total disregard for humanity that reigned on the border between Kansas and Missouri. Lee had listened to Cole, and Jefferson Davis, the Confederate president, had listened long and carefully to him, too. Judah P. Benjamin, secretary of war, had taken his advice and when Quantrill had demanded a promotion and recognition, his request had been denied.

Cole wondered briefly if the violence would ever stop. He wondered if he would ever be able to cleanse his own heart of hatred.

Suddenly he forgot the war, forgot everything.

He could see the well to the left of the house, near the trough, and he could see Kristin standing there. She had just pulled up a pail of water.

Her hair was in braids, but a few golden strands had escaped from her hairpins and curled over her shoulders. She was dressed in simple gingham—no petticoats today—and she had opened the top buttons of her blouse. She dipped a handkerchief into the bucket and doused herself with the cool water, her face, her throat, her collarbone, then flesh bared by the open flaps of her blouse. Hot and dusty, she lifted the dipper from the pail and drank from it. Then she leaned back slightly and allowed the cool water to spill over her face and throat.

Cole's stomach tightened, and he felt his heartbeat in his throat, and he wondered what it was about the way she was standing, savoring the water, that was so provocative, so beguiling, so sensual. He nudged his horse again, eager to greet her.

He came in at a gallop. She spun around, startled. The water spilled over her blouse, and the wet fabric outlined her young breasts. Her eyes widened at the sight of him, first with panic, he thought, then with startled recognition. He drew up in front of her and dismounted in a leap. Her blouse was soaked, and her face was damp. Her lips were parted, and her face was streaked with dust. She was beautiful.

"Cole..." she murmured.

He pulled her hard against him. He found her lips, and he kissed her deeply, and she tasted even sweeter than he remembered. She was vibrant and feminine. He choked out something and touched her breast, feeling her nipple hard as a pebble beneath his palm. She melted against him. She gasped, and she trembled beneath his touch. Her lips parted more fully, and his tongue swept into the hot dampness of her mouth.

Then, suddenly, she twisted away from him with another choking sound. Startled, he released her. She shoved hard against his chest, backing away from him, wiping her mouth with her hands as if she had taken poison. Her eyes remained very wide and very blue. "Bastard!'' she hissed at him. She looked him up and down. ''Stupid bastard! In a Confederate uniform, no less! Don't you know this whole area is crawling with Yankees?''

''I'll take my clothes right off,'' he offered dryly.

She shook her head stubbornly. She was still trembling, he saw. Her fingers worked into the fabric of her skirt, released it, then clenched the material again. Her breasts were still outlined by her wet blouse, the nipples clearly delineated. He took a step toward her. ''For God's sake, Kristin, what the hell is the matter with you? You're my wife, remember—''

''Don't touch me!''

''Why the hell not?''

''You're a bushwhacker!'' she spat out. ''You're his—you belong to Quantrill, just like Zeke.''

That stopped him dead in his tracks. He wondered how she had found out. A haze fell over his eyes, a cool haze of distance. It didn't really matter. He'd had his reasons. And though he wasn't with Quantrill anymore, if he'd found the right man when he had been with him, he would have been as savage as any of them.

''A friend of yours stopped by here right after you left in the fall,'' Kristin informed him. ''Bill Anderson. You remember him? He remembered you!''

''Kristin, I'm not with Quantrill any longer.''

''Oh, I can see that. You got yourself a real Reb uniform. It's a nice one, Cole. You wear it well. But it doesn't cover what you really are! Who did you steal it from? Some poor dead boy?''

His hand slashed out and he almost struck her. He stopped himself just in time.

''The uniform is mine, Kristin,'' he said through clenched teeth. ''Just as you're my wife.''

He didn't touch her. Her face was white, and she was as stiff as a board. He started to walk past her, heading straight for the house. Then he spun around. She cringed, but he reached for her shoulders anyway.

''Kristin—'' he began. But he was interrupted by a man's voice.

''You leave her alone, Johnny Reb!''

Cole spun around, reaching for his Colt. He was fast, but not fast enough.

"No!" he heard Kristin scream. "Matthew, no, you can't! Cole, no—" She threw herself against his hand, and he lost his chance to fire. She tore her eyes from his and looked over at the tall man in the Union blue coming toward them with a sharpshooter's rifle raised. Kristin screamed again and threw herself against Cole. He staggered and fell, and he was falling when the bullet hit him. It grazed the side of his head. He felt the impact, felt the spurt of blood. He felt a sheet of blackness descend over him, and wondered if he was dying. As he railed against himself in black silence for being so involved with Kristin that he never heard or saw the danger, Cole heard the next words spoken as the man who had called to him, the man who had shot him, came forward.

"Oh, no! Oh, my God—"

"Kristin! What's the matter with you? I'm trying to save you from this jackal—"

"Matthew, this jackal is my husband!"

As he slowly regained consciousness, Cole realized he wasn't dead. He wasn't dead, but he'd probably lost a lot of blood, and it seemed as if he had been out for hours, for it was no longer daylight. Night had fallen. An oil lamp glowed softly at his side.

He was in the bedroom they had shared, the bedroom with the sleigh bed. Everything was blurred. He blinked, and the room began to come into focus. He could see the windows and a trickle of moonlight. He touched his head and discovered that it had been bandaged. He drew his fingers away. At least he couldn't feel any blood. Someone had stripped off his uniform and bathed the dust of the road from him and tucked him between cool, clean sheets.

Someone. His wife. No, not his wife. Kristin. Yes, his wife. He had married her. She was his wife now.

She had stopped him from killing the man.

But she had stopped the man from killing him, too.

A sudden pain streaked through him. He was going to have one terrible headache, he realized. But he was alive, and he was certain that the bullet wasn't embedded in his skull. It had just grazed him.

He heard footsteps on the stairs, and then on the floor outside his door. He closed his eyes quickly as someone came into the room. It was Delilah. She spoke in a whisper. "Dat boy is still out cold." She touched his throat, then his chest. "But he's living, all right. He's still living, and he don't seem to have no fever."

"Thank God!" came in a whisper. Kristin. Cole could smell the faint scent of her subtle perfume. He felt her fingers, cool and gentle, against his face. Then he heard the man's voice again. Matthew. She had called him Matthew. Of course. The brother. The one he had told her to write to just so that this wouldn't happen.

"A Reb, Kristin? After everything that happened—"

"Yes, damn you! After everything that happened!" Kristin whispered harshly. "Matthew, don't you dare preach to me! You left, you got to go off and join up with the army! Shannon and I didn't have that luxury. And Zeke came back—"

"Moreau came back?" Matthew roared.

"Shut up, will you, Matthew?" Kristin said wearily. She sounded so tired. So worn, so weary. Cole wanted to open his eyes, wanted to take her into his arms, wanted to soothe away all the terrible things that the war had done to her. He could not, and he knew it.

She probably didn't want him to, anyway. She would probably never forgive him for his time with Quantrill. Well, he didn't owe anyone any apologies for it, and he'd be damned if he'd explain himself to her. And yet...

"Kristin," Matthew was saying huskily, "what happened?"

"Nothing happened, Matthew. Oh, it almost did. Zeke was going to rape me, and let every man with him rape me, and then he was probably going to shoot me. He was going to sell Samson and Delilah. But nothing happened because of this man. He's a better shot than Shannon or me. He's even a better shot than you. He happened by and it was all over for Zeke."

"Zeke is dead?"

"No. Zeke rode away." A curious note came into her voice. "You see, Matthew, he won't murder a man in cold blood. I wanted him to, but he wouldn't. And after that, well, it's a long story. But since he's married me, none of them will harm me, or this place. They're—they're afraid of him."

"Damn, Kristin—" He broke off. Cole heard a strangled sound, and then he knew that brother and sister were in one another's arms. Kristin was crying softly, and Matthew was comforting her. Cole gritted his teeth, for the sound of her weeping was more painful to him than his wound. I will never be able to touch her like that, he thought. He opened his eyes a fraction and took a good look at Matthew McCahy. He was a tall man with tawny hair and blue eyes like his sisters. He was lean, too, and probably very strong, Cole thought. He was probably a young man to be reckoned with.

He shifted and opened his eyes wider. Sister and brother broke apart. Kristin bent down by him and touched his forehead. Her hair was loose, and it teased the bare flesh of his chest. "Cole?"

He didn't speak. He nodded, and he saw that her brow was furrowed with worry, and he was glad of that. She hated him for his past, but at least she didn't want him dead.

"Cole, this is Matthew. My brother. I wrote him, but the letter never reached him. He didn't know that—he didn't know that we were married."

Cole nodded again and looked over at Matthew. He was still in full-dress uniform—navy-blue full-dress uniform. As his gaze swept over Matthew, Cole couldn't help noticing that Matthew McCahy's uniform was in far better shape than his own, and in much better condition than that of the majority of the uniforms worn by the men of the South. The blockade was tightening. The South was running short of everything—medicine, clothing, ammunition, food. Everything. He smiled bitterly. The South had brilliance. Lee was brilliant, Jackson was brilliant, Stuart was brilliant. But when a Southerner fell in battle, he could not be replaced. Men were the most precious commodity in war, and the Confederacy did not have nearly enough.

The Union, however, seemed to have an inexhaustible supply of soldiers, volunteers and mercenaries.

Cole knew a sudden, bleak flash of insight. The South could not win the war.

"Reb—Sorry, your name is Cole, right? Cole Slater." Matthew came around and sat at the foot of the bed. He swallowed uncomfortably. "You saved my sisters' lives, and I'm grateful to you. I wouldn't have shot you if I'd known. It was the uniform. I'm with the North.'' He said it defensively. It was not easy for a Missourian to fight for the North.

"You had just cause," Cole said. His voice was raspy, his throat dry. His mouth tasted of blood.

Matthew nodded. "Yes. I had just cause." He hesitated. "Well, I'm home on leave, and I guess that you are, too."

"Something like that," Cole said. Kristin made a little sound of distress, but she quickly swallowed it down. Cole didn't glance her way. He smiled at Matthew and reached for her hand. She was playing the loving wife for her brother, he knew, and he wondered how far she would go. She let him take her hand, let him pull her down beside him.

"We'll have to manage while we're both here," Matthew said. He stretched out a hand to Cole, and Cole released Kristin's long enough to take it. "Does that sound fair to you, Reb?"

"It sounds fine to me, Yankee."

Matthew flushed suddenly. "Well, maybe I'd best leave the two of you alone." He rose quickly.

Kristin was on her feet instantly. "No! I'm coming with you!"

Matthew's brow furrowed suspiciously. "Kristin—"

"Sweetheart..." Cole murmured plaintively.

"Darling!" Kristin replied sweetly, syrup dripping from her tone, "I wouldn't dream of disturbing you now. You must rest!"

She gave him a peck on the forehead, and then she was gone, practically running out of the room.

Matthew smiled at Cole. "Too bad there's a war on, ain't it?"

"Yeah. It's too damn bad," Cole agreed.

"She's stubborn," Matthew said.

"Yeah. I've noticed."

"Just like a mule."

"Well, I guess I agree with you there, Yankee."

Matthew laughed, then left and closed the door behind him.

Three days later, Cole was feeling damned good, and damned frustrated. Kristin had managed to elude him ever since his return, sweetly pleading his weakened condition. She had spent her nights in her own room, leaving him to lie there alone. But as night fell on his third day back, Cole jerked awake from a doze to realize that Kristin had come into the room.

He heard her breathing in the darkness, each breath coming in a little pant. Her back was against the door, and she seemed to be listening. She thought he was sleeping, he realized.

Cole rose silently and moved toward her in the dark. He clamped a hand over her mouth and pulled her against the length of his naked body. She gave a muffled gasp and stiffened then began to struggle to free herself.

"Shush!" he warned her.

She bit his hand, and he swore softly.

"Let me go!" she whispered.

"Not on your life, Mrs. Slater."

"Bushwhacker!"

His mouth tightened grimly. "You're still my wife, Kristin."

"Try to rape me and I'll scream. Matthew will kill you. You don't even have a gun up here!"

"If I touch you, Kristin, it wouldn't be rape," Cole assured her.

"Let go—"

He did not let go. He kissed her, plunging his tongue deep into her mouth, holding her so firmly that she could not deny him. He caught her wrists and held them fast behind her back, pressing his naked body still closer to hers. She wore a thin white cotton nightgown buttoned to the throat. It was so thin that he could feel all the sweet secrets her body had to offer.

He raised his lips from hers at last, and she gasped for breath. He pressed his lips to her breast and took the nipple into his mouth through the fabric, savoring it with his tongue.

"I'll scream!" she whispered.

"Scream, then," he told her. He lifted her into his arms and carried her to the bed, searching feverishly for the hem of the gown. He found it and pulled it up, and then they were together, bare flesh touching bare flesh. He seared the length of her with his lips, and she raged against him with husky words and whispers. But then she rose against him. She wrapped her arms around him and pulled his head down to hers and kissed him again. And then she told him he was a bastard, but she gasped when he caressed her thighs, and she buried her face against him when his touch grew intimate and demanding.

"Scream," he whispered to her. "Scream, if you feel you must..."

He thrust deep into her. She cried out, but his mouth muffled the cry, and then his tongue filled her mouth.

It had been so very long, and she had dreamed of him so many times.

He stroked and caressed her insides until she was in a frenzy. Then he drove into her with all the force he possessed, and she felt the familiar sweetness invade her once, and then again and again. Then, suddenly, he was gone from her. She was cold, and she was lost, but then he was kissing her again, her forehead, her cheeks, her breasts, her thighs.... He turned her over gently, and his lips trailed a path of fire down her spine. Then she was on her back again, and his silver-gray eyes were upon her and she swallowed back a shriek of pleasure as he came to her again....

The night was swept away.

Later, as she lay awake in the ravaged bed, Kristin berated herself furiously for her lack of principles. She reminded herself again that he had been with Quantrill, and she fought back tears of fury.

She slept with her back to him, and he did not try to touch her again. In the morning, she avoided him. At dinner she was polite, though she wanted to scream. She was disturbed to see that her brother and Cole talked about the cattle and the ranch easily, like two old friends. Shannon had talked to Matthew, and Shannon thought Cole was a hero, no matter what.

He's a bushwhacker! she wanted to shriek to her brother, but of course she could not. Matthew would want to kill Cole, if he knew. And Kristin had never seen anyone as talented with a gun as Cole. No one. If Matthew tried to kill him, Matthew would be the one who died.

Later that evening, when it was time for bed, Matthew walked upstairs with them, and Kristin had no choice but to follow Cole into her parents' bedroom. When the door closed behind them, Kristin stared at it. Cole was behind her, so close that she could feel his warm breath on the back of her neck.

"I hate you," she told him.

He was silent for a long time. She longed to turn around, but she did not.

"I don't think you do, Kristin," he said at last. "But have it however you want it."

He stripped off his clothes and let them lay where they fell, and he crawled into bed. She stayed where she was for a long time. She heard him move to blow out the lamp, and still she stood by the door. Then, finally, she stripped down to her chemise and climbed gingerly into the bed. She knew he was still awake, but he did not try to touch her. She lay awake for hours, and then she drifted off to sleep. While she slept, she rolled against him, and cast her leg over his. Their arms became entwined, and her hair fell over him like a soft blanket.

They awoke that way. Her chemise was up to her waist, her shoulders were bare, and her breast was peeking out. She gazed over at Cole and saw that he was awake and that he was watching her. Then she felt him, felt him like a pulsing rod against her flesh. He moved toward her, very, very slowly, giving her every chance to escape. She couldn't move. Her flesh was alive, her every nerve awake to shimmering sensation, and when he came inside her she shuddered at the pleasure of it, of having him with her, of touching him again, of savoring the subtle movement of his muscles, of feeling the hardness of him as he moved inside her.

And yet, when it was over, she could still find nothing to say to him. She rose quickly and dressed, aware all the while of his brooding eyes upon her.

"Where have you been?" she demanded at last.

"In Richmond."

"Not with—"

"You know I wasn't with Quantrill. You saw my uniform."

Kristin shrugged. "Some of them wear Confederate uniforms."

"I wasn't with Quantrill."

Kristin hesitated, struggling with her buttons. Cole rose and came up behind her, and she swallowed down a protest as he took over the task. "How long are you staying?"

"I've got another week."

"The same as Matthew," she murmured.

"The same as Matthew."

"And where are you going now?"

"Malachi's unit."

She hesitated. Liar! she longed to shout. Tears stung her eyes. She didn't know if he was lying or not.

He swung her around to face him. "I'm a special attaché to General Lee, Kristin. Officially, I'm cavalry. A major, but the only man I have to answer to is the grand old man himself. I do my best to tell him what's going on back here."

Kristin lifted her chin. "And what do you tell him?"

"The truth."

"The truth?"

"The truth as I see it, Kristin."

They stared at one another for a moment, enemies again. Hostility glistened in her eyes and narrowed his sharply.

"I'm sorry, Cole," Kristin said at last. "I can't forgive you."

"Damn you, Kristin, when did I ever ask you to forgive me?" he replied. He turned around. He had dismissed her, she realized. Biting her lip, she fled the room.

She avoided him all that day. She was tense at dinner as she listened to the conversation that flowed around her. Matthew, puzzled by her silence, asked if she was unwell, and she told him she was just tired. She went up to bed early.

She went to bed naked, and she lay awake, and she waited.

When Cole came to bed, she rolled into his arms, and he thought she made love more sweetly than ever before, more sweetly and with a greater desperation.

It went on that way, day after day, night after night, until the time came for Matthew to ride away again.

And for Cole to ride away again.

And then they were standing in front of the house, ready to mount up, one man she loved dressed in blue, one man she loved dressed in gray. Both handsome, both young, both carrying her heart with them, though she could not admit that to the man in gray.

Kristin was silent. Shannon cried and hugged them both again and again.

Kristin kissed and hugged her brother, and then, because there was an audience, she had to kiss Cole.

Then, suddenly, the audience didn't matter. May was over. They had heard that Vicksburg had fallen, and Kristin thought of all the men who would die in the days to come, and she didn't want to let either of them go.

She didn't want to let Cole go. She couldn't explain anything to him, couldn't tell him that she didn't hate him, that she loved him, but she didn't want to let him go.

She hugged him fiercely, and she kissed him passionately, until they were both breathless and they both had to step away. His eyes searched hers, and then he mounted up.

Shannon and Kristin stood together and watched as the two men clasped hands.

Then one rode west, the other east. Cole to Kansas, Matthew deeper into Missouri.

Shannon let out a long, gasping sob.

"They're gone again!" she said, and pulled her sister closer to her. "Come on. We'll weed out the garden. It's hot, and it'll be a miserable task, and we won't think about the men at all."

"We'll think about them," Shannon said. She was close to tears again, Kristin thought. Shannon, who was always so fierce, so feisty. And Kristin knew that if Shannon cried again, she would sob all day, too.

"Let's get to work."

They had barely set to work when they heard the sounds of hooves again. Kristin spun around hopefully, thinking that either her brother or her husband had returned.

Shannon called out a warning.

It was Zeke, Kristin thought instantly.

But it was not. It was a company of Union soldiers. At its head was a captain. His uniform was just like Matthew's. They stopped in front of the house, but they did not dismount.

"Kristin Slater!" the captain called out.

He was about Matthew's age, too, Kristin thought.

"Yes?" she said, stepping forward.

He swallowed uncomfortably. "You're under arrest."

"What?" she said, astonished.

His Adam's apple bobbed. "Yes, ma'am. I'm sorry. You and your sister are under arrest, by order of General Halleck. I'm right sorry, but we're rounding up all the womenfolk giving aid and succor to Quantrill and his boys."

"Aid and succor!" Kristin shrieked.

She might have been all right if she hadn't begun to laugh. But she did begin to laugh, and before she knew it, she was hysterical.

"Take her, boys."

"Now, you just wait!" Delilah cried from the porch.

The captain shook his head. "Take Mrs. Slater, and the young one, too."

One of the soldiers got down from his horse and tugged at Kristin's arm. She tore it fiercely from his grasp.

The young man ruefully addressed his captain. "Sir..."

"My brother is in the Union army!" Kristin raged. "My father was killed by bushwhackers, and now you're arresting me...for helping Quantrill? No!"

The soldier reached for her again, and she hit him in the stomach. Shannon started to scream, and Delilah came running down the steps with her rolling pin.

"God help us, if the Rebs ain't enough, Halleck has to pit us against the womenfolk!" the young captain complained. He dismounted and walked over to Kristin. "Hold her, men."

Two of them caught her arms. She stared at him.

"Sorry, ma'am," he said sincerely.

Then he struck her hard across the chin, and she fell meekly into his arms.

Chapter Twelve

"Y'all have just the blondest hair! And I do mean the blondest!"
Josephine Anderson said as she pulled Shannon's locks into a set of
high curls on top of her head. She was a pretty young woman herself,
with plump cheeks and a flashing smile and a tendency to blush
easily. She never smiled when their Yankee captors were around,
though. Josephine was a hard-core Confederate. She and her sister
Mary had been brought in a week after Kristin and Shannon, and
they all shared a corner of a big room on the second floor of a
building in Kansas City. Josephine and Mary were both very sweet,
and Kristin liked them well enough, despite their fanaticism. They
had both wanted her and Shannon to meet their brother Billy—who
turned out to be none other than Bill Anderson, the Bill Anderson
who had stopped by the house to make sure that Kristin knew about
Cole's position with Quantrill's raiders.

That was all right. At the very beginning, Kristin had sweetly told
the girls that she did know their Billy. She also told them what had
happened to her father—and that she wished that she were anything
other than what she was: a citizen of a country whose people tore
one another to shreds.

Josephine and Mary had turned away from her in amazement, but
then the next day they had been friendly. They respected her right
to have a passionate stand—even if it was a strange one.

And when Cole's name was mentioned, Mary acted just the way
Shannon did. "Ooh! You're really married to him?" she gushed.

It seemed that Cole had been to dinner once at their house with
Bill when he had first started out with Quantrill. But they didn't

know very much about him, only that there was some deep secret in his past.

"He can be real quiet like, you know!" Mary said.

"But, oh, those eyes!" Josephine rolled her own.

"It's such a pity he left Quantrill!" Mary told her fiercely. "Why, he'd have cleaned out half of Kansas by now; I just know it."

Kristin assured them that Cole was still with the Confederate Army—in the cavalry, like his brothers. Then Shannon went on to tell them about their brother Matthew and how he had gone off to join up with the Union Army after their father's death.

Mary and Josephine thought that was a terrible tragedy, but they understood that, too. "I'm surprised he didn't become a jayhawker, because that's how it goes, you know! They say that old John Brown was attacked way back in '55, that one of his sons was killed. So he killed some Missourians, and some Missourians went up and killed some more Kansans. But you two—why, I feel right sorry for you! Missourians, with a brother in blue and your husband in gray. It's a shame, a damned shame, that's all."

It was a good thing they were able to come to an understanding. All summer long, General Ewing, the local Union commander, had women picked up so that their men couldn't come to them for food or supplies. There were a great many of them living at very close quarters. The authorities holding them weren't cruel, and the women weren't hurt in any way. A number of the young officers were remarkably patient, in fact, for the women could be extraordinarily abusive when they spoke to their captors. But though the men behaved decently toward their prisoners, the living conditions were horrid. The building itself was in terrible shape, with weak and rotting timbers, the food was barely adequate, and the bedding was full of insects.

Kristin wanted desperately to go home. At first she had been angry. She had fought and argued endlessly with various commanders, and they had all apologized and looked uncomfortable and shuffled their feet, but none of them had been willing to let her go. And finally she had become resigned.

She grew more and more wretched. She had often been sick in the first weeks of her captivity and she had thought it must be the food. She was still queasy much of the time, but, though she hadn't told anyone, she knew why now. She was pregnant. Sometime in February of the following year she was going to have Cole's baby. She had been stunned at first, but then she had taunted herself end-lessly. Why should she be surprised, after all. Children were the result of a man being with a woman.

She wasn't sure how she felt. Sometimes she lay there and railed against a God that could let her have a baby in a world where its blood relations were destined to be its mortal enemies, in a world where murder and bloodshed were the order of the day.

Then there were nights when she touched her still-flat belly and dreamed, and wondered what the baby would look like. And then, even if she was furious with Cole, even if she had convinced herself that he was as evil as Zeke, she knew she loved him. And she did want his child. A little boy with his shimmering silver eyes. Or a girl. Or maybe the child would be light, with her hair and eyes. Whoever the child took after, it was destined to be beautiful, she was certain. Cole's baby. She longed to hold it in her arms. She dreamed about seeing him again, about telling him.

And then there were times when she sank into depression. Cole probably wouldn't be the least bit pleased. He probably intended to divorce her as soon as the war was over, she thought bitterly. She was imprisoned for being the wife of a man who intended to divorce her.

Then not even that mattered. She wanted the baby. She wanted the baby to hold and to love, and she wanted it to be born to peace. The war could not go on forever. She didn't care who won. She just wanted it to be over. She wanted her baby to be able to run laughing through the cornfields, to look up at the sun and feel its warmth. She wanted peace for her child.

And most of all, she wanted it to be born at home. She did not want to bear her baby here, in this awful, crowded place of degra-dation.

Kristin looked up from the letter she was writing to her brother asking if there was anything he could do to get the authorities to free Shannon and herself. The three other women in the room looked as if they were preparing for a ball.

Josephine stepped back. "Oh, Shannon, that just looks lovely, really lovely."

"Why, thank you, ma'am," Shannon said sweetly. Then she sighed. "I wish I could see it better."

Mary dug under her pillow and found her little hand mirror. "Here, Shannon."

Suddenly the room fell silent. One of the young Federal officers, a Captain Ellsworth, had come in. The women looked at him suspiciously.

His dark brown eyes fell on Kristin. "Mrs. Slater, would you come with me, please?"

She quickly set aside her paper and pen and rose, nervously folding her fingers in front of her and winding them tightly together.

A middle-aged woman called out to the captain, "Don't walk too hard on this here floor, sonny! Those Yankee boots will make you come right through it!"

He nodded sadly to the woman. "Sorry, Mrs. Todd. The place is awful, I know. I'm working on it."

"Don't work on it!" Mary Anderson called out gaily. "You tell them to let us go home. You tell them that my brother will come after them, and that he'll kill them all."

"Yes, miss," Captain Ellsworth said, staring straight at her. "That's the problem, Miss Anderson. Your brother already does come to murder us all." He bowed to her politely. Then he took Kristin's elbow and led her out of the room. He preceded her down the groaning staircase to the doorway of the office below. Kristin looked at him nervously.

"It's all right, Mrs. Slater. Major Emery is in there. He wants to talk to you."

He opened the door for her, and Kristin walked in. She had never seen Major Emery before. He was a tall, heavyset man, with thick, wavy, iron-gray hair and great drooping mustache to match. His eyebrows were wild and of the same gray, and beneath them his eyes were a soft flower blue. He seemed a kind man, Kristin thought instantly, a gentleman.

"Mrs. Slater, sit, please." Kristin silently did so. The major dismissed Captain Ellsworth, then smiled at Kristin. "Can I get you some tea, Mrs. Slater?"

"No, thank you." She sat very straight, reminding herself that, no matter how kindly he looked, he was still her captor. He smiled again and leaned back in his chair.

"Mrs. Slater, I'm trying very hard to get an order to have you and your sister released."

A gasp of surprise escaped Kristin. Major Emery's smile deepened, and he leaned forward again. "It will take a few days, I'm afraid."

Kristin and Shannon had been here almost three months. A few more days meant nothing.

"Because of my brother?" Kristin said. "Did Matthew find out that we were here? I didn't want to tell him at first because I didn't want him going into battle worrying, but I was just writing to him—"

"No, no, Mrs. Slater. I haven't heard anything from your brother at all."

"Oh, I see," Kristin murmured bitterly. "You've finally decided that a woman who had her father killed by some of Quantrill's men is not likely to give aid and comfort to the enemy, is that it?"

Major Emery shook his head. "No. Because of your husband," he said quietly.

"What?" Kristin demanded suspiciously. "Major, I'm in here because I'm married to Cole Slater. No one seems to believe me when I say that he isn't with Quantrill anymore."

Major Emery stood and looked out the window. Then he turned back to Kristin. "Do you believe it yourself, young lady?"

"What?" She was certain she was blushing, certain her face had turned a flaming red.

"Do you believe in him yourself, Mrs. Slater?"

"Why...of course!" she said, though she was not at all sure she did.

Emery took his seat again and smiled. "I'm not sure, Mrs. Slater, I'm not sure. But that doesn't really matter. You see, I do have faith in your husband. Complete faith."

Kristin stared at him blankly. She lifted a hand in the air. "Do go on, major. Please, do go on."

"I'm wiling to bet I know your husband better than you do, Mrs. Slater. In certain ways, at least."

She tightened her jaw against his mischievous grin. He was a nice man, she decided, a gentle, fatherly type, but he seemed to be having a good time at her expense at the moment.

"Major..."

His smile faded. He looked a little sad. "He was a military man, you know. He went to West Point. He was in the same class as Jeb Stuart. Did you know that?"

Yes, he had said something to Shannon about it. To Shannon. Not to her.

"I know that he was in the military, yes."

Major Emery nodded. "Cole Slater was one of the most promising young cavalrymen I ever knew. He fought in Mexico, and he was with me in the West. He's good with the Indians—fighting them and, more importantly, talking with them, making truces. Keeping truces. Then the war came."

"And he resigned," Kristin murmured.

"No, not right away. He didn't resign until they burned down his house and killed his wife."

"Killed? His wife?" She didn't realize that she had gotten to her feet until Major Emery came around the desk and gently pushed her back into her chair. Then he leaned against the desk and crossed his arms over his chest, smiling down at her kindly. "I reckoned you might not know everything. Cole is a closemouthed man. Tight-lipped, yes sirree. He was an officer in the Union Army when South Carolina seceded from the Union. That didn't matter none to the jayhawkers. He was a Missourian. And Jim Lane had sent out an order that anybody who was disloyal to the Union was to be killed. The boys got pretty carried away. They rode to his place and they set it on fire. Cole was out riding the range. I imagine he was giving his position some pretty grave thought. Anyway, Jim Lane's jayhawkers rode in and set fire to his place. His wife was a pretty thing, real pretty. Sweet, gentle girl from New Orleans. She came running out, and the boys grabbed hold of her. Seems she learned something about gunfire from Cole, though. She shot up a few of them when they tried to get their hands on her. Cole came riding in, and by then she was running to him. Only some fool had already put a bullet in her back, and when Cole reached her, she was dying. She was expecting their first child right then, too. She was about five months along, so they tell me. Of course, after killing his pregnant wife, none of the men was willing to let him live, either. Someone shot Cole, too, and left him for dead. But he's a tough customer. He lived.''

"And he joined up with Quantrill," Kristin whispered. She swallowed. She could almost see the fire, could almost smell the smoke, could almost hear the screams. She suddenly felt ill. As if she were going to throw up.

"Oh, my God!" she whispered, jumping to her feet. Major Emery, too was on his feet in an instant, yelling for a pail and some water.

To her horror, she *was* sick. Major Emery was a perfect gentleman, cooling her forehead with a damp cloth and then insisting that she have tea with lots of milk to settle her stomach. When it was over and they were alone again, he said to her, "You are expecting a child, Mrs. Slater?"

She nodded bleakly.

"Well, my point exactly. I just don't think you should be here anymore. And I don't think Cole is still with Quantrill, because it just isn't his style. Ma'am, I want you to know that I find our jayhawkers every bit as loathsome as the bushwhackers. They're all murderers, pure and simple. Cole isn't a murderer. I think he went with Quantrill to try to get the man who led the attack on his ranch, and only for that reason. Only he wasn't easy to find, because he retired along with Lane. Hell, Lane is a U.S. senator! But the man who attacked Cole's place is back in the center of Kansas, and like Lane, he owns a lot of things, and a lot of people. Cole knew he couldn't get to him, not with Quantrill. And he knew that what Quantrill was up to was murder. He's regular army now, all right."

Kristin swallowed some of her tea and nodded painfully. She hurt all over, inside and out. She had despised Cole, despite everything that he had done for her, just because Bill Anderson had told her that Cole had ridden with Quantrill. She desperately wanted to see him again. She wanted to hold him. She wanted to make him forget, if only for a moment, what had been done to him.

It made men hard, this war did. It had made her hard, she knew, and it had made him harder. She realized anew that he did not love her, and now, she thought, he never would. He had loved his first wife.

"Mrs. Slater?"

Kristin looked at the major. "Yes...yes I think that he's in the regular army. That's—that's what he said."

The major frowned suddenly, his hands flat on his desk. He looked up at the ceiling.

Then Kristin felt it. There was a trembling in the floor beneath her, in the very air around her.

"Hellfire and damnation!" Major Emery shouted. He leaped to his feet, hopped over his desk and pulled her out of her chair. He dragged her over to the door and kicked it open, then huddled with her beneath the frame, shielding her with his bulk.

Suddenly floorboards and nails were flying everywhere and great clouds of dust filled the room. Dirt flew into Kristin's mouth and into her eyes, and she heard screams, terrible screams, agonized screams.

The whole building was caving in. The awful place had been faulty structurally and decaying and now it was actually caving in.

"Shannon!" Kristin screamed. "Shannon!" She tried to pull away from the major, but she couldn't. He was holding her too tightly. The rumbling continued, and inside was chaos. Boards were falling and breaking and clattering on the floor. A woman's body fell right next to Kristin, who was able to pull away from the major at last to kneel down by the girl.

It was Josephine Anderson, and Kristin knew instantly that she was dead. Her eyes were wide open, glazed as only death could glaze them. "Jo!" she cried out, falling to her knees. She touched the still-warm body and closed the pathetic, staring eyes. Then she looked up from the body to the gaping hole above her. "Shannon!" she screamed. She twisted around to look at what had been the hallway and the stairs. Only the bannister was left. Everywhere, the floor had crumbled. Tears and screams filled the air. "Shannon!"

"Mrs. Slater! You must remember your child!" the major urged her, grabbing her arm.

"Please!" She shook herself free and stumbled through the wreckage that littered the floor. She found Mary, her body grotesquely twisted beneath a pile of boards. "Mary!" After clawing away the debris, Kristin knelt and felt for the other woman's pulse. Mary was alive. She opened her eyes. "Jo?"

"It's Kristin, Mary. Everything…everything is going to be all right." She squeezed the girl's hand and turned around, searching for someone, anyone. "Get help here!" Kristin shouted, suddenly choking back tears. Where was Shannon? The girls had all been together.

Several young medics rushed in. Kristin moved away as they knelt over Mary. There were clanging bells sounding from outside, and the sound of horses' hooves was loud as a fire hose was brought around.

"Mrs. Slater!"

The major was still trying to get her out.

"Shannon!"

An arm was protruding from a pile of lumber. Kristin began to tear away the planks. This was the worst of it. The woman beneath was dead. Kristin inhaled on a sob and turned away.

"Kristin!"

She looked up. Shannon, deathly pale, was clinging to a board that looked as if it were just about to give way.

"Shannon! Hold on! Just hold on a little longer—"

There was a cracking sound. The board began to break. Shannon's toes dangled ten feet over Kristin's head. "Hold on!"

"No, Miss McCahy, let go now! I'm here. I'll catch you!"

It was Captain Ellsworth. He stepped in front of Kristin and reached out his arms to Shannon. Shannon still clung to the board. "Come down, now! Please, before it breaks!"

Kristin saw the problem. If the board broke, Shannon could fall on a splinter in one of the beams that had been exposed, and she would be skewered alive.

"Shannon! Where the hell is your courage? Jump!" Kristin called out. She watched as Shannon's eyes fell on the splintered beams below her. But then Shannon looked down at her and she grinned. "What the hell! We can't all live forever, now, can we? Thumbs up, Kristin. Say a prayer."

Shannon released her hold on the board. She fell, her skirts billowing out around her, and suddenly, Captain Ellsworth was falling, too. He had caught her and the impact had brought him down with her.

"Get them both out of here!" Major Emery shouted. He picked Kristin up bodily and carried her outside. Captain Ellsworth swept Shannon up and followed. When they were finally out in the street, Kristin and Shannon hugged each other, sobbing.

"Jo—"

"Jo is dead," Kristin said softly. Then they stared at one another as they realized how lucky they were to be alive. And they just hugged one another again and sobbed, and listened to the chaos as more women were carried from the building, some alive, some injured...and some dead.

A week later, Kristin and Shannon were in the home of Captain Ellsworth's sister, Betty.

Four women besides Josephine Anderson had been killed. Rumor had it that Bill Anderson had gone berserk, foaming at the mouth, when he had heard that one of his sisters had been killed and the other had been seriously injured. Many Confederates were saying that General Ewing had purposely ordered that the women be incarcerated in the ramshackle building so that just such a tragedy might occur. There would be repercussions. To make matters worse, General Ewing had issued his General Order Number Ten, ordering all wives and children of known bushwhackers to move out of the state of Missouri.

That night, Major Emery rode out to the small house on the outskirts of the city with Captain Ellsworth beside him. It was quite apparent that an attachment was forming between Shannon and the captain, and Kristin didn't mind at all. After all, the young captain had come valiantly to her rescue. Kristin liked him herself. He was quiet and well read and unfailingly polite. And Shannon was eighteen, a young woman who already knew her own mind.

But though both the captain and the major were charming in Betty's parlor, Kristin knew that something was very wrong. The major called her onto the porch.

He looked at the moon, twirling his hat in his hand. "Quantrill attacked Lawrence, Kansas, yesterday."

"Oh, God!" Kristin murmured.

"It was a massacre," Major Ellsworth said grimly. "Almost the entire town was razed to the ground. At least one hundred men were killed...one twelve-year-old boy was shot down for being dressed up in an old Union uniform. And Quantrill only lost one of his boys. A former Baptist preacher named Larkin Skaggs. He was too drunk to ride away with Quantrill. An Indian found him and shot him dead, and then the survivors ripped him to shreds." Major Emery was silent for a moment. "What is it coming to? None of us, not one of us, it seems, is any better than a bloody savage."

Kristin wanted to say something to comfort him. A lot of good men were experiencing the same despair, she knew. But she could think of nothing to say.

He turned around and tipped his hat to her. "You're free, young lady. I'm going to see to it that an escort takes you and your sister home.

"But how—"

A grin tugged at his lower lip. "Someone got through to your brother, and he raised all kinds of hell with the higher-ups. And then..."

"And then?"

He shrugged. His eyes twinkled. "Well, you see, Kristin, I know Cole. And a lot of other cavalry boys know Cole, so we know damned well that he isn't any outlaw. But people who don't know him, well, they're still convinced that he's a bad 'un. At the moment, that's all right, because there's a rumor out that he's heard about you and Shannon being held up here and that he's steaming. After everything that's happened, well...we can't have troops everywhere. Some folks are afraid he might ride in here and destroy the town just to get to you. I decided not to dispute that with any of them. I thought you deserved the right to go home if that was what you wanted."

Kristin stared at him a long time. Then she kissed him on the cheek. "Thank you."

"You see Cole, you tell him I sent my regards. You tell him I miss him. I never did meet another man who could ride or shoot like him."

She nodded. "Thank you. Thank you so much. For everything."

"Be there for him. He probably needs you."

Kristin smiled ruefully. "He doesn't love me, you know. You see, he only married me because he felt he had to. To protect me."

"Love comes in a lot of ways, young lady. You give him a little time. Maybe this war will end one day."

He tipped his hat to her again, and then he was gone.

In retaliation for the attack on Lawrence, General Ewing issued General Order Number Eleven, which forced almost everyone in Missouri to leave. People were given fifteen days to leave their property. The exodus was a terrible thing to watch, one of the worst things Kristin had seen in all the years since the fighting had begun. Poor farmers were forced to leave behind what little they possessed, and others were shot down where they stood because they refused to leave. Because the McCahy ranch belonged to Matthew, a soldier serving in the Union army, Major Emery was able to keep his promise and send Kristin and Shannon home, however.

The young lieutenant who escorted them was appalled by what he saw of the evacuation. Once he even told her that it was one of the cruellest measures he had ever seen taken. "This war will never end," he said glumly. "We will not let it end, it seems. The people who do not fight are ordered to leave, and the bushwhackers will come through here when they're gone, stealing whatever they leave behind!"

It was true, Kristin discovered. Even when they were home, when it seemed that they had returned to something like a normal life, Peter often came to her at night to tell her that he had seen another house burning somewhere, or that he had found cattle slaughtered, a sure sign that guerrillas had been in the area, living off the land.

In the middle of September they had a letter from Matthew. He was trying to get leave to come and see them, but so far he hadn't been able to manage it. He explained:

But the Rebels are in worse shape than we are. I think that perhaps by Christmas I will be able to come home. There was a battle fought in a little town in Pennsylvania called Gettysburg. Kristin, they say it was the most awful yet, but General Lee was stopped, and he was forced to retreat back to the South. Since then, there has been new hope that the war may end. Some of these fellows say that they will force the South to her knees. They do not know Southerners. I cannot imagine your husband on his knees, nor do I ever quite forget that I am a Missourian myself. But I pray for it to end. I watched another friend die yesterday of the dysentery, and it seems that we do not even have to catch bullets to drop off like flies. John Maple, who was injured in our last skirmish, had to have his leg amputated. Kristin, if I am caught at all by shot, I hope that the ball passes straight to my heart, for those operations are fearful things to witness. There was no morphine, but we did have some whiskey, and still, John screamed so horribly. Now we must all pray that the rot does not set in, else he will die anyway.

Kristin, forgive me, I wander again into subjects that do not fit a lady's ears, but you are my sister. I am still so grateful that you and Shannon are home. Every man who heard of the incident in Kansas City was appalled, and none was proud. That you might have been killed there chilled me to the bone, and I waited very anxiously for the news that you were safe.

As I said before, the Rebs are hurting badly. They have good generals, and good men, but those that die cannot be replaced. I am telling you this, aware that you must be worried for your husband. If you do not see him, you must not instantly fear the worst. They have probably refused to give him leave. They are desperate now to hold on to Virginia, and perhaps they are keeping him in the East.

Kristin set her brother's letter down and stared out the window. She wondered if Cole would come if she thought hard enough about him. Then she wondered, not for the first time, if he had been at the battle of Gettysburg. They talked of it constantly in Kansas City. It seemed that the death toll had been terrible there, but she had read the lists endlessly, looking for his name, and she had not found it. She had thought, too, that he might have been with John Hunt Morgan, along with Malachi, but she had read that Morgan had been captured in July, though what had become of his men was unknown. She had checked the lists of the dead again and again. Once her heart had nearly ceased to beat when she had read that a Slater had been killed, but it had been Samuel Slater from South Carolina, no relation, she hoped, to Cole.

Looking out the window would not bring Cole back to her. Wishing for him to appear would not help, either.

Every night she left a light burning in the window, hoping he would return. Even if he were to try, it would be hard for him to do so, she knew. The Union was getting a firm grip on the area. There were almost always patrols somewhere in the vicinity.

Every night she stood on the steps before going up to bed, and she lifted her chin, and she felt the breeze, and she waited. But it was all to no avail.

All to no avail...

Until one night in late September.

There had been no breeze all day, but there was the slightest whisper of one now. The night had been still, but now a tumbleweed lifted from the ground. Fall was coming, and in the pale glow of the moon the world was dark brown and pale gold and rich orange.

She thought she had imagined the sound at first. The sound of hoofbeats. But she had learned how to listen, and she closed her eyes, and she felt the wood beneath her feet shiver.

She stumbled out onto the porch and down onto the bare earth. She felt the hoofbeats more clearly. A rider was approaching, a single rider.

She needed to run into the house. She needed to grab one of the Colt six-shooters, or her rifle. The breeze was cool, and she was standing there barefoot on the cold ground, dressed only in a white cotton nightgown. The wind swept the gown around her and molded it to her breasts and hips and thighs. The breeze picked up the tendrils of her hair and sent them cascading behind her.

Then she saw the horse, and saw the rider, and she was exhilarated and incredulous and jubilant.

"Cole!"

"Kristin!" He reined in his horse, cast his leg over the animal's haunches and slid quickly to the ground. He frowned at the sight of her there, but she ran to him, laughing, and threw herself into his arms.

They closed around her.

Cole felt her, felt her soft and fresh and fragrant and clean, the way he had dreamed her, the way he had imagined her, the way he had feared he would never feel her again. The road home was always long and hard and dangerous. He had been riding for days, trying to avoid the Union patrols that were all over the place.

But now she was in his arms. There were no questions, no answers. She was in his arms, whispering his name. He began to shake. Her hair spilled over his hands like raw silk. She pressed against him, and she was so feminine and sweet that he nearly lost his breath. He breathed deeply, and her scent filled him, and it made his heart pound and his loins quicken.

"Kristin—"

She caught his face in her hands and kissed him. She kissed him as if she had starved for him, she kissed him deeply, passionately, like a woman. She kissed him with the fullness of her mouth and with the fullness of her body. Her tongue was wickedly sensual, touching all of him, plunging deep into his mouth. When his tongue invaded her mouth in turn, she moaned and fell against him, suddenly weak. After a long time he lifted his head to stare down into her eyes, eyes as blue as sapphires beneath the moon.

"What are you doing out here?"

"Waiting."

"You couldn't have known I was coming."

"I'm always waiting," she told him, and she smiled. It was just the slightest curve of her mouth, a rueful admission that left him feeling as if the earth trembled beneath his feet. He swept her hard against him again, heedless of whether she felt the emotion that racked him.

"I heard about Kansas City. I tried to come for you. Malachi and Jamie knocked me flat. Then I heard about the building, and I heard they let you go at the same time—"

"Hush!" She pressed a finger to his lips. She smiled again, and it was a dazzling smile. She was so soft, all of her. Her arms wound around him. Her thighs molded to his, naked beneath the gown. Her breasts pressed against his chest, against the gray wool of his uniform. "It's all right. We're home. Shannon and I are home, and you've come home now, too."

It wasn't his home. He could have told her that. But he didn't want to. Not tonight. She might not understand.

He wove his fingers into her hair, savoring the feel of her. Then he swept her up into his arms and stumbled up the steps, somehow keeping eyes locked with hers.

It seemed to take forever to reach their room, and it was not until much later that he wondered if his poor horse had managed to wander to the trough and into the barn. If not, the animal had known much worse nights upon the road.

For the moment, all that he knew was the woman in his arms and the sweetness of his homecoming.

When they were alone in their room he set her down. With trembling fingers, he undid the buttons of her nightgown and let it float to the floor. He stared at her. He wanted this moment to be etched in his memory forever, and he wanted the memory to be as incredible as the reality. Her eyes luminous. Her smile welcoming. Her breasts full and round and firm, more entrancing even than he had remembered. Her legs long and beautifully shaped.

Then he touched her.

And he wanted, too, to remember the feel of her skin against his fingertips, and so he touched her again and again, marvelling at the softness of her. And he kissed her, for he had to remember the taste of her. He kissed her lips, and he kissed her forehead, and he found the pulse at the base of her throat. He kissed her breasts, and the desire inside him grew. He savored the taste of her shoulders, of the little hollows there. He turned her around and kissed her back, trailing his fingers down the beautiful line of her spine and over the curve of her buttocks. He had to touch and taste and feel all of her. He went on and on, drinking deeply of her, until the whole of his body shook and trembled, until she cried out his name with such anguish and passion that he came to his feet, crushed her in his arms and lifted her again, bearing her to the bed.

Whispering to him, telling him how much she wanted him, how she needed him, how she desired him, she feverishly helped him out of his clothes, desperate to touch him as he had touched her. Soft as a feather, gentle as a breeze, sensual as the earth, she touched and petted and loved him. Then, at last, they came together, a man and a woman meeting in a breathless fusion.

All that night she felt she was riding the wind, an endless, sweet, wild wind that swept away the horrors of the world and left her drifting on the clouds of heaven. Anticipation had sown its seeds, and their first time together was erratic and wild and thunderous for them both. Barely had they climaxed before he touched her again, and again the clamor of need rose quickly in them. They were slower this time, easier, for the first desperate hunger had been appeased.

And still the night lay ahead of them.

She never knew just how many times they loved that night, never knew when she slept and dreamed, never knew when she awakened to find that he was holding her again. She only knew that it was heaven, and that however long she lived, however old she grew, she would never, never forget it, or the crystalline beauty of the desire that surged between them.

It was morning before they spoke.

Dazed and still delighted, Kristin lay in his arms, wondering lazily how to tell him about the child. She wondered if he could tell by the subtle changes in her body. He hadn't said anything. She smiled. His need for her had been too great for him to have noticed anything. She thought to speak then, but he was speaking already. He was talking about the war, and his tone was cold.

"Stonewall Jackson was the greatest loss. Lee might have taken Gettysburg if he hadn't lost Stonewall. It was the first battle he had to go into without Jackson. God, how I shall miss that man!"

"Sh..." she murmured. She drew a finger across the planes of his face, and she felt the tightness there, and the pain. It was a strong face, she thought, a striking face. And it was so hard now.

"And Morgan...God help Morgan. He has to escape." He shook his head. Then he turned to her and took her in his arms, whispering, "How can I say these things to you? You've been through so much already, you've witnessed so much. That horror in Kansas City..."

"The deaths were terrible," Kristin admitted. She drew away, smiling at him. "But Major Emery was very kind."

Suddenly Cole was stiff as steel, and every bit as cold. "Emery?"

She didn't understand the abrupt change in him. "Yes. He said that you had been with him, before the war. He—"

He sat up and ran his fingers through his hair. "He what?" She didn't answer, and he turned, setting his hands firmly on her shoulders. "He what?"

"Stop it! You're hurting me!" Kristin pulled away from him. "He told me about—he told me about your wife."

Cole smiled suddenly. It was a bitter smile. "I see," he said softly.

"What do you see?" she demanded.

"Nothing, Kristin, nothing at all." He tossed the covers aside and stood and wandered around the room, picking up his clothes.

"Cole!"

He stepped into his gray trousers and pulled on his shirt. Still ignoring her, he sat and pulled on his boots. She frowned when she realized that he was putting his uniform back on—something he wouldn't be doing if he was staying.

"Cole, you can't be leaving already?"

He stood up, buckling on his scabbard. He nodded gravely. Then he walked to her and stroked her chin. "I only had five days. It took me three to find my way through the Federal troops. I have to pray I can make it back more quickly." He bent down and touched her lips lightly with his own. "You are so very beautiful, Kristin," he murmured to her. But he was still distant from her. Very distant.

"Cole—" She choked on his name. Her heart was aching. There were so many things that needed to be said, and none of them mattered. She had said or done something to offend him and she didn't even know what it was. "Cole, I don't understand—"

"Kristin, I don't want your pity."

"What?"

"Pity, Kristin. I don't want it. It's worthless stuff, and it isn't good for anyone. I wondered what last night was all about. You were barely civil to me when I left in May. Hate me, Kristin. Hate me all you want. But for God's sake, Kristin, don't pity me!"

Incredulous, she stiffened, staring at him, fighting the tears that stung her eyes.

"I've thought about having you and Shannon move to London until this thing is over with. I had a little power with Quantrill, but I'm afraid my influence with the Yankees is at a low ebb. This is a dangerous place—"

"Go!" Kristin said.

"Kristin—"

"Go back to your bleeding Confederacy!" Kristin said heatedly. "I've already met with the Yankees, thanks, and they were damned civil."

"Kristin—"

"I'm all right here! I swear it. We are fine."

He hesitated, then swept his frock coat over his shoulders and picked up his plumed hat.

"Kristin—"

"Cole, damn you, get out of here! You don't want my pity, you want my hatred! Well, then, you've got it! Go!"

"Damn you, Kristin!"

He came back to the bed and took her in his arms. The covers fell away, and she pressed against the wool of his uniform, felt the hot, determined yearning of his kiss. She wanted to fight him. She wanted to tell him that she really did hate him. But he was going away again, going away to the war. And she was afraid of the war. The war killed people.

And so she kissed him back. She wound her arms around him and kissed him back every bit as passionately as he did her. And she felt his fingers move over her breast, and she savored every sensation.

Then he lifted his lips from hers, and their eyes met, and he very slowly and carefully let her fall back to the bed.

They didn't speak again. He kissed her forehead lightly, and then he left her.

PART 4

The Outlaw and The Cavalier

Chapter Thirteen

June, 1864

He never should have come to Kansas.

Cole knew he should never have come to Kansas. A scouting mission in Kentucky was one thing. He could slip into Virginia or even Maryland easily enough. Even in Ohio he might be all right. In the East they were slower to hang a man as a spy. In the East they didn't shoot a man down where he stood, not often, not that Cole had heard about anyway.

He should never have come to Kansas.

But the war effort was going badly, very badly. First General Lee had lost Stonewall Jackson. Then Jeb Stuart had been shot, and they had carried him back to Richmond, and he had died there. Countless men had died, some of them brilliant men, some of them men who were perhaps not so brilliant but who were blessed with an endless supply of courage and a fine bravado, even in the face of death.

Jeb was the greatest loss, though. Cole could remember their days at West Point, and he could remember the pranks they had pulled when they had been assigned out west together. The only comfort in Jeb's death was the fact that his little daughter had died just weeks before. They said that when he lay dying he had talked of holding her again in heaven. They had buried him in Hollywood Cemetery. Cole had been with Kristin when they had buried him, but he had visited the grave when he'd come to Richmond, and he still found it impossible to believe that James Ewell Brown Stuart, his friend, the dashing cavalier, could be dead. He had visited Flora, Jeb's wife, and they'd laughed about some of their days back in Kansas, but then Flora had begun to cry, and he had thought it best to leave. Flora had just lost her husband, a Confederate general. Her father, a Union general, was still fighting.

The war had never been fair.

Cole had to head out again, this time to the Indian Nation, to confer with the Cherokees and Choctaws who had been persuaded to fight for the Confederacy. The Union armies were closing in on Richmond, and Lee was hard pressed to protect the capital without Jackson to harass the Federals as they made their way through the Shenandoah Valley.

When he had left Virginia Cole had gone to Tennessee, and from Tennessee he had been ordered to rejoin his brother's unit. The noose was closing tighter and tighter around the neck of the Confederacy. John Hunt Morgan had managed to escape his captors, and he needed information about the Union troops being sent into Kentucky and Tennessee from Kansas City. Cole had taken the assignment in the little town outside the big city for only one reason—he would be close to Kristin. He had to see her. It had been so long, and they had parted so bitterly. He'd received a few letters from her, terse, quick notes telling him that they were all fine, telling him that the Union was in firm control of the part of Missouri where the ranch sat, that he was better off away and that he should take care.

Jamie and Malachi had received warmer letters. Much warmer letters. But still, even to his brothers, Kristin had said very little. Every letter was the same. She related some silly little anecdote that was sure to make them laugh, and then she closed, telling them she was praying for them all. She thought there might be a wedding as soon as the war was over or maybe even before. Shannon was corresponding regularly with a Captain Ellsworth, and Kristin said she, too, thought he was a charming gentleman. He was a Yankee, but she was sure the family would forget that once the war was over. They would all have to, she added forcefully, if there was to be a future.

Cole wasn't sure there could be. There was that one part of his past that he couldn't forget, and he never would be able to forget it, not unless he could finish it off, bury it completely. Not until the redlegs who had razed his place and killed his wife were dead could he ever really rest. No matter how sweet the temptation.

Sitting at a corner table in the saloon, his feet propped and his hat pulled low, he sipped a whiskey and listened to the conversation at the bar. He learned quickly that Lieutenant Billingsley would be transferring eight hundred troops from Kansas to Tupelo and then on to Kentucky by the following week. The saloon was crowded with Union soldiers, green recruits by the looks of them—he didn't think many of the boys even had to shave as yet—but they had one or two older soldiers with them. No one had paid Cole much heed. He was dressed in denim and cotton, with a cattleman's chaps and silver spurs in place and a cowhide vest. He didn't look much like a man who gave a damn about the war one way or the other. One man had asked him what he was doing out of uniform, and he'd quickly invented a story about being sent home, full of shrapnel, after the battle of Shiloh. After that, someone had sent over a bottle of whiskey and he'd set his hat low over his forehead and he'd listened. Now that he had his information, it was time to go. He wanted to reach his wife.

His wife.

He could even say it out loud now. And only once in a while did the bitterness assail him. His wife... His wife had been slain, but he had married a little spitfire of a blonde, and she was his woman now. His wife.

He tensed, remembering that she knew, knew everything about him, about his past. Damn Emery! He'd had no right to spill out the past like that for her. Now he would never know...

Know what? he asked himself.

What her feelings were, what her feelings really were. Hell, it was a damnable time for a marriage. He could still count on his fingers the times he had seen her....Kristin. He'd been impatient with her, and he'd been furious with her, but he'd always admired her courage, no matter what, and from the beginning he'd been determined to protect her.

Then he'd discovered that he needed her.

Like air. Like water. Like the very earth. He needed her. When he'd been away from her he'd still had the nightmares, but time had slowly taken them away. When visions of a woman came to haunt him while he slept, it was Kristin's delicate features he saw, her soft, slow smile, her wide, luminous eyes.

He'd never denied that he cared for her.

He just hadn't wanted to admit how much.

He didn't want a wife feeling sorry for him. He didn't want her holding on, afraid to hurt a traumatized soldier. The whole thing made him seethe inside. He'd swear that he'd be quit of her as soon as the war was over, and then he'd panic, and he'd pray that everything was all right, and he would wish with all his heart that he could just get back to that little patch of Missouri on the border where he could reach out and just touch her face, her hand....

And if he did, he wondered glumly, what good could it do him? He could never stop. Not until one of them lay dead. Him or Fitz. Maybe Fitz hadn't fired the shot that had killed his wife, but he had ordered the raid on Cole's place, and he had led it. In the few months that he had ridden with Quantrill, Cole had managed to meet up with a number of the men who had been in on the raid.

But he'd never found Henry Fitz.

His thoughts suddenly shifted. He didn't know what it was that told him he was in danger, but suddenly he knew that he was. Maybe it was in the thud of a new pair of shiny Union boots on the floor, maybe it was something in the air. And maybe he had lived with the danger for so damned long that he could smell it.

He should never have come to Kansas.

It wasn't that he wasn't armed. He was. And the poor green boys in the saloon were carrying muzzle-loading rifles. He could probably kill the dozen or so of them in the room before they could even load their weapons.

He didn't want to kill them. He'd always hated that kind of warfare. Hell, that was why Quantrill had been able to run circles around the Federals for years. Quantrill's men were so well armed that they could gun down an entire company before they could get off a single shot.

He prepared to leave, praying that the newcomer wasn't someone he knew. But when he saw the man's face beneath the brim of his hat, his heart sank.

The man was his own age, and he wore a lieutenant's insignia. He had dark hair and a long, dark beard, and the lines that furrowed his face said that he should have been older than thirty-two.

It's been a long hard war for all of us, Cole thought bleakly.

The Union officer's name was Kurt Taylor, and he had ridden escort and trails out in the Indian country with Cole when he had been with Stuart. Another West Pointer. They'd fought the Sioux side by side many times.

But now they were on opposite sides.

When Cole stood, Taylor saw him. The men stared straight at one another.

Cole hesitated. He wasn't going to fire, not unless he had to. He didn't cotton to killing children, and that was about what it would be. He looked at the boys standing at the bar. Hell, most of them wouldn't even have started school when the trouble had started in Kansas.

Do something, Taylor, Cole thought. Say something. But the man didn't move. The two of them just stood there staring at one another, and it was as if the world stood still.

Then, miraculously, Taylor lifted his hat.

"Howdy," he said, and walked on by.

Taylor had recognized him. Cole knew it. He had seen the flash of recognition in his eyes. But Taylor wasn't going to turn him in.

Taylor walked up to the bar. The soldiers saluted him, and he told them to be at ease. They returned to their conversations, but they were no longer as relaxed as they had been. They were in the presence of a commissioned officer now.

But Kurt Taylor ignored the men, just as he was ignoring Cole. He ordered himself a brandy, swallowed it down quickly and ordered himself another. Then he turned around, leaned his elbows on the bar and looked out over the room.

"You know, boys," he said, "war itself, soldiering, never did bother me. Joining the army seemed to be a right noble position in life. We had to defend American settlers from the Indians. We had to keep an eye on Mexico, and then suddenly we had our folks moving into Texas. Next thing you know, our great nation is divided, and we're at war with our Southern cousins. And even that's all

right, 'cause we all know a man's gotta do what a man's gotta do."
He paused and drained his second brandy. He didn't look at Cole,
but Cole knew damned well that Taylor was talking straight to him.

"Bushwhackers!" Kurt Taylor spit on the floor. Then he added,
"And bloody murdering jayhawkers. I tell you, one is just as bad as
the next, and if he claims to wear my colors, well, he's a liar. Those
jayhawkers we've got up here, hell, they turned half of Kansas and
Missouri against the Union. Folks that didn't own no slaves, that
didn't care one way or another about the war, we lost them to the
Confederacy because they so abhorred the murder that was being
done. Quantrill's boys started up after Lane and Jennison began their
goddamn raiding."

"Pardon me—" one young man began.

"No, sir! I do not pardon you!" Kurt Taylor snapped. "Murder
is murder. And I hear tell that one of the worst of our Kansas murderers is right here, right here in this town. His name is Henry Fitz.
He thought he could make himself a political career out of killing
Missourians. He forgot there were decent folk in Kansas who would
never condone the killing of women and children, whether it was
done by bushwhackers or jayhawkers." He stared straight at Cole,
and then he turned his back on him.

He knew Cole wouldn't shoot him.

He knew Cole wouldn't shoot a man in the back.

Cole was trembling, and his fingers were itching. He didn't even
want to draw his gun. He wanted to find Fitz and wrap his fingers
around the bastard's throat and choke the life out of him.

"Give me another brandy there, barkeep. Boys, you watch your
step while Fitz is around. He's down Main Street at the McKinley
barn with his troops. I'd say there's about a dozen of those marauders. Yep, I think you ought to steer clear of the area."

He tossed back another brandy, and then he turned and looked at
Cole again.

And then he walked out of the saloon.

Cole left a few minutes after Taylor did. He wondered if his old
comrade in arms had put on the performance he had so that Cole
would get out of town or so that he would stay in it.

He came out on the steps and looked up at the noonday sun, and he smiled. He came out to the hitching post and mounted his horse, a bay he had borrowed from Malachi because he had been afraid his own stallion was too well known here.

Taylor had even told him where to find Fitz. Straight down Main Street.

Cole started the bay at a walk. Within seconds he had urged the horse to a trot, and then to a canter, and then to a gallop. The barbershop whizzed by him, then the savings bank, the newspaper office and Ed Foley's Mercantile. He passed rows of neat houses with white picket fences and summer gardens, and then he was on the stretch of road leading to the farms beyond the town limits.

He must have headed out in the right direction, because suddenly there was a line of troops coming toward him. Redlegs, so called for the color of their leggings. Raiders. Murderers. Jim Lane had led them once. Now Senator Jim Lane was in Washington, and even Doc Jennison, who had taken command of them after Lane, had gone on to new pursuits. But Henry Fitz was still leading his band, and still striking terror into the hearts of innocent men, women and children.

Cole slowed the bay to a walk as the men approached. Henry Fitz sat atop a piebald, dead center. He had narrowed his dark little eyes, and he was staring down the road at Cole.

Cole kept moving. He had to do this. He had to kill Fitz. And if he died, too…

Would Kristin care? he found himself wondering. He had never doubted her gratitude, but he wondered now what she would feel if she heard that he had been gunned down on a Kansas road. Would she shed any tears for him? Would she miss him? Would she revile him for dying a senseless death, for leaving her alone?

He closed his eyes for a moment. He had to do this. If they were to have any kind of a future together, he had to do this. Now.

For a moment he remembered the flames, remembered them clearly. He remembered the crackling of the fire and he remembered the acrid smell of the smoke. And he remembered her, running, running to him. He remembered reaching out and touching her, and he remembered the way she had looked into his eyes and smiled and died. And he remembered the blood that had stained his hands…

I loved you! his heart cried out. I loved you, Elizabeth! With all my heart and with all my soul.

And in that moment he knew at last that he loved Kristin, too. He had to bury the past, because he longed for a future with her. He had been afraid to love again. He had not wanted to destroy Elizabeth's memory by loving again. Yet he knew now that if Elizabeth could speak to him she would tell him to love Kristin, to love her deeply and well, in memory of all they had once shared.

He brought the bay to a halt and watched the road. The redlegs were trotting along easily, none of them expecting trouble from a lone man atop a single bay horse. But in the center of the group, the frown upon Henry Fitz's face was deepening. Another five feet—ten—and he would recognize Cole.

"Howdy, there," Fitz began, drawing in on his reins. The rest of the party stopped along with him. His hat was tilted low over his thickly bearded face, and his eyes seemed to disappear into folds of flesh. "I'll be damned!" he said suddenly. Then he laughed. "Come all the way to Kansas to die, boy?"

And he reached for his revolver.

Cole had been fast before the war. He had been fast in the West. He was faster now.

Fitz had been the inspiration that had taught him how to draw faster than sound, faster than light. He had always known that someday, somehow, he would meet up with this man.

And he did now, guns blazing. Holding the reins in his teeth, he tightened his thighs around the bay and rode into the group.

He watched Fitz fall. He saw the blood stain his shirt crimson, and he watched him fall. The rest of it was a blur. He heard men and horses screaming as he galloped through their midst. A bullet struck his saddle, and then the bay went down beneath him. Cole tasted the dust roused by the multitude of horses. He jumped away from the fallen bay, grabbed his rifles and fired again. The gunfire seemed to go on forever.

Then there was silence. He spun around, a cocked rifle in either hand.

Three men remained alive. They stared at him and raised their hands. Their faces meant nothing to him.

He hurried away from his fallen horse and leaped into the saddle of a large, powerful-looking buckskin. Warily eyeing the three men, he nudged the horse forward. The buckskin had been a good choice. It surged forward, and Cole could feel the animal's strength and sense its speed. He raced forward, his heart pounding, adrenaline pumping furiously through his system.

He was alive.

But as he raced toward the town he saw the soldiers. Rows of blue uniforms. Navy blue. On both sides of the road. He slowed his horse to a walk. There was nowhere to go. It was over. They would build a gallows in the middle of town, and they would hang him as a bushwhacker.

Suddenly Kurt Taylor was riding toward Cole. "Hear there's been some shooting up at the end of town, stranger. You might want to hurry along and let the army do the picking up."

Cole couldn't breathe. Taylor lifted a brow and grinned at him. Cole looked down at his hands where they rested on the pommel. They were shaking.

He saluted Taylor.

Taylor saluted back. "Someone ought to tell Cole Slater that the man who killed his wife is dead. And someone also ought to warn him that he's an outlaw in these parts. Someone ought to warn him that he'd best spend his time way, way deep in Dixie. I know that the man isn't any criminal, but there aren't many who served with him like I did. The rest think he ought to wear a rope around his neck."

"Thank you kindly, sir," Cole said at last. "If I meet up with him, I'll tell him."

He rode on, straight through the ranks of blue uniforms. He kept riding. He didn't look back, not even when he heard a cheer and realized that the Union soldiers were saluting him, that Kurt Taylor had won him a few friends.

His thigh was bleeding, he realized. He had been shot after all, and he hadn't even known it. It didn't matter much. He had to keep riding. He wanted to get home. Night was falling. It was a good time to ride.

A little farther down the road he became aware that he was being followed. He quickly left the road and dismounted, whispering to the buckskin, encouraging it to follow him into the brush.

He was being followed by a single horseman. He hid behind an oak tree and listened to the hoofbeats. He waited until the rider was right by his side. Then he sprang up and knocked the man to the ground.

"Damn you, Cole Slater! Get off me."

"Taylor!"

Cole stood and dragged Taylor to his feet.

"You son of a bitch!" Taylor laughed, and then he clapped Cole hard on the shoulders. "You damned son of a bitch! Hasn't anybody told you that the South is going to lose the war?"

"It wouldn't matter what they told me," Cole said. "I can't much help what I am." He paused a moment, and then he grinned, because Kurt really had been one damned good friend. "Thank you. Thank you for what you did back there. I've seen so many men tearing one another to shreds. The truth meant more to you than the color of a uniform. I won't forget that, Kurt. Ever."

"I didn't do anything that God wouldn't call right," Kurt said. "You got him, Cole. You got that mangy bastard. 'Course, you do know they'll shoot you on sight now and ask questions later."

"Yes, I know that."

"You're heading south, I hope?"

"East, and then south."

"Don't stay around the border too long," Taylor warned him. "Even to see your boy. Major Emery said that if I ever came across you I was to warn you—"

"What?" Cole snapped, his hands on Taylor's shoulders.

"I'm trying to tell you. Major Emery said—"

"The hell with Emery! What boy?"

Taylor cocked his head, frowning. "Why, yours, of course. Born last February. A fine boy, I understand. Captain Ellsworth gets out there now and again, and he reported to the major that both mother and child were doing fine. Don't rightly recall what they named him, but Ellsworth says he's big and healthy and has a head of hair to put many a fine lass to shame. Cole, let go, you're about to snap my damned shoulder blade. Oh, hell! You mean you didn't know? Listen to me now. Don't you go running off half-cocked after everything that happened here today. You move slow, and you move careful, you hear me, Slater? Most of the Union boys would shoot me if they knew I let you slip through my fingers. Cole?''

"I'll move careful," Cole said.

Yes, he'd move careful. He'd move damned careful. Just to make sure he lived long enough to tan Kristin's sweet hide.

Why in God's name hadn't she told him?

It was hot and humid on the Fourth of July, 1864. Scarcely a breeze had stirred all day.

It had been a difficult day for Kristin. She had learned long ago to keep her mind off her worries, to try not to think too much, to concentrate on her tasks. Anything was better than worrying. If she worried all the time she would drive herself mad.

But the fourth was a particularly difficult day.

There were celebrations going on everywhere. Union soldiers letting off volleys of rifle fire, ranchers setting off fireworks. Every gunshot reminded Kristin that her husband could meet her brother on the field of battle at any time, that they were still at war, that the nation celebrating its birthday was still bitterly divided.

There was smoke in the air, and the noise was making the baby restless. She'd had him with her down in the parlor, and Delilah's Daniel, almost three years old now, had been laughing and entertaining the baby with silly faces. But then Cole Gabriel Slater had decided enough was enough, and he had jammed one of his pudgy little fists into his mouth and started to cry.

"Oh, I've had it with the entire day anyway!" Kristin declared to everyone in the room and to no one in particular. She picked up the baby and started up the stairs. Delilah, sewing, stared after her. Shannon, running her fingers idly over the spinet, paused. Samson rolled his eyes. "Hot days, yes, Lordy, hot days," he mumbled. He stood up. "The hands will be back in soon enough. I'll carry that stew on out to the bunkhouse."

Upstairs, Kristin lay down with her fretful baby and opened her blouse so that he could nurse. She started, then smiled, as he latched on to her nipple with a surprising power. Then, as always, an incredibly sweet feeling swept through her, and she pulled his little body still closer to her. His eyes met hers. In the last month they had turned a silver gray, just like Cole's. His hair was hers, though, a thatch of it, blond, almost white. He was a beautiful baby, incredibly beautiful. He had been born on the tenth of February. Stroking his soft cheek, she felt her smile deepen as she remembered the day. It had been snowing, and it had been bitterly cold, and she had been dragging hay down for the horses when she had felt the first pain and panicked. It would have been impossible for Dr. Cavanaugh to come out from town, and it would have been impossible for her to reach town. Pete had been terribly upset, and that had calmed her somehow, and Delilah had assured her that it would be hours before the baby actually came.

Hours!

It had been awful, and it had been agony, and she had decided that it was extremely unfair that men should be the ones to go off to war to get shot at when women were the ones stuck with having babies. She had ranted and raved, and she had assured both Delilah and Shannon in no uncertain terms that she despised Cole Slater— and every other living soul who wore britches, as a matter of fact— and that if she lived she would never do this again.

Delilah smirked and assured her that she was going to live and that she would probably have half a dozen more children. Shannon waltzed around in a daydream, saying that she wouldn't be complaining one whit if she were the one about to have the baby—if the baby belonged to Captain Ellsworth.

The pain subsided for a moment, and Kristin had smiled up at her sister, who was pushing back her soaked hair. It was "colder than a witch's teat," as Pete had said, but she was drenched with sweat.

"You really love him, don't you, your Captain Ellsworth?"

Shannon nodded, her eyes on fire. "Oh, Kristin! He saved my life. He caught me when I fell. He was such a wonderful hero. Oh, Kristin! Don't you feel that about Cole?"

She hesitated, and she remembered how happy she had been to see him. And she remembered how they had made love, how tender he had been with her, how passionate. With a certain awe she remembered the way his eyes had fallen upon her, how cherished that look had made her feel. And she remembered the ecstasy...

But then she remembered his anger and his impatience, and how he had grown cold and distant when she had mentioned his past. He was in love with another woman, and though that woman lay dead, she was a rival Kristin could not best.

"Cole was a hero!" Shannon whispered. "Kristin, how can you forget that? He rode in here and he saved our lives! And if you think you're having a difficult labor, well, then...that is God's way of telling you you had no right to keep the information about this baby from your husband!"

I meant to tell him.... Kristin almost said it. But if she did she would have to explain how he had acted when she had mentioned his past, and she would have to think about the fact that he didn't love her, right in the middle of having his child. She shrugged instead. "What can he do? There is a war on."

A vicious pain seized her again, and she assured Shannon that Cole was a rodent, and Shannon laughed. And then, miraculously— for it had been hours and hours, and it was nearly dawn—Delilah told Kristin that the baby's head was showing and that it was time for her to push.

When he lay in her arms, red and squalling, Kristin knew that she had never imagined such a love as swelled within her.

And she prayed with all her heart that her son's father was alive, that he would come home to them all. She vowed that she would ask no questions he could not answer, that she would not ask for anything he could not give.

Lying with the baby, nursing him as she did now, was the greatest pleasure of her life. Kristin forgot the world outside, and she forgot the war, and she even forgot that his father probably did not know he existed. She loved his grave little eyes, and she loved the way his mouth tugged on her breast. She counted his fingers endlessly, and his toes, and she thought that he was gaining weight wonderfully and that he was very long—even Delilah said he would grow to be very tall—and that his face was adorable. He had a little dimple in his chin, and Kristin wondered if Cole had a dimple like it. She had seen all of his body, but she had never seen his naked chin. He had always had a beard.

Delilah had warned her to let Gabe, as they called him, nurse only so long at one breast. If she did he would ignore the other, and she would experience grave discomfort. Consequently she gently loosened his grasp on her left breast, laughing at his howl of outrage.

"Heavens! You're more demanding than that father of yours!" she told her baby, cradling him against her shoulder and patting his back. Then, suddenly, she realized that she was not alone. She had been so engrossed with her son that the door had opened and closed without her noticing it.

A peculiar sensation made its way up her spine, and suddenly she was breathless. She dared to look at the door, and found him standing there.

Her hero.

He was in full dress uniform, tattered gray and gold, his sword hanging dangerously from its scabbard. He was leaner than she remembered him, and his face was ashen, and his eyes...his eyes burned through her, seared into her.

"Cole!" she whispered. She wondered how long he had been standing there, and suddenly she was blushing, and it didn't matter that he was the child's father, she felt awkward and vulnerable and exposed.

He pushed away from the door and strode toward her, and despite herself she shrank away from him. He reached for the baby, and she clung to her child. Then she heard him speak, his voice low and hoarse.

"My God, Kristin, give him to me."

"Cole—"

She had to release the baby for Cole meant to take him. She nervously pulled her dress together but he had no eyes for her. He was looking at the baby. She wanted to shriek his name, wanted to run to him. It had been so long since she had seen him last, and even that had seemed like a dream. But she couldn't run to him, couldn't throw her arms around him. He was cold and forbidding. He was a stranger to her now.

He ignored her completely, setting the squalling child down on his back at the foot of the bed, freeing him from all his swaddling so that he could look at the whole of him. Kristin could have told him that Gabe was perfect in every way, but she kept silent. She knew he had to discover it for himself. Suddenly she was more than a little afraid of her husband. Should she have written to him? What good would it have done? Cole shouldn't be here even now. There were far too many Union troops around. Was that the real reason? she wondered. She had hesitated once because he had made her angry, because she had realized that he did not love her. But she hadn't written, she knew, because she had been afraid that he would be determined to come home, and that that determination would make him careless.

For a moment Gabe quieted and stared up at his father. He studied Cole's face as gravely and as purposefully as Cole studied him. His little body was perfectly still.

Then he had had enough of his father. His mother was the one he wanted. He lifted up his chubby little legs and screwed up his face and kicked out and howled in outrage all at once. The cry brought a surge to Kristin's breasts that soaked the bodice of the gown she held so tightly against her. Cole covered his son again, then picked him up and set him against his chest. Kristin reached out her arms.

"Please, Cole, give him back to me. He's...he's hungry."

Cole hesitated, staring at her hard. Then he handed the baby to her. Kristin lowered her head and wished he would go away, but then she remembered that he had just come, and that if he went away again he might be killed this time. Color spilled over her cheeks, and she remembered just how they had gotten the baby, and she touched the baby's cheek with her finger and let her bodice fall open and led his little mouth to her breast. He latched on with an awful, pigletlike sound, and she found that she couldn't look up at all, even though she knew that Cole was still in the room and that his eyes were still on her.

The room was silent except for the baby's slurping. Then even that stopped, and Kristin realized he had fallen asleep. She lifted him to her shoulder and tried to get him to burp, but he was sleeping too soundly. Biting her lip, she rose and set him in the cradle that Samson had brought down from the attic. All the while she felt Cole's eyes on her.

Still, he didn't touch her, and he didn't speak to her. He stood by the cradle and stared down at the child. He was going to touch him again. Kristin bit her lips to keep from protesting. She watched in silence as Cole's long fingers tenderly touched the tiny cheek. She tried to button her bodice, then realized that she was drenched and that it was a foolish gesture. Flushing, she hurried to change her gown, but it didn't matter. Cole didn't seem to have noticed. She wondered if she should tiptoe away and leave him alone, but the moment she started for the door he was on his feet, and she realized that he had noted her every movement.

"Where do you think you're going?"

His voice was low, but there was real anger in it, and real menace.

"I thought you might be hungry."

He was silent. His gaze fell over her. Then he took a step toward her, and she almost screamed when his fingers gripped her arms and he shook her. "Damn you, Kristin! Damn you a thousand times over! You knew! You knew—and you didn't tell me! What right did you have to keep him from me?"

She tried to free herself, but she could not. She looked in his eyes, and she hated what she saw there, the uncompromising hardness.

"What rights have you got!" she choked out. "You ride in whenever you choose.... You may feel you have obligations, but that is all you have! I—"

"I ride in when I can get here!" he snapped, shaking her again. Her head fell back, and her eyes, glazed suddenly with tears, stared into his. "Lady, there is a war being fought out there! You know that. Of all women, you know that. I have done everything that is humanly possible, I have given you everything—"

"No! No, you have not given me everything! You have never given me the least little part of your—"

"I could have been killed. I don't know how many times I could have been killed on some stinking battlefield, and I wouldn't even have known I had a son!"

"Let me go!"

"No!"

"Please!" He was so close to her, and he felt so good. He was so warm, and she could feel the hardness of his body, and the touch of his hands. She wanted to touch his face and soothe away the lines around his eyes, and she wanted to fill the emptiness in his heart. She wanted to see his eyes alight with passion again. As she thought of the passion they had known together, her breasts seemed to fill again, but it was not for her child this time, it was for him. She needed to be held, to be touched.

To be loved.

"Please!" she repeated softly. She was so glad to see him, and their time together should be a precious respite against the war that raged on around them.

"Cole, I wanted to tell you when you were here, but all of a sudden we were fighting, because Major Emery had committed the horrible sin of telling me that you had been hurt. Mr. Cole Slater had been hurt, cut open and left bleeding, and he just couldn't bear that! Well, you are human, Cole, and you're supposed to bleed! And I should hurt for you, too, because damn it, what happened was awful!"

"Kristin, stop—"

"No! No, I will not stop! What have you got now? One week, one day? One lousy hour? Not long, I'll warrant. There are too many Federals around. So you stop, and you listen to me! I am grateful to you, Cole, eternally grateful. And I've been glad of this bargain of ours, heartily glad. You have fulfilled every promise you ever made me. But don't you dare yell at me now! I didn't write because I didn't want you getting killed, because I was afraid of your temper."

"My temper! I would never—"

"Yes, you would! You would have taken foolish chances to get here. You would have been afraid because of what happened to you with—"

She broke off, remembering that Emery had said that his wife had been pregnant when she had been killed.

"Oh, God, Cole, I'm sorry. I just realized that you would probably rather that she...that I..."

"What the hell are you saying?" he asked hoarsely.

Kristin shook her head miserably. "Your wife, your first wife...

You were expecting a child. I'm sorry, you must be thinking of her, that you would prefer—''

"That she had lived? That you had died? My God, Kristin, don't you ever say such a thing, don't you even think it, do you hear me?'' He caught her against him. He threaded his fingers roughly through her hair, and suddenly he lowered his head and buried his face in the fragrant strands. "Don't you ever, ever think that!" he repeated. Then he looked at her again, and he smiled. It was a weary smile, and she saw how much the past few years had aged him, and her heart ached.

"He is a beautiful boy. He is the most wonderful child I've ever seen. And he is mine. Thank you. Thank you so very much.''

"Oh, Cole!'' she whispered. She was dangerously close to tears. He saw it and his tone changed.

"I'd still like to tan your hide for keeping the truth from me!''

"Cole, I really didn't mean to. I was afraid. I'm always afraid, it seems.''

"I know, I know.'' He held her against him.

"Cole, you must be starved. Let me go down and have Delilah—''

"No, not now.''

"Cole, you must need—''

He stepped away from her.

"I need my wife,'' he said. "I very, very badly need my wife.''

He bent his head and kissed her, and then he lifted her into his arms and they fell upon the bed together.

"We have a son, Kristin,'' he said, and she laughed. "We have a son, and he's beautiful, and...and so are you.''

It was a long, long time before either of them thought of any other kind of sustenance.

Chapter Fourteen

The days that followed were glorious for Kristin. It wasn't that anything had been settled between them. It was just that for a time they seemed to have achieved a private peace, and it was wonderful.

They did not stray far from the house. Cole explained how hard it had been to elude the patrols to reach her. But Kristin knew her own land, and she knew where they could safely travel. They picnicked on the banks of the river with the baby, and while he slept they splashed in the deliciously cool water. Kristin was first shocked and then ridiculously excited to dare to strip away her clothes in the broad daylight and make love in the water.

In the evening they sat beneath the moon and felt the cool breezes play over them. Kristin listened while Cole and Samson talked about what was left of the herd, and it seemed that everything that was said began with the words "When the war is over…"

At night, lying curled against her husband's body, Kristin asked him if he thought the war would ever end. He hesitated a long time, stroking her hair.

"It's ending now, Kristin. We're being broken down bit by bit, like a beautiful animal chewed to bits by fleas. We never had the power. We never had the industry. We never had the men. It's going to end. If the Confederacy holds out another year I'll be surprised. Well, we went a long way on courage and tactics. But that Lincoln is a stubborn cuss. Tenacious. He's held on to his Union, so it seems."

He sounded tired, but not bitter. Kristin stroked his chest. "Can't you just stay here now? If you know you're losing…"

"I can't stay, Kristin. You know that."

"I don't know anything of the kind! You've done your best for the Confederacy! You can't—"

"Kristin, Kristin!" He caught her hands. "I'm an outlaw as long as the war is on. If I stay here, I'll be in terrible danger. If some glory-seeking commander hears about it, he might just waltz in and string me up. If I'm going to die, I'd rather it be fighting than dangling from the end of a rope!"

"Cole, stop it—"

"And it isn't over, Kristin. I'm in the game and I have to stay with it. If I don't go back, Malachi will come here and shoot me for a traitor."

"He would not!"

"Well, someone would," he said.

"Cole—"

"Kristin, I have to go back."

"Cole—"

He rolled over and swept her into his arms and kissed her and then looked into her eyes. "When I ride now, I will think of my son. Thank you for Gabe, Kristin. Thank you." He nuzzled her lips and kissed her forehead and her throat and the valley between her breasts. She tried to keep talking, to keep arguing, but he nuzzled his way down the length of her torso, and she grew breathless and couldn't speak. When he had finished she couldn't remember what she had wanted to say, only that it was terribly important that she hold him as long as she could.

The next day Kristin was overjoyed when Matthew arrived unexpectedly. He quickly warned her that both he and Cole could be shot if they were caught together. Still, for a few hours, it was a wonderful homecoming. Matthew admired his nephew, and Shannon clung to her brother, and Delilah managed a fine feast. Then Cole and Matthew shut themselves up in the library together. Kristin finally had to force her way in.

"You're discussing me, I know it, and I will know what is going on!" she insisted.

"Cole has to leave," Matthew told her. "Right away. Tonight."

"Why?"

Matthew looked unhappily at Cole. Cole shrugged and gave her the explanation. "Matthew is putting the ranch under the protection of a Federal troop."

"But—"

"I can't be here, Kristin. And Quantrill's group has split up."

"What?"

"During the spring," Matthew explained, "Quantrill and his men got into some heavy feuding in Texas. Bill Anderson has some men under him, and George Todd has a group, too. Quantrill still has his followers. Bill attacked some Federals during the summer, and Archie Clements scalped the men he murdered. The situation is frightening, and no one knows where Zeke Moreau is, or who he's with. So you see, Kristin, Cole has to get out of here. And you have to be protected."

Tears stung her eyes, and she gritted her teeth to keep from spilling them. She turned away from the men.

"I fixed the tear in your frock coat, Cole. And Delilah has been washing everything. The two of you, sometimes your clothes smell as if you'd been sleeping with skunks for a year. I'll see that you're packed up and have Shannon wrap up a supply of jerky."

She stumbled into the hallway. Cole found her there and swept her into his arms and took her upstairs to their room. She cried the whole time they made love, her tears spilling over his shoulders and his chest and dampening his cheeks.

Then he kissed her and held the baby tightly. She insisted on coming down with him, and when he was mounted he leaned down to kiss her again. Holding their child close to her breast, Kristin waved as he left.

That night some Union soldiers moved into the bunkhouse. Kristin supposed it was necessary. But it was still hard.

The bushwhacker situation grew much worse. On the thirtieth of September Kristin was surprised when she came out on the porch to see that Major Emery was riding toward her. She stood and smiled, ready to greet him, but her smile died when she saw his face. She went pale herself, and the world spun, and she was afraid that she was going to faint.

"Oh, my God, it's Cole—"

"No, no, Mrs. Slater," he assured her hastily, taking Gabe from her. "He's a fine boy, ma'am. A fine boy." He looked around uncomfortably. "I don't think your sister should know the whole of this, ma'am, but...Captain Ellsworth is dead."

"Oh, no!"

"That damned Bill Anderson! Since his sister died they say he froths at the mouth every time he fights. Fights—bah!" He spat into the dirt. "He tore up Centralia. He made twenty-five unarmed soldiers strip, and then he shot twenty-three of them dead. The troops that went out after him fared worse. It was a massacre. At least a hundred killed. Stripped, scalped, dismembered, their bodies mutilated as they died—"

"Oh, God! Oh, God!"

They both heard the scream. Kristin turned around to see that Shannon was standing in the doorway. She had heard every word. She knew.

"Oh, God! No!" she shrieked. Major Emery took a step toward her, barely managing to catch her as she pitched forward in a dead faint.

"Could you take her to her room for me, please?" Kristin whispered.

Major Emery nodded and carried Shannon upstairs. "We've a company surgeon out in your bunkhouse. I'll send him over and see that he gives her something."

The doctor didn't come soon enough. Shannon awoke, and she started to cry. She cried so hard that Kristin was afraid she would hurt herself. Then she was silent, and the silence was even worse. Kristin stayed with her, holding her hand, but she knew that she hadn't reached her sister, and she wondered if anyone ever would again.

* * *

Fall came, and with it more tragedy for the South. General Sherman was marching to the sea through Georgia and the Carolinas, and the reports of his scorched earth policy were chilling. In the west, the Union bottleneck was almost complete.

On the twenty-first of October George Todd died when a sniper caught him in the neck. Five days later Bill Anderson was killed in the northwestern corner of Missouri.

Kristin was alarmed to see how eagerly Shannon received the news of their deaths.

Thanksgiving came and went. It was a very quiet affair. Kristin was Matthew McCahy's sister, but she was also Cole Slater's wife, and so it didn't seem right to invite any of the Union men in for a fancy supper.

Matthew made it back for Christmas Day, and Kristin was delighted to see him. She asked if he had heard anything, and he told her that the last he had heard, Cole Slater was still at large. John Hunt Morgan, the dashing cavalry commander, had been killed late in the year, and Matthew hadn't heard anything about where Cole or Malachi or Jamie had been assigned.

She cried that night, cried because no news was good news. It seemed so long since she had lost her father, and she could hardly remember Adam's face. She didn't want to lose anyone else. She could hardly stand to see Shannon's pale face anymore. She hadn't seen her sister smile since Captain Ellsworth had been killed. Not once.

After Christmas dinner, Kristin sat before the fire in the parlor with her brother and her sister. She began to play a Christmas carol on the spinet, but Shannon broke down and ran upstairs to her room. Kristin sat staring silently at her hands for a long time.

Finally Matthew spoke.

"Kristin, nothing's going to get better, not for a long, long time, you know."

"They say it's almost over. They say the war is almost over."

"The war, but not the hatred. I doubt they'll fix that for a hundred years, Kristin. It isn't going to be easy. The healing will be slow and hard."

"I know," Kristin whispered.

"You just make sure, Kristin, that if Cole comes around you get him out of here fast. He isn't going to be safe anywhere near this place, not until some kind of a peace is made, and then only if amnesty is given."

Kristin's fingers trembled. She nodded. "He won't come back. Not until...not until it's over."

Matthew kissed her and went upstairs. Kristin stared at the fire until it had burned very low in the grate.

In February Gabriel had his first birthday. The news that month was good for the Union, grim for the Confederacy. Sherman had devastated the South. Robert E. Lee was struggling in Virginia, and Jefferson Davis and the Confederate cabinet had abandoned Richmond half a dozen times.

By March, everyone was talking about the campaign for Petersburg. Grant had been pounding away at the Virginia city since the previous summer, and the fighting had been fierce. The Union had tried to dig a tunnel under the Confederate lines. Mines had exploded, and many Confederates had been killed, but then they had rallied and shot down the Union soldiers who had filled in the crater. The soldiers shuddered when they spoke of it.

Kristin had become accustomed to the men who had made their headquarters on her land. They were mostly farmers and ranchers, and more and more she heard them speak wistfully of the time when the war would be over, when they could go home. The Confederate general Kirby-Smith was still raising hell in the West, and the Southern forces were still fighting valiantly in the East, but the death throes had already set in for a nation that had never had a chance to truly breathe the air of independence. Major Emery came one day and sat with them on the porch while the first warmth of spring touched them. Morosely he told Kristin that the death estimates for the country were nearing the half-million mark. "Bullet, sword and disease!" He shook his head. "So many mothers' sons!"

When he left her that afternoon, Kristin had no idea that she would never see him again alive.

* * *

April came. General Lee's forces were gathering around Richmond for a desperate defense of the capital. Gabe was learning to walk, and Kristin had agreed with Samson and Pete that he might be allowed to try sitting on top of a horse.

Kristin came outside one April afternoon, and she knew instantly that something was wrong. There was a peculiar stillness in the air.

There should have been noise. There should have been laughter. The dozen or so Union troops billeted on the ranch should have been out and about, grooming their horses, hurrying here and there in their smart blue uniforms with their correspondence and their missives.

Pete was nowhere in sight, and neither was Samson.

"Samson?" Kristin called out.

Then she heard the barn door creak as if the breeze had moved it, but there wasn't any breeze. She looked toward it, and she saw a hand. Its fingers were curled and crumpled, and it was attached to a bloodstained blue-clad arm. Kristin felt a scream rising in her throat, but she didn't dare release it. She wrenched Gabe into her arms and ran for the house as fast as she could.

"Shannon!" she screamed. In the hall she found a gun belt with the two Colt six-shooters Cole had insisted she keep loaded and ready. With trembling fingers she wound the belt around her waist and reached for the Spencer repeating rifle Matthew had brought at Christmas.

"Shannon!" she called again.

Her sister came running down the steps, her eyes wide, her face pale.

"Something is wrong. Take Gabe—"

"No! Give me the rifle!"

"Shannon, please—"

"I'm a better shot than you are, damn it!"

"Maybe, yes! But I'm not as desperate and reckless as you are!" Kristin snapped. "Shannon, for God's sake, you are the best shot! So for the love of God take Gabriel and get upstairs and try to pick them off if they come for me."

"Who?"

She didn't know how she could be certain, but she was.

"Zeke is back. He's out there somewhere. Shannon, please, don't let them get my baby!"

With that she pushed Gabriel into her sister's arms and started out the door again. Shannon watched her. Gabriel began to cry, and she pulled him close and hurried up the stairs.

"Holy Mary!" Private Watson muttered. "Will you look at that? Fool Yankee, he's all alone and coming right at us!"

Cole looked up from where he sat polishing the butt of his rifle. His eyes narrowed as he watched the trotting horse. Judging by the way the man riding it sat, he was injured, and injured pretty badly.

"Should we shoot him?" someone murmured uncertainly.

"Somebody already done shot him," came the wry answer.

"Leave him be, boys," Cole said, rising curiously. Cole had been promoted to Colonel, which made him the highest-ranking officer in the group. Malachi was now a major and Jamie a captain. The three of them were with a small company of men simply because small companies were all that was left in their sector of the West. They had decided to find Kirby-Smith, wherever he was, and join forces with him, but for the last month they had kept a field headquarters in this abandoned farmhouse deep inside an overgrown orchard.

"I know that man," Cole muttered suddenly. He hurried forward, his brothers and his ragged troops at his heels.

He reached the horse, and the Yankee fell right into his arms. Cole eased him down to the ground, wresting his own scarf from around his neck to soak up the blood pouring from the wound beneath the man's shoulder blade.

"Matthew McCahy, what the hell happened to you, boy?" he said gruffly. He looked at Captain Roger Turnbill, the company surgeon, and then he looked down at Matthew and wondered how the hell his brother-in-law had found him. Then he decided it didn't matter, not until Matthew was looked after.

"Let's get inside the house," Captain Turnbill said.

The men started to lift him. Matthew opened his eyes, huge blue eyes that reminded Cole painfully of his wife, so very close by, so endlessly far away. Matthew reached up and clutched the lapel of Cole's frock coat.

"Cole, listen to me—"

"You know this blue belly well, colonel?" Captain Turnbill asked.

"He's my wife's brother. I know him well enough."

"Then let's get him inside. He's bleeding like a stuck pig."

"Matthew—" Cole gripped the hand that clutched him so tightly. "Matthew, the captain is going to help you. I swear it." Cole wondered if Matthew was delirious, or if he was merely wary of the Confederate surgeon. Doctors on both sides had been known to boast that they had killed more of the enemy than all the artillery shells in the service.

"Cole! For God's sake, listen to me!" Matthew rasped out. His fingers held Cole's like a vise. "It's Zeke—"

"What?"

Matthew swallowed painfully. "We met up with him southeast of here, in a little two-bit place called James Fork. We were a small detachment, thirty of us, heading over to Tennessee. I went down, I was knocked out and they took me for dead. I heard him talking over me. Said he couldn't wait to get to the McCahy place and tell Kristin McCahy that he'd managed to murder her brother now, too. They spent the night at James Fork. I waited till they were drunk and I found a horse, and here I am—"

Cole was ashen and tense. He didn't realize how hard he was gripping Matthew's shoulders until Captain Turnbill said softly, "Ease off, colonel."

"How did you find us?" Jamie asked carefully. He was the only one who seemed to be capable of rational thought at the moment.

Matthew smiled. "Your location isn't exactly a secret, gentlemen. Kurt Taylor was out here with a scouting party a few weeks ago. Some of the higher-ups know where you are.... They're just hoping the war will be over before they have to come in and clean you out." His smile faded, and he choked and coughed and then groaned in pain.

"Get him up and in the house!" Turnbill ordered. A half-dozen men quickly obeyed him, Jamie Slater tensely and carefully taking Matthew's head and his wounded shoulder.

"Slater! You've got to get there. You and your men, you've got a chance. Riding straight west—"

Cole followed after him. "There's a dozen Yankees on the ranch," he said tensely. "I know it."

"So does Zeke Moreau," Matthew gasped out.

Then he was suddenly silent.

"Is he dead?" Malachi asked tonelessly.

Turnbill shook his head. "Passed out from loss of blood. It's amazing that he made it here."

Cole didn't follow any farther. He paused in the yard in front of the farmhouse and looked around at the men who remained with him. Besides his brothers and the doctor, he had one sergeant, two corporals and twenty-two privates. They had survived a hell of a lot. How could he ask them to die at this point?

"I've got to leave you, boys," he said. The soldiers who hadn't helped carry Matthew into the house ranged silently around him. "This is a private battle, and some of you might say it's being waged against one of your own—"

"Hell, Quantrill and his kind were never one of my own," Bo Jenkins, a shopkeeper in peacetime, said. "My kind of Southerner ain't never shot down a man in cold blood."

"Glad to hear it, private," Cole said quietly. "But still, I can't rightly ask you to come along and get killed—"

"Hell, colonel, how's this any different from all the other times?" Jenkins said.

His brother John stepped up beside him. "Seems like we've been following you a long time, sir. We'll keep on doing that. I mean, what the hell, colonel? You think we all want to live forever?"

Cole felt a smile tug at his lips. "Then let's get ready. We've got to ride fast. We've got to ride like the wind."

Armed and ready, Kristin came out of the house and moved quickly toward the barn, toward the bloody hand lying in the spring sunshine.

She paused at the gaping doorway and flattened herself against the wall. Then she kicked open the door and stepped inside, both her Colts cocked and ready to fire.

She heard nothing, saw nothing. She blinked in the dim light, then she saw that at least five men in Yankee blue lay on the ground and in the hay. Their killer or killers had interrupted them in the middle of a poker game. The cards were still sitting on a bale of hay in the center of the barn.

Someone had been holding a full house.

Kristin swallowed painfully.

"Drop 'em," came a sneering voice from behind her. It was one of Zeke's men. She didn't know his name, but she recognized the voice from its jeering tone. She had heard the man's raucous laughter when her father had died.

She froze, aware that she hadn't a chance in hell of turning quickly enough to kill the man. She wondered whether she shouldn't turn anyway and die quickly. Zeke surely no longer desired her. All he wanted was revenge.

Suddenly there was an explosion right over her shoulder. She screamed, stunned, wondering if she'd been hit. She hadn't. She stared toward the center of the barn, and there lay one of the Yankee soldiers she had thought were all dead. Blood was pouring from his temple, but he was smiling at her, and his pistol was smoking. She whirled around. The man behind her lay dead, very dead. There was a black hole burned right into his chest.

She slammed the Colts back into the gun belt and ran over to the Yankee who had saved her life, falling down on her knees beside him. "Bless you! What can I—"

"Lady, you can save yourself!" the man whispered, and he winced. "If all goes well, then you come back for me. Damn it to hell, but I can't help you no more now. My leg is all busted up. You go careful. He's in the house."

Chills swept up her spine. "He's...where?"

"Moreau, their leader. He's up in the house."

He was in the house, with her sister and her child. Kristin raced for the doorway. She found Samson and Pete slumped against the far wall of the barn. Pete was dead, his eyes wide open and staring. Samson was still breathing, a thin stream of blood trickled from his forehead.

She paused for a split second to tear apart her skirt and dab at the wound. She lowered him to the ground and pressed the hastily made bandage against his forehead. Then she raced into the yard, across the paddock and toward the house, easing the Colts from the belt once again.

Suddenly there was a shot. She stopped where she stood, feeling the dust rise around her feet where a bullet had bitten into the earth. She looked up, way up, to her bedroom window.

Zeke was standing there, a handful of Shannon's hair caught in his filthy fingers.

"Drop the guns, Mrs. Slater," Zeke drawled. "Drop 'em right now, else I'll let this pretty gold stuff in my fingers run red with McCahy blood."

Kristin stared up at him in despair. She heard a shuffling around her, and she knew that his men were emerging from the bunkhouse, from the far side of the house, from behind the watering trough. She looked around, and the faces spun before her. How many of them were there? Twenty? Thirty? It was hard to tell.

"Drop 'em in the dust, Kristin, slow and careful!" Zeke laughed then, fingering Shannon's hair. "She sure did come along nicely, Kristin. Why, I think she's even prettier than you are. Hard to tell, though. You're both nasty as rattlers."

Shannon cursed and bit Zeke's hand savagely. Zeke swore in turn and cuffed her hard. Suddenly Gabe began to cry. Kristin cried out involuntarily and bit her lip.

Shannon screamed as Zeke tore at her hair. Zeke, shouting insanely, addressed Kristin again.

"Drop the guns or else I'll kill the kid first. Slow. I'll blow off his legs one by one, and then his arms and then, if he's still alive, I'll cut off his ears!"

Kristin set the Colts on the ground. She heard Zeke's wild laughter, and then he and Shannon disappeared from the window. The shuffling around her began again. She closed her eyes and tried to ignore the soft jeers and the horrible smell as the men moved closer and closer.

The door to the house burst open, and Zeke appeared, shoving Shannon before him. Shannon was white, but Kristin was, perhaps ridiculously, glad to see that her sister's hatred seemed to outweigh her fear. There would be plenty of time for fear.

Zeke, keeping his punishing grip on Shannon's hair, forced her into the center of the circle. He came close to Kristin, and he smiled. "I'm going to tell you about the afternoon, Kristin. Just so you can anticipate it all. Every sweet moment. See Harry over there? The guy with the peg leg and the rotten teeth? He's had a real hankering for you, so he gets to go first. I'm going for little sister here. Fresh meat. Then, well...hell, we've learned to share and share alike. We are going to make sure you stay alive, though. At least until we've had a chance to fire the house and the barn. You should get to hear the horses scream. That's a real fine sound. Then—maybe—Harry will scalp you. He learned the art real well from little Archie Clements himself. But we'll see how the afternoon goes. We may not have time for everything. There's lots of Yankees in these parts. Did you know that, Mrs. Slater? Sure you did. Your brother's a turncoat Yankee, ain't he? But don't worry about him none. I killed him last night."

Kristin's knees sagged, and she fell into the dirt. Matthew! It couldn't be. No!

Zeke started to laugh.

Something inside her snapped. She catapulted from the ground, flying at him in a fury. Shannon screamed but quickly rallied, and together they fell on him, biting him, tearing at him with their nails. Zeke screamed but none of his men moved to help him at first. And they couldn't shoot. They might kill him.

Then they heard it. The unmistakable sound of hoofbeats pounding the Missouri earth, pounding like thunder, coming closer and closer.

"Take cover!" one of the bushwhackers shouted.

Zeke let out a terrible growl and threw Shannon down hard in the dirt. He slammed the back of his hand against Kristin's cheek, and when she reeled, stunned by the blow, he caught her by the hair and dragged her up the steps to the porch and behind the oak rocker.

The hoofbeats came closer, thundering like a thousand drums. "Bastard!" Zeke muttered. "How could they know..."

It was only then, as Zeke aimed his gun through the slits in the back of the rocker, that Kristin got her first glimpse of the riders.

They were dressed in gray, and they might have been a sorry sight had they not ridden with such grace and style. A rebel yell suddenly rose up in the air, and the horses tore around the front of the house. Dust flew everywhere. Gunfire erupted, and Kristin bit back a scream.

Cole was leading them, whirling his horse around, his head held high. Malachi was there, too, and Jamie.

The Union army had failed endlessly against the bushwhackers because the bushwhackers were so well armed and so fast. But now they were fighting a man who knew their ways. A man who was faster. A man with a company of soldiers who were every bit as well armed as they were, a company of soldiers who were determined to salvage something of honor and chivalry from a war they were destined to lose. They fought their own kind, for their own kind had defied the very code of the South that so many had fought to preserve.

Kristin couldn't see for the clouds of dust the horses and the gunfire had churned up. All she knew was that Zeke was dragging her viciously along the porch.

She fought him. He swore he would turn around and shoot her, but she didn't really care. He had murdered Matthew, and he had murdered her father, and he was probably going to murder her. All she dared hope for was that Delilah had hidden somewhere, and that she had found Gabe. She wanted her son to live. She wanted something good to rise from the dust and ashes of this war. She wanted her child, Cole's child, to live, to remember, to start over.

"Damn you!" Zeke screamed. He twisted her arm cruelly behind her back, and she cried out in pain. He pushed her to the front door and then into the house. He pushed her toward the stairs, and the pain in her arm was so piercing that she had to stumble up the steps.

"Maybe we do have a little time. Maybe they'll all stay real busy out there for a long, long time. I wouldn't mind having you on Cole Slater's bed while he chokes on his own blood down below."

Suddenly the front door flew open and Cole was standing in the doorway. Zeke whirled, and Kristin stumbled and almost fell, but Zeke caught her and held her in front of him.

Framed by the doorway, the sunlight behind him, Cole was frightening and yet strangely beautiful. In his left hand he held his cavalry saber, and with his right he aimed his Colt.

"Put it down nice and easy, Slater, nice and easy," Zeke said. He pulled Kristin close against him, so close that she could breathe in the reek of his breath and feel the sweat of his body.

"You get your filthy hands off my wife, Zeke."

"You know, Slater, I started in with Quantrill late. That's why I didn't remember you the first time we met here. But now I remember you real well. And I've thought about this moment. I've dreamed about it. So you put the gun down. See how I've got this beautiful silver barrel aimed right at her throat? Think about how her blood will pour out where the artery's cut...."

Suddenly they heard a cry. It was Gabriel, crying in fear and rage. Delilah must have him in a closet close by, Kristin thought.

Her stomach twisted, and she saw that Cole had gone white. She sensed that Zeke was smiling. Now Cole was forced to think not only about her but about his son.

"That's a real fine boy you got there, Slater," Zeke drawled. He moved the barrel of the gun against Kristin's cheek. "A real fine wife, a real fine boy. You want to see them live, you'll set that gun down, slow and easy. No fast moves."

"No fast moves," Cole echoed tonelessly.

Gabe was still crying. Kristin bit into her lip. As soon as Cole set the gun down, Zeke would shoot him, and there was so much she had to tell him. Gabe was walking now, could say so many words. She had taught him to say papa. He had the most wonderful laugh in the whole world, and his eyes were so very much like his father's....

"Cole, no!" she cried out.

He smiled at her. "I have to do this, Kristin."

Zeke laughed. "Yeah, he has to."

Cole was looking at her. A curious smile touched his lips. "I never got a chance to tell you that I loved you, Kristin. I do, you know. With all my heart."

"Oh, God, Cole!"

"I love you. I love you. Duck, Kristin."

"What?" she gasped,

He didn't drop his Colt. He aimed it right over her head. She screamed, and the world exploded.

Chapter Fifteen

Kristin fell, and it was as if the earth had opened up beneath her feet. All she knew was that Cole had fired.

And that Zeke had not.

Zeke's body was tumbling down the stairs after hers. Kristin came to a halt at the landing, and something fell hard on top of her. She stared up at Zeke, at his wide, staring eyes, at his forehead, where flesh and bone had been ripped away. She pushed away from him, desperate to get him away from her.

"Kristin, Kristin!"

Strong arms were around her, pulling her up from beneath him. She couldn't tear her eyes away from him. His face was still frozen in a sneer, even in death.

"Kristin!"

Cole turned her into his arms. "Kristin!" She looked up and saw his face, his eyes. Concern furrowed his brow as he eased his knuckles over her cheek. "Are you hurt?" he asked anxiously.

She shook her head. She couldn't speak. She stared at him blankly, and then she shrieked out his name and threw herself against him and started to cry. He stroked her hair and murmured comfortingly to her. Then he held her away from him and studied her anxiously. She struggled desperately for control.

"Oh, Cole! How did you know to come? They slaughtered all the Yankees.... Oh, no, a few of them might still be alive. You have to help them. Him. One of them saved me." Tears flooded her eyes.

No matter how hard she tried, she couldn't keep from crying. "Cole! He killed Matthew! He found my brother and he killed him."

"Hush, Kristin, hush," Cole murmured. He pulled her against his body again and smoothed back her hair. Then he tilted her chin and sought her eyes. He had to make sure she understood. "Kristin, Matthew is fine. Well, I'm sorry, I suppose he's not fine. He's injured, but he's alive, Kristin. I would never have known——" He was suddenly unable to speak. It was all over, and now he was suddenly paralyzed by the fear. His hands trembled as he held her. "Kristin, Matthew's company was attacked. Zeke left him for dead, but he wasn't dead, and he got away in the night. Thank God, the Yanks knew where I had my men all along, and Matthew knew the area so well that he came straight to me."

Her eyes were wide with hope, with a joy she dared not feel. "Oh, Cole! Please, don't tell me that unless——"

"It's the truth, Kristin, I swear it."

"But they didn't come after you? The Yankees, they let you be?"

"I have a few friends in the right places," Cole said with a wry smile. "It gives me hope. Maybe, when this thing is over, some of the hatreds will be patched up. Some of them won't be. But, oh, God, I want it to end. I want it to be over!"

He pulled her against him again and she felt the beating of his heart. The rough wool of his frock coat tickled her cheek, and she had never been so glad of anything in her life. She wanted to look at him again. She wanted to study his features, and she wanted to see him smile, because he was young again when he smiled. She wanted to see the silver light in his eyes when he held her, and most of all she wanted to hear him speak again. She wanted to hear him say he loved her.

Of course, this wasn't really the right time. There was a dead man at her feet, and though the guns had gone silent outside the house, dead men littered the earth there, too, and—please God—a few living men, too. She had to go back to the barn for the young Yankee who had saved her life, and she had to find her son.

"Kristin——" Cole began, but he was interrupted by an outraged cry.

"Miz Kristin! Mister Cole! Why, thank the Lord," Delilah called. She was at the top of the stairs with Gabe, who was struggling fiercely to free himself from her grasp. Cole stared at his son with the awe of a parent who has not seen his child in a long, long time. Gabe might have been a grown man the way Cole was staring at him.

Kristin's eyes twinkled. "He walks now. And he talks. I taught him how to say papa."

Delilah hurried down the stairs. She saw Zeke's body, but she didn't pause. She spat on it and stepped over it, and then she set Gabriel down. He tottered for a moment. Kristin watched Cole as he went down on his knees and reached out for the boy. Gabe waddled carefully over to inspect the stranger.

"Say papa!" Kristin urged him.

Gabriel wasn't interested in saying anything. He turned away from the stranger who was his father and buried his face in his mother's skirts. He reached out his arms, and Kristin laughed and picked him up. Then, suddenly, she crushed him against her, so hard that he cried out in protest. "Oh, Gabriel!" she murmured, holding him tight.

Cole came to his feet and rescued his screaming son. He lifted Gabriel very high and silver eyes gazed into silver eyes. "I'm your papa, little man!" He laughed. "And you'd best get used to the idea."

Gabriel couldn't possibly have understood what Cole had said to him, of course, but he smiled anyway, as if he had decided to accept the stranger in gold and gray. Cole lowered him at last and set him on his hip, smiling at Kristin.

Suddenly there was an awful commotion at the door.

"Put me down, you piece of trash!" Shannon shrieked.

Malachi—Shannon thrown over his shoulder—came through the doorway, his face dark and thunderous. "I don't mind bushwhackers, and I don't mind the damn Yankees, but Cole, I will be damned if I'll be responsible for this brat!"

"Put me down!" Shannon screamed.

He did. He dumped her in front of Cole, and she was thrashing and flailing, trying to get her balance. She rolled over and came face-to-face with Zeke Moreau's body.

"Oh!" she gasped, and fell silent at last.

Kristin looked at Malachi and arched a brow.

He sighed with great patience. "Kristin, I didn't know what the hell was happening in here. I didn't want her barging in to get shot, or to cause you or Cole to get shot. Mainly. It would be her own damn fault if she did get shot, but since she is your sister, I thought I'd try to save her sweet, darling, precious little life!"

For once Shannon didn't reply. She was still staring at Zeke's face. She began to tremble uncontrollably, and then she burst into tears.

Kristin started toward her sister, but Cole pulled her back. Malachi was kneeling beside Shannon, and he pulled her up and away from the body.

"It's over! It's all over!" he told her roughly. "Don't go falling apart now."

Shannon stiffened momentarily, and then she hiccuped. Malachi gave her his handkerchief, and she dried her face, nodding an acknowledgement. Then she jammed it back into his hand.

"I never fell apart, you backwoods bastard!"

"Well, good. Get your derriere out there and start helping!"

"Helping?"

"There are injured men out there. Unless you're too damned prissy to help the men who were willing to die to save your miserable life."

"Miserable?"

"Go!"

"I am going, Malachi Slater! I'm going because those are fine men out there—even the rebels! I'm going for them, and I'm going because I choose to go, and I'll never, never do anything because you tell me to, do you understand?"

With an elegant toss of her golden curls, she swept past him. It was a splendid exit except for one thing. Malachi smacked her rump soundly as she went past. She yelped in outrage and slapped him hard across the face. He caught her by the elbow and turned her toward him, his face dark with rage.

"Malachi! Please! She is my sister," Kristin reminded him sweetly.

Slowly, his eyes narrowed, he released Shannon. "Why, thank you, kind sir!" she said. Then she kicked him hard in the shin and raced out the door.

Kristin began to smirk, and then Cole laughed, and the baby giggled. Delilah laughed along with them, but then her laughter faded, and she gasped, "Samson! My man! Oh, Mister Slater—"

"The barn," Kristin said quickly, her eyes on Cole. "He was breathing—"

Cole ran out the door, Delilah hard on his heels. Kristin followed but when she stepped out on the porch she stood there stunned, her son in her arms, staring at the scene of destruction.

There were bodies everywhere. Men in gray were collecting them, dragging them away. A weary-looking young man nodded to her in grim acknowledgment as he passed her. She swallowed and caught his arm. "Thank you. Thank you for coming here."

He smiled and tipped his hat. "I'd go anywhere Colonel Slater invited me, ma'am. I'm right glad we got here in time."

He had work to do, and he went back to it. Dazed, Kristin stepped down into the yard.

Then someone called out, asking for water. She hurried over to the trough and found one of Cole's boys behind it, clutching his shoulder and trying to stand.

"Here, here!" she whispered, ladling up some water. Gabe gurgled. He seemed to think they were playing.

"Thank you, ma'am," the soldier said. Then he winced, and she saw that he had a ball lodged in his flesh.

"Help me over here!" she called. Another soldier lifted the wounded man, and within minutes she had him in the house and on the couch and she had Cole's men scurrying around, boiling water, ripping up sheets for bandages, setting up the parlor as a temporary infirmary.

Gabriel refused to sleep, so she set up a little playpen in the parlor and busied herself with the injured. Shannon was at her side and Delilah, too, now that she knew that Samson was all right. He had been knocked cold, and he had a blinding headache, but otherwise he was none the worse for wear.

Samson was out on burial detail now. Zeke Moreau's body had been removed from the house.

There had been a scene when that had happened. Shannon had followed them out. She had stood on the porch and begged the men, "Please...please! Don't bury that man's body anywhere on this property!"

"Miss McCahy—"

"Please! Let the vultures eat him, let the wolves finish him, but I beg you, don't bury him near here!"

And so some of the men had set out with a wagon, and they were taking Zeke and the bodies of the other bushwhackers far, far away. Pete was dead, and he was family, and three of Cole's men had fallen, and there were the Yankees that the bushwhackers had killed. They were being laid to rest with infinite tenderness in the family plot, beside Kristin's mother and father.

By nightfall, most of the traces of the gun battle had been cleared away. Delilah managed to produce a hearty stew in abundance to feed everyone.

At ten they heard the sound of a wagon creaking along. Cole had just finished eating, and he was sipping a brandy on the porch. Gabriel was in bed, and Kristin was sitting at Cole's feet, listening to a sad tune being played on a harmonica somewhere nearby.

She felt Cole stiffen. Then she realized that he had sentries posted, for there was something like a Rebel yell in the darkness, and then the wagon came through.

"Cole?" Kristin murmured.

"It's a surprise," he said, squeezing her shoulder. She followed him down the steps and out to the yard. There was something lumpy in the back of the wagon, something cried out plaintively, "Kristin, Shannon?"

"Matthew!" She screamed her brother's name and flew to the wagon. She kissed him, and she held him so tightly that he muttered,

"Kristin, I survived being shot, you're going to kill me here in my home at last with kindness!"

"Oh, Matthew!"

Then Shannon was flying down the steps. The three McCahy's greeted one another, and the men looked on, and then the harmonica player started up again, with "Lorena" this time bringing tears to eyes that had nearly run dry in all the years of bloodshed.

Matthew was brought in and put to bed in his own room. Once he was tucked in, he caught his sister's hand, and Kristin smiled and kissed him on the forehead again and told him to rest.

"Kristin!" He pulled her back. "Kristin, there'll be a bunch of Yankees here soon. They'll find out that Major Emery and his men were slaughtered, and they'll know that Cole and his men came in for the cleanup, and they'll be damned glad. But there's still a war on. They'll have to take them prisoner, or else they'll have to fight, and a lot of men will die needlessly. They're true heroes—to both sides, probably—but that won't make any difference. Kristin, are you understanding me?"

No, she wasn't. Or perhaps she was and she wanted to deny it. She couldn't have her husband taken away from her so soon.

"Kristin, Cole is considered an outlaw. Worse than ever before."

"Why? What do you mean?"

"He'll have to explain that to you himself. But be prepared. They need to sneak away now, tonight."

She felt weak, as if she had been drowning and she had reached and reached for a rope and it had been viciously wrenched away.

"Thank you, Matthew," she told her brother.

She blew out the lamp and left him. She hesitated, leaning against the door.

When she came back downstairs, she quickly discovered that everything that Matthew had said was true. The Confederate surgeon who had so carefully tended to her brother was checking the men she had sutured and bandaged—and preparing them for travel. He smiled at her when he saw her.

"Your brother is going to be just fine. Keep the wound clean. Never use the same sponge twice when you're cleaning out a wound.

I'm becoming more and more convinced that rot travels that way. Seems we have been doing better with sanitation than the blue bellies.'' He paused, and she thought that he, too, looked weary. "He's a fine young man, your brother. You take care of him.''

"Thank you, Captain Turnbill,'' said Kristin. He was about to turn away, but she stopped him with a hand set lightly upon his arm. "Captain, are you sure these men are fit to travel?''

"The worst wounded are the Yankees we found in the bunkhouse and the barn, and they don't have to travel anywhere. My men have one broken arm, a broken leg, some shot in the shoulder and two concussions. They'll be all right.'' He paused, looking at her unhappily. "Mrs. Slater, they'll be a lot better off traveling now than they would be in a Yankee prison camp. I'm not a man to say that all Yanks are butchers, but there's not much good to be said about prison camps, whether they're Yankee camps or Confederate camps.''

The able-bodied men were walking past her, making ready to leave. Kristin couldn't see her husband anywhere.

Malachi came around behind her and squeezed her shoulders. He turned her around. "Hope Cole won't mind,'' he said, and he hugged her and gave her a kiss on the cheek. "Hell, I don't care if Cole does mind!'' he said, and he kissed her again. She didn't know there was a tear on her cheek until he wiped it away.

"Oh, Malachi…''

"It's all right. We won't be far away.''

"Not far away at all.''

It was Jamie who spoke. He was right behind Malachi, and he took her from his brother and kissed her cheek, too. "You take care of yourself, little sister, you hear? Take good care of that nephew of mine, too.''

She nodded, unable to speak for a few seconds.

"Cole—''

"Cole is right here,'' her husband said. Tears blurred her vision. He took her in his arms. "Hey!'' he whispered, his lips nuzzling her throat. "Stop that! You can't send my brothers away with tears in your eyes.''

"Your brothers..."

She whirled around in his arms. Cole looked over her head. Malachi tipped his hat and grinned, and Cole grinned back. The two of them went out, and the house slowly fell silent. "I'm not leaving tonight, Kristin."

"What?" she whispered.

There was a bit of a commotion outside. Shannon was saying goodbye nicely to Jamie, and not so nicely to Malachi. Cole grinned, and Kristin grinned back, her eyes searching his. Then the door slammed, and Shannon whispered. "Oh, excuse me!"

Neither of them turned around. They heard Shannon tiptoe into the parlor to stay with the Union injured.

He was beautiful, Kristin thought. He was the most beautiful man she had ever seen. He was leaner than he had been that first day she had seen him. Strands of gray were creeping into his hair and into his beard, but somehow they were beautiful, too. They went well with the silver light in his eyes, with the handsome, dignified planes of his face.

"Oh!" she whispered heatedly. "You have to leave! Matthew says they consider you an outlaw—"

"They won't know I'm here, Kristin. My men are gone. They've taken my horse. They've learned how to disappear with the night. And for now I'm staying with my wife."

"Oh!"

"If she'll have me."

"Oh!" She touched his cheek, tenderly moving her fingertips over the coarse beard there. "Oh, she will have you!" she breathed.

He caught her hand and kissed her fingertips. Silently he led her up the stairs and through the doorway to their bedroom. Then he leaned against the door, and she smiled as she watched him.

"I never thought I would be here with you now!" he whispered.

"But you are," she said.

"Yes, I am."

Kristin walked over to him. She lifted off his hat and tossed it on the floor, and she unbuckled his scabbard and his gun belt and cast his weapons aside. Studiously, she unbuttoned his frock coat and his uniform shirt, and when his shoulders and chest were bare she felt the sweet thrill of anticipation invade her. Her fingers grew awkward, and she found that she was trembling. She whispered his name, and she pressed her lips to his chest and to the pulse at the base of his throat. He caught her lips and kissed her hungrily, tasting and tasting her mouth, trembling with ever-greater ardor. She was breathless when he released her and turned her around to work at the tiny buttons of her dress. He was shaking as badly as she, but was more practiced, and more determined, and she was startled when the dress fell quickly away from her, and then her chemise, and then her petticoats. He lifted her up with her stockings and shoes still on and carried her quickly to the bed, pausing with a rueful laugh to check on Gabriel, who was sleeping sweetly in the little bed in the corner.

Then he tossed her on the bed and fell upon her, and she threaded her fingers joyously through his hair. He groaned and kissed her again, and then he kissed her breasts, staring at them, savoring them, easing his tongue over each nipple, then his teeth, then the fullness of his mouth.

"Oh, Cole!" Her head tossed from side to side, and lightning swept through her, embedding a sweet, swirling heat at the apex of her thighs, a dizzying need for him. He filled it, touching her with a light and tender stroke and then with a demanding one, watching her eyes, watching her body, feeling the thunder of the desire that grew and grew within him.

He kissed her belly, and he stroked her thighs, and he played his touch over the golden triangle at their juncture, and then he delved within it. He made an incredibly sensual act of taking off her shoes, peeling away her garters and hose. Then he rose boldly above her. He drew a steady pattern with the searing tip of his tongue from her throat down the valley between her breasts to her navel and into the very heart of her fire. And she cried out for him, and he came to her.

Then he hovered, just above her, and she opened her eyes wide, waiting, pleading, wondering why he denied her. A great sound of agony escaped him, and he buried his head against her breasts.

"I do love you, Kristin. I do love you."

"Oh, Cole!" she said, clinging to him. "Please..."

He pushed away from her, and stared at her. "Well?"

And then it dawned on her what he wanted, and she pressed hard against him, arching to meet his need. "Cole, I have loved you for ages! I love you so very much. I could never admit it, I was so afraid, I knew you didn't love me."

"I just didn't dare admit it," he said softly.

"Say it again!" she demanded.

"I love you. I love you, Kristin McCahy Slater, and I swear that I will do so until the end of time."

"Oh, Cole!" She buried her face against his chest. It was hot and sleek and damp with perspiration. And he chose that moment to plunge deep, deep within her, and even as he did he was whispering again, the sweet words over and over again.

He loved her.

Later that night—much later, for making love took on a sweet new dimension when the words were spoken, and they were tempted to explore that dimension again and again—Cole held her in his arms and told her everything. First he told her about the day the jay-hawkers had come, and how they had burned down his home and killed his wife. She heard the agony in his voice, but she didn't stop him, because it was important that he say everything, that he lay his soul bare for her, as she had hers. He needed to trust her in that way, and, Kristin thought, he needed the healing power of words. His heart needed the cleansing.

She listened, and she was not afraid of the past, merely saddened. Then she listened as he told her what had happened in Kansas, how his old friend Kurt Taylor had been there and how he had purposely alerted Cole to the fact that Henry Fitz was in town with his jay-hawkers.

"I killed him, Kristin. I knew what I was doing. I knew exactly what danger I was riding into, but I had to face him." His arms tightened around her. "If we were to have a future, I just had to do it. Can you understand that?"

She didn't really have to answer him. She planted little kisses over his chest, and he groaned, and his hands rode roughly over her hair, and then they were in one another's arms once again. They were still so desperate, so hungry, so determined to have all that they could of one another, to cherish, to hold, to keep always for their dreams.

It was near dawn before they dozed off. Kristin was startled when she awoke almost before she had slept. Day was breaking, bright and fresh as a rainbow. Pink light fell upon her.

She heard the sounds of hoofbeats below.

With a soft gasp, she rose and raced to the window.

Down by the well she saw a single Union officer. She glanced at Cole, and he seemed to be asleep. He seemed at peace, the lines of strain erased from his features at last.

Kristin struggled into her gown and left the room without stockings or shoes, closing the door behind her. She padded silently down the stairs and hurried out to the well.

She couldn't imagine how she looked to the man, her face pale, her blue eyes wide, her hair in complete and lovely disarray around her fine-boned, very worried face.

He smiled at her and looked her up and down. He suddenly envied Cole Slater very much.

"Good morning, ma'am. This the McCahy ranch?"

"It is. My brother, a Union officer, is inside, recovering from wounds."

And your husband, a Southern officer, is inside, too, I'd wager, he thought, but he was silent.

"This is sweet, clear water. Thank you."

"You're very welcome to it."

"Zeke Moreau came here and gunned down most of the men?"

Kristin swallowed and nodded.

"There's a detachment of medics coming for the injured later today."

"That's fine. We're doing our best."

"I'm sure you are."

"Would you like to come in?"

He shook his head. "No thanks. I'm not here officially." He spoke softly. "I came here to tell you that the war is over. Well, all but the shouting. I'm sure it will take a while for all the troops to surrender. Kirby-Smith is a tenacious soul. Proud man, fine fighter, but—''

''The...the war is over?'' Kristin breathed.

''Yes, ma'am, like I said, all but the shouting. Two mornings ago, on April twelfth, General Robert E. Lee surrendered the Army of Northern Virginia to General Ulysses S. Grant at a little place called Appomattox Courthouse. Word has it that President Lincoln is determined that this great nation must unite in peace and brotherhood as quickly as possible, and he seems determined that there be brotherhood between North and South again.''

She was shaking. She had to sit down. He saw her lips and her limbs tremble, and he came around to her and helped her over to the porch. He gave her a sip of water, and she nodded her thanks.

''The war...is really over?''

''Really over.'' He smiled. ''I hear tell that Colonel Slater and his men came in here yesterday. Yep, I hear tell they cut down Zeke Moreau and his bloody bushwhackers. That must have been a fine piece of work, yes, ma'am. I'd have liked to have been here. No doubt the Union commanders—and the law—will hear about it.'' He smiled at her again. '''Course, Slater's men are gone, I take it?''

Kristin nodded. ''Yes...they're gone.''

''You his wife?''

''I'm his wife.''

''Someone ought to tell him that the war is over. 'Course, they should warn him that he needs to take care. Some people still don't take kindly to a few of his exploits. Once with Quantrill, you know, and then there was Kansas...'' He shrugged. ''If you should happen to see him, Mrs. Slater, you might warn him to lie low for a while. Ride on to Texas, maybe. Fitz had a brother, and he's sure to make an outcry. But tell him that he has to remember—the war is over. It will all come right. You hear? Tell him Kurt Taylor said so.''

Kristin nodded.

''Thanks for the water. That's mighty good water.''

''You're welcome, sir. Mighty welcome.''

Kristin stood and waited. She waited until the Union officer in his blue uniform had disappeared on the dusty Missouri horizon.

Then she turned and screamed, ''Cole! Cole!''

She tore up the stairs. He was up. He had been watching her and the officer from the window. Kristin threw herself at him, sending him flying across the room.

''It's over, it's over! The war is over! Lee has surrendered! Oh, there are still troops that haven't surrendered yet, but they're saying it's over! Oh, Cole!'' She caught his face between her hands, and she kissed him. She kissed his throat and his shoulders, and she was so alive and vibrant that even though he had been worried and wary he had to laugh.

''Kristin, Kristin, it can't be that easy—''

''No, it isn't that easy,'' she said solemnly, and she told him what the man had said. ''His name was Kurt Taylor, and he said you should head for Texas.''

''I will,'' Cole said.

Kristin corrected him. ''We will.''

''We will?'' he asked her, arching a brow. ''I do seem to recall that there was once a woman who would not leave this ranch. She sold her honor to a disreputable rebel in order to stay right here on this property.''

Kristin smiled at him. She had never felt so deliciously alive and sensual and vibrant and aware of all the world around her. It was spring—and the war was over. Over.

''It isn't my ranch. I was just holding on to it for Matthew, and Matthew is here now. You see, it's time to move on, anyway. And I consider that my honor was sold for a fair price. It was rather useless, you see, while my son—he's just magnificent. And—''

''And?''

''Well, there is this other minor thing. I fell desperately in love with that disreputable rebel. Even when I wanted to hang him myself, I was very much in love.''

''Very much?''

''Incredibly, inestimably, most desperately in love.''

''Really?'' He laced his fingers through hers and bent his head and kissed her. She felt a shudder rake through him, and she sought his eyes.

"Cole?"

"We really have a future."

"Yes!"

"We can watch Gabriel grow, and we can have more children. And I can hold them when they are little tiny infants—"

"And you can change their little bottoms, too," Kristin informed him sweetly.

He smiled, and he kissed her again, and she let out a sweet, shuddering sigh. "Cole?"

"My love?"

She smiled, slowly, lazily, sensuously. "If you go to Texas, I will follow you wherever you may lead. But for the moment..."

"Yes?"

"We've never made love in peacetime before. Never," she told him with very wide eyes. "We've never made love in peacetime, whispering that we love one another!"

He threw back his head and laughed, and his eyes sizzled, silver and mercury, into hers, and she thought that he would always be her cavalier, the tall, dark stranger with the plumed hat who had stepped into her life like a hero, taking her from darkness into light. They weren't clear of the darkness yet. There would be pain. There would be time to mourn Pete, who had always been her friend, always at her side. There would be time to mourn Major Emery, who had been their friend, too, noble and caring, until the very end.

For now, though, they had one another.

Cole grinned wickedly. "Then," he said, "we must make love at peace, and whisper that we love one another. Kristin!"

"Yes?"

He came close against her lips, his mouth a breath away from hers.

"I love you!" he whispered fervently. "I love you, I love you, I love you!"

And though they were at peace they soared into the sweetest tempest, and through it all they never ceased to whisper the words.

The sun entered their room, and a new day had truly dawned.

Cole stroked his wife's beautiful hair, luxuriating in the sweet satisfaction she brought him. He stared at the ceiling, at the new light of day.

It would take the country a long time to heal, he knew. A long, long time. A long time to unite.

But she had brought healing to him, and his heart was united with hers now. "A new age," he murmured.

"What?"

"I said I love you!" Cole lied, and he turned to her again.

The war wouldn't end as easily as Kristin thought. Life was never as easy as that. But they did have a future.

And Texas could wait just a little while longer.

Author's Note

The war did not end easily, and especially not in the West, on the Kansas-Missouri border where it had really begun, long before shots rang out at Fort Sumter.

General Kirby-Smith was determined, and he held out with his troops until the twenty-sixth of May, holding the last Southern command to stand in the field.

William C. Quantrill died on June 6, 1865, fatally wounded by Union troops while conducting a raid on Louisville, Kentucky. On his deathbed he swore that if he had captured Jim Lane, leader of the jayhawkers before Doc Jennison, he would have burned him at the stake.

Jim Lane himself fired his last shot on July 1, 1865—with his revolver in his own mouth.

Frank and Jesse James and the Younger brothers—Quantrill's men—went on to find a separate infamy.

For Cole and Kristin, all those things were in the future. Cole was to have his own problems.

But those are really part of Malachi and Shannon's story, and must be told by them.

RIDES A HERO

Prologue

May 30th, 1865
Kentucky
The Road Home

"It's him, I tell you. It's Captain Slater! Captain Malachi Slater!" The young man seated on the wagon that blocked the road could hardly control his excitement. "We done got him, Bill," he cried.

Startled, Malachi pulled back on the reins of the bay mare that had taken him through numerous battles, and stared ahead. Two young Union sentries were guarding the road that eventually led to his own home. The sight of the sentries here in Kentucky didn't surprise him. The war was over. The Yankees had won. Yanks were everywhere now, and that was the way it was.

At least he no longer had to be wary. His fighting days were over. He was going home. His unit had surrendered, and he had put his own signature on the paper, swearing an oath of allegiance to the Yankee flag. He should have been bitter, but right now he was just tired. He had seen the death toll, and he was just damned glad that it was all over.

So he didn't need to fear hostility from the sentries. And hell, seeing them, he couldn't feel much fear. The Yanks, it seemed, had been dipping into the bottom of the barrel as the war ended, almost as much as the Confederates had. These boys were teenagers, green-gilled, and he was certain that neither of them had ever shaved.

Except there was something…something about the way they said his name.

"Captain Slater, you just hold on there," the first boy said nervously.

They shouldn't have known his name. His rank, of course, was apparent from the worn gold braid on the shoulders of his gray wool cavalry greatcoat. But his name...

"You're under arrest," the second boy—the one called Billy—began, and then his mouth started to work hard as if he couldn't seem to remember the right words to say.

"Under arrest?" Malachi roared out in his best voice of command. "What in hell for? The war is over, boys. Haven't they told you yet?"

"You're a murderin' outlaw, Captain Slater!" the first boy said. Malachi frowned and the boy quickly added, "Sir!"

"Outlaw, murderer? I know that you don't give the Rebels much credit, but our cavalry fought as soldiers, same as yours."

"Captain, the poster that's out on you has nothing to do with the cavalry!" Billy said. "And that's a fact. You're wanted for murder in Kansas—"

"I've never been in Kansas!"

"It says right on the poster that you and your brothers are part of the Slater gang, and that you rode into Kansas and murdered private citizens. Yes, sir, you are under arrest!"

Kansas?

Hell.

He'd not been in Kansas for years. But his brother Cole had been in Kansas, and he had waged a single-handed battle against the cutthroat who had murdered his first wife.

Malachi hadn't been anywhere near Kansas during that time, but that was only part of what was taking him aback. Cole was no murderer either. Someone must be out for them. The Slater gang indeed! That must mean that someone wanted his younger brother, Jamie, dead, too.

The Union boys were trying to ready their breech-loading rifles. They were both so nervous they couldn't seem to rip open their powder bags, not even with their teeth.

Malachi's cavalry saber was at his side and he had a Colt stuffed into the holster beneath his greatcoat. He had enough time to fill them both full of holes. "Listen to me, fellows. I am not going to let you put me under arrest," he said.

The boys looked green. They glanced his way, but they kept trying to get to their powder. When they did get to it, they spilled most of it trying to get it into the well of the gun. They glanced at him again with terror, but they still moved to their pouches for balls, and tried to ram them down according to proper military procedure.

"Confound it," Malachi said irritably. "Do your mothers know where you are?"

The boys looked up again. "Hank, you got him?"

"Hell, no, Billy, I ain't ready. I thought you were ready."

Malachi sighed deeply. "Boys, for the love of God, I don't want your deaths on my conscience—"

"There's a big, big bounty out on you, Captain Slater! A Mr. Hayden Fitz in Kansas is fierce and furious. Says if'n somebody don't shoot you and your brothers, he's going to see you all come to justice and hang by the neck until dead."

"Oh, hell!" Malachi swore savagely. "Damn it!" He dismounted, sweeping his hat from his head and slamming it against his thigh as he paced back and forth before the two. "It's over! The war is over! I fought off the Kansas jayhawkers before the war, and then I fought all those damn years in the war, and I am tired! I am so damned sick and tired of killing people. I can barely stand it! The bounty isn't worth it, boys! Don't you understand? I don't want to kill you."

They didn't understand. He stopped and looked at them, and they might be still green, but they'd gotten their muskets loaded. Billy started to aim his.

Malachi didn't wait any longer. With a savage oath escaping him, he charged the boy, pulling out his saber.

But he was sick and tired of killing. As he leaped atop the wagon where the boys sat, he could have skewered them through, both of them. But he didn't. For some damned reason, he wanted them to grow old enough to have the wisdom not to pull such a stunt again.

He sliced his saber against the boy's musket and sent it flying.

"Run, Bill, run!" Hank suggested wisely.

But Hank was holding tight to his own rifle. Malachi swore at him and leaped from the wagon and hurried for the bay mare. He leaped on the horse and just barely nudged her. Like a true warrior, she soared forward like the wind, straight for the wagon.

She carried him up and up and they were sailing. But just as they were over the top of the wagon, a burst of pain exploded in his thigh.

Hank had apparently managed to shoot his rifle. Amazingly enough, he had struck his target.

Malachi didn't dare stop. He kept the bay racing, veering into the woods. She was a good old horse, a fine companion, and she had been with him through many a battle. When pain and exhaustion claimed him and he slunk low against her, she kept going, as if she, too, knew the road home, the long, long road home.

Finally the bay stopped before a stream. For a long moment, Malachi clung to her, then he fell and rolled until he could reach the water. He drank deeply before falling back. His leg was burning; his whole body was burning. Surely it wasn't such a deep wound. He needed to keep moving. He had to get to Cole as quickly as possible.

But it wasn't going to be that night. Despite the strength of his will, his eyes closed.

It seemed to him that a fog swirled up from the stream. Pain no longer tormented him, nor hunger, nor exhaustion. The stream was inviting. He stood and shed his worn uniform. Balancing his way out on the rocks, he dived in. The water was cool and beautiful, the day warm with a radiant sun, and birds were singing. There was no smell of burned powder near him, no screams of the dead or dying; he was far, far from the anguish of the war.

He swam through the coolness, and when he surfaced, he saw her.

An angel.

She was standing on the shore, surrounded by the mist, her hair streaming gold and red, sweeping down and around her back. She was a goddess, Aphrodite emerging from the sparkling beauty of the stream. She was naked and lithe and beautiful, with sultry sky-blue eyes and ink-dark lashes, ivory cheeks, and lush, rose-colored lips.

She beckoned to him.

And he came.

Looking at her, he knew that he must have her. Naked, he tried to hurry, thrashing through the water. He had to touch her. To feel the fullness of her breast beneath his hands, caress her with his whisper and his kiss. But even in the strange seduction of the dream, he knew she was familiar. She was his Circe, calling him with magical promises of unimaginable pleasure, but he also knew her.

Nearer, he drew nearer to her, nearer and nearer...

He started to cough. His eyes flew open.

The only Circe that awaited him was the faithful bay mare, snorting now upon his soaking cheek. Malachi staggered to his feet and looked from his sodden clothing to the stream. He had fallen in, he realized, and nearly drowned.

He had been saved by a dream. The dream of a lush and beautiful woman with golden hair that streamed down her back, and eyes to match a summer's day.

He touched his cheek. At least the stream had cut his fever. He could ride again.

He should find attention for his leg, he thought. But he couldn't spare the time. He had to reach Missouri. He had to warn Cole.

"Come on, Helena," he told the mare, securing the reins and leaping upon her back. "We need to head on west. Home. Only we haven't got a home anymore. Can you believe that? All these damned years, and we still aren't at peace yet. And I get shot by a kid who still has to have his mother tell him to scrub behind the ears. And I dream about beautiful blond temptresses." He shook his head, and Helena whinnied, as if she doubted the sanity of her rider.

Maybe he wasn't sane anymore.

He grinned as he kept riding through the night. It had been a funny dream. Curious how his Circe had seemed so familiar. His sister-in-law, Kristin, was a beautiful blond, but it hadn't been Kristin...

Malachi was so startled that he drew in sharply on his reins and the bay spun around.

"Sorry, old girl, sorry!" Malachi told the horse. Then he went thoughtfully silent, and finally laughed out loud.

It hadn't been his sister-in-law in the dream, but it had been Shannon, Kristin's little sister. Kristin's obnoxious little sister! Willful, spoiled, determined, proud...obnoxious! He'd itched to take a switch to her from the moment they had first met.

But it had been Shannon in the dream. Shannon's eyes had beckoned him, sultry and sweet. Shannon's hair had streamed in a burst of sun and fire around the slender beauty of her form. Shannon's lips had formed to issue whispers of passion.

And he had thought when the dream ended that he had lost his temptress! he told himself dryly.

Well, he had not. He was riding toward the spitfire now, and he could almost guarantee that their meeting would not be sweet, nor would she beckon to him, or welcome him.

If he knew Shannon, she wouldn't be waiting with open arms.

She'd be waiting with a loaded Colt.

"Doesn't matter much, Helena," he told his horse. "Damn it!" he swore out loud to the heavens. "When will this war be over for me?"

There was no answer. He kept riding through the night.

Chapter One

June 3rd, 1865
The Border Country, Missouri
The McCahy Ranch

Someone was out there.

Someone who shouldn't have been out there.

Shannon McCahy knew it; she could feel it in her bones.

Even though the sunset was so deceptively peaceful!

It was peaceful, beautiful, quiet. Radiant colors soared across the sky, and sweetly kissed the earth. There was a silence and a stillness all around. A soft breeze just barely stirred, damp and sweet against the skin. The war was over, or so they said.

The night whispered tenderly of peace.

Peace...

She longed for peace. Just ten minutes ago she had come outside to watch the night, to try to feel the peace. Standing on the wide veranda, leaning idly against a pillar, Shannon had looked out over the landscape and had reflected on the beauty of the night.

The barn and stables stood silhouetted against the pink-streaked sky. A mare and her foal grazed idly in the paddock. The hills rolled away in the distance and it seemed that all the earth was alive with the verdance and richness of the spring.

Even Shannon had seemed a part of the ethereal beauty of the night. Elegant and lovely, her thick hair twisted into a knot at her nape, little tendrils escaping in wisps about her face. Tall and slim, and yet with curved and feminine proportions, she wore a luxurious velvet evening gown with a delicate ivory lace collar that fell over the artfully low-cut bodice.

She was dressed for dinner, though it seemed so very peculiar that they still dressed every evening. As if their pa was still with them, as if the world remained the same. They dressed for dinner, and they sipped wine with their meat—when they had wine, and when they had meat—and when their meal was over, they retired to the music parlor, and Kristin played and Shannon would sing. They clung so fiercely to the little pleasures of life!

There hadn't been much pleasure in years. Shannon McCahy had grown up in the shadow of war. Long before the shots fired at Fort Sumter signaled the start of the Civil War in April 1861, Missouri and Kansas had begun their battling. Jayhawkers had swooped in from Kansas to harass and murder slave owners and Southern sympathizers, and in retaliation, the South had thrown back the bushwhackers, undisciplined troops who had plundered and killed in Kansas. Shannon McCahy had been only a child when John Brown had first come to Missouri, but she remembered him clearly. He had been a religious man, but also a fanatic, ready to murder for his religion. She had still been a child when he had been hanged for his infamous raid on the arsenal at Harper's Ferry.

So she really couldn't remember a time of real peace.

But at least the thunder now no longer tore at the earth. Rifles and pistols no longer flared, nor did swords clash in fury. The passion of the fight was over. It had died in glorious agony and anguish, and now every mother, sister, lover and wife across the nation waited...

But Shannon McCahy hadn't come outside to await a lover, for she had the questionable luxury of knowing that her fiancé lay dead. She even knew where he was buried. She had watched the earth fall, clump by clump, upon his coffin, and each soft thud had taken a bit more of her heart.

The war had robbed her blind. Her father had been brutally murdered in front of her by bushwhackers, a splinter group of Quantrill's infamous Raiders. And in the summer of 1862 Zeke Moreau and his bushwhackers had returned to the McCahy ranch to take her sister, Kristin. But that had also been the day that Cole Slater had walked into their lives, his guns blazing. He had saved them from being murdered and eventually married Kristin. After that his name kept them safe from the bushwhackers, but the war had still gone on. And ironically, she and Kristin had then been arrested by the Yankees for giving aid and succor to Cole, just because once upon a time Cole had briefly ridden with Quantrill.

But Shannon had fallen in love with the Yankee officer who had pulled her from the wreckage of their prison when the faulty old building had literally fallen to pieces. For a brief time, she had believed in happiness.

Until Robert Ellsworth had been slain by the bushwhackers.

In the end, Zeke Moreau and his bushwhackers had come back to the ranch one last time. Cole had ridden in with his brothers and their Confederate cavalry company, and Shannon's brother, Matthew, had brought his Union compatriots. For one sweet moment, there had been no North, and no South, just a fierce and valiant stand against injustice.

But the war was over now.

No...never. Never in her heart, she thought. Then she stiffened, suddenly alert and wary.

There was a movement out by the stables. She blinked and stared again, and felt a quickening in her stomach, a streak of cold along her spine.

Now she was sure.

Someone was out there.

Someone who shouldn't have been out there.

Someone furtive, stealthy, sneaking around the stables.

"Cole? Kristin?" she whispered. She cleared her throat and called their names again a little louder.

Where were her brother-in-law and sister? They should have been in the house, but no one was answering her. She bit into her lower lip, wondering what she should do. There was a pair of Colt six-shooters over the cabinet just inside the hallway; Cole had set them up the very night they heard the war was over.

After that last fight, Malachi and Jamie Slater had ridden back to the war, not knowing that it was already over. Matthew McCahy had known it was over before he left, for he had stayed until his injury had healed, but then he had left also, to return to his Union Army unit. The war might be over, but he knew that peace was yet to be assured. The aftermath of the war would follow them.

And Cole Slater knew that he would eventually have to flee Missouri. He *had* ridden with Quantrill, although only briefly, and certain Yanks with power might consider him ripe for hanging. But Cole intended to wait for Matthew to return home before leaving the ranch. It wouldn't be safe to leave Kristin and Shannon alone. He had friends who would warn him if danger threatened.

Meanwhile, Cole had hung the Colts and had given Shannon some stern advice. "Most of the men coming home will be good ones," he had told her, hammering nails into the wall. "Yep, lots of good men, both blue and gray. Those who have fought with heart and soul for their ideals. And all that those men want to do now is come home. They want to pick up their plows again, open their shops again, start up their businesses once more. They want to hold their wives, and kiss their children, and lick their wounds and try to find a future. They'll come through here. They'll want water, and they'll want meals. And we'll help them when we can, both Union and Confederate."

"So what are the guns for?" Shannon asked, not even wanting to think of helping Confederates, men like the bushwhackers who had killed Robert.

"Because there are men whom the war has maimed, Shannon. Not in body but in mind. Dangerous men. Deserters and vultures. And I can assure you that as many of that type fought for the Union as for the Confederacy. Mind your step, Shannon. You know how to use these guns. Use them well. If anyone threatens you at all, be ready to defend yourself."

"Yes. I will. I can shoot."

"The bad guys, Shannon. Not just some poor farmer in a gray uniform."

"Cole, I have fed and cared for the Rebels passing this way."

"Yes, you have. But not with a great deal of pleasure."

"You make me sound cruel and unreasonable—"

She saw a strange light of pity in his eyes as he answered. "I don't think that, Shannon. The war has done things to all of us."

But he shook his head as he walked away, and she could tell that he really did think she was heartless. He knew that she could never forgive what had happened, even now that the South had been broken. She would never, never forget Robert Ellsworth, his gentle love, his simple honor. Nor could she ever forget his death. She had seen him buried. He had never been laid out in a proper wake, for there had not been enough of him left for the undertaker to prepare. The brutality had made her hard, and very cold.

Cole was wrong, though, if he thought she could no longer feel. She could still feel way too much, it seemed at times. But it was so much easier to be cold, and it was easier to hate. Cole was wrong if he thought she would kill just any Rebel soldier, but she could very easily gun down the men who had so callously gone out and brutally slaughtered Robert and his men. She thought she could have faced it if Robert had died in battle, but what the bushwhackers had done to him had been worse than murder.

Cole was disappearing around the corner, and she longed to call out to him. She did love him, even if he was a Rebel. He had saved Kristin and Shannon from certain rape and probable death, and he was as dear to her as her blood brother, Matthew. But she didn't call out. It wasn't something she could explain.

Cole's first wife had been killed by Kansas jayhawkers, yet now he seemed to have come to terms with life. Maybe Kristin had taught him forgiveness. But Shannon didn't know how to forgive, and it wasn't something she thought she could learn. She just knew that she still lived with the anguish of the past, and she could not put it behind her.

For Cole's sake, though, she would bite her lip and hand out water to the Rebs heading home. This was Missouri; most of the state was Confederate. She might have been a Rebel herself, since the ranch stood on the border between Kansas and Missouri, and the McCahys actually had leaned toward the South at first. But then Pa had been murdered. Matthew had joined up with the Union Army, and everything that followed after that had conspired to make Shannon an avowed Yankee, through and through.

But that didn't matter now.

Over the past days they had been handing out water and meals to boys in blue and to boys in gray. She reminded herself that Matthew was still out there somewhere. Maybe some Reb girl was giving him a cup of water or a piece of bread.

Shannon had handed out water and hot soup without a word. She had bandaged up Rebs, just as she had done on the day when the two cavalry units—Matthew's Federals and the Slaters' Confederates—had joined forces and beaten Zeke Moreau's marauders. For Matthew's sake, she cared for the weary soldiers who passed the house. Somewhere out there, he would be wandering the countryside. And Cole's brothers, too. Perhaps some young woman was being kind to them.

Shannon hoped that someone would deal gently with Jamie.

But if Malachi passed by some strange farmhouse, well, then, she hoped they gave him salt water!

Both Cole's brothers were Rebels. Jamie she could tolerate.

Malachi, she could not.

From the time they had first met, he had treated her like a bothersome child. She didn't know quite what it was that lurked between them, she only knew that it was heated and total and combustible. Every time they met, sparks flew and fury exploded.

She tried. She tried very hard not to let him creep beneath her skin. She was a lady. She had great pride, and tremendous dignity. But Malachi had the ability to strip her quickly of both. She would be pleased with her composure and the calmness of her temper, but then he would say just one word and she would lose all poise and restraint and long to douse him with a pail of water. And when she lost her temper at his needling, he would taunt her all over again, pleased that he had proven her to be a child, and a brat at that.

Not so much now, she assured herself. And it was true. She had grown colder since Robert Ellsworth had died. No one could draw much of a reaction from her anymore.

She thought Jamie might return soon. But Malachi wouldn't.

Malachi had probably thought to join up with General Edmund Kirby-Smith and fight to the bitter finish. But even Kirby-Smith had surrendered now. Maybe Malachi would head for Mexico, or for Central or South America. Good riddance to him. It was difficult to forget the last time they had met. It had been on the day when all hell had broken loose, when Moreau's band had been broken. Even then, in the midst of chaos, Malachi had managed to annoy her. In the thick of it all, he had ordered her around and they had very nearly come to blows. Well, she *had* slapped him, but Kristin and Cole had been there, and Malachi had been forced to calm his temper. Shannon hoped the Federals had picked him up and placed him in a prison camp. It would be good for him to cool his heels for a while. He was going to have to accept the truth.

The Confederacy was bested and broken, and the Glorious Cause was lost.

It was over.

But not yet ended. Some drifter was crawling around in the stables.

Shannon didn't stop to think a moment longer. She stepped back through the doorway to the entry hall and plucked one of the Colts from its crossed position. She reached into the top drawer of the secretary beneath it for the shells and quickly loaded the gun.

"Kristin! Cole! Samson, Delilah, someone!" she called out.

But the house was silent. Where were they all? She didn't know. She was on her own.

Shannon slipped back onto the porch.

The colors of the night were growing darker, deeper and richer. The sky seemed to have turned a deep purple; the land itself seemed to be blue. The outline of the stables stood black against the horizon, and the two loft windows looked like dusky, evil orbs, staring at her menacingly.

Her heart was beating hard, she realized. The coldness remained near her spine.

She should not be afraid. She had been under attack in one form or another several times now. She should have learned courage.

She was still frightened.

But not frightened enough that she would sit like a wounded lamb and wait to be assaulted, she assured herself. No, she would turn the tables. No honest man skulked and loitered in stables. No sincere fellow, Reb or Yank, hid, waiting for the coming of darkness.

She raced from the porch to the paddock, then paused, breathing fast. She listened intently, and heard nothing, but still, she knew.

Someone was there. She could feel it in the air now. She could sense the danger.

She leaned against the paddock fence. She was good with a Colt. Damned, deadly good. Cole claimed that she could hit the eye of a fly from a distance of a hundred feet, and that wasn't far from the truth. As long as she held the weapon, she would be safe.

Don't ever tarry, Cole had warned her once. Make your decisions quickly. And if you decided to shoot, shoot to kill.

It shouldn't be too hard, she thought. She had lived through so many years of hell; she had grown up under the fire. In the world she knew, it was kill or be killed, hurt or tortured. She could manage any situation. She always had.

Shannon drew in a deep breath and pushed away from the paddock fence. Where was Cole? He had been born with a sixth sense. He should have known that there was trouble by now, yet he wasn't here. She couldn't depend on Cole. She had to depend on herself.

Shannon raced for the door to the stables. It stood as dark as the windows in the coming night, gaping open like a dark pit.

And she could feel the evil lurking and waiting inside.

She gritted her teeth and carefully flattened herself against the paneling by the stable door, then swiftly, flush against it, she stole inside.

The darkness was complete. For several long moments she stood where she was, her heart thundering, her fingers like steel around the Colt, her breath coming too fast and seeming to rasp more loudly than a twister. He would hear her, she thought. He would hear her, and find her.

She forced herself to be calm; she was not as loud as she thought. But she had to adapt to the darkness, or she would accomplish nothing.

One horse whinnied and a second one snorted. She tried to envision the place with light. The stalls were large and well constructed; there were fifteen of them across from her, but only nine of the horses would be in their stalls, for the men were still out on the range after the cattle. The tack room was to her immediate right, and to her left was a pile of fresh hay and the grain bags. There was more hay up in the loft above her head.

She caught her breath suddenly, barely daring to breathe.

That's where he was—in the loft.

She wasn't in a very good position if the intruder lurked right over her head.

She cocked her Colt and sank low to the floor, then began inching toward the bales of hay. They could provide her with some cover, and make her position a mystery in this stygian darkness, too.

But even as she moved, she heard the soft, careful shuffling above her. A board creaked, and then the building was still again.

Shannon waited.

There was no further movement. Time seemed to tick on endlessly.

All of a sudden she realized what she had to do. Move the ladder.

She ran for it with an impetuous burst of speed, determined to capture the intruder atop the loft.

"Hold!" a voice commanded.

She ignored it and continued racing for the ladder, then wrenched it away from the opening. It rattled to the ground, leaving no means of escape from the loft above.

A shot rang out. It whizzed high over her head and was imbedded into the wall far behind her. Was it a warning shot? Or did the man in the loft have extremely bad aim?

She shot back, aiming for the voice. She heard a low rasp of swearing, and knew then where her target was.

If you shoot, she had been warned, shoot to kill.

She had seen blood and death in wanton numbers...

And still she hesitated. The man was trapped in the loft. What could he do?

Even as she asked the question of herself in silence, the answer came to her, and in a most unexpected manner.

He leaped from the loft like a phantom in the night and landed softly in the hay.

Shannon screamed, whirling around and lifting her Colt, aiming toward the bales of hay. She could not see him. He had landed hard, but he had rolled in a flash, and now he hid behind the many bales.

She took aim and fired at the first bale. The shot exploded, loud and crystal clear, in the night.

Why had nobody come from the house? Surely they had heard the shots. But perhaps the noise was muffled by the barn walls and the hay.

And neither could she seem to hear anything from the house or from beyond the stables. She was pitched into a desperate world where she was on her own.

No noise had come from the intruder. No thud, no cry, no gasp of fear or anger or dismay. There was nothing at all.

Had she killed the man?

Shannon stepped forward, moving as silently as she could upon the earthen floor. She moved slowly, pausing with each step. She must have killed him. She heard nothing, nothing at all.

She took another step toward the hay, peering around the side of the tied bale. There was nothing there. She thought she heard something from the stalls. She swung around and realized that it was only the horses moving restlessly.

Then she sensed a movement in the corner. But that was impossible. No one could have gotten by her, not even in the darkness...

It was a mouse in the corner. A mouse, and nothing more. She had shot and probably killed the intruder, and he lay there, somewhere in the hay.

Shannon moistened her lips and tried to still the fear that swept along her spine. She still sensed danger. He wasn't dead. He was hiding, lurking in the darkness. She wanted to shriek and scream and turn and flee in terror. She didn't dare. She had to find him before he found her.

She turned once again and hurried to the next stack of hay, piled higher than the first. She looked to the rear and each side of it...and then a rustle came from just above her head.

She inhaled and jerked back, looking up, trying to aim her Colt. It was too late.

He leaped upon her.

They fell to the ground together. Shannon's Colt went flying through the darkness. He fell hard upon her and she was assailed with the scent of leather and fine pipe tobacco. His hard-muscled arms held her and a wire taut body covered her. A scream bubbled and rose within her.

His hand clapped hard over her mouth.

"Stop," he hissed.

She interrupted him with a savage kick.

He swore in the night, but his hold went slack.

She shoved against him with all her might, and found her escape. She leaped to her feet and dashed toward the door, inhaling for a loud, desperate scream.

"No!" The voice thundered behind her. He caught her by an elbow, wrenching her around. Her scream died in her throat as they crashed to the ground again. This time, he held her with force. He thrust his frock coat back and straddled her prone and dazed form. Shannon lashed out madly with her fists, thudding them furiously against his chest.

"Stop it, Shannon!"

His use of her name did not register in the raw panic that had seized her. She had not come this far to be raped and murdered in her own stables. She gasped for breath to scream again and raked out with her nails, seeking his eyes.

"Stop it!" He caught her wrists and pulled them high above her head. She started to scream, and he secured her with one hand, clamping the other hard over her mouth. She bit him. He swore in a white rage, but did nothing more than grip her jaw so hard between his thumb and forefinger that she could scream no more for the pain that it caused her.

"For the love of God, will you stop it, brat!"

She froze. She wondered how it was that she had not recognized his voice until he used that particular term.

Malachi!

Malachi Slater had come home.

Chapter Two

She stopped struggling and looked up at him. The moon must have come out, for some light was now filtering into the stable. He leaned very close against her, and she began to make out his features.

They were handsome features. She would grant Malachi that much. He was a striking man. His forehead was high and broad, his eyes were large, cobalt blue, sometimes nearly as black as the darkness that now surrounded them. His mouth was full and well defined, his jaw square beneath the gold and red sweep of his mustache and beard, and his nose and cheekbones chiseled in strong, masculine lines. He was a tall man, made lean by the war, and made hard by it, too.

With his face so close to hers, she realized that his beard was not so neatly clipped as it had always been before. There were shadows beneath his eyes. The rough wool of his Confederate uniform was tattered and torn in many places, and the gold braid, the insignia of his rank in the cavalry, was nearly worn away.

She should have known him much sooner. They had tangled often enough. She knew the strength of his arms and the deep tenor of his voice, and the bullheaded determination of his anger. She should have known him.

But he was different tonight. He was still Malachi, but more fierce than ever. Tonight, he seemed brutal. Tension lived and breathed and seethed all around him.

"You gonna be quiet now, brat?" he asked her harshly.

Shannon gritted her teeth. She could not begin to answer him. The gall of the bastard! He had known that it was her. He must have known that it was her from the moment she had entered the stables, and he had knocked her down and dragged her around—twice!—and had no apology for it.

She squirmed hard against him, fighting his hold. His hand pressed more tightly upon her, his breath warmed her cheeks, and she felt a new wave of his ruthless determination.

"Well?" he repeated. His teeth flashed white in the darkness as he smiled with a bitter amusement. "Shannon, are you going to be quiet now?"

He lifted his hand from her mouth. Her lips felt bruised and swollen from his casual disregard.

"Quiet!" she said, and her tone was soft at first, deceptively soft. She knew she should use some restraint. At the best of times, he had little patience with her.

Well, she had no patience with him. Her temper ignited like a fuse. "Quiet?" Her voice rose, and then it exploded. "Quiet? You scurvy, flea-ridden son of a jackass! What the hell do you think you're doing? Get off me!"

His lips tightened grimly and his thighs constricted around her hips.

"Miss McCahy, I'll be happy to do so. Just as soon as you shut that lovely little mouth of yours."

"Get off!" she whispered furiously.

"Shh!"

He was too close to her. His eyes were like pits of blue fire boring into hers, and she was acutely aware of him as a man. He leaned so close that his beard brushed her face. His thighs were hot and tight around her, and his arms, stretched taut across her as he maintained a wary grip upon her wrists, were as warm and threatening as molten steel.

"Malachi—"

"Shannon, I am waiting."

She closed her eyes and ground her teeth. She waited, feeling her heart pound, feeling the seconds pass. Then she smiled with savage sarcasm, but remained silent.

Slowly, he eased his hold. He released her wrists and sat up. He still straddled her hips, but he was no longer pinning her with his touch. Shannon tried counting to keep her smile in place. She longed to explode and shove him far, far away from her.

And still he kneeled there. He crossed his arms over his chest, and watched her through narrowed eyes.

She waited. She could stand it no longer.

"I have been quiet! Now get the hell off me!"

In a flash, his hand landed on her mouth, and he was near her again, so near that this time the warm whisper of his breath touched her cheek, and sent hot, rippling sensations seeping throughout the very length of her. He was tense, so tense that she wondered if she really knew the man at all, and she was suddenly afraid.

"I have been fighting blue bellies a long, long time, and you are the worst of them. Now, I am not going to wind up in prison or swinging from a rope at the end of this because of you. I do swear it. Shut up, Shannon—"

"Don't you threaten me!"

"Threaten! I'll act, and you know it!"

She didn't realize until it pulled and hurt that he had a grip upon her hair. She clenched her teeth, swallowed and tried to nod. Even for Malachi, this was strange behavior.

It was the war, she decided; he had finally gone insane.

"I'll be quiet!" she mouthed.

"Do so, Shannon, I'm warning you."

She nodded again.

He seemed to realize that he was hurting her. He stared at his hand where he gripped her hair, and he dropped it as if it were a golden fire that truly burned. He sat back again, then watched her.

"No sudden movement, no screams."

"No sudden movement," she repeated in a solemn promise. "No screams."

Seeming satisfied at last, he rose, finding his plumed cavalry hat on the floor nearby and dusting it off upon his thigh. He swept it low before her, and Shannon curiously caught her breath.

He was a charismatic man, a tall and arresting one. She knew he rode with elegance and finesse, as if he had been born to it. It sometimes seemed that he embodied some spirit of chivalry, something of a certain gallantry that had belonged to a sector of the deceased, prewar South. He had grace, and he had courage, she did not deny him those. He would never think of personal safety if something threatened someone he loved. He was loyal and devoted to his brother, and to her sister, Kristin.

He also seemed to have gone quite mad, and she needed desperately to escape him at the first opportunity. She didn't know whether to be terrified or furious.

"Miss McCahy," he murmured, reaching for her hand. "Please accept my hand. I admit, my manners were poor..."

It was too much. He had wrestled her to the ground twice, threatened her, bullied her and acted as if he belonged in an asylum. Now he was acting like the last of the cavaliers. She wanted no part of him; she had to escape.

She stared at his hand, creeping away on her elbows and haunches. "You must be completely out of your mind," she told him flatly. Then she leaped to her feet and spun around to run.

"Damn you!"

The oath left him in a fury. This time, when he caught her and dragged her back, he did not throw her to the floor. He curved one hand over her mouth and brought her flush against his chest with the other, his fingers taut beneath her breast. He whispered against her ear.

"Shannon, I am tired, I am bone tired. It has been my belief since I first had the pleasure of your acquaintance that a switch in the barnyard would have done you a world of good. Now, I am going to ask you one more time to behave, and then I am going to take action against you, as I see fit."

Rage and humiliation boiled inside her. "Malachi Slater, don't you ever talk to me like that, ever!"

"Don't push it."

She brought her heel against his leg with a vengeance. It wouldn't do much damage against his boot, she thought regretfully, but it did incite him further.

She gasped as he swung her around to face him, locking her against his body, his arms around her, her fingers laced tightly through his and held taut at the small of her back, as if they were involved in a close and desperate waltz. She opened her mouth to protest, but something in his eyes silenced her, and she stared at him in stony silence instead.

So much for dignity. So much for pride. She did manage to lift her chin.

"Shannon, behave," he said, then paused, watching her. Then he said with a trace of amazement, "You really meant to kill me!"

She inhaled, and exhaled, and tried to count. She tried to stop the trembling in her body, and the thunder in her heart. She was going to speak softly, and with bold, sheer reason. She could not stand being this close to him. She despised her vulnerability, and she hated the shivers that seized her and the way her blood seemed to heat and steam and sizzle throughout her. She hated the hardness of his body, like warm, living rock that she could lean against, when he was every inch the enemy.

"You would have!" he repeated. "You would have shot me. I wonder, did you or did you not know who I was?"

"Malachi, I'd love to shoot you. In both kneecaps, then right between the eyes. But you are Cole's brother, and because of that fact alone, I would never seek to take your miserable life. Besides, you lost, Malachi. I won." She paused, savoring the words. "The war, Malachi. I am the victor, and you, sir, are the loser."

He grinned, slowly, and shook his head. He leaned closer so that his eyes streaked blue fire straight into hers. His lips were almost against hers, the hair of his mustache teased her flesh, and she felt his words with every nerve of her body. "Never, Shannon. You'll never, never be the victor over me."

"You've already lost."

"We've yet to play the game."

"Malachi, you're hurting me!"

"You were trying to kill me."

"I was not! Every deserter and drunk and cutthroat and thief across the country thinks that this is playtime. I didn't know who you were! It's your fault. You should have come straight to the house. You shouldn't have been skulking around in the stables. I wouldn't have come out here if—" She broke off, frowning. "You Reb bastard!" she hissed. "You knew that it was me! You knew that it was me, but you jumped me anyway."

"You were wandering around with a Colt. I know what you are capable of doing with one, Miss McCahy."

"You could have called out—"

"Hell, ma'am, now how did I know that you wouldn't have been damned pleased to use the thing against me, and with such a good excuse."

She smiled, savagely gritting her teeth, trying to elude his hold. He would not release her. "Pity I don't have it now. I could be tempted."

"But you don't have it, do you? My point exactly."

"Malachi Slater—"

"Stop, Shannon. I told you. I'm exhausted. I'm bleeding and starving and exhausted and—"

"Bleeding?" Shannon interrupted, and then she wondered irritably why she cared. "Why didn't you come straight to the house?"

He twisted his jaw, watching her suspiciously. "I thought there might be a Yank patrol there."

"You saw that it was me—"

"Yes. But I didn't quite take the chance that you wouldn't just be thrilled to tears, little darlin', to turn me over to a patrol."

"Why, Captain Slater, you sound as if you believe I hate you."

"Miss McCahy, I am just fully aware that the sisterly love you offer to my brother does not extend to me. So you see, Shannon, at first I had to take care that you did not shoot me with pleasure, then I had to assure myself that you did not have a pack of blue-belly friends awaiting me in the house."

"My brother is a blue belly, you will recall," Shannon told him acidly.

"I said a patrol, and that's what I meant."

"A Yank patrol?" Startled, Shannon quit struggling and spoke curiously. "Why? Matthew isn't even back yet. Why would there be a Yank patrol at the house?"

He stiffened, his hold easing on her a bit. "You mean...you haven't heard?"

"Heard what?"

He stared at her for a moment longer and pulled her even closer.

"Swear to me, Shannon, that you're on the level. That you're not going to scream, or run, or try to shoot me again."

"If I had meant to shoot you, Malachi Slater, believe me, you'd be dead right now."

"Shannon, I'm going to let you go. If you scream or move or cause me another problem, I promise, you will live to regret it with all of your sweet heart. Do you understand?"

"There is no bloody patrol at the house!" she told him. Then she lowered her eyes and sighed. "I swear it, Malachi. You're safe for the moment."

Then she gasped, suddenly realizing that Cole's behavior had been a bit strange that afternoon. A friend of his had stopped by, and after that Cole had mentioned very casually that he might have to leave for a day or two to find a hiding place. Just in case, he had assured them. Just in case of trouble. Had Cole known something? It was his nature to be quiet and not alarmist. And he would have played any danger down for fear that Kristin would insist on accompanying him. He would just slip away, and then hurry back once he knew he could keep her safe...

"What?" Malachi demanded sharply.

"There's no patrol. It's just that...an old friend of Cole's stopped by today. And then Cole began to act strangely. Perhaps he does know something he's not telling us." Her heart felt as if it were sinking. Perhaps Cole was already gone. He could have slipped away already, looking for a place to take them. He had wanted to head to Texas before, but he wouldn't leave them for that length of time, Shannon knew. If he had gone off, it would be just for a few days, to find a hiding place deeper into Missouri.

Malachi tilted his head, watching her curiously, but he seemed to believe her. He released her and turned aside. With an uncanny agility in the darkness, he went to the door and found the lantern that hung there and lit it, bringing the flame down low.

And Shannon saw that Malachi was in worse shape than she had at first imagined.

His coat was indeed tattered, his braid frayed. He was very lean, and his handsome features were taut with fatigue. A deep crimson bloodstain marred his trousers high on the inner left thigh.

"You've been hit!" she cried, alarmed. "Oh, my God, I did hit you in the hay—"

He shook his head impatiently, sinking down upon one of the bales of hay. "You didn't hit me. A Union sentry hit me when I passed through Kentucky." He paused, and a gray cloud of memory touched his eyes as he stared into the shadows at nothing. "I could have taken them down," he mused, "but it didn't seem to make any sense. I thought that I could outrun them. They were just kids. They couldn't have been more than seventeen. More killing just didn't seem to make much sense."

None of it was making sense. He must have been in terrible pain, and yet he made his spectacular leap from the loft despite his injury. He must have been desperate indeed.

Curious, Shannon moved carefully over to him. "Malachi, the war is over. Why were they—"

"You really don't know?"

"Know what?" she demanded, exasperated.

"It isn't over. It isn't over at all." He hesitated. "Cole went into Kansas, you know. He killed the man who killed his wife."

Shannon nodded. "I know," she said stiffly. Malachi kept staring at her. "So?" she asked. "Cole knows that he's going to have to leave Missouri for a while. When Matthew comes home, Cole and Kristin will head for Texas."

Malachi leaned against the hay. He winced, and she thought that his leg must be hurting him very badly for him to display even a hint of pain. "Cole can't wait for Matthew to come home. He hasn't got the time. They've got wanted posters up on him. You see, the man he killed has a brother. And the brother seems to own half the property in Kansas. He virtually controls his part of the state. Anyway, he's calling Cole a murderer. He wants him brought in, dead or alive. And he's got enough influence—and money—to see that things are done his way."

Shannon felt weak. She wasn't terribly sure that she could stand. She staggered. She couldn't believe it. Cole had fought long and hard for a chance. He had battled a million demons, and now he had found his peace. He had Kristin and the baby, and with them the promise that there could be a normal life.

And now he was branded outlaw—and murderer.

"He's going to have to head out and hide, Shannon, right away," Malachi said softly. "They'll know to come for him here."

She nodded, thinking that this was what Cole had heard earlier. He had quite possibly left already. But in a second, she was going to go back to the house to check. She would at least have to tell Kristin that the world of peace and happiness that she had just discovered was being blown to bits by the thunder of revenge.

"Why—why were they shooting at you? You weren't in Kansas with Cole," Shannon said.

Malachi grinned, a lopsided, caustic grin. "Why, darlin', I'm the man's brother. A Slater. According to the powers that be, I ran with Quantrill, and I butchered half the population of Kansas."

"But you were never with Quantrill. You were always regular cavalry," Shannon said.

"Thanks for the vote of confidence. I didn't think that you would rush to my defense."

"I wouldn't," Shannon said coolly. "Facts are facts."

Malachi shrugged, leaning wearily back again. "Well, it doesn't matter much anyway. You go on up to the house and get Cole. We'll ride out tonight. You seen Jamie?"

Shannon was sorry to have to shake her head. She liked Jamie. He was always calm and quiet. The peacemaker of the three brothers, she thought. The Slaters were close; she could understand that. She and Kristin were close. Too many times, Kristin had been all that she had had left.

Too many times...

In the days after Robert had died, she had wanted to die herself. She had lain there without eating, without speaking, without the will to move. Kristin had been there. Kristin had given her the desire to survive again.

She lowered her head, almost smiling. Malachi had even helped her then. It had been unwitting, of course. He had never allowed her the peace of silence, or the chance to dwell in self-pity. Since she'd met him he'd been demanding, a true thorn in her side. But his very arrogance and his endless determination to treat her like a wayward child had brought out her fury, and with that her passion to live.

"I'm sorry. I haven't seen Jamie," she told him softly.

"Well," Malachi said softly to the lamp. "Jamie is no fool. He'll lay low. He'll find us."

His words were a lie, Shannon thought. He was worried sick. She didn't say so, though, for there was nothing that either of them could do.

"You were in the same company," she said. "Why aren't you together?"

"Jamie set out a day or two before I did. He wanted to stop by to see some old friends who had lost a son." He gritted his teeth. "We've got to run. He'll know how to lie low."

"You're not running anywhere, not the way that you are," Shannon told him. She couldn't bear seeing the blood on his leg. She didn't know why. Most of the time she thought that not even the Comanches could think up a cruel enough death for Malachi. But tonight the sight of his blood disturbed her.

"What do you mean?" he asked her warily.

"Your leg."

"I can find a doc south of here to take out the ball—"

"The ball is still in it?" Shannon said.

He stiffened as he held his breath for several seconds, watching her. "Yeah, the ball is still in it."

Shannon whirled around and headed for the tack room. They kept some rudimentary surgical supplies there; it was a necessary precaution on a cattle ranch.

"Shannon!" he called to her. "What do you think you're doing?"

"I'll be right back."

She found the surgical box in the lower left hand drawer of the desk. She paused. They had no morphine; nothing for pain. Nobody did, not in Missouri. Not in most of the South.

She pulled open the next drawer and found a bottle of Kentucky whiskey. It would have to do.

Then, as she came out of the tack room, she paused, wondering why she was thinking of doing this for Malachi Slater.

Maybe she didn't hate him so much.

No...she hated him. He was Cole's brother, and if his leg wasn't fixed up, he might slow Cole down. That was it, surely.

She swept back to his side and kneeled down. She opened up the box and found a pair of scissors. She needed to slit his pants and find the extent of the wound.

"What do you think you're doing?" he asked her harshly.

"I'm going to cut your pants."

"If you think that I'm going to let you anywhere close—"

"The wound is in your thigh, you fool. Here." She handed him the whiskey. "Drink some of this."

He didn't hesitate to swallow a good shot of the whiskey. He closed his eyes, wincing when he was done. "That was good. It was an inestimable piece of kindness from a Yank to a Reb. Now forget it, I'll find—"

"Sit still, Malachi, and quit whining."

"I'll be damned if I'm whining. Shannon! Shannon, stop!"

He clenched his teeth, but when he went to grip her wrists, he was too late. He hesitated. She already had the shears snipping at his pants, and to make a move might have been dangerous. He inhaled sharply.

She paused and met his eyes. She smiled sweetly. "Sit back now, Captain Slater. Relax."

"You move carefully there, Miss McCahy, or I swear, I'll make you sorry this very night!"

"Why, Captain Slater, I would take great care with those silly threats of yours at this particular moment."

He caught her arm and her eyes once again. "Shannon, I don't make silly threats. Just promises."

"You aren't in any position to make...promises, not at this moment, captain."

"Shannon—"

"Trust me, Malachi."

"The way I would a black widow, Shannon."

She smiled and stared at his fingers, which were still locked around her arm. She looked at him again. His eyes remained clear and deep and blue upon hers. Slowly, he eased his fingers, releasing her.

She felt him inhale as she carefully snipped at the bloodstained wool. Seconds later, she pulled the material away from the wound.

She could see the ball. It was sunk in just far enough that a man wouldn't be able to remove it himself. One swift slice with a scalpel and a quick foray with the forceps and it would be gone. Then she could douse it with some of the liquor and bind it, and his chances of a clean recovery would be very good indeed.

"Take another swig of the whiskey," she told him, staring at the wound because she didn't dare look into his eyes. "I'll just get the scalpel—"

His hand landed hard upon her wrist, and her eyes were drawn to his. "I don't trust you with a scalpel, Shannon."

She smiled sweetly. "You have to trust me. You have no choice."

"You bring it too close to any part of my anatomy that I consider near and dear, and you will regret it until your dying day."

"Alas, the ladies would be heartbroken!" she taunted in turn. "I will take the gravest care."

He released her wrist, but continued to watch her. There was a warning sizzle in his eyes that brought tremors to her heart. She had to steady her hands. "What the hell," she muttered. "Mr. Ego Reb. Were I to wound anything near and dear there's a likelihood that nobody would even notice."

It was a good thing that the knife had yet to touch his flesh. He caught her wrist again, pinning it, drawing her eyes to his once more. "Sometime, darlin', I just might let you find out."

She jerked away. "Darlin', don't even dream of it. Not in your wildest thoughts."

"Couldn't handle it, huh?"

"I'll handle it right now, if you're not careful, Captain Slater."

"Is that a promise, Miss McCahy?"

"No, a threat."

"Your hands better move with the skill of an angel, got that, Miss McCahy?"

His grip on her wrist was tight. But it wasn't the pain that gave her pause. It was his agony, for all that he concealed it so well.

She nodded. "Give me the bottle."

"What for?"

"To clean the scalpel." She doused the small sharp knife with the alcohol, and then he took the bottle back from her. He swallowed heartily. "Ready?" Shannon asked him.

"You are eager to take a blade against me," he said.

"Right."

"I can't wait to take one against you." His speech was slurred just a bit. When she glanced his way, she saw his grin, lopsided, heartstopping. She closed her eyes tightly against it, against the searing cobalt of his eyes, and the charisma of that smile. He was making her tremble tonight, and she couldn't falter.

She brought the scalpel against his flesh, holding his thigh to keep it steady. He didn't start or move at the swift penetration of the knife, but she felt his muscles jump and contract, and the power was startling.

He didn't make a sound. He just closed his eyes and clamped down on his jaw, and for a moment she wondered if he was conscious, and then she hoped that he was not. She quickly finished her cut, and brought the small forceps out. She had cut well. She quickly secured the ball and dug it from his flesh, then liberally poured whiskey over the wound and began to bind it with linen bandages. There weren't enough to finish the job. She glanced at his face, then lifted her skirt and tore her petticoat.

One of his eyes opened and he looked at her. "Thanks, darlin'." He wasn't unconscious.

"I don't want you getting Cole killed," she said flatly. She came up on her knees, and wrapped the linen around his thigh, moving higher and higher. Both his eyes were open now. She wished that her elegant bodice weren't cut quite so low. He was staring straight at her cleavage, and he was making no gentlemanly move to look away.

"Quit that," she ordered him.

"Why?"

"You're supposed to be a Southern gentleman," she reminded him.

He smiled, but the smile held pain. "The South is dead, haven't you heard? And so are Southern gentlemen. And you be careful right now, Miss McCahy. You're moving real, real close."

She was. She pulled her fingers back as if she had been burned.

"You did a good job," he told her, tying off the bandage.

"Because everything is intact?" she said caustically.

"I do appreciate that. But then, you wouldn't have dared do me injury, I'm certain."

"Don't be so certain."

A soft, husky chuckle escaped him. "Some day, I promise, I'll make it all worth your while."

"What does that mean?"

"Why, we'll have to wait and see, won't we?"

"Don't hold your breath, Captain Slater. And besides—" she widened her eyes with a feigned and sizzling innocence "—I'm just a child, remember? The McCahy brat."

She started to turn away. He caught her arm and pulled her back. She almost protested, but he moved with a curious gentleness, lifting a fallen tendril of hair, smoothing it. And his eyes moved over her again, over the rise of her breasts beneath the lace of her bodice, to her flushed cheeks, to the curve of her form where she knelt by his feet.

"Well, brat, it was a long war. I think that, maybe, you've begun to grow up."

"I had no choice," she said, and she was suddenly afraid that she would start to cry. She gritted her teeth and swallowed the tears harshly. She felt his eyes upon her, reading her thoughts and her mind and her heart.

"I was very sorry about your Captain Ellsworth, Shannon," he said. "I know what it did to you. But be careful. If you're not, you'll have scars on your soul, like Cole did when the jayhawkers killed his wife."

"Malachi, don't—"

"All right, Miss McCahy, I won't talk about sacred territory." He smiled, a devilish smile, taunting her, leading her away from the memory of pain. "You are maturing, and nicely. Thank you, Shannon." He paused, his eyes searching her, his smile deepening with a sensual curve to his lips. She thought that he was going to say something else, but he repeated himself. "Thank you, you did a good job. Your touch was gentle, nearly tender."

"I told you—"

His knuckles brushed her cheek. "Definitely growing up," he murmured softly.

She didn't know what to say. It should have been something scathing, yet she didn't feel that way at all, not at that moment. She just felt, curiously, as if she wanted to be held. As if she wanted to burst into tears and be assured that yes, indeed, the war was over, and peace had come. She wanted to feel his arms around her, the heat of his whisper as he caressed her tenderly and assured her that all was well.

But she had no chance to respond at all.

For at that moment, the quiet of the night beyond the stables was shattered. The thunder of hoofbeats sounded just outside, loud, staccato, a drumroll that promised some new portent of danger. Even through the closed door, she could feel the beat she knew well.

Shannon rose quickly, the blood draining from her face.

"Riders, Malachi! Riders coming to the house!"

As if in answer to her worried exclamation, she heard a faint scream of horror from the house. Shannon ran to the door, wrenching it open. The scream came again. Shrill now, then higher and higher.

"Kristin!" Shannon cried. "It's—it's Kristin! Oh, my God, it's Kristin!"

"Wait!" Malachi called.

Shannon barely heard him. Horses had come galloping down upon the ranch again. Numerous horses. The sound of those hoofbeats told her that the uneasy peace that had so briefly settled over the ranch would now be shattered once again.

She started to run.

"Shannon!" Malachi thundered.

She ignored him, unaware that he was behind her, swearing, raging that she should stop.

"Damned fool brat!" he called. "Wait!"

She didn't wait. She burst into the night, staring at the house. In the glow of the light from the house she could see twenty or so horses ranged before the porch. Most of them still carried their riders. Only a few of the men had dismounted.

"No!" Shannon breathed, but even as she ran, she saw her sister.

A tall husky man with unruly dark whiskers was coming out of the house with Kristin tossed over his shoulder.

Kristin was dressed for dinner, too, in a soft blue brocade that matched the color of her eyes. Her hair had been pinned in a neat coil, but now it streamed down the giant's back, like a lost ray of sunshine.

Stunned, Shannon stopped and stared in horror.

"I've got her!" the man said sharply. "Let's get the hell out of here!"

"What about Slater?" someone asked.

Shannon couldn't hear the reply, but her heart seemed to freeze over. If Cole wasn't gone, then he was dead. If there was a single breath left in his body, the burly man wouldn't have his hands on Kristin.

Kristin was screaming and fighting furiously as the man walked hurriedly to his horse. Kristin bit him, hard.

He slapped her in return, harder. Swearing. Then he tossed a dazed Kristin onto his horse, and mounted behind her.

"No!" Shannon shrieked, and she started to run in a panic toward the house once again. She leaped one of the paddock fences in a shortcut to the house. She had to stop them. She had to save her sister.

Her feet flew over the Missouri dust, and her heart thundered. She had no thought but to reach the man before he could ride away with her sister. In terror, she thought only to throw herself at the man in a whirlwind of fury.

Suddenly, she was, in truth, flying. Hurtling through the air by the force of some rock-hard power behind her, and falling facedown into the red dust at her feet. Stunned, she inhaled, and dirt filled her lungs. Dizzy and gasping, she fought against the force now crawling over her, holding her tight. Panic seized her. It was one of the men, one of them...

"Stop it, Shannon!"

No! It was Malachi again. Damn Malachi. He was holding her down, holding her prisoner, when the men were about to ride away, ride away with Kristin...

"Let me go, you fool!"

He was lying over her, the length of his body flat on hers, hard and heavy. His chest lay on her back, and his hands were flat upon hers, pinning them down. She could barely raise her head to see.

She could only feel the tension and heat of his whisper as he leaned low against her in warning.

"You fool! You're not—"

"Damn you! Get off of me! He has my sister!" She couldn't even begin to fight; she couldn't twist away from him.

"Shannon! He has twenty armed men! And you're running after him without so much as a big stick!"

"He has—"

"Shut up!" One of his hands eased from hers, but only to clamp over her mouth. He kept them down, almost flat upon the earth. A trough lay before them. It hid them from view, Shannon realized, while they could still see the men and the house two hundred yards away.

"He has Kristin!" Malachi agreed. "And if you go any closer, he's going to have you, too! And if you don't shut up, he'll be after the two of us. We could try shooting down twenty men between us without killing your sister in the fire, but we'd still need our weapons—those wood and steel things back in the hay—to do it with!"

She went still, ceasing to struggle against him.

"My only hope is to follow them. Carefully," he said hoarsely. He eased his hand from her mouth. He did not lift his weight from hers, but pinned her there with him with a sure pressure.

She hated him for it.

But he was right. She had no weapon. She had panicked, and she had run off with nothing, and she could do nothing to help Kristin.

She would only be abducted, too.

"No!" she whispered bleakly, for the horses were moving. The men were all mounted, and the horses were beginning to move away.

With the same speed and thunder, they were racing away, into the night.

And red Missouri dust rose in an eerie fog against the darkness of the night...

And slowly, slowly settled.

Chapter Three

When the horses were gone, Malachi quickly stood and reached down for Shannon. She would have ignored his hand and risen on her own, but he didn't give her a chance. All the while, he kept his eyes fixed on the house. As soon as she was standing, he dropped her hands to start limping for the porch. He climbed over the paddock fence.

"Where are you going?" Shannon demanded, following him.

He didn't seem to hear her. He kept walking.

"Malachi!" Shannon snapped. He stopped and looked back at her as if she was a momentary distraction—like a buzzing fly. "Malachi! We have to get guns and horses; we have to ride after them. You're wasting time! Where are you going!"

"I'm going to the house," he said flatly. "Excuse me." He started walking again.

She ran after him and caught his elbow, wrenching him around to face her. Stunned, frightened and furious, she accosted him. "What? You're going to the house. Just like that. Sure, we've got all the time in the world! Let's take a rest. Can I get you dinner, maybe? A drink? A cool mint julep, or something stronger? What the hell is the matter with you? Those men are riding away with my sister!"

"I know that, Shannon. I—"

"You son of a bitch! You Rebel...coward! Good God, I wish to hell that you were Cole! He rode in here all alone and cleaned up a small army on his own! You didn't even fire a shot. You yellow-bellied piece of white trash—"

"That's it!" He stepped back, and his arm snaked out. He caught her wrist and held her in a bruising grip, speaking with biting rage. "I'm damned sorry that Cole isn't here, Miss McCahy. And I'm damned sorry that I didn't have the time to dig through the hay to find my gun or your gun or even my saber. If I had had my gun, I probably could have killed a few of them before they gunned me down. So I'm real, real sorry that I don't feel like dying like a fool just to appease your definition of courage. And, Miss McCahy—" he paused for a breath "—as for Cole, I really, honest to God can't tell you just how much I'd like to see his face. And that, to tell the truth, is what I'm trying to do right now. Those men are riding away with your sister. Well, my brother was in that house, and I—"

He paused again, inhaling deeply. Shannon had gone very pale and very still. She had forgotten Cole in her fear for Kristin. Malachi had not.

He dropped her arm, pushing her from him. "I want to find out if Cole is alive or dead," he said flatly, and he spun on his heels.

It took Shannon a few seconds to follow him, and when she did so, she did in silence. Dread filled her heart. She hoped Cole had left already. But the second that she learned something about her brother-in-law she would be gone. Maybe Malachi could let those men ride away with Kristin—she could not.

He heard her following behind. He spoke without turning around. "I am going after Kristin. If you don't mind, I will arm myself first."

"As soon as we...as soon as we find Cole," Shannon said. "I'll get everything we need. We can leave—"

"*We* aren't leaving. I'm leaving."

"I'm coming with you."

"You're not coming with me."

"I am coming—"

"You're not!"

Shannon opened her mouth to continue the argument, but she didn't get the chance. The porch door swung open again as Delilah came running out. Tall, black and beautiful, with the aristocratic features of an African princess, she was more family than servant, and no proclamation had made her free. Gabriel McCahy had released both her and her husband, Samson, years before the war had ever begun.

Now her features were wretchedly torn with anguish.

"Shannon!" she cried, throwing out her arms. Shannon raced to Delilah, accepting her embrace, holding her fiercely in return. Delilah spoke again, softly, quickly. "Shannon, child, I was so afraid for you! They dragged Kristin from here so quick—"

"Delilah," Malachi said harshly, interrupting her. His voice was thick. "Where is my brother? What happened? Cole would never— Cole would never have allowed Kristin to be dragged from his side."

Delilah shook her head, trying to get a grip on her emotions. "No, sir, Captain Slater," she said softly, "Cole Slater never would have done that. He—"

"He's dead," Malachi said, swallowing sickly.

"No! No, he isn't dead!" Delilah said with haste.

Relief flooded through Shannon. She couldn't stand any longer. She staggered to the porch and sank down on the lowest step. "Where *is* Cole, Delilah?"

"He rode out before—"

"When?" Shannon cried. "I didn't see him go!"

"Let's come inside. You both look as if you could use a little libation," Delilah said.

Shannon shook her head and stood with an effort. "I'm going after Kristin—"

"You're not going after anyone," Malachi said. "I'm going, and I'll do so as soon as I'm ready."

"Don't tell me what I can and can't do, Malachi Slater!"

He walked over to her, his eyes narrowed, his irritation as apparent as his limp. "Shannon McCahy, you are a willful little fool, and you will get us both killed, as well as your sister. I will tell you what to do, and if you don't listen to me, I'll lock you in your room. No, that wouldn't do, knowing you, you'd come right through the window. I'll tie you to your bed. Are we understood?"

She wasn't going to get into another test of strength with Malachi, not at that moment.

Nor was she about to listen to him.

But she inhaled and raised her chin with what she hoped was a chilling dignity. She walked up the steps to the porch and paused before the door. "Yes, let's do go in. I'll get Malachi some of Cole's breeches, and we'll all have a shot of whiskey. Delilah, you can tell us what happened. We do need to move quickly. Malachi needs to get going.''

She smiled at him sweetly. She saw his lashes fall as his eyes narrowed, and she saw the cynical curl of his lips beneath his mustache. He didn't trust her. Not a bit. It didn't matter.

She entered the house with a serene calm, walking quickly through the Victorian parlor toward the office. It had been her pa's office; recently, she had begun to think of it as Cole's office. One day, she hoped, Matthew would reclaim it. The country would rebuild after the war, and Matthew's children would come and crawl on his lap while he went over accounts or the payroll.

Delilah and Malachi followed her. She opened the bottom drawer of the desk and drew out a bottle of Kentucky bourbon. With steady hands she found the shot glasses on the bookcase and poured out three servings, then handed one to Delilah and one to Malachi. She took her father's place behind the desk. ''All right, Delilah, what happened?''

Malachi was watching her. He perched on the edge of the desk, waiting.

Delilah didn't sit. She swallowed the bourbon neat, and paced the floor.

''Cole left here about an hour ago. He came to speak with Samson and me, explaining that he thought things were going to get hotter a lot sooner than he expected. Some guy called Fitz wanted revenge. Cole didn't think that this Fitz would want to hurt the McCahys—but he knew that Fitz wanted all the Slaters, and just to be safe, he wanted to move Kristin and the baby right away. He didn't want to say anything to Kristin until he had a place to take her and little Gabe, and, well, you know your sister, Shannon, she wouldn't have let him get away. She'd have risked anything, herself and even little Gabe, I think. He meant to come back within a day or two. He didn't want her risking that child or herself.'' She paused.

''Go on, Delilah,'' Malachi prodded her. He leaned over the desk and opened the top drawer, reaching for a cigar. ''Excuse me,'' he said to Shannon, smiling politely. She didn't care for the slant of his smile, nor for the touch of blue fire that sparkled in his eyes.

He was, indeed, watching her. And he wasn't about to trust her.

"I gave Cole some food. He gave me a kiss on the cheek, and said that he'd be back, and that everything would be fine. He also said that I shouldn't be surprised to see you coming here mighty soon, Captain Malachi, and that Jamie might be on his way, too. And he left a letter to Kristin on his desk. I brought it up to Kristin right away. She had guessed that he was gone. She ripped the letter open and read it quick, and then she let it drop to the floor. She just sat there, staring at me with her pretty face white as a sheet."

Delilah sighed, slumping down into the leather-covered sofa before the desk. "Then finally she started to cry. 'I knew that he'd have to run, but we meant to run together. He must be desperate, to have gone without me, without the baby! He knew, he knew...that I would follow him anywhere. But he was afraid that they might hurt me or the baby to get to him. Oh, Delilah!' she cried. She cried out my name, just like that. It hurt so bad to hear. I told her that he'd be back for her, just as soon as he could find a place...'"

Shannon nodded. So she had been right. Cole had been gone all along. Cole would have heard Malachi in the barn. He would have heard the shots. He would have come to her. Not that it mattered now.

Delilah paused, shaking her head, staring blankly at the desk before her. "Then the horses came."

"And the Red Legs took Kristin?"

"They swept right in here. But Kristin was so glad to tell them that they were too late. Cole was gone, long gone. Then that bearlike bastard brought his knife so tight against her throat that he drew blood. Thank God he didn't seem to know anything about the baby."

"The baby!" Shannon and Malachi cried in unison, jumping up in alarm.

Delilah smiled. If there was one thing in the world that Malachi and Shannon could agree upon, it was their nephew, Gabriel. They both doted on him, and their alarm was clearly written upon their faces. "Gabe is just fine. He's upstairs sleeping with my boy in my room. They fell asleep on the bed together, and so I left them there. I don't think those men even know that he exists." She stared straight at Shannon. "They know about you, though, missy. They were going to look for you, tear the place apart for you, but the dark-haired fellow with the beard said that they should hurry, they had Kristin Slater, they didn't need anyone else.''

Shannon inhaled and exhaled slowly. She looked down at her hands. Maybe she had been lucky. If she hadn't been out at the stables with Malachi, she might have been taken, too.

Or she might be dead now, because she would have tried to fight them. She might have shot some of them down, but there had been an awful lot of them. Red Legs...

She jumped to her feet, staring at Malachi in renewed horror. "Red Legs! They were Red Legs!"

Malachi shrugged. "The Red Leg units are all part of the army now, Shannon. Lane and Jennison were stripped of their commands long ago.''

His words didn't help her much. Shannon had learned to hate the Southern bushwhackers, but she'd always had the good sense to despise the jayhawkers as they had butchered and plundered and murdered and robbed and raped and savaged the people and the land with every bit as much—if not more—ruthless energy than the bushwhackers.

The Red Legs, as the men were called, were infamous for their brutality. She had seen the uniforms worn by the men in front of the house. But in the darkness, she had not realized who they were. But Malachi had seen them clearly, and he had known right away. He had good reason to know them. A unit of Red Legs had killed his sister-in-law, Cole's first wife.

"We have to get Kristin back," she said.

Malachi rose, too. "I will get Kristin back, I promise you."

"Malachi—"

"Shannon, damn it, you cannot come."

"I'm an ace shot, and you know it."

"And you also panicked just a little while ago. You started racing after them with your mouth wide open and your hands bare. Shannon, the only way I'm going to get Kristin away from those men is to sneak her out of their camp. I can't go in with guns blazing—they will kill her if I even try it."

"Malachi, please just let me—"

"No."

"You don't even know what I'm going to say!"

"Shannon, you listen. Stay here. Take care of Gabe. Wait, maybe Cole will come back, or will try to get a message through to you, or maybe Matthew will come home. Who knows, Matthew just may have some influence with these people. He fought long and hard in the Yank army. If he can get to the right authorities, maybe he can get Kristin back through legitimate means."

She gritted her teeth, staring at him. "Meanwhile they could kill, torture, rape or maim my sister."

He sighed, hands on his hips, and gritted his teeth in turn. "Shannon, you may not come with me."

She lowered her head quickly, trying not to let him see her eyes. She was going about this all wrong. She knew Malachi. He was as stubborn as a worn-out mule. He wasn't going to say yes, and she was an idiot to argue it out.

She should let him leave and then follow his trail. He didn't ever have to know that she was near him. And if he didn't manage to get Kristin away from the band of Red Legs, she'd find a way herself.

"Well," she said, "let me go and get you a pair of Cole's breeches."

"Never mind," he told her. "I know where the room is." He turned on his heel and started out of the room.

"Captain Malachi, you'd better have some supper in you before you leave," Delilah said. "You wash up and dress and come on down, and eat something first. And I'll pack you up a little something for your saddlebag."

"Thanks, Delilah."

"He needs to hurry, Delilah," Shannon said sweetly.

Malachi's eyes met hers across the room, sharp and icy and blue, and he smiled. That chivalrous slant of a grin across his features might have been heart-stopping, she thought, if he had just been some other man.

"Oh, I think I have time to grab a bite," he said.

"Certainly. We wouldn't want you to go off hungry."

"I'm sure that you wouldn't."

He kept staring at her, so she kept smiling pleasantly. "You go on then, Malachi. I'll help Delilah see to some dinner."

"Fine," he said. "Thanks." He tipped his hat to her. The brim fell over his eyes, and she wondered once again what he was thinking. But he was quickly gone. She listened to the sound of his boots hitting the parlor floor, then moving up the stairway.

Delilah stood up quickly, eyeing Shannon warily. "What you got on your mind, missy?"

"Nothing that you need to worry about, Delilah."

"Oh, I'm worried," Delilah assured her. "I'm plenty worried." She rolled her eyes Shannon's way.

Shannon ignored her. "Let's go see to something to eat," she said hastily.

Delilah sniffed. "There's plenty to eat out there. Cold roast, cold potatoes and cold turnip greens. Not very nice anymore, but there's plenty. I'll set a plate over the fire. You come pack up some food for Captain Malachi."

Shannon followed Delilah from the office through the elegant little parlor and past the entry to the stairway. She paused, looking up the steps. Malachi would be changing. Then he would eat and leave. She would have to follow quickly. She wouldn't have time to change her clothing. She'd have to roll up a pair of trousers and a cotton shirt, grab a hat and be on her way.

"Shannon?" Delilah looked at her from the doorway to the dining room. "You comin'?"

"I'm right behind you, Delilah," she said, and meekly walked through the dining room to the kitchen. "Is the smoked meat in the pantry?"

"Yes'm, it is," Delilah said, slicing roast beef on the counter and watching Shannon from the corner of her eye. Shannon ignored her and pulled two clean cloths from the linen drawer. She found strips of smoked beef and pork and began to wrap them carefully. Delilah had just baked bread, so there were fresh loaves to pack, too. She turned around just as she was finishing. Delilah was leaning against the door frame, watching her.

"And what are you doing?"

"Packing food."

"I can see that. You're packing up two bundles."

"Malachi is a very hungry person."

"Um. And you're going to give him both of those bundles, right?"

Shannon exhaled slowly. "Delilah—"

"Don't you wheedle me, Shannon. You've been wheedling me since you came up to my knees. You're grown now. I know what you're going to do."

"Delilah, I have to go after Kristin—"

"Malachi will go after Kristin."

"And what if he fails?"

"You think that it will help Kristin if they take you captive, too?"

"Delilah—"

Delilah threw up her hands. "Shannon McCahy, I can't stop you. You're a grown woman now."

"Thank you, Delilah."

"Anyway," Delilah said with a sly smirk, "I don't need to stop you."

"Oh?"

"No, missy, I sure don't. I don't need to at all."

"And why is that?"

"Why, darlin', he's gonna stop you, that's why."

"Don't you dare say anything to him, Delilah."

"I won't. I promise you that I won't. And I can tell you this, it ain't gonna matter none!"

Without waiting for a reply, Delilah turned her back on Shannon, and went to work making up a plate for Malachi, humming as she did so.

Shannon wrinkled her nose at Delilah's back. She knew darned well that Delilah couldn't see, but she might have done so, her next words came so quickly.

"You've got hay in your hair, Shannon McCahy. Lots of it. And hay stuffed right into your cleavage, young woman. You might want to do something about that before dinner."

Instinctively, Shannon brought her hand to her hair, and she did, indeed, pluck a piece of hay from it.

"I thought you weren't terribly partial to Captain Malachi?" Delilah said sweetly.

Shannon found the hay sticking from her bodice. She plucked that out, too, spinning on her heels and walking toward the door. "I'm not, Delilah. I'm definitely not."

"Hm."

She didn't have to defend herself to Delilah. She didn't have to defend herself to anyone.

Then why was she doing so?

"We had an accidental meeting in the stables, and that is all, Delilah. You were right—I'm not at all partial to Captain Slater."

Lifting her chin, she swept out of the kitchen. She paused, biting her lower lip as she heard Delilah's laughter following her. She shook her head and pushed away from the door. She needed to hurry.

She went up the stairs to her room. Beneath her bed she found a set of leather saddlebags. Dragging them out, she quickly stuffed one side with clean undergarments, a shirt and sturdy cotton breeches. The other side she would save for food and ammunition. She made a mental note to bring plenty of the latter, then shoved the saddlebags under the bed.

She stood quickly and hurried to her washstand, pouring clean water into the bowl. She washed her face and hands and realized that she was trembling. She dried off quickly, then moved to the mirror to repair her fallen and tumbling hair. Swearing softly, she discovered more hay. She brushed it out quickly and redid her hair in a neat golden knot at the nape of her neck.

When she was done, she stepped back. Subdued? Serene? She wondered. That was the effect she wanted. It wasn't to be. Her cheeks were very red with color, her eyes were a deep and sparkling blue, and despite herself, she felt that she looked as guilty as hell.

"I'm not guilty of anything!" she reminded herself out loud. "They've taken my sister..."

That thought was sobering. Where was Kristin now? Had they stopped to rest yet? They were heading for Kansas, she was certain. Surely they would keep her safe—until they had Cole. And Cole was no fool. When he heard that they had Kristin, he would take care, of course he would...

Her eyes gazed back at her, very wide and misty now. She blinked and stiffened. She needed to find strength. She couldn't possibly sit around and wait. She had to do something to bring Kristin home again.

There...not too bad. She folded her hands before her, and a mature young woman with wise blue eyes and a slender face and soft wisps of blond hair curling around her face gazed back at her. A serene young woman, soft and feminine—with no more hay protruding from the bodice of her elegant dinner gown. She was ready.

Shannon started to run swiftly down the stairs, then she realized that Malachi was standing at the foot of them, waiting for her. She quickly slowed her pace, and her lashes swept low over her eyes as she tried to gaze at him covertly. He had that twisted grin of his again, that cocky, knowing grin.

"Miss McCahy, I was waiting to see if you were joining me for supper. We're all set, and all alone, so it seems. Delilah has gone out back to wait for Samson."

She had come to the foot of the stairs. He was very close, watching her face. She swept by him. "Of course, Malachi."

He followed behind her and pulled out her chair. Delilah had already set their dishes on the table. When Shannon sat, Malachi pushed her chair in to the table. He hovered behind her. She wished that he would sit.

He did not. He reached over her, pouring her a glass of burgundy. She look up at him.

"What is dinner without a fine red wine?" he said lightly. Then he gazed at the bottle, and she saw his handsome features grow taut. "I haven't had any in quite some time," he murmured.

Shannon quickly looked away, feeling that she intruded on some intimate emotion. He did not seem to remember that she was there, but if he had, she thought he would not want her watching.

He poured his wine and sat across from her. He sipped it and complimented the fine bouquet. He cut off a large bite of roast beef, and chewed it hungrily and cut another.

"You're not eating," he told Shannon.

"And you're eating too slowly," she muttered.

He looked up, startled, and smiled. "Shannon, I will catch up with them. I'm probably going to have to follow them for several days to learn their ways and find the best time to sneak in among them. Don't begrudge me one hot meal. I haven't had one in ages.''

She felt a twinge of guilt. She knew that the Rebel soldiers had been down to bare rations at the end of the war, moldy hardtack and whatever they could find on the land. She lifted her wineglass to him. ''Enjoy,'' she said softly.

Malachi paused in the midst of chewing, lifting his glass to hers, suddenly mesmerized by the girl before him.

Woman. It had been a long war, and she had grown up during the painful duration of it.

And in the soft candlelight, she was suddenly every bit the glorious image he had seen in his dream. Her lips were softly curled, her cheeks were flushed, her eyes were a crystal and beautiful blue, soft and inviting. Golden strands of hair escaped the knot at her nape and curled against the porcelain clarity and softness of her cheeks, down the length of her slender neck and over her shoulders. Her breasts pushed against the low bodice of her elegant gown. She might have been a study of wisdom and innocence, for her smile was soft and young, but her eyes seemed ancient.

Malachi swallowed a sip of wine. She was still smiling. The little wretch. She was up to something. She planned on following him.

He raised his glass in return. ''To you, Shannon.''

''Why, thank you, sir.''

Just as gracious as a Southern belle. He was definitely in trouble if Shannon was being charming.

''You're welcome.'' His eyes were warm as he gazed at her. He lowered his head, hiding a smile, then he allowed his hand to fall upon hers. She almost jumped a mile.

''Did I thank you for treating my leg?''

''It was my pleasure.''

''Oh, I'm sure it was.''

Shannon didn't know quite what he meant by that, but she was determined not to argue.

It might be nice not to do so, she thought suddenly.

He was such a striking man. He had washed quickly, and his hair was slightly damp, and he had trimmed his mustache and beard. He had donned a pair of Cole's gray trousers, and a clean cotton shirt, which lay open in a V at the neck, displaying a hint of the bronze flesh of his chest, and the profusion of red-gold hair that grew there. He was achingly masculine in the muted glow of the candles, and she was stunned that his wry smile could bring about a curious beating in her heart.

She had not thought of any man as really attractive...

As sexually attractive...

Not since Robert had died. Then she had dreamed.

For so long those dreams had seemed like dust in the tempest of the wind. She could barely remember Robert's kisses now, or the excitement they had elicited within her. She could scarcely recall the lovely satin and lace gown that Kristin had made for her. Kristin had laughed with mischievous pleasure, assuring her that it would be the perfect gown for her wedding night...

She had ripped the gown to shreds.

When Robert had died, she had ceased to lie awake at night and ponder the things between a man and a woman. The soft, exciting stirrings within her had died.

She had thought that they had died.

But with Malachi's hand so softly atop hers, his eyes with their devil's sparkle so close, his knee brushing hers, she was suddenly feeling them again.

Her cheeks flamed crimson, and she jerked her hand from beneath his, nearly knocking over her wineglass. He cocked an eyebrow at her, and it seemed to her that he was still secretively smiling.

"Something wrong, darlin'?"

"I'm not your *darlin'*."

"Excuse me. Is something wrong, Miss McCahy?"

Wrong? It was horrid. And on a night when Kristin had been so savagely taken...

Kristin, remember Kristin, she told herself. That was why she was here, trying to be charming.

"No," she said quickly. "No, nothing's wrong. I'm just so tired. I mean, it's been such a long day. No, no, nothing is wrong at all. What am I saying? Everything is wrong!"

"Hey!" He leaned across the table and caught her chin with his forefinger. She sensed a tremendous warmth within him that she had never seen before, and it touched her, and embraced her. She didn't pull away when he held her, or when he sought out her eyes.

"I will find her, Shannon. I will find her. They—they aren't going to hurt her—"

"They are a Red Legs unit."

"They aren't going to hurt her. Fitz wants her alive. Why do you think they took Kristin?"

"Because they want Cole."

"Right. So they won't hurt her, or else they won't have her to use against my brother. It's going to be all right."

Shannon nodded. He released her, but his eyes stayed on her with a curious speculation, and it seemed that he had to force himself to return his attention to his meal.

And she had to force herself to forget his haunting touch.

"Is—is everything good?" she asked him.

"Delicious," he said briefly.

"I do hope so. More wine?"

"Thank you, Miss McCahy."

"My pleasure."

He sat back, sipping the wine that she had poured. He lifted his glass, and the speculation remained in his eyes. "No, my pleasure, Miss McCahy." He sighed, finished the wine, set his glass down and rose. She jumped up along with him.

"You're going now?"

"I'm going now."

"I'll get your food. And your coat and cavalry jacket." She paused. "You probably shouldn't ride into Kansas with that jacket. Do you want another one?"

He took his jacket and coat from her. "Why, haven't you heard, Miss McCahy? The war is over. Or so they say."

"Or so they say," Shannon echoed.

He grinned. He touched her cheek, and she quickly turned away. "I'll get your food."

"Thanks," he drawled, but when she started to walk away, he caught her hand and pulled her back.

He had put his plumed hat atop his head, and his Confederate greatcoat lay over his shoulders. His eyes were heavy-lidded and sparkled with a lazy sensuality and humor.

"It was a nice dinner, Miss McCahy. You were a beautiful companion. I enjoyed it. Whatever comes, I want you to know that. I enjoyed it."

It was very peculiar talk, coming from Malachi. She nodded nervously and pulled away from him. "I'll...I'll just get your food."

"I'll meet you out front. I want to take a last peek at Gabe, and tell Delilah goodbye."

"Fine."

She fled to the kitchen. She hurriedly secured his bundle of food, adding a bottle of her father's old Irish whiskey from the cupboard. Then she went outside and nervously waited.

Soon he passed by her on the porch. "Just need to get the bay," he told her.

"Of course."

She watched him walk to the stable, a tall figure, dominating the night, with his greatcoat falling from his shoulders and his plumed hat touching the sky.

He was swallowed up by the darkness.

Moments later he reappeared, a masterful horseman, cantering toward her on the bay.

He reined in before he reached the porch and waited as she approached him with the bundle of food and the liquor.

"Is your leg all right?" she asked him with a little pang of guilt. He should have had some rest, but he seemed to be doing well with the wound. As long as infection didn't set in, he should be fine.

But it was true that he should have rested.

"The leg feels good, thanks." He buckled the food into his saddlebag. The bay mare shuffled nervously, wanting to be gone.

Shannon stepped back. Malachi nodded to her, lifting the reins. "Take care of Gabe. I'll be back with Kristin as soon as I can. I hope Cole will hear of this and come back, but we can't rely on that. Be ready. We'll have to take her somewhere. She'll have to hide now, too, or they'll come after her again."

Shannon nodded. "I'll be ready."

"I'll bet you will. Goodbye."

She lifted a hand and waved. He saluted, swung the bay around and rode into the night.

Shannon could barely stand still. The second he was out of sight, she swung around and raced up the steps. She burst into the house and ran up the stairway. She didn't pause to change, but wrenched her saddlebags from beneath the bed and tore down the stairs again and into the kitchen.

Delilah was there. Shannon ignored her as she packed her own food, then she hurried over and hugged Delilah fiercely. "Take good care of Gabe, Delilah."

"Shannon, Shannon, you shouldn't be going! I thought that he would know, I thought that he would stop you—"

"No one can stop me, Delilah. You know that. Please, please, promise to take good care of the baby!"

"You know that I will, missy, you don't need to say a word."

"I know that. Oh, Delilah, you and Samson were God sent! I don't know what we'd ever have done without you."

"You might not be able to run off like this."

"Delilah, she's my sister. I have to go for her."

Shannon kissed Delilah quickly on the cheek, swept up her bags and left the kitchen.

In the hallway she plucked the second Colt from the wall and stuffed her bag full of ammunition. Delilah hovered behind her.

"Shannon, you take care, young lady. Don't go off impetuously and get yourself in trouble, you hear?"

Shannon nodded and threw the door open. She started to hurry out, and she hurried straight into Malachi's waiting arms.

"Malachi!"

"Shannon!"

He set her back on her feet, a broad, smiling barrier in the doorway. He took her saddlebags from her hands. "Going somewhere tonight, Miss McCahy?"

"Yes!"

She tried to snatch the bags from him. His smile faded from his face, and he tossed the saddlebags on the floor of the porch. The sound reverberated, but neither of them heard it. Their eyes were locked.

"Malachi Slater—"

"You aren't coming, Shannon."

"Damn you, you can't—"

"I am sorry, Miss McCahy, but what I can't do is let you get yourself killed."

"Malachi—" She cried out in soft and wary warning. He stepped forward anyway and dipped low, catching her in the midriff and throwing her over his shoulder.

"Put me down, you damn Reb!" she ordered him. He just kept walking. She pummeled his back. "Malachi, Slater, you—"

"Shut up, Shannon."

"Scurvy bastard—"

His hand landed firmly upon her derriere. "This is such a delectable position!" He laughed, his footsteps falling upon the stairs.

She burst out with every oath she knew, beating savagely against his shoulders. He didn't seem to feel a thing, protected as he was by the heavy padding of his greatcoat.

Despite her wild fight, they came quickly to the second floor. His long strides brought them down the corridor to her room. He pushed the door open, and a second later tossed her hard upon her bed. Her skirts and petticoats flew around her, and she scrambled first for some dignity, pressing them down.

"Temper, temper, Shannon," he murmured.

"Temper!" She jumped to her knees, facing him. He arched a brow but didn't take a single step back. He seemed to be waiting for her next move, just waiting.

Shannon smiled and sank down on her pillows, comfortably crossing her arms over her chest. "Go ahead. Lock me in."

"I intend to."

"Aren't you forgetting?" she said sweetly. "This is so very foolish. The second that you're really gone, I will crawl right through that window. Now, it would just make so much more sense if you would be a reasonable man and—what are you doing?"

Shannon sat up, tensing, for he had turned away from her and was prowling through her drawers.

"Malachi?" She rose to her knees again, then leaped from the bed, accosting him. She pulled his hand out of her top drawer. A pair of her knit hose dangled from his hands.

"You're letting me come?" she said curiously. Then she realized from the grim determination on his features that he had no intention of letting her come. She still wasn't sure just what he meant to do.

Then he reached for her, sweeping her off her feet and plopping her down on her bed once again.

"Malachi, no!"

"Shannon, darlin', I'm sorry, yes!"

She let out a spate of oaths again, struggling fiercely against him. She didn't have much chance. He quickly had a grip on her wrists. No matter how she swore and raged and resisted, he tied them to the bedposts with her own knit stockings.

"I'll get you for this, Malachi Slater!"

"Maybe you will."

"I hope that your leg rots and falls off. Then I hope that the infection spreads, and that everything else rots and falls off."

Leaning over her, securing the last of the knots, he smiled. "Shannon, I don't think that was a very ladylike comment."

She narrowed her eyes. "This is no gentlemanly thing to do."

When he was done, he sat back, satisfied. She stared at him in trembling fury. A frightening and infuriating vulnerability drove her to try to kick him. He laughed and inched forward. He touched her cheek gently, almost tenderly.

"You're not coming, Shannon. I tried to warn you."

"Don't you dare touch me. Let me loose."

"You look lovely in bed."

"Get off my bed!"

"All that passion! It's quite—stirring, by God, Shannon, it is. I hope it remains if I'm ever tempted to take you into my bed."

"Malachi Slater, I promise you," Shannon grated out, straining at the bonds that tied her wrists and staring at him with rage and tears clouding her eyes, "the only way you'd ever get me into your bed would be to knock me out cold and then tie me to it!" She jerked hard upon her wrist.

He laughed, rose and bowed to her deeply, sweeping down his

plumed hat. Then he came very close, and suddenly teased her forehead with the briefest touch. It might have been a kiss.

"Miss McCahy, I promise you. If I ever decide to bring you to bed, no ties or binds will be needed."

She gritted her teeth. "Get out!"

He swept his hat atop his head and offered her his slanted, rueful smile.

"Take care, Shannon. Who knows? Maybe the possibilities are worth exploring." He paused for a second. "And I promise you, darlin', that I will not let anything rot and fall off."

With that, he turned and left her.

Chapter Four

"**Y**ou can't just leave me tied like this!" Shannon called in amazement to him as the door closed in his wake. She bit lightly into her lower lip. "*I* could rot and fall off and die!"

She heard the husky sound of his easy laughter—and the twist of the key in the door. "Delilah will be up in a few hours. You won't die, Shannon." He seemed to hesitate. "And you might well do so if you were to come with me. Delilah isn't going to let you go until my trail is as cold as ice, so just behave."

"Malachi!"

It was too late. He had gone. She could hear his footsteps as he pounded down the stairs.

With a cry of pure exasperation, Shannon jerked hard upon her wrists, then slammed her head against her pillow. Tears formed in her eyes.

How could she have been so incredibly stupid?

She tried to breathe deeply, to regain a sense of control. She stared at her left wrist, then tried to free it. He was good with knots, she determined. The ties did not hurt her, but they seemed impossible to loosen.

She fell back in exasperation.

There had to be some way out of it. There had to be.

She stared at the ceiling for several long minutes. The best she could come up with was a fairly dirty trick, but she had to try it.

She waited. This time, she wanted to make sure that he was gone. She waited longer.

Then she screamed, high-pitched, long and hard and with a note of pure terror.

Within seconds, Delilah burst in upon her, her dark skin gray with fear. "Shannon! What is it?"

"Beyond my window! Right outside! There's someone here, oh, I know it, Delilah!"

Shannon lowered her lashes quickly. She wondered if God would ever forgive her for the awful scare she was giving Delilah, then she figured that most men and women who had survived the war had a few sins on their consciences—God was just going to have to sort them all out. He would understand, after all they had been through, that she had to go after her sister herself, come what may.

"Outside, now?" Delilah whispered.

"Let me up before someone gets in!" Shannon urged her. She was whispering, too, and she didn't know why. It didn't make much sense, not after her blood-curdling scream.

Delilah hurried over to the bed, clicking her tongue as she worked on Shannon's left-hand knot. "Lord, child, but that man can tie a good knot!"

"Get a knife. There's a little letter opener in my top drawer. It's probably sharp enough."

Delilah nodded, hurrying. She came back and started sawing away at the stocking. "Yes, he sure can tie a knot!" she murmured once again.

"I know," Shannon said bleakly. Then she looked up, and her eyes met Delilah's.

Delilah jumped back, dropping the letter opener and shaking her finger at Shannon. "Why, you young devil! This whole thing was a ploy!"

Delilah had nearly severed the knot. Shannon yanked hard and managed to split the rest of the fibers. The letter opener was within her reach on the bed. She grabbed it before Delilah could reach it, and quickly severed the second bind.

Then she was free.

"Shannon McCahy—"

"I love you, Delilah," Shannon said, quickly hugging her and giving her a kiss on the cheek. "Take care of Gabe."

"Shannon, don't you go getting yourself killed! Your death will be on my conscience! Oh, Lord, but your poor pa must be rolling over in his grave!"

"Pa would understand," Shannon said, then she hurried from the room. She had lost a lot of time. Malachi would ride hard at night. It wouldn't be easy to catch up with him. Not that she wanted to meet up with him tonight. She just wanted to find him so that she could follow along behind him.

She hurried down the stairs. Delilah had picked up her saddlebags from the porch and dragged them into the hallway. Shannon knelt and checked her belongings. She reached into the top drawer beneath the empty Colt brackets and found matches and added them to her bags.

Delilah had followed her downstairs. Once again, Shannon hugged her.

"Come home soon," Delilah said.

"If Matthew comes, you tell him what happened. Maybe, maybe Matt can do something if the rest of us fail."

"Shannon—"

"We're not going to fail." She gave Delilah a brief, hard hug and hurried out of the house.

Entering the stables seemed strange, even just seeing the hay bales where she had fallen beneath Malachi.

She was startled to discover that she had paused and imagined the two of them as they had been that night, so very close in the hay. A curious heat swept over her, because she was remembering him as a man. The touch of his hands, the curve of his smile. The masculine scent of him. The husky tones of his voice.

She pressed her hands against her cheeks with shame. She wasn't in love with Malachi Slater. She didn't even like him. She had hated him for years.

But that wasn't what disturbed her. What disturbed her was a sense of disloyalty. She had been in love. Deeply in love. So in love that when she had heard of Robert's death, she had wanted to die herself. She had ceased to care about the war; she had ceased to care about the very world.

And now her cheeks were heating because Malachi Slater had spent the night touching her...

In anger, she reminded herself.

But with laughter, too, and with a new tension. And he had teased and taunted her.

And promised her things.

He had whispered against her flesh, and his words had often been husky and warm. She had never denied him his dashing charm or, in her heart, his bold masculinity.

She had just never realized how deeply it could touch her as a woman.

Her breath seemed to catch in her throat and she emitted a soft sound of annoyance with herself. He was a Rebel, and he was Malachi, and she would never forgive him for being either. She needed him tonight. And she would find him.

She quickly assessed the horses in the stables. She chose not to take Arabesque, her own mare, for the horse was a dapple gray, a color that glowed in the moonlight. She patted the mare quickly. "Not this time, sweetheart. I need someone dark as the night, and fleet as a bullet. Hmm..."

She had to hurry.

Without wasting further time, she decided on Chapperel, a swift and beautiful animal, part Arabian, part racer, nearly seventeen hands high and able to run like lightning.

He was also as black as jet, as black as the night.

"Come on, boy, we're going for a ride," she told the gelding, as she quickly saddled and bridled him and led him from the stables.

She looked at the sky. There was barely a sliver of a moon, but the stars were bright. Still, the trail would be very dark. It would be almost impossible for her to track Malachi.

But maybe it wouldn't be so hard to track the twenty horses that had raced before him. They had headed west—that much she knew for a fact.

And they would be staying off the main roads, she thought.

The Red Legs who had taken Kristin might still be a part of the Union army, and then again, they might not. No Union commander in his right mind was going to sanction the kidnapping of young women. No, these people had to be outlaws...

And they wouldn't be taking the main roads. They would be heading west by the smaller trails, and that was what she would do, too.

How much of a lead did Malachi have on her? An hour at most.

Shannon nudged the gelding, and he broke instantly into a smooth and swift canter.

And seconds later, he was galloping. The night wind cooled Shannon's face and touched her with the sweet fragrance of the earth. The darkness swept around her as she crossed the ranch and then the open plain.

Then it was time to choose a trail. She ignored the main road where the wagons headed west and where, over the past years, armies had marched by with their cannons and caissons. There was a smaller trail, rough and ragged and barely discernible, through the trees.

She reined in and dismounted and moved close to the ground, picking up a clump of earth. There were hoof marks all around.

She rose and felt a newly broken branch.

This was the trail she would take.

Malachi knew Missouri like the back of his hand.

He knew the cities, and he knew the Indian territories, and the farmlands and ranches. He could slip through Kentucky and Arkansas and even parts of Texas with his eyes nearly closed.

But these boys were moving west into Kansas. In another hour, they'd be over the border.

And he was an ex-Confederate cavalry captain, still wearing his uniform jacket.

He should have changed it. He should have accepted Shannon's offer of a civilian jacket, but somehow, he had been loathe to part with the uniform. He'd been wearing it for too many years. He'd ridden with too many good men, and he'd seen too many of them shot down in the prime of life, to forget the war. It was over. That was what they said. Abraham Lincoln had said that they must bind the wounds. "With malice towards none, with justice for all."

But then Old Abe had been gunned down, too, and in the blink of an eye, the South had begun to see what was going to be.

She was broken; she was laid to waste. Northern opportunists and plain old crooks swept down upon the fine manors and mansions, and liquor-selling con men were stirring up the ex-slaves to wage a new kind of war against their former masters. Homes and farms were being seized; men and women and children were starving in much of the devastated South.

No...

He probably shouldn't be heading into Kansas in a Confederate jacket. It was just damned hard to take it off. They didn't have a whole lot left. Just pride.

He had fought in the regular cavalry. Fought hard, and fought brilliantly. They had often hung on against impossible odds. They had a right to be proud, even in defeat.

And maybe, even in Kansas, he might have been able to ride through in his uniform if he wasn't who he was. If there hadn't been wanted posters out on him. But if he found himself picked up by the law because of his pride, he wouldn't be able to do Kristin any good, he would probably be hanged, and his pride would definitely be worthless stuff.

Tomorrow, he would pick up some clothes someplace. He'd be much better off traveling as a simple rancher. Displaced, maybe. An ex-Reb. He wouldn't be so damned obvious.

Not that he meant to be in Kansas long. He would get Kristin and get out. There would be plenty of places, deep in Missouri, to hide out until he found Cole and Jamie and decided what to do.

A swift gray shadow seemed to fall over his heart.

They would probably have to leave the country. Head down to Mexico, or over to Europe. The thought infuriated him. The injustice of it was absurd, but no one was going to give any of the Slater brothers a chance to explain. That son of a bitch Fitz had branded them, and because they were Rebs, the brand was going to stick.

Malachi reined in suddenly. In the distance, far ahead, he could see the soft glow of a new fire.

The Red Legs had stopped to make camp for the night.

He nudged the bay mare forward once again. He had been riding hard for hours, and it was nearly midnight, but they still had a certain distance on him.

Carefully, warily, Malachi closed that distance.

When the crackling fires were still far ahead of him, he dismounted from the bay. He whispered to the horse and dropped the reins, then started forward on foot.

The Red Legs had stopped in a large copse right beside a slim stream. Coming up behind them through the trees, Malachi found a close position guarded by a large rock and hunkered down to watch.

There were at least twenty men. They were busy cooking up beans and a couple of jackrabbits on two separate spits. A number of the men had lain down against their saddles before the fire, but a number of them were on guard, too. Three men were watching the horses, tethered to the left of the stream. As he looked across the clearing, Malachi could see two of them against the trees.

They were armed with the new Spencer repeating rifles. They would be no easy prey.

Looking around again, he saw the worst of it.

Kristin was tied to a tree near the brook. Her beautiful blond hair tumbled around her face, but her skin was white and her eyes were closed. She was exhausted, and desolate...

And guarded by two men.

Even as Malachi watched, the situation changed. The tall, burly man who had taken her from the house was walking her way. He bent beside her. Her eyes flew open and she stared at him with stark hatred. The man laughed.

"Sweet thing, I just thought that you might be hungry."

"Hungry for the likes of you, eh, Bear?" shouted a tall, lean dirty blond with a scruffy mustache. He stood up and sauntered toward the tree. He leaned down by Kristin, too. "Sweet, sweet thing. My, my, why don't you come on over and have dinner with me? Roger Holstein, ma'am—"

Kristin spit at him. A roar of laughter went up, and the young man's face darkened with fury. He lunged for her.

The man he'd called Bear pulled him back. "You keep your hands off her."

"Why? We weren't even supposed to bring her back. We were supposed to find Cole Slater. So you tell me why I can't have the woman."

Another man by the fire stood up. "Why should you have her, Holstein? What's the matter with the rest of us?"

"No one's gonna have her, and that's the way I say it is!" Bear bellowed, and Malachi slumped against the rock, relieved. Bear took a step toward Roger Holstein, shaking his fist. "You listen, and you listen good. The woman is mine. I took her. And I'm still the law in this unit—"

"Hell!" Roger Holstein muttered. "We ain't no unit anymore. The war is over."

"We're a unit. We're a unit because we belong to Fitz, just like we always have. And I was there that day Cole Slater shot down Henry and half a troop. He ain't no fool. If he hears that she's already been abused by you pack of trash, he'll take his time. He'll come after us slow and careful. And he won't be alone. He's got a pair of brothers who can pick the eyes out of hummingbirds in the next damn state with their Colts." Bear hesitated, looking at Kristin. "We don't hurt the woman."

"Hell, Bear, I wasn't going to hurt her!" Roger complained. "I was gonna make her have a hell of a good time!"

"You don't touch her. Fitz decides what to do with her. By my mind, leaving the lady her tender flesh and sweet chastity will come in real handy as bargaining power."

For a moment, Malachi thought that fighting was going to break out right then. He prayed silently that it would not; he would never be able to slip away with Kristin if it did.

He didn't think that his prayers would be answered. The tension among the men was as thick as flies on a steer carcass. It escalated until every man in the place was silent, until only the sound of the crackling fires could be heard.

Then Roger Holstein backed down.

"Have it your way, Bear. We'll see. When we get back to Fitz, we'll see."

"Damned right, we will," Bear agreed.

Malachi looked at Kristin. Her eyes were closed again. She was silent and probably grateful that the situation had calmed.

Thank God it was Kristin there and not Shannon. Shannon was

incapable of keeping silent. She would be raging and fighting and biting and kicking and creating complete disaster.

Malachi sank against the rock, closing his eyes, exhaling slowly. He wondered what had made him think of Shannon.

The whole damned night had been filled with Shannon, he reminded himself wryly. But she was safe. Delilah would just be releasing her sometime around now. And she would know that there would be no way in hell to follow a trail that cold.

Thank God it wasn't Shannon? he queried himself. Hmph! If it had been Shannon, he wouldn't be here now. He wouldn't be sneaking into Kansas in his Confederate uniform. He'd be headed south. If it had been Shannon kidnapped, he would have pitied the damned Red Legs.

No, she surely hadn't been a Circe this evening. She had been a complete spitfire, stubborn, willful and...

Beautiful.

Just like the woman in his dream, the sweet vision who had brought him from the brink of death. She was beautiful, perhaps even more beautiful than Kristin, for she was a searing flame, with a life so vibrant that her golden hair was touched by the fire, as were her eyes, brilliant, sparkling, searing. Her voice was like a lark's, sweet and pure...even when she yelled.

Actually, he wasn't thinking about her eyes.

He was thinking about her hands, and the tenderness in her fingers when she had cleansed and bound his wound.

No...

He wasn't even thinking about that.

He was thinking about the provocative swell of her breasts when she leaned over him, when she brushed against him. He was thinking of the lithe and shapely heat of her body, the slimness of her waist, the softness of her flesh, the full sensuality of her lips.

Shannon had grown up.

He slunk down into the rock, pulling his hat low over his forehead. She was still Shannon McCahy. The little brat who had been on his tail since he had first walked onto the McCahy ranch. She had fired at him that very first time, and she was firing at him still.

He smiled and leaned back.

He had kissed her once. To shut her up. They were all playing innocent when a Yank officer had come by the ranch, and Shannon, bless her sweet, sweet hide, would have gladly handed him right over.

And so he had kissed her.

It did seem to be the only way to shut her up.

But the kiss had been sweet. Her passion then had been that of anger, but passion nevertheless, and it had feathered against his senses until he had realized who she was, and what he was doing.

But now, tonight, he remembered that kiss.

He opened his eyes and clamped his teeth together. He knotted his fingers into fists and then slowly released them, suddenly aware that he wanted her. That he desired her, hotly, hungrily and completely.

Wanting a woman wasn't so strange, he reminded himself. Over the years, he had wanted a number of women, and, during the war, when lovers were quickly won and lovers quickly lost, many young women, like many men, were quick to seek the solace of the moment. The women he had wanted he had often had. The widow in Arkansas, the desolate, lonely farm woman in Kentucky, the dance-hall girl in Mississippi.

Once, it seemed like a long, long time ago now, there had been a girl he had loved. Ariel Denison. Ariel... He had even loved the sound of her name. They had been very young. The sight of him could bring a flush to her cheeks, and the warmth of her dark eyes upon him alone could bring forth all the ardor in his heart and soul. Her father had approved, and they were to have been married in June. They spent what May days they could together, hand in hand, racing down to the stream, daring to swim together, daring to come to the shore and lie naked in the sweet grasses, making love. He'd never known anything so deep, or so wonderful...

But by June, she was gone. A cholera epidemic swept through the countryside, and Ariel, smiling to the last, had died in his arms, whispering her last words of love with the last of her breaths. He had not cared then if he contracted the disease. He hadn't cared at all, but he had lived. Since then, he hadn't fallen in love again. He had given his passion to his land; his loyalty had been to his family and, once the war came, to the Confederacy.

He didn't remember much about love...

But no man lived long without desire. He was used to that. So it was strange to discover with what depth and fervor he desired Shannon.

The brat. His foremost enemy. The ardent, fanatical Unionist. The bane of his every trip to the ranch. Shannon...

"Hey!" came a sudden, loud shout. "Did you hear that?"

Malachi turned around, looking over the rock toward the camp. The guards by the horses were moving. Half the men had begun to settle down for the evening.

Now they were waking up.

Bear strode toward the guards. "What? What is it? I don't hear anything."

"There's something there. Something out in the bushes."

They had seen him. They had heard him, Malachi thought.

But they hadn't. The guard was pointing in the other direction.

"You scared of a bobcat or a weasel?" Bear sneered.

"It weren't no weasel!" the guard protested.

Bear paused, then shrugged. He looked at two of the men. "You, Wills, and you, Hartman, go take a look around. The rest of you, keep your eyes open."

Hell! Malachi thought. If they went snooping around too far, they would find the bay. He cursed whatever creature had been sneaking around the camp. If it was a weasel, he hoped some poor bastard ate the creature.

He sank against his rock. They weren't going to look for him there, not right beneath their noses. He was going to have to sit tight and wait. If they would just settle down for the night, even with the guards on duty, he would be able to reach Kristin. Once the camp was quiet, he would be able to circle around and come at her from the stream. He would have to kill the guards by the horses; he wouldn't have any choice.

Malachi frowned suddenly, feeling the earth beneath his hands. He lay against the ground and listened to the tremors of the earth.

Someone else was out riding that night. Not too far distant, a group of horsemen was coming toward them.

A Union patrol?

He thought they were still in Missouri, but they might have crossed over the border. They had really headed south as much as they had headed west. Not that it mattered much. Union patrols were everywhere.

But it could also be a Southern outfit, heading home.

Maybe it didn't matter. Maybe it did.

He tensed, waiting.

Then a shrill and furious scream caught his attention. He swung around, looking into the center of the Red Legs camp.

"Son of a bitch!" he swore beneath his breath, staring. "If they leave behind just a piece of her, I'm going to skin her alive!"

Shannon had just been thrown into the center of the camp. Hartman and Wills had brought her, and with laughter and gusto cast her with force into the den of rogues.

Wills was limping, swearing away.

"She shot off my toe!" he howled.

"Thank God she can't aim," Roger said, chortling.

"I did aim, you stupid ass," Shannon said with venom. "If I'd have wished it, I'd have shot out your heart."

Wills went silent; even Roger went silent. There was a chill around them all, as if they knew her words to be the truth.

"Get down there, witch!" Wills swore savagely. He shoved her down, hard.

She landed on her knees. She had changed clothing, and wore tight black trousers, a gingham tailored shirt and a pair of sturdy brown boots. She'd worn a hat, a broad-brimmed hat, but now it lay several feet from her in the dust. Her hair had been pinned, but the pins were strewn around her, and her hair was falling, like a golden sunrise, in delicate rays down her back.

Malachi bit hard into his lip as she raised her chin to face Bear, all her heat and fury and passion alive in her eyes. She shouldn't have changed. The perfection of her form was even more apparent in the tight breeches and man's shirt, and he was not the only one to notice. The Red Legs were all rising, one by one, creating a circle around her.

"My, my, my," Roger Holstein drawled. He moved his tongue over his lips. "What have we here?" He stepped out of the circle, coming toward her. Shannon struggled quickly to her feet. Malachi tensed, watching the sizzle in her eyes.

"Don't be stupid, Shannon!" he muttered to himself. "Be quiet, be good, let them tie you up and I can get you out...don't be stupid!"

But she was going to be stupid. Roger reached for her, and Shannon moved like lightning, sinking her teeth into his hand. He screamed with pain, then caught her with his backhand, sending her spiraling into the dirt. "Bitch!" he roared.

The men laughed like hyenas. "Least she didn't shoot you, Roge!" Wills said.

Roger came forward again, sucking at his sore hand.

"Get away from her," Bear ordered, coming into the center of the ring.

"Oh, no, you don't," Roger said with hostility. "That one is for Fitz. Fine. This one is mine."

"I'll die first, I swear it!" Shannon hissed from the ground. She seemed to sense that her only hope was Bear. Holding her cheek, she rose and raced behind him. "I'll kill you—"

"Yeah, watch it, man, the little lady will bite you to death!" someone jeered.

"Get out of my way, Bear!" Roger howled. "She's mine!"

"No!"

"You've got Slater's wife—"

"This is his sister-in-law, you idiot."

Roger paused to look from one woman to the other. It was impossible to miss the resemblance. "So they're sisters. So what of it?"

Kristin called out then. "You touch her, and I'll kill myself, you bastard! Then you'll have nothing, nothing at all—"

"Kristin!"

Shannon burst through the throng of men, racing for her sister. Bear caught her just before she could get to Kristin's side. He swept her up by the waist, laughing. "Little darlin'!" he exclaimed. "If you go to anybody, sweet pea, you go to old papa bear!"

He reached up with one of his great hands and clutched the front of her shirt, tearing. Shannon screamed and savagely swung a kick his way.

She did know how to aim.

With a tremendous groan, Bear dropped her and doubled over. Shannon pulled his gun from his holster and swung around, facing the men, who were all on their feet.

"Don't take a chance," she warned them, backing carefully toward Kristin. "I know what I'm doing with this thing."

"You can't kill us all," Roger told her, but he didn't take another step her way.

"I can castrate at least six of you," Shannon promised, and at least six of the men took a step backward.

"Now, all that I want is my sister," Shannon began. She kept talking, but Malachi no longer heard her words because there was movement behind her. One of the guards watching the horses had drawn his knife and was sneaking up behind her.

"Damn!" Malachi mouthed. He couldn't shoot at the man; Shannon was in the way. If she would move...just a hair.

She didn't. The guard came up behind her and slipped the knife around her quickly, right at her throat, against her jugular.

"Castrate us!" Roger chortled as she dropped the gun. "Why, honey, we're all going to make you glad that you didn't—"

The man with the knife moved. Just enough.

Damn her, damn her, damn her, Malachi thought. They were probably all dead now. But he couldn't wait any longer.

He rose and he fired. He got the guard right between the eyes. The man fell.

Shannon reached down for the gun she had dropped. Confusion reigned as men rushed toward her, as men looked around, anxious to discover who had fired the shot.

Malachi kept shooting. He didn't have any choice. He tried to aim and focus and to keep a good eye on Shannon, too. Men fell, and men screamed, and dust flew. But there were too many of them, just too many of them.

Shannon had been holding her own. But in the midst of the melee, Bear stumbled to his feet. He staggered toward Shannon from the rear while another man approached her from the front. She aimed forward...

And Bear took a firm swipe against her arm, sending the gun flying. She turned to fight, and he punched her hard in the mouth. Her eyes closed and she slumped to the ground.

"Get him! Get that varmint in the woods!" Bear ordered.

"Varmint?" Malachi stood up, staring at Bear. "Excuse me, you jayhawking jackals. Captain Malachi Slater, late of Hunt's magnificent cavalry, and still, my friends, a Southern gentleman. Shall we?"

"It's a damned Reb!" one of the guards shouted.

"It's more than that. It's a damned Reb Slater!" Bear roared. "Kill him!"

Well, this is it, Malachi thought. Shannon had wanted him to die for honor, and he would just have to go down that way. He stood, firing again and again as the Red Legs raced toward him, trying to fire, but failing. He ran out of bullets as a pair of them charged over the rocks, but he had his saber with him, and he drew that. He charged in turn, and managed to kill the first two men, but more of them were coming for him, more and more...

He was engaged with one fighter when he noticed a carbine aimed his way. He wasn't even going to have time to ask forgiveness of his sins, he thought. No time to mourn...

A blast sounded.

It was the Yank holding the carbine who fell, and not Malachi. Amazed, he looked around.

Hoofbeats! He had heard the hoofbeats! And now the riders were upon them.

"It's a pack of Red Legs!" shouted a man leaping into the scene on a dapple gray stallion. "Red Legs! Bloody, bleeding, murderin', connivin' Red Legs!"

"Reg Legs!" came another shout.

And they all let out with a sound near and dear to Malachi at that moment.

A Rebel cry went up. Savage, sweet, beautiful to his ears.

He watched as the six horsemen charged the scene. They were in plumed hats and railroad coats, no uniforms, and yet he thought he knew who they were. He was sure that he recognized the young man on the dapple gray mare.

He did. These boys had been with Quantrill. He knew two of them. Frank and Jesse James. Jesse had been a bare kid when he had tasted his first blood, but then lots of boys had become men quickly in the war.

Now this little group was probably headed home, toward southern Missouri. They still seemed young. Even with the war over. But then, Quantrill had depended on young blood, youthful, eager, savage raiders.

Quantrill was dead now. Bloody Bill Anderson was dead, and Little Archie Clement was dead. Archie who had loved to scalp his enemies. Archie had been with the bushwhackers who had so savagely mowed down the contingent of Union officers sent to catch them, the contingent that had included Shannon's fiancé...

Well, Malachi didn't think much of bushwhackers, but these boys had come just in time. Maybe Shannon would accept rescue. Maybe she would keep her mouth closed. But he had to get to her.

He could barely see through the tangle of fighting men and horses, bushwhackers and jayhawkers. He rose, staring over the wavering light of the fires.

He heard a high-pitched scream, and his heart thudded painfully.

He looked between a pair of horses as they danced, a deadly dance for their riders. In the gap he could see Bear. The man was cutting Kristin loose from the tree and throwing her over his shoulder.

Roger Holstein broke away from the battle and joined Bear. Wills, with his bloody toe, ran after them, too.

"Damn it, no!" Malachi swore. Where was Shannon? He couldn't see her. Did the bushwhackers have her, too?

No, they didn't, not that group, anyway. Bear and Holstein and Wills had mounted and pulled away. They were heading fast for the trail, heading west.

"Damn it, no!" Malachi raged again, pushing his way through the warring bushwhackers and jayhawkers, racing toward the Union horses. Bear was gone with Kristin, long gone before he could reach them.

"Malachi!"

It was Shannon. He whirled around in time to see one of the James brothers racing along beside her and sweeping her up onto his mount.

"Hey, you got yourself a girl, Frank!" One of the other riders laughed.

"Not just a girl, Jessie! D'you know who this is?"

"Who?"

"That Yankee-lovin' McCahy brat! Had herself hitched up to one for a while, before we did him in—ouch!" he screamed, looking down at the girl thrown over his saddle, then up at his brother again. "She bites."

"Yellow-bellied bushwhackers!" Shannon screamed. But Malachi sensed something different in her screams, in the sound of her voice.

He heard the pain.

She knew now that these men had been there the day when Robert Ellsworth had been killed, and she would never ask for their mercy.

"Shannon!" he thundered her name over the clash of steel and the explosion of gunfire.

"Let's go!" Frank shouted. He fired a number of shots into the air.

Malachi had swung around, racing toward Frank, when one of the Red Legs jumped in front of him, his sword drawn.

He didn't have time for a fight!

The mounted bushwhackers were gathering together. They had come, they had done their damage. Now they were riding away.

The Red Legs with the sword lunged toward Malachi.

"Ah, hell!" Malachi swore, engaging in the battle. The fellow wasn't a bad swordsman. In fact, he did damned well.

He grinned at Malachi as their swords locked at the hilt. "West Point, class of '58."

"Good for you, ya bloody Yank!" Malachi retorted. He pulled away, parrying a sudden thrust, ducking another.

The riders were pounding farther and farther away, into the night.

"You're good, Reb!" his opponent called.

"Thanks, and you're in my way, Yank," Malachi replied.

"In your way? Why, you're almost dead, man!"

"No, sir, you are almost dead."

Always fight with a cool head...

It had been one of the first rules that Malachi had ever learned. His comment had provoked his opponent. It was the advantage he needed.

The Red Legs lifted his sword high for a smashing blow. Malachi thrust straight, catching the man quickly and cleanly through the heart.

He fell without a whimper.

Malachi pulled his sword clean and leaped away from his fallen foe, swinging to counter any new attack.

But he was alone.

Alone with a sea of corpses.

At least twelve of the Red Legs lay dead, strewn here and there over their camp bags, over their saddles, over their weapons; some shot and some thrust through by swords. Only one of the raiders lay on the ground. A very young boy with a clear complexion.

He groaned. Malachi stooped beside him, carefully turning him over. Blood stained his shirt. Malachi opened it quickly. There was no way the boy could live. He'd been riddled with shot in the chest. Malachi pressed the tail ends of the shirt hard against him, trying to staunch the flow of blood. The boy opened his eyes.

"I'm going to die, captain, ain't I?"

He might have said something else, but the boy already knew. Malachi nodded. "The pain will be gone, boy."

"I can't die. I got tobacco in my pocket. Ma would just kill me. That's a laugh, ain't it? But she'd be awful, awful disappointed in me."

"I'll get that tobacco out, boy," Malachi said.

The youth's eyes had already closed again. Malachi thought that the boy had heard him, though. It seemed that his lip curled into a grateful smile just as the life left his eyes.

Malachi eased the boy to the ground. Someone would come, and someone would find him.

This was border country still. He might be sent to his home.

Malachi dug the tobacco out of the boy's pocket and tossed it over one of the older Red Legs. "Your ma won't find no tobacco, boy," he said softly. Then he stood and he looked around at the sea of dead again.

The clearing was absurdly silent and peaceful now. Its inhabitants all lay quiet, tumbled atop one another as if they rested in a strange and curious sleep. He walked among them quickly, cursing to himself, but he couldn't just leave a man if he was wounded, whether he was a Reb or a Yank.

He needn't have worried. Every one of the Red Legs in the clearing was dead. Dead, and growing cold.

Malachi stepped from the clearing and looked down the road. He stared up at the night sky. The silence was all around him. The sound of horses' hooves had died away in the distance.

"Damn!" he swore.

The Red Legs had taken Kristin in one direction.

The raiders had taken Shannon the opposite way.

Which the hell did he follow?

He didn't take long to decide. He would get Shannon first. He could bargain with the James boys, he was sure. If Shannon could keep quiet for about two seconds he could get her back quickly. He would go after Shannon first.

Though for the life of him, he wasn't at all sure why.

Chapter Five

Shannon could not remember a more miserable night in her life.

The raider party traveled through what remained of it. Somewhere, at the beginning, she had said something that the men really hadn't liked—though she couldn't see where they would like anything that she had to say to them—and she had been bound hand and foot and gagged and tossed over the haunches of the horse.

Then they had begun to ride, in earnest.

They knew their territory. They followed no specific route. They traveled over plains and through tangles of bracken and brush.

They talked about going home, and they talked about the friend they had left behind.

"Willie was dead, shot in the chest, there wasn't nothing that we could do. He went down fighting."

"Yeah, he went down fighting. Well, the war's over. Someone ought to find him and give his body to his ma."

"Yeah, someone ought to find him."

"God help him."

"God help us all."

For a while, Shannon listened to their words, but she couldn't believe that they would try to invoke God's aid, and then, as they kept on quietly conversing, she began to weave in and out of reality. She couldn't understand them anymore. She knew who they were. The remnants of Quantrill's Raiders. They had ridden with Quantrill. They had ridden with Bloody Bill Anderson, and with little Archie Clement.

They might well have been with the raiders on a bloody awful day outside Centralia when the bushwhackers had massacred the small contingent of green recruits sent after them. When they had dismembered the corpses and the dying, scalped them and sliced off ears and noses and privates to be stuffed down their throats...

It was how Captain Robert Ellsworth had died. And as she lay trussed and tossed over the haunches of the horse, it made her feel faint, and it made her feel ill.

The night went on and on.

Then Shannon realized that it wasn't night anymore, it was day. They had traveled miles and miles without rest, or if they had paused to rest, she had been unconscious when they had done so.

It was no longer night. It was day. The sun streamed overhead, and the songs of larks could be heard on the air. Somewhere nearby, a brook bubbled and played.

They had come so far. So very far. She wondered bleakly where Kristin was. She had been so certain that when the Red Legs had settled down and slept, she would have been able to slip in and free her sister.

But then the men had come for her.

And now Kristin was being taken one way, and she was being taken another.

And where was Malachi? He had been there. She had seen him firing and fighting, and then he had disappeared. And then she had seen him again just when she had been swept up into the arms of the bushwhacker.

He had probably followed Kristin, she thought. He had gone for his brother's wife. And she was glad of it, Shannon thought. She was so glad of it, because the men might well hurt Kristin...

What were these men going to do with her?

The gag choked her, making her feel ill all over again. They knew her. They knew that she was old McCahy's daughter, and that her sympathy had been with the North. They surely knew that she was Cole Slater's sister-in-law, but that probably wouldn't count for much. She had been engaged to marry a Union officer, she was the sister of a Union officer, and they knew that she hated them with every breath in her body.

What would they do to her?

And what could be worse than this torture she had already endured, hanging hour after hour over the horse this way, her face slamming against the sweaty flesh and hair and flanks of the animal? She ached in every muscle of her body. It would never, never end.

Then suddenly, at last, they stopped.

Hands wound around her waist, pulling her from the horse. Had she been able to, she would have screamed at the sudden agony of the movement; it felt as if her arms were breaking.

"There you go, Yank," the man said, setting her down beneath a tree. The others were dismounting. They formed a semicircle around her, all of them staring at her.

"What are we going to do with her, Frank?"

The man who asked the question stepped forward. His name was Jesse, Shannon knew that much. And he was Frank's brother. The two of them had spoken occasionally during the endless ride.

Neither of them was much older than she, but they both carried a curious coldness in their eyes. Perhaps they had ceased to feel; perhaps they had even lost a sense of humanity in all the violence of their particular war. She didn't know. And at that moment, she was so worn and exhausted, she wasn't even sure that she cared.

"I wonder what the Red Legs wanted with her," Jesse mused.

"Same thing any man would want with her, I reckon," someone spoke up from the rear. Shannon blinked, trying to see him. He was tall and dark-haired with a pencil-slim mustache, and he smiled at her in such a way that she felt entirely naked.

She closed her eyes. At that particular moment, she just wanted to die. Bushwhackers. The same men who had brutalized Robert might be about to touch her. Death would be infinitely better.

"Better loosen up that gag," the one named Jesse said. "We're losing her, I think. She's going to pass out on us."

Frank stepped forward, slipping the gag from her mouth. Shannon fought a sudden wave of nausea. He leaned over her and slit the ropes tying her wrists and ankles. Her blood started to flow again, but she could still barely move. She rubbed her wrists, backing against the tree, staring at the lot of them. There were five of them left. Jesse and Frank, Jesse with a round young face and dark, attractive eyes, Frank taller and leaner, older. There was the dark-haired man who taunted, and two smaller, light-haired men. Maybe they were brothers, too, she didn't know.

"What's your name?" Jesse asked.

She stared at him in furious silence. They seemed to know everything else. They ought to know her name.

"Shannon. Shannon McCahy," the tall, dark-haired one said. "She was picked up with her sister when the Federals decided to put all the families away. She was there when the house fell apart, when Bill's sister and those other girls were killed and wounded."

"Then she's a Southerner—" Jesse began.

Frank snorted and spit on the ground. "She ain't no Southerner, Jesse. You heard her. She's Yank through and through. Just like her blue-belly pa with the yellow streak down his back—"

Movement came back to her. She felt no pain. Like a bolt of lightning, Shannon flew at the man in a rage. She did so with such force that he went flying to the ground. "You murderers!" she hissed. "You hideous rodents...murderers!" Pummeling the startled man who couldn't seem to fight her fury, Shannon then saw the gun in his belt. She grabbed it and aimed it straight at his nose. The others had been about to seize her. She swung around with Frank's Colt, aiming it right at Jesse. He lifted his hands and backed away.

"We didn't kill your pa, little girl," Jesse said softly. "We weren't there. Zeke Moreau had his own splinter group. You know that."

She gritted her teeth, thinking about Robert, trembling inwardly at the depth of the hate that seared her. She could have pulled the trigger. She would have happily maimed or wounded or killed any one of them. When she thought about Centralia...

Jesse knelt in front of her, speaking earnestly. "You're just seeing one side of it, you know. One side. They came in—the jayhawkers, the Red Legs—they came in and ripped us all up really bad, too, you know. We all got farms burned down or kin slain. It always did work two ways—"

"Two ways!" Shannon exclaimed. "Two ways!" She was choking. "I never heard of anything as bad as Centralia. Ever. In the town, unarmed men were stripped and shot down. And outside the town, the things you people did to the Union men shouldn't have been done to the lowest of creatures, much less human beings—''

"You obviously haven't seen much of the handiwork done by your friends, the Red Legs," the tall, dark man said dryly.

"You ain't gonna change her mind," Frank said from the ground.

The dark-haired man moved closer, a wary eye on the Colt. "My name is Justin Waller, Miss McCahy. And I was there, at Centralia—''

"Bastard!" Shannon hissed.

"Justin—'' Jesse warned sharply, but Shannon already had the gun aimed straight between Justin Waller's eyes. She pulled the trigger.

And she heard the click of an empty chamber.

"Son of a bitch!" Justin swore. He reached for Shannon. She couldn't escape him quickly enough and he dragged her to her feet. She screamed as he twisted her arm hard behind her back.

"Justin—'' Jesse began.

"That bitch meant to kill me!"

"Don't hurt her. We don't know what we're doing with her yet."

"I know what I'm gonna do with her," Justin growled savagely. His free hand played over her throat and the rise of her breasts, which had been left bare when the Red Legs had ripped her shirt. The little pink flowers and white linen of her corset were absurdly delicate against the tattered fragments of the man's ranch shirt.

Shannon recoiled, kicking out desperately. Justin pulled harder upon her arm and she choked back another scream of pain. He pressed her to her knees. "Get me some rope, Jesse. I'm too damned tired to truly enjoy what I intend to do with this little beauty. And she can't be trusted an inch.''

Jesse lifted a length of rope from his saddle pommel, but he stared at Justin contemplatively as he walked toward him. "We ain't decided about her yet, Justin.''

"We ain't decided what?" Justin had his knee in Shannon's back as he looped the rope around her wrists.

She gritted her teeth against the pain.

"She's kin to Cole Slater," Jesse said softly. "And I never did cotton to the idea of rape and murder, Justin.''

"You rode with Quantrill."

"Quantrill didn't murder women."

"All right, Jesse. All right. I ain't gonna murder her."

"You're right, you ain't. I'm in control here."

"War's over, Jesse."

"I'm still in control here, you understand that."

Justin jerked hard on the rope, then shoved Shannon flat on the ground. She tasted dirt as he grasped her ankles and began looping a knot around them.

"Maybe we oughta just let her go," one of the light-haired men said. "Hell, Justin, we ain't supposed to rape our own kind—"

"She ain't our own kind. And if we just let her go, she'll have the law down on us so fast our heads will spin. That is, if she doesn't get hold of another gun. She shot at me, you fools. She meant to kill me. And you all say what you want, she's going to pay for that."

He jerked hard on the last of his knots. He reached for Shannon's shoulders and dragged her face up close to his. "Bitch, when I wake up, we're going to have some real, real fun."

Shannon spit at him.

Swearing, he wiped his face and tossed her down hard beneath the tree. He stared at the four others, who were looking his way. "And you all can watch, join in or turn the other way, I just don't give a damn."

Shannon watched Jesse James set his jaw hard. "I'm in control here, Justin. We agreed. Don't you forget that."

Justin ignored Jesse and went to his horse. He loosened his saddle and pulled it off and threw it beneath the tree next to Shannon. He fumbled through his saddlebags for a canteen. Looking furiously at the other men, he walked down a grassy slope to the fresh-running spring water of a stream.

"Water," Frank James muttered, following Justin.

Jesse remained, staring at Shannon. She didn't know what he was thinking. "Lots of people lost in this war," he told her quietly. "Hell, ma'am, I do not like half the things I learned to do, but I doubt that I'll ever forget them. We all want to remember the weddings and the christenings and the flowers in the fields on a Sunday.

Hell, I never really wanted to get so damned good at killing. I just did." He paused. "You shouldn'ta shot at Justin. It was a mistake."

"He's an animal. He was there—at Centralia. You heard him."

"You still shouldn't have tried to kill him. You got his temper up way high."

He turned away from her. Justin was back, drinking water from his canteen. It spilled over his face and trickled down his jaw. It reminded Shannon just how desperately thirsty she was. He stared at her, and she saw he knew of her thirst. He smiled and drank more deeply.

She wasn't going to beg. Not of a man like that.

Frank James was back by then, too. He was drinking from a wooden Confederate-issue canteen with his initials engraved into the wood. He looked at her, then knelt by her, lifting her head.

"Don't give her no water!" Justin said irritably. "I'll give it to her." He smiled, nudging at Shannon's rump with an evil leer. "If she's good, if she's real good, she'll get some water. You'll see, my friends. Old Justin knows how to take a Yankee shrew."

Frank ignored him, lifting Shannon's head, allowing a trickle of water to cool her face and seep into her mouth. She drank it thirstily.

"Frank!" Justin swore.

Frank told Justin what he should do with himself, and Justin jumped to his feet. Shannon watched the two men with interest, her heart thundering. If they would just rip each other to shreds...

Jesse, who was now leaning against the tree, paring off a bite of dried beef from a strip he'd taken from his saddlebags, spoke sarcastically. "That's good, you two. Real good. Kill each other. She's enjoying every minute of it."

Both men stopped. They stared at her.

"Let's all get some sleep," Jesse said. "You want her that bad, Justin, the girl's yours. But don't kill her. I ain't no murderer of women and children, and I ain't ever gonna be."

He stretched out on the ground, leaning his head upon his saddle. Frank swore and chose another tree.

The two light-haired men found their own shade, and Justin smiled as he settled down beside Shannon. She stared at him, her face against the earth, hating him. He laughed and reached out, slipping his arm around her, twisting her over and pulling her close against him. She squirmed and struggled, choking on the tears that threatened to stream down her face. "Bastard, I swear I'd just as soon die!" she hissed vehemently.

Justin laughed at her futile efforts. Tied hand and foot as she was, she wasn't going to do anything.

His hand hooked beneath her breasts as he pulled her against his chest and the curve of his body. His fingers played over her breasts and rested there. He whispered against her ear. "Just a few hours of sleep, honey. I apologize for being so exhausted. But just a little bit of sleep...I wouldn't want to disappoint you. I want to hear you scream and scream and scream..." Laughing again, he leaned his head back against his saddle, seeking sleep.

Shannon closed her eyes and set her teeth. She gave him time to fall asleep, then tried to edge away from him.

His hand tightened around her like a clamp. "Not on your life, my golden Yank. Not on your life." His fingers moved through her hair. Shannon held her breath, praying that he would stop.

He did. He dug into his saddlebags for another length of rope and grimly tied her wrists to his own. Shannon watched him in bitter silence. When he was done, he smiled and touched her cheek. "You're a beautiful Yank-lover, you know that?"

She ignored him. He lay down to sleep again, chuckling.

Shannon lay awake in misery until absolute exhaustion overwhelmed her. Despite her hunger and thirst and discomfort, she closed her eyes, and sleep claimed her.

To the best of Malachi's knowledge, there was no one on the lookout for the James boys.

But they were riding as if their lives depended on getting into the heart of Missouri just as fast as possible.

And they were hard to track. By the time he'd reached his bay and found Shannon's big black gelding, the raiders were already well ahead of him.

And they knew where they were going. Thank God they had turned southward, deeper into Missouri. It was land he knew. If he hadn't been accustomed to the terrain, he'd never have managed to follow them. They cut a course right through forest lands, knowing unerringly where they could take shortcuts and pick up roads again and disappear back into the forests again.

By midmorning he realized that they were following the course of a small stream. Malachi stuck with it.

He was exhausted. His leg was aching, and he was afraid that the fever might be searing through him again. An hour's worth of sleep just might make it a bit better...

But he didn't dare take an hour. He knew Frank and Jesse James only slightly. He'd met them once in the short time that Cole had ridden with Quantrill, and he'd found them to be reckless, sometimes ruthless kids. He thought it might be the Younger brothers traveling with them, another set of reckless youths.

He didn't think that the James boys were especially cruel or brutal. They were still sane, at least, he thought. Like the Younger brothers. They were probably still sane, if nothing else.

But the other man...

His name was Justin. Malachi knew who he was. Cole had seen him in action early on in the war, and the malice with which the man killed and the pleasure he took from his brutal actions had turned Cole away from Quantrill's gang completely.

But to the most decent bushwhacker out there, Shannon would be quite a tonic to swallow. And she wouldn't keep quiet. She wouldn't be able to do so. He had already heard her ranting and raving.

He didn't have time to rest, not for ten damn minutes.

He paused only to give the horses water, and to douse himself with it, and drink deeply. He chewed on the dried meat he had brought, and swallowed some of the liquor Shannon had packed him. It was good, and it helped to keep the pain in his leg at bay.

It was almost night again when he came upon them at last.

He was still a little distance away when he saw the horses grouped in the trees. There were no cooking fires laid out in the camp; in fact, it was barely a camp at all. The bushwhackers had merely stopped along the road.

Malachi was pretty sure that he'd be able to reason with the men; hell, at least they had obstensibly fought on the same side. But the war had taught him to take nothing for granted, so he dismounted from the bay and tethered her with the black gelding some distance down the stream from the raiders. Then he approached them again in silence, coming close enough this time to see the layout in the camp.

They must have been sure of themselves; very sure. No one was left on guard. Each and every one of the bushwhackers was curled up, sound asleep.

Or maybe they weren't so sound asleep. Men like that learned to sleep differently, with one eye open. If a fly buzzed through that camp, the men would probably be aware of it. He'd be a fool to go sneaking in, no matter how silently he could manage it.

And as he had suspected, Shannon was in trouble.

The Younger brothers were stretched out in front of an oak; the others were all laid out beneath other trees, thirty yards apart, and perhaps fifty yards up the grassy slope from the stream.

Shannon was bound hand and foot, and tied to Justin.

He swore inwardly, thinking she must have fought them tooth and nail, because she seemed to have lost Jesse's protection. Jesse, like many other bushwhackers, despite their savagery, still put Southern womanhood on a pedestal. If she had just kept her mouth closed and acted out the part of the Southern belle…

But she hadn't.

Sweat broke out on Malachi's forehead and his hands went clammy as he watched her. She was pale and smudged with dirt, but even so, her features retained their angelic beauty, and her tangled hair swept around her face like a glorious halo. Where the sun fell upon it her hair glowed like golden fire.

She was tied to Justin—but at least she was decently clad. She seemed to sleep the sleep of the dead, but even in that sleep, it seemed she strained with all her heart against the man holding her prisoner.

He hadn't touched her yet. Justin hadn't touched her, Malachi assured himself. But he meant to do so.

At the periphery of the circle, Malachi inhaled and exhaled deeply, deciding what plan of action to take. He could try shooting them all, but the bushwhackers were damned good shots, and if he didn't kill

Justin right away, he was certain that Justin would kill Shannon for the pure pleasure of it.

No. This wasn't the time to go in blazing away. He needed to play diplomat.

He stood at the periphery of the camp, his saber and his pistols at his side, but his arms relaxed. "Jesse. Jesse James!" he called out sharply.

They moved as one. As soon as he called out, the five of them were awake, staring at him down the length of their Colts and revolvers.

He lifted his hands. He saw five pairs of eyes look over his gray uniform jacket.

By the tree, Jesse stood.

"Malachi!" Shannon called out. "Malachi!" She struggled to rise. Justin jerked on the rope and clamped his hand hard over her mouth.

Malachi nodded toward Justin, trying to burn a message into Shannon's fool head with the strength of his eyes.

"Hey! It's the fool Reb who was taking on the whole of that Red Legs camp by himself!" One of the Younger brothers called out.

"Malachi. Malachi Slater," Jesse said. He walked forward, wary still, but a smile on his face. "You're Cole Slater's brother, right? Hey, they got a whole pack of wanted posters out on you, did you know that?"

"Yeah, I know it. But thanks for the warning."

"What are you doing here about? Heading south? It might be best if you were to take a hike into Mexico."

"Well," Malachi said, "I can't rightly do that yet, you know. I got to tie up with my brothers somewhere. And the Red Legs have got Cole's wife. That's what was going on when you fellows showed up there today. Those men report to a man named Hayden Fitz, and he wants my brother dead. We Slaters stick together; I can't leave yet."

One of the Younger brothers stood up. "Hey, Captain Slater. I seen Jamie. About two weeks ago. He knows about the posters, and he's making his way south. Thought you ought to know."

"Thanks. Thanks a lot. That's real good to hear."

Malachi smiled at the Younger brothers, then turned his eyes on Justin. He strode across the clearing between the trees and lowered himself down on the balls of his feet, staring straight into Justin's eyes.

"I've come for her."

"Well, now, Captain Slater, I'm rightly sorry. She's mine."

Shannon bit his hand. Justin let out a yelp, freeing her mouth, bringing his sore palm to his own mouth.

"Malachi—"

"Shut up, Shannon."

"Malachi—"

"Shut up, Shannon," he said again, smiling with clenched teeth. He stunned her by sending her a smart slap right across the face. She gasped. Tears that she would never shed brightened the blue beauty of her eyes.

"Justin, I don't prowl the countryside for just any woman. This one is mine. We're engaged to be married."

Shannon gasped, and Malachi glared at her.

Justin laughed crudely. "That won't wash, captain. That won't wash one little bit. I know all about this feisty little Yank lover. She hates Rebs. I don't think she even knows the difference between the bushwhackers and the regular army, captain. She just hates Rebs. I thought that I should give her a good taste of Johnny Reb, how about that, captain?"

There was no respect in his tone. There was an underlying hint of violence.

"She'll get a good taste of Reb. She's my fiancée, and I want her back now."

Malachi leaned across Justin with his knife and quickly slit the ropes holding Shannon down. She leaped to her feet, rubbing her wrists, and ran behind him. Malachi stood quickly as Justin leaped to his feet. The men stared at one another.

Malachi reached his hand behind him. "Come here, Shannon. Shannon—darlin'!—get your sweet...soul over here, ya hear?"

He grabbed her hand and jerked her up beside him. "Tell them, darlin'."

"What?" she whispered desperately.

"Tell them that you don't hate all Rebs."

She was silent. He sensed the turmoil in her, even as he breathed in the soft sweet scent of her perfume, still clinging to her despite the dirt that smudged her face.

He was ready to strangle her himself.

"Tell them!"

"I—" She was choking on the words, really choking on them. "I—I don't hate all Rebs."

"She ain't your fiancée!" Frank James said.

"She is!" Malachi insisted, his frustration growing. He swung Shannon around, none too gently, and brought her into his arms. "Darlin'!" he exclaimed, and he pulled her close. He stared into her sky-blue eyes, his own on fire.

Her eyes widened; it seemed that at last that she had discovered her own predicament, and realized that her freedom might well hinge on her ability to act.

"Yes! Yes!" She threw her arms around him. Her breasts pressed hard against his chest and her fingers played with the hair at his nape.

And her lips came full and soft and crushing against his.

There was a curious audience before them, and their very lives were hanging in the balance.

And at that instance, it didn't seem to matter.

He locked his arms around her, setting his hands upon the small of her back and bringing the whole of her body hard against his. His lips parted over hers, and in the breath of a second, he found himself the aggressor, heedless of the men watching. He thrust his tongue deep into the sweet crevice of her mouth, feeling the warmth and fever of her reach out and invade him. He held her tighter and tighter, and raped her mouth with the sheer demand of his own. The tension of it seared into the fullness of his body. Then she brought her hands between them, pressing hard against his chest, and he finally lifted his lips from hers, and stared into her wide, startled and glimmering eyes.

Glimmering…with fury, he thought. He only prayed that she had the sense to keep silent until they were away.

If they did get away.

One of the Younger brothers laughed. "Hot damn, but I believe him. That was one of the most sultry kisses I've ever seen. Set me burning for a bit o' lovin', that's for sure."

Shannon's lashes fell over her eyes. Malachi heard her teeth grate together as he swept her around him. "Jesse, she's mine. And I'm taking her."

"You got my go ahead," Jesse said. "Frank?"

Frank shrugged. "The man is still wearing a gray uniform, and he says that the girl is his. Guess it must be so."

There was a sound like a growl from Justin. "Well, captain, I don't say that it's so. The girl tried to kill me. I got a score to settle with her."

"She tried to kill you?" Malachi repeated, playing for time. He didn't doubt one bit that Shannon had tried to kill any of them.

"That's right," Jesse said, sighing. "Why, Justin would be dead right now if Frank's gun hadn't been empty."

Malachi smiled, arching a brow. "What was she doing with Frank's gun?" he asked politely.

Every one of the bushwhackers flushed, except Justin, and he kept staring at Malachi with hatred in his eyes.

"I untied her," Frank James muttered. "I felt sorry for her, gagged and tied. She jumped me."

"She jumped you?"

"Captain, if you know that woman so well, you know that she's a damned hellcat, a bloody little spitfire." He swore again. "She's more dangerous than the whole lot of us."

Malachi lowered his head, adjusting the brim of his hat to hide the smile that teased at his lips. They weren't in the clear yet.

He looked up again, gravely, at Jesse. "Not much harm done, was there? I mean, the gun was empty. Justin looks alive and well and healthy to me."

"You ain't takin' her, Slater," Justin said.

Malachi inhaled deeply. "I am taking her, Justin."

"Maybe she ought to apologize to Justin," Jesse suggested. "Maybe that will smooth things over a bit."

"Oh, yeah," Justin said, tightening his lips, and leaning back with a certain pleasure. "Sure. Let's see this. You get her to apologize, captain."

"Shannon, apologize to the man."

She had been silent for several minutes, a long time for Shannon. She had stood behind him and at his side, quiet and meek. He gripped her fingers, drawing her in front of him. He hissed against her ear. "Shannon! Apologize."

"I will not!" she exploded. "He is a bloody, vicious, sadistic murder—"

Malachi's hand clamped over her mouth. Justin stood in a silent fury. Frank James laughed, and Jesse didn't make a move or say a word at all.

"Your woman don't obey you real well, Captain Slater," Frank observed.

Malachi swept his arm around her, jerking her beneath his chin, laying his fingers taut over her rib cage and squeezing hard. "She's gonna obey me just fine." He lowered his voice, whispering against her earlobe. "'Cause if she doesn't obey me damned fast, I'm going to leave. I'm going to tell Justin to go ahead and enjoy himself to his heart's content—"

"He is a cold-blooded murderer!" Shannon whispered back. He sensed the tears in her voice, but he couldn't afford to care.

"Apologize!" he told her.

She inhaled deeply. He felt the hatred and the fury that swept from her in great waves, and he wondered if he would always be included in that pool of bitter hatred and rage. "I'm sorry that I tried to kill you," she spit out to Justin. She lowered her head. "And I'm sorry that I failed!" she whispered miserably.

Malachi tightened his hold upon her so that she gasped, but as he looked around, he realized, thankfully, that he was the only one who had heard her last words.

He smiled. "All right?"

He didn't want to give them all time to think. "Thanks, boys. I never would have made it against the Red Legs without your help. Be seeing you."

He adjusted his hat and shoved Shannon around, daring to bare his back to the raiders. They wouldn't shoot a Confederate officer in the back.

Even bushwhackers had a certain code of ethics.

He walked several feet, hurrying Shannon ahead of him.

"Slater!"

He stopped, pushing her forward, turning around.

Justin was walking toward him. "Captain Slater, they're letting you take the woman. I'm not."

Malachi stiffened. He stared at Justin. It was a direct challenge, and there was no way out of it.

"No, Malachi!" Shannon cried, racing to him. He shoved her back again, not daring to take his eyes off Justin.

"Then I guess it's between you and me," he said softly.

"That's right, captain. That's what it boils down to."

"Swords or pistols?"

"Draw when you're ready, captain—" Justin began, but he never finished. His eyes suddenly rolled up in his head and he fell to the ground with a curious, silent grace.

Jesse was standing there. He had just clobbered Justin with the butt of a Spencer repeater. He smiled at Malachi.

"I don't know what would have happened, captain, but you've got a powerful reputation as a crack shot. Of course, Justin is pretty damned good himself. One of you would have died. And I'm just sick of the bloodshed, you know. I figure the Yanks killed enough of us that we don't need to run around killin' one another, not now, not when we're all trying to get home for a spell. So you take your little hellcat and you go on, Captain Slater. Head for Mexico, as fast as you can. The best of luck to you, captain."

Malachi turned from the man on the ground to Jesse. He nodded slowly. Then he turned around. Shannon was still standing there, and he grasped her elbow firmly and pulled her along with him. "Come on!" he whispered to her when she seemed to be balking.

Jesse was still watching them. Malachi put his arm around Shannon's shoulder and pulled her close against him. She looked back once and didn't seem to want to protest, not one bit.

He hurried them down the slope to the embankment of the spring, then rushed along the embankment.

Darkness was coming once again. He wanted to sleep...badly. But he wanted to put some mean distance between them and Justin before he paused to sleep.

He didn't need to urge Shannon along. As soon as they had left the raiders behind, she broke away from him and started to run. Her hair streamed behind her, and in the darkening twilight, he heard the soft, sobbing gasps of her breath as she hurried.

Groaning, he ran after her.

She meant to put distance between herself and the raiders, too. She ran so hard and so fast that she was quickly past the spot where he had tethered their horses.

"Shannon!"

He hurried after her. It was almost as if she hadn't heard him. She was probably furious, he thought wearily. She was angry because he had made her apologize. Because he had kissed her.

He had more than kissed her. He had kissed her and touched with an invasion so deep that the intimacy invoked could never be forgotten.

Nor, for her part, he was certain, forgiven.

"Shannon!"

Cursing the pain in his leg, he ran after her with greater speed. At last he caught up with her. She stumbled and fell, rolling down the grassy slope until she was nearly in the water. Malachi followed, dropping down beside her. Her eyes were huge and luminous and moist, a beautiful, glittering blue, still wet with tears. She stared at the sky unblinkingly while he knelt by her.

"Shannon! Damn it, I'm sorry. You fool! You damned bloody little fool. Didn't you understand? I had to get you out of there. Justin is a murdering sadist, and that's exactly why you don't mess with a man like him." He sighed. "All right, hellcat. Stay angry. Tear me up again whenever you get the chance. But for now, we've got to get on the road. We need to ride—"

"Malachi!"

She shot up suddenly and ran straight into his arms. She laid her cheek against his chest, and he felt the terrible beating of her heart and the shivering that seized the whole of her body. The soft cream mounds of her breasts rose above the pink-flowered white cups of

her corset, brushing against the rough material of his wool greatcoat.
Her hands seemed frail and delicate where they fell against him.

"Oh, Malachi!"

And she burst into tears.

He put his arms around her and he kissed the top of her head. He
held her tight against him.

Hellcat. It was an apt name for her, but his little hellcat had broken. The war had made her build an impenetrable shield around
herself. She was strong as steel and tough as nails, and no one, no
one commanded Shannon McCahy.

But now...

Her shield had shattered and broken, and he wasn't sure that he
could stand up to the soft and delicate beauty beneath it.

"It's all right. It's over. It's—"

"Malachi, thank you. Oh, my God, you came for me. You—you
took me from him. Thank you!"

He curved his hand around her cheek, and he smoothed the tears
from her face with his thumb. She stared at him, and her eyes were
earnest and glorious, her hair a shroud of gold, cloaking her half-
bared shoulders and breasts.

He swallowed hard and managed to stand. He reached down for
her, lifting her high into his arms. "We have to ride," he told her.

She nodded trustingly. Her head fell against him. His boots
sloshed through the stream as he walked toward the horses.

Chapter Six

When she was set on the black gelding, Shannon seemed well and eager to ride. Malachi was glad of it. He didn't know how long he could stay awake himself, but as long as they could, they would ride.

They crossed the stream, then followed along it. No words passed between them. When Malachi looked back in the darkness, he saw her slumped low in the saddle, but she didn't complain or suggest they stop. He had given her his greatcoat; her shirt was nothing but tatters now, and he didn't want to take the time to dig through his belongings for a new shirt for her. He wanted to move.

It was too late to steal Kristin back before the Red Legs left Missouri. They would have to travel deep into Kansas. The only benefit to that situation was that it was unlikely Justin would follow him into Kansas. There might be a bounty out on Malachi, but at least he had been regular army, not a bushwhacker. A man recognized as a bushwhacker in Kansas might not stand much of a chance.

"Shannon?"

"Yes," she called softly.

"You all right back there?"

"Yes."

"We'll go another hour."

"Fine."

They plodded onward. Where the stream forked, he took the westward trail, telling her to walk the black gelding behind his bay mare in the rocky, shallow water. That way there would be no footprints for the bushwhackers to follow.

With the first light, he reined in. There was a perfect little copse beside the water. It was sheltered by magnificent oaks, and grass grew there like a blanket. On one side of the stream, the water deepened in a small natural pond. It was just like the swimming hole back home where he and Cole and Jamie had roughhoused after working hours, and where the neighborhood girls had come to watch and giggle from the trees, and where, sometimes, the young ladies had boldly determined to join them. He smiled, thinking about those days. They had been so long ago.

Malachi realized that Shannon had reined up behind him. "This is it," he said softly. "We'll rest here."

Nodding, she moved to dismount and missed her footing. She fell flat into the water on her rear and lay sprawled, apparently too tired to move.

Malachi dismounted and hunkered down in front of her, smiling. "Hey. Come on out of the water."

She nodded, barely. Her eyes fell on his, dazed.

He flicked water on her face and saw the surprise and then the anger spark her eyes. "You do need a bath," he told her. Dirt still smudged her face. "Badly. But this doesn't seem to be the right time. Come on, I'll help you out."

His greatcoat had fallen open, exposing the lace and flowers of her corset. When he went to take her hand, his fingers brushed over the lace, and over the firm satiny flush that rose above the border. Warmth sizzled straight to his loins, and he paused, stunned by the strength of the feeling. He shook his head, irritated with himself, and grabbed her hands. "Up, Shannon, damn it, get up."

Sensing the sudden anger in him, she staggered to her feet, using his hand for support.

"You're soaked. Let's get up on the bank."

Thank God he was exhausted, he told himself. Really so exhausted that he couldn't even think about what the sight of her did...

She sighed softly as they cleared the water, throwing his coat from her shoulders and sinking down to remove her boots. Her hair, touched by the pale, new light of the coming morning, glowed with a fiery radiance and teased the flesh of her shoulders and breasts. He didn't touch her at all, but the warmth sizzled through him again, making his heart pump too fast and his tired body come alive.

Maybe it was impossible to be too exhausted.

He gritted his teeth and swore.

She paused in surprise. "Malachi, what's wrong?"

When had she learned to make those blue eyes so innocent and so damned sultry all in one? And her hair, just falling over one eye now...

"What's wrong?" he yelled at her. "All I was trying to do was get Kristin back from the Red Legs, and instead I'm running over half of Missouri to get you back from a pack of bushwhackers. And did you try to use one ounce of sense in the hands of death? No, Shannon, you just provoke them further, and almost get us both killed."

She jumped to her feet. She was trembling, he saw.

"You don't understand. You don't understand and you can't understand. You weren't there when my pa was killed, and you didn't get to hear, in rumor and in truth, day after day after day, what was done to the men outside Centralia. You don't—"

"Shannon, I fought in the war. I know all about dying."

"It wasn't the dying!" Tears glittered brightly in her eyes, but she wouldn't shed them, she wouldn't break down again, and he knew it. "It wasn't the dying. It was the way that they died. He admitted it; that bastard admitted that he had been there, outside Centralia. He might have been the one who—who...Malachi, they had to pick up his pieces! They had to pick up Robert's pieces. I loved him, I loved him so much."

Her face was smudged but her chin was high, and her eyes were even more beautiful fevered with emotion. He felt her pain, and he wished heartily that he had never spoken to her. She still didn't understand. Justin just might want to do the same damned thing to her, if he could get his hands on her again. She'd fought Justin anyway. Or maybe she had understood, and hadn't cared.

She stared at him, her head high, her hands on her hips, her passion like an aura around her. "I loved him, and that bastard helped dismember him!"

"It can't matter!" Malachi told her curtly. "You can't allow it to matter right now!"

"You don't understand—"

"Maybe I don't understand, but you're not going to explain anything to me. No Yank is ever going to explain the horror of this war to a Confederate. We lost, remember? Oh, yes, of course, you're the one who likes to remind me of that fact."

"Maybe you do understand dying and killing. Maybe you just don't understand what love is."

"Shannon, you're a fool, and my life is none of your damned business."

"Malachi, damn you—"

"I don't want to listen right now, Shannon. I'm tired. I have to have some sleep," he said wearily. He didn't want to fight with her. He just didn't want to look at her anymore. He didn't want to see all the fire and excitement and beauty…and the pain and misery that haunted her.

He didn't want to desire her.

But he did.

He turned away from her, heading for the horses. For a moment he thought that she was going to run after him and continue the fight. But she didn't. She stayed still for several long minutes, tense, staring after him. Then she walked down to the water. He tried to ignore her as he unsaddled the horses and rolled out his bedroll and blanket beneath the largest oak. He hesitated, looked at her bedroll, rolled behind the seat of her saddle. He unrolled it, too, beside his own. He didn't want her too far away. He knew that he would awaken if footsteps came anywhere near them, but he was still wary of sleeping. Justin struck him as the type of man who worked hard toward vengeance.

He could hear her, drinking thirstily, splashing water, washing her face. Scrubbing her face and her hands again and again.

He threw himself down on the bedroll, using his saddle as a pillow and turning so he could keep an eye on her. Day was coming fast now. Sunlight played through the leaves and branches, caressing her hair and shoulders and arms. It rippled against the water in a magical dazzle.

"What are you doing?" he demanded.

"Scrubbing. Scrubbing away that awful bushwhacker!" she retorted.

"You can throw your whole body in later and scrub to your heart's content!" he called to her irritably. "Get out now. Let's get some sleep."

She turned around and saw him stretched out, then opened her mouth as if she was about to argue with him.

Maybe she was just tired. Maybe, just maybe, she was still a little bit grateful. Whatever, she closed her mouth and walked toward him.

She hesitated by her bedroll, looking at him. Strands of damp hair curled around her face, and its planes were delineated, soft and beautiful. Water beads hovered over her breasts.

He groaned inwardly and tipped his hat over his face. "Good night, Shannon."

"Perhaps I should move this." She indicated her bedroll.

"Lie down."

"I've never had to sleep this close to a Reb before."

"You slept with Justin just about on top of you yesterday."

She smiled with sweet sarcasm and widened her eyes. "I've never willingly slept this close to a Reb before."

"Willing or other, lie down, brat!"

He watched her mouth twist. He was too damned tired to argue, and if he touched her at that moment, he wasn't at all sure what it would lead to. "Please! For the love of God, lie down, Shannon."

She didn't say a word until she had settled down beside him, but then heard a tentative whisper. "Malachi?"

He groaned. "What?"

"What…what are we going to do now?"

He hesitated. "I should spank you, brat," he said softly. "And send you home."

"You—you can't send me home. You know that." There was just the touch of a plea in her voice, and the softest note of tears. "You can't send me back."

"That's right," he muttered dryly. "Justin is out there somewhere, waiting for you. Maybe I should let him have you. The two of you could keep on fighting the war, from here until doomsday."

"Malachi—"

"I'm not sending you back, Shannon. You're right about that; I can't."

"Then—"

"We're going to go onward for Kristin."

"But how will we find her? We'll never pick up the trail again. There's only a few of them left now, but they're so long gone that it would be impossible to find them."

"We don't need to find them."

"But—"

"Shannon, I know where they're taking her. They're taking her to Fitz. And I know how to find the town. We all know something about it, Cole, Jamie and I." He hesitated. "You forget, we've had dealings with the Red Legs before." He was silent for a moment, thinking back to when Cole's place had been burned down and his beautiful young wife killed. Malachi's jaw tightened. "I'm not sure if we can head them off quickly enough, or if we'll have to—figure out something else. We'll find her. We'll reach her."

"Do you think—do you think that she'll be all right?"

He lifted his hat and rolled toward her. She was staring at him so earnestly. Her eyes seemed old, so very wise and world-weary, and their tiredness added a curious new beauty and sensuality to her features.

He propped himself up on one elbow, watching her across the distance of the mere two feet that separated them.

"Shannon, they're going to take good care of Kristin. She is all that they have to use against Cole. Now, please, go to sleep." He lay back down, slanting his hat over his face.

"Malachi?" she whispered.

"What?" he asked irritably.

"Thank you—really."

Her voice was so soft. Like a feather dusting sweetly over his flesh. His muscles tightened and constricted and ached and burned, and he felt himself rising hard and hot.

"Shannon, go to sleep," he groaned.

"Malachi—"

"Shannon, go to sleep!"

She was silent. So silent then. She didn't try to speak again.

It was going to be all right. She was going to go to sleep; he was going to go to sleep. When he woke up, he wouldn't be so damned tired. He'd have so much more control over his emotions and needs.

A sound suddenly broke the silence of the morning.

He threw his hat off, leaping to his feet. She stared at him, startled.

She sat on her bedroll, cross-legged like an Indian, chewing on a piece of smoked meat. She had bread and cheese spread out before her, too, just like a damned picnic.

"What the hell are you doing?" he demanded.

"Eating!"

"Now?"

"Malachi, I haven't eaten in ages! It's been almost two full days."

His temper ebbed. He hadn't thought to stop for food last night, and she hadn't said anything, either.

"Just hurry it up, will you, please?"

"Of course," she said indignantly. She stared at him with reproach. He threw up his hands, issued a curt oath and plopped back down on the ground.

He just had to have some sleep.

He didn't sleep. He listened as she finished with the food and carefully wrapped it up to pack in her saddlebags. He listened as she stretched out on the ground, pulling her blanket tight around her shoulders.

Then he just listened to the sound of her breathing. He could have sworn that he could even hear the rhythmic thumping of her heart.

When he closed his eyes, he could see her. Could even see the pink satin flowers sewn into the lace of her corset. He could see her flesh, silky soft and smooth, and he could see the length of her, and the beautiful blue sizzle of her eyes...

He didn't even like her, he reminded himself.

But then again, maybe he didn't dislike her quite so much, either.

Somewhere in time, he did sleep.

He slept well, and he slept deeply. Warmth invaded him. He felt more than the hard ground beneath him, more than the coldness of the earth.

He felt flesh.

He awoke with a start.

He had rolled, or she had rolled, and now she lay curled against his chest. His chin nuzzled her hair; his arm lay draped around her. He was sleeping on her hair, entangled within it. Her features in repose were stunning, a study in classical beauty. Her cheekbones were high and her lips were full and red and parted slightly as she breathed softly in and out. Her lashes lay like dusky shadows over her flesh, enticing, provocative. The scent of her filled him deliciously. His arm was over her breast, the fullness of one round mound...

He jerked away from her, gritting his teeth. He should wake her up. He should shove her from him, as hard as he could.

He bit hard into his lip, then carefully eased her from him. She didn't whimper or protest. It he hadn't felt her breathing, he might have been afraid that she had died, her sleep was so deep and complete.

He sat up and pulled off his boots and socks and walked down to the water. It was cool and good, and just what he needed. He shucked his shirt, and let the water ripple over his shoulders and back. He came back to his bedroll stripped down to his breeches.

He sighed and laid back. He looked up at the sky. It was midafternoon now. They should ride again by night.

Damn her. He was the one who needed sleep so badly.

He closed his eyes. They flew open almost instantly.

She had rolled beside him again.

He looked at her and then sighed, giving up. He slipped his arm around her and held her close to the warmth of his body. He didn't listen to her heart but he felt it, beating sweetly.

It was so much worse now. He felt her with his naked flesh, and it was good to hold her as a woman. Too good. But he didn't release her. He held her and swallowed back his darker thoughts.

Knowing Shannon, he thought wryly, she would rise in a fury, accusing him of all manner of things. She would probably never believe that she had come to him in her sleep.

Come to him for the simple warmth and caring that she could not seek when she was awake.

We all need to be held, Malachi thought.

He sighed, shuddering against the fragrance of her hair. He would sleep again, he would sleep again. And she would never know just how fully he had played the gentleman, the cavalier...

He would never get back to sleep.

But finally, he did. Perhaps the very rhythm of her breath and heartbeat finally lulled him to sleep. Perhaps abject exhaustion finally seized him.

When he slept, he dreamed again.

He was remembering, he realized. Remembering the day when he had been shot. To the day when he had fallen into the brook.

He was seeing things. Illusions. Soft sunlight playing down from the sky, glittering upon the warm, rich earth. Sunlight touching the earth...and touching upon the woman.

She had risen from the center of the brook like a phoenix reborn from the crystal-clear depths. She seemed to move with magic, bursting with gentle beauty from the depths. Her arms, long and graceful, broke the water first, then her head, with her hair streaming wet and slick, and then her shoulders and her breasts with tendrils of her hair plastered around them. And she continued to rise, rise and rise, until the full flare of her hips and the shapely length of her legs arose.

Venus...arising from her bath.

She was perfection, her breasts lush and ripe and full and firm and achingly beautiful with their rouge-tipped, pebbled peaks. Her waist was supple and slim, her hips...

She was illusion, illusion moving in slow motion. She was the product of a dream, of too many sleepless nights. Maybe she was a spirit of twilight, a creation of sunset. She blended with the colors of the sky, gold and red and soft magenta.

She dipped down again, cupping her hands, dashing the water up within them. She straightened, tossing it upon her face, and the little droplets fell and streamed from her hands like a cascade of diamonds.

He wasn't dreaming.

He was wide awake, he realized. Wide awake and staring at the stream. Obviously, she had thought he would stay asleep.

He rose and walked down to the water.

She paused, seeing him.

Their eyes met across the water, across the sky touched by sunset in gold and magenta and red.

She froze, as if some spell had been cast upon her there. She didn't drop down to the water, nor did she cover herself with her hands. She simply stared at him, her lips slightly parted, some words, perhaps, frozen upon them. She just watched him.

She just watched him.

And he didn't pause or hesitate.

He walked straight over to her. And when he reached her, he put his arms around her, lifted her chin and studied her face and her lips and her eyes, his fingers moving over the ivory softness of her face.

Then he lowered his head slowly over hers, capturing her lips with his own.

And still, she didn't move...

His arms tightened around her. He ran his fingers gently down her cheek to her throat, and he sent his tongue deeply into her mouth, stroking the insides. Desire burst upon him like the crystal shards of sunlight that sprinkled diamondlike upon the water. There would be no turning back for him now. Not now...

He moved his hand over her breast, massaging the fullness, teasing the nipple between his thumb and forefinger and encompassing the fullness of the weight again.

Her lips broke from his. A startled gasp escaped from her, but she didn't fight him. She slipped her arms around him, clinging close to him. Her lips settled upon his shoulder, and her fingers splayed across his back. He continued to play with her breast and she cast her head back as he pressed his lips against her throat, again and again and again. Then he moved downward, and lifted her breast to take it into his mouth, sucking upon the nipple and spiraling his tongue around the aureole.

She cried out, holding his shoulders. He rose to take her lips again, seizing them with hunger, plundering them apart, and seeking her mouth with a fire of passion. She pressed against him, trying to free herself. Her lips rose from his.

"We shouldn't..."

"For God's sake, don't tell me that now!" he said hoarsely, and his mouth closed over hers again, and this time, she made no protest at all. Her arms curled around his neck. He kissed her until he felt her tremble with the same deep desire that burned within him. Until he thought that she would fall.

Then he moved back, and drank in the sight of her again. He reached out and placed his hands around the enchanting fullness of both her breasts, awed by the sensual beauty of their deep-rose pebbled peaks. He touched her breasts, moving his fingers lightly over them, then possessing them with the fullness of his touch.

He stepped even closer, and swept her into his arms.

Splashing through the water, he carried her toward the grassy bank. Her eyes were closed. He knew he should have wondered if she dreamed of another man. He should have wondered if she had any experience with what she was doing, but he didn't wonder about anything at all. Holding her, carrying her to the shore, seemed to be the most natural thing to do, and he would not have ceased with his intent had lightning come from the sky to strike him down.

He laid her upon the soft grass embankment. Her eyes remained closed as the last rays of sunlight played over the beauty of her body again. He fell down beside her, and when the light shadowed magenta upon her, he kissed her, and then where the rays fell golden, he kissed her, too. The beautiful colors and musky light were broken by the dappling patterns of the oak leaves, waving above them in the softness of the breeze.

Holding his weight above her, he kissed her lips gently, then moved down between the valley of her breasts. He ran his hand over the lush curve of her flank as his tongue laved her flesh. She tasted of the water, and of the deep, rich colors of the sun.

Malachi stood, looking down at her, feeling the pulse that lived inside of him, increasing erratically with each touch against her. He stripped away his breeches, watching her still, watching the play of the sunset over her supple form. The world receded; the echoes of gunfire could not touch him here. There was nothing but the glorious, magenta sunset, and the girl, as golden and beautiful as the wavering rays of the falling sun, as naked and primitive as the simple earth where they lay.

He lay down beside her again, half covering her with the blanket of his naked flesh. Her eyes remained closed, and she was nearly motionless. He kissed her temple, whispered against her earlobe, trailed his lips down the snowy length of her throat and over the slender line of her collarbone. His hands teased her breasts again, and she arched against him, a curious cry coming from deep within her throat. He watched with fascination, seeking to judge the responses of her body. The shaft of his desire lay naked against her thigh, warmed there by her flesh and grazed by the evening air, so that the burning ache to have her beneath him soared high and fevered, and still he held himself in check.

He wondered if she even remembered who he was. He wanted her to open her eyes. To see his face, to know his name.

He moved his hands to lazily draw circles along her inner thigh, rising higher and higher. He buried his face against her throat and between her breasts, and feathered her flesh with the soft hairs of his beard. She whimpered slightly and began to undulate against him.

With bold and deliberate purpose, he parted her thighs. A certain resistance met him at first, but he caught her lips again, and his kiss seared and invaded and seduced. He wanted to slide down between them, but he kept his eyes hard upon hers instead. He stroked surely along her thigh until he came to the juncture of it, and swiftly, surely penetrated her with an intimate touch.

Her eyes flew open at last and met his. Wide and blue and beautiful and dazed. He knew how to make love, and his stroke moved with tender, sensual finesse.

"No..." she murmured softly, color flooding her cheeks.

He leaned close against her, speaking a breath away from her lips and keeping her eyes locked with his.

"Whisper my name, Shannon."

"No..." she murmured, and he knew that she didn't protest what they did, but only that he forced her to see the reality of it.

That he forced her to look his way, and say his name.

He found the most erotic places of her body and teased her, then plundered ruthlessly within her once again. She cried out, trying to twist from him, trying to elude his eyes. He shifted, burying his weight deep inside her, and holding himself just slightly away from her. She moved, she moved so sweetly against him even as she denied him.

"Put your arms around me, Shannon, tightly around me!" he urged her, and she did so. It was easy for her to cling tightly against him. Her fingers moved over his shoulders, over his back. Tentative, hesitant, seeking to hold him close as he held her, and seeking to give him a certain pleasure.

"Whisper my name, Shannon," he insisted. He hovered over her, teasing her with the fire of his own body. "Say my name. Open your eyes, and say my name."

Her eyes flew open again. There was a shimmer of fury deep within them. "Malachi!" she whispered tensely.

"Now..." He lowered his head to hers once again, and a ruthless grin touched his features. "Tell me what you want me to do."

She stared at him in astonishment, and a flush as crimson as the sunset touched her cheeks and seeped over her breasts. He couldn't bear it much longer. He had to have her soon. But they had always waged war between them, and this one, at least, he would not lose.

"Tell me what you want."

"No..."

"It's easy." She started to press against his shoulders. He caught her hands, and he laced his fingers with hers, and he drew them high over her head. "Say that you want me. I want you, Malachi." He kissed her. He slid his tongue into her mouth and withdrew it and then raked it along her lips. He drew her hands down and held her firm as he moved low against her, lazily taking her breast in his mouth again, slinking lower and lower against her. She escaped his grasp, and her nails raked into his shoulders. He heard her gasp and felt her fingers on his head when his kiss teased her belly.

She was alive with passion. Her head tossed and her hips moved, and she whispered something, moistening her lips. Her eyes were closed again, and her face lay to the side. They were both entangled in her hair.

"I can't hear you, Shannon."

"I—I want you."

"I want you, Malachi."

"I want you...Malachi."

Her voice was breathy, barely a whisper. It was all that he wanted, all that he needed. She moved against him with grace and exquisite sensuality, and a burst of triumph and fever took hold of him as he shifted, touching her, thrusting deep, deep inside her.

She stiffened, and screamed, and he realized then that he had believed her experienced because he had wanted to believe it. He had been deceived, but only because he hadn't wanted to think...

But he felt. He felt the tear within her body, and the constriction of pain, and the trembling that filled her. He started to jerk from her, but her hands pulled him back.

Her eyes were open now. Tears touched them, but they met his with a curious honesty. "No, no—I said that I wanted you. I said I want you...Malachi."

"Damn it, you didn't tell me that you were a—"

"You didn't ask," she reminded him softly. "Please..."

Her voice trailed away. He realized that it was too late to undo any harm, and yet perhaps not too late to recapture the magic.

He began to move very carefully. Slowly he entered fully within her, and just as slowly he withdrew. Then he plunged again, slowly...slowly.

Minutes later she cried out, straining high against him.

Innately, she seemed to know the craft of womanly art. Supplely, exquisitely, she moved beneath him. He matched his rhythm to hers, to the soft magic of the evening. The breeze rustled the leaves and silently caressed them. Birds cried out, and the water rippled and dazzled still. Malachi cried out hoarsely, giving himself free rein at long last, burying himself again and again with speed and fever within the moist and welcoming nest of her body.

The pressure built in him explosively, and still he held himself in a certain control, whispering to her, touching her bare flesh with kisses, urging her ever onward.

She cried out, straining hard against him, collapsing.

He allowed his own climax to come, and when it seized him it was sweet and violent; he shuddered as wave after little wave of pleasure shook him, and rippled anew. When he had finished at last he gazed down at her.

Her eyes were closed again, her lips were parted, and her breath still came swiftly...and he felt the little tremors that touched her. She seemed white, very pale.

"Shannon?" He stroked her hair, smoothing damp tendrils from her face. She moved, trying to free herself from the burden of his body. He shifted his weight, and she curled against him.

"Shannon—"

"Don't. Please, don't...not yet," she whispered.

While the twilight darkened, he held her, staring at the trees and watching the silhouette of the leaves against the sky until it was too dark to see them.

Then suddenly, in silence, she pushed away from him. She rose, and her hair fell over her eyes, obscuring them. She walked quickly to the water, and did not pause at the edge, but hurried to where it was deep, and ducked beneath it. Malachi watched her pensively, thinking that the action wasn't much different than the one she had taken that morning when she washed her hands and face as if to wash away the scent and memory of Justin.

He rose and followed her into the water. "Shannon!" She ignored him, and he caught her arm, turning her around. She jerked away from him.

"Shannon, what are you doing now?"

"Nothing."

"Then why won't you talk to me?"

"I don't want to talk."

"Shannon, what just happened—"

"Shouldn't have happened. It shouldn't have happened!" she repeated fiercely. She sat in the water, pursing her lips, scrubbing her thighs and behaving now as chastely as a nun. She sank even lower into the water until the surface rippled against her breasts, and for some reason, the sight irritated him more than her perverse denial.

"Shannon—"

"Malachi, damn you! Could you at least have the decency to leave me alone now?"

"Could I have the decency?" He caught her elbow, pulling her to her feet. He was furious and she was distant. And yet, something was irrevocably and forever changed between them. It seemed natural now to hold her this way, to have her against him sleek and bare and intimate. She couldn't make love the way that she had and pretend that the moments hadn't existed.

"Decency?" he asked sarcastically. "Oh, I see. It was all my fault—"

"I didn't say that."

"It's what you mean."

"Well, you're just one hell of a Southern gentleman! You know something? That's what Kristin always called you. You were the perfect Southern knight, the hero, the magnificent cavalier! Riding to a lady in distress! Well, she's wrong; you're no gentleman. You may have seen me bathing, but you might have turned your back."

"Oh? And you, I suppose, were the perfect lady? Naked as a jay and strutting like a dance-hall girl out there—"

"You could have turned around. I thought that you were a gentleman!"

"Don't ever think, Shannon. Every time you do, someone gets into trouble. And don't you ever deny me, or—"

"Malachi, it was your fault."

"My fault. Right. I didn't exactly drag you screaming from the water."

She lowered her head.

He caught her chin, lifting it. "You just wanted to indulge in a little fantasy. You never made it into bed with the Yank when he was alive, so now you're willing to take on a Rebel captain just to see what it might have been like—"

She struck out at him like lightning, slapping his cheek with a stinging blow, then ducked, afraid that he would extract retribution. Every time she had touched Malachi in anger before, he had repaid her in some way.

But that night, he did not. He touched his cheek, then spun around. "You're right, Shannon. It never should have happened."

He sloshed through the water to the shore and, ignoring her completely, dressed at his leisure. He heard her, though. He would always hear her, he realized. Hear her, and imagine her. Her eyes like the sky. Her grace and energy, her supple beauty. He would hear her, and imagine her, clothed and...unclothed.

He heard her coming to the shore, and imagined her slipping into her thin cotton pantalets and beautiful corset with the pink roses sewn into the lace. He sneaked a glance, and saw she had plunged into her jeans, and now sat on her bedroll pulling on her boots.

He dug into his saddlebags and found a clean checked cotton shirt. He tossed it to her.

"Thank you. I don't—"

"Put it on. If you ride around in that corset thing, every man jack we run into will fall under the illusion that you're ready and willing, too."

She slid the sleeves of the shirt over her arms and began to work on the buttons. Her head was high. "I wasn't going to refuse the shirt, Captain Slater. I was going to suggest that you should wear something similar. That Confederate coat of yours is pretty distinctive."

Malachi didn't reply. He turned around to pack up his bedroll, setting his greatcoat and jacket in with his blanket. His trousers were gray, but his shirt was plain blue cotton.

He couldn't quite part with his hat yet, so he set it atop his head, and stared at Shannon, waiting. When she had buttoned her shirt, she dug into her bag for a comb. She started trying to untangle the long strands of her hair.

Malachi saddled the horses, and she was still struggling. He walked over to her impatiently, snatching the comb from her fingers. "Get down on your knees," he told her gruffly.

"I won't—"

"It's the only way that I can handle this mane!"

She complied in silence. He quickly found the tangles, and eased them out. When he was done, he thrust the comb back to her. "May we go now, Miss McCahy?"

She nodded, lowering her head. They mounted and started out.

Malachi rode ahead of her, silent as death, wrapped up with his own demons. He felt as if they had been on the road for hours when she finally tried to catch up with him, calling to him softly.

"Malachi?"

"What?"

"I—I want to explain."

"Explain what?"

"What I said. I didn't mean to deny—"

"That's good. Because I won't let you deny the truth."

"That's not what I meant. I want to explain—"

She was still behind him. He couldn't see her face, and he was glad. It was easier to be cynical and cool that way. "Shannon," he said, with a grate to his voice, "you don't have to explain anything."

"But you don't understand—"

"Yes, I know. I never do."

"Malachi, before the war, I was always a lady—"

"Shannon, before, during and after the war, you always were a hellion."

"Malachi, damn you! I just meant that...I never would have done...what I did. I shouldn't have..."

He hesitated, listening to her fumbling for words. He could sense tears in her voice again, and though he ached for her, he was bitter, too. He didn't like playing substitute for a ghost. He might have forced her to admit that she had desired him, but the thought of her Yankee fiancé enraged him.

The ghost had never had what he had had, he reminded himself. He cooled slightly. "The war has changed lots of people," he said softly to her. "And you *are* a lady, brat. Still, I'm sorry."

"I don't want you to be sorry, Malachi. I just—it shouldn't have happened. Not now. Not between us."

"A Yank and a Reb. It would never do," he said bitterly.

She cantered up beside him, veering into his horse so that he was forced to look at her. She was soft and feminine now, her beautiful features and golden hair just brushed and kissed by the pale dusky moonlight.

"Malachi, please, I didn't mean that."

"I hope you meant something," he told her earnestly. "Shannon, you changed yourself tonight. Forever. You cast away something that some men deem very precious. You can't just pretend this didn't happen."

Even in the dim light he saw her flush. She lowered her face. "I know that. But that's not at all what I meant. What I meant is that..." She hesitated.

"Shannon, I did not drag you down, I did not force you into my arms. I seduced, maybe, but not without your ready cooperation."

He thought she might hit him. She didn't move. Only the breeze stirred her hair. They had both stopped, he realized.

She looked up at him, smiling painfully. Tears glazed her eyes. "I did want you, Malachi. I shouldn't have. I knew it was you, and I wanted you...and I shouldn't have. Because I did love Robert, with all of my heart. And it hasn't even been a year. I..." She shook her head. "I...I'm the one who is sorry."

She moved ahead of him. He suddenly felt exhausted, tired and torn to shreds.

He had never imagined, never, through hellfire, war and his meager taste of peace, that Shannon McCahy could come to brew this tempest in him. Anger, yes, she had always elicited his anger...

But maybe, just maybe, she had always aroused this fever in his loins, too. And maybe he was just beginning to see it now.

She was searing swiftly into his heart, too.

Maybe they could be friends. Maybe every war deserved a truce now and then.

"Shannon."

She reined in and looked to him.

"Let's camp here and get some sleep. We'll move more westerly tomorrow night, away from the water, so let's take advantage of it now."

He thought she raised her eyebrows, and he remembered clearly just what advantages the water had given them. "To drink and bathe," he told her dryly.

She nodded and dismounted, removing her saddle. He would have helped her, but she had grown up on a ranch and knew what she was doing, so he decided to leave her alone. They both needed some privacy right now.

He unsaddled his horse, set her to graze, and hesitated. At last he decided it was safe, and he moved close to the water to build a small fire. Shannon watched him as the flames caught. He looked at her. "I need some small rocks. I've got a pan; we'll have coffee." And brandy, he added to himself. Lots of it.

He was the one who needed to keep away from her. This was going to be hard, damned hard now. He couldn't look at her, have her near, and not imagine her in his arms again. Maybe if she hadn't known how to move and arch and undulate and please a man, all by instinct...

She came back with the rocks, and he arranged them around his fire and set the pan so that the water would boil without putting out the flame. He stared at the water while she undid the bedrolls, setting them up for the remainder of the night.

The coffee was soon done; Shannon laid out bread and cheese and smoked meat. They barely spoke to one another as they ate, and when they were done, silence fell around them again.

"Why don't you go to bed," he told her.

She nodded. "Yes. I guess that I will." She rose and started for their bedrolls, then paused, looking at him.

She seemed angelic then. Soft and slim and wistfully and painfully feminine. She smiled at him awkwardly. "Malachi?"

"What?"

"Does it matter to you?"

"Does what matter to me?"

"A—er—a woman's..."

"Virginity?" He offered.

She flushed, and shook her head. "Never mind—"

"Shannon—"

"Never mind. Forget it. Sometimes I forget consequences and..."

He took a long sip of coffee, watching her over the rim of his cup. "Have you forgotten them this time?"

"What?" she murmured. It was her turn to be confused.

He stood and walked over to her. Malachi was irritated by the touch of malicious mischief in his own heart. He would set her to thinking and worrying for days, he thought.

But then he had spent these last hours in a type of hell, and he would surely spend all their moments together in torment from this day forth.

"Consequences. Procreation. Infants. Sweet little people growing inside a woman's body..."

Her eyes widened. She hadn't thought about it at all, he saw, and he was right—now she would worry for days.

He kissed her on the forehead. "Good night."

She was still standing there when he walked back to the fire.

Chapter Seven

"What do you think?" Shannon murmured. It was late the next afternoon, and they had spent the day riding westward, avoiding the major roads, and had slipped quietly through the countryside.

"I think it's Kansas," Malachi replied flatly, turning toward her.

They sat on their horses looking down a cliff to a small, dusty town. On the distant rolling plains they could see farmhouses and ranches. Before them they could see a livery and a barbershop and a saloon. A sign stretching across the top of a long building advertised Mr. Haywood's Dry Goods and Mercantile, and next to it was a smaller sign, advertising Mrs. Haywood's Haywood Inn, Rooms to Let by the Day, Month, Year.

"Haywood, Kansas," Shannon murmured. She could still feel Malachi looking at her, and she couldn't bring herself to look his way. She'd had trouble looking at him ever since...

She couldn't believe what she had done. She hadn't had a single drop of liquor inside her. She hadn't been dragged, forced or coerced. She had done it all of her own free will, and if it were possible to live a thousand years, she would never be able to forget it. Or Malachi...

She could not look at him anymore and not remember everything. When his eyes touched her now she started to tremble deep inside. When she watched his hands resting on the reins, she remembered them against her body. The low male tenor of his voice moved against her now as if it touched her every time, as if it stroked the length of her back, just brushing over her flesh. And too often, way too often, she would grow hot and shivery all at once, and at the very core of her, and she would be ashamed to remember the feeling of unbelievable ecstasy that had burst upon her at the end.

She had never denied him his appeal, even in her moments of most vehement hatred. Even as the war had waged on and on, even as he dismissed her again and again as a child. And now she knew even more about him that she could not deny. That he was wonderfully muscled and sleek and bronze. His back was riddled with scars, and she knew that they were the result of cavalry battles, that he had been nicked time and again, and that he fought on, because a man just didn't walk away from a war, or from his duty as he saw it.

She knew that his chest was tufted with short red and gold hair, and that the hair narrowed enticingly at his hips, and that it flared out again to frame a demanding...masculinity.

He was an attractive man.

But she should have never been attracted, and each time she thought of her own behavior, it hurt. She knew that he thought that she had wanted to see him as a substitute for Robert. But he hadn't allowed it, and by then...she hadn't cared. She could make excuses. Maybe she had been striking out against the loss. Maybe she had just felt the need to be held.

No, the need to be loved.

But there really was no excuse. They hadn't even been friends. Passionate enemies, at best. What he must really be thinking of her, deep down inside, she couldn't even imagine...

And then she suddenly knew what her greatest fear was—that it had been a swift, casual fling for him, when for her it was a nightmare that changed her entire life and left her wondering if she had any morality whatsoever. And of all men to humiliate her so, it just had to be Malachi...

She had to be mature about it. She had to learn to forget it, and she had to learn to...quit worrying. Malachi had brought up a consequence that hadn't even passed through her mind. She'd never been that innocent, not on the ranch. She always knew what men and women did to create sons and daughters. It was just that she couldn't afford to think about it. She had to put it behind her now as well. Kristin was out there, somewhere. And Shannon did need

Malachi's help. She didn't know the first thing about Kansas, or the awful man, Fitz. She needed Malachi.

"We need to go down," he said slowly, reluctantly. "We need to buy some food, if there's any to be had. And I'd give a hell of a lot to see a newspaper and try to find out what's been going on in the world."

"I'll go—" Shannon began.

"Don't be a fool," he told her impatiently. "I can't let you go down alone."

"I would be perfectly safe, and you wouldn't be."

"No one is safe anywhere around here. It wasn't safe before the war, and it surely isn't safe now."

"But I'm a Yank, remember?"

"Yeah, but they may not see it like that. To some, anyone from Missouri is a bushwhacker. Anyone at all."

"So what do you suggest?"

He gazed at her, lifting a brow. "Why, we pretend like hell, Miss McCahy, what else. We go in together—man and wife. Our place has been burned out. We're looking to keep on moving westward. Don't mess up, you hear?"

She eyed his hat pointedly. "You're riding in with a lantern of truth atop your head, captain," she said sweetly.

He swept the hat from his head and looked at it for a long moment, then dismounted and walked toward some bushes. He set the hat carefully in the midst of them.

"Is this a funeral?" Shannon asked sarcastically. "Maybe we should run down and bring the preacher out to mutter a few last words."

His face was savage when his eyes lit on hers. She swallowed, wishing that she hadn't spoken. He didn't reply. He walked around and mounted the bay again and reached out for her horse's reins, holding the horse there before him. "Follow my lead, Shannon. I don't mind dyin' for Kristin, and I don't even mind dying for you— when it can't be helped. I will be bloody damned, though, if I'll die just because you can't keep a civil tongue in your body."

His words fell into silence. Shannon stared at him without a word for what seemed like an endless time. She had only been teasing him. She hadn't realized how her words might wound, and she didn't know how to explain that or apologize.

"What about your saddle?" she asked him coldly. "Are there any Confederate markings on it, or on any of the other trappings on your horse?"

"My saddle came off a dead Ohioan's plow horse," he said. "And the bridle is from your ranch. No markings at all."

"Shall we go then?" she said tautly.

He released her horse's reins and they started down the slope. "We're going to buy some supplies and get some information," he told her. "You keep careful."

"Me?" she inquired sweetly. "You should be grateful to have me along, Malachi Slater. They aren't going to take your Confederate currency here. I've got Yankee dollars."

He turned to stare at her. "You keep your Yankee dollars, Shannon."

"Oh?"

"I've got gold, Miss McCahy. Last I heard, they're still taking that stuff everywhere. Come on now, I want you close."

He continued down the slope. Their horses broke into smooth canters as they crossed the empty plain and entered the town by the single road that cut through the line of buildings. Malachi reined in, nodding to Shannon to do the same. They dismounted in front of the mercantile and tethered their horses on the wood rail that ran the length of the place, then started up the two dusty steps to the open doorway.

There was a portly, balding man behind a counter that stretched in front of a wall with rows and rows of just about everything. There were rolls of fabric, mostly cottons and linens, but there were brocades and silks and satins, too, and smaller rolls of elegant laces. There were sacks of flour and coffee and tea and sugar, and there were sewing goods and farm supplies, leather items, blankets, sheets, canteens. The whole store was composed of shelving, and Shannon saw jars of jams and preserves, pickled vegetables and smoked and dried meats. As small as this town was, it seemed to be a prosperous place.

"Howdy," the portly man said to the two of them.

Malachi grinned broadly, walking up to the man. "Howdy, sir."

"What can I do for you, young man?"

"Well, the wife and I are heading out west. We just need ourselves some food supplies."

"We can take care of that, Mr.—"

"Uh, Sloan," Malachi said.

"Gabriel," Shannon said quickly at the same time.

Malachi frowned at her, his jaw locking. The balding man looked from one of them to the other. "It's Sloan Gabriel, sir," Malachi said. He jerked Shannon over to his side. "And this is my wife, Sara."

The man looked from Malachi to Shannon. Shannon smiled and escaped Malachi's punishing grip, wandering away to look over the merchandise in the store. "Nice to meet you, Mrs. Gabriel."

"Likewise, I'm sure," she murmured demurely.

The man leaned toward Malachi. "My wife's got herself a little tea parlor next door, young man. Maybe the lady would like a cup?" He winked. "And you could take a walk on over to the saloon and have yourself a pint or two."

"That sounds mighty nice," Malachi told him. A saloon was always the best place to hear whatever news was passing around. He looked at Shannon.

"Sweetheart." She was looking at a roll of calico and didn't pay him the slightest heed. He walked over to her, catching her hands and spinning her around and into his arms. "Darlin'! That nice man, Mr.—"

"Haywood," the balding man supplied.

"That nice Mr. Haywood says his wife has a little tea shop next door. Wouldn't you like to have a cup of tea, complete with milk and sugar? It's been a long, hard road."

She smiled sweetly. "Are you going to have a cup of tea, darlin'?" she asked him. She came up on her toes, slipping her arms around his neck.

"I had reckoned that I might have a beer across the way," he told her, his jaw twisting. Her smile had been dazzling, and her eyes were absurdly large and innocent. Her body was pressed tight to his and he could feel all the curves and soft slopes that he had recently come to know so well.

His eyes narrowed. "Careful!" he mouthed. She couldn't be that innocent. She had to know what she was doing to him.

"Why, darlin'," she drawled sweetly. "I don't mind. I'll come over to the saloon with you." She wrinkled her nose up prettily. "I don't rightly care for that nasty old beer, but—"

He untangled her arms from around his neck. "Sweetheart," he said firmly, "you go on and have tea. It might be a rough place. There might be some...talk...I don't want you to hear."

"If you're there, my love, I'm sure that I'll be safe."

"You'll be much safer, sweetheart, having tea."

"But I don't mind hearing talk, beloved."

He was losing control. There was a definite note of irritation in his voice. "Honey love, sometimes a man just don't talk as freely when there's a lady present. You'll have tea."

"But, darlin', I—"

He didn't let her finish. He could hear Mr. Haywood snickering behind him, and he'd had about enough. She was the one pressing it. He pulled her even closer and slammed his lips down hard upon hers in a bruising, punishing kiss. He held her so tightly that she could barely breathe, and that was what he had intended. When he released her, she was silent, gasping for breath. He spun her around so that his back was toward Mr. Haywood and he whispered with vehemence. "Go over and have tea. Now. You ruin this—"

"But I want to hear, too—"

"Go. Now. Smile, kiss me sweetly, and damn you, go have a cup of tea. I mean it, Shannon."

He could hear her teeth grinding, but she went still. Malachi spun around. "Next door, you say, Mr. Haywood?"

"Sure thing. The little lady can go right through this door here."

Shannon didn't see a door. Then she realized that even the door was lined with shelves that were filled with merchandise.

"See you soon, sweetheart." Malachi pulled her into his arms, kissing her on the forehead. She longed to slap him, hard. She smiled instead, and threw her arms around him again, rising up on her toes, and quickly threading her fingers through the hair at his nape. She kissed him...

She kissed him with purpose...and with menace, pressing her lips fully against his, and teasing his lip with the thrust of her tongue. Startled, he gave way. She pressed her tongue fully into his mouth, slowly, provocatively, filling it.

Then she withdrew, dropping back on her heels with her body tight to his, rubbing him with the length of it. She saw a dark sizzle in his eyes, but ignored it despite her own breathlessness. She turned to Mr. Haywood and smiled brightly. "Newlyweds, you know!" she explained, flushing and batting her lashes. "I can't bear to see him go, even for a second. It's just been so hard, what with the war and all. The cows scattered, then the fields were trampled, and then the whole ranch was burned down one day. But now we're finally together, heading west, and it is just so hard to let my darlin' out of my sight..."

Both men were silent. Malachi was as stiff as a poker, not saying a word. But when she looked at him, his eyes were narrowed. Real narrow. The way he looked at her caused her heart to jump and shiver, and she decided then to make a hasty retreat. She offered Mr. Haywood another smile and quickly passed through the shelved door that he held open for her.

She found herself in a large parlor. For a moment, it reminded her so much of her home that she inhaled quickly, feeling a little dizzy. It was lovely. A piano stood on a braided rug before a polished wood staircase. Beautiful Victorian chairs sat all around the piano in pleasant angles, a grouping of three here, two there. There was a grouping around the fireplace, and there were lovely little marble-topped tables all around.

"Hello?"

A short, buxom woman with small brown eyes, iron-gray hair and warm, rosy cheeks came through a doorway, wiping her hands on a towel. She smiled at Shannon, then eyed her outfit.

She didn't fit in the beautiful little parlor, Shannon realized. Not in her dusty breeches and checked shirt.

But the woman didn't hesitate long. It was ranch country, farm country, and Shannon's outfit was not completely alien here.

"Hello, miss..."

"Uh—Gabriel," Shannon said quickly. "Sh—Sara Gabriel, Mrs. Haywood. Your husband sent me over."

"Oh, how lovely. Well, do sit down. I'll bring you in some of our finest, young lady." She extended her arm around the parlor. "As you can see, we're not terribly busy at the moment."

Shannon nodded, wondering if they were ever busy. It seemed to be such a small town to support the shop and boardinghouse.

"Sit, sit!"

She shooed Shannon into one of the chairs by the fireplace and disappeared. Shannon barely had a chance to get her breath and look around before Mrs. Haywood was back, carrying a large silver tray. She set it down on one of the marble-topped tables. She poured tea from a pot through a strainer and looked at Shannon. "Sugar, cream?"

"Yes, please," Shannon said.

As Mrs. Haywood continued fixing the tea, Shannon looked over the curve of her chair toward the street. Malachi was just going into the saloon, pushing his way through a set of swinging doors.

"Is that your husband, dear?" asked Mrs. Haywood, following Shannon's eyes.

"Yes," said Shannon, a little grimly.

"Now, now, don't worry about him, Mrs. Gabriel," Mrs. Haywood advised her. She sighed with an expansive smile and patted Shannon's knee. "You're such a pretty young thing, you needn't worry a bit. Newlyweds, eh?"

"Er, yes ma'am. How did you know?" Shannon said.

"The war, my girl, the war. Young ladies here and there are snatching up their fellers the second the boys come home. Too many young men dead. Too many young women left without husbands or intendeds. Those who can are marrying quick. Did your husband fight in the war, Mrs. Gabriel?"

"Yes—yes, he did," Shannon said quickly. She prayed that Mrs. Haywood wouldn't ask her any more questions.

She didn't. She pointed to the pastries on the plate. "Meat pies and cinnamon swirls and raisin muffins. And I'm the best cook this side of the Mississippi, I promise you. Help yourself, young lady."

Shannon hadn't known how hungry she was until she bit into the first pie. It was still warm from the oven, and the pastry was fluffy and light and delicious, and the meat was tender and seemed to melt in her mouth. She hadn't had anything nearly so good in ages, and it felt as if she and Malachi had been on the road forever, despite the fact that this would only be their fourth night away. Everything about the parlor felt good, from the elegance of the chairs to the fine food and sweet tea. It was nice to stop, even if Malachi had been his usual dictatorial self when he had refused to let her go to the saloon.

Mrs. Haywood kept talking as Shannon ate. She explained that Haywood was kept busy by the traffic that went through. There were roads all around the town. Some of them went south, Texas way, and some of them went to Missouri, and some of them headed toward the north, while an awful lot of them headed out west. "People are headin' for California, right and left, already. Almost as much as back in '49. The war...it left so many without a home, or without a home they could call their own anymore."

Shannon nodded vaguely. She found herself looking over the rear of the chair, out the curtained windows and across the street to the saloon. Heat suffused through her as she thought of the way she had kissed Malachi in the store, and she wondered why she had done so. If she were playing a game, it was a dangerous one. If she was hoping to taunt him or hurt him, she was risking herself by doing it. She didn't know what had seized her; she didn't seem to know herself at all any more.

Nor did she understand why she was so anxious over the length of time he was staying at the saloon. What was he doing over there?

Drinking it up with the whores, no doubt, she thought, and a flush of anger filled her. She didn't care; it was none of her business.

But she did care. It made no sense. She did care. Maybe it was the idea that he could move on from her to a whore so quickly. Maybe it left her with doubts about her abilities.

She almost bit through her cup with that thought, and she reminded herself fiercely that she really loathed Malachi, loathed him with all her heart, and she had never set out to please him, she had never set out to be with him at all. And she didn't want to be with him now; it was a matter of necessity.

Maybe he wasn't being entertained by a woman at all. Maybe he was in trouble, Shannon thought.

"You two staying the night?" Mrs. Haywood asked her.

"Uh—no, I don't think so," Shannon said. "Ma—my husband, Sloan, wants to keep moving. He says the sooner we get where we're going, the sooner we'll get settled down."

"But a little rest never did nobody any harm, either," Mrs. Haywood said. "Pity, I've got the coziest little room upstairs. Pretty lace curtains, a big wool comforter, a fireplace and—" she winked, leaning toward Shannon "—I got the most unbelievable hip bath you ever seen up there. It's a two seater, wood and copper, just right for a young mister and his new missus."

Shannon nodded, her face growing red despite herself. "I'm sure it's very, very nice, Mrs. Haywood—"

Mrs. Haywood jumped up, grabbing her hand. "Do come on. Your young man seems to be enjoying himself. You come on up here, and I'll show you my honeymooners' retreat!"

Shannon didn't have much choice. She stared across the roadway one more time, wishing she could give Malachi a good punch right in the gut. What did he think he was doing? Was he enjoying himself at her expense, or...

Was he in trouble?

She wished she knew.

It was a typical saloon, the type that had been cropping up in Kansas ever since the white man had first started to claim the land. Two men served behind the bar, and a beautiful brunette with a feathered hat and shoulderless gown played tunes at the piano. There were two lone drinkers at round tables, and a poker game going on in the rear of the room. Three of the players were ranchers; they had come with their dusty hats and kerchiefs and chaps and spurs, and they were swigging on whiskey bottles. A fourth man seemed to be a clerk or a banker. He was wearing a neat pin-striped suit with a crooked tie and white shirt.

The other two had a somewhat professional air about them. Both wore vested suits and tall hats. One was lean with a thin curling mustache, and the other was heavier set with small, very dark and very alert eyes.

Malachi wandered over to the bar, and one of the barkeeps hurried to serve him. "Beer," Malachi said briefly, throwing a coin on the bar. The man smiled and drew a foaming brew from the tap. Malachi nodded his thanks.

"Passing through?" the barkeep asked.

Malachi nodded again. From the corner of his eye, he saw that the gamblers were being served by a tall, buxom redhead. The sight of the woman gave him a start, and he almost forgot to answer the barkeep. "The wife and I are heading out for California. Seems the only thing to do now." He remembered Shannon's words and added, "We were burned out. End of the war, you know. Seems to make sense to up and start all over."

"Yep, seems to make sense. Lots of people heading west these days. You staying in town long?"

"Nope. Just came in to wet my whistle."

The barkeep smiled. "And your wife is over at Mrs. Haywood's having tea."

"Yeah, how'd you know?"

"Cause this is Haywood's saloon. His town, really. He entertains the lady folks on that side of the street, and the men on this side. Darned good scam, ain't it, Mr.—"

"Gabriel. Sloan Gabriel."

"Matey. Matey MacGregor. It all seems to come out clean in the wash here. The Haywoods are right nice folks themselves, and that seems to make it all right."

Malachi grimaced. "Yeah, maybe it does." He turned around, leaning against the bar, watching the tall red-haired woman again. He swore inwardly. It was Iris Andre from Springfield, and he did know her.

He thought he should turn around and hurry out of the saloon, but just at that moment, the woman looked up and saw him. Surprise and pleasure appeared on her attractive features, and she straightened, ignoring the poker players, and hurried toward him. She was going to call out his name, he knew it.

"Iris! I'll be damned!" He went to her quickly, hugging her and squeezing the air from her before she could speak. He picked her up to swing her around, whispering in her ear, "Sloan. Sloan Gabriel. Please."

She nodded swiftly—Iris always had been a bright woman. She meant to have her own business one day, and Malachi was sure that when she did, it would be a financial success.

"Sloan!" she said enthusiastically.

"You two know each other, Iris?" the barkeep called.

"Sure do, Matey. We're friends from way back. Sloan, grab your beer and come over here to a table for a moment."

He'd always liked Iris. She might be a whore, but she was a whore with class. He didn't miss a beat. She was almost as tall as he was, and though she wasn't beautiful, she was attractive with her strong features, blazing red hair, green eyes and regal height.

"Come on!" she urged him, pulling him farther and farther into the back. She sat him down at one of the small tables, far away from the others, far away from probing eyes. "Malachi! What the hell fool thing are you doing in Kansas? Wait a minute, don't answer that. Buy me a drink so this will look like business. Matey!" she called out. "We'll take a bottle of whiskey over here. The good stuff."

"Coming right up."

Iris dangled her fingers sensually over the back of Malachi's hand while they waited for Matey to come over with the whiskey. When he was gone, Iris lowered her head close to Malachi's. "Malachi! They've got wanted posters up all over the country! They say you were in on a raid with your brothers, that you went into Kansas and shot some guy named Henry Fitz, and that you're wanted on all kinds of other bushwhacking activities, too. I heard about what Fitz did to your brother, so I wasn't too surprised—"

"Iris, I wasn't with Cole, not that I wouldn't have gone with him if I could. But the war was ending right then. I had a whole contingent of men under me, and I couldn't just go running off to Kansas. Cole was a scout. I was regular cavalry. I went where I was ordered to go."

"Malachi." She moved even closer to him. "I know that none of you has done anything to be hanged for, but you don't know Hayden Fitz.''

''And you do?''

Iris nodded. ''Never met a meaner son of a bitch in my entire life. There's something evil about him. He likes bloodletting, and he likes to watch men die. He's worth money, too, Malachi. Big money. He invested with arms manufacturers during the war and made himself even richer. He owns Sparks—''

''Sparks?''

''The town where he lives. I mean, he owns it.'' She smiled, waving a hand around. ''All right, so the Haywoods own Haywood. But this is a two-bit rest stop, Malachi. Sparks is big. The stagecoach goes through. It's always filled with Conestogas. There's a jail and a circuit court, and if he manages to get you into that jail, he'll hang you, too. You fool! You gotta get out of Kansas.''

Malachi shook his head. ''I can't. Hayden Fitz sent men to my sister-in-law's place. Cole wasn't there, so they carried her away. I've got to find her.''

Iris sat back. ''At least you got rid of your Reb uniform,'' she said softly. ''You don't look like the poster so much anymore.''

''I still have the uniform,'' he said, pouring out shots of the whiskey. ''It's stuffed in my saddlebags. And my hat—well, I left it out in some bushes. It was kind of hard to part with, you know?''

She nodded. ''Old times,'' she murmured, then she looked at him. ''Oh, Malachi!''

''What, Iris?''

''Malachi, I did hear something about Fitz holding a woman. Just the other day, some of the boys were talking about Fitz having a blond woman in his jail. Said she was part of a conspiracy to murder Union soldiers.''

His heart sank, but it was what he had been expecting to hear. The Red Legs would have carried Kristin straight to Fitz. And Fitz surely knew that he was holding the key to Cole's whereabouts.

''You think he'll—hurt her?'' Malachi asked.

She shook her head strenuously. ''I—uh—I don't think so. He could kill her, Malachi, if he does anything. But hurt her? Not if he's using her for bait.''

"You hear anything about my brothers?" he asked her.

She shook her head. "Not a word. Sorry, Malachi." She was silent for a minute. "But I can help you."

"What?"

"Like I said," she told him dryly, "I know Hayden Fitz. I know his sheriff, Tom Parkins, real well. The town ain't twenty miles from here, Malachi. I can take a trip over and bring you back some information."

"Iris, that's good of you. That's real good, but I can't stay here—"

"You can stay here if you can stay anyplace on God's good earth. I tell you, Malachi, for Yanks, these are real good people here. Stay. Just give me one or two days. I can ride over tomorrow, spend some time and ride back.

"I can't have you do that—"

"I do it now and then anyway, Malachi."

He hesitated. If anything happened to Iris, he would never forgive himself. But if she could help him free Kristin and he didn't let her, he'd never forgive himself, either.

"Iris, I can't believe I'm saying this, but all right. You think I'm really safe here?"

"As safe as you're going to be."

He exhaled slowly.

"I won't let nothing happen to me, Malachi, I swear it," she insisted. "It's all right. It really is."

He still hesitated, then he sighed. "All right. It's good to see you, Iris. So good. You stayin' on here?"

"Don't look at me like that—I'll feel like I want to stand up and sing 'Dixie,' and that just ain't no good anymore. No. I'm going to California. The war is too close here, Malachi. I want to leave it behind. My father fought with Grant, and he's dead. My brother was with General E. Kirby-Smith down south, and now he's dead, too. I want out of this hatred, Malachi. It ain't going to end here. Not in my lifetime."

He laced his fingers through hers and squeezed them. They were very close and intimate, two friends who had run the same gamut.

That's how they were sitting when the saloon doors burst open and Shannon came into the room.

She had a Colt shoved into her belt, and she looked around the saloon carefully, looking for any danger. He saw from the position of her hand that she could have grabbed the gun in a split second, and fired, with great accuracy, in less time than that.

Her eyes fell on his.

"Ma—Sloan!" she said, startled. Her eyes took in the two glasses, the whiskey bottle and his hand, his fingers interweaved with Iris's on the table. She took in Iris, from the little flare of her hat to her black petticoats peaking out from beneath her crimson gown. She looked from the poker players to the bar, where Matey was staring at her expectantly.

Her eyes narrowed, dark lashes falling over her brilliant blue eyes. Her hair was loose and beautiful, spilling all around her shoulders. It was one of those occasions when her masculine apparel made her look all the more feminine, for her slender legs seemed very long, and her derriere was defined by her trousers just as her breasts were full and defined by her cotton shirt.

She was furious. Malachi wondered why. Just because he had left her for so long, hadn't allowed her to take an equal part in this venture? Or was there, maybe, just maybe, more to it than that?

Thinking about it made a pulse beat hard against his throat. He wanted to be with her somewhere alone, then, at that moment.

He swallowed down his desire and fought the tension. She was striding his way. They were going to do battle again. Her claws were bared; he could almost see them. He nearly smiled. A woman didn't get that way unless she was jealous. At least a little bit jealous.

"Darlin', I'm so very sorry to interrupt," she drawled. Her voice dripped with honey. She smiled sweetly at Iris. Then she knelt close to Malachi. "You son of a bitch! You left me over there scared to death...never mind. Bastard! Well, darlin', at least the whole town will be expecting a marital dispute. I'm checking into Mrs. Haywood's. I assume you have other arrangements." She stood. "Nice to meet you, Miss—" she said to Iris.

"Iris, honey. Iris Andre. And you're...?"

"I'm—" Shannon paused and shot her very sweet and dazzling

smile at Iris once again. "I'm Mrs. Sloan Gabriel," she said, and she picked up Iris's shot glass and tossed the whiskey into her face.

Matey inhaled in a massive gasp; even the poker players went dead silent.

Malachi leaped to his feet, reaching for Shannon. Iris was on her feet, too. Malachi knew Iris, and Iris didn't take that kind of thing from anybody. He jerked Shannon around behind him. "Iris, I do apologize for my wife's manners—"

"Don't you dare apologize for me to any who—"

He spun around, clamping his hand hard over Shannon's mouth. "Iris, I apologize with all my heart." He jerked Shannon's wrist and twisted her arm around so that she couldn't possibly fight him without feeling excruciating pain. "Darlin', please, Iris is an old friend, and we just have a few things to say to one another." He dropped his voice and whispered against her ear. "Darlin', you are acting like a brat, and I promise you, if you don't act grown-up real quick here, I'm going to peel those breeches and tan your hide, just to prove that the man wears the real pants in this family. I'll do it, Shannon, because I'll have to." He hesitated. "She knows something about Kristin. She can help us, Shannon!"

He released her, very slowly. He waited expectantly, ready to snatch her back into his arms if need be.

For once in her life, she seemed to have believed his threat. Perhaps she was so concerned that she would grab at any scrap of information about her sister. She faced Iris.

"Miss Andre, it was a pleasure," she said. Her voice was the softest drawl, her manner that of a charming, well-mannered belle. She swept from the saloon like a queen.

A cheer went up from the poker crowd. One of the ranchers stood. "Mister, I sure salute you! That's one heck of a spirited filly, beautiful to boot, and you handled her like a man!"

"Buy him a drink!" the heavyset professional gambler called. "If I'd been able to manage my wife like that, I might be a rich man by now!"

Malachi laughed, sitting down and waving a hand in the air. "She's going to be mighty mad later, gents. We'll see how I handle her then." He looked at Iris. She sat beside him. He gave her his

kerchief to wipe the whiskey from her face. She seemed more confused than angry.

"Malachi, that really was your wife?"

He shook his head. "Iris, she is my sister-in-law's sister. She
wants Kristin back. I couldn't seem to stop her from coming with
me, and that's another long story, too."

Iris sat back, smiling. Malachi poured her more whiskey, and she
swallowed it.

"Thanks for not ripping her hair out."

"Don't kid yourself, Malachi. I saw that Colt in her pants. I'm
willing to bet she knows how to use it."

"Like a pro—except that she has a bad time aiming at people."

Iris was smiling at him with a peculiar little grin. "She might not
make you such a bad wife after all, my friend."

Malachi frowned. "Iris—"

"She's got spirit, and she's got courage. A little raw around the
edges, as if she's got some scars on her. But we've all got scars. I
can't see you with a namby-pamby woman, and she ain't that."

"No, she isn't that. She's a pain in the damned—"

"Butt!" Iris broke in, laughing. "Yes sir, she's that. But I can
see something in your eyes there, Malachi. She ain't going to be
checking into Mrs. Haywood's place alone, is she?"

Malachi smiled, idly twirling his whiskey around in his glass. Miss
McCahy had seen fit to comment upon his actions and whereabouts.
He was damned ready to comment upon hers.

"I think I should give her time to check in and settle down and
get real, real comfortable. What do you think?"

Iris laughed at the sizzle in his eyes.

She wished that it was her. But it wasn't. He was more like a
married man than he knew. The beautiful little blonde with the delicate features and the tough-as-nails stature had those golden tendrils
of hers wrapped tightly around him.

Still, Mrs. Sloan Gabriel's manners did need a little improvement.

"Let her get real, real comfortable," Iris advised him sagely. "A
game of poker might be right in line here. Come on over, I'll intro-
duce you to the boys."

"All right. I'm glad to meet the boys."

The heavyset gambler was Nat Green. The slimmer man with him was Idaho Joe, and the ranchers were Billy and Jay Fulton, Carl Hicks and Jeremiah Henderson. It was a good game. Iris held onto his shoulders, laughing, while he played. She brought him drinks.

Around supper time, she disappeared and came back with big plates of steak and potatoes and green beans.

He lost at cards—a little bit—and the meal cost him almost as much as the liquor, but he didn't care much. He had a good time.

And through all of it, he anticipated his arrival at Mrs. Haywood's Inn, Rooms by the Day, Month or Year.

He was just dying to see his darlin' wife.

Just dyin' to see her.

Chapter Eight

He knew that the door would be locked.

He even suspected that Shannon might have gone to Mrs. Haywood with quite a sob story about being ignored so that her husband could play around with another woman.

Shannon was a good little actress. He was learning that quickly.

And he was learning, too, that things had changed between them, irrevocably. Maybe they would always be at battle, but the battle-grounds were subtly changing. He might still spend ninety percent of his time thinking Mr. McCahy should have dragged his daughter into the woodshed a number of times at a far younger age, but he couldn't deny what she had done to him. Exactly what that was, he wasn't sure yet. And he didn't want to think about it; he didn't want to analyze it. He fixed it in his mind that Shannon had started this one. Either down in the store when she had kissed him with that pagan promise, or when she had come striding across to the saloon to douse Iris in whiskey. This one, she had begun.

But he was going to finish it.

He had his own fair share of acting ability.

"Mr. Gabriel!" Mrs. Haywood said with censure when Malachi came to ask for a key to the room. "Now, I know, sir, that a man has got to have a few simple pleasures of his own. And a saloon's a good place for a man to have whiskey and a cigar—keeps the scent out of his own parlor, you know. But when it comes to other things...when he leaves a beautiful little bride..." She shook her head in reproach.

"Iris is just an old friend, ma'am." Mr. Haywood was in the

kitchen, eating his supper. Malachi raised his voice a hair, determined to work on them both. "I don't know what my wife told you, Mrs. Haywood, but there was nothing going on. I had a few drinks, and I lost a few hands of poker. Ma'am, you got to understand. If a man lets his wife make a fool of him like that, well, then, he just ain't a man anymore."

"That's right, Martha." Mr. Haywood dropped his napkin on the butcher-block kitchen dining table and strode to the door. "Martha, if the man wants a key to his own room, we'd best give it to him. She's his wife, and that's that."

Mrs. Haywood was still uncertain. "Mr. Gabriel, I probably ain't got no right to keep man and wife apart, but—"

"I'm going to try to make her understand, Mrs. Haywood. Honest, I am."

"You give him the key, Martha," Mr. Haywood said.

"You're right, Papa, I suppose. Oh, Mr. Gabriel, I was just giving my husband a piece of apple pie. Won't you have some?"

"Why, that's mighty kind of you. Thank you, ma'am."

He had the key, and he had a cup of good strong coffee and some of the best apple pie he'd tasted in his entire life. And it was the middle of summer.

"I jar and preserve all my own fruits," Mrs. Haywood told him proudly.

"Well, it's the finest eating I've done, ma'am, since way before the war."

As Mrs. Haywood blushed, the door to the parlor opened. A pretty young girl in a maid's cap and smooth white apron walked in. She bobbed a nervous little curtsy to Malachi and looked at the Haywoods. "Mrs. Gabriel is all set for the night, Mrs. Haywood. She had me fetch her some of the lavender soap, and asked if we'd be so good as to put the price on the bill. She thanks you kindly for the use of the tub."

His heart started ticking a staccato beat. If he'd gone by instinct, he would have knocked the table over, brushed the maid aside, burst through the door and raced up the stairs.

Primitive, he warned himself reproachfully.

That wasn't what he wanted. Slow torture was what he had in mind.

He sipped his coffee like a gentleman. "My wife's in the bath?" he inquired innocently.

"Oh, why, yes, Mr. Gabriel," Mrs. Haywood said. "Don't worry, young man, you're welcome to stay here in the kitchen if you're worrying about disturbing her."

"Why, ma'am, I was thinking that I might steal a little of her water, and save someone having to haul more up the stairs." He spoke sincerely, rising.

"That's thoughtful of you, Mr. Gabriel," Mrs. Haywood said. Around her ample figure, Mr. Haywood looked up at Malachi with his brow arched and a skeptical smile slipping onto his lips.

"Mighty thoughtful, son," he said dryly.

Malachi flashed him a quick grimace. "Mr. and Mrs. Haywood, thank you again. Good night, now."

He nodded to the young maid and swept by her. He forced himself to walk slowly through the parlor and up the stairs. He glanced at the key. Room five.

It wasn't hard to find.

He took a deep breath outside the doorway, smiled again, and slipped the key into the lock. He heard her key fall out of the door on the other side as he pressed his in. He pushed open the door.

The most outrageous bathtub he'd ever seen sat before the fire. It was a long wooden tub with headrests rising up at both ends. It was decorated with copper and delft tiles, and at that particular moment, it was laden with bubbles...and with Shannon.

Her hair was curled high on top of her head, leaving the slim porcelain column of her neck bare. Her shoulders and just a peak of her breasts rose out of the bubbles.

She turned on him, her eyes wide and startled and very blue. She almost leaped up, but then seemed to realize how much worse that would be. "Get out!"

"Darlin'!" he said softly, with taunting reproach. And he stepped into the room, closing the door behind him, leaning against it. His eyes stayed on her while he twisted the key in the lock.

She must have put on one hell of a performance with the Haywoods, he thought. She hadn't expected him that night. It was a pity that he hadn't gotten to see it.

Shannon sank farther into the tub, watching him as he sauntered coolly into the room.

"Don't you dare get comfortable," Shannon warned him. She felt herself burning all over, and it wasn't from the steam in the bath. It was caused just by the way his eyes fell upon her.

The nerve of him. How dare he be here. How dare he look at her like that. When he had just left his redheaded slut!

He tossed the key onto the side table and dropped down on Mrs. Haywood's beautiful crocheted bedspread, lacing his fingers behind his head and staring right at her. He smiled.

"Don't let me disturb you."

"You are disturbing me." She narrowed her eyes. "You've no right in this room. The Haywoods—"

"The Haywoods know that a man has a right to be with his wife—beloved."

"The Haywoods know that the man is a scoundrel and cad, seducing women from the Mississippi to the Pacific. They understood completely that you deserved a night in the livery stables."

"Tsk, tsk." His apparent relaxation had been deceptive. He moved all of a sudden, sleek and easy, twisting to stretch out on his stomach, facing her from the foot of the bed. There was no more than six feet between them. She could see the tension in his features and the pulses beating furiously against his throat and temple. There was a dangerous gleam in his eyes, and she was aware that he was angry with her—furious, probably, for her behavior in the saloon—and that he seemed to have forgotten any rules of fair play for the night.

She sank lower in the tub. He wouldn't force her into anything. She knew him, and she knew that he would never force any woman.

But what would he do?

And what would she do? If he touched her, she would scream, she thought, and not with horror, but because her flesh seemed to cry out to know his hands again. She was hot inside and out, and trembling fiercely. The scent of the lavender soap was all around her, the softness of the bed awaited...

And he had just spent hours and hours with a whore.

"Malachi—" She paused. "Sloan," she hissed. "This is my room. Get out."

He smiled, giving her a flash of white teeth against the golden strands of his mustache and beard. "I'm sorry, sweetheart. I may be a cad, but I wouldn't dream of leaving my sweet young wife alone for the entire night."

He rose and sat at the foot of the bed, nonchalantly kicking off his boots and peeling away his socks. Shannon watched him, stunned, as he proceeded to pull the tails of his shirt from his pants and unbutton his shirt and cast it aside.

"What are you doing?" she asked him quickly.

"I'm going to take a bath."

"No, you're not. This is my bath."

"Darlin', we've got to talk, and it looks like it's just the right place, to me."

"Malachi, if you touch me, I'll scream."

"You're my wife. They might shake their heads a bit downstairs, but they won't interfere."

"I'm not your wife!" Shannon swore, panicking. The look in his eyes caused shivers to streak along her spine. The sight of his bare chest, sleek and gleaming, brought her body alive with memory. She lowered her head, determined not to look at him.

But she could hear him.

She heard his pants fall to the floor, and she heard his footsteps as his bare feet padded behind her. He dropped to his knees and his lips touched her shoulders like a burning brand. She jerked away from him and wished she hadn't, for when she turned to him she saw his hungry eyes on her newly exposed breasts. Her nipples hardened instantly and flames seemed to rise to her cheeks, then sink back and lie deep in her core. She sank into the water. She wanted to be angry, indignant. Her voice came out as a husky whisper. "Malachi, I am not your wife!"

He was on his feet, naked as a jay, and his manhood flying proud and firm. She was determined not to stare, but her teeth were chattering, and she felt compelled to watch him, like a marionette jerked by strings. She loved the look of him, she realized. She felt some ancient and instinctive fascination, which lay deep below the level of her mind, something that caused her blood to race and heat and her breath to catch and come too quickly and that made her flesh come alive at the very thought of him. She could not draw her eyes from him. She could not help but respond to the naked length of him. She found him magnificent. From the breadth of bronzed shoulders to the lean hardness of his thighs, she found him so boldly and negligently male that she could not turn away.

He stepped into the tub, sitting behind her so that his feet brushed her bottom. He leaned back against the rim of the tub and sighed deeply. "This is just wonderful." He closed his eyes in complete comfort.

Hating him, hating herself, Shannon swore furiously. "Malachi, I am not your wife!"

His eyes flew open, glittering and dangerous. "That's not what you told Miss Andre when you so rudely doused her."

"I—I had to appear upset."

"Did you now?" He leaned forward. His hands dangled over his knees. His fingers almost brushed the flesh of her breasts. She leaned against the tub, as far as she could go. It made no difference. "You're lucky she controlled her temper."

"You're damned lucky that I'm controlling mine right now."

"Am I? Why, beloved, is that a threat?"

She didn't answer him. She was shaking all over and she only hoped she had the bravado to make an escape. "If you're going to stay, Malachi, then I'm going to go." She started to rise. He was on his feet in an instant. He set his hands on her shoulders and pressed against them with relentless determination. Water and bubbles swished all around them. Her rear landed hard against the bottom of the tub, and he followed her quickly back down.

"Sit. You're not going anywhere."

"Don't you dare manhandle me! I've had it. I've simply had it! I'm not going to sit—" She tried to rise again. He caught her foot this time. She felt his free hand roaming the water for the soap. His fingers brushed her thighs and her rear and her flank and she gritted her teeth to keep from screaming out.

"Malachi—"

"Sit," he said pleasantly. "Just sit, darlin'."

"Malachi, you son of a bitch!" She tried to pull away. His grip upon her foot was firm. Softly humming "Dixie," he washed her foot with the lavender soap.

She leaned back and spoke through a clenched jaw. "Malachi, I want you out of here! Now! You left me cooling my heels to run off to a saloon. You spent the whole afternoon and evening with a whore. I had to act the way I did—"

"Jealous, darlin'?" He taunted huskily. She opened her eyes. Her foot was free and he had come close to her. Very close. Their limbs were all entangled. She could feel the shaft of his sex against her ankle, the hardness of his thighs against her toes. It was unbearable.

And she could see the pulse beating, beating, against his throat. His lips were close to hers as he spoke.

"Never!" she promised him in a heated panic. "I just can't stand the thought of being sullied by your touch."

"No?" He cocked his head, and his lashes fell lazily over his cheeks. "You didn't mind down in the store this afternoon."

"That was—that was necessary."

"No, I don't think so. I don't think so at all. Shannon, I haven't ever, not even by the most practiced whore, been kissed so provocatively in my entire life."

She leaped up. It had gone too far. Her cheeks were blazing and her breasts were heaving. The bubbles and water sluiced from her, bathing her in a seductive white foam.

Malachi leaned back. His eyes fell on the hardened dark peaks of her breasts as they thrust through the white foam of the bubbles. She saw that look in his eyes again, and she cried out softly as she stepped from the tub. She grabbed for the towel, but she had barely dried her face before he was up behind her. He lifted her cleanly from the ground and tossed her upon Mrs. Haywood's crocheted spread. She gasped for breath, trying to rise. It was impossible. He was down beside her within a split second, a leg cast over her hips and thighs, his arm a bar of steel across her.

"That kiss wasn't necessary at all," he told her.

"I am going to scream, Malachi. I'm going to scream so loudly that you'll be sorry."

"If you scream," he promised her, "it isn't going to be for help."

"You bastard!" She surged against him. "You can't come from a fancyhouse to me—" She broke off, straining against the muscles that held her. She tossed like a wild creature, but it served no purpose. It just put their bodies more fully in contact. Her breasts rubbed against his chest, and her limbs became more and more entangled with his. She felt the hard, searing heart of his desire against her thighs, against her belly. She tried to kick him and failed, but he swore softly, knowing her intent. He straddled her, keeping himself safe from her rancor, and caught her hands, pinning them to her sides. Exhausted, she twisted her head from his, gasping desperately for breath.

She heard him chuckle softly and she opened her eyes, staring at him in fury. "I will scream, Malachi! You bastard!" Tears glazed her eyes. "Gentleman! Southern cavalier! The last of the flower of knighthood—"

"Shannon, I didn't touch her."

"What?" she breathed.

"She's a friend, and a good one. She's going to do some spying on Fitz for me."

"Fitz?"

"We're not far, not far at all now. Fitz has Kristin. She's in jail."

"Oh, no, Malachi!" She surged against him, bit her lip and fell back.

"But she's all right. Iris is going to go see her. She's going to help us."

"Or else turn you in," Shannon said softly.

He shook his head with irritating confidence. "She's a friend."

"I'll bet she is."

He lay over her, his head close to hers. "You are jealous, Miss McCahy. I told you; I didn't touch her."

"That—that doesn't mean anything at all," Shannon whispered against his lips. "I don't—"

His mouth closed upon hers with a curiously tender force, parting her lips, searing them, causing them to part sweetly beneath his. She lost contact with everything but the fire of his tongue, so hot and hard, thrusting into the depths of her soul and desire. She didn't feel the bed beneath her, or know that gentle candlelight filled the room. She could only taste the fever of his kiss.

She ceased to fight him. Her fingers curled around his. His mouth lifted from hers, and touched down again upon the column of her throat. The brush of his mustache and beard feathered softly over her flesh, and she moaned, arching hard against him. He lowered his head, sweeping his face over her breasts, slowly encircling one mound with the tip of his tongue, then taking in the fullness of her nipple with the whole of his mouth. His teeth grazed the pebbled peak as he licked it in slow and leisurely fashion.

Her heart was beating like thunder; her blood seemed to hiss and boil and cascade through her, and she could not think of anything but the exquisite pleasure of his touch. Something deep inside her tried to warn her that it was wrong, that no great and everlasting love lay between them, that theirs was the heated and tempestuous passion forged from the hatred borne between sworn enemies.

But she did not hate him. Not at all...

She craved his touch with a basic, undeniable need. She felt the huge pulse of his passion, thundering against her, and she was sweetly excited, pleased that this time there would be no pain at all. She wanted to touch him. She wanted to explore his shoulders and run her fingers over his chest, and she even wanted to venture decadently downward, and touch with fascination the place from which his darkest desire sprung...

His lips moved over her, down to her belly. His tongue laved her with hot moisture, and his beard continued to caress her flesh and evoke a greater surge within her. She wanted him so desperately...

Suddenly he rose above her. His features were tight, but he smiled and he spoke lightly. "Good night, Shannon."

She stared at him in utter disbelief, then the color surged to her face and she tried to strike him in a raw fury. Once again, he secured her hands. He fell to her side and swept her against him. "We need to get some sleep."

"Sleep! I will never sleep with you, you Confederate snake! You rodent, you knave, scalawag! You bastard, you—"

"Enough, Shannon."

"Vulture, diseased rat! Rabid dog!"

"Enough!" He managed to land his hand on her derriere in a sharp slap. She swore again with the venom and expertise of a cowhand, and this time his hand landed over her mouth. "Darlin', let's go to sleep, or I will forget that I'm a gentleman."

"Gentleman!"

"A gentleman," he repeated. "You're the one who wants to be left alone," he reminded her gruffly.

She was quick and twisted around to see his face. His eyes were unreadable, his features taut, his jaw locked. And his eyes...he stared at her as if he hated her, and she found herself lowering her eyes in misery.

It was true. She had wanted to be left alone because...

"Oh, Malachi!" she said miserably, a sob catching in her throat. He was the one who had brought them to their present untenable position, but she had provoked him earlier. She had meant to stir him down in the store, and she had meant to provoke him over at the saloon. She had been sick, imagining him in the arms of the redhead...

"Malachi, I did love Robert," she whispered. "And if I did, then it can't be right, it just can't be right... I don't mean by Sunday-school morals, I mean in the soul, in the heart..."

She was near to tears. She couldn't possibly be speaking to Malachi this way, especially not when she lay naked in bed with him.

But something in his eyes softened, and his touch was very gentle as he drew her against him. "Shannon, I know that you loved him. You've taken nothing away from him by needing to feel warm again." He sighed. His beard brushed the top of her head. His hand lay against her midriff, but it was a tender touch, and not meant to seduce or capture. "Tell me about him."

"What?"

"Tell me about him. When did you meet? What was he like?"

She shook her head. She couldn't begin to imagine Malachi being interested in her deceased Yank fiancé. But he whispered against her hair softly. "Talk to me. It may feel good. You met when the house in Kansas City fell down."

She nodded, absurdly content to lie there, held by him. "I was arrested along with Kristin—for my relationship with Cole. I was arrested for harboring bushwhackers!''

"The Slater men haven't done much for you, have they?'' he murmured quietly.

"I didn't mind that. Cole saved us. I always liked Cole. From the first moment I saw him.''

Just like she always hated me, Malachi thought. He smoothed back a strand of her hair. What the hell was he doing here? He'd never been that much of a gentleman. Why had he let her go when she was welcoming him against her? He sighed softly.

"It was awful,'' Shannon said, shivering. "They had so many of us, stuffed into that terrible decrepit building. When the roof collapsed...'' She paused. "I thought I was going to die. I was just hanging through the roof when the rafters broke apart. I could hear everyone screaming. And then Robert was there. He and Kristin made me jump. And he caught me. He was so brave and wonderful—a hero. I'll never forget looking into his eyes then. And then...then we heard all the screams again. Five of the women were killed. So many were hurt badly... It was odd. We were friends then, all of us. The other girls knew where my sympathies really lay, and they understood. Josephine Anderson was my friend. When she died, her brother went mad. That's when he really became Bloody Bill, after she died. Oh, Malachi! So many people died!''

"It's all right,'' he said softly. She was crying. Not sobbing hysterically, just crying very quietly. "It's all right,'' he said again.

He kept stroking her hair. She didn't speak again, and he didn't speak, either. He closed his eyes, just holding her. It was too painful for any of them to think of the war. Northerner, Southerner, it was just too damned painful to look back. Great men, kind men, good men, all of them dead. Gallant men, alone and moldering in gallant graves. He sighed and closed his eyes. He couldn't let it go on any longer. He had to find some way to free Kristin.

And then he had to find his brothers.

And run.

He opened his eyes. The candles were burning low. He had drifted to sleep. The room was cast in very soft shadows, and the light was pale and ethereal.

He wondered why he had awakened. Then he knew.

Her fingers were moving over his chest. Her nails lightly raked his flesh, and her hair fell over him like a brush with angel's wings. She traced tentative, soft patterns over him, exploring his rib cage and breast and collarbone.

He lay still. He kept his eyes open a slit, watching her. She rose slightly, watching him, watching the movement of her fingers. Her breasts peeked out from the golden glory of her long hair, and as she watched her fingers moving over him, she lightly moistened her lips with the tip of her tongue.

I'll be damned if I'll be a gentleman, he thought. Even cavaliers and knights of old surely had their needs.

He reached out, catching her hand where it lay over his heart. Her eyes darted to his in alarm.

"Go on. Touch me," he whispered.

"I—I didn't mean to wake you," she stuttered. They were both whispering. She must have known that he could not let her go, not this time. She was exquisite in the light, her breasts full and firm and ripe and her skin silky, shining in the candles' pale glow. Her eyes were so very blue...

"I'm awake," he told her.

"I've disturbed you—"

"Disturb me further, darlin'...please." His eyes remained locked with hers. He drew her hand along the length of his body. He heard her breath go ragged in her throat and her eyes followed the motion of their hands with a deadly fascination. Her fingers trailed over his flesh, over the soft hair that nestled around his sex. She tensed, and he felt her trembling. He sensed a certain fear within her, but he held her tight. She curved her hand around it hesitantly.

Rockets seemed to burst within his head and into his body. She gasped softly as she felt him swell huge and hard. She cried out softly. He reached up, slipping his hand around her neck to cup her head. He rose up on an elbow and kissed her slowly and fully, taking her lips, releasing them, hovering over them again just to brush them with the taste of his mouth and the seductive jut of his tongue.

Then he laid her flat and crawled aggressively over her. He kissed her again, easing away her hesitance.

He felt her fingers upon his shoulders again. Her body found a slow undulation beneath his. He set his hand upon her breast, and followed his touch with his kiss. He stroked her thighs and invaded her intimately with his touch.

With raw purpose he moved his body in a slow, bold sweep down the length of hers. He kept his eyes hard upon hers until he came to the juncture of her thighs, when he replaced his intimate touch there with the searing violation of his tongue.

She called out his name in a gasp as he brought her to the very edge of ecstasy, then withdrew. He found her eyes once more and she choked out incomprehensible words, reaching for him. She pulled him to her, seeking his shoulders with her lips and teeth. He pushed away again, demanding that she meet his eyes as he parted her thighs with the wedge of his knee and thrust deep and swiftly inside her.

She shuddered and whispered his name again.

That night, he gave little heed to finesse, and passion rose like a tempest within him. He caught her lips again with a savage passion, and as their bodies arched in an urgent rhythm, he caressed her with rough and demanding hunger.

Her legs wrapped high around him and her kisses fell upon him as she tasted the textures of his face and his throat. Her fingers trailed down his back to knot into the rigid muscles of his buttocks. At the end he cast back his head as a fierce shudder gripped his body, a hoarse cry escaping his lips. She sobbed out in turn, barely aware of the night, of time or place, barely conscious of reality.

Seconds later, she felt his touch, so absurdly gentle once again. Their harsh breathing could still be heard, and they were both covered in a soft sheen. "Malachi—"

"It's all right," he said gently. "You don't have to say anything." He lay back, bringing her down beside him. He whispered softly against her ear. "Just don't think to hop up and leave me. Don't deny me."

She lay there in silence. The darkness closed around them as the last of the candles burned out.

Much later, they crawled beneath the sheet. Shannon knew a moment of panic at this new intimacy, but then she relaxed again. There was nothing left to fear for that night. She hadn't meant what had happened. At least she didn't think that she did. She had thought he slept soundly, and she had not been able to resist temptation.

And temptation had definitely led to sin, she thought.

With his arms closed around her, she felt as if she might start crying again, because it felt so good. His arms offered warmth and security and a steel-hard strength, and she found she loved that. Just as she was coming to love the slant of his grin. And the way he would never let a man—or a woman—down. He had his code of honor.

And in his sweeping way, he was a cavalier.

She loved his courage, and his daring, just as she was coming to love the bronzed power of his arms, holding her close now. Just as she was coming to love the breadth of his golden-matted chest, and the hard, muscled length of his thighs...

And his impossible, immoral intimacy. She could not believe the way that he had touched and caressed her, and neither could she believe the sweet, unbearable ecstasy that he brought her with his sheer decadent purpose and determination. She was coming to care for him too much...

"Malachi," she whispered softly.

"What?" He moved his hand gently against her, beneath her breasts, idly, tenderly upon them.

"Have you ever been in love?"

He went still, then he moved away from her, his arm over his forehead as he rolled to his back, staring at the ceiling. "Yes. Once. Why?"

"I just...wondered."

He grunted, giving her no further answer.

"Malachi?"

"Yes?"

"Who was she?"

"A girl." It was a short, terse answer. He sighed. "It was a long, long time ago."

"What happened?"

"She died."

"The war—"

"A fever."

"I'm so sorry."

"I told you, it was a long, long time ago."

"It hurt you, though. Badly."

"Shannon, go to sleep."

"Malachi—"

"Shannon, go to sleep. It's night, and I'm tired." He started to rise. In the darkness, she saw the glitter in his eyes. "Unless you plan on entertaining me again, I suggest you go to sleep."

She closed her eyes quickly, turning from him and hugging her pillow. She couldn't...do it again. Not that night. She had to hug what had happened to herself, and she had to try to understand it, and live with it.

She felt him as he eased back down.

And later, when she was drifting off to sleep, she felt his arm come around her again, strong and sure, bringing her body close against his. It was warm, and it felt better than she ever might have imagined.

It felt...peaceful.

She opened her eyes and looked down at his hand, brown against the whiteness of her flesh in the moonlight.

It felt right, and though it might not be, she was tired. She was tired of the war, and tired of fighting. She didn't want to worry anymore. She wanted to take moments like these, and cling to them.

Her pa would be twisting and turning in his grave if he knew anything about her behavior in bed with this man, she thought ruefully. Gabriel McCahy had been a strong man—in his beliefs, in his ideals, in his morality. He'd liked his Irish whiskey, and he'd always been able to spin a fine tale, but he'd loved their mother, and when she had died, he'd been determined that his daughters would be ladies.

Of course, he'd never reckoned on the war.

And then, she reflected wistfully, maybe he wouldn't be so upset after all. He'd had an ability to judge men, and he might have understood that she had stumbled upon a good one, albeit, he came clothed in gray.

She closed her eyes and slept, her fingers falling lightly over Malachi's where they lay across her midriff.

"It is him! I told you it was him, Martha!"

Malachi woke abruptly, his eyes flashing open.

The bore of a sawed-off shotgun was stuck right beneath his nose. He jerked up. Shannon, curled against his chest, moaned in protest and went silent again. Instinctively, Malachi pulled the sheets high over her naked form as he stared respectfully into the face of the man carrying the shotgun.

"You're Malachi Slater," Mr. Haywood said. He barely dared glance at his wife, plump and pink in her nightgown and cap behind him. "Martha, you look now. It is him."

"Do you make a habit of bursting into your guests' bedrooms in the middle of the night?" Malachi demanded icily.

Beside him, Shannon stirred. Her eyes flew open and she saw the shotgun. "Oh!" she gasped, grasping the covers. She stared from Malachi to Haywood, and past him to his wife. She stiffened, raising her chin, and her voice came out as imperiously as a queen's. "What is the meaning of this?"

"There's wanted posters out on him all over the countryside," Haywood said. "You're a dangerous man, Captain Slater. Captain! Hell! Bushwhackers shouldn't get no titles or rank!"

Shannon leaped from the bed, dragging the covers with her, and heedlessly leaving Malachi bare. "He isn't a bushwhacker!" she swore. "It's all a lie! You want to shoot somebody, you ought to go out and shoot Fitz!"

Malachi grimaced at her sudden, passionate loyalty and pulled his pillow around to his lap. "Mr. Haywood, what she's saying is true. I was never a bushwhacker. I was a captain under John Hood Morgan until he died. I signed surrender forms with my men, and we were all allowed to keep our horses, and I was even allowed to keep my arms. I didn't know anything about this until some Union sentries shot at me." He indicated the wound on his leg. The bandage had been lost during his impromptu swim in the stream, but the evidence of Shannon's quick surgery was still there, a jagged red scab.

"Well, I don't know, young man. You're worth an awful lot of money, you know. If this is the truth, you can tell it to Mr. Fitz,'' Haywood said.

"Fitz will hang him and ask questions later," Shannon said.

Both the Haywoods looked at Malachi again. Malachi barely saw Shannon move, but suddenly she was behind the chair and she was aiming her Colt at the two of them.

"Drop the shotgun," she said.

Mr. Haywood frowned. "Now, come on, little girl. You put that thing down. Those Colts can be mighty dangerous."

"You ever seen close hand what a shotgun does to a man?" she inquired sweetly.

Malachi was afraid of the outcome.

"Can she shoot that thing?" Haywood asked him.

"Better'n General Grant himself, I'm willing to bet," Malachi replied sagely.

He still didn't think it wise to wait. He leaped from the bed.

Shannon watched in amazement as he swooped down on Mr. Haywood, bare as birth, and procured the shotgun. Mrs. Haywood gasped in astonishment, but didn't look away from the swaggering male body. Malachi bowed in response to her gasp. "Ma'am, excuse me." He tossed the shotgun to Shannon, reached for his pants and quickly limped into them.

"Oh, my goodness!" Mrs. Haywood gasped again. Her eyes closed and she promptly passed out.

"Oh, no!" Shannon wailed. Wrapping the sheet around herself, she hurried over to the fallen woman. Malachi stopped her, grabbing the Colt from her fingers. Shannon dropped down by Mrs. Haywood. "Malachi, Mr. Haywood, I need some water."

Mr. Haywood moved suddenly, as if rousing himself from shock. "Water. Water." He hurried to the washstand and brought over the pitcher. Nervous and disoriented, he poured the water over his wife's face. She came to, sputtering and coughing. She looked up at her husband. "Mr. Haywood!" she said reproachfully.

"Are you all right?" Shannon murmured.

"We've got to get out of here, Shannon!" Malachi warned her gruffly.

She ignored him. "Mrs. Haywood, I swear to you, I was telling you the truth. You've got to understand the whole story. Mr. Fitz had a brother who led a unit of jayhawkers, Mrs. Haywood—''

"I never could abide jayhawkers," Mr. Haywood said. "Never could abide them! Why, they were just as bad as the bushwhackers themselves.''

Shannon nodded. "They killed Cole Slater's wife, Mrs. Haywood. She was expecting a child. She was innocent, and they came and they killed her, and they burned down the ranch... And, well, Cole ran into Henry Fitz toward the end of the war. It was a fair fight— even the Yanks there knew it. Cole killed him.''

"So now Hayden Fitz wants the whole lot of you Slaters, is that it?'' Mr. Haywood asked Malachi.

Malachi nodded. "But that doesn't matter. I want Hayden Fitz. He has Shannon's sister, Cole's new wife, in his jail. He's going to use her, another innocent woman, to lure my brother out of hiding. I'm sorry, Mr. Haywood, but I ain't going to be hunted down and murdered by the likes of Fitz. And I'm mighty sorry, 'cause you and your wife are fine people, but I'm going to have to tie you up so that Shannon and I can get out of here.''

"Shannon?'' Mr. Haywood looked her way, then sank down on the bed. He looked to his wife. "What do you say, mother?''

"I never could abide those jayhawkers. Killing women and innocent children. And that poor dear girl, locked in a jail cell. It ain't decent!''

"Ain't decent at all.''

Malachi looked uneasily from Shannon, kneeling by Mrs. Haywood, to Mr. Haywood, calmly sitting on the bed.

"What—''

"You don't need to tie us up, Captain Slater.''

"I'm sorry, but—''

"You're going to need us, I think. We're not going to turn you in. If what you tell us is true, we'll try to help you.''

"Why?''

"Why?'' Mrs. Haywood stood up, strangely noble despite the water that dripped from her nightcap over her bosom. "Why? 'Cause somewhere, Captain Slater, the healing has to start. Somewhere, it has to quit being North and South, and somewhere, we have to stand against the men going against the very rules of God!''

''Malachi!'' Shannon urged him. ''We need them, if they will help us. We need this base. We need...we need the information that we're supposed to get in the next few days.''

Malachi thought furiously. Iris said that these were good folks. And Iris said that she could get to Fitz, and she could probably help him with information that he could never get on his own.

''Malachi! We have to trust them.''

Slowly, he lowered the Colt. Then he tossed it onto the bed.

''Shannon, I pray you aren't going to get us both killed,'' he said savagely.

''Hmph.'' Mr. Haywood stood, as stout and proud as his wife. He went over and picked up his shotgun. He didn't wave it at Malachi, but he held it in his hand, shaking it.

''So you ain't a bushwhacker and you don't deserve to hang for that! But you aren't this young lady's husband, either, and you should be strung up for seducing an innocent, and that's a fact.''

Shannon was surprised to see the flush that touched Malachi's cheeks. ''That's none of your business, Mr. Haywood,'' he said.

''It is our business, captain,'' Martha Haywood warned him severely. ''You were living in sin, right beneath our roof. What do you say, Papa?'' she asked her husband.

''I say that he hangs.''

''What?'' Malachi exploded. He made a dive for the Colt. Mrs. Haywood moved faster. She grabbed the gun and aimed his way. ''Now, captain, where are your manners? I never did meet a more gallant boy than a cavalry officer, and a Southern gentleman at that. You should be ashamed of yourself.''

''Ashamed! Where have the values gone?'' Mr. Haywood said fiercely. ''Pride and gallantry and good Christian ethics. The war is over now, son.''

''Sir—'' Malachi took a step forward. A shot exploded in the room, and he stood dead still. Mrs. Haywood knew what she was doing with a Colt, too, so it seemed. The ball went straight by Malachi's head, nearly grazing his ear.

"Shannon," he said through his teeth, keeping his eyes warily upon Mrs. Haywood. "Shannon, I am going to wring your neck!"

"No, captain, you're not. You're going to marry that girl, that's what you're going to do."

"I'm not going to be coerced into any marriage!" Malachi swore.

"Well, son, you can marry her or hang," Mr. Haywood guaranteed him. "Mrs. Haywood, would you like to go for the preacher? A Saturday morning wedding seems just right to me."

"No!" Shannon called out.

Malachi looked at her, startled. She was wrapped in the sheet, her hair a wild tangle around her delicate features and beautiful sloping shoulders.

Her eyes were filled with flashing blue anger. "Don't bother, Mrs. Haywood. I won't marry him."

"Well, well, dear, I'm afraid that you'll have to marry him," Mrs. Haywood insisted. "Right is right."

"That's right, young lady. You marry him, or we'll hang him."

Shannon smiled very sweetly, glaring straight at him. "I will not marry him. Mr. Haywood, you'll have to go right ahead. Hang him."

"Shannon!" Malachi swore. He swung around to stare at her in a fury. He was unaware of Mr. Haywood moving around behind him. He really did want to throttle her. His fingers were just itching to get around her neck.

His fury did him in.

He didn't see Mr. Haywood, and he certainly didn't see the water pitcher.

He didn't see anything at all. He simply felt the savage pain when the pitcher burst as Mr. Haywood cracked it hard over his skull.

He was still staring at Shannon, still seeing her standing there in white with her hair a golden, glowing halo streaming angelically all around her...when he fell to the floor.

And blackness consumed him.

Chapter Nine

Two hours later Shannon found herself in the store, standing on a stool, while Martha Haywood fixed the hem of the soft cream gown that Shannon wore.

It was a beautiful, if dated, bridal gown.

It had been Martha Haywood's own. A lace bodice was cut high to the throat with a delicate fichu collar over an undergown of soft pure satin. Ribands of blue silk were woven through the tight waistline, and the lace spilled out over the full wide skirt. Tiny faux pearls had been lovingly sewn into much of the lace.

"Mrs. Haywood, you don't understand," Shannon said urgently. She dropped down at last, catching the woman's nimble hands upon the hem. "Mrs. Haywood, you and your husband can't keep threatening Malachi. I don't want to marry him. And I don't believe you. You can't hang him if I refuse to marry him."

"We can, and we will," Mrs. Haywood said complacently.

"But I don't want to marry him. Please!"

Mrs. Haywood stared at her with her deep brown eyes. "Why? Why don't you want to marry him? You seem to be with him by choice."

"I am with him by choice. No...I mean, yes! But it's more circumstance than choice."

"That still doesn't explain why you don't want to marry him."

"Because...because he doesn't love me. I mean, I don't love him. It's just all—"

"Love comes," Mrs. Haywood told her. "If it isn't there already," she muttered. "The way you two came in here, the way we found you together... You explain yourself to me, young woman."

"I..."

"You just crawled into bed with him just like that...because of circumstances?" Martha Haywood's tone sent rivers of shame sweeping into Shannon. She felt as if she was trying to explain things to a doting and righteous aunt.

"You must have felt something for him. But then again, I'm not arguing that. Did you hear what you told me? You said that he didn't love you. So maybe you do love him. And maybe you're just afraid that he doesn't love you."

Shannon shook her head vehemently. "I promise you that he does not love me. And I do not love him. I was in love, once, during the war. I was engaged to marry a Yankee captain. He was killed... outside Centralia."

Mrs. Haywood finished with the hem and stood. "So you can't love again, and that's that. Why? You think that young man who did love you would want you spending your life in misery." She shook her head slowly and gravely. "The world has a lot of healing to do. And you should maybe start with your own heart. This Captain Slater seduced you under my roof, young lady. And you were curled up to him sweet as a princess bride this morning, so you're halfway there."

"Mrs. Haywood—"

"Papa has gone for the preacher. He is the local magistrate, so he's the law here. Oh, don't you worry none. Papa and me won't ever let on to anyone that we know your man's really a Slater. And the reverend will keep the secret, too. That is, if you two do the decent thing and marry up."

"You can't hang him for not marrying me!"

Mrs. Haywood laughed delightedly. "Maybe not, but there ain't no law against hanging a criminal. Captain Slater understands. Papa explained it to him real clearly."

"Mrs. Haywood—"

"Lord love us, child, but you do look extraordinarily fine!" She stepped back from the stool, gazing over Shannon and her handiwork with rapture. Tears dampened her eyes.

"Mrs. Haywood, this dress is beautiful. Your kindness to me is wonderful, but I still can't—"

"I had meant to see my own daughter in it one day. She was such a pretty little thing. Blond, with blue eyes just like you. And if I'd a caught her in bed with a Rebel captain, it'd have been a shotgun wedding, too, I promise."

"You...had a daughter?"

"Smallpox took Lorna away," Mrs. Haywood said softly. She wiped a tear from her cheek. "Never did think I'd put a young lady in this dress, so it's quite a pleasure."

Shannon sighed deeply. She should have just run away. She should have run from the house, screaming insanely, and then maybe the Haywoods would have understood.

But she just couldn't tell if they really intended to hang Malachi or not. If they weren't going to hang him for being a wanted man, surely they wouldn't for not being the marrying kind.

Still, she couldn't just run away. Not when they had locked him up. Not when they were holding all the weapons.

"Mrs. Haywood, please try to understand me—"

"Did you ever stop to think that Hayden Fitz just might get his hands on your man?" Martha asked her.

"What...do you mean?"

"Your man is going after your sister, his brother's wife. He ain't going to stop until he has her. He'll succeed with his mission, or he'll die in the attempt. I know his type. I saw all kinds during the war. Men who would run under fire; men who carried their honor more dear to their hearts than life. Your boy is one of the latter, Miss Shannon. So you tell me, what if Fitz gets his hands on the boy?"

"He...he won't," Shannon said.

"He could. I promise you, lots of folks wouldn't have paused like Papa and me. Fitz has power in these parts. Lots of it. He owns the mortgage on a dozen ranches, and he owns the ranchers, too. He owns the sheriff and he owns the deputies. So you tell me, what if Fitz gets his hands on this boy and kills him? What if you were free of us, and Fitz caught him and killed him anyway?"

"I don't...I don't understand what you're trying to say," Shannon protested.

"What if you're carrying that man's child and they hang him? What'll you tell your son or your daughter?"

Shannon felt herself growing pale, and she wasn't sure just what it was that Mrs. Haywood's grim words did to her. She had known all the while that they were entering into a dangerous world.

She knew that people died. She had been watching them die for years.

She felt ill and flushed and hot. Was she such a fool? Did everyone else think so rationally? The odds seemed so foolishly against them...

She still couldn't marry him. Not if she carried ten of his children, not if they were both about to be hanged in a matter of seconds. And suddenly she realized why.

She did feel for him. He had created a tempest deep within her heart, and it was with her always.

She didn't know how to put a name on the feeling. She didn't know if it was love or hatred or a combination of both. The thought of him with another woman had made her insanely jealous, and it had been humiliating to see how quickly he could still arouse her in the wake of her anger. Maybe their hatred had been mixed with love from the very beginning. Maybe circumstances were letting all her emotions explode here and now.

But she couldn't marry him.

She had heard herself. He didn't love her. And if he was forced into marrying, he would never forgive her. Not in this lifetime, or the next, and he would escape her as soon as he possibly could. She didn't want the misery for either of them.

If she was ever to have him, it had to be of his own free will.

"Mrs. Haywood, I can't—"

"Let's go into the next room. I hear voices. Papa must be in there with the preacher, and it's high time that we got on with the ceremony."

"Mrs. Haywood—"

The woman stopped and turned to her, her hands folded serenely before her. "Papa is not a patient man, young lady. And I'll wager he's got the shotgun aimed right at your Captain Slater's heart. Don't tarry, now. I don't want him getting nervous. The poor fellow might move in the wrong direction and Papa might decide to shoot him in the kneecap just to make sure that he sticks around.''

With a smile she turned and opened the shelved door and proceeded into the parlor. Shannon hurried behind her. They didn't mean it. They wouldn't shoot Malachi, and they wouldn't hang him, either.

Would they?

She stopped short when she came to the entrance of the parlor.

Malachi was there. He was standing right in the center of the parlor.

Mr. Haywood had apparently decided to dress Malachi for the occasion, as well. He was wearing a ruffled white shirt and a pinstriped suit with a red satin vest and a black-lapelled frock coat. She'd never seen him dressed so elegantly, and her breath caught in her throat as she saw him. The beauty of his costume was offset by the raw menace in his eyes and the rugged twist of his jaw. She had never seen him so coldly furious, nor had his eyes ever touched upon hers with such glaring hatred and with such a raw promise of revenge.

For a moment she couldn't move farther. She couldn't breathe, and she believed that her heart had ceased to beat. Panic made her seize hold of the doorway, meeting the savage fury of his glare.

''Come in, come in!'' Mr. Haywood called.

She still didn't move. Then she realized that the preacher was moving behind Malachi. He was a tall thin man with a stovepipe hat and black trousers and a black frock coat. He nodded to her grimly.

She heard a peculiar sound and looked at Malachi again...and saw that his wrists were shackled by a pair of handcuffs.

''Oh...really, please,'' she murmured. ''Please, you all must understand...''

''Talk to her, captain. Talk to her quick,'' Mr. Haywood advised Malachi. He, too, was all spruced up in a silk shirt and brown trousers, which gave him a dignity he had lacked earlier. One arm was around his wife's shoulders; in the other, he carried the shotgun.

''Get over here!'' Malachi snapped to Shannon.

The deep grate of his voice brought her temper surging to the fore. "Malachi, damn you, I am trying—"

She broke off with a gasp because he was striding her way with purpose and hostility. He might have been shackled but he managed to get a grip around her wrist, jerking her hard against him. She shivered as she felt the fire and tension and fury within him and felt his heated whisper against her cheeks.

"Get over here and marry me."

"Malachi, I don't believe them. I don't believe that they'll hang you if we don't marry."

He glared at her. "So you want to wait—and see?" he asked her slowly.

"I don't think—"

"You don't think! Do you want to wait until they tie the rope around my neck? Or maybe we should wait until I'm swinging in the breeze!"

"We could—"

"Shannon! Get over here and marry me now!"

"No! I will not—"

"You will, damn you!"

"I won't! Malachi, it wouldn't be right—"

"Right! You're talking about right? At a moment like this you're worried about right?"

"I don't love you!"

"And I don't love you, so maybe we're perfectly right!" His eyes narrowed to a razor's edge, raked hers with contempt. "They'll hang me, you bitch! Get over here and do it."

"What a wonderful way to ask!" she hissed sweetly.

His jaw twisted and set. "I'm not asking you, I'm telling you."

"And I'm afraid I'm not listening."

His fingers tightened around her wrist with such a vengeance that she cried out softly again.

"Captain Slater!" Martha Haywood protested, calling from the center of the parlor.

He didn't ease his hold. She found herself watching the pulse at the base of his throat with a deadly fascination. She felt weaker than she had ever felt in her life. She had thought she knew how to match her temper to his.

But maybe she didn't.

He pressed her up against the door frame, hard. "Shannon, you can get out of this later. You can say that you were coerced. But for the love of God, get over there now."

Some demon steamed inside her then, and she didn't know quite how to control it. All of her seemed awhirl in a tempest of hot blood and raw emotion. His anger fed her own. And for once, he was powerless against her.

"I don't like the way you're asking, captain," she told him icily.

He wasn't powerless, not in the least. With a swift turn on his heel, he dragged her along after him into the center of the room. She was stunned when he fell down on one knee, maintaining his firm grip on her before the preacher and the Haywoods. "Miss McCahy!" he hissed, the words dropping like sharp icicles from his mouth. "Dear Miss McCahy—beloved. Do me the honor this day of becoming my lawful wedded wife!"

"That wasn't exactly voiced the way I always thought that I'd hear the words!" Shannon retorted.

"Please, please, please, my beloved darlin'!" he said, rising swiftly, his eyes like knives that sliced through her. She was shaking, knowing that she pushed him. But he could have protested, too. He could have done more than he was doing.

"One more please, captain. And make it a good one."

"Please," he said. She had never heard anything that sounded less like an entreaty. He looked like some savage creature, and he didn't just want to chew her all up, he wanted to skin her alive first. But her demons told her they shouldn't be doing this.

He didn't wait for her answer, but turned to the reverend. "Go ahead, preacher man," he said dryly. "Get to it."

"No!" Shannon protested.

Mr. Haywood cocked the shotgun. The preacher began the ceremony.

Shannon listened to him in a daze. She could no longer run screaming into the street, because Malachi held her in a vise. Nor could she really risk it. Maybe Haywood would hang Malachi. She just didn't know.

The preacher was nervous. Looking at Malachi would probably make anyone nervous. Only the Haywoods seemed complacent.

Malachi answered the preacher in a cold raw fury, biting off each of his words. He spoke loudly and with a vengeance, enunciating each word. Love, honor and cherish. Till death did them part.

When her turn came, Shannon couldn't answer. She turned to him with one last fervent plea.

"Malachi, we can't do this—"

"Love, honor and obey!" he snapped at her.

"Malachi—"

"Say it!"

Shivering, she turned to the preacher. She stuttered out the words.

"The ring," the preacher said, clearing his throat.

"The ring?" Malachi said blankly.

"I've got it, Reverend Fuller," Mr. Haywood said. He stepped forward and placed a small gold band in Malachi's hand. Malachi stared at the man for a moment, fingering the gold. Then he slipped the ring on Shannon's finger, despite the fact that she was shaking so badly that her hands weren't still at all.

"We owe you again, Mr. Haywood," Malachi muttered.

"Don't worry. Price of the ring will be on your bill," Mr. Haywood said complacently.

"Hush, Papa! This is a beautiful rite!" Mrs. Haywood murmured.

It fit her tightly, snugly. Shannon felt the gold around her finger as smoothly and coldly as Malachi must feel the steel of the cuffs around his wrists. His eyes touched hers with a searing blue hatred and she thought that she could not wait to remove the ring.

Seconds later the preacher was saying that by the authority vested in him by the law of the great State of Kansas, and the greater authority vested in him by the glory of God on high, he now pronounced them man and wife.

Mrs. Haywood let out a long sob, startling them all. They stared at her. She blew her nose and smiled wistfully. "Don't mind me, dears, I always cry at weddings. Papa, release the groom from those shackles. He probably wants to kiss his bride. Reverend Fuller, could you do with a touch of Madeira? We've no champagne, I'm afraid. Maybe we've some across the way.''

Reverend Fuller said that Madeira would be just fine. Malachi stared at Shannon venomously as Mr. Haywood came to him with a small key and freed him from the handcuffs.

"Captain Slater, a glass of Madeira?'' Mrs. Haywood began.

But Malachi, freed, paid her no attention. He dragged Shannon into his arms and forced his mouth hard against hers with brutal purpose. His fingers raked her hair at her nape, holding her still for his onslaught. His tongue surged against her lips and forced them apart, raked against her teeth and invaded the whole of her mouth with ruthless abandon. Finally his mouth left hers and his lips touched her throat where it lay arched to him with deliberate possession. Then his mouth demanded hers again. His fingers trailed over the white lace of her gown with idle leisure and abandon, cupping lightly over her breast. The savage fury and heat of his kiss left her breathless, and with a searing sense of both clashing, tempestuous passion, and of deep, shattering humiliation that he would touch her so before others.

She felt the wrath in him deeply. It burned around him, and emitted from him in waves. She was amazed that he had married her; that he hadn't told the Haywoods to go ahead and hang him, and be damned. She hadn't thought that Malachi could be coerced into doing anything that he didn't want to do, but it seemed that they had managed to coerce him.

She tore away from him; he let her go. The back of her hand rose to her lips, as if she could wipe away his touch. "They should have hanged you!'' she hissed.

He blinked, and opaque shadows fell over his eyes. He bowed to her in a deep mockery of courtesy.

"You were trying hard enough, weren't you?''

He didn't give her a chance to answer. He swung around to Mrs. Haywood. "I thank you for your hospitality, ma'am,'' he drawled with a sure trace of sarcasm, "but I think I've a mind for something a little stronger at the moment.'' He strode toward the front door, then paused, looking back. "I have fulfilled your requirements to escape the hangman, haven't I?''

"Sign your name on the license, and you're free to go," Mrs. Haywood said.

Malachi walked to the marble-topped table where the license lay. He signed his name with an impatient scrawl and looked at Mr. Haywood, his jaw twisted hard, his hands on his hips.

Mr. Haywood nodded to him grimly. Malachi cast Shannon one last glare and then he threw open the door, slamming it in his wake. Shannon stared after him as cold fingers seemed to close over her heart.

"Madeira?" Mrs. Haywood offered her with a winning smile.

Shannon mechanically accepted the glass of wine. She cast back her head and swallowed it down in a single gulp. It wasn't enough. Malachi was right about one thing—they both needed to head straight for the whiskey.

She set her glass down. The wine tasted like bitter acid in her present mood. "I'll give you your dress back, Mrs. Haywood," she said simply. She turned, nodded to the preacher and to Mr. Haywood, and ran up the stairs. She found both keys on the bedside table, and picked them up, biting into her lower lip with such force that she drew a trickle of blood.

Malachi might really be her husband now, but he wasn't coming into this room again. Ever.

Ever!

She couldn't admit it, not even to herself, that her fury came mainly from the fact that she was afraid that he wouldn't even try.

He had slipped a ring upon her finger, forcing her to issue vows, and then he had left her.

For a red-haired whore.

No, he wouldn't be coming in the room again. Ever...

"Why, Ma—Sloan!" Iris called out to him as he entered the saloon. She never would get accustomed to calling him by another name.

He nodded her way and walked up to the bar, tossing down a coin. "Whiskey, Matey, if you would, sir. Whiskey, and lots of it."

Iris, pretty as a picture in a quiet gray dress and blue shawl, hurried over to him. She slipped her arm through his. "I was about to leave. I'm going to take the buggy and head for Sparks and see what I might find out about your sister-in-law. Is it still safe for me to leave? What's happened?''

He looked at Iris, at the concern naked in her eyes. He felt her soft touch on his arm, and some of the anger eased out of him.

"It's safe." He caught her to him and tenderly kissed her forehead. "You're a fine woman, Iris. Funny, ain't it? You really are such a fine damned woman no matter what your vocation. And her…''

"Your…traveling companion?''

"The little darlin'…yes. Shannon." He grimaced, staring at the ceiling, then he laughed bitterly. "My traveling companion. The curse of my life! The sweet little—hellcat!''

"What did she do now?''

"Damned little witch. I should have let you floor her yesterday, Iris. Hell." Matey put the whiskey bottle in front of him and he took a long, long swallow, gasping as the liquor sizzled its way down his throat to his stomach. He looked at the bottle reflectively. "I should have floored her myself.''

"Malachi…'' Iris realized that she had used his name, and she looked quickly around. The saloon was nearly empty. Only Matey might have heard her, and Matey minded his own business. "Let's go to my room, Mr. Gabriel,'' she said softly.

Malachi looked at her speculatively and picked up the whiskey bottle. "Yes, Iris, let's go to your room.''

She led him up a flight of stairs in the rear and opened the first door.

She had a real nice room for a working girl, Malachi thought. There was a big bed with four carved posters and a quilted spread, a braided rug on the floor, a handsome dresser and a full-length mirror on a stand.

"Nice,'' Malachi murmured. He drank more of the whiskey. He drank deeply, then he crashed down on the bed. He reached out for Iris with a slow smile curving into his lips. She sat down by his side, but watched him speculatively. He stroked her arm, and soft, feathery tendrils of desire swept along her flesh. She wanted to be touched by him. She had almost forgotten the feeling of wanting to be touched.

She pulled her arm away. He swallowed more whiskey, leaving one last slug in the bottle. Then he just lay there, staring at the ceiling.

"I want to kill her, Iris. I want to close my fingers right around her lovely white throat, and I want to squeeze until she chokes. I want to take my hand..." He raised his right hand as he spoke, studying the length of his fingers and the breadth of his palm, flexing his fingers. "I want to smack my hand against her flesh until it's raw...I want to shake her until her damned teeth crack!"

"Malachi, what happened?" Iris asked him softly.

His eyes fell upon her. His lip curved into a twisted, wry grin. "I married her. For real."

Iris lowered her eyes, swallowing. "Why?"

"They said they'd hang me if I didn't. They're convinced that she's a sweet young innocent and that I seduced her."

"Didn't you?"

"No. Yes. Hell, she's almost twenty now, she's as sweet as raw acid, and as to her innocence..."

"Yes?"

"She seduced me equally. No one innocent has a right to look the way she does...naked."

Iris would have laughed if she didn't feel such a peculiar hurt deep inside.

It wasn't that he had married the girl. It was the way he spoke about her.

"Now who is it who thought that you weren't married to begin with? Who thought that she was...seduced?"

"The Haywoods. They said they'd hang me."

"Of course they would want to hang you! You're worth a lot of money, dead or alive. There's a bounty on your head. If they know that you're not married, then they know—"

"They don't care who I am. They don't intend to let the knowledge go past themselves—and the reverend, of course," he added bitterly.

Iris exhaled softly. "Thank God for that!"

Malachi grimaced. "They weren't going to hang me for being a Confederate, a bushwhacker, or Cole's brother. They wanted to hang me because I seduced Shannon!"

Iris inhaled deeply. She couldn't believe that she was going to defend the other woman, that beautiful young woman with the sky-colored eyes, alabaster skin and the sun-drenched fall of long, curling hair.

But she was.

"Malachi, if the Haywoods forced you into a marriage, you can't really blame her." She paused, frowning. "Did she tell them…who you really are? Did she demand that you marry her? I mean, they are real God-fearing folk. Did they do it? Or did she force and coerce you?"

"What?" He stared at her blankly.

"Malachi, you can't hate her if they forced it. Maybe you can't even really hate her if she did make them force you into it. She isn't…well, she isn't my kind of woman. If you took advantage of her, maybe she had a right to force you—"

"She didn't force me."

"Then—"

"The bitch!" he exploded. "They're sitting there swearing up and down that they will hang me—and she's refusing! She's sitting there arguing with a shotgun. I was barely able to make her spit out the words! She would have made me hang."

"Then…"

"She's a witch, Iris," he said softly. He swallowed the last slug of whiskey. Iris hoped he wasn't heading for one heavy drunken stupor; even an experienced drinker like him would have trouble with the amount he had swallowed in the last ten minutes. "She's a witch," Malachi continued. "I mean to touch her, and I'm furious, and I want to hurt her. And I don't quite understand it, 'cause I'm hurting myself. I dream of her eyes. I dream of her reaching out to me. And then sometimes she touches me and I feel everything in me exploding just to touch her back, to feel her softness, to see her smile, to see her eyes glaze with wanting… She teases and she taunts, and she loves like a wildcat, like a pagan temptress, then she bares her claws and she swipes out and she draws blood, Iris, blood."

Iris smiled slowly. He still wasn't looking at her. He was staring at the ceiling. He turned around and suddenly grasped her hand. He kissed her fingers, and she shivered, feeling the sensual movement of his lips and beard against her flesh. "She's not like you, Iris. She's not like you at all. You can't ever talk to her, you can't reason with her. She's a witch…I've been fighting her forever and forever, Iris. Always fighting. She would have let me hang, can you believe that?"

"They wouldn't have hanged you," Iris said.

"She didn't know that."

"Maybe she did."

"She didn't, and that's a fact." He sat up. His eyes glittered. "Well, she has married me now. And she's going to pay for it!"

"Malachi, you were mad because she wouldn't marry you."

"She wanted them to shoot my kneecaps, the witch! But now, now she's mine…"

He fell back. His eyes closed.

Iris watched him for a minute. He was asleep. She smiled ruefully. "She may be a witch, but you're in love with her," Iris said softly.

She set the empty whiskey bottle on the dressing table, and decided to leave him where he was. Let him sleep off the bottle of whiskey he had swallowed in ten minutes, and maybe he'd go back to his tender young bride in a better state of mind.

She picked up her portmanteau and hat, walked to the door and blew him a kiss sadly. "I'll be back tomorrow, captain," she said softly. "Even if you do love her, I've got to help you."

She turned around and left him. If she hurried, she could make it to Sparks, spend plenty of time there and still be back in Haywood by the morning with all the information she could gather. She had friends in Sparks. Friends of the best variety for what she needed now. They were smart, beautiful women. And they knew the men of Sparks.

She looked back with a wistful smile.

Malachi slept peacefully.

Iris shrugged. He probably needed the rest.

She left, letting him sleep on.

And on…

* * *

Shannon changed and returned Martha Haywood's gown immediately, thanking her. She didn't want to wear Malachi's shirt any longer than she had to, so she determined to go into the mercantile and find another. Martha followed beside her, talking about her own early years of marriage.

"They were a hoot and a holler, I do tell you. Why, we were madder 'n wet hens at each other time and again, but then, I don't really remember what one of those arguments was about."

Shannon found a pretty soft blue blouse with teal embroidery along the bodice. She set it on the counter with boxes of ammunition. "First off," she told Martha Haywood softly, "we've got the same conflicts between us that just set a whole country to war."

"The war is over," Martha reminded her.

"Secondly, I knew a man once who was always gentle. He never had a temper about him."

"You'd have been miserable in a year."

Shannon gasped in horror. "That's not true! I was in love with him, I was deeply in love with him—"

"And you can't let it go. Still, it's true. You'd have been miserable in a year. Now, I don't think that you and Captain Slater will be getting along real well for a long time to come. But I think you'll come to realize that you have more in common than can be seen."

Shannon flushed. She set her hands on her hips. "He's been over at the saloon all day, Mrs. Haywood."

"Well, go on over and get him then. If you want him back, go on over and get him."

Shannon bit her lip, pretending to study the beautiful new blouse. "It's wonderful embroidery," she said softly. Then she smiled at Mrs. Haywood. "I don't want him, Mrs. Haywood. I don't want him near me again, and I mean it. He's been over in that saloon all day…" She swallowed fiercely. "Mrs. Haywood, could I have a tray sent up to me? I think that I want to retire early."

"It was a hard tonic for him to swallow, Shannon, being manipulated by us and all. I'm amazed that he was as docile as he was. And it must have been darned hard on him when you turned him down—"

"He didn't want to marry me."

"You refused to marry him when we might have hanged him!"

"You wouldn't have hanged him. Thank you for trying, Mrs. Haywood. I need to lie down for a while."

"It's very early," Martha told her anxiously.

"Yes, I know. Now, you're running a tab on everything, right? I should be ashamed. We came out of the war much better than many folks. I do have money."

"We're running a tab, Mrs. Slater."

Mrs. Slater. The name sounded absurd, and she hated it!

Malachi had been in the saloon for hours and hours now. And if he tried to tell her that he wasn't with the redhead this time, she'd probably scream and go mad on the spot.

Impulsively, she kissed Mrs. Haywood on the cheek. "I really need to lie down," she said softly. "Thank you so much for everything."

Shannon stepped into the parlor. She realized that she was absently twisting the ring around her finger. She tried to wrench it off. It was too tight. Soap might take it off.

On impulse, she hurried to the door to the street and pushed it open. Things were quiet, very quiet. An old bloodhound lifted his head from his paws across the way on the saloon veranda. He looked at Shannon, then dropped his head again. Two men idly conversed down the way before the barber's shop, and that was it.

Shannon strode down the steps and across to the saloon. She entered the building, assuring herself that she wasn't going to do anything but order herself a brandy.

She pushed through the swinging doors. The saloon, she saw, as her eyes adjusted to the darkness, was almost as quiet as the street. A lone rancher sat in the back, his hat pulled low over his eyes, hiding his face. A blond harlot in crimson silk sat upon the bar, absently curling a strand of hair around her finger.

The barkeep was drying glasses. He looked at Shannon warily.

"May I have a brandy, please? And could you put it on my husband's tab?"

He shrugged uncertainly, found a glass, filled it and set it before

Shannon. She nodded her thanks and swallowed the brandy down. She looked around the saloon again. Malachi was definitely not there.

Kristin would be horrified that she was standing in the saloon, Shannon thought. But then Kristin had always been more conventional, and Kristin had always had a better hold on her temper. Well, maybe not. Kristin had waged a few battles with Cole, and Cole was such a lamb in comparison with Malachi. None of that would matter to Kristin. A lady shouldn't be in a saloon like that.

Even if she was wondering what her husband of five hours was up to.

He wasn't in the saloon.

"Have you seen, er, Mr. Gabriel?" she asked the bartender sweetly.

The blond woman answered, looking her up and down and smiling sweetly. "He's still sleeping up in Iris's room, last I heard."

Shannon felt dizzy. It was as if the whole room went black, then seemed to be covered in a red haze.

"Thank you very much," she said pleasantly. "When you do see him again, please tell him that he is most welcome to remain where he is, and that he will not be at all welcome elsewhere. Thank you."

"Wait," the woman began.

But Shannon cut her off with a clipped, commanding tone, her chin high, her eyes a cutting, crystal blue. There was a note of warning in her voice. "Please, just see that he gets my message." She'd had no idea that she could speak quite so commandingly, but the woman's next words died on her lips and Shannon turned and left the saloon. In the middle of the street, she suddenly paused, doubled over and let out a deep, furious, and anguished scream.

Martha Haywood came running out of her parlor. "Oh, dear, oh dear, what is it?"

Shannon straightened. "Nothing. I'm fine, Mrs. Haywood."

"You're fine!" Mrs. Haywood exclaimed. "That didn't sound at all like fine to me!"

"Well, I wasn't fine until I did it. Now, I am fine. I promise you." She wasn't fine at all. She felt as if she was being ripped apart on the insides by sharp talons. She wanted to kill Malachi. Slowly. She wanted to stake him out on the plain and allow a herd of wild buffalo to trample him into the dust. She wanted to watch the vultures come down and chew him to pieces. She wanted...

She wanted him to come back so she could tell him just how furious she was. And how hurt. How deeply, agonizingly...hurt.

"I am fine, Mrs. Haywood," she repeated, smiling, stiffening. She clung to her temper. She would never forgive him. Never. She stood as tall as she could, straightening her shoulders. "Just fine. If you'll excuse me... Can you please see to it that I'm not disturbed until the morning?" She pushed past Martha and hurried into the house. She raced up the stairs and went into her room, locking the door and assuring herself that she had both keys.

She gasped, trembling, as she looked around.

Martha Haywood had tried so hard to make it welcoming!

Hot water steamed in the bath and there were fresh flowers beside the bed. A silver tray with cold meat and pastries sat on a table, and across the bed lay one of the most beautiful white satin nightgowns she had ever seen. There was a note on it. Shannon picked it up. "Every bride deserves a new thing of beauty. Wear it with our warmest wishes. Martha and Hank."

She set down the note and sank onto the bed, and suddenly she was softly sobbing. Every woman harbored and cherished dreams of just such a gown on her wedding night. And every woman cherished her dreams of a man, magnificent and gallant and handsome. A man who would hold her and love her...

She had the gown, and she had the man. But the dream had dispersed in the garish light of reality.

Malachi did not love her.

She lay on the bed and gave way to the flood of tears that overwhelmed her, and then, when her tears dried, she stared at the ceiling and she wondered just how long she had really been in love with Malachi. They'd never had a chance to be friends. From the start the war had come between them.

But she would never forgive him for this. Never. Come what may, he would never touch her again.

Whether he'd been coerced into marriage at gunpoint, it hadn't been her doing; she'd tried her best to stop it all. He'd had no right to go straight to the red-haired whore, and she would never forgive him.

After a while, the shadows of twilight played upon the windows. The bath had grown chilly, but she decided to indulge in it. She carefully set a chair under the doorhandle first; she wasn't taking any chances.

There was a bottle of wine with the food on the table. Shannon sipped a glass as she bathed quickly.

She even donned the beautiful satin gown.

In time, she stretched out in bed. She closed her eyes and she remembered him the evening before, coming into the room with a vengeance and a purpose. Sweeping her up, holding her.

Claiming his rights, when they weren't in truth married.

But now she was his bride.

Eventually, she closed her eyes. She had her Colt by her side, fully loaded. If he tried to return, she would demand that he leave quickly enough, and she would enforce her words.

But this night, their wedding night in truth, he did not return.

Toward dawn, she cried softly again.

He was her husband now. He did have certain rights.

But he wasn't coming back. Not that night.

Chapter Ten

At two in the morning, Malachi stirred. His head was killing him; his mouth tasted as if he had been poisoned, and his tongue felt as if it was swollen in his throat. A clock ticked with excruciating, heavy beats on the mantel.

He staggered out of bed and peered at the clock. When he saw the time he groaned and looked around the room. Iris was gone. She was a good kid. She had gone to Sparks, trying to help him. He was sleeping in her room, while Shannon...

Oh, hell.

His head pounded with a renewed and brutally savage fury. Shannon...

Shannon would be sleeping, too, by then. If she wasn't sleeping, it was even worse. She'd be furious, hotter than a range fire.

He threw himself back on the bed. The hell with her. They were going to have one fabulous fight, he was certain. It couldn't be helped.

He was going to be a rational man, he promised himself. He was going to be level and quiet. He was going to be a gentleman. Every bit as much a gentleman as the Yank she mourned.

The hero...

Well, hell, at this moment, it was easier for a Yank to be a hero. Rebs weren't doing very well. Just like she liked to tell him—they had lost the war.

Darlin'...the South will rise again, it will, it will, he vowed to himself. Then he remembered that he had just promised himself that he was gong to be reasonable.

They were married to one another.

His head started pounding worse as his blood picked up the rhythm, slamming against his veins. He was married to her...for real. If he had a mind to, he could walk right across that street and sweep her into his arms. He could do everything that the rampant pulse inside him demanded that he do. He could meet the blue sizzling fire in her eyes and dig his hands through her hair and bury his face against her breasts. He could touch her skin, softer than satin, sweeter than nectar, he could...

Rape his own wife, he thought dryly, for she sure as hell wasn't going to welcome him.

She would have let him hang! He was the one with the right to be furious. Granted, he would have come for Kristin with or without Shannon—he had meant to come without her—but it was still her sister he had traveled into enemy territory to save.

He could have been in Mexico by now. He could have been living it up in London or Paris. There was no more cause, no South left to save. It was over.

It should have been over.

He exhaled. He wasn't going to go to her now. She'd surely bolted the door against him. And the house would be silent. Dead silent. It just wasn't the time for a brawl, which is what it would be.

If she didn't just shoot him right off and get it over with.

She wouldn't shoot him. She was his wife now.

Yeah, a wife pining for a divorce, or pining to become a widow quick as a wink.

The turmoil and tempest were swirling inside him again. He didn't want to start drinking. He rose and went to the washstand and scrubbed his face and rinsed out his mouth, availing himself of Iris's rose water to gargle with. He felt a little better. No, he felt like hell. He felt like...

Racing across the street and breaking the door down and telling her that she was his and that she would never lock a door against him again, ever...

He groaned, burying his head in his hands. They were just a pair of heartfelt enemies, cast together by the most absurd whims of fate. She was in love with a dead man, and he wasn't in love at all. Or maybe he was in love with...with certain things about her. Maybe he was just in love. Maybe there really was a mighty thin line between love and hate, and maybe the two of them were walking it.

He walked to the window and stared at the night.

The new moon was coming in at long last, casting a curious glow upon the empty street.

They were forgetting their mission. Kristin...they had come all this way and met with physical danger, culminating with the last encounter with the Haywoods. They had come together in a burst of passion, and they had exchanged vows, and now they were legally wed, man and wife, and despite it all, they were still enemies, and despite it all, he could still never forget her, never cease to want her.

He walked over to the bed and lay down, folding his hands behind his head, staring at the ceiling. Iris would come back, and then he would have a better idea of what to do next. Cole must have heard what was happening by now. Jamie, too. And once they had heard about Kristin, they would have started moving this way.

He and Shannon had to start moving again. They had to cease the battle and come to a truce and worry about their personal problems later.

It was the only logical move...the only reasonable one.

He gritted his teeth hard against the fever and tremor that seized him again. He steeled himself against thoughts of her. He wanted her so badly...he could see her. He could see her as she had been in his dream, rising from the water, glimmering drops sluicing down her full, full breasts...water running sleek down the slimness of her flanks, down her thighs...

He could see her eyes, dusky blue, beautiful as they met his in the mists of passion. He could almost feel her moving against him, sweetly rhythmic. He could hear her whispering to him... whimpering, crying out softly and stirring him to a greater flame, a greater hunger...

Logical, reasonable. This was insane.

He was a gentleman, he reminded himself. He had been raised to be a Southern gentleman; he had fought a war to preserve the Southern way of life, perhaps the great Southern myth. He didn't know. But he had been taught certain things. He loved his brother; he would always honor his brother's wife. He believed in the sanctity of honor, and that in the stark horror of defeat, a man could still find honor.

Logic…reason. When the morning came, he would defy the very fires within him. She would not be able to ask for a more perfect gentleman. As long as she didn't touch him, he would be all right.

The perfect gentleman.

If not quite her hero.

Someone was turning the knob of her door.

Shannon didn't understand at first just what was awakening her. Something had penetrated the wall of sleep that had come to her at last.

She lifted her head and she listened. At first, she heard nothing.

Then she heard it. The knob was twisting. Slowly. Some weight came against the door. Then the knob twisted and turned again and again. Someone was trying to be quiet; stealthy.

She rose, biting into her lower lip.

It was Malachi, at last.

She leaped out of bed and ran to the Haywoods' lovely little German porcelain clock. She brought it close to her eyes and looked at the time.

It was almost three in the morning.

She spun around. The knob was twisting…

Malachi. Damn him! He had finished with his whore, and now he wanted to come back to her to sleep! On her wedding day!

Oh, granted, it was no normal wedding day!

But still…

She hated him! She hated him with a vengeance! With everything inside her. How could he? How could he drag her—force her!—into this horrid mockery of marriage, and then spend the day with a harlot. After last night…

It was foolish to give in to him, ever.

She hadn't meant to give in to him.

Ever.

She had simply wanted him, and therefore, it had never been so much a matter of giving, it had been a matter of wanting. Of longing to touch, and to be touched in turn. Of needing his arms. Of needing his very height, and his strength. Of hearing his voice with the deep Southern drawl, of feeling his muscled nakedness close to her...

She had loved once.

And she loved now, again. Perhaps he could never understand. And if she valued not only her pride but her soul and her sanity, he could not know.

Not that it mattered. She could never let him in; she could never let him touch her again. He couldn't come straight from his whore to her. Whether emotion entered into it or not. He just couldn't do it, and that was the way that it was.

Her eyes narrowed; she was ready for battle.

But the doorknob twisted one last time, and then she heard footsteps—soft, soft footsteps!—moving away from her, down the hall and then down the stairs, fading away into the night.

"Malachi!" she murmured in misery.

So there would be no fight, and no words spoken. She could not go to battle, and she could not give of herself or take, for he was gone, leaving her again.

She lay down and cast her head against the pillow in misery. She stared straight ahead and ached for what seemed like hours and hours.

He had gone back to her. Back to his old friend. Back to the red-haired harlot.

She could not sleep. She could only lie there and hurt.

At three in the morning, the last of the locals threw down their cards, finished off their beers or their whiskeys and grunted out their good-nights to Matey and to Reba, the golden blonde who played the piano at the Haywood saloon.

Reba started collecting glasses. Matey washed them, telling Joe, his helper, to go on and clear out for the night. Joe had a wife and new baby, and was grateful to get out early for the evening.

Reba tucked a straying tendril of her one natural beauty, her hair, back into the French knot she wore twisted at her nape. She looked across the saloon to the dark shadows and paused.

They had both forgotten the stranger. It was peculiar; she had thought that he had left earlier.

But he had not. He was still there, watching her now. She could feel it.

He raised his face, tilting back his hat.

He was a decent-looking fellow, Reba thought. Sexy, in a way. He was tall and wiry and lean, with dark hair and strange, compelling light eyes. The way he looked at her made her shiver. There was something cold in that look. But it made her grow hot all over, too, and there weren't many men who could make her feel anything at all anymore.

This one made her skin crawl. He also made her want to get a little closer to him. There was something dangerous about him. It was exciting, too.

"Mister," she called to him. "We're closing up for the night. Can I get you anything else?"

He smiled. The smile was as chilling as his eyes.

"Sure, pretty thing. I'll take me a shot and a chaser..." His voice trailed away. "A shot and a chaser and a room—and you."

"You hear that, Matey?" Reba called.

"Got it," Matey replied with a shrug. The drinks were his responsibility. It was Reba's choice, if she wanted to take on the drifter this time of night.

Reba brought the shot and the beer over to his table. He grasped her wrist so hard that she almost cried out and pulled her down beside him. She rubbed her wrist, but thought little of the pain. Lots of men liked to play rough. She didn't care too much. Just as long as they didn't get carried away and mar the flesh. If he wanted to be a tough guy, though, he could pay a little more.

"You got a room?" he asked her.

"That depends," she said.

"On what?"

He was a blunt one, Reba decided. She flashed him a beautiful smile, draping one long leg over the other, and displaying a long length of black-stockinged thigh. She ran a finger over the planes of his face, and found herself shivering inside again. His eyes were strange. They were so cold they might have been dead. They calculated every second. They were filled with something. She didn't quite recognize what it was.

Cruelty, maybe...

She shook away the thought. A lot of men looked at women that way. It made them feel big and important. Still...

She started to pull away from him. She almost forgot that she made her living as a whore, and that she didn't mind it too much, and that the pay was much better than what she had been making as a backwoods schoolteacher on the outskirts of Springfield.

Should she? She was tired; she wasn't in any desperate need for money. She should just tell him that it was too darned late for her to take a man in for the night.

"I got gold," he told her. "Is that what it depends on?"

Gold. He wasn't going to try to pawn off any of that worthless Southern currency, and he wasn't even going to try to pay her with Union paper. He had gold.

"All right," she told him at last.

And unknowingly sealed her fate.

He stroked her cheek softly, and looked toward the stairs. He smiled at her, and Reba silently determined that she had been mistaken—he was just a tough guy, not a cruel one. And he was handsome. Not nearly as handsome as Iris's friend Sloan, but he had all his teeth, all his hair and all his limbs. And that wasn't so common these days.

A working girl could always use a little extra cash.

"Where's your friend?" he asked her.

"Who?"

"The redhead."

Strange, he was talking about Iris. Reba started to answer, but then she paused, stroking his arm. "Iris is occupied for the evening." She smiled.

The stranger lifted his glass toward the saloon doors. "The husband, eh? That the blushing little bride was looking for."

Reba chuckled. "It's a good thing the groom is occupied. The maid over at the Haywoods' told Curly—Curly's the barber—that Mrs. Gabriel has bolted down for the night. Sloan Gabriel would need four horses to ram the door down."

"Is that a fact?"

"'Course, Iris says he'll do it. When he—when he's good and

ready, he'll go over and break right in. Determined type. He doesn't take nothing off of her.''

"Doesn't he, now?''

"Not Sloan Gabriel.''

The stranger's lip curled. "Sloan Gabriel, eh?''

"That's right. That's the man's name. Why?''

"No matter. It's just a good story. I watched the woman earlier. She needs a lot of taming.'' He paused, sipping at his whiskey. "You think Mr. Gabriel will just break the door on down to get to her, eh?''

"To teach her a lesson.''

"And he's here now. Right here in this fine establishment.''

"Ain't that a laugh.''

"Yeah. It's a laugh. But, hey, now...'' He swallowed the whiskey in a gulp, then drained his beer. He set the glass down on the table hard. "No matter at all. What matters now is you and me. Let's find that room of yours, all right?''

Reba nodded swiftly, coming to her feet. She took the stranger's hand and called good night to Matey as they walked up the stairs. She passed by Iris's doorway and hid her smile of secret delight.

Sloan Gabriel was in there, all right. Still sleeping away, after consuming his own bottle of whiskey. Iris had asked her to look in on him now and then, and she had been glad to comply. He was still sleeping peacefully, and his golden wife assumed he was enjoying the daylights out of himself. She didn't know why she didn't tell the stranger. It was a funny story. It was great.

But Iris had acted as if she didn't want too many people to know where she was going.

Reba shrugged and hurried to her own door.

When they entered her room, the stranger closed the door. Reba turned around, smiling at him. "Want to help me with a few buttons, honey?'' she asked. She sat down at the foot of the bed, a woman practiced with her craft, and slipped off her shoes. When that was done she slowly slid off her garters and started peeling away her stockings one by one. He watched her, standing by the door. Reba smiled with pleasure, certain that she had this drifter well in hand.

"What's your name, honey?'' she asked him.

"Justin," he said.

"Justin what?"

"Justin is all that matters."

"All right, Justin, honey." She smiled and licked her tongue slowly over her lips, as if she gave grave attention to her stockings. He was quiet, then he spoke suddenly, pushing away from the door.

"Turn over," he told her.

"Now, honey, no funny stuff," she said. He didn't smile. She added nervously. "Honey, any deviation—any slight, slight deviation—will cost you a fortune." Little pricks of unease swept along her spine, but she kept smiling anyway.

Her smile faded when he suddenly strode across the room and jerked her around by the arm, pressing her down into the bed, face first. He tore at her chemise and petticoats, ripping them from her with a vengeance. Gasping, smothering, she tried to protest.

"Shut up," he warned her.

"No! No, please—"

Reba tried to twist around. He slapped her hard on the cheek, sending her head flying against the bedpost. Stunned, she still tried to resist. She hadn't the power. He shoved her over and down.

A scream rose in her throat when he sadistically drove into her. But her scream went unheard, muffled by her pillow.

In time, either the pain dulled, or she passed out cold.

When she awoke, it was morning. She felt the sun coming in through the window.

She tried to move, but everything about her hurt. Her cheek and eye were swollen where he had beaten her. She hurt inside, deep inside. She would have to see the doctor, and pray that nothing was busted up too bad. God, she was in agony.

She was afraid to open her eyes; he might still be there. She didn't feel him, though. She lifted her lashes just slightly. Then she dared to twist around.

He was out of the bed. He was dressed, and he was staring out her window, toward the Haywoods' store and hotel across the street.

Suddenly, he stiffened and straightened. She saw him set his hand on his gun at his hip.

"There he goes," he murmured. He swung around, as if sensing that Reba was awake. She closed her eyes, but not fast enough. He came over to her, wrenching her up. "You shut up, bitch!"

"I didn't say—"

He slapped her again. Reba gasped, screaming for all that she was worth. Matey would be up and about; someone would hear.

"Oh, no you don't!" He slammed her pillow down on her face, pressing hard. Reba twisted and gasped, and the pain entered her lungs as she could draw no air. He kept talking. As she grew dizzy, she could hear him. "You ain't ruinin' it for me, honey." He started to laugh. "What's one little whore, when the golden girl is right across the street? If you're right, Slater is in there, getting through to her for me right now. I tried to get to her last night, but I was afraid to bust the door down myself. I might have had the whole town down on me. I slipped out, and I slipped back in, and nobody knew it at all. I came back to the saloon...and to you, too, honey. I'm gonna kill Slater, and I'm gonna make her wish that she was dead. You can imagine how good I am at that, huh, honey?" Dimly, she heard him laugh. "You can imagine. You can just imagine." He pressed harder and harder upon the pillow.

Her struggles ceased.

Finally, he tossed the pillow aside. She was still and silent. "I wouldn't have had to kill you if you'd just known how to keep that whore's mouth of yours closed." He tipped his hat to her. "It's closed now, honey. Sure am sorry. It's just that you don't compare. No, ma'am, no way, you just don't compare. I'm gonna have me that girl, and I'm gonna kill that man."

He looked outside. Malachi Slater was heading across to the livery stable. Looked like time to take a walk himself.

"Shannon!"

She had awoken, hearing him call out her name in annoyance. He banged on the door. She pressed her fingers against her temple and ignored him.

"Shannon, open this door."

"No!"

"Don't give me a hard time now, Shannon McCahy. I've got to get in."

"It isn't McCahy anymore, is it?" she demanded bitterly through the door. "Get away from here!"

She waited. There was silence for a moment. "Shannon, open the door. Now."

"You arrogant Reb bastard!" she hissed at him. "Go away. I'll never open the door."

She heard his sigh even through the door. "Shannon, I am going to try not to fight with you. I am going to do my best to get along with you, Shannon, because—"

"Your best! Malachi, go!"

"Shannon, I really am trying. Now, open the door and—"

"You're an ass, Malachi. A complete ass!"

"Shannon, I am trying—darlin'. But keep it up, and you'll pay. I promise," he said very softly.

"Go away!"

"Shannon, I'm giving you ten seconds. One—"

"You should have knocked when you came last night."

"I didn't come here last night. You're dreaming."

"Nightmare, Mr. Slater. If I was dreaming, it was a nightmare." She paused, then said with disgust, "You liar!"

"I didn't come near you last night, Shannon. But so help me, I'll come near you now!"

It was a threat. A definite threat. After everything that he had done!

She spat out exactly what he should do with himself.

He slammed into the door. The noise brought her flying up in panic, searching for the Colt. The wood splintered and sheared around the lock, and the door soared open.

Malachi stood in the doorway, looking much the worse for wear. His clothing was rumpled, his eyes were red, and his temper hadn't improved a hair.

Not that the night had done much for Shannon's.

She lifted the Colt and aimed it straight at his heart. "What do you think you're doing here?" she demanded huskily. She couldn't quite find her voice.

He eyed the Colt but ignored it. He stepped into the room, kicking the door shut behind him. "Shannon, I am going to try and talk reasonably. I—"

"Malachi, get out of here. Or else I will shoot you. I will not kill you. I will aim—"

"Don't you dare say it!" he snapped at her.

"Say what?"

"You know what!"

"All right! I'll shoot at—"

"Shannon!"

"Malachi, I don't want you here. I married you to save your damn neck and you can't even stay with me for two seconds."

"I had to beg you to—"

"You forced me to say those words."

"You know, I'm remembering right now just how bad it was. Dropping down on my knees to beg you to—"

"Beg! You get out, now! Or I will put a bullet right where it might count the most!"

"Why, darlin'," he drawled. "You are my beloved wife, and I can come to you whenever I choose."

"The hell you can."

"The law says I can," he told her softly.

"The law plans on stringing you up—darlin'. Maybe we ought not tempt fate."

"Well, then, Mrs. Slater, I say that I can." He crossed his arms over his chest, leaning back against the broken door. His lashes fell with a lazy nonchalance over his eyes, but she could see the slit of blue beneath them, wary and hard.

She was trembling. She couldn't let him see it. She kept her hand as steady as she could manage on the Colt.

"You chose your bed, captain. You just go on back to it."

"Darlin', I'm tired of you spying on me, and I'm damned tired of your being a brat. I didn't come to fight—"

"You shouldn't have come at all."

"Put the gun away, Shannon."

"Get out!"

"I can't, not now—"

"Malachi, get away from me, now!"

"Put the gun away, Shannon. Put it away now! I'm warning you as nicely as I can, but I mean it." It sounded as if he was growling at her. She gritted her teeth and smiled sweetly.

"Malachi, since I am the one with the gun, I'm warning you."

"You'll be damned sorry when you don't have the gun."

"Don't threaten me."

"You vowed to obey me."

"You vowed to cherish me. It was all lies. So no, captain, you go on back across the street to your whore. You're not going to touch me."

"You're one Yank I do intend to touch, my love."

She pulled back the trigger on the Colt, letting him hear the deadly click. "Get out. You know that I can aim."

"I haven't come to do anything to you. I've come because this is my room, and you are my wife. Put the gun down. I have every right here, and you won't shoot me."

"You have no rights here, and I will shoot you!"

He took a step toward her. She fired, with deadly accuracy. The bullet whizzed by his face, so close that it clipped his beard before embedding itself into the thick wood of the door behind him. He stopped, staring at her, the muscles in his jaw working. He was surprised, but he was not afraid. "You shot at me!" he said, his voice harsh and low. "You actually shot at me!" He took another step toward her.

"You fool!" Shannon warned him, backing away. She fired again, and drew blood this time, nicking his ear.

But it did no good. He was upon her, wrenching the Colt from her hand. His fingers dug around her upper arms with a trembling force, and he picked her up and tossed her like a sack of wheat upon the bed. She struggled to rise, but he caught her and pushed her back. He straddled her, pinning her down, and she saw the naked amazement and wrath in his eyes. "You little bitch! You really would have killed me!"

She wriggled and kicked, struggling fiercely. "If I'd meant to kill you, you'd be dead, and you know it."

He eased his hold on her to touch his ear, feeling the trickle of blood. She used the opportunity to surge against him, freeing her hands and swinging at him. She caught him on the jaw with a good punch, and he swore savagely, securing her beneath him again. The beautiful white satin bridal nightgown was twisting higher and higher around her hips with every fevered moment. "Let me go, Malachi."

"Oh, no, Shannon, you're the one who wanted to play rough. Well, let's play rough, shall we?"

And he wrenched the gown up high on her thighs with his free hand. He released her to unbuckle his trousers, and she screeched, jumping up. He caught her arm, twisting her down.

"You shot at me!" he hissed at her.

She swung forward, trying to hurt him, trying not to cry. "And you slept with the red-haired harlot, so leave me alone!" She slammed against his chest and thrashed out with her legs. She heard him groan in pain and she knew that she had gotten him good.

But he fell against her again, and her hair caught and pulled in his fingers. "I didn't sleep with her—"

"Oh, no! Don't try to play me for a fool, Malachi."

"I did not sleep with Iris. She's a real friend, an old friend. I should sleep with her. She is kind, and caring. And warm. But I wasn't with her last night. I slept in her bed, but not with her."

"Liar!"

"No!"

He pushed her flat against the bed. Tears stung her eyes and she writhed and struggled against him. "Liar!" she accused him again. But his lips met hers, and she didn't understand what happened at all.

"I am not lying!" he swore, and his hatred contoured and marred his features.

"Please..."

He assaulted her...but she met his fury with her own. His mouth forced down hard upon hers...but her lips parted to his, and she met the invading thrust of his tongue with the passionate fury of her own. When his lips broke from hers, she cried out his name. She didn't know if it was a plea, a broken whisper, a beseechment that he leave her...or a prayer that he stay with her.

Whatever it was, it changed his touch. He went very still. Shannon was amazed that she had freed her hands, only to wind her arms around him, only to rake her fingers through his hair. She felt the touch of his fingers, slowly curling around her breasts over the satin of the gown.'

"I am not lying!" he vowed again, and softly. He rubbed her nipple between his thumb and forefinger and felt it swell to his touch. She felt the softness of his beard, and the sweet, burning tenderness of his kiss. He ravaged her body still, but with care, with passion, but with some strange lust gone, so gentle that she arched and writhed and twisted toward him, maddened to feel more and more of it...

Then he thrust into her, deep, full, grinding, and defying all his previous gentleness. Bold, determined, sure, his fingers and his eyes locked with hers as he claimed her completely and cast her shuddering to her depths with the ecstasy of feeling his body within her own, burning within her, a part of her mind, her heart, her frame...her soul.

"Malachi." She whispered his name again as he began to move within her. She held him, embraced him, caressed him. Fever and tempest were with them as they whirled and whirled in a dark and furious and timeless storm that stripped away pretense...

And even hatred...

Satisfaction burst upon them, as volatile as the burning cannon fire of the war that had raged around them.

He pulled from her when it was over. She lay silent; he lay looking at the ceiling.

"What are we doing to one another?" he said softly. But he didn't look her way. He rose. Shannon could not move, not even to adjust the satin of the gown over her hips. She heard him doffing his borrowed clothes, donning his own trousers and shirt and boots. She still did not move.

He paused at last. "We've got to go. Get up. Get dressed. I'll explain when you come down, but I've got some good news as far as freeing Kristin is concerned. Hurry. We need to get moving."

He walked to the door. When he reached it, he paused for several seconds.

"I'm sorry, Shannon. Really sorry. It...it won't happen again."

He was gone. She listened dully as his footsteps faded away on the staircase. Listlessly, she curled into herself. She had to get up. She had to get dressed and ready. They were going after Kristin. This was what it was all about...

She dragged herself up. Then she leaped up from the bed, anxious to call him back because she realized now she could still hear his footsteps. She had to tell him that she was sorry, too, so very sorry...

"Malachi!"

He was coming up the stairs, coming back to her. She raced to the doorway.

A man was coming up the stairs. He was wearing a feather hat, and his head was bowed low, and the brim covered his face. But it wasn't Malachi. A sense of danger suddenly sheared along her spine.

At that moment he reached the top step and raised his head.

She stared straight into the evil leering face of the bushwhacker, Justin Waller. "Howdy, Shannon. Excuse me—howdy, Mrs. Gabriel," he said softly. "My, my, my, I have been anxious to catch up with you. And you do look particularly pretty this morning."

"You!" she cried, swinging around to dive for the Colt.

"Me! Justin Waller, Mrs. Gabriel. Why, yes'm, I've turned up again, and I am...anxious!"

The Colt was on the floor somewhere. She groped frantically, opened her mouth to scream. The sound that issued from her was a breathy gasp. He caught her around the waist. She opened her mouth to scream again, and his hand clamped tight over her mouth. "No, no, my little darlin'," he crooned, his face taut against hers, his pleased grin displaying his teeth. "You do have to hush! The captain might have gone for the horses, but the Haywoods are downstairs, and I planned to leave kind of quiet like. I do want to deal with Malachi Slater, but not here. Not now. You're going to be real, real quiet for me."

Shannon tried desperately to inhale and bite his hand. He laughed, reaching into his pocket with his free hand, and produced a soaking, foul-smelling scarf. He removed his hand from her mouth. She gasped in quickly to scream, but before she could issue a sound, he dropped the scarf upon her face, and she inhaled the potent drug upon it.

The room spun and faded and went opaque, and then disappeared entirely from view.

Justin Waller waited. Her eyes fell shut; she went limp beneath him. He pulled the scarf from her face at last, and lifted her dead weight over his shoulder.

At the top of the staircase, he hesitated. He heard Slater talking in the kitchen.

Quickly, quietly, he ran down the stairs and out the front door. The street was quiet. He smiled. He walked calmly to his horse, tossed Shannon over the animal's flanks, and mounted behind her lolling body.

And rode serenely out of town.

Chapter Eleven

When Malachi returned with the horses, Iris was already waiting for him, seated in a small buckboard wagon. She was wearing green brocade with a cocky little feathered hat, and the green went exceptionally well with her red hair.

Malachi tethered the horses and looked at her. "You're a beautiful woman, Iris," he told her.

She smiled and didn't flush. "Thanks, Malachi. You didn't need to say that."

"You don't need to come."

"Yes, I do," Iris said. "You don't know anything about the back entrance to Cindy's house. And you won't be able to run around in the town of Sparks, I promise you. You won't be able to do your brother one bit of good if you're arrested along with his wife."

"I don't like putting you into danger," he said softly.

"I won't be in any danger. Cindy's a friend of mine. I come into Sparks often enough. I'm known there."

"Still—"

"Malachi, I swear that I will be in no danger.

Malachi still didn't like it, but he knew he had no right to dictate to Iris. And her trip to Sparks had been monumentally important.

She had found Cole. He'd been sitting in the local saloon, his hat pulled low over his head. She hadn't recognized him herself at first, not until she'd leaned back and seen his silver gray eyes. He'd been wearing ranch clothes and a Mexican serape and his face had been covered with the rustic start of a beard and mustache. He hadn't looked at all like Cole.

He'd recognized Iris, though. Before she could talk to him, he'd come up quickly to buy her a drink, then he had told her he was going by the name of Jake Egan.

Iris had brought him to Cindy's place, a big gabled house her friend owned on the outskirts of town. It was a cathouse, of course, and Shannon was sure to hate it, but that was where they were going now.

Cole told Iris that Jamie was just over the border, and he had gotten word to him. The three of them planned to converge in Sparks, and take matters from there. Thanks to Iris and her friends, they would have a good place from which to plan and work.

Iris glanced toward the Haywoods. "Your wife ain't pleased, I take it?"

He shrugged. "I haven't told her yet."

Iris frowned. "But—"

"We had an argument. We didn't get that far," Malachi said briefly.

Iris lowered her head and a smile stole over her lips. "I hope you told her that I wasn't with you—"

"Iris, it doesn't matter—"

"It matters to me! I'd just as soon she not shoot me."

"She's not going to shoot you, Iris."

"Malachi—"

"Iris, the matter is solved."

"I don't think so, Malachi."

"And why is that?"

"Well, as you might have noticed, Mrs. Slater isn't out here yet."

Malachi swore softly. He started up the porch steps toward the front door.

"Malachi!" Iris called to him. "I'm going to run back in. Reba might be up by now and I want to thank her for covering things for me yesterday."

Malachi nodded to her and hurried up the steps and opened the door to the parlor. Mrs. Haywood was just coming out of the kitchen with a big parcel in her hands. "Here you are, Captain Slater. Some of my best summer sausages and biscuits. And when you're heading back through, you make sure to come and see us."

Malachi nodded stiffly. "Surely, ma'am," he said, and he looked up the stairway. "Has she come down yet?"

Mrs. Haywood shook her head. "Maybe you should go on and hurry her along."

He nodded again. Mrs. Haywood was still staring at him.

"We wouldn't have hanged you, captain, you know."

"I'm glad to hear that, ma'am."

"And we couldn't have forced you into marrying your lady—not unless you wanted to."

He hesitated, staring at her. "Now, Mrs. Haywood—"

"Never mind. Maybe you're not ready to admit that. You go up and hurry her along. I'll take the vittles out to the buckboard. Iris is going with you?" Mrs. Haywood's eyes danced with merriment. "What a lively trip. I wish I were going. I wish that I was twenty years younger!" she said, and she laughed.

A slow smile curved Malachi's lip. He saluted her. "Yes, ma'am, it would have been nice to have you along."

Mrs. Haywood, chuckling, headed toward the door. Malachi went to the steps and started up them, two at a time.

He came to the door and noticed the splinters around the broken lock. He had already paid Mr. Haywood for the damages, but seeing the door made him feel ill. He had sworn he wasn't going to lose his temper, and he had. He had sworn that he wouldn't touch her in anger...and he had. He wanted to leave this place now. More than anything, he wanted to leave this place. Nothing could really be solved between himself and Shannon until Kristin was rescued, or...

Until they all died in the attempt.

"Shannon!" he called out sharply.

He stepped into the room. She was nowhere around. Other than that, the room was exactly as he had left it, not half an hour ago. "Shannon?" he called out again.

Damn her. She was angry, and she was playing some trick. Never! He never could trust her, not for one damned moment! He thought she had understood how close they were coming to Kristin.

He wandered to the foot of the bed and sank down upon it with a weary sigh. Where had she gone? Mrs. Haywood hadn't seen her downstairs. And...

He looked across to the hall tree. Shannon's shirt and trousers were still hung on it.

He rose, a frown knitting his brow. He went over to their saddlebags and ripped hers open. Her dress was still there. Wherever she had gone, she had gone wearing the slinky satin nightdress she had worn this morning.

He jumped up, trying to tell himself that she might have run into the mercantile store to buy something. More underwear, a new shirt, perhaps. Another one of the embroidered blouses like the one on the hall tree...

Malachi ran down the steps. Just as he reached the parlor, he heard screaming from the street. He burst out of the door and ran down to the street, his booted footsteps clattering over the wood of the steps until he hit the dust.

Iris was in the middle of the street, her arms around the blond, Reba.

Reba was lying in the dust, wrapped in a blanket, and held tenderly by Iris. Her eyes were closed. Her face was parchment white. A trickle of blood seeped onto the blankets.

The Haywoods were there, bending over.

"What happened?" Malachi demanded.

"She shouldn't have moved. She was trying to get to you. She wants you to kill him," Iris said, her voice rising hysterically.

"Kill who?" He looked from Iris to Reba. Her eyes remained closed. He leaned down and picked her up. He glanced at Martha Haywood for assent, but the sturdy matron was already shooing him toward the house. "Right into the parlor, Malachi. Bring her to the couch. I'll send Papa for the doctor."

He hurried inside with the blond whore and laid her carefully on the sofa. He knelt beside her as Iris followed, smoothing back her hair. She had been beaten. Her lip was swollen, and one of her eyes was almost shut.

Her other eye opened slowly. She almost smiled, a caricature of a smile. "He wanted your wife, Mr. Gabriel. He wanted your wife."

"What?"

His heart thudded, then seemed to stop for a moment. Cold fear fell harshly upon him. He took Reba's hand in his. "Please, we know you're...hurting.'' The way the blood seeped from her, she was probably dying. Maybe she knew it; maybe she didn't. "Try to tell me."

She moistened her lips, nodding. "Kill him. You have to kill him. I saw him watching you. He was waiting for you to get to her; he couldn't make the noise to reach her. He tried...last night. Then he came up to my room with me." She paused. Tears trickled down her cheeks. "He's got your wife, Mr. Gabriel. He thinks I'm dead. He thinks he's safe... Get him. Kill him. He—" She tried to find breath to speak, and made one final effort. "He said that his name was Justin."

Malachi shot up. Iris and Mrs. Haywood stared at him. "Justin Waller," he said. "He followed us. I underestimated him. I thought I'd lost him."

He turned and strode toward his horse, checking that his Colts were in his gun belt. When he reached the bay, he leaped upon the animal, and then just sat there. He didn't even know which way to ride.

East. Back the way they'd come.

Justin Waller wouldn't dare head farther west into Kansas. He'd killed a lot of men in Kansas. Maimed and wounded them. Someone might recognize him.

East. He had to return eastward.

He set off at a gallop, and realized a second later that he was being followed. He turned and saw that Iris had mounted Shannon's big black gelding. With her skirts and petticoats flying, her fine green dress bloodstreaked and ruined, she was racing after him.

He reined in. "Iris, go back! What do you think—"

"Malachi, she's dead. Reba just died."

"So go back! This man is an animal. I'm better off alone."

"Your wife may need me," Iris said quietly.

Malachi locked his jaw, he was suddenly shaking so hard. That Shannon might be touched by the madman hurt...hurt so badly that he couldn't help her...

"All right, come on," he told Iris.

He leaned forward over the bay's neck, urging the animal forward, and they galloped eastward again at a breakneck pace. How much time did Justin Waller have on him already? How much time did Justin Waller need?

He didn't dare think. He rode.

It was the sickness in Shannon's stomach that finally woke her. She didn't know what he had used in his scarf to knock her out, but the smell of it had invaded her system, and her mouth tasted horrible, and she was certain that she was going to be sick any minute. She didn't care much about being sick. It might make her feel better. Except that there was a gag in her mouth, tied so tightly over her lips that she was afraid that she would choke to death upon her own fluids.

She tried opening her eyes carefully. The sunshine shot into them like knives. She had thought that she was moving; she was not. Her wrists hurt her because she was tied to a tree. The sun was overhead, streaking through the leaves. She was in a copse, surrounded by rocks and foliage and trees. She couldn't move at all, for rough nooses looped both of her wrists, and her arms were pulled taut around the circumference of the tree.

She closed her eyes again. The dizziness still assailed her. She willed it to go away.

There was a sound in the woods. She opened her eyes quickly. Justin Waller was coming through the bushes. There was nothing she could do. Absolutely nothing but stare at him, and hate him with everything in her.

"Hello, little darlin'," he crooned. He hunkered down by her, smiling as he tossed his rifle down at her side. He ran his hand over her thigh, moving the satin of her gown upward to her hip. She kicked and thrashed at him, and the motion almost made her sick. He laughed, enjoying her inability to really do anything, anything at all.

"I'd like to remove that gag, honey, and hear everything that you have to say to old Justin. You're going to apologize, do you know that? You're going to tell me how sorry you are for everything you ever did to me. And then you're going to tell me that you'll never leave me again. And you're going to tell me how much you want me, you're going to ask me to be nice to you."

He lifted his hand to her cheek, and ran a finger down her throat. He idly stroked a line down to the rise of her breast, and he laughed again at the rage that filled her eyes when he cupped the mound.

"You're thinking that Slater will come and kill me, aren't you? Well, he's going to come. That's why you're here. I'm going to meet him on the road, and then I'm going to kill him. And then I'm going to come back for you. But do you know why you're here in this nice little cove? 'Cause if I die, Miss McCahy, you're going to die, too. He'll never find you. Only the snakes and the buzzards will know where you are. Maybe a rattler will come by. And maybe not. Maybe you'll just bake slowly in the sun...and you'll be glad to die, you'll want water so badly. Then the birds will come down and you know what they like to do first? They like to pluck out eyes..."

He sighed, letting his hand drop. "I'd really like to stay. But—"

He broke off, listening. From somewhere, Shannon could hear the sound of hoofbeats.

Justin's face went dark. "How the hell did he know so damned fast?" he muttered. "Must not have done in that whore properly..." He stared at Shannon. "No matter, darlin'. Don't fret. Don't miss me too much. I will be back."

He rose, clutching his gun, and thrashed his way through the undergrowth. The sound of the hoofbeats was coming closer and closer. Shannon closed her eyes.

Malachi.

He would never abandon her, she thought. No matter how mad she made him, no matter how they fought...

Even if he hated her. He would never abandon her.

But would Malachi be expecting Justin to ambush him? And Justin meant to do just that. Sit in wait to prey upon Malachi, shoot him down in cold blood from the shadows of the bracken on a summer's day.

Malachi was coming closer. Shannon could feel the hoofbeats pounding the earth. There was more than one horse. He wasn't alone. Maybe that was something that Justin hadn't counted on.

She tugged at the ropes that held her, but Justin could tie a secure knot. The more she twisted, the more hopelessly tightly she was bound. Tears stung her eyes. If she could just call out. If she could warn him that it was going to be an ambush.

Willing herself not to panic, not to give up, she twisted her head, biting at the gag. At first, she felt nothing.

Then she felt it loosening.

The sound of hoofbeats had slowed as the riders had entered the narrow trail through the forest. Shannon bit desperately against the material slicing her mouth. There was a give and then a tear. She twisted and spit again. The gag slipped enough for her to draw in a huge gulp of sweet air, and then scream for all she was worth.

"It's a trap, Malachi! Don't come any closer! It's an ambush! Be careful, for the love of God—"

As she screamed, Justin Waller suddenly appeared through the shrubs, and she saw the murderous hatred in his eyes.

"Stupid bitch!" he swore. His palm cracked across her cheek so hard that she was dazed.

She felt a little trickle of blood at her lip but that didn't deter him in the least. He stuffed the gag into her mouth and secured it, winding a strip of rawhide tightly around her head. It cut searingly into her mouth, and she could barely breathe, much less issue the softest cry.

He smiled, pleased with his handiwork. "Our time is coming, sweet thing," he promised her.

He jumped to his feet, carelessly holding his repeating rifle. The sound of hoofbeats had ceased. The forest seemed quiet.

"Slater!" Justin screamed.

Shannon took some small pleasure in realizing that she had ruined his original plan. He couldn't possibly ambush anyone. He was the one whose whereabouts were now known.

"Slater, I'm going to shoot her. Right through the head."

She couldn't help the shivering that seized her. Justin Waller would do it. He would shoot a human being just as quickly and easily as he would swat a fly. There would be very little difference to him.

He aimed the rifle at Shannon. She caught her breath, and her heart seemed to cease to beat. She wanted to pray; she wanted to ask God to forgive her all her sins, but she didn't seem to be able to think at all.

Malachi's face filled her thoughts. His slow, cynical smile curling into his lip beneath his mustache. His eyes, bluer than teal, deeper than cobalt, secretive beneath the honey and gold arches of his brows. In those seconds, she imagined his face. And she wished with all her heart that she could see him. She prayed at last, and she prayed that he not be fooled into giving his life for hers...

The rifle exploded with a loud blast. Dust flew up, blinding Shannon. But she wasn't hit. He had aimed at the ground, right beside her feet. He aimed again, and she quickly closed her eyes as pieces of bark sheared from the tree and flew around at the impact of the explosion. Shannon choked and screamed deep in her throat. More shots exploded against the tree. She almost longed for him to hit her so that the torture of waiting for a bullet would end.

"Come on out, Slater. One of these shots is going to hit her! Or maybe one of them already has. Maybe she's screaming deep, deep down inside, and you can't hear her...but you can hear me. Come on out, Slater, you coward, damn you!"

There was a rustling sound behind them. Justin swung around, shooting at the bushes. Bracken broke and flew, and the earth was spewed up in a rain of dirt. But when the noise died away, there was nothing. Nothing at all.

Justin hunkered down in the dirt, looking anxiously around. The silence was awful. It dragged on forever.

Shannon thought that she might have passed out again. It seemed that she closed her eyes and opened them again, and the sun was falling. The sky was streaked with beautiful, dark colors. Twilight was coming on.

And she was still tied to the tree. Justin was less than ten feet away from her, his rifle over his knee. He still stared out into the bracken as the night fell.

A fly droned around Shannon's face, and landed on her arm. She leaned against the tree, desolate, despairing.

"I think I've killed him. I thought he was out there, but maybe I've killed him," Justin muttered to himself.

He twisted around and looked at Shannon and saw that her eyes were open. Low on the ground, he crawled to her. He reached up with his knife toward her head, and she wondered with horror what he intended to do. She tried not to shrink from him, but she was terrified, and she couldn't help it. He smiled, liking her fear.

But he didn't cut her. He slipped the blade into the rawhide tie that he had bound so tightly around her head. He slid it, and let the scarf gag fall from her face. She inhaled, gulping in air. She would have screamed, but it seemed like such a foolish thing to do. There was probably no one to hear her.

Maybe Malachi *was* dead. Justin had mowed down half the foliage around him, and sheared away rock and trees. He could easily have hit Malachi. He could be out there anywhere, lying injured, dead, dying...

Justin stretched his length against her body. She didn't kick him and she didn't speak. She stayed still, her head against the tree, and stared at him. He was insane, she decided. Some men would come back from the war and tremble through the night at the memories of the horrors they had seen...of the death they had themselves delivered. But Justin Waller had used the war. He had loved it, reveled in it. It had allowed him to rape and murder freely. And now it seemed that he had learned murder and rape as a way of life.

She would give him no satisfaction, she swore.

"You've nothing to say, sweet thing?" he whispered against her flesh. He touched her cheek and ran his hands down to her breast again. "Our time has come. Your lover is dead, and we have the whole night ahead of us. Your mouth is free. You can scream and scream and scream..."

She gazed at him. "You're pathetic," she said softly.

He grabbed her thigh, pinching it mercilessly. She wasn't going to cry out, but the pain came so fiercely that she did.

"Talk to me nicely, little girl. Talk to me nicely. Tell me that you won't take off again. No more tricks. And maybe, just maybe, if you're good, real, real good, I'll let you live."

She lifted her chin. She ignored his hand upon her thigh, inching up the satin of her gown. "Death might be very simple, Justin," she said.

He started to laugh again. "Yeah, it just might be. But you ain't going to die. Not until I'm through with you.'' He cupped her chin in a cruel grip and moved his face close to hers.

She managed to twist away. "I will throw up on you," she threatened. "I swear, I will throw up all over you. That drug is heaving up and down inside of me."

He jerked away from her as if he had been burned. He stared at her, and then he chuckled and stroked her chin again. "You are a one, Miss Shannon McCahy. I've waited a long time for a woman the likes of you. A long time."

He leaned toward her again. She prayed that the earth would open up and swallow them whole.

The earth did not open up, but there was suddenly a massive rustling in the bushes near the road. Justin jerked away from her and stood up on the balls of his feet with his rifle ready. Shannon watched him with renewed fear. "Son of a bitch! Sit tight, sweetheart. I'll be back, and we won't waste any more time." He jumped close to the tree, then bent down and disappeared into the low brush.

Shannon strained frantically against the ropes that bound her. Maybe Malachi lived. Maybe he was out there thrashing around, needing help. Justin would hunt him down. He would hunt him down and shoot him between the eyes. Justin Waller might be a raving lunatic, but he had fought with the bushwhackers, and he had learned a lot about guerrilla warfare. He was wiry and athletic. He was an able opponent. And Malachi...

"Watch out!" she screamed aloud. "Malachi! If you're there, watch out!"

Justin did not return to shut her up. She bit her lip, looking into the bracken. Night was just starting to fall.

Suddenly, from around the tree, a hand fell over her mouth. Fear curdled within her again. With wide, startled eyes she twisted around.

It was Malachi. He had found his hat. It sat jauntily atop his head, the brim low, sheltering his eyes. He brought a finger to his lips, and she exhaled, so dizzy with relief that she nearly fell. Hunched down low beside her, he smiled the crooked, rueful smile that had stolen her heart.

"Are you all right?" he asked her swiftly.

She nodded. "Malachi—"

"He didn't—he didn't hurt you?"

"He hasn't had much time. He's been watching for you through the day. Oh, Malachi! Be careful! Please, just get me out of here. He's dangerous. He's sick. He's—"

"Shh!" He brought his finger to his lips again. He seemed to hear something that she could not. "Can you make it just a few minutes longer?"

"Malachi—"

"Can you?"

"Yes, of course, but—"

"Shh!" He didn't untie her. He slunk back into the brush behind the tree.

"No!" Shannon whispered. She heard the branches breaking and a soft tread upon the earth. Justin Waller was returning. He was returning, and Malachi had left her for him...

"Weren't nothing," Justin said. "Weren't nothing at all but a rabbit or a squirrel. I left you for a rabbit. Can you beat that? My nerves are raw, honey, but you're gonna fix that."

Laughing, he dropped the rifle. He fell down on his knees beside her, and he stroked her calf. She kicked out in a rage. He fell upon her, the whole of his length covering her, smothering her. She started to scream and writhe, and Justin smiled, bringing his leering features level with hers.

"Moment of truth, honey darling mine—"

He broke off at the sound of a gun cocking, right at the base of his ear.

"Moment of truth," Malachi said harshly. "Get up. Get off my wife."

Shannon watched as Justin Waller went as stiff as a poker and slowly rose. Malachi didn't miss a beat. The barrel of his Colt remained flush against the man's head.

"She ain't your wife. Not for real—Mr. Gabriel."

"She is my wife—for real, Mr. Waller. And I don't take kindly to you touching her. In fact, I don't take kindly to much that you've done."

There was another rustle in the trees. Malachi didn't move a hair.

Justin sneered, and despite herself, Shannon stiffened. Iris Andre stepped in among them. She had a small pearl-handled knife in her hands. She hurried toward Shannon, knelt beside her and started sawing the ropes that held her.

"Just how many woman do you need, Slater?" Justin taunted.

Malachi walked around in front of him, aiming the Colt at his heart. Shannon looked gratefully to Iris as the red-haired woman freed her. Maybe she was a whore. Maybe she had been sleeping with Malachi. But they had come together to save her, and for that, she had to be grateful.

Iris flashed her an encouraging smile. Shannon rubbed her wrists.

"Can you stand, honey?" Iris asked.

"I—I think so."

But she couldn't. When she tried to rise, she fell back upon the tree. She was parched; she hadn't had water in hours. The nauseating taste of the drug remained.

Iris lent her an arm.

"Boy, captain, you do have it made. A whore and a wife, leaning on each other. That's mighty cute, Miss McCahy."

"It's Mrs. Slater," Shannon told him.

"Poor little fool. Can't you see what he's doing to you?"

"Iris, tie up his hands," Malachi directed.

Iris nodded, leaving Shannon against the tree. Shannon stood there, chafing her wrists, shivering as darkness fell and the coolness of the night came upon them. She watched as Iris walked toward Justin with firm purpose. Malachi tossed her a skein of rope.

But before Iris could reach him, Justin reached out, and grasped her and pulled her against him. He produced a knife from his calf, and caught it against her throat.

"Malachi, shoot him!" Iris called out.

Malachi didn't dare shoot; Justin would have slit her throat as easily as he breathed.

"Drop it, Slater," Justin advised.

Malachi reached out and dropped the Colt. But as he did so, he lunged.

Justin thrust Iris away from himself just as Malachi stormed against him. Justin had his knife; Malachi was unarmed. They rolled together. Malachi leaped to his feet. Justin swiped at him with the knife, and Malachi leaped again. The knife sliced through the air.

Malachi landed a blow against Justin's chin, but then Justin was swinging with the knife again.

Malachi was good. He was fast on his feet; he could whirl with the wind. But Justin was armed. Unless he was disarmed swiftly.

Shannon could barely move. She shook her head, trying to clear it, needing strength. Iris lay on the ground before her, trying to stagger up.

"Iris!"

The woman turned to look at her.

"The Colt. Give me the Colt."

"You'll hit...Malachi."

Shannon shook her head. She had to clear it. She crawled past the tree before falling to the ground. She couldn't quite reach Malachi's Colt.

Iris reached for it and swept it along the dirt to Shannon. For a brief moment their fingers touched. Shannon bit her lip, then smiled swiftly, encouragingly. Her fingers curled around the butt of the gun.

The men were still locked in deadly combat. Justin was on top of Malachi; Malachi was straining to hold the man's arm far above him, to escape the deadly silver blade of the razor-edged knife. Shannon blinked against the darkness and against her trembling fear and the nauseating aftereffects of the drug.

She aimed carefully, and then she fired.

She was a crack shot, and she proved it that night. She hit Justin right in the hand. His knife went flying as he screamed in pain, his fingers shattered.

Malachi pushed him away and reached for the knife. Stunned, he came up on the balls of his feet and looked at Shannon. He smiled slowly, smoothing back a lock of hair that had fallen over his eyes.

"Thanks...darlin'," he murmured.

He stood, dusting off his pants. Justin Waller was rolling on the ground screaming.

"Bitch! I'll kill you, I swear, I'll kill you—"

"You aren't killing anyone else, Waller," Malachi said softly.

"We're taking you back to Haywood, and they'll see that you hang."

"There ain't no wanted posters out on me, Slater."

"They're going to hang you for murder. Reba died this morning," Malachi said.

Justin let out a howl. "Your wife wanted it, Slater. She was smooth as silk to touch. She was better than that blond whore back in town. She screamed and cried and asked me for more and more."

Malachi stood still.

"But then, you can't imagine that whore. She wanted to live so badly. She begged me to stop."

"I'm not going to kill you, Justin," Malachi said. He walked over to where the man lay. "I'm not going to kill you. The war is over. I'm done killing. They'll hang you, and you aren't going to say anything to make me kill you now and cheat the hangman."

"You shoulda seen her scream."

Malachi ignored him. He started walking toward Shannon again.

"I'm going to kill you, Slater!" Justin raged. He stumbled to his feet and came running toward them. Cupping his bleeding hand beneath his good arm, he stumbled toward them and fell upon his rifle where it lay by the tree. Malachi started to spring for him.

Then a shot rang out. Justin Waller fell down dead.

Malachi and Shannon stared at one another, then turned and looked at Iris. She had a little ivory-handled pistol in her hand. A small waft of powder floated from it.

She looked from the dead man to Malachi. "You couldn't kill him, Malachi. I had to."

Malachi nodded at her. He walked over and retrieved his hat from where it had fallen in the dust, then he came back to Shannon.

"Can you ride with me?" he asked her.

She nodded.

"What about him?" Iris asked, referring to Waller.

"We'll put him on his horse and bring him back to Haywood. They can do what they want with him there. If they happened to know that he was at Centralia, they might butcher him up and feed him to the crows. I don't know. We're done here. We've got to get moving."

Iris nodded. Malachi brushed Shannon's forehead with a kiss, then nodded to Iris. Iris came forward and slipped her arm around Shannon while Malachi picked up the dead man, throwing him over his shoulder.

Shannon looked at Iris sickly. "He—he killed a woman?"

"A friend of mine," Iris said.

"The blond woman?"

Iris nodded. "Come on, honey. Let's get out of these woods. It's been a long day, and it's going to be a longer night."

Arm in arm with Iris, Shannon made her way through the bracken and trees. Malachi walked ahead of them.

They came to where a trail showed in the moonlight. The bay and her black gelding were there. Malachi tossed Justin's body over the bay and looked at the women. "I'm going to give the woods a look for his horse. Will you be all right?"

"Of course, sugar—er, uh, I mean, sure, Malachi," Iris said.

"I'm fine," Shannon added. She wasn't fine at all. She was sick to death and cold and shivering, but Justin was dead, and the danger was over. And Malachi had cared enough about her to come for her.

She had loved Robert Ellsworth. She had loved him very much.

But that didn't stop her from loving Malachi now. No matter what his relationship had been with Iris.

She couldn't even hate Iris anymore.

Malachi walked into the bushes and disappeared. Shannon must have weaved in the night breeze, because Iris quickly made a clucking sound. "Let's sit. It's all right here, I'm sure. We'd hear a rattler if there was one around anywhere."

"Iris," Shannon said softly, sitting down beside the redhead.

"What? I'm sure that there's really nothing to worry about—"

"Iris, I'm really sorry about the whiskey."

Iris inhaled sharply and her eyes fell on Shannon. "It's all right." She grimaced ruefully. "Most ladies do feel that way about whores."

"Oh, Iris, trust me! I didn't act like a lady!" She smiled, and then she laughed, and she realized she was glad because she had wondered if she would ever laugh again. Then she was afraid, because perhaps her laughter sounded hysterical. "Too bad you couldn't have met my pa, Iris. He would have explained in no uncertain terms that a lady wouldn't do things like that.'' She hesitated, then she smiled. ''Pa would have said that you were quite a lady, Iris. Thank you for coming for me. You don't owe me anything. Even if you—even if you do sleep with my husband.''

Iris squeezed her hand in return. ''I didn't sleep with your husband. Well, not now, anyway. I had a thing on him once, years ago, in Springfield. It was before the war. It was—it doesn't matter what it was. It's over.''

''You know that we're not really married,'' Shannon said softly.

''You are really married now, if I understand things right.''

Shannon flushed. ''He had to marry me or hang.''

Iris shook her head, and her sage green eyes glittered knowingly. ''You don't know your man very well, Mrs. Slater. No one ever forced Malachi to do anything that he wasn't willing to do already, deep down inside.'' She brought her finger to her lips. ''Sh! He's coming back. And men are funny. They just hate to have women talk about them.''

Shannon smiled. Malachi thrashed his way through the bushes with Justin Waller's buckskin horse.

''Shannon, can you ride with me?''

''Yes.''

''Iris? You'll be all right on Shannon's black?''

''Yes, Malachi.''

The two of them were meek, Malachi thought. Damned meek, for a pair of hellcats.

He walked over to Shannon and reached down to her, wishing that his hands would quit shaking. It had been the longest day of his life. He'd had to wait and watch and steel himself to be patient lest Waller killed them both. He had barely managed to keep still when Waller had started shooting at the tree and the ground.

He pulled Shannon to her feet. The once beautiful satin nightdress was mud-stained and torn. ''We'll get you into a warm bath and dressed as soon as we get to the Haywoods',' he said gruffly.

She smiled tremulously and stumbled against him. Her eyes shone with their own crystal-blue radiance, and he couldn't look away from them. They had never been so softly blue upon him. They carried a look of innocence and knowledge, older than the hills, and they had never carried such tenderness.

He swept her into his arms. Her eyes remained locked with his. Her arms curled trustingly around his neck.

He set her atop his horse and mounted behind her. She leaned against his chest, and they were a silent party as they rode back to Haywood.

Chapter Twelve

Shannon was certain, upon their return to Haywood, that she had never been more cherished in her life.

They had been met on the steps of the inn by Martha and Mr. Haywood and what seemed like half the town. Cheers went up as they rode in. Malachi handed Shannon down to Matey. A woman quickly brought a blanket to wrap her in, and Martha Haywood brought her water, which she gulped down until Malachi warned her that she must go slowly. That was the last she saw of Malachi. The men dragged him off to the saloon.

It was the last she saw of Iris for the moment, too, but she didn't dwell on the thought.

Martha clucked like a mother hen and took her immediately beneath her wing. She fed her roast beef with hot gravy, potatoes and carrots. Hot tea was made with brandy, and the bathtub was filled with steaming water and French bubble powder.

Shannon bathed with a vengeance. She wanted to wash away so much. The dirt, Justin's touch upon her...and the blood that marred not only the night, but so much of the countryside. She scrubbed her flesh and her hair, and she wasn't happy until she had scrubbed both a second time. Martha stayed with her, helping her rinse out her hair. And when Shannon stepped out of the tub at last, Martha was there with a huge fluffy towel to wrap around her. When she was dried, Martha offered her a new nightgown.

It was entirely different from the first. It was soft flannel with little pink flowers and it buttoned all the way to the neck. It was warm and comfortable, and Shannon loved it. Combing out her clean but snarled hair, Shannon thanked Martha. "You've been so very good to us."

Martha waved a hand in the air. "We haven't done a thing, dear."

Shannon laughed. "You're harboring a man whose face graces dozens of wanted posters and you've treated me like a daughter."

Martha looked at the bed as she straightened the sheets and plumped the pillows. "I'd like to think that if my girl had lived, dear, she would have been a great deal like you."

Shannon came over and kissed her cheek. "Thank you. That's so very sweet."

Martha blushed. "Crawl in here now. Someone wants to see you."

Her heart fluttering, Shannon crawled into the bed. Malachi was coming. There were things she wanted to say to him. Things that she needed to say.

Martha smiled and left the room, closing the door behind her.

It didn't lock anymore.

Shannon sat back against her pillow, biting her lower lip and smoothing her fingers nervously over the covers. She heard a slight sound as the door opened and she looked up with anticipation.

Iris Andre walked into the room.

Shannon tried not to show her disappointment. She smiled as Iris came to the bed, pulling a chair over from the hearth. "How are you feeling?" Iris asked her. She smiled, and her eyes were bright with concern.

A moment's jealousy rose within Shannon, and she tried to swallow the feeling. Iris had such lovely flame-colored hair and bright green eyes. She had changed into a soft blue cotton dress, high-necked, decorated with rows of soft white lace. She looked beautiful and worldly and sophisticated, and somehow angelic, too. And once, Malachi had had a love affair with her. Iris denied that she had slept with him this time, but he had been with Iris far more than he had been with Shannon.

"I feel fine, Iris, thank you. The nausea has all gone away. Food helped."

"So you're none the worse for wear?"

Shannon ruefully pulled the sleeves back on her gown and showed where her wrists were chafed. She shivered, and her smile faded. "He killed your friend. I am so sorry."

"So am I," Iris said softly. "No one deserved to die that way, not even a...whore."

"Oh, Iris!" Shannon sat up and reached out for the woman's hand.

Iris smiled. "You are very sweet, do you know that?"

Shannon flushed. "There isn't a sweet bone in my body." She hesitated. "Ask Malachi. He'll tell you."

"Malachi!" Iris said, laughing. There was a sparkle about her eyes.

"Why are you laughing?" Shannon demanded.

"I'm enjoying this, I suppose," Iris said, and then she sighed. "He does say that you have a temper. And you are good with a Colt. I'm glad I never tempted you to shoot."

"I was very tempted to shoot when we met," Shannon admitted.

"I'm glad that you didn't," Iris said. She stood up abruptly. "I guess I had better go. Malachi is anxious to see you—"

"Iris?"

"Yes?"

"I don't understand." She had to force herself to look at the other woman. "He didn't come back here last night..." She couldn't help it. She lowered her eyes, and her voice trailed away.

"I wasn't here, honey. I went over to Sparks."

"Oh!" Shannon looked at her again.

"It's a long story. I'm sure that he wants to explain it to you himself. I'll see you tomorrow. Malachi is anxious to get on his way tonight—"

"He's leaving?"

"There I go again. He'll explain—"

"He's leaving me here?"

"No, not exactly. Please, let him explain." Iris didn't give Shannon another chance to question her. She smiled and hurried out of the room. Shannon's mind began to race. Something had happened, something that she didn't know about. They were getting closer and closer to Kristin, and Malachi meant to leave without her.

She started to crawl out of bed. If he was leaving that evening, so was she.

She started at the sound of a tap on the door. Malachi? She glanced at the door, remembering what had happened when she tried to keep him out. And now he was tapping quietly?

He didn't wait for her answer. He stepped into the room. Shannon quickly glanced his way. He had been at the saloon, but he hadn't been drinking, not much, anyway. He still wore his cavalry hat. He was taking chances here, she thought. But then, maybe it didn't matter in Haywood. Maybe the war had really ended here.

She loved him in that hat. She loved the way the brim shadowed his eyes and gave mystery to his face, and she loved the jaunty plume that flew with Rebel fervor.

She loved him...

His shirt was torn at the sleeve and covered with dirt from his fight with Justin Waller on the ground. His shoulder was visible through the tear, bronzed and muscular. There was a masculine appeal to him that made her heart ache to look at him—mussed and torn in her defense, ramrod straight and tall and lean and rugged. She felt that she stared at him for ages, but it could have been no more than seconds. He frowned as he realized that she had been about to crawl out of bed. "What do you think you're doing?"

"I'm going to get dressed. If we're leaving—"

"I'm leaving."

"But—"

"Shannon, I'm just going ahead of you by a day. I have to go tonight." He smiled, and his lip twisted with a certain amount of amusement rather than anger. He strode across the room to her and caught her by her shoulders, pushing her gently back down on the bed and sitting by her thigh. She opened her mouth to say something, but no words would come to her. She didn't feel like fighting him at that moment. She didn't feel like fighting at all.

She reached up and stroked his cheek, feeling the softness of his beard.

He caught her hand and kissed her fingers. "I was so damned scared today," he told her.

She smiled. "So was I."

"Are you really all right?"

She nodded. "You came in time."

He folded her fingers and set them down upon her midriff. He stood and wandered idly over to the window, leaning against the wall and staring out at the street. "Did Iris tell you? She found Cole."

"What?" Shannon shot up with pleasure. "Oh, Malachi, I'm so very glad. Where? Is that what—"

He turned around and walked back to her. She was kneeling at the end of the bed. Her hair was drying in soft, waving tendrils that curled over her shoulders and breasts and streamed down the length of her back. Her eyes were beautiful with enthusiasm. She looked completely recovered from the day, and exquisitely alive and vital.

She loved Cole, she reminded herself. She always had loved Cole. The bright enthusiasm in her eyes was for his brother.

"Cole is in Sparks."

"Oh, no!"

"It's all right. He's safe. Iris has a friend there named Cindy who has a—er—house...on the outskirts of town. Cole is there. He's safe. He's gotten word to Jamie. That's why I have to leave tonight."

Shannon started to crawl out of bed again. "Whoa!" he told her, catching her arm. "You aren't coming. Not tonight."

"But Malachi—"

He caught her chin and lifted it. He met the dazzling sapphire blue of her eyes, and smiled. "I'm not leaving you, Shannon. It's too much trouble to try. But I want you to stay here tonight, please. I want you to get one good night's rest. Iris will bring you in the morning with the buckboard. All right?"

"But Malachi—"

"Shannon, we have to figure out a way to free Kristin. There isn't going to be anything that you can do until we form some kind of a plan. Please, get some rest tonight. For me."

The last words were softly spoken. They were husky, and they seemed to touch her with tenderness.

If he had yelled or ordered her around, she would have fought him. But he wasn't yelling; he wasn't angry. His hand upon her was light, and she longed to grip it and kiss his fingers in return.

"Stay?" he said.

She nodded. He stroked her cheek before turning away from her. He tossed his hat onto the chair.

"Will you take good care of that for me? Bring it tomorrow in the buckboard. Pack it. They probably won't think too much of it in Sparks."

"I'll pack it carefully."

"Thanks."

He started to unbutton his shirt, then realized that it was torn beyond salvation. Grinning at her, he ripped open the buttons. "This one has bit the dust, don't you think?"

She nodded. She didn't care in the least about his shirt. She cared about his shoulders, bronze and hard and glimmering in candlelight. And dried blood showed on a cut on his arm.

Shannon leaped out of the bed. He started to frown at her again.

"Your arm," she told him softly, as she hurried past him to where a clean cloth lay over the rim of the bath. She picked it up and wet it and came back to his side, suddenly hesitant to touch him. She looked up, meeting his eyes, and she flushed.

"It's nothing," he told her. She nodded, then gently started to bathe the wound. It wasn't deep. She wiped away the blood, then she found herself rising on her toes to press her lips against his back, against his shoulder. He twisted around to look at her. She kept her eyes upon his, and kissed his upper arm, then jutted the tip of her tongue to spiral it slowly upward to his shoulder.

He turned and caught her elbow and pulled her against him. Against the flannel of her gown and through his breeches she felt the pulsing hardness of his body. She laid her head against his chest and touched the mat of hair that lay there. She brought her palm against his chest, over the muscle, and found his hard nipple amidst the mat of gold hair. She teased it between her fingers, then tentatively reached forward with her tongue and bathed it with warmth. His groan gave her new courage and a soaring, exciting sense of her own power. She pressed her lips against the furiously beating pulse in his throat, and over the width of him and breadth of him, burrowing low against him to tease the steel hardness of his midriff, and delve her tongue into the fascinating pit of his navel.

He groaned again, dragging her back to her feet, winding his fingers into her hair.

"You've had a rough day," he said jaggedly. "You're supposed to be in bed."

She smiled wickedly. "I'm trying to be in bed."

It was all the invitation that he needed. He smiled in response and swept her up high, depositing her on the bed. He leaned over her, working upon the nightgown's dozen tiny buttons. They gave at her throat, and she arched back as he kissed and stroked the length of the soft column while working away at the next buttons, those that went lower and lower against her breasts.

There would never be another night quite like it for her. Soft moonlight played through the window and a soft cool breeze caressed her flesh. He made her warm despite it.

He made love slowly, with a leisurely abandon. She touched him and he caught her hands. He kissed each finger individually, and he raked his tongue between them, and then suckled them gently into his mouth. He kissed her arms, and her knees. He loved her feet, and cherished her thighs, and he ravaged her intimately with his touch and with his tongue until she cried out, shaking, soaking and glistening with her release. Then he touched her again...

And they sat and stared at one another, their bodies glowing in the soft light. When they reached out again, it was like tentative strangers, allowing slow exploration. She knew she could dare anything, and found the thrill of feminine power. She shivered and died a little bit with the delight of hearing him groan as she possessively stroked his body, and held him with her hands, and with her kiss, and with all the warmth and welcoming heat of her body. Time lost all meaning. His whispers were sweet, and often urgent. Passion was stoked to a never-ending flame, but for that night, tenderness reigned.

Somewhere in it all, she fell against her pillow, and in exhaustion, she slept. She awoke, though, when he moved away from her.

She watched him dress in the moonlight, loving the length of him. His shoulders, broad and gleaming, his legs, long and muscular, his buttocks, tight and hard...

She smiled as her thoughts continued to his most intimate and personal parts, then her smile faded, because he was leaving her, and she was suddenly very afraid.

"Malachi."

Startled, he looked at her. He pulled on his breeches and went over to the bed. "I'm glad you're awake," he said softly. He kissed her lips. "Do you mind coming with Iris?"

She shook her head. "I mind that I'm not coming with you."

"You'll be safer coming with Iris." He rose and donned a clean shirt, buttoning it quickly and tucking the tails into his pants. "Shannon, I'm a wanted man. You're not, and neither is she. Just in case there turns out to be trouble."

"Malachi—"

"Shannon, we'll be staying in a brothel, you know."

"And that's where you're going now?"

He nodded.

She didn't say a word. She watched him finish dressing. He kept his eyes on her, and when he had pulled on his boots, he came over to her with the Colt. "If anyone bothers you on the way, shoot him. Don't hesitate, and don't ask questions, just shoot. You understand?"

She nodded, her lashes hiding her eyes. He caught her hands and pulled her into his arms. He kissed and touched her, as if he memorized her flesh and curves. Then he kissed her again and slowly released her. Shannon picked up her pillow and watched him as he walked to the door.

"Behave," she whispered softly at last.

He turned back, grinning slowly. "Why, ma'am, I'm a married man. I intend to be an angel."

She smiled, wanting to send him on his way without worry. It was difficult to smile. She didn't feel good about his leaving. She didn't know why, but she was scared.

"Be careful," he warned her.

"You be careful yourself."

"I'll be careful," he promised. He hesitated, as if he was going to say more. "I'll be very careful," he said after a moment, and then he turned away.

"Malachi!"

She leaped out of bed and raced to him naked. She didn't want him to go because there were so many things to say. But suddenly, she couldn't say them. She simply threw herself against him and he held her very tightly for a moment.

"I'm afraid," she told him.

"Afraid, vixen?" he whispered. "The hellcat of the west is afraid?" he teased in a husky voice. "Darlin', if you had just been on our side, the South might have won the war."

"Malachi, I am afraid."

"We're going to get Kristin, and then we'll all be safe," he vowed softly. Then he kissed her swiftly on the lips again and was gone.

Shannon closed the door in his wake and slowly, mechanically went to the bed and slipped into the flannel nightgown. She sat on the bed, then stretched out, and she tried to tell herself that she would be with him soon. Her eyes would not close; she could not sleep. She stared at the ceiling, and gnawed upon her lower lip, and worried regretfully about all the things she had not said. She was in love with him. It would have been so easy to whisper the truth. To tell him that she believed in him...

He was on his way to a whorehouse, she reminded herself dryly, and he had spent two nights in a saloon. But Shannon believed Iris, and she believed Malachi, whether it was foolish or not.

That wasn't what mattered, she thought, staring out the window at the moonlit night. What mattered were the things that lay between them. He had been forced to marry her, and his fury had been obvious. She couldn't whisper that she loved him because he didn't love her. She might have forgotten her hatred of the past, but she didn't think that he could forget the years that had gone before. She was his wife, and they had exchanged vows, but that wasn't enough for a lifetime. She couldn't hold him to a marriage.

She didn't mind loving him; she craved to be with him. But she couldn't hold him to the marriage.

She twisted around, determined that she would sleep. She started to shiver. All of a sudden, she was very afraid. She didn't like him out of her sight.

He was safe, she told herself.

But no matter how many times she repeated the words, she could not convince herself, and it was nearly dawn when she slept.

* * *

Mrs. Haywood was perplexed to see her go in the morning.

"You don't need to go traipsing off, young lady. Let the men settle things. You should stay right here, in Haywood."

Iris was already in the buckboard and they were packed. Chapperel was tied to the rear of the wagon, and they had a big basket of food and canteens of water and even a jug of wine.

"We're going to be just fine, Mrs. Haywood," Shannon assured her. "Iris and I can both take care of ourselves."

"Hmph!" Martha sniffed, and she wiped away a sudden tear. "You come back when things are all right again, you hear?"

Shannon nodded and gave her a fierce hug. "We'll come back, Martha, I promise." She hurried down the steps then and over to the buckboard. It was going to be a long ride.

She climbed into the buckboard and waved to Mrs. Haywood. Mr. Haywood was with her now, his arm around her. "You send for us if you need us!" Mr. Haywood called.

"Thank you! Thank you both so much!" Shannon returned. She smiled. What more could they possibly do for her? No one could help a man condemned as an outlaw without so much as a trial.

"Ready?" Iris asked her.

"Ready," Shannon said. Iris lifted the reins. They started off. Shannon waved until they had left the little one-road town behind them, and then she turned and leaned back and felt the noon sun on her face.

She felt Iris watching her and she opened her eyes. "Are you really all right?" Iris asked her.

"I am extremely well, really. I've never felt healthier. Never. Honest."

"It's a long ride, that's all."

"I've already come a very long way," Shannon told her.

They rode in silence for a while. Then Iris asked her about her home, and about the war, and Shannon tried very hard to explain the tangled events that had led her to be living in the South—and being a Union sympathizer.

Iris was silent when she finished. Shannon looked at the other woman curiously. "You knew Malachi before. And if you found Cole, I assume that you knew him before, too."

Iris smiled. "And Jamie. They all used to come into a place where I worked in Springfield. Before the war."

"I see."

Iris looked at her curiously. "No, you probably don't see. You were raised by a good man, and you loved him, I hear it in your voice when you talk about your pa. I was raised by a stepfather who sold me to a gambler on my thirteenth birthday. You can't begin to see."

"I'm sorry, Iris. I didn't mean to presume to judge you." She hesitated. "You speak so beautifully, and when you dress like you so often—"

"I don't look like a whore, is that it?"

Shannon flushed, but she didn't apologize. She looked at Iris and smiled. "I just think that you are too good and too fine a woman to end up...like Reba."

"You're going to try to make me go straight, huh?" Iris asked.

"You could, you know."

"And do what?"

"Open up an inn."

"Miss Andre's Room and Board for Young Ladies?" Iris asked. "Why not?"

Iris laughed and flicked the reins. "All right. I'll think about it. And what about you?"

"What do you mean?"

"When it is over, what about you?"

"I—er—I'll go home."

"Alone?"

Shannon lowered her face. "You know he didn't mean to marry me," she murmured.

Iris was quiet for a minute. "I know that you're in love with him."

"He doesn't love me."

"How can you be so sure?"

"He—he's never said so. And...Iris, you can't imagine, we were enemies. I mean bitter enemies. Remember, the North and South will still clash for years to come. His favorite name for me is brat. There isn't a chance…''

Iris laughed delightedly. "You listen to me, young woman. If he were mine, if I had this chance, I would hang on for dear life. I would fight like a tiger. If you've any sense, and if you do love him, you'll do the same.''

"But, Iris, I can't force him to stay with me!''

"Then sleep with your pride. Lie awake night after night, and remember that you have the cold glory of your pride to lie with you instead of the warmth of the man you love.''

Shannon fell silent. They rode awhile longer, then Iris suggested they stop for lunch.

They found a brook, and as they dangled their feet in it, Shannon entertained Iris with stories about growing up with Kristin and Matthew.

"You'd like my brother,'' she said impulsively.

Iris sniffed. "A Yankee.''

"I'm a Yankee, remember? And you're living in Kansas. Yankee territory.''

"No. The whole country is Yankee territory now,'' Iris said. "And I'm a working girl. Confederate currency doesn't put much food on the table these days.''

They left soon after.

They didn't pass a single soul on the road. Close to sunset, they came to a rise overlooking a valley. Shannon climbed down from the buckboard to look down at the town of Sparks.

It was obviously thriving. There were rows of new houses, and more rows of businesses. Ranches spread out behind the town, and the fields were green and yellow and rich beneath the sun. In the distance, she could see railroad tracks, and a big station painted red. Iris told her that the town was a major junction for the stagecoaches, too.

She came back to the buckboard and looked at Iris. "It's a big place,'' she murmured uneasily. "A very big place. And Hayden Fitz owns it all now?''

Iris nodded gravely. "He owns most of the land. And he owns two of the stagecoach lines. And the saloon and the barbershop. And the sheriff and the deputies. Come on. Climb back in.'' She pointed down the valley to a large house surrounded by a stable and barns. It was a fair distance from the town. ''Cindy's place.''

''Cindy's place,'' Shannon echoed. She shrugged, and a smile curved her lips. ''Let's go.''

In another thirty minutes they reached the house on the plain.

It was a beautiful, elegant place with cupolas and gables, numerous stained-glass windows, and even a swing on the porch. It looked like the home of a prosperous family.

But when Iris reined in, the front door opened and a woman burst out, running down the stairs and dispelling any vision of family life.

She was clad in high heels and stockings and garters and little else but a short pink robe. She had midnight-black hair and a gamine face, and it wasn't until she was almost at the buckboard that Shannon realized that she was not a young girl at all but a woman of nearly fifty. She was beautiful still, and outrageous in her dress, and when she laughed, the sound of her laughter was husky and appealing.

''Iris! You did make it back. And this must be Malachi's blushing little bride.''

''I'm not little,'' Shannon protested, hopping down from the buckboard. She extended a hand to Cindy. She might be slim, but she was taller than Cindy by a good inch or two.

''I stand corrected,'' the woman said. ''Come on down, Iris. Do come in before someone notices that Mrs. Slater here is a newcomer.''

''You're right. Let's go in,'' Iris said.

They hurried up the steps to the house and came into a very elegant foyer. Shannon could hear laughter and the sounds of glasses clinking. Cindy cast her head to the right. ''That's the gaming room, Mrs. Slater. I don't imagine you'll want to wander in there. And there—'' She pointed to the left. ''That's the bar. Don't wander in there, either. Not that you're not welcome—the men just might get the wrong idea about you, and I don't want to have to answer to Malachi. Come on, and I'll show you to your room. Then I'll show you the kitchen. You're perfectly safe there. It's Jeremiah's domain, and no male dares tread there.''

Cindy started to lead them up a flight of stairs. Shannon caught her arm, stopping her.

"Excuse me, but where is Malachi?"

"He's, er, he's out at the moment," Cindy said. "Come on now, I've got to get you settled—"

Shannon caught her arm again. "I'm sorry, but he's out where? Is Cole here? Has Jamie slipped in yet?"

"Cole is just fine, and Jamie looks as good as gold," Cindy said. She came to the second-floor landing and hurried down the hall, pushing open a door. "It's one of the nicest rooms in the house. See the little window seat? I think that you'll be very comfortable in here, Mrs. Slater."

Shannon stood in the center of the room. It was a beautiful room with a large bed, a marble mantel, chairs, and the promised window seat. It was missing one thing. Her husband.

"Thank you for the room, and for your help and hospitality, for myself, my husband and my brothers-in-law. And excuse me for being persistent, but where is my husband, please?"

Cindy looked uneasily from Iris to Shannon.

"He's..."

"You might as well answer her," Iris advised. "She won't give up asking you."

"I won't," Shannon said.

"He's holding up a train."

"What?" Shannon gasped in astonishment.

"Wait a minute, I said that badly, didn't I?"

"Is there a good way to announce to his wife that a man is holding up a train?" Iris demanded.

"Well, he isn't really holding it up—"

"What are you saying!" Shannon demanded.

Cindy sighed and walked over to where a pretty little round cherry-wood side table held brandy and snifters. There were only two snifters—the room was planned for a party of two, and no more.

"We'll share," Cindy told Iris, and she drank a glass of brandy before pouring out two more and handing one glass to Shannon and the other to Iris.

"Cindy, explain about Malachi," Shannon insisted.

"All right. All right. Kristin is being held in the Hayden house. They've got bars on the windows, and at least twenty guards in and around the house. There was no way for the three men to break in and carry her away." She hesitated. "The boys just might have some friends around here, but we don't really know that yet. A lot of decent folk aren't pleased that Hayden Fitz is holding a lady, no matter what legal shenanigans he tries to pull. Anyway, Jamie heard tell that some bushwhackers on the loose were planning to hold up the train south. And there's a Federal judge on that train. They're going to seize the train from the bushwhackers and then try to explain the whole story to the judge."

"Oh, those fools!" Shannon cried. "They're going to get themselves killed."

Iris slipped an arm around her. "Honey, come on! They aren't fools. They know what they're about."

"If the bushwhackers don't shoot them, the judge will!"

"Well," Cindy said dryly, "you can be sure of one thing."

"What's that?"

"If Cole Slater is killed, Hayden Fitz won't need your sister any more. He'll let her go."

"I don't know," Iris murmured miserably, staring at her glass. "Knowing the perversions of Hayden Fitz, I imagine—"

"Iris!" Cindy said.

Iris quickly looked at Shannon and flushed. "Oh, honey, I'm sorry. I really am..."

"It's all right, Iris. You don't need to hide the truth from me," Shannon said. She sank down on the bed. "Oh, God!" she murmured desperately. "He said that we'd be together tonight. He said that we'd be back together."

Iris and Cindy exchanged looks over her head. Shannon leaped up suddenly. "Iris, I can't just sit. here. Let's go into town."

"What?"

"Iris, you can get in to see Kristin, can't you? I would feel so much better if you saw her."

"Shannon, I don't know—"

"Iris, I can't just sit here. What if—" She hesitated, feeling her heart thunder hard against her chest. "What if Cole and Malachi don't make it? Iris, we have to discover some other way!"

"Malachi would hang me if—"

"Iris, I'm going with or without you."

Cindy shrugged, lifting her brandy glass. "You both look like respectable young women right now. Can't see how a ride into town could possibly hurt. Besides, if Hayden is around, he probably will let you in to see Kristin, Iris."

"Iris, I'm going with or without you. Iris, please. I'll go mad sitting here wondering about Malachi and Jamie and Cole and that stupid train!"

Iris sighed. "All right," she said at last. "All right. Shannon, I hope to God that this works out! He'll flay me alive if it doesn't."

"We'll be fine," Shannon assured her. "Just fine."

She would have plenty of time later to rue her confident words.

Maybe, if Shannon could have seen Malachi, seated comfortably in the club car of the train along with both his brothers, she might have felt a little better.

The three Slater brothers were seated in velvet-upholstered chairs around a handsome wood table drinking whiskey from crystal glasses at the judge's invitation. Cole was intense, straddled across his chair, leaning on the back, his eyes silver and his features taut as he spoke. Malachi leaned back, listening to his brother, more at ease. Jamie was, for all appearances, completely casual and negligent, accepting his drink with ease. He wore a broad-brimmed Mexican hat, chaps and boots, and looked every bit the rancher. Only the way his eyes narrowed now and then told Malachi that his younger brother was every bit as wary this night as he and Cole.

Two friends of Jamie's from Texas were playing lookout while the brothers spoke with Judge Sherman Woods. Cole, seated to Malachi's left, was earnestly explaining what had happened at the beginning of the war, how his wife had been killed, how the ranch had been burned and how, sick with grief, he had joined up with the bushwhackers for vengeance.

"But I never gunned down a man in cold blood in my life, judge," Cole said simply. "Never. I always fought fair. I wasn't with Quantrill more than a few months, then I went regular cavalry. I was assigned as a scout. I took my orders directly from Lee. I was in Kansas, and I did kill Henry Fitz, but it was fair. Any man who was there could tell you that.'' Judge Woods lit up a cigar and sat back. Malachi liked the man. He hadn't panicked when the masked bushwhackers had seized the train, and he had barely blinked when the Slaters had reseized it from the robbers at gunpoint, sending them on their way into the night. He was a tall thin man with a neatly trimmed mustache and iron-gray hair. He wore a stovepipe hat and a brocade vest and a handsome black frock coat and fancy shoes, but he seemed to be listening to Cole. He looked from one brother to the other. ''What about you?'' he asked Jamie.

Jamie smiled with innocent ease. ''Judge, this is the first time I've been in Kansas since 1856. I was damned stunned to hear that I was a wanted man. And amazed that any fool could think that my brother was a murderer.''

The judge arched one brow. He turned to Malachi. ''And what about you, captain?''

Malachi shrugged. ''I wasn't in Kansas. I spent most of the end of the war in Kentucky, then in Missouri. I would have come to Kansas, though, if I had thought that Cole might need me. Fitz was a murderer. He killed my sister-in-law. He killed lots of other people. And it seems to me, sir, that if we're really going to call a truce to this war, we have to prosecute all the murderers, the Yank murderers, too. Now Hayden Fitz is holding an innocent woman. God alone knows what he could want with her, and so help me, I can't understand what law he is using to get away with this legally.''

The judge lifted his hands. ''You do realize that what you're doing right now is illegal?''

''Yes, it is,'' Cole admitted.

''But we did stop those other fellows from robbing you blind,'' Malachi reminded him.

''Of course. All right, I've listened to your story. And God knows, gentlemen, I, for one, am anxious to see an end to the hostilities! I'm afraid we won't live to see it, but I'm a father of four, and I keep praying that maybe the next generation will see something good come to this land. You had best slip off this train and disappear into the night, the same way that you came. I give you my word of honor that I will look into this situation immediately. If you're patient, I'll see that your wife is freed, Cole Slater. But I suggest that the three of you remain out of sight for the time being. Understood? And, oh—stay away from Fitz. We don't want him finding you.''

Malachi looked at Cole, and Cole looked at Jamie. They all shrugged. They *were* in hiding. Just because they were hiding right beneath Fitz's nose…

They shook hands with the judge. Outside the club car, Jamie waved to his friends, and they jumped from where they were standing on the engine platform and the mail car. The five men hurried quietly for their waiting horses, then galloped away into the darkness of the night.

A half mile from the train, they left Jamie's friends, Cole and Malachi voicing their thanks earnestly. The two men had served with Jamie during the war. "Don't mind helping a Slater," said the older of the two. "Jamie pulled me out of a crater in December of '64. I owe him my life."

"Thanks just the same," Jamie said, tilting his hat. Malachi and Cole echoed the words.

Then the brothers were alone together, riding through the night.

Malachi flashed Jamie a smile. "Well, I admit, it seemed like a reckless plan to begin with, but it went fairly well."

"Nothing really gained," Jamie murmured.

"Nothing lost," Cole said, sighing. Malachi saw his brother's frown in the moonlight. "And we're close enough. If Fitz does threaten Kristin…"

"Then we are close, and we just get a little more reckless," Malachi said. He urged the bay along a little faster.

"Hey!" Jamie called out to him. "What's your hurry now? We're not being pursued."

Malachi reined in. "I…Shannon is supposed to be coming in tonight."

Jamie started to laugh. "That hellcat in a whorehouse? You're right. Let's hurry."

Cole grinned. "It will be good to see her," he said softly. "I've missed Miss McCahy."

Malachi hesitated, then he muttered. "Mrs. Slater."

"What?" Both brothers queried him.

"Mrs. Slater," he repeated. He looked from Jamie to Cole. They stared at him in amazement.

"They were going to hang me," Malachi explained lamely. "I— er, we kind of had to do it."

"She married a Reb?" Jamie demanded.

"She married—you?" Cole said.

"I told you, they were going to hang me if we didn't. Damn it, quit staring at me like that!" He swore. He urged the bay forward. "It's a long, long story and I'm not in the mood for it tonight."

"Cole, come on now, hurry!" Jamie laughed. "I am anxious to hear this! The hellcat married to my brother! Mrs. Sweet-little-hellcat Slater, holed up in a whorehouse! I can't wait."

Malachi ignored his brother and urged his horse faster. He wanted to see Shannon. His heart was pounding; his body was aching. They would have to take some time. She would need to see and hug and hold Cole, and she would laugh and maybe cry and then hug Jamie fiercely, too. But then they would be alone.

And he was realizing more and more that he had come to live for the moments when they could be alone.

She was his wife...

And he was very anxious to lie down beside her that night.

He had no idea until they rode into the yard in the darkness of the night that he would be denied that simple pleasure.

Chapter Thirteen

Shannon breathed a sigh of relief as they reached town. No one thought to molest two women riding in a buckboard, and when Iris reined in just to the right of Hayden Fitz's massive dwelling, with its barred windows and guards, they were still left entirely alone. The man before the door raised a hand to Iris, and a grin broke out on his features.

"Why, Miss Andre. Nice to see you."

"Herb Tanner," Iris told Shannon with a sniff. She reached in back of her for the basket of food they had packed. "I think that you should sit tight—"

"Who's that you got with you?" the man called out.

"Never mind," Iris said beneath her breath. "You keep quiet. Let me do the talking." Iris looked at her and shook her head mournfully. "A beautiful young blue-eyed blonde. You could be in trouble just by being here. I wish I had a sheet to put over your head. Keep your mouth shut, you hear?"

"I'll be silent as a mouse," Shannon promised.

She crawled out of the buckboard behind Iris and followed the older woman toward the house. Herb Tanner was holding a repeating rifle, but he seemed to consider his guard duty a bit of a joke. He set the gun down to sweep his hat off to Iris.

"Hello, Herb," Iris said sweetly.

"Hello, Iris!" Herb said happily. "The boss man is engaged this evening, if you come to see him." He spoke to Iris, but he looked over her shoulder to Shannon, offering her a broken-toothed and lascivious grin.

"Well, Herb, I really came for curiosity's sake."

Herb's grin widened. "You curious about me, Iris?"

Iris laughed and patted his chest and moved close to him. "Why, Herbie, you could make a woman just as curious as a prowling cat, you know that, boy? But that wasn't what I meant. Not at this particular moment." She moved closer against him. "I want to see the woman that old Fitz has locked up in the house. I have a bet with my friend Sara here that we can get in to see her. They say that she's the wife of that awful outlaw, Cole Slater. What do you think, Herbie? Could we get in? Just to give her some apple pie and chicken from Cindy's house."

"I don't know, Iris," Herbie said.

"Oh, Herbie, come on! Isn't it funny? A couple of girls from Cindy's place bringing vittles to that little bushwhacker's lady? Why, it's just plain ironic, it is. Fitz would laugh himself silly, I'm certain."

"Iris, Fitz is in a meeting with some of his boss people—"

"Herbie, I could promise you a real good time."

Shannon saw that Herb jumped and trembled like a dog with a juicy new bone, just from the sound of Iris's voice. She clamped a hand on Iris's arm. Annoyed, Iris turned to her. Shannon pulled her down the steps.

"Iris! I don't want you promising that man sexual favors to get us into that house!"

"It's probably the only way, Shannon."

"Iris—"

"Shannon, it's what I do for a living!"

"You told me you just might think about changing occupations."

"Honey—"

"Iris, don't make any promises, please."

Iris grinned and shrugged. "All right, honey. You can promise him the sexual favors."

"What!"

"Oh, for heaven's sake. I'll promise him for a later date, and we'll never get to it, all right?"

Shannon exhaled slowly. "All right."

They hurried back to Herb. "Little financial negotiation," Iris said sweetly to him. "Sara doesn't think I should be giving the business away. But if you can get us in to visit that bushwhacker's woman, I'll promise you...I'll promise you the time of your life next Friday night. What do you say, Herbie?"

Herb's Adam's apple bulged and he exhaled in a rush. "Gee, Iris, I didn't think I could ever afford you. Not in a month of Sundays!"

"Well, curiosity, you know..."

Herb's eyes narrowed in calculation. "It's a deal, Iris. But I want you both." He looked over at Shannon like a cat who had swallowed a mouse, a pleased gloat on his face.

"What?" she gasped.

Iris elbowed her in the ribs.

"Sure, Herbie. Let us in, huh?"

"Let me see your basket," Herb said. Iris produced the basket. Herb searched through it. Satisfied, he nodded. He stepped aside, opening the front door.

There was another armed man in the entryway. "Let 'em in, Joshua. They're all right. They're just bringing the prisoner a bite of food."

"All right, Herb."

Joshua nodded to them. Iris dazzled him with a sweet smile, and he pointed them up the steps.

Shannon ran alongside Iris. On the landing was another man sitting in a chair reading the newspaper. Joshua called up to him. "Fulton, it's just a pair of—er, ladies to see the prisoner."

Fulton looked up and spat tobacco into a brass spittoon. "Herb say it was all right?"

"Honey chile, Herbie let us in," Iris told him sweetly.

Fulton stood up and moved close behind her. "Is there anything left that you can promise me?" he asked with a yellow-toothed smile.

"We'll see, darlin'," Iris promised. "Now, if you'd just show us the bushwhacker's wife..."

Fulton shrugged and produced a set of keys. He walked down the hall to a door and twisted a key in the lock. "You're looking good, Iris. So is your friend." He paused, staring at Shannon. "You new in town, girl?"

Shannon nodded.

"Learning the ropes of the business," Iris supplied.

Fulton's eyes swept over Shannon. "Well, I'll be savin' up my dimes, young lady. You can bet on that."

"Fulton, for you, there will be a big discount," Iris promised.

Fulton smiled and pushed open the door. "Company!" he called. Iris hurried into the room. Fulton caught Shannon's arm. "I'll be expecting a big discount, little lady."

Shannon wrenched her arm away, then remembered to smile. "Sure, sweetie," she promised, and batted her lashes his way. Iris grasped her arm and jerked her into the room. "Enough is enough, Shannon!" she hissed. "You want to wind up serving the man right here in the hallway?"

But Shannon wasn't listening. While Iris closed the door, Shannon stared across the room.

Kristin was standing by the foot of the bed, tall, stiff and proud, and every inch the lady. Her facade broke as she saw Shannon. Both women cried out and raced across the room and into one another's arms.

"Shh!" Iris begged them. "They'll hear you!"

Shannon and Kristin went dutifully silent, but continued to grip each other fiercely. Finally Kristin drew away. Shannon surveyed her sister as anxiously as Kristin studied her.

Kristin seemed to be all right. Someone had supplied her with a change of clothing, and she wore a cotton day dress in a soft rich burgundy with a cream lace collar. She was thin and pale, but she was smiling, and there didn't seem to be a mark on her.

Kristin held Shannon's hands as she made her sit down at the foot of the bed. Amazed, she looked from Shannon to Iris. Then she whispered, "What are you doing here? Shannon, I have been ill with worry! I saw the bushwhackers take you away—"

"Malachi rescued me," Shannon said quickly, not wanting to talk about that experience or Justin Waller.

"Oh, Shannon, you see, he has a good heart."

"Yes, Kristin—"

"Shannon, you shouldn't be here," Kristin said anxiously.

"Kristin, if I hadn't followed, Malachi might have slipped you away from the Red Legs. So I have to make up for that. Iris and I had to come!''

Kristin looked at Iris again, smiling. She stood up and offered Iris her hand. "How do you do? I'm Kristin Slater," she said softly. "Whoever you are, thank you!''

"Iris Andre," Iris offered.

"How did you get in here?" Kristin asked.

Shannon looked at Iris and Iris looked at Shannon. "We made a few deals," Shannon said ruefully.

"What? Oh," Kristin said. Her eyes, wide and very blue, fell upon Iris.

"I'm sorry, Mrs. Slater, but you should know. I'm a whore. And your husband and her husband have been staying out at Cindy's place. It might not be fittin', you two being ladies and all, but we're willing to help, and—''

"Sh!" Kristin cautioned, hurrying to Iris with a crooked smile. "I don't care what you do, Miss Andre. I thank you for caring. Did you say my husband? Cole? Is he there? He can't be!" She whirled around and stared at Shannon. "Nor Malachi. They wouldn't allow Shannon to do such a foolish thing as come here."

A small smile teased Iris's lips. "Mrs. Slater, I'm willing to bet that both Cole and Malachi are aware that there is not much that can stop your sister when her mind is set. But, yes, Mrs. Slater, your husband has been in town. So has Shannon's and so's your brother-in-law Jamie. They went out tonight to try to un-hold-up a train.''

"What?"

"Kristin, I had to come. I had to see you. We must come up with a way out of this awful situation!" Shannon said.

Kristin was still staring at Iris, a frown marring her features. "My husband," she murmured. She stared at Shannon. "And her husband...Miss Andre, what husband?"

"Why, Malachi."

"Malachi!"

"Shh!" Shannon jumped to her feet.

Kristin sat at the foot of the bed, staring at Shannon incredulously. "Malachi!" she gasped. "Shannon, that's impossible! The two of you are incapable of sharing a room for ten minutes without all hell breaking loose. You and...Malachi?''

Shannon smiled uneasily. ''It—er—it seemed like the thing to do at the time.''

''They had threatened to hang him,'' Iris supplied with a shrug.

''But—'' Kristin began.

''I'll tell you all about it at some other time,'' Shannon promised quickly. ''Kristin, are they treating you well?''

''Well enough.''

''No one has—''

''No one has physically abused me,'' Kristin said flatly. ''Fitz thinks that if he can't get Cole to come out of hiding by just holding on to me, he'll pass a rumor that he's willing to deal.'' She hesitated. ''So Cole is here. Oh, God, Shannon, don't let him do anything stupid! What is this about a train? Please, talk to him. Make him see that he can't win. Tell him to go home and get the baby and leave the country. Tell him—''

''Kristin! You know that he'll never do that.''

''I have the perfect plan,'' Iris said softly.

Kristin and Shannon spun around to look at her. She smiled. ''It will be easy enough to find another night when Fitz is occupied. And if not, I know how to occupy Fitz. Then we come with more of the girls. And we bring a few shawls and the like. And we all leave together. We just walk away, all of us, together. I guarantee you, none of the men will feel like moving.''

Kristin stared at her in silence, then burst into laughter. ''Oh, Iris, it's wonderful. But I couldn't let you do something like that! Fitz would surely get even with you—''

''With all of us? What could he do?''

''Fitz would find something.''

''No. Because he would never be able to prove it. He wouldn't discover you missing until the next morning, and you could all be halfway to Texas by then. He wouldn't know which of us were involved, and it would be hard to hang a whole whorehouse. I think the men of this town would finally rebel.''

''Neither Cole, Malachi or Jamie will let you do it, either,'' Kristin warned.

"They won't know!" Shannon said.

"But—" Kristin began.

"Shh! We'll be back," Shannon told her.

"Be ready," Iris warned Kristin. She grabbed Shannon's arm and pulled her to her feet. "We've got to move now, or they'll suspect us of something tonight, and we don't want that."

"Take care!" Shannon warned her sister, and hugged her fiercely again. "We'll be back."

"Come on!" Iris tugged on her sleeve.

They hurried to the door together. There was no one on the upstairs landing and they hurried down the steps. When they reached the bottom, Fulton was blocking their way. Iris smiled at him. "Thanks, Fulton. We'll be seeing you soon."

"You bet you will, Iris."

"Why, Fulton, what's wrong with you, honey?"

Fulton stepped aside. Shannon gasped, stunned.

Bear stood there. He was the massive jayhawker who had carried Kristin away after the fighting between the jayhawkers and the bushwhackers, and it was obvious from the glint in his eyes that he remembered his brief glimpse of Shannon.

"What's going on?" Iris asked uneasily.

Shannon didn't say anything. The big man walked toward her with a wide grin plastered against his beefy features. "It is her," he said flatly. His arms crossed over his chest, he walked around Shannon. "Saw you when I was coming down the street, little miss. I thought I recognized you." He spun in a sudden fury and banged Fulton on the head with his hat. "Couldn't you see how much she looked like that Slater woman? They're as like as two peas from the same pod, you damned fool."

"Don't go beating at me, Bear!" Fulton protested. "Herbie said that the women were all right."

"Well, Herbie's going to have to answer to the boss, and that's that," Bear said. He grinned at Shannon and Iris. "Let's go and see the boss man, little lady."

Bear grasped Shannon by the arm. Iris slunk back against the wall. Shannon bit hard into Bear's fingers. When he screamed, Iris pulled out her small pistol.

"Let her go, Bear," Iris said.

Bear lifted up his hands. Shannon grabbed the Colt she was carrying from her skirt pocket. She drew the gun and held it on Fulton. "We're going to walk away. I'm going to go back up and get my sister out, and we're going to walk away."

"I think not, ma'am," a deep male voice called out.

Shannon spun around and looked up the stairs.

Kristin stood on the top step now, biting into her lip.

Behind her stood a tall, lean man with snow-white hair and cold gray eyes. He wore an elegant brocade vest and a frock coat and he held a small silver pistol to Kristin's skull. "Drop the gun," he told Shannon.

"Don't do it!" Kristin charged her. "Get out, Shannon, just get out—oh!"

The man cracked Kristin hard upon the head and she fell at his feet. He smiled at Shannon and aimed the gun toward her sister's back. "Drop it."

"Do it, Shannon," Iris advised wearily. "That's Fitz. And he will shoot her, without a thought."

"Why, thank you, Iris," Fitz drawled softly, "for that fine commendation. Girl, drop the gun."

Shannon inhaled and exhaled. Fitz cocked the gun. Shannon slowly bent and lay down her Colt.

"That was a very fine idea, young woman." He nodded to Bear. "Bring her to my office."

Bear set his arms upon Shannon. She tried to shake him off. "I can walk on my own!" she spat out.

"Fitz, you can't hold this girl—" Iris began.

"Iris, I am so disappointed in you!" Fitz said, shaking his head with a half smile. "Fulton, escort our friend Iris to my chamber, will you? Iris, I don't know what promises you made to get in here, but we'll just discuss them all. Later. And you will pay up."

Fulton grabbed Iris, sweeping her little pistol from her hands and jerking her around. "Come on, Iris. You heard the boss."

"Fitz, you can't hold her! Fitz, you—"

"I can, and I will, Iris," Fitz said. He stepped over Kristin and started down the stairs. "Get her out of here, Fulton. You'd better start worrying about yourself, Iris. Harboring a known criminal like this one here. Why, we could just shoot you down on the spot, Iris, and no court of law in the country could have a thing to say about it. Fulton, get her out of here!''

"Fitz, you'll pay!'' Iris vowed as Fulton wrenched her arm behind her back. Iris cried out in pain. Shannon couldn't bear seeing Iris so hurt on her behalf. She flew at Fitz, her nails gouging his flesh.

"Let her alone, you bastard!'' she hissed.

She didn't expect the iron grip of the man. He caught her flailing fists and pressed her against the banister. When she tried to kick him he lashed out, slapping her so hard that she staggered to her knees. He jerked her to her feet and prodded her before him. He threw her through a door in the foyer, and she fell to the ground.

He followed her into the office, stepping over her skirts. He closed the door behind him and walked around his desk to sit, idly watching her for several moments.

Shannon barely dared move. She stared at the man and waited.

"Well, well, well,'' he murmured at last. "My net is closing fast around all the little fishes.''

"I don't know what you mean,'' Shannon said.

"Don't you?'' he said, arching a distinguished white brow. "I think that you do. After all, my dear, you are here now, aren't you?'' He smiled. "I hear things, you know. Nothing much happens in these parts that I don't hear about. Captain Malachi Slater was with you in Haywood.''

Shannon shrugged. "I'm here on my own.''

"Come, come, my dear. Malachi Slater gunned down half my men in the woods along with his bushwhacker friends. Bushwhackers. You never can trust them. I even heard that Malachi Slater gunned down a fellow Reb just the other day.''

"He didn't gun down anyone,'' Shannon said.

"Ah, but he is near!'' Hayden Fitz said. He smiled. "And your name is Shannon, and you're a Slater now, too. Is that true?''

Shannon shrugged. "Malachi despises me. If you hear everything, you must know that he and I are enemies. We were on different sides during the war, Mr. Fitz. Perhaps you should know, too, that my brother is a highly respected Union officer. When he gets his hands on you, you'll be really sorry.''

Fitz laughed, delighted. ''Don't fret, girl. Your brother will be too late to help you. Oh, young lady! I can't tell you just how happy I am to have you. The net does draw tighter and tighter. And I know you *are* Mrs. Malachi Slater.'' He stood up, coming around the desk. He looked down at her. ''You're even prettier than your sister, and I didn't think that possible. My men would really enjoy you. And they just might, you know. I could enjoy an evening with you myself—'' He broke off, shrugging. ''But I want the Slaters first. I want every last one of them dead.''

''You'll never do it,'' Shannon said defiantly. ''They'll kill you, and you know it. You're so damned afraid of them that you can barely stand it!''

''Those Slaters are cold-blooded murderers!''

''The Slaters! Your brother swept in and murdered innocent women! How dare you talk about cold-blooded murder?''

''Bushwhackers deserved to die.''

''There weren't any bushwhackers back when Cole's wife was killed! Just bastards like your brother!''

Fitz clenched his teeth and struck out at her with his booted foot. She screamed with the sudden pain.

The door burst open. Bear and Fulton rushed in.

''Trouble, boss?'' Bear asked. Fulton was frowning, staring at Shannon.

''Boss, you know you can't hold another woman here. Someone will protest—''

''Shut up, Fulton.''

''But boss, if this gets out, too, now…''

''Mary Surratt was hanged for complicity in the Lincoln assassination,'' Fitz said quietly, staring at Shannon. ''I'm sure that I can pin complicity on these lovely ladies, too.''

''But boss, what about Iris?''

''Fulton, are you questioning me?''

''Sir, it's just—''

''Bear, go out, will you? Check the street and see if we've got any other visitors running around tonight.''

"Yes, sir."

Bear ran out. Fulton asked, "Mr. Fitz, should I go out with him?"

Shannon should have seen the curious cold light in Fitz's strange gray eyes, but she wasn't prepared for what happened next.

"No, Fulton, you stay here," Fitz said. "I need you." Then he pulled out his little pistol and aimed it at Fulton.

"No!" Fulton gasped, his eyes widening with horror.

Fitz fired. Fulton dropped to the floor.

And Hayden Fitz threw himself on top of Shannon, pretending to struggle with her.

The door burst open. Bear was back.

"She shot him!" Fitz cried. "The little bitch came flying at me and stole my pistol and shot Fulton, shot him down dead, in cold blood."

"Liar!" Shannon raged, trying to free herself. Fitz held her tightly, meeting her eyes with a cold smile.

"Murderess!" He stood and dragged her to her feet. "Damned bushwhacker's murderess!" he swore. He held her very close in a deadly challenge. "You'll hang for this!" he promised, and shoved her toward Bear. "Lock her up. Lock her up with her sister. They can both hang for murder, and for conspiracy to do murder!"

"You can't get away with this!" Shannon cried.

"Watch me, Mrs. Slater. Just watch me. You'll feel the rope around your neck and then you'll know."

She escaped from Bear and flew at Fitz with such a rage that she managed to rake bloody scratches down his cheeks with her nails. He hissed out something, and Bear came up behind her. He struck her hard on the head with the butt of his gun.

Hayden Fitz went hazy before her. Then the world went black.

"Lock them both up," Fitz said. "And make sure poor Fulton is brought over to Darby's funeral parlor. See that he's done up right. Stupid, murdering bitch."

"Yes, sir, yes, sir," Bear said. He scooped Shannon up into his arms and left the office.

Hayden Fitz stepped over Fulton's body. He walked to the stairs and looked up them. He smiled.

Iris had yet to pay for her part in the night's proceedings. She had yet to pay...

But she would pay very dearly.

He set his hand upon the banister and started up the stairs.

"That's—that's all I know," Cindy said unhappily, staring at the three Slater brothers. "A friend of Bear's come in here about midnight, and told everyone what happened. We've got to move the three of you—they'll come here looking for you, and I'm gong to have to pretend to be innocent. I—"

Malachi stood up. "Cindy, you don't have to do anything. I'm going in tonight," he said softly.

"No! Malachi, no, that's just what Fitz wants!" Cindy protested. "If you go raging in—"

"He's got my wife," Malachi thundered.

Cole stood and clapped Malachi on the shoulder. "He's had my wife, Malachi, don't forget that. I admit, bursting in, guns blazing, was my first thought. But Fitz will kill them, Malachi."

Malachi slunk back into his chair. He stared across the room.

"We have to bide our time," Jamie murmured.

"There will be some kind of a trial," Cindy said. She looked unhappily at Malachi. "But Hayden's telling everybody that Shannon McCahy Slater shot one of his men in cold blood. The trial will be rigged. She'll be condemned, and unless he gets his hands on you, he will hang her. He'll hang them both."

Malachi stood again. He strode across the room and came back to stand before Cole.

"A hanging. A big crowd, ropes. Lots of confusion."

Cole smiled slowly. "A few sharpshooters could do a fair amount of damage in a crowd like that."

Malachi grinned his slow, crooked smile. Cole laughed, and as Cindy watched, even Jamie smiled with a leisurely pleasure.

"You've all lost your minds!" she told them.

"No, darlin'," Malachi drawled softly. "I think we've just found our way out of this mess."

"What are you—"

Cindy broke off. Someone was knocking at the door. A voice called, "Cindy! It's Gretchen. I need to see you."

The Slaters quickly stood. Malachi came around behind the bar. Cole and Jamie sank against the pillars. Gretchen pushed open the door. She was followed by a tall man clad in the dark blue uniform of the Union cavalry man.

"Cindy, this man insists he get to you!" Gretchen said, rubbing her wrist and looking at the stranger in the shadows. "He said that he knows the Slaters are around here somewhere, and he wants Cole to know that the baby is fine." Pretty, sandy-haired, freckle-faced Gretchen looked at the man resentfully. "He said something about a house shouldn't be divided, not a family, and that the Slaters ought to know what he was talking about."

Malachi came around the bar. He looked closely at the stranger. He started to laugh. "Matthew! Matthew McCahy! How are you?"

Matthew stepped forward. "Well, Malachi!" Matthew pumped his hand firmly. "What in God's name is going on? I've been following a trail of the most absurd stories to get here. Red Legs and bush-whackers, corpses all over. I've got friends investigating Fitz, but I don't seem to be able to get to my sisters. What the hell is going on? I hear tell that they arrested Shannon today, too, for murder."

"It's all right," Malachi said. "We've got a plan."

Cole and Jamie stepped out of the shadows. Cindy sighed with relief. "Well, I think that this calls for drinks all around," she murmured.

"Drinks, then we've got to get out of here before we cause Cindy any trouble," Cole said.

He took a seat at the round table. The other men followed him. Matthew McCahy looked hard at Malachi. "All right. What's the plan?"

"It's dangerous, Matthew. We might get ourselves shot up."

"They're my sisters," Matthew said. "My flesh and blood. I'll darned well get shot up for them if I feel like it." He narrowed his eyes. "Kristin is Cole's wife. But I've got more of a stake in this thing than either of you have, Malachi and Jamie."

Malachi shook his head. "Shannon is my wife," he said, finding with surprise that breaking this news got easier with practice.

"What?" Matthew said incredulously.

"Malachi married Shannon," Jamie answered, smiling with amusement.

"Yes, I married Shannon!" Malachi said dryly. "Now, if you all don't mind, think we could get on with this?"

"Sure," Matthew said.

Malachi leaned across the table and started talking. Matthew listened gravely. When Malachi was done, he sat back, nodding. "Think we'll have any help on it?" he asked.

"Jamie's got a couple of friends from Texas here," Malachi said.

"And I've met some people in the area," Cole added. "Maybe they won't take a stand against Fitz alone, but if we give them half a chance, they'll help us."

"It doesn't matter what we do or don't have," Malachi said. "As far as I see it, it's our best shot. Are we agreed?"

All around the table, they nodded to him one by one. Jamie lifted his whiskey glass. "What the hell. A man's gotta die sometime," he said cheerfully.

Malachi stood. "Let's get out of here. Cindy, you'll keep us up on everything that happens. Everything."

"Of course, Malachi. You know that."

An hour later, the Slaters and Matthew McCahy had slipped away into the night.

When Fitz's men came to the house, there was no sign that they had ever been near.

The only benefit to being held was that she was with her sister.

For the first day, Shannon nervously paced the room, but she was grateful that they had at least been kept together. She hadn't really meant to say much about her own strained relationship with Malachi, but the hours dragged on and Shannon found herself telling her sister almost everything.

Almost...

She didn't tell her how easily she had fallen into her old enemy's arms, or how she had longed for him to touch her again and again. She didn't tell her that even as they waited now, prisoners in the room, she thought of her husband, longing to be with him, aching to see his slow, lazy grin and the spark it ignited in his eyes. She didn't speak about that longing...

But watching Kristin's smile, she thought that her sister read her mind, and her heart, and that she knew.

"Actually," Kristin said mischievously, "I think you just might be perfect for one another."

Shannon shook her head. "Kristin, I don't know. I should let him out of the marriage. But Iris says that I'm a fool if I don't fight for him."

"I agree with Iris," Kristin said. She took Shannon's hands. "I'll never forget how miserable I was about Cole! I was tied up in knots, hating him, loving him. But it worked out for us, Shannon. I didn't think that he would ever forget his first wife, but he did fall in love with me. Shannon, even when I gave birth to Gabe, I was so afraid that Cole would never, never love me. You have to fight sometimes, for anything in life that is good. Look at the two of us now. Things have worked out—"

She broke off and Shannon bit her lip, watching her sister. Nothing had worked out for any of them. They were in the midst of disaster.

"I'm so scared!" Kristin said softly.

Shannon threw her arms around her. "It's all right. It's going to be all right!"

The two sisters hugged one another, shivering. They didn't know if it would be all right at all.

The next day was the mock trial, which took place in the town courthouse. Hayden Fitz sat on the bench as judge; the jurors were selected from among his men. Shannon was accused of murder. She stood at the witness stand and listened silently to the charge, then turned scornfully upon Fitz.

"I didn't murder anyone. You shot down your friend, Mr. Fitz. You shot him down in cold blood because he was protesting your cruelty to me. You may own this town, Mr. Fitz, but I can't really believe that you own everyone in it. Someone will get to you. The war is over, Hayden Fitz. No one will let you do murder endlessly!"

There was a murmur among the crowd. Fitz stood, pointing his gavel at her. "You murdered Fulton. I saw you with my own eyes. You murdered him to free your outlaw sister. You shot down men in Missouri, too. You're in league with your husband, and the two of you rode around the country in Cole Slater's gang, bushwhacking, murdering innocent Union women and children.''

"Never," Shannon said quietly.

Fitz slammed his gavel against his desk. "You may step down, Mrs. Slater.''

She didn't step down; she was dragged down. Kristin was brought up. Kristin denied everything, and threw at Fitz his brother's activities as a jayhawker. She described graphically how Cole's first wife had died.

A murmur rose in the courtroom, but Fitz ignored it. Kristin was handcuffed and led back to Shannon. They were both returned to the room with the barred windows at Fitz's home while the carefully selected jury came to their decision.

By night, the verdict was brought back to them. They were both convicted of murder and conspiracy against the Union.

They were to be hanged one week from that night at dawn.

"One week," Kristin told Shannon bitterly. "They want to make sure to give Cole and Malachi and Jamie a chance to show up.''

Shannon nodded. One week. She looked at her sister. It had already been three days since she had been captured.

"Kristin?''

"Yes?''

"Where do you suppose they are? I'm scared, too, Kristin. They *were* in town. And now it's so silent! What if they've already been caught, and been taken..." Her voice trailed away miserably.

"They haven't been taken," Kristin told her dryly. "Fitz would have men walking through the streets with their heads on stakes if he'd caught them.''

That was true, Shannon thought.

But as the days passed, they still heard nothing. An ominous silence had settled over the town. A harsh, brooding silence, as if even the air and the earth waited...

And prayed.

Slowly, excruciatingly slowly, the week passed. Finally, the night before the scheduled hanging came. Kristin sat in the room's one chair; Shannon stood by the window.

The scaffold had been built beneath the window, right in the center of the street, because Fitz had wanted them to watch its building. Shannon stared at it with growing horror.

It was a long night.

Morning finally came. "I—I can't believe that they haven't tried to rescue us!" Shannon told Kristin.

Kristin stared at the ceiling. "I was wrong. They must be dead already," she said softly.

Shannon felt as if icy waters settled over her heart and her body. She had endured too much. If Malachi was dead, then so be it. She wanted no more of this earth, of the awful pain and suffering. He had just taught her how to live...

And now, it was over.

When Bear came for them, he tied their hands behind their backs and led them out. Kristin smiled at her sister as they walked into the pearly gray dawn. It was going to be an absurdly beautiful summer's day. "Pa will be there, I'm certain," she said. "It won't be so hard to die. Mother will be there, too. And Robert Ellsworth. Oh, Shannon! What about Gabe, what will happen to him?"

"Delilah will love him. Matthew will come home, and he will raise him like his own."

"Shannon, I love you."

"Courage!" Shannon whispered. She was going to start to cry. Courage was easy in the midst of safety. But as they walked up the steps of the scaffold and beneath the dangling nooses, it was much harder to find.

Fitz sat in front of the scaffold on his horse. "Have you any last words, ladies?" he asked them.

Shannon looked over the crowd. The people weren't smiling or cheerful; they looked troubled. "Yes!" she called out. "We're innocent! Your hatred and your vengeance have made a mockery of justice, Hayden Fitz. And if you do not pay, sir, in this lifetime, I am certain that you will pay in the next, in the bowels of hell forever!"

Fitz's cold eyes narrowed. "Hang them!" he ordered.

The ropes were fitted over their heads and around their necks.

Shannon bit back tears as she felt the rope chafe the tender flesh of her neck. In a second, it would be pulled taut. She would dangle and choke. If God were merciful, her neck would snap. And if he were not merciful, she would die slowly of suffocation. Her tongue would swell and protrude and she would die hideously...

Hayden Fitz lifted his hand. The executioner walked over to the lever that would snap open the trapdoor.

Hayden Fitz read off the charges, and the order that Kristin and Shannon Slater be hanged by the necks until dead.

He lifted his hand...

And let it fall.

The executioner flipped the lever, and the floor gave beneath them.

Suddenly, the street was alive with explosions.

Shannon was falling, but the rope did not tighten around her neck. Someone had cut it. She kept falling, and crashed hard upon the ground. Cindy was there, slitting the rope that bound her wrists. Shannon twisted around in the dust.

"Get up! Get out of here!" Cindy cried.

"Kristin—"

"I'm freeing Kristin. Get up, go! Both of you!"

Kristin did not ask questions. She grabbed Shannon's hand and the two of them crawled out from beneath the scaffold. Shannon peered through the rain of gunfire. The streets had gone mad. People were screaming and running.

And a group of horsemen was bearing down on them.

She raised her hand over her eyes to shade them from the sun.

Malachi rode straight at her on his bay mare, his cavalry sword glinting in the sun, a Rebel cry upon his lips. He wore his plumed hat, and his full gray and gold Confederate cavalry dress.

He was coming for her, fighting his way down the street. Any man fool enough to block his way was cut down. As he neared her, she saw his teal-blue eyes blazing.

"Shannon! Get ready!" he yelled, striking down the last of Fitz's men to stand between them. He was a golden hero, riding to save her.

The bay was rearing over her. He reached down and swept her up onto the saddle before him, and they thundered down the street together.

Chapter Fourteen

The morning had burst into madness as they fled the town. There were explosions of gunfire. Women were screaming; men were shouting. Held tight against Malachi on his bay, Shannon was dimly aware of a number of horses riding beside them. Her hair kept whipping against her face, blinding her, but she managed to see at last. Cole was to her left with Kristin, her brother Matthew was to her right, and numerous men she'd never seen before were riding behind her. Some of them were in tattered remnants of uniforms, both blue and gray. Some were dressed as ranchers.

They all rode grimly, not stopping until they were miles from the town. Then Malachi reined in, shouting over Shannon's head to Cole. "We'll kill the horses if we keep this up. Think we've come far enough?"

Cole shrugged, his arms tight around his wife, and looked back along the trail they had just taken. "Here's Jamie," he said.

Jamie Slater, on a huge dapple gray stallion, raced up behind them. He waved his hat in the air, a look of triumph on his face.

"Fitz is dead. And there isn't the first sign of pursuit. I think we can take it easier now."

"Not too easy!" A woman called. Shannon gasped as she saw Iris on a dark roan, riding up behind Jamie. "Fitz may not have been tremendously popular, but someone may seek to avenge him."

"Iris!" Shannon gasped when the redhead looked her way. She was, as always, impeccably dressed, and her hair was unrumpled. She looked unscathed by her imprisonment, except for the large blue circle beneath her right eye.

"I'm all right, honey," Iris said softly. "Thanks to Jamie. He pulled me away from Fitz."

"Jamie, bless you!" Kristin said.

"Always willing to oblige," Jamie drawled softly.

Shannon leaped down from in front of Malachi and ran over to Jamie, who also hopped down off his horse to meet her. "Hey, brat!" He laughed, sweeping her up in a fast hug. Matthew and Kristin dismounted as well, and they all hugged one another with laughter and relief.

"Shannon, get back over here!" Malachi commanded sharply. She glanced at him and saw that his features had become as threatening as a winter storm. She stiffened. Cole wasn't yelling that way. She stared at Malachi, defiant and hurt at once. Safe in the warmth of his arms, she had felt that the war between them was over. But now it seemed that nothing had changed. Did he still hate her?

"We do have to keep moving," he said.

Kristin turned and hurried back to Cole. He lifted her up before him. Jamie and Matthew mounted up again.

Shannon turned to the strangers who surrounded them. "I don't know who you are, but thank you, all of you. With all my heart, I thank you."

"We all thank you," Kristin echoed.

Malachi looked around at the curious assortment of men with them. "Shannon is right—thank you all." He pointed to the right. "These are Sam Greenhow, Frank Bujold, Lennie Peterson and Ronnie Cordon—all friends of Jamie's from General Edmund Kirby-Smith's command down in Texas. And those boys there—" he pointed to the left "—are from Haywood."

"Howdy," said one of the Confederates to Shannon, and he tipped his hat to Kristin. "I don't mean to be telling you all your business, but you were right, Malachi. You should keep moving. You need to put some mean space between you and Sparks."

Malachi nodded. He and Cole and Matthew thanked the men. Then Malachi called to Shannon again. "Shannon, get over here."

She didn't like his tone, but she could acknowledge he was right. She lifted her head and walked back to Malachi. He reached down for her, encircling her waist with his arm and pulling her up before him. They waved to the men who had risked their lives to fight against the corrupt rule in Sparks.

A silence fell as their curious little party started off: Cole and Kristin, Matthew, Jamie, Iris and Malachi and Shannon. Jamie rode in the lead, taking them south.

Shannon waited as the morning wore on, wanting to speak, not knowing what to say. She stared at Malachi's hand where it rested on her knee, and thought of how she had come to love that hand, how the texture of the bronze skin, the tiny tufts of gold hair on his long fingers now meant everything in the world to her.

She thought of the warmth of the man behind her, and she thought of the danger they had faced together time and time again. When she remembered the past she wanted to cry out all her pent-up fears and sorrows, but her recollections also made her think gravely of the future, too. Life was precious. It was dear, and could be so swiftly stolen away.

She and Malachi had life. This morning, they both had life. They had the sun over their heads, and the radiance of the blue sky, and they rode with people near and dear to them. God had been good to them that morning.

But Malachi was still as stiff and cold as steel. Shannon thought that perhaps he had decided that now he had carried out all obligations to her. He was angry, that much she knew. Maybe he was anxious, too, to be free.

But Iris had told her to fight for him. Could she do that?

Shannon moved her fingers gently over his hand. "Thank you," she told him softly.

He grunted in return. She thought that he would say no more, but then he growled in her ear. "I should thrash you within an inch of your life, young woman."

"What?" she demanded, startled.

"You were told to come to Cindy's. But oh, no, that wasn't good enough for you. You had to put yourself and Iris into a damn fool dangerous position—"

"*I* was foolish! You three were out holding up a train—"

"We went to un-hold-up that train—"

"There is no such thing as un-holding-up a train, Malachi Slater.

If you had been killed, Kristin would have been on her own. I would have had to have done something—"

"You did real well," he drawled sarcastically.

Shannon clenched her teeth, trying not to break into ridiculous tears. She stared down at his hand, and noted that he was shaking. With anger, she assumed. "I was doing fine," she stormed. "Ask Iris. Then that horrible Bear recognized me."

"You could have been killed."

"And you could have been killed—un-holding-up a train!"

"I know what I'm doing, and you don't!"

"Lower your voice. Everyone can hear us."

"Can they now?"

"You're humiliating me, Malachi Slater."

"Humiliating you? I wish I had a switch."

"You're the one who should be taken to a woodshed, Captain Slater. Let me down."

"Let you down? You going to walk to Texas?"

"I'll go and ride with my brother."

"You'll ride with your husband, Mrs. Slater," he said, and the words were hard but the husky tension in his voice swept sweetly over her. There was a note of possession in his words that captivated and thrilled her. She didn't mind the demand in it at all.

She looked down at her own hands. They were trembling, too.

Jamie pulled up suddenly in front of them, extending his arm to point. "There's a river up here, and a natural cove. Shall we take a break and ride with the cooler air in the evening?"

"Yes, please!" Kristin answered him. They had ridden so hard at first, and now they had been in the saddle for hours and hours.

"All right with you, Matt? Malachi?" Cole asked.

Malachi nodded. Shannon leaped down quickly. Malachi dismounted behind her.

"Someone get a fire going," Jamie said. "I'll see if I can find something in the woods to cook."

He nodded to them all, pulled his rifle from his saddle and started into the woods.

"I'll join you," Matthew called after him. He looked at Iris, eyeing her from head to toe. "Start the fire."

"I don't know how to start the fire."

"Learn," Matthew said curtly. He started off after Jamie. Iris kicked the dirt.

"Learn!" she muttered. "Damned—Yank!"

Shannon started toward Iris, wanting to assure herself that the woman was all right and to help her build the fire. She didn't get far. Malachi caught her by the arm. She stared at him indignantly.

"We're going for a walk," he told her.

"But I don't want to go for a walk," she began.

She broke off with a startled scream as he swept her up into his arms. "I said that we're going for a walk."

Stunned, Shannon remained silent, staring up into his teal-blue eyes. In the background, Kristin laughed softly. She'd obviously heard the exchange.

Stung by her elder sister's amusement, Shannon started to protest, but Malachi was already carrying her off. With long strides he followed the river's edge, beneath the shade of the huge old oaks. The sun rose high above them, the sky was blue, and the water was tinkling a delightful melody.

Shannon's arms had curled around his neck for self-preservation. She kept staring at him as he moved, unhurriedly but with purpose.

"Malachi...let me down!" she entreated him softly. They were far out of sight of the camp now, around a curve in the river. There might not have been a living soul in miles, and there was no sound except for the melody of the rushing water and songs of the birds and the whisper of the breeze through the leaves of the oaks.

"Malachi, put me down!"

This time he responded, laying her on a grassy spot upon the slope, and immediately throwing himself down next to her. He placed his knee casually over her legs, supported his weight on an elbow, and touched her cheek.

"I should tan your hide," he said softly. His fingers trailed over her flesh. He stroked her face and her throat. He leaned against her and kissed first her forehead, then the tip of her nose. He buried his face against hers, and kissed the lobe of her ear, nibbling the soft flesh, warming it with the heat of his breath.

She wrapped her arms around him, holding him close.

"Malachi..."

"I should...I should really tan your hide."

His face rose above hers. His eyes searched hers, and she smiled slowly, her own eyes wandering over his beloved features, his clipped beard, his mustache, seeing the fullness of his lips, the character in his eyes.

"Malachi..."

She reached up and threaded her fingers through his hair and pulled his head down to hers. She kissed him, then broke away, then teased his mouth with the tip of her tongue, then kissed him passionately once again. His lips parted to hers, and he took control with a tender and savage aggression that swept through her like heat lightning across a summer's sky.

She felt the passion deep within him, simmering, threatening to burst. He leaned over her intimately, his fingers trembling as he worked at the tiny buttons of her bodice.

Shannon caught his hand. Her lashes fell low and sultry over her eyes. "Malachi, you are something, you know. You're always yelling at me."

"I'm not always yelling at you." He shook away her hand. She made no further protest as he peeled back her bodice and kissed her breasts above the froth of her chemise. Shannon stroked his shoulders, inhaling swiftly as shivers of delight cascaded along her spine.

"You are always yelling at me," she corrected. She placed her hands on either side of his face and lifted his eyes to her.

"You are always doing foolish things," he said softly. "And if I yell at you..."

"Yes?"

He smiled slowly. "What do you want? A signed confession?" Shannon nodded.

"If I yell at you..."

She caught her breath, waiting.

"It's because I love you."

"Oh, Malachi!" She threw her arms around him and they rolled in the grass, laughing. "Malachi, say it again!"

He caught her beneath him and laid his hand upon her breast over the thin material of the chemise. He stroked the nipple with his thumb until it hardened to a coral peak, and she moaned softly. "Malachi…"

"You were willing to let me hang rather than marry me!" he told her reproachfully.

"I didn't want you to be forced to marry me!"

"You didn't want to marry me."

"But I did. I really did."

"You were in love with a ghost. Are you still?"

She shook her head, biting into her lower lip as she met his eyes. His hands were still roaming sensually across her body. "I did love him. But…even on the awful day that we were married…I did want to marry you."

"Did you?"

He laid his head against her breast and used his tongue to stroke her through the soft fabric. Shannon forgot the question. Malachi did not.

"Did you?" he repeated.

"What?"

"Love me. You haven't said it, you know."

She smiled, trembling beneath him. "I love you, Captain Slater. I think I loved you all along."

"From that very first time you tried to shoot me?" he teased.

"Maybe. Malachi…"

"What?"

"Love me."

"It's been forever," he said huskily, lacing his fingers with hers, stretching out over her.

"It's been a week."

"A long week," he corrected her. And when he took her lips with his own, she saw he spoke the truth.

"Love me," she whispered to him once again.

So he did. The sound of the river came as the sweetest melody, and the grass beneath offered up the softest bedding. He laid his coat upon the ground and stripped her of her clothing piece by piece. She barely dared to move while he touched her, feeling as if time had come to a standstill between them, and that she might shatter some fantastic spell if she were to breathe. She waited. She waited for him to finish with her, and then to doff his own clothing, and to lie down beside her.

She wondered if anything would ever again be as beautiful as that day at that moment. The sun was warm upon her and the air was cool, and his body was a fervent flame of fire within and around her. He touched her with tenderness, and with searing passion. He led her to the brink of ecstasy, and back down, merely to stroke the flames one more time.

Then there was nothing while she soared. Climax burst upon her, and she felt the sweet rush of his release.

Once again, the earth existed. The sky, the river, the ground beneath them.

Shannon looked to her side and saw that his hat lay upon the ground, his fine, plumed Confederate cavalry captain's hat. She smiled, wondering how she had ever allowed the war to stand between them. She realized then that she loved him for everything that he was. A man, a Rebel, a knight in shining armor.

A hero.

No matter how many times she had needed him, he had come for her. He had never let her down.

She touched his cheek. "I do love you. I love you, Malachi Slater."

"Captain Slater."

She smiled.

"I can't change my part in the war, Shannon. Nor do I want to. I fought for what I believed."

"I know."

He hesitated, pulling her close beneath his chin. "The fighting isn't over, Shannon. Fitz is dead, but they'll still come for us." He paused again. "Matthew is going to ride for home tomorrow, Shannon. I'm going to send you with him."

"No!" she protested, sitting up.

He smiled and lazily ran a finger over her bare breast. "Shannon, Cole and Jamie and I have to leave the country. I don't know where we're going. I don't—"

"Kristin will go with Cole."

He shook his head gravely. "Kristin is going home to the baby, Shannon."

"Malachi—"

"No!" he said firmly. Standing up, he started to dress, tossing her her stockings. "Shannon, I have to know that you're safe. Do you understand? Get dressed. We should get back to the others."

"And what are we supposed to do?" Shannon demanded bitterly. "Just go home and wait for the years to go by?"

"We'll find a way to return."

"When?" Shannon demanded, wrenching her dress over her head. "Malachi, I don't mind—"

He caught her against him and kissed her. He broke away from her, smiling ruefully. "That is the only way to shut you up, you know."

"Malachi—"

"No." He kissed her again, then caught her hand, pulling her along.

"Wait!" Shannon cried. She pulled back, flushing as she did up the numerous little buttons on her gown.

He paused, looking around. Shannon was about to argue again when he suddenly went very tense and brought his fingers to his lip. He drew his gun, and pulling her behind him, crept along the trees.

A few minutes later, Shannon began to hear the sounds as well. There were men and horses deeper in the woods. She crept along beside Malachi until they neared a small encampment.

There were about fifteen of them, all dressed in clean blue uniforms. They were a cavalry unit, and a young group at that. Two of the men were cleaning their carbines; one leaned against a tree reading, and the others were finishing a meal, laughing and talking idly.

"Damn!" Malachi muttered. "We've got to slip back and get the others to move."

Shannon nodded. She turned around to hurry with him, then hesitated and looked back, anxious to see if they had been spotted. They had not. The men didn't even look up. She turned again to follow Malachi, well ahead of her now and running in a half crouch through the bracken. Suddenly, she screamed, crashing straight into a blue-clad soldier who appeared from behind a tree.

He gasped, as startled as she, and she realized that he had been taking care of personal business in the bushes.

"Excuse me!" Shannon muttered.

"Excuse me, ma'am," the man apologized. Then his eyes narrowed. "Hey, wait a minute," he began, his hand falling upon her shoulder.

"Let her go!" Malachi called out. He stood ahead of them, leveling his gun calmly at the man.

But by then all the young cavalry boys were up and stumbling around looking for their weapons, and the most prepared were already through the trees.

"Let her go!" Malachi insisted.

"Slater!" Someone called suddenly. Shannon saw that it was the officer in charge. And he must have known Malachi, because he raised his hands, displaying that he carried no weapon, and he walked forward.

"Captain Slater," the officer called, "I know you—"

"I don't know you."

"I know your brother Cole. I'm Major Kurt Taylor. We were together in the West before the war broke out." He hesitated. "I saw him in Kansas. Before he went up against Henry Fitz."

"Ain't that nice," Malachi drawled softly. "I don't want to hurt anybody, major. Tell him to let my wife go."

"Captain Slater, I know that you could shoot down half my boys in a matter of seconds."

"That's right. So let her go."

"Captain, we were sent to find you."

"What?" Malachi asked warily.

"Judge Sherman Woods sent us out. I can't make promises—"

"I wouldn't trust a promise from a Yank anyway," Malachi interrupted.

"You've got a beautiful wife, captain. Do you really want to spend the rest of your life running? Or do you want to take a minute and listen to me?"

"Start talking."

"I can't leave, captain. So to get away from me, you're going to have to kill these men. If you come in with me, I'll promise you and your brothers a fair trial.''

''What's to make me think the Union will keep this promise?''

''You'll have to trust Judge Woods, Captain Slater. You went to him for help, and he wants to help. But you have to give him the chance to do so.''

''I'm sorry—'' Malachi began.

''Malachi!'' Shannon cried in anguish. ''Please! For God's sake, please! Give us this chance.''

He was very still for a long time. Tall, proud, his Confederate greatcoat over his shoulders, his plumed hat waving in the breeze. His jaw was hard, his eyes cold, his chin rigid and high.

Then he exhaled and tossed his gun down.

''I couldn't shoot those boys anyway,'' he said quietly. ''I just couldn't kill any more damned children. They say that the war is over. Major, we'll have to see if it is.''

Major Taylor nodded. ''Captain, will you do something for me?''

''What's that?''

''Go talk to your brothers. If I can, I'd like to avoid being a target for a Slater.''

Malachi nodded. He reached out a hand to Shannon, and she ran to his side. Together, they walked through the woods with Major Taylor behind them.

When they reached the others, Jamie instantly drew his gun. Cole and Matthew followed suit.

''Kurt!'' Cole said, slowly lowering his Colt. ''What's going on?'' he asked Malachi.

''You do know this fellow?'' Malachi asked Cole.

Cole nodded. ''What—''

''Judge Woods sent me out to find you. We'll give you a fair trial in Missouri. It will be fair, I swear it on my honor.''

Cole looked at Malachi, a question in his eyes.

''I'm tired of running,'' Malachi said. ''And honor is honor. Blue or gray. I believe this man has some. I've already surrendered to him.''

''Well,'' said Cole, ''it's what we wanted when we talked to Judge Woods. Jamie?''

Jamie shrugged his shoulders. "I don't trust Yankee honor much, but I'll go with you and Malachi, Cole."

The two men dropped their guns on the ground.

"I just hope I don't end up hanging," Jamie muttered.

"You won't hang!" Shannon cried. She clung to Malachi's hand. She wouldn't let him hang. She couldn't.

Malachi turned to her. He swept off his hat and took her into his arms and kissed her long and deep for everyone to see. Then he broke away from her, replacing his hat on his head. He strode over to the bay and mounted. "Whenever you're ready, major. Your prisoner, sir." He saluted sharply.

Major Taylor saluted in return.

Cole kissed Kristin, and he and Jamie followed Malachi's lead, mounting their horses.

Then they rode away, without looking back.

Kristin started to sob. Matthew came up to her and put his arm around her, and then he gathered Shannon to him, too. "It's going to be all right. I swear to you, it will be all right."

"It will be!" Shannon agreed fiercely. "It has to be."

Iris cleared her throat. "I managed to make the fire, and Jamie managed to shoot the rabbits. Let's sit down and eat. And then we can head back and plan some strategy."

"She learns really fast," Matthew said with a grin. "Let's eat."

She tried to smile. She could not. But she slipped her arm around Kristin's waist and led her to the fire.

They did eat. When they were done, Kristin mounted with Matthew and Shannon sat behind Iris, and they started their cold, lonely trek back home to Missouri.

Chapter Fifteen

The trial took place in Springfield. The courthouse was crowded with spectators, and with artists from *Harpers* and from every other leading paper and magazine.

Shannon had visited Malachi in jail, and she hated the experience. He was distant from her there. She knew that he loved her, and that he was in jail for her sake. But not even for her would he deny any of his brothers, and he explained to her that the brothers had determined to stand together. They would not opt for separate legal representation, nor would Jamie and Malachi seek lesser charges.

Malachi smiled ruefully to Shannon through the heavy iron bars of the jail. "We are all innocent."

"Cole wouldn't want you to hang because he rode with Quantrill."

"Tell me, Shannon, could you bear it if Cole were to hang because he sought to avenge the death of a beautiful and innocent bride? His wife, a woman carrying his child? She was my sister-in-law. I would have joined Cole at any time; I was already in the Confederate cavalry."

"Malachi—"

"If you love me, Shannon, you must love me for the man that I am. My brothers and I stand together."

She turned away, tears in her eyes. Cole already would have tried to convince Malachi and Jamie to save themselves. The Slaters were a stubborn lot.

And no…she could not bear it if Cole were to hang! They had all paid enough; the war was over. She could not accept any further horror—they had to win.

The first day of the trial was wretched, although their lawyer, Mr. Abernathy, was a skilled defender, with a sure belief in the Slater brothers' innocence. Shannon was pleased with him, even if he didn't pressure the men to stand alone. But Taylor Green, the prosecuting attorney, scared her. He seemed to personally want the Slater brothers to hang, all three.

When the trial started, Green immediately struck upon Cole Slater's association with William Quantrill. There were dozens of witnesses to testify to that association. But they weren't necessary, for at the end Cole quietly admitted to it. In a low, controlled voice he described the scene at his own ranch, years before, at the very outbreak of the war, when the jayhawkers had come to kill his wife. Shannon listened to him, and ached for him. He did not break or falter, but she saw it all through his eyes. She saw his young wife, she heard the woman screaming, and running, running, trying to reach her husband. He made them feel what it was like, to catch her as she fell, to feel her blood upon his hands...

The court was still when he finished. Not even Mr. Taylor Green managed to speak for several seconds.

And then there was a recess for the day.

Kristin came to the witness stand the next day and described in graphic detail how Zeke Moreau had murdered their father, and how Cole Slater had ridden to their rescue.

"Against the bushwhackers?" the prosecuting attorney asked her scathingly. "You want us to believe, Mrs. Slater, that your husband rode against his old comrades at arms? Maybe they just made a deal there instead, isn't that possible?"

"No, sir, it isn't possible at all," Kristin said. "He came and saved our lives. And he returned with Malachi and Jamie Slater to save the lives of half a Union company when Zeke Moreau came back again."

Kristin was fierce and beautiful and unfaltering. Taylor Green did not care to have her on the stand long.

Malachi was called.

He walked to the witness stand in full dress uniform, and Shannon's heart felt as if it had been torn. He was tall and straight, distinguished and ruggedly indomitable, and he was the handsome cavalier who had captured her heart.

"Captain Slater—well, of course, you are a civilian now, aren't you, sir?"

"The war is over," Malachi said flatly.

"But you choose to wear that uniform."

"We fought with honor."

"You still deny the Union?"

"The war is over," Malachi repeated.

"You would like it to continue? You still think that the South can rise again and whip the North, eh, captain?"

"No, sir. I think that the war is over, and I damned well would like it to end for good!"

A loud murmur rose in the courtroom. Shannon smiled. It seemed the first ray of hope. The people were with her husband.

"Did you ride with Quantrill?"

"No."

"Never?"

"No, never. But I would have ridden with my brother. If you'd seen his wife, lying in a pool of innocent blood, you'd have ridden, too."

"Captain, you seem to be an ornery sort."

"I'm telling you the truth, and that is all. This is a court of law, and we are sworn to the truth, right?"

"You're bold with your brand of truth."

"I have to be. And I have to believe that there is still justice in this land. If justice has not been lost, then my brother Cole is innocent, and so are James and I."

"You were regular army."

"Southern cavalry. Under John Hunt Morgan."

"Sounds like you avoided the border war, captain. So tell me, why don't you come clean, and give us the truth about Cole Slater."

"The truth is, Mr. Green," Malachi said, his eyes narrowed sharply, "that my brother is one of the finest men I've ever met in my life. In the North or the South. And if Cole is guilty for wanting to hunt down the man who murdered his wife, then I'm guilty, too. I would have been with him if I could have been.''

"An admission, gentlemen of the jury, there you have it! You may step down, Captain Slater!''

"Admission!'' Shannon didn't know that she was the one who had shouted until everyone turned to look her way. "Admission! Why, you Yankee bastard!''

There was an instant uproar. Some people were laughing, and some, the northern sympathizers, were offended. The judge slammed down his gavel. "Young woman, one more such outburst and I shall hold you in contempt! Are we understood?''

She sank into her chair. Only then did she realize that Malachi was watching her, too, and that a smile curled his lip. She lowered her eyes, then met his once again, and the smile warmed her and gave her courage.

Malachi walked down from the stand, and Jamie was called up for questioning. He was barely civil, but Taylor Green didn't manage to get a single rise out of him. Jamie could be as stubborn and proud a Slater as either of his brothers.

Shannon sat in the court with Kristin and Matthew and Iris, listening to it all. When the session broke, she was allowed to see Malachi for a few minutes.

"Yankee bastard?'' Malachi teased her, his eyes dancing. "Did I hear you say that? You, Shannon McCahy Slater, called that man a Yankee bastard?''

"Malachi!''

"I could die happy, hearing those words upon your lips!''

"Don't you dare talk of dying!''

"I'm sorry.''

"Damn your pride!'' she told him savagely, tears glistening in her eyes. "You are innocent, and it's as if you're trying to make yourself sound guilty!''

He smiled, tilted her chin and kissed her. "I can only tell the truth, Shannon.''

She wanted to say more. She wanted to argue and hit him and make him see reason, but an officer of the court came and took him away, and she wasn't able to say anything more.

The days went on, and the situation began to appear bleaker and bleaker.

It wasn't that it didn't seem to be a fair trial. It was just that Taylor Green seemed to know how to make a simple statement of fact sound like a full confession. And the fact remained that Cole *had* ridden with Quantrill. No matter how briefly he had done so, it was enough to condemn him in many hearts. Still, she knew that his first speech had also touched the hearts of many. The brutal slaying of a young woman was a heinous act to any ordinary man, be he a Yankee or a Rebel.

On the fourth night of the trial Shannon went to see Mr. Abernathy. He was at dinner, and his housekeeper nearly stopped her from reaching him, but she pushed by. He was just about to start eating his dinner—a lamb chop, peas and a roasted potato.

"What are you doing?" Shannon demanded. She was so distraught that she picked up his plate and tossed it into the corner of the room.

He arched his snowy brows, and cleaned his fingers on the napkin that was tied about his throat and covered his chest. He smiled slowly at her and glanced remorsefully toward his lamb. "Mrs. Slater, I could call this assault! At the very least, it's a case of assault against a very fine lamb chop!"

"I'm sorry," Shannon murmured swiftly. She was sorry. She drew up a chair at the table. "I'm just so worried—"

Mr. Abernathy smiled again and took her hand, patting it. "Trust me, Mrs. Slater. Trust me."

"They could hang, sir!"

"I'm not going to let them hang. Now you'll see, you'll see."

"When?"

"Why, tomorrow, I do believe. The prosecution seems to have finished. I'll start with my case tomorrow. And I'll wager you two lamb chops that I'll need but a day!"

Shannon couldn't believe that he could possibly undo all the harm that Mr. Green had done. But he gave her a glass of sherry, and shooed her out the door.

Shannon went back to the hotel, where she found Kristin red-eyed and puffy-faced from crying. Shannon hugged her sister and lied through her teeth. "It's going to be all right. Mr. Abernathy has it all well in hand. Why, he says he can have them freed by tomorrow!"

"He can?" Kristin wanted so badly to believe.

In the morning, Mr. Abernathy stood before the court and addressed the judge. "My defense is simple. I will prove that we've no case against any of these men, no foundation for a charge of murder. And, your Honor, I will request that the case be dismissed!"

The judge invited Mr. Abernathy to proceed. Mr. Taylor looked up in protest, and Mr. Abernathy bowed very politely to him. He looked around, opening his arms to the court.

Then Shannon realized that the courtroom was curiously filled with men, officers in blue and gray.

One by one they stood and addressed the judge.

"Sir, I'm Corporal Rad Higgins, U.S. cavalry. I came here to say that I rode with Malachi Slater back in April, against a horde of bushwhackers. I rode with Jamie and Cole Slater, too. I'd like to testify, sir, that I ain't ever rode with better men."

"Sir, I'm Samuel Smith. First Sergeant, Darton's brigade, Union army. I'd been left for dead when these fellows came riding in. The fought and beat Quantrill's offshoots, and they offered me the finest medical care. Their doc even saved my arm, and it had been shot up mighty bad."

From a man with the stripes of an artillery sergeant on his arms: "I knew Cole Slater in Kansas before the war. I never met a finer officer."

One by one, the men stood. Soldiers in blue, soldiers in gray.

Then a woman stood up, plump, dignified, gray-haired.

"I'm Martha Haywood, and this is my husband, and I come to say that I ain't ever met finer people than Captain Malachi Slater and his bride, and that's a fact. And my husband will testify to that fact, too." Mr. Haywood stood alongside her.

Shannon looked around, incredulous. They were all there. Jamie's Confederate friends from Texas, the people from Haywood, even the professional gamblers from the saloon. And one by one they testified with moving stories to the honesty and honor of the Slater brothers.

When it was over, the judge stood. He slammed his gavel against his desk.

"I dismiss these cases," he told the prosecution. "Lack of evidence," he said flatly.

And he walked away.

Silence reigned for a moment. Then there was a Rebel war whoop as hats were thrown high into the air. The crowd rushed forward to congratulate the Slaters.

Shannon pushed her way through until she reached Malachi. He drew her into his arms, and he kissed her warmly.

"It's over," he said softly. "The war is really over."

"All of our wars are over," she promised him. She slipped her hand into his hands, then turned around, searching for Mr. Abernathy. She hurried over to him and gave him a tremendous kiss on the jowl. "Bless you! And I promise you a dozen lamb chops every year, as long as I live!"

"That would be right nice, Mrs. Slater, mighty nice."

"What's this?" Malachi demanded, shaking hands with his attorney.

"That's a mighty fine little woman you have there, captain." Mr. Abernathy said. "Some temper, though, huh?"

"It's a ghastly temper," Malachi agreed.

"Malachi!" she protested.

"I love it, though," he told Mr. Abernathy. "I wouldn't have her any other way. She's full of fire and sparks."

"Malachi—"

"In fact, I'm going to take her right home and see if we can't get a few sparks a-flying." His eyes fell on her. "Seems like a long, long time since I've been away."

"Scat!" Mr. Abernathy told them.

They still had to fight through the crowd. Malachi had to kiss Kristin, and Shannon had to kiss and hug Jamie and Cole, and the brothers embraced, and then Malachi and his brothers thanked each and every man and woman who had come to their defense. Shannon hugged Martha Haywood fiercely, and Martha told her with shimmering eyes that she should go. "And be happy, love! Be happy."

They came out into the sunshine at last.

Then Malachi kissed her. Slowly, surely, completely. He broke away. "Come on. We can go home. We can really go home."

"And start sparks flying?" she teased him.

"No," he whispered.

"No?"

His eyes danced, as blue and clear as the sky above them. "Sparks are already flying."

She smiled slowly, meeting his eyes, curling her fingers within his while he sun beat down upon them, warm and vibrant.

"Yes, let's go home!" she agreed in a fervent whisper.

Because they could. They could really go home.

Life and love were theirs, and they were only just beginning.

The war was more than over. Peace had truly begun.

Epilogue

June 18th, 1866
Haywood, Kansas

Martha Haywood had just locked up the house for the night. There were no guests at the hotel, so she thought she might as well lock up early. She wished that someone would come through. It was summer, and it was beautiful, and it would be nice to be busy and have company.

She felt a surge of nostalgia for the previous year. She smiled, remembering all the hustle and bustle when Captain Slater had come with his Miss McCahy. Maybe she had been wrong. Maybe she and Papa shouldn't have forced the two to enter into marriage.

People had a right to make up their own minds.

She hoped things had worked out. Captain Slater and Miss McCahy had been the perfect couple. A handsome, dashing hero and a damsel in distress. But she hadn't heard from the two of them in a while, not since the letter at Christmas…

Martha started, hearing a fierce pounding at the door. She hurried over as fast as she could, muttering to herself. "People should have more courtesy. Why, I have half a mind not to open the door. Stopping this late along the way…"

But she threw open the door anyway.

For a moment, she just stared, stunned.

"Martha, may we come in?" Shannon Slater asked her. She

looked like an angel on the porch, in her light blue traveling dress with a white lace collar. She held a big, blanketed bundle in her arms, and she stood next to her husband. He was as dashing as ever. His Confederate gray was gone, and he wore a well-tailored dark frock coat and a stovepipe hat. He was carrying a valise and held a squirming bundle as well.

Shannon didn't wait for an answer. Smiling, she stepped into the house, pressing her bundle into Martha's arms. "We are awfully late, aren't we? I'm so sorry. It's much harder traveling with the children."

"Children?" Martha sputtered at last.

"This one is Beau. And this—" she smiled, pulling back the blanket on Malachi's bundle "—is Nadine."

"Oh!" Martha said at last. "Oh, twins!"

"Twins," Malachi agreed, and he pressed his bundle, too, into Martha's arms.

"Twins!" Martha repeated, as if she could think of nothing else to say.

Malachi winked at Shannon, enjoying the woman's flustered pleasure. "This is our wedding anniversary, you know, Martha."

"Yes," Shannon said, stripping away her gloves. "So we've come back, eager for our honeymoon suite."

"Your honeymoon suite—of course!"

Beau gurgled. Martha laughed with delight. "Oh, he is precious!"

"Well, you see, Shannon's brother Matthew and Iris were married last week—"

"No!" Martha gasped.

"Oh, yes. We were all just wonderfully pleased. But they're setting up housekeeping now."

"And we've done what we can to pull the McCahy ranch together," Malachi said.

"So," Shannon continued, "Cole has gone to Texas with Kristin and Gabe and Jamie and Samson and Delilah."

"We're going to join them down that way, too," Malachi said.

"Malachi has been offered a job as sheriff in a little town west of Houston," Shannon said.

"Cole is ranching, and Jamie is—believe it or not—scouting for the cavalry."

"Oh, how wonderful!" Martha said. She looked from one of the squirming babies to the other. "Oh! They're just both so beautiful."

Malachi pinched Martha's cheek. "We're so glad that you like them, Martha."

"Like them? Why, captain, I love them!"

Shannon smiled sweetly and kissed Martha's cheek. "Good." She laughed mischievously. "Because we're going to sneak up to our honeymoon retreat."

"Oh, of course!" Martha giggled. "You two go right ahead."

Malachi swept Shannon off her feet, striding to the stairs. "Oh, we'd like to baptize them tomorrow, if we could. If you and Mr. Haywood wouldn't mind. And we want you and Mr. Haywood to be the godparents."

"Oh!" Martha would have clapped like a child except that her arms were full of squirming babies. She looked at them more closely. They both had soft ringlets of gold and immense blue eyes. Nadine was going to be a beauty like her mother, and Beau would be as handsome as his sire. "My godchildren!" Martha cried. She turned around quickly. "We won't mind. We won't mind at all."

She wasn't sure that Malachi and Shannon heard her. Their eyes were locked with one another's as he carried her up the stairs. She was glorious, with her hair streaming over his arms, and he was wonderful in his dark coat, tall and striking. It was so romantic, the way he held her.

"Of course, of course!" Martha repeated.

Shannon had heard her. She looked over her husband's shoulder and winked. Martha waved. A second later the door—now repaired—closed at the top of the stairs.

"Oh, my!" Martha said. "Papa! Papa, wake up, Mr. Haywood. We've responsibilities tonight!"

She sat down with her two little bundles.

And she smiled. She had been right—she had been ever so right. They were the perfect couple, and it was just like a fairy tale... Ending happily ever after!

* * * * *

APACHE SUMMER

Chapter One

Western Texas, 1870

"Look, Lieutenant! Fire, rising high to our left!"

Jamie Slater reined in his roan stallion. With penetrating silver-gray eyes he stared east, where Sergeant Monahan was pointing. Across the sand and the sagebrush and the dry dunes, smoke could indeed be seen, billowing up in black and gray bursts. Tendrils of flame, like undulating red ribbons, waved through the growing wall of smoke.

"Injuns!" Monahan breathed.

To Jamie's right, Jon Red Feather stiffened. Jamie turned toward him. The half-breed Blackfoot was a long way from home, but he was still one of the best Indian scouts around. He was a tall, striking man with green-gold eyes and strong, arresting features. Thanks to a wealthy white grandfather, Jon Red Feather had received a remarkable education, going as far as Oxford in England.

Jamie knew that Jon resented the ready assumption that trouble meant Indians, even though he admitted readily to Jamie that trouble was coming, big trouble. The Apache hated the white man, the Comanche despised him, and Jamie was convinced that the great Sioux Nation was destined to fight in a big way for all the land that had been grabbed by the hungry settlers.

Through Jon, Jamie had come to know the Comanche well. He didn't make the mistake of considering the Comanche to be docile, but, on the other hand, he'd never known a Comanche to lie or to give him any double-talk.

"Let's see what's going on," Jamie said quietly. He rose high in his saddle and looked over the line of forty-two men presently under his command. "Forward, Sergeant. We ride east. And by the look of things, we'd best hurry."

Sergeant Monahan repeated his order, calling out harshly and demanding haste. Jamie flicked his reins against the roan's shoulders, and the animal took flight with grace and ease. His name was Lucifer, and it fitted the animal well. He was wild—and remarkable.

That was one thing about the U.S. Cavalry, Jamie reckoned as they raced toward the slope of the dune that led to the rise of smoke. They offered a man good horses.

He hadn't had that pleasure in the Confederate cavalry. When the Confederacy had been slowly beaten into her grave, there hadn't been many mounts left. But the war had been over for almost five years now. Jamie was wearing a blue uniform, the same type he'd spent years of his life shooting at. No one, least of all his brothers, had believed he would last a day in the U.S. Cavalry, not after the war. But they had been wrong. Many of the men he was serving with hadn't even been in the war, and frankly, he understood soldiers a whole lot better than he did politicians and carpetbaggers.

And he had liked the life in the saddle on the plains, dealing with the Indians, far better than he had liked to see what had become of the South. This was western Texas, and the reprisals from the war weren't what they were in the eastern Deep South. Everywhere in the cities and towns were the men in tattered gray, many missing limbs, hobbling along on crutches. Homeless and beaten, they had been forced to surrender on the fields, then they had been forced to surrender to things that they hadn't even understood. Taxes forced upon them. Yankee puppets in place where local sheriffs had ruled. The war was horrible—even after it was over.

There *were* good Yanks, and Jamie had always known it. He didn't blame good men for the things that were happening in the South—he blamed the riffraff, the carpetbaggers. He liked his job because he honestly liked a number of the Comanche and the other Indians he dealt with—they still behaved with some sense of honor. He couldn't say that for the carpetbaggers.

Still, he never deceived himself. The Indians were savage fighters; in their attacks, they were often merciless.

But as Jamie felt the power of the handsome roan surge beneath him as he raced the animal toward the rise of fire and smoke, he knew that his days with the cavalry were nearing an end. For a while, he had needed the time to get over the war. Maybe he'd needed to keep fighting for a while just to learn how not to fight. But he'd been a rancher before the war had begun. And he was beginning to feel the need for land again. Good land, rich land. A place where a man could raise cattle in wide open spaces, where he could ride his own property for acres and acres and not see any fences. He imagined a house, a two-story house, with a great big parlor and a good-sized kitchen with huge fireplaces in each to warm away the winter's chill. Maybe it was just time for his wandering days to be over.

"Sweet Jesus!" Sergeant Monahan gasped, reining in beside Jamie as they came to the top of the rise of land.

Jamie silently echoed the thought as he looked down upon the carnage.

The remnants of a wagon train remained below them. Men had attempted to pull the wagons into a defensive circle, but apparently the attack had come too swiftly.

Bodies lay strewn around on the ground. The canvas and wood of the wagons still smoldered and smoked, and where the canvas covers had not burned, several feathered arrows still remained.

Comanche, Jamie thought. He'd heard that things were heating up. Seemed like little disputes would eventually cause a whole-scale war. Monahan had told him he'd heard a rumor about some whites tearing up a small Indian village. Maybe this was done in revenge.

"Damnation!" Sergeant Monahan breathed.

"Let's go," Jamie said.

He started down the cliff and rocks toward the plain on which the wagon train had been attacked. It was dry as tinder, sagebrush blowing around, an occasional cactus protruding from the dirt. He hoped there was no powder or ammunition in the wagons to explode, then he wondered what it would matter once he and his men looked for survivors. The Indians had struck sure and fast, then disappeared somewhere into the plain, up the cliffs and rock. Like the fog wisping away, they had disappeared, and they had left the death and bloodshed behind them.

"Circle carefully!" he advised his men. "A half-dead Comanche is a mean one, remember!"

Riding behind him, Jon Red Feather was silent. Their horses snorted and heaved as they slowly came down the last of the slope, trying to dig in for solid footing. Then they hit the plain, and Jamie spurred his horse to race around and encircle the wagons. There were only five of them.

Poor bastards never had a chance, he thought. He reckoned that someone had been bringing some cattle north, since there was at least a score of dead calves lying glass-eyed and bloody along with the human corpses.

There was definitely no one around. And there was not a single Indian left behind, not a dead one, or a half-dead one, or any other kind of a one.

He dismounted before the corpse of an old man. There was an arrow shaft protruding from his back.

Jamie touched the man's shoulder, turning him over. He swallowed hard. The man had been scalped, and a sloppy job had been done of it. Blood poured down his forehead, still sticky, still warm.

It hadn't happened more than a half hour ago. If they had headed back just a lousy thirty minutes earlier, they might have stopped this carnage.

His men had dismounted too, he realized. At a command from Sergeant Monahan, they were doing the same as he, searching through the downed men for any survivors. Jamie shook his head, standing. Hell. He had just been to see the local Comanche chief. Running River was the peace chief, not the war chief, of the village, but the white men and Running River's people had been doing just fine together for years now.

Jamie liked Running River. And though he had never kidded himself that any Comanche couldn't be warlike when provoked, he couldn't begin to imagine what in hell would have provoked an attack like this one. If the Indians were hungry, they would have stolen the calves, not slaughtered them.

Jon Red Feather was next to him, investigating the body.

"No Comanche did this," he said.

Jamie frowned at him. "Then what do you think? A band of Cheyenne? Maybe a wandering tribe of Utes. We're too far south for it to be the Sioux—''

"I promise you, Lieutenant, no self-respecting Sioux would ever do such a careless job. And the Comanche are warriors, too. They learn from an early age how to lift the hair."

"Then what?" Jamie demanded impatiently. His blood ran cold as he realized that Jon was insinuating that it hadn't been Indians who had made this heinous attack.

It wasn't possible, he told himself. No white man could have killed and mutilated his own kind so savagely.

"Hey, Lieutenant!" Charlie Forbes called to him. Jamie swung around. Forbes was on the ground beside one of the dead men, an old-timer with silver-gray whiskers.

"What is it, Charlie?"

"Looks like this one was hit by an arrow, tried to rise and got shot with a bullet, right in the heart."

He could feel Jon standing behind him. Jamie adjusted his plumed hat and twisted his jaw. "Don't try to tell me the Comanche don't have rifles."

"Hell, I'm not going to tell you that. They get them from the Comancheros—the Comancheros will sell rifles to anyone. Of course, you've got to bear in mind that the Comancheros do buy them from your people."

Jamie didn't say anything. He stepped past Jon and stared at the one wagon that seemed to have had little damage done to it. He thought he heard something.

He had to be imagining things. The job here had been very thorough. Still, he watched the wagon as he straightened his back, trying to get out all the little cricks and pains.

He felt queasy about this thing. And he hadn't felt queasy about anything in quite some time.

He'd grown up on bloodshed. Before he had been twenty, his sister-in-law had been slain by Kansas jayhawkers. Then war had been declared, and though he had fought in a decent regiment under the command of John Hunt Morgan, he had never been able to escape the horror of the border war. From his brother Cole he had learned that the Missouri bushwhackers could behave every bit as monstrously as the jayhawkers.

And a Southern boy called Little Archie Clements had gone around doing a fair bit of scalping in his day. He and his men had stripped down men in blue and shot them without thought, and when they'd finished with the killing they'd gone on to scalping.

He had no right to think that the Indians were any more vicious than the white men. No right at all.

He exhaled slowly. Knowing that the Southern bushwhackers had been every bit as bad as the Northern jayhawkers was one of the reasons he was able to wear this uniform now. A blue cavalry uniform, decorated in blue trim, with a cavalry officer's sword at his side. He didn't carry a military-issue rifle, though. Through four years of civil conflict he had worn his Colts, and he wore them to this day.

His eyes narrowed suddenly. He could have sworn that something in the wagon had moved.

He glanced over his shoulder. Jon was behind him. Jon nodded, aware instantly of Jamie's suspicions. He circled around while Jamie headed straight for the opening at the rear.

He looked in. For a second he could see only shadows in the dim light. Then things took form. There were two bunks in the wagon. Ironically, they were neat and all made up—with the sheets tucked in, the blankets folded back at an inviting angle and the pillows plumped up. Beyond the bunks were trunks and boxes. Everything seemed to be in perfect order.

But it wasn't. He felt just a flicker of movement again. He didn't know if he really saw it or if he felt it, but all his senses were on edge. He hadn't worked in Indian country and spent all this time with Jon Red Feather not to have learned something of his senses. There was someone near. He could feel it in his gut, and he could feel it at the nape of his neck, and he could feel it all the way down his spine. Someone was very near.

"Come on out of there," he said softly. "Come on, now. We don't want to hurt anyone here, we just want you to come on out."

The movement had ceased.

Jon was moving up toward the front of the wagon. The horses, still smelling smoke, whinnied and nickered nervously. Jamie leaped to the floor of the wagon.

His eyes flickered to the left bunk. There was a long, soft white gown lain out by the side. It was sleeveless, low-bodiced and lacy, a woman's nightgown, he thought. And a pretty piece for the dustiness of the road. It did belong with the perfectly made and inviting beds, but it didn't really belong on a wagon train. Was she alive? Had she been some young man's bride? He hadn't seen a woman's corpse, not yet, but then his men were still moving among the bodies.

"Is anyone in here?" he said, moving past the bunks. There were boxes and trunks everywhere. There was a coffeepot, cast down as if someone had been about to use it. There was a frying pan in the middle of the floor, too. He paused, crouching on the balls of his feet, looking at the floor. Coffee was spilled everywhere.

"Come on out now," he said softly. "It's all right, come on out."

He kept moving inward. The shadows in the wagon made it difficult to see. There seemed to be a swirl of soft mauve taffeta, fringed in black lace, set in a heap before him. He reached down carefully, hoping he hadn't come upon another corpse.

He touched a body. He touched warmth. He moved his hand, and it was filled with fullness and living warmth. Instinctively his fingers curled over the full, firm ripeness of a woman's breast. He could feel the shape and weight and the tautness of the nipple with his palm right through the taffeta. She was warm, but very still. Sweet Jesus, let her be alive, he thought, still stunned by the contact his fingers had made.

She was alive. Beyond a doubt, she was alive. She burst from her hiding place with a wicked scream of terror and fury. Startled, he moved back. He had been prepared for danger, for a wounded Comanche, but when he had touched the softness and striking femininity of her form, he had relaxed his guard.

Foolish move.

He backed away, but she screamed again, high and shrill and desperate, a sound like that of a wounded animal. He started to reach for his Colt, but his hand fell quickly as he reminded himself that it was just a woman. A small, delicate woman.

"Ma'am—"

She cast herself upon him with a vengeance, pitting her body against his with a startling ferocity and strength.

"Hey—" he began, but she didn't heed him. She slammed her foot against his leg and brought a fist flailing down upon his shoulder, trying to throw him off balance. He braced himself as she slammed against him, but still she brought them both down upon the floor.

"Hey! Damn, stop!" he yelled, aware of her fragile size, her wild mane of honey-colored hair. Nor could he forget the full feel of her breast within his hand. She was exquisite. He had to be gentle.

Her foot slammed against his shin again. She thrashed with the fury of ten Comanche. Her flailing fist caught his jaw so hard that his teeth rattled.

Gentle...hell!

She was a monster. There was no way in hell a man could possibly be gentle and survive. Gritting his teeth harshly he caught her wrists, trying not to hold them in a painful vise.

She screamed again incoherently, freeing her hands to grope on the bunk. He should have held her in a vise! There was just no being nice here. She was like wildfire atop him, raging out of control. He saw a smile of triumph light her features as her fingers curved around something, and she lifted it high.

"Whoa, wait a minute, ma'am—" he began, seeing that she held a long-bladed and lethally sharp bowie knife. Damn! She was going from fists to steel. "Lady, I'm warning you, stop!"

She didn't pay the least bit of attention to him. Rather, she fought on with desperation, drawing up her arm again, preparing to slash the blade across his throat.

Jamie swung out, catching her by the middle, his hands resting beneath the swell of her breasts. He cast her far away from him and struggled to his feet. "I'm the cavalry!" he snapped out. "Damn it, I'm the good guy."

She didn't seem to hear him, or really even see him. Her huge, violet-blue eyes were glazed, he saw, and she barely blinked at his words. She certainly didn't seem to understand them. She screamed again and flew at him. The blade slashed the air uncomfortably close to his windpipe.

He clamped down grimly on his jaw and caught her arm with a stunning blow, sending the blade flying out of the wagon. She gasped, but when he lunged for her, she was ready to fight again, her nails gouging for his eyes. He swore again, capturing her wrists and falling down hard with her upon the floor of the wagon. Struggling to hold her still, he looked up to see that Jon Red Feather was looking in from the driver's seat of the wagon.

"I could have used some help here, you know!" he thundered.

Red Feather grinned. "You—against one little honey-haired girl? Honestly, Lieutenant."

She was no little girl. Lying atop her, Jamie was very aware of that. She was small and slight, but the sweet, provocative fullness of her breasts was now crushed lushly against his cavalry jacket, reminding him that it had been some time since he'd last been to Maybelle's House of Gentlemanly Leisure Pursuits. She fought him still, writhing like a wildcat, and with every twist and turn of her body, he realized more fully just how grown up the woman was, how evocatively mature. She stared at him with death-defying hatred, and as he gazed at her, she lunged against him again, trying to bite his shoulder.

"For the love of God!" he snapped, rolling with her to retain his hold without bringing bodily injury to her or losing a hunk of flesh himself. She freed one wrist from his grasp and began tearing at him again. Their momentum was taking them closer and closer to the rear of the wagon, and then suddenly they were outside it, plunging down to the dirt together.

She shrieked, and he realized then that she was fighting to free herself from his hold rather than fighting to harm him. But he wasn't about to let her go. She was too unpredictable. Their limbs entangled, and her petticoats rode around them. He could feel the slender length of her legs, warm and alive, scantily clad in pantalets, against his own. She reached up to strike him again, and he caught her hand with a serious fury as his patience snapped.

"Enough!"

He drew her hands high over her head and straddled her hips, pinning her down at last. Her hair lay spread out over the dirt in a majestic fan while the Texas sand smudged her beautiful features. She gasped desperately for breath, her breasts rising and falling with her effort. She was down, subdued at last. He released her wrists, remaining straddled upon her, careful to maintain his own weight.

"It's all right—" he tried to tell her, but to no avail. She tried to twist, lashing out, clawing for his face. She caught his chin and drew blood.

"Woman, no more!" he shouted. His hand raised high and with determination, and he caught himself right before he could slap her in return. He saw her eyes close tightly in expectation of the blow, but it did not fall. He held her tight, trying to check his temper, staring at her hard. Then he caught her arms and dragged them high above her head, leaning close and hard against her. His anger faded at last as he saw her eyes go damp with tears she fought to control. She was hysterical, he realized, and yet she had really come at him with an attempt to kill.

She shuddered and gasped, and a trembling rippled through the entire length of her body. Still, he could not trust her to release her. "We're the damned cavalry!" he repeated. "Listen to me! No one is going to hurt you. The Indians are gone. We're the cavalry. We want to help you. You do speak English, don't you?"

"Yes!" she snapped furiously, and the trembling ceased. "Yes, yes, I understand you!" Her eyes beheld him, then glazed over again. "Bastard!" she hissed to him, "Murdering, despicable bastard."

"Murdering bastard? I'm trying to help you."

"I don't believe you!"

Startled by her words, Jamie fell silent. Her eyes remained locked with his, the tears she would not shed highlighting the deep blue color. Her hair fell in tangled streams around them both, like a pool of sunlight just before twilight fell. Watching her, he nearly forgot why he straddled her.

She didn't believe him. He had come to rescue her from the Comanche, and she didn't believe him.

"Listen, now, lady, I am with the cavalry—these men, all of us, we're with the United States Cavalry—"

"Your uniform doesn't mean anything!"

"Lady, you are crazy!" That was it, she had lost her mind. She had watched the savage attack and she had retreated into some fantasy world of fear. "You're all right now, or you will be if you quit trying to hurt me."

"Hurt you! Oh!"

"The Indians are gone—"

"There never were any Indians!"

"No Indians?"

"They dressed like Indians, but they weren't Indians. And you were probably in on it! The law is corrupt, why not the cavalry?"

"Lady, I don't know what you're talking about. I'm Lieutenant Slater out of Fort Vickers, and we've just stumbled upon your present difficulty."

She blinked, and her gaze went guarded. He still held her locked beneath him. His men were coming near, alerted by the commotion.

She gazed around her, past his head, and it seemed that she slowly realized that they really were a cavalry company. Everyone was staring at her with silence, with sympathy.

She looked at Jamie, and a slow flush spread into her features. They were now both painfully aware of the way their bodies came together. Her legs and hips burned against his, bare beneath the thin cotton shield of her pantalets. She wore no corset, he knew that very well, and her breasts seemed to swell, as if with realization of their intimate contact against his chest. She touched her dry lips with the tip of her tongue, and even that seemed an intimate gesture. She squirmed beneath him, but he wasn't about to give her any quarter. He had tried to be as gentle as possible and he was bleeding as if he had been gouged by a mountain cat because of it. A drop of blood from his chin fell upon her bodice even as he thought that he should show her some mercy.

"Lieutenant, let me—"

"What's your name?"

"If you would just—"

"What's your name?"

Her eyes flashed with a silver-blue annoyance as she realized that he was going to hold her until he chose to let her go. "Tess," she snapped. "It's Tess."

"Tess what?"

Her eyes narrowed. "Tess Stuart."

"Where were you going and where were you headed from?"

"Wiltshire. We were bringing some cattle and a printing press. We were heading home from a small town called Dunedin, nearly a ghost town now. That's why we bought the printing press. They didn't need it anymore."

"You said we. Who were you riding with?"

"My—" She hesitated just a moment, her lashes rising and falling swiftly. Tears burned behind her eyelids. She must know that everyone was dead.

She wasn't going to shed those tears. Not in front of him. "My uncle and I. We were heading home to Wiltshire."

He eased himself up a little. He saw her swallow as his thighs tightened against her hip, then she lifted her chin, determined to ignore him, determined to be as cool as if they were discussing the matter over tea in a handsome parlor. She had inestimable courage. No matter how she was beaten, she would never surrender but would fight it out until the very end. It was there in her eyes. All the silver-blue fire a man could imagine. She was either a complete fool or one of the most extraordinary women he had ever met. Despite her warm honey spill of hair, her large, luminous eyes and her perfect fragile features, she had a spine of steel.

Courage could kill out here in the West. That, he told himself, was why he held to her so tightly. She needed to learn that she could be beaten.

"You're lucky as hell that the Indians didn't see you, you know," he told her hoarsely.

She lifted her chin. "I told you—they weren't Indians."

"Who were they?"

"Von Heusen's men."

"And who the hell is von Heusen?" He was startled when he heard a curious rumble in someone's throat behind him. Still holding her, he whirled around. He looked at the faces of the young men in his company.

"Well? Does someone want to answer me?"

It was Jon Red Feather who drawled out a reply. "Richard von Heusen. Calls himself a rancher sometimes, an entrepreneur at others. You never heard of him, Lieutenant?"

"No, I never heard of him."

"You spend all your time on Indian affairs, Lieutenant," Jon said. "You've been missing out on the shape of things down here."

It was true, Jamie thought. He hadn't wanted to know a lot about the ranchers. He didn't want to see the carpetbaggers, or talk to them.

"You're telling me a guy named von Heusen did this?" he said to Jon.

Jon shrugged. "I can't tell you that."

"I can tell you that he owns a hell of a lot of Texas," Monahan said softly. "It's a good thing it's a big state, else he might own a good half of it."

Jamie looked curiously at the girl. Tess. Her eyes were upon him as she watched him in silence, scathingly. Then she hissed with all the venom of a snake. "He's a carpetbagger, Yank. You ever heard tell about the carpetbaggers down here? They're vultures. They came down upon a defeated and struggling South, and they just kicked the hell out of us. Bought up land the Southern boys couldn't pay their taxes on 'cause the Union didn't want any Confederate currency. Well, Lieutenant, von Heusen bought up Wiltshire."

"You're trying to tell me that a Yankee named von Heusen came out here and shot your wagon train full of arrows? In broad daylight, just like that?"

"No, not just like that," she retorted. "And I doubt that he came out here himself. He had his men all greased down and painted up like Comanche, just in case someone didn't die."

"So you did see Comanche attack the wagon."

"No. That's not what I'm telling you at all. I'm no fool, Lieutenant. I was born and bred out here and I know a Comanche when I see one. And I know a fraud when I see it, too."

"You're saying a group of white men came out here and did this to their own kind?"

"Yes, Lieutenant, how wonderfully perceptive of you. Why, you must have studied at West Point! That's exactly what I'm telling you." Her lashes flicked again. "Von Heusen masterminded this whole thing. You need to arrest him, Lieutenant. Arrest him for murder."

"You said yourself, von Heusen himself probably wasn't even here."

Her eyes widened, her fury seemed to deepen, but she kept her voice low and controlled. "You're not going to arrest him?"

"I'm not a sheriff to begin with, Miss Stuart. And if I were, I'd have to have some kind of proof."

"I'm your proof!"

"It would be your word against his!"

"He wanted our land!"

"Lots of men try to buy land. It doesn't make them murderers!"

She looked as if she wanted to scream, or at least gouge out another pound of his flesh.

"You're a fool!"

"Thank you kindly, ma'am," he retorted.

She gritted her teeth. Tears stung her eyes again. "Get the hell off me."

He realized he was still lying against her, still holding her down. She wasn't trying to kill him anymore. She just looked as if she wanted to escape him, the touch of him, the sight of him.

"I can't go bringing in a man for something without some kind of proof!" he told her furiously. "And not at the word of a half-crazed girl."

"Oh!" She raked out at him again. He caught her hand, then he rose to his feet, dragging her up with him. His jaw twisted hard against the loathing he saw in her eyes.

"Lady—"

"Lieutenant!" Charlie called to him, walking around from the field of corpses. "Shall I start a burial detail?"

She was staring past Charlie, staring at the white-haired man who had been hit by the arrow then shot through the heart.

"Oh, God!" she gasped. She stumbled forward, trying to reach the corpse. The blood fled from her face, and her beautiful features became as ashen as the smoke-charred sky. She paused suddenly, unable to go any farther. "Oh, no, oh, God. Uncle Joe," she whispered, reaching out a hand.

She did not take another step. Even as she reached out, she was falling. Her lashes fluttered over her beautiful eyes, and she began to sink toward the ground.

Instinctively, Jamie rushed forward. He caught her as she fell, sweeping her into his arms. She was as cold as death itself, and remained every bit as pale as he stared down at her.

There was silence all around him. His men looked on.

"Charlie, yes! For God's sake, yes! Get a damned burial detail going, and get it going quickly!"

The men turned around, hustling into action.

And Jamie stared at the girl, wondering just what in hell he was going to do with her. He needed to set her down, to let her lie somewhere. She was a slight burden, weighing practically nothing, or so it seemed.

Yet she was a burden. A definite burden.

He hurried toward her wagon, maneuvered up to the floor of it and laid her on the bed. He meant to turn around and leave her and call for the company surgeon, but for some reason he paused and found himself smoothing out her sun-and-honey hair and brushing her cheek with his knuckles.

He felt a sensation down his back and looked up quickly. Jon Red Feather was just below him, looking into the wagon. "She's still out cold."

"I'll call Captain Peters. He doesn't have much hope, but he's still checking to see if there is any breath remaining in any of the bodies."

"Maybe she's better off being out for a while anyway," Jamie said softly.

"Yeah, maybe." Jon hesitated. "What are we going to do with her?"

"Take her back to the fort. Then someone can escort her on home."

Jon nodded. He smiled suddenly. "Someone, right?"

"Yeah, that's right. Someone."

"She's your responsibility," Jon said. "Your burden—she fell into your arms."

"What? She's a burden I've just set down, Jon."

Jon shook his head. "I don't think so. I don't think so at all. I think that you've taken something upon yourself, Jamie, and I don't think that you can ever really let it go."

Jamie arched a brow. "Yeah? Well, I don't believe you, Jon, and I don't believe her. This von Heusen may be a carpetbagging monster, but I don't believe he can be guilty of this."

"You're just going to have to find out, aren't you?"

"That's not my job, Jon."

"That's not going to matter, is it? 'Cause you see, if the girl is right, then she's in danger. You're going to have out the truth—or you'll be signing her death warrant."

"That's ridiculous, Jon."

"No, it's not. You really can't let her go."

"The hell I can't."

"Oh?" Jon arched a raven-dark brow. "Is that so?" He inclined his head toward Jamie. "Your fingers are still all tied up in her hair, Lieutenant. All tied up. Silken webs maybe, but seems to me that you're all tied up."

Jamie gazed at his hand. His fingers were still hovering over her hair. It was truly the color of honey just kissed by the sun. Much deeper than blond. Too touched by light to be brunette. Golden red.

He pulled his hand away and turned toward Jon with a denial. But Jon, smiling serenely, had already turned away.

"Doc Peters should be free by now," he said quietly, then he was gone.

Jamie stared at the girl. Silken webs...

He clenched down hard on his jaw because Jon was right about one thing. Someone would have to discover the truth about her accusations. He didn't believe them. He couldn't believe them.

And yet...

If they were true, to leave her alone in the town of Wiltshire might very well be to sign her death warrant.

He swore softly and leaped from the wagon. His leg still hurt from where she had kicked him, and his chin still ached. He could feel it bleeding. Damn her. She was as quick as a sidewinder, as ornery as a mean bear. He could still remember her fury...

He paused, for he could remember more. The alluring fullness of her breast beneath his fingers, the softness of her hair, the warmth of her legs entangled with his.

He clenched his fists at his sides and unclenched them, knowing Jon was right, that he was going to have to somehow stick beside her until he could find the truth. She was a hostile little witch...

And he already wanted her. Craved her. Ached to touch her, feel more of her.

He swore softly, determined to behave like an officer and a Southern gentleman and solve this dilemma with no more thought for his unwilling companion.

Then he heard her...weeping, crying very, very softly as if she were muffling the sound in her pillow. She had come back to consciousness, and it seemed to be a bitter awakening. She cried and cried. He felt her agony, felt it rip and tear into him, and it was terrible. The horror of it reached inside him and touched his heart as it had not been touched in years. He had thought his emotions were stripped away by war.

The girl's wrenching sobs brought them back.

He started to turn, to go to her. He stopped himself.

No. She would not want him.

He stiffened his shoulders and walked on.

Chapter Two

By dusk, all the graves had been dug. By the light of lanterns and camp fires, Reverend Thorne Dryer of Company B read services over the graves.

Tess Stuart stood near the reverend. Her eyes were dry now, and she was silent. Something about her very quietness touched Jamie deeply; she was small, but so very straight, her shoulders square, her lustrous hair hidden beneath a black hat and sweeping veil, her form encompassed in a handsome black dress with gray pearl buttons on the sleeves and at the throat. Dust to dust, earth to earth, ashes to ashes. The reverend called on God to claim His own, to show mercy upon their souls, to give solace to those who remained behind.

Tess stepped forward to drop a single flower on her uncle's grave. She was still silent, and not a tear marred the perfect and tragic beauty of her face.

Then she swung around and headed for her wagon. Jamie didn't mean to follow her, he just discovered that he was doing so. She sensed him just before she reached the wagon and swung around.

"Yes, Captain?"

"Lieutenant, miss. Lieutenant Slater."

"Whatever," she said coolly. "What do you want?"

Hostile! he thought. More hostile than any full tribe of Indians he had come across. She made him itch to set a hard hand against her behind, but she had experienced great pain today. He was a fool to have followed her. He should let her be. He didn't want her as a burden, and she didn't want him as her protector. If she needed a protector.

"Miss Stuart, I just came by to offer my condolences. To see if you were all right, if you might need anything for the night."

"I'm just fine, Lieutenant." She hesitated. "Thank you." She whirled around in her black skirt, then crawled into the wagon. Jamie clenched his hands tight at his sides and returned to the group. The funeral was just about over. Jon and Monahan and a few of the others were stamping down the last of the dirt and erecting wooden crosses over the graves.

The crosses wouldn't stay long. The wind would take them, the dust would wear them away, and in time animals then men would tramp upon them. The West was like that. A man lived and died, and little but bones could be left behind. Bones and dreams.

"I ordered the men to set up camp, Lieutenant, just like you said," Monahan told him.

"Thank you, Sergeant."

"Is that all, Lieutenant?"

"No. Split them even, Monahan. Half can sleep while the second half stay on guard. Just in case."

"In case the Injuns come back," Monahan said.

"In case of anything. This is the cavalry, Sergeant!"

"Yes, sir!"

Monahan saluted sharply. He shouted orders, his voice loud in the night. The men at the graves hurried after Monahan as he started toward the fires where the others were already setting up camp. As Jamie watched, he saw his men melt into the rocks and crevices around them. They were a crack troop. They had campaigned through the most rugged Indian territory in the West and they had all learned their lessons well. They could walk as silently as any brave, shoot with the same deadly accuracy and engage in lethal knife play with ease.

It hadn't been easy for Jamie, not at first. Some of the men had resented the Rebel who had won his promotions so easily. Some hadn't thought a Reb ought to be given a gun, and many had had their doubts about Jamie in Indian country. He had been forced to prove his way at every step, in battle or in negotiations. They'd met up with a tribe of warring Apache once near the border, and he had shown them something of his mettle with his Colts as the battle had begun. Later he found out there had been some whispering about all the Slater brothers, and how deadly he and Cole and Malachi had been during the war. Overnight, it seemed, his reputation had become legendary.

He smiled in the darkness. It had been worth it. He had gained a loyal following, and good men. Nothing would come slipping through his lines tonight. He could rest with ease.

If he could rest at all.

Despite himself he felt his eyes drawn toward the wagon that stood just outside the circle of small cavalry-issue A-frame tents.

"What a burden," Jon said quietly from behind.

Jamie swung around, arching a brow. Jon wasn't the usual subordinate, nor did Jamie expect him to be. "Why don't you quit making the comments and start telling me something about this von Heusen fellow."

"You really interested?" Jon asked.

"Try me. Come on. We'll get some coffee and take a walk up by the ridge."

Monahan gave them coffee from a tin pot at the fire, then the two men wandered up the ridge. Jamie found a seat on a flat rock and rested his boots on another. Jon stood, watching the expanse of the prairie. By the soft light of the moon, it was a beautiful place, the mountains rising like shadows in the distance, the sage rolling in ghostly fashion and the camp fires and stars just lighting up the darkness around them.

"She's telling the truth," Jon said.

"How can you know?" Jamie demanded.

Jon shrugged, scuffed his boots against the earth and turned to hunker down near Jamie. "I know because I've heard of this man before. He wanted land further north during the war. He was a cattle baron up there then, and he was ordered by the government to provide members of the Oglala Sioux on reservation land with meat. He gave them maggot-riddled beef that he wouldn't have fed to his own sows. The Indians formed a delegation to speak with the man. He called it an Indian uprising and soon every rancher in the area was at war with the Sioux. Hundreds, red and white, died. Uselessly, senselessly. And von Heusen was never punished."

Jamie was quiet for a moment. He stared toward the remnants of the wagon train.

"So he's got property now in Wiltshire. And he wants more. And he likes to rile up the Indians. I still can't do anything, Jon. Even if I believed Miss Stuart, there wouldn't be anything I could do."

"Because you can't prove anything."

"Exactly. And no sane white man is going to believe it."

"That's too bad," Jon said after a moment. "That's really too bad. I don't think Miss Stuart can survive very long."

"Come on, Jon, stop it! No matter how powerful this von Heusen is, he can't just out-and-out murder the woman! The whole town would be up in arms. He can't own the whole damned town!"

Jon shrugged. "He owns the sheriff. And we both know that he doesn't have to out-and-out murder the girl. There are ways."

"Damn!" Jamie stood up, dusting the dirt off the rump of his breeches with his hat.

"So what are you going to do?"

"I told you. We're riding back to the fort—"

"And then?"

"Let's get there, eh?"

Jon stood. "I just wanted you to know, Jamie, that if you decide to take some of that time the government owes you, I'll go with you."

"I'm not taking any time."

"Yeah. Sure. Whatever you say, Slater."

Jamie paused, grinning. "Thanks, Red Feather. I appreciate it. But believe me, I'm sure I'm not the escort Miss Stuart has in mind."

Jon pulled his hat low over his eyes, grinning. "Well, Jamie, me lad, we don't always know just exactly what it is that we need, now, do we? Good night." Without waiting for a reply he walked down the ridge.

Jamie stayed on the ridge a while longer, looking at the camp fires. He'd stay up with the first group on watch; Monahan would stay up with the second.

But even when he saw the guard change and the sergeant take his place silently upon a high ridge, he discovered he couldn't sleep. The cot didn't bother him—he had slept on much less comfortable beds—nor did the night sounds, or even the nightmare memories of the day.

She bothered him...

Knowing that she slept not far away. Or lay awake as he did. Perhaps, in private, the tears streamed down her face. Or perhaps she was silent still, done with the past, determined to think of the future. She believed what she was saying to him. She believed that the wagon train had been attacked by white men dressed up like Indians. She wouldn't let it rest.

He groaned and pulled his pillow over his head. It wasn't exactly as if she was asking for his help. She'd made it clear she didn't even want to hear his voice. He owed her nothing, he owed the situation nothing.

Yes, he did.

He owed the people who had died here today, and he owed the Comanche, who were going to be blamed for this. And he owed all the people who would die in the bloody wars to follow if something wasn't proven one way or the other.

Still, he didn't sleep. He lay awake and he wondered about the woman with the sun-honey hair who lay not a hundred yards away in the canvas-covered wagon.

Sometime during the night Tess slept, but long before dawn she was wide awake again, reliving every moment of what had happened. Her grief and rage were so deep that she wanted to scream aloud, but screaming again would do no good, and she had already cried until she felt that her tears were a river that had run as dry as the plain with its sagebrush and dust.

She cast her feet to the floor and stared across the darkened wagon to the bunk where her Uncle Joseph should have been sleeping, where he would sleep no more. Joe would lie out here in the plain for eternity, and his body would become bone, and in the decades to come, no one would really know that a brave and courageous man had died here fighting, even if he'd barely had a chance to raise a weapon. Joe had never given in, not once. He couldn't be intimidated. He had printed the truth in the *Wiltshire Sun*, and he had held fast to everything that was his.

And he had died for it.

Tess pulled on her shoes and laced them high up her ankles, then silently slipped from the wagon. The cavalry camp fires were burning very low. Dawn couldn't be far away. Soldiers were sleeping in the

A-frame tents, she knew, and more soldiers were awake, on guard, one with the rocks and cliffs that rose around the edge of the plain.

They were on guard—against Indians!

She clenched her jaw hard, glad of the anger, for it helped to temper the grief. What kind of a fool did they think she was? Not they—him! That Yank lieutenant with the deep, soft drawl.

The one she'd like to see staked out for the ants.

Walking silently through the night, she came upon the graves at last. She closed her eyes and she meant to pray, but it wasn't prayers that came to her lips. Goodbye, Joe, I loved you! I loved you so very much! I won't be able to come back here, I'm sure, but you're the one who taught me how special the soul was, and how little it had to do with the body. Uncle Joe, you were really beautiful. For all that grizzled face of yours and your broken nose, you were the most beautiful person I ever knew...I won't let you have died for nothing, I swear it. I won't lose. I'll keep the paper going, and I'll hold onto the land. I don't know how I'll do it, but I will, I swear it, I promise. I promise, with all my heart...

Her thoughts trailed off and she turned around, uncannily aware that she wasn't alone.

She wasn't.

The tall lieutenant with the wicked force to his arms was standing not far behind her, silent in the night. In the haze of the coming morning, he seemed to be a towering, implacable form. He wasn't a heavy man, but she had discovered in her wild fight with him that his shoulders were broad, that his arms and chest were well and tautly muscled, that he was as lean and sleek and powerful as a puma, agile and quick. His eyes were a most interesting shade of gray, remote, enigmatic, and yet she felt their acuteness each time they fell upon her. She realized, in the late shadows of night, that he was an arresting man. Handsome...but not because of perfect features or any gentleness about him. His face was ruggedly hewn, but with clean, strong lines. His jaw was firm and square, his cheekbones were high, his eyes were wide and well set, his forehead was broad. He had a look of the west about him, and a look of the war, perhaps.

Something seemed to stir within her, startling her. He was compelling in his very masculinity, she decided. His mouth could be hard, controlled, grim, but then again, when his lips did move, they were strikingly sensual. And then there was the color of his eyes, and the way they could fall upon her. She discovered that her palms were damp and her lips were dry. It was difficult not to wonder about the man. She'd already touched him. She knew the hot feel of his muscles beneath her fingers, she knew the warmth and tension of his body stretched over hers. She hadn't realized it until this moment. She had been fighting him.

But now she remembered. Every sensation.

She clenched her fingers into fists at her sides, remembering that this was the man in charge. The man who refused to believe her. She'd lived here all her life. She knew the difference between a white man and a Comanche. She definitely knew the difference between von Heusen's men and Comanche.

The Comanche had morals—and a sense of honor.

"What are you doing here?" she asked, determined to keep her chin high, her voice level, her dignity intact. She'd already scuffled with him once—but he wouldn't find her in such a tempest ever again. He could doubt her from here to eternity. She'd give him no opportunity to find her hysterical or babbling.

"I heard you come here. I didn't mean to intrude, I just wanted to make sure that you were all right."

She couldn't help it—she felt as if the hackles rose on her neck just like those of a wolf, as if every nerve ending in her body had come alive to scream. Things seemed to snap and crackle in the air, and she longed to kick him in the shin again. He was worried about her. Because he considered her to be unhinged!

"I'm just fine, Lieutenant."

"Look, Miss Stuart—"

"You look, Lieutenant. You have your opinions, I have mine. And they don't seem to coincide in any way. I'm fine. Your men are guarding the camp. I'm quite sure that a ferret couldn't slip by them. They are, after all, your men, and I'm quite sure that they've got the fear of God whipped deeply into them."

"Oh, really? The fear of God is whipped into them?"

He cocked his head at an angle, and his mouth moved. Sensual. When it wasn't cast into one of those grim lines, it was wide and generous, and she discovered that she was staring at his lips.

Tess stepped back, almost as if he had reached out to touch her, which he had not. He was keeping his distance. His feet were firmly planted on the ground, his arms were crossed over his chest, and the look he gave her was one of amusement.

"Yankee discipline," she said sweetly. He didn't answer her, but something seemed to fall over his eyes, something very hostile. Well, they'd all survived the war. Hostility died hard.

She hadn't meant to continue hating the North. The war had been exhausting. It had been good to hear that it was over, that no one else was going to die. But then the carpetbaggers had descended. Von Heusen, in particular, and more of his ilk. Men who bought the land from decent people who couldn't pay their taxes.

Von Heusen went further. When he wanted a ranch, the cattle had a habit of disappearing. When the rancher tried to buy feed, it was moldy and bad. And sometimes even the rancher disappeared. Von Heusen had hired guns to go with him every time he moved.

Hired guns...who could be painted bronze and wear buckskin and attack with tomahawks and rifles.

She was hostile, she realized. Really hostile. Maybe this Yankee lieutenant wouldn't do the things von Heusen had done, but he hadn't promised her a lick of help in righting things. He didn't care.

The only people who cared were the citizens of Wiltshire, and there weren't really all that many left. Even the sheriff was one of von Heusen's men, put into office during one of the shadiest elections imaginable.

It was light, Tess realized. The daylight had come as they had stood there, staring at one another. Against the pink of the sky, Lieutenant Slater suddenly seemed a towering menace. A pulse beat at the base of his throat as he watched her. His jaw seemed cast into a slight twist, then locked as if it held back his temper. There was a good ten feet between them, and still she felt his heat, body heat. Her heart was beating too quickly, and something warm churned deep within her abdomen while little touches of mercury seemed to dance along her back. She needed to break away from him. She despised his attitude; she couldn't help but despise him for the blue uniform that reminded her so completely of the war.

He wore it well, his dark, plumed hat pulled low over his eyes, his shoulders broad in the navy blue cavalry shirt, his legs long, his hips trim...

She had to walk past him. She swallowed hard and forced herself to smile. "If you'll excuse me, Lieutenant, I'm sure that you're anxious to ride as quickly as possible."

She started to walk. The closer she came to him the harder her heart beat. She was almost past him.

Then his arm snaked out and he caught her elbow. Her heart slammed against her chest as she looked into his smoke-gray eyes, sizzling into hers beneath the sun. His eyes were still shadowed by the brim of his hat.

"I am sorry, Miss Stuart. I'm very sorry."

She wanted to speak. Her throat was dry. She felt his fingers upon her as if they burned. She was acutely aware of the warmth and strength of his body.

She stared at his hand upon her and pulled from his grasp. "Thank you, Lieutenant," she managed to say, then she forgot her dignity and fled.

In an hour they were ready to start out. Lieutenant Slater ordered the downed and useless wagons burned. He almost ordered her new printing press burned, but Tess forgot all about a low-toned and well-modulated voice and dignified behavior and came bursting from her wagon to demand that the press be carried into something that was still capable of rolling.

"What in hell is it?" the lieutenant demanded impatiently.

"A press! A printing press! I need it for the *Wiltshire Sun*!"

"Your uncle's newspaper? But he's—dead, Miss Stuart."

"The *Wiltshire Sun* is not dead, Lieutenant, nor do I intend to let it die. I will not take a step without that printing press."

A spark of silver touched his eyes as they narrowed upon her. "Don't threaten me, Miss Stuart."

"I'm not threatening! I'm telling you what will and will not happen."

He took a step toward her and spoke very quietly. "Miss Stuart, you will move when I say so, ma'am, because I'll set you upon your pretty little—er—rump within the wagon, and one of my men will drive."

"You wouldn't dare! I'll tell your superiors—"

"You tell them anything you want. Want to test me?"

She gritted her teeth and stared into his eyes. "I need that press, Lieutenant."

He stood still, hard, cold, immobile.

"Lieutenant, please! I need that printing press! It would only take your men a few minutes. Please!"

For a moment he continued to stare at her. Then he turned around, calling to Sergeant Monahan. The men were ordered to move the press into one of the wagons that could still roll. "Private Harper!" Slater called. "Hitch your horse to the rear and drive the extra wagon."

"Yes, sir!"

Tess exhaled slowly. Lieutenant Slater cast her a hard glare, then turned around. He strode away, calling for his men to see to the last of the fires, then mount up.

When he had gone, Tess realized that the handsome Indian with the striking eyes was silently watching her. He saluted with a smile, as if she had managed very well. Then he, too, turned away.

Tess was certain it was a long day for the cavalry. The men were accustomed to moving quickly—now they were burdened down by the wagons. The landscape was beautiful—and monotonous. The land was a constant pale, dusty brown, the little bit of color against it the dull green of sage and cactus.

She was determined not to complain, but the dust soon covered her, and after endless hours of driving the six mules that pulled her wagon, she was exhausted. Her arms hurt in places where she hadn't realized she had muscles. She could have said something, she was certain. The majority of the young cavalry men were kind and solicitous, riding by her whenever they could, asking her if she needed anything.

But each time a man drove by, she saw Lieutenant Slater in the distance beyond him, and so she smiled sweetly and said that she was doing very well.

He had to stop. He had to stop sometime.

He finally called a halt when the sun began to fall into the horizon and the whole world went pink again. He stayed away from her, but she knew he was watching her. Was he judging her? Trying to decide if she was crazy or if she was having female whimsies? She had to keep a tight lid on her temper. No matter what he did or said, she had to keep quiet. When she reached his fort she would speak calmly and rationally with the commander, and she would make him understand.

"Miss Stuart!" Sergeant Monahan rode over to her, then dismounted from his horse. "Let me help me you down, miss. I'll see to your mules and the wagon."

"Thank you, Sergeant. I can really—"

She broke off, nearly falling as he helped her from the wagon. He held her steady as her feet touched the ground, and she smiled for him. "Thank you again. I guess I do need some help."

"At your service."

She felt she was being watched. She looked over Monahan's shoulder and there was Slater, still mounted on his huge horse, overseeing his men as they broke their formation to make camp. He tipped his hat to her, and she felt something run hot and liquid inside her. He was watching her in Monahan's arms, and very likely acknowledging a feminine ability to draw others to handle her own responsibilities. Her temper started to soar.

Monahan stepped back, and his wide baby blue eyes were full of gentleness and kindness and maybe just a bit of adoration. He was a wonderful man, just like a great big shaggy bear. The devil to Lieutenant Slater. If his men wanted to behave like gentlemen, she had no intention of stopping them.

"Miss Stuart, Lieutenant Slater rode this far because we know this place. If you go just past that ridge yonder, there's the prettiest little brook. It's mostly surrounded by dry rock, but the water runs pure and clean. There's an area up there far from where we'll water the horses. You can take a walk up there and find all the privacy you might desire."

"Thank you again, Sergeant," Tess said. "I would dearly love a bath. I'll take you up on your suggestion." She hurried to the back of the wagon and found clean clothing, a bar of soap and a towel. When she emerged again, Sergeant Monahan was unharnessing the mules. He pointed toward the ridge. She could see that some of the soldiers were headed in the other direction. She smiled again and hurried toward the ridge. She was puffing slightly when she walked over it, but then she gasped with delight.

The brook was surrounded by boulders and high rocks, but there were little tufts of grass growing between the rocks, and a few wildflowers had managed to eke out an existence there. The evening was pink and gold and very beautiful, and she could hear the sound of the water as it ran. It looked so cool and delicious after the dry dust of the day.

She clambered down the rocks to a broad ledge, dropped her towel and soap and clothing and sat down, hurriedly untying her shoes. Staring at the clean, fresh water, she pulled her blouse from her skirt and quickly shed it, then her skirt and shift and pantalets and hose. She stepped down the rock, so entranced by the water that she never once realized she wasn't alone.

Barefoot and bare-chested, his cavalry trousers rolled above his ankles, Jamie Slater sat in the shadow of a rock, swearing softly. His own bath had just gone straight downhill. And he didn't mean to be a voyeur, but she had stripped so damned quickly, and he'd been so darned surprised that he had just stayed there.

Watching.

She was like a nymph, an angel cast out from the evils of the heat and the plain. Her skin was alabaster, her breasts perfect. Her waist was very trim, her derriere rich and lush and flaring out from that narrow waist, and her legs were so long and shapely that they suggested the most decadent dreams, the most sensual imaginings. Angel...vixen...her hair streamed around her like the sunset, thick and cascading, falling over her bare shoulders, curling around her breasts, haunting, teasing, evocative.

He fell back, groaning slightly.

Tess didn't see him. She plunged into the water, amazed that she could still draw such simple pleasure when the pain of Joe's loss was still so strongly with her. But she was still alive, and the water was so cool and clean after the dust and filth of the plains. It came just to her ankles at first, and there were little rocks and pebbles beneath her feet, so she had to be careful walking. Then the water became deeper, and she sank into it, stretching out, soaking her hair, floating, shivering, delighted. The sun was still warm, the water almost cold, and together they were marvelous. She swam around in the shallows, careful not to hit her arms and legs on the pebbles, then found a smooth shelf to stand on and scrubbed herself thoroughly with the soap, rising to form rich suds, sinking beneath the surface again to rinse them away. She scrubbed her hair, feeling wonderful as she removed the dirt and grime from her scalp. Finally she rose from the water. She paused, ringing out her hair, then hurried to where she had left her things. She picked up her towel and studiously rubbed herself dry, then sat upon the ledge to dry her hair before donning her clean clothing.

She stretched, closing her eyes and leaning against the rock, which was still warm from the sun. The last of the dying rays touched her body, and she closed her eyes for a moment.

When she opened them, she nearly screamed.

Lieutenant Slater was standing above her. His shirt hung open over his chest, and he was barefoot and grim. She opened her mouth to protest. She was stark naked, and he was staring down at her without the least apology.

But when she opened her mouth, he suddenly drew his gun and fired off several shots.

She'd never seen a gun move so fast or heard anything like the way the Colt spit and fired in fury.

She didn't gasp; she didn't scream. She thought he had lost his mind, but when she twisted to grasp her towel, she paused, stunned, staring at the carcass of the dead moccasin that had been barely a foot away from her.

She looked up at the lieutenant, unable to speak, unable to move. He had saved her life, she realized. She had been completely unaware of the snake that she had so carelessly disturbed.

He didn't say anything, just looked at her, his gray eyes sliding over her body, and everywhere they touched her, she felt fire coursing through her. She felt her nipples harden, and she was horrified that they did so, but still she didn't manage to say a word.

He slid his Colt into his hip holster and spoke at last. "You need to be more careful about the rocks you choose, Miss Stuart," he said.

She heard running footsteps. He quickly reached for her towel and handed it to her. She clutched it to her breasts as a young private suddenly appeared.

"Lieutenant! I heard the shots!"

"It's all right, Hardy. It was me. A snake. Nothing that could shoot back."

The private was staring at them, wide-eyed.

"That's all, Hardy."

"Yes, sir, Lieutenant."

The private saluted. Slater saluted in return. Then he tipped his hat to her and turned around. Tess reddened to a dark crimson and watched as he picked his way upstream. She saw his socks and boots on a flat boulder, and her breath seemed to catch in her throat. He had been there all the time.

She leaped to her feet and hurried into her fresh clean clothing with shaking fingers. She could barely tie her pink-ribboned corset, and she had to do the buttons on her blouse twice. She pulled on clean hose and her shoes and looked at the rock.

He was waiting. Waiting for her to leave. He sat on the ledge, his toes in the water.

He looked up as if he felt her watching him. "It's almost dark, Miss Stuart, if you don't mind."

"If I don't mind! You—you sat there through my bath, Lieutenant!" she sputtered.

"Lucky I did," he replied pleasantly.

She was alive. Maybe she was lucky. But that wasn't the point, and he knew it.

He shrugged, rising, casting off his shirt. "It really doesn't matter that much to me, Miss Stuart. You're welcome to stay. Maybe you'll even want to join me...?"

She swung around, furious. He was ready to strip down with her standing right there. He'd sat and stared at her while she had been completely naked, assuming she was alone...

She'd given him a whole damned show in the water!

Swearing softly, she plodded away, anxious to quit the brook. She hurried to her wagon and sat on the bunk, hugging her arms to her chest.

Damn him. Just remembering his eyes upon her made her breasts swell again and her nipples harden to taut peaks. When she closed her eyes it didn't help. She remembered the way that his shirt had hung open over his chest, and the sandy dark hair that grew in rich profusion there, the ripple of tight muscle on his abdomen, the swell of it at his breast and shoulders.

"Miss Stuart?" It was Sergeant Monahan.

"Yes?" She almost shouted the word.

He was at the rear of the wagon, smiling. "Wasn't that just the prettiest little brook you've ever seen?"

"Absolutely beautiful," she said evenly. But it didn't matter— apparently word of the shots had gotten out. Another one of the men stepped behind Monahan, nodding respectfully to her.

"Monahan! Hardy says she almost got it from a moccasin. Luckily the lieutenant was near and blasted the thing to kingdom come. Ma'am, it is the prettiest little brook around, but you be careful from here on out, you hear? You've become pretty important to all of us."

"Thank you, that's very kind," she murmured, but she knew that she was blushing again. Everyone knew what had happened.

But they didn't really know. They didn't know what it had felt like when his eyes had touched her naked flesh...

"Rations aren't much, ma'am, but one of the boys brought in a few trout. May I fix you a plate and bring you some coffee?" Monahan asked her.

"Please," she agreed. "That would be very nice."

Monahan brought her a plate of food, the other young man brought her coffee. She thanked them both. Then, as she ate, it seemed that every man in the company came by to see how she was, if she would like anything, if she needed anything, anything at all, for the night.

She thanked them all, and when they left, and the darkness fell, and the camp became silent, she smiled. They were Yanks, but a good group of them. Maybe there was hope. She believed again. There were von Heusens in the world, but there were others, too, good people. She just had to keep fighting. She had to hold on to the ranch and she had to keep the Wiltshire newspaper going.

"Miss Stuart."

She started, feeling every nerve within her body come alive. She knew the voice. Knew the deep tone, low and husky and somehow capable of slipping beneath her skin. It was a sensual, sexy voice, and it awakened things in her she was certain had died beneath the rifle fire of the last years of the war.

She inhaled quickly. If she was silent, he might just walk away. He might believe that she slept and just walk away.

But he wouldn't. He knew she was awake. She sensed it, and she resented him for his easy knowledge of her.

"Yes?" she asked crisply.

"I just wanted to make sure that you were all right."

"I'm fine, Lieutenant."

"Is there anything you need?"

"I want you to believe me, Lieutenant. And you're not offering me that."

He was silent. She hoped he would turn away, but she sensed he was smiling.

"You didn't thank me. For saving your life."

"Ah, yes. Thank you for saving my life." She found herself crawling the length of the bunk, then defying him over the rear edge of the wagon. "Lieutenant?"

"Yes?"

"Come closer, please."

He took a step nearer. Tess let her hand fly across his cheek. He instantly caught her wrist, and she was glad of the surprised and furious fire in his eyes as they caught hers. She kept smiling, even if his fingers did seem to be a vise around her, even if the air seemed charged with electricity.

Even if she was just a little bit afraid that he was going to drag her out of the wagon and down beneath him into the dirt.

"I do thank you for saving my life, Lieutenant. But that was for the ungentlemanly way in which you did so."

She pulled on her hand. He didn't let go. His eyes glittered silver in the moonlight.

"I'll try to remember, Miss Stuart, that you are most particular about the way a man goes about saving your life," he told her.

"You know exactly what I'm saying."

"I never meant to give you offense."

"Never?"

"I do swear so, Miss Stuart. I kept my presence quiet because you were as bare as a baby before I realized it. And then, well, I do admit, I was caught rather speechless."

"You weren't speechless on the rock!"

He smiled slowly. "No."

"Oh, you...Yank!"

She tugged on her wrist again. He didn't release her at first, then his fingers slowly unwound. He was smiling, she realized. And his eyes fell over her again, and she felt as if he was burning the sight of her into his memory. A flame shot high within her, and she didn't know if she was horrified—or fascinated.

"Good night, Miss Stuart," he said softly.

Then he did walk away. She didn't move, and after a moment he turned back.

"Miss Stuart?"

"What?"

He hesitated. "You're a very beautiful woman. Very beautiful."

He didn't wait for an answer. He walked away and disappeared into the night.

Chapter Three

Two days later, they reached the fort.

It was, Tess thought, a typical military fort in Indian country. The walls of the stockade were high, maybe twenty-five feet high, and built of dark sturdy logs. She heard the sound of a bugle while they were still some distance from the fort, then the huge wooden gate swung open to allow their party to enter. Looking up as they went into the compound, Tess saw armed guards in their cavalry blue lined up on all the catwalks and staring down at them.

She was grateful to have reached the fort. She was driving her mules, swearing to them beneath her breath, and wondering if the calluses would ever leave her fingers. She'd gotten them right through Uncle Joe's heavy leather gloves. She was sweaty, salty and sticky, and her hair was coming loose from the neat braid she'd twisted at her nape. She had said that she could manage—and Lieutenant Slater had let her do just that.

His men had continued to be very kind, and she had continued to smile and be as gracious as she could in return. He had kept his distance since he had left her that night, but she had felt his eyes on her.

Always…his eyes were on her. When she drove the wagon, she would suddenly feel a warmth, and she would look around to discover that he was no longer at the head of the column, but had ridden back and was watching her. And at night, when one of the men would bring her coffee or food, he would stare across the distance of the camp fire. And by night she heard footsteps, and she wondered if he wasn't walking by to determine if she was sleeping. If she was safe. Or did he walk by to discover if she might still be awake?

He infuriated her, but she was also glad, and she realized that she felt safe. Not because she was surrounded by thirty or so cavalry men, but because he was walking by, because he was near.

But now they had come to the fort. He would turn her over to his commander and disappear from her life. Someone would be assigned to see her to Wiltshire, and she need never see him again. Never feel his eyes again, the touch of smoke gray and insinuation that warmed everything within her and seemed to caress her as if he saw her again as he had by the brook.

They were in front of the command post. Tess pulled hard on the reins, dropped them and started to leap from the driver's seat. She smiled, for Jon Red Feather was there to help her. She had grown to like the man very much: his striking, sturdy appearance, his silence and his carefully chosen words. And she sensed that he believed her when others might not.

He set her upon the ground. She thanked him then looked at all the confusion around her. Wives, children and perhaps lovers had spilled from the various buildings in the compound to greet the returning men. Monahan had called out an order dismissing them all, and the band was quickly breaking up. Lieutenant Slater was striding up the steps to the broad porch that encircled the command post, saluting the tall, gray-haired man who awaited him. Jon indicated the steps. "Miss Stuart, I believe the colonel will want a statement from you as soon as possible. I'll see to your accommodations for the evening and return shortly."

He walked her to the porch. Apparently Slater had already explained something about her, for the colonel was quick to offer her a hand and guide her up the steps. "Miss Stuart, our most sincere condolences on the loss of your uncle, but may I say that we are heartily glad that you have survived to be here today."

"Thank you," Tess said. It was strange. It already seemed like the whole thing had happened in the distant past. Days on the plains could do that, she decided. And yet, when the colonel spoke so solicitously of Uncle Joe, all the pain and the loneliness rushed back.

She tried to swallow them down. She needed to impress this man with intelligence and determination, not a fit of tears. She didn't want to be patted on the back. She wanted to be believed.

"Miss Stuart, if you would be so good as to join us inside, the colonel would like to speak with you," Slater said. There was a startling light in his eyes as they touched her. Not amusement, but something else. Almost a challenge. He wanted to see if she would back down, she thought.

Well, she wouldn't.

She walked past both men and into a large office with file cabinets and a massive desk and a multitude of crude wooden chairs. Slater pulled out a chair for her, and she sat down as regally as she could manage, pulling off her rough leather gloves and letting them fall into her lap. She felt Slater's eyes, and she looked up then looked quickly away. He had seen the blisters and calluses on her hands.

The colonel took his seat behind the desk. He was an elderly man, whose gentle blue eyes seemed to belie his position as a commander of such a post. His voice, too, was gentle. Tess thought he was genuinely grateful to see her alive, even if he had never met her before. "Would you like coffee, Miss Stuart? I'm afraid I've no tea to offer you—"

"Coffee will be just fine, thank you," Tess said.

She hadn't realized that there was another man in the room until a silent young corporal stepped forward to bring her a tin mug of black coffee. She thanked him and an awkward moment followed. Then the colonel sat forward, folding his hands on the desk. "Miss Stuart, Lieutenant Slater informs me that you have claimed that it was not Indians who set upon your band."

"That's right, sir."

"Then who?"

"White men. Hired guns for a man named von Heusen. He is trying to take my uncle's property and—"

"He'd have men attack a whole wagon train to obtain your uncle's property? Think now, Miss Stuart, is that logical?"

She gritted her teeth. Slater was watching her politely. She wanted to kick him. "It wasn't a large wagon train, Colonel. We've had good relations with the Comanche in our area, and my uncle wasn't afraid of the Comanche! We were traveling with a very small party, a few hired hands, my uncle—"

"Maybe, Miss Stuart, the Indians weren't Comanche. Maybe they were a stray band of Apache looking for easy prey, or Shoshone down from the mountains, or maybe even an offshoot of the Sioux—''

"No Indian attacked that wagon train."

Tess swung around. Jon Red Feather had come into the room. He helped himself to coffee, then pulled up the chair beside Slater. He grinned at his friend, then addressed the colonel. "I'm sure that Miss Stuart does know a Comanche when she sees one, sir. And it wasn't Apache. Apache usually only scalp Mexicans—in retaliation." He turned and smiled at Tess. "And I can promise you that what was done was not done by the Sioux. A Sioux would never have left Miss Stuart behind."

A shiver ran down Tess's spine. She didn't know if Jon meant that the Sioux would have taken her with them—or that they would have been sure to kill and scalp her, too.

The colonel lifted his hands. Even with Jon corroborating her story, he didn't seem to believe her. Or if he did believe her, he had no intention of helping her. "Miss Stuart, I have heard of this von Heusen. He has big money, and big connections, and I understand he owns half the town—''

"Literally, Colonel. He owns the judge and the sheriff and the deputies."

"Now, Miss Stuart, those are frightful charges—''

"They are true charges."

"But don't you see, Miss Stuart, you'd have to go into a court of law against this man. And you'd have to charge him in Wiltshire, and like you said…'' His voice trailed away. "Why don't you think of heading back east, Miss Stuart?"

She was up on her feet instantly. "Head back east? I have never been east, Colonel. I was born here in Texas. My grandparents helped found Wiltshire. And the little bit of town that von Heusen doesn't own yet, I still do. I have no intention of turning it over to him! Colonel, there's nothing else that I can tell you. I have had a rather trying few days. If there's some place where I might rest, I'll be most grateful to accept your hospitality for a night or two. Then, sir, I have to get home. I have a ranch and a paper that need my expertise."

The colonel was on his feet, too, and she sensed that, behind her,

Jon and Slater had also risen. She spun around, feeling Slater's eyes, certain that he was laughing at her again.

But he wasn't laughing. His eyes were upon her, smoky and gray and enigmatic. She sensed that she had finally gained a certain admiration from him. What good it could do her, she didn't know. The colonel had been her last hope. Now the battle was hers, and hers alone.

"Miss Stuart, I'd like to help you if I could—"

"Nonsense, Colonel. You don't believe a word I'm saying," Tess told him sweetly. "That's your prerogative, sir. I am very fatigued..."

"Miss Stuart can take the old Casey place while she's here," Jon said. "Dolly Simmons is there now, with linens and towels."

"I shall be most grateful to the Caseys," Tess said.

"No need," Slater drawled. "Casey is dead. Caught a Comanche arrow last year. His wife went on back east."

He was taunting her, and she smiled despite it. "I have told you all, Lieutenant, I've never been east—"

"Oh, not that east, Miss Stuart. Mrs. Casey and the kids went to live in Houston, that's all."

"Well, I rather like the area I live in," she said sweetly, then she turned to the colonel. "If I may, sir...?"

"Of course, of course! Jamie, you and Jon will please escort the young lady to her quarters. And Miss Stuart, if it's Wiltshire you're insisting on reaching, I'll arrange you an escort just as soon as possible."

"Thank you."

Jon opened the door. Tess sailed through it. Slater followed her. "It's this way, Tess," Jon told her. He'd never used her first name before, and certainly not as he did now, intimately, as if they were old friends. There was a bright light to his striking green eyes, and she realized that it was for the benefit of Jamie Slater. Jamie. Silently, she rolled the name on her tongue. "Lieutenant" seemed to fit him better.

Not always...Not that day he had looked down at her on the rocks after shooting the snake. His hair had been ruffled, his shirt had fallen open, and she had wanted to touch him, to reach out and feel the vital movement of his flesh, so bronze beneath the setting sun. Then,

then the name Jamie might have fit him just right. It was an intimate name, a name for friends, or for lovers.

He was behind her still. Jon Red Feather was pointing things out to her. "That's a general store, and there's our one and only alehouse, we don't dare call it a saloon. And down there is the coffeehouse for the ladies. We've a number of women at the fort here. The colonel approves of the married men having their wives with them, and since the fort is strong and secure..." He shrugged. "Then, of course, we have the stores and the alehouse and the coffeehouse, so we've a few young and unattached ladies, which makes it nice for the soldiers at the dances."

"Dances!"

"Why, Miss Stuart, we do try to be civilized out here in the wilderness."

"Desert," Jamie Slater said from behind them. "I think it's really more a desert than a wilderness, don't you, Jon?" He didn't wait for an answer, but continued, "There's the Casey house right there." He strode up three steps to a small house that seemed to share a supporting wall with the structure beside it.

The door burst open suddenly. There was a large buxom woman standing there. She had an ageless quality about her, for her features were plump and clear, her eyes were dark and merry, and it was difficult to see if her hair was blond or silver. "You poor dear! You poor, poor dear! Caught up in that awful Indian attack—"

"Miss Stuart doesn't believe that it was Indians, Dolly," Jamie Slater said evenly.

Dolly waved a hand in the air. "Don't matter who it was, does it? It was awful and heinous and cruel and this poor girl lost her friends and her uncle. It was your uncle, right, dear?"

"Yes," Tess said softly.

Dolly had a hand upon her shoulders, drawing her into the house. Jon and Jamie Slater would have followed except that Dolly inserted her grand frame between them and the doorway. "Jon, Jamie, get on with you now. I'll see to Miss Stuart. I'm sure you were right decent to her on the trail, but she's had a bad time of it and I'm going to see to it that she has some time to rest, and I'm going to give her a nice long bath, some home-cooked food, and then I'm going to put her to bed for the night. She needs a little tenderness right now, and I'm not so sure you're the pair to provide it!''

"Right, Dolly," Jon said. Amused, he stepped back.

Jamie Slater tipped his hat to Tess over Dolly's broad shoulder. His lip, too, was curled with a certain amusement, and Tess felt that, for once, she could too easily read the message behind his smoke-gray eyes. He thought that she needed tenderness just about as much as a porcupine did.

"Good evening, Miss Stuart. I do hope that you'll be feeling better soon."

"If you're lucky, Jamie Slater, she'll be up and about for the dance tomorrow night."

"If I'm lucky—" Jamie started to murmur.

"Well, hell, there's no lack of young men around here, Lieutenant!" Dolly said.

Tess could feel a brilliant crimson flush rising to her cheeks. She wasn't sure who she wanted to bat the hardest—Dolly for so boldly putting her into an awkward situation, or Jamie Slater for behaving as if escorting her to a dance would be a hardship.

"There's absolutely no need for anyone to concern himself," she said quietly, a note of steel to her voice. There—she'd given Slater his out. "I consider myself in mourning. A dance would be completely out of the question."

"Would it?" There was a core of steel to Jamie's voice, too. He managed to step past Dolly and catch her shoulders, and she thought he was furious as he gazed into her eyes. She couldn't understand him in the least. "I don't think so, Tess. Your uncle was a frontiersman, a fighter. I don't think he'd want you sitting around crying about what can't be changed. He'd know damned well that life out here was hard, and sometimes awfully darned short and sweet, and he'd want you to live. And that's what you're good at, isn't it? Fighting—living?"

"Lieutenant Slater, really, I—"

"Maybe it's just the fighting that you're so good at. Maybe you don't really know how to live at all."

She cast back her head, ignoring the grip of his fingers upon her shoulders. She gritted her teeth hard, then challenged him hotly. "And you think you're the one who could teach me how to live,

Lieutenant? Why, I'm not sure that you're more than a perfect Yankee mannequin yourself, Lieutenant.''

His lip curled. His grip on her shoulders suddenly relaxed. ''Why don't you test me then, Miss Stuart?''

''Jamie Slater, that young girl is vulnerable right now—'' Dolly started to warn him, but Jamie and Tess both spun on her.

''As vulnerable as a sharp-toothed cougar,'' Jamie supplied.

''Never to the likes of him!'' Tess promised.

Dolly was silent. Soft laughter sounded, and Tess saw that it was Jon Red Feather laughing, and that he seemed quite pleased with the situation.

''No wonder white men don't like Indians!'' Jamie muttered darkly.

''Sure. Keep the white folks at war with themselves, and half the battle is solved,'' Jon said pleasantly. ''Jamie, come on. It's settled. You can pick up Miss Stuart right after sunset.''

''Nothing is settled—'' Tess began.

''Sunset!'' Jamie said. He seemed to growl the word. And he didn't give her another second to protest, but slammed his way out the door. It closed with such a bang that even Dolly jumped, but then she smiled benignly.

''I do just love that man!'' Dolly said.

Tess stared at her blankly. ''Why?'' she demanded.

''Oh, you'll see, young lady. You'll see. And that Jon! He does like to stir up trouble. But then, maybe it's not trouble this time. Jon can be plain old silent as the grave when he wants, too. I think that he's just delighted to put Miss Eliza's nose out of joint. She thinks she just about has her claws into Jamie, and who knows, it is lonely out here. But she isn't right for him, she just isn't right at all. You'll see.''

''Miss Simmons—''

''Dolly. We're not very formal out here. 'Ceptin' the men, when they're busy playing soldier, that is.''

''Dolly, I have no intention of going to a dance with Lieutenant Slater. I don't really like him. He's self-righteous and hard as steel and cold as ice—''

''Hard maybe, cold, no. You'll see,'' Dolly predicted.

''But—''

"Come on, I've got a steaming bath over there in the corner. You just hop in, and I'll make you some good strong tea, and pretty soon dinner will be ready, too. And you can tell me all about yourself and what happened, and I'll tell you more about Lieutenant Slater.''

"I don't want to know anything more about Lieutenant Slater,'' Tess said firmly. But it was a lie. She wanted to know more about him. She wanted to know everything about him.

And she did want to go to the dance with him. She wanted to close her eyes and feel his arms around her, and if she thought about it, she wanted even more. She wanted to see him again as she had seen him that morning with his shirt hanging open and his hair tousled and his bare feet riding the rocks with confidence and invincibility.

"Let me help you out of those dusty travel clothes,'' Dolly said. She was quick and competent, and Tess felt immediately at home with her, able to accept her assistance. In seconds she was out of her dirt-coated clothing and into a wooden hip tub with a high back that allowed her to lean in comfort. Dolly tossed her a bar of rose-scented soap and a sponge, and she blissfully squeezed the hot water over her knees and shoulders.

"What did you do to your hands, young lady?'' Dolly demanded.

Tess looked ruefully at her callused palms. "Driving. I can do it, of course. It's just Uncle Joe usually did most of the driving.''

She didn't know what it was about saying his name, but suddenly, tears welled in her eyes.

"You should cry it out,'' Dolly warned her. "You should just go right on ahead and cry it out.''

Tess shook her head. She couldn't start crying again. She started talking instead. "He raised me. My parents died when I was very young, both caught pneumonia one winter and they just didn't pull through. Joe was Father's brother. He sold Father's land and put the money into trust for me, and he took me to live with him, and he made me love the land and reading and Texas and the newspaper business, and most of all, he made me love the truth. And he never gave up on the truth or on fighting. And that's why I have to keep it up. He always gave me everything...''

Her voice trailed away. So much, always. She remembered learning how to ride, and how to ink the printing press, and then how to think out a story, and what good journalism was, and...

And what it was like to live through pain, and stand up tall despite it, and to learn to carry on. Joe had been there when she had fallen in love with Captain David Tyler back in '64, when his Confederate infantry corp had been assigned to Wiltshire. She had been just seventeen, and she'd never known what it was like to love a man in that mercurial way until she'd met David. They'd danced, they'd taken long walks and long rides and they'd had picnics out by the river, and he had kissed her, and she had learned what it was like to feel her soul catch fire. They'd known the war couldn't go on much longer, and they planned to marry as soon as it was over.

But then David's company had been assigned to Kirby-Smith. Most of the other men, Rebels and Yanks, had lain down their arms and started on the long trek home, but David had been killed by cannon fire because Kirby-Smith fought to the bitter end. And when Tess had felt as if her heart had really broken and that there was no way to go on any longer, Joe had been there. He had been silent. He hadn't tried to tell her that she was young, that she would get over it, that she would love again. He had just held her, and he had been there to comfort her whenever she had needed him. And he had given her more and more assignments on the newspaper. She had discovered that although she never forgot David, she could learn to live with the pain, that she could even smile at his memory. There had been warm, good things between them, and she never wanted to forget them. Because of Joe, she had learned that she could remember them with a smile.

But now Joe was gone, too. And in his way, Jamie Slater was right. Joe wouldn't have wanted her to stop living.

Stop living...

Who did the Slater man think he was? She had always lived, and lived hard and with boldness and determination!

Maybe it had been a while since she had had fun. She was twenty-four years old. Most men would consider that rather over the hill, she realized. But then, times had changed. Many women were over the hill these days. The war had taken so many of the young men the women her age would have married.

She'd never cared about that. She'd never believed that marriage was a market, that a woman had to be married. Joe had given her her independence, too. She could manage the paper without him— she had done so often enough when he had traveled. He had taught her to take care of things herself. And when David had died, she hadn't wanted anyone else; she had wanted to work, and to listen to Joe. Then it had become all-fired important to fight von Heusen. Just as it was important to fight him now.

She touched her cheek with her damp fingers, and despite herself, she wondered if she looked old, like a spinster. She hadn't given her appearance much thought in a long time, and yet she had still known how to play the sweet young girl with Slater's men. She had even managed to do a little innocent flirting to irritate him. Not that he seemed to notice. He'd never come around insisting that she needed help...

But he had asked after her, he had walked by her wagon. And he had looked at her in that way.

In the warmth of the water, she felt her body grow hot and she wondered with some dismay at the effect that thoughts of the man had upon her. She hadn't felt this surging pulse of heat when she had been in love with David.

She wasn't in love with Slater. She disliked him. He was self-righteous, and he didn't believe a word she was saying. He was the type of man she needed to fight, a Yankee carpetbagger, scalping what he could from Texas.

"You all right now, Tess?" Dolly asked her.

Tess opened her eyes and smiled. "I'm fine, Dolly, I'm really just fine. I appreciate your caring, and your help."

"Oh, maybe I have a bit of Jon Red Feather's streak of mischief in me. You're a beautiful young thing—"

"Miss Simmons—"

"But you are!" Her dark eyes sparkled. "And by tomorrow night we'll have that pinched look gone from your face and your hair all clean and in ringlets and you'll be a rare challenge to Miss Eliza!"

"Dolly, I don't want to be a rare challenge to Miss Eliza. I've work to do. I must return to Wiltshire just as soon as possible. I've got a good foreman at the ranch, and the paper has a fine editor, but the ranch and the paper are both mine now, and I've got to make them work."

Dolly sniffed, apparently uninterested in a woman running a paper or a ranch. "There's things a young lady should be doin', and things she shouldn't! Now you, you need to be married. You need yourself a man."

Tess sank back into the water wearily. "I need a hired gun, that's what I need."

Dolly was quiet for a moment, then she said enthusiastically, "Well, then, you really do need Lieutenant Slater."

"What?"

Dolly came around the side of the tub and perched on a stool. "Why, he was claimed to be an outlaw, him and his brothers! There was a big showdown, and the three of them shot themselves out of an awful situation. Then they surrendered, and all went to trial, and the jury claimed them innocent as babes! But those Slater boys— why, it was legendary! He's as quick as a rattler with his Colt."

He was, Tess thought. She couldn't forget the way he had killed the snake. She might have died, except that he was so fast with that gun.

She shivered suddenly. Maybe he wasn't what she needed. He was what she wanted. A man good with a gun. A man with hard eyes and a hard-muscled chest and hands that were strong and eyes that invaded the body and the soul.

"Someone's got to escort you to Wiltshire," Dolly said flatly. "And Jamie, he's got time coming. And he really ain't no fool. I know there's this big thing going on about whether it was Indians or white men attacked you, but Jamie, he'll find out the truth."

"He didn't believe a word I said."

"Oh, but he could discover the truth! He knows the Shoshone, the Comanche, the Cheyenne, the Kiowas and even the Apache better than most white men—most white men alive, that is! Why, he speaks all their languages! He can tell you in a split second which tribes are related to which, and he knows their practices, and how they live. Sometimes he even knows the Indians better than Jon Red Feather, 'cause you see, Red Feather is a Blackfoot Sioux, and he thinks that the world begins and ends with the Sioux! If you're telling the truth—oh, my dear! I didn't mean that! I know you're not telling fibs! But if you're right about it being white men, why, Jamie will find that out. He won't let the Comanche be blamed for some atrocity they didn't commit!''

Tess was silent. Dolly spoke again, softly. "If it isn't Lieutenant Slater who takes you, it might be the colonel himself. His wife was killed by Pawnees before the war, and he ain't ever forgiven any Indian since. Or else there's Sergeant Givens, and he's an Indian hater, too. Or Corporal Lorsby, and he's a lad barely shaving, he won't be too much good to you. Oh, wait just a minute, I've got some shampoo here, all the way from Boston.''

"I don't want to use your good—''

"Come, come, what good does it do to this old head of mine? Use it! Your hair will smell just like spring rosebuds, and every bit as sweet as sunshine.''

Tess accepted the shampoo. She disappeared beneath the water to soak her hair, then she scrubbed and rinsed it. As she rose from the water again, Dolly was still talking to her.

"Lieutenant Lorsby, he's a good boy. He's just untried. He's never been in a battle. He came from the east, and I'm sure he's a bright and wonderful boy, but he don't know a Kiowa from a Chinaman, and that's a fact. You really need to think about this, you know.''

Tess nodded, feeling a chill as the steamy water cooled. Maybe she did need Lieutenant Slater after all. She smiled at Dolly. "Could I have the towel, please?''

Dolly held it, and Tess stepped from the bath, wrapped the towel around her and took a seat before the fire as she started to dry her hair. "All right, Dolly, so tell me, please, just what is it about this Miss Eliza that's so horrible.''

"Why, I'm not quite sure. 'Ceptin' she seems to think that she's God's gift to the men of the cavalry. Jamie's the only one who's never fawned over her, and I think that's exactly why she's set her cap for him! He seems to be amused most of the time, but the woman does have a wicked fine shape, and a wicked heart and mind to go along. You'll see. Now sit back, and I'll bring you your tea, and then some of the finest Irish stew you'll ever taste. Then I'll see to getting the rest of your things brought in. I have a nightgown for you, right over there on the bed. Once you're all tucked in, I'll see to the rest. You need to get some sleep.''

Dolly brought her tea, then the stew, and it was delicious. Tess hadn't felt so warmed and cared for since...

Since Joe had died. The thought brought her close to tears again, but she didn't shed them. She finished eating and put on the nightgown Dolly had provided for her. She crawled into the bed, more exhausted than she had imagined. As Dolly started to leave the darkened room, Tess called her back.

"Thank you, Dolly. Thank you, so very much."

"It's nothing, child."

Tess sat up. "Dolly?"

"Yes?"

"I didn't take you from your family, did I?"

She smiled. "Me? No, child. I sit around most of the day and remember Will. My husband. He was with the cavalry, killed just a few years ago. He made it home, though. Jamie Slater brought him home to me. He rode through an ambush to bring Will home. So now I mind the store a few hours a day, and I try to look after the soldiers that need a little mothering. And now you. It's been my pleasure, dear, so you go on and get some sleep."

Dolly was gone then. Tess yawned in the luxurious warm comfort of the clean bed. She stretched out, thinking that she would sleep. If she wasn't plagued with memories of Joe.

But it wasn't memories of Joe that kept her from sleeping. Even in the darkness and the warmth, she felt strange chills snake along her body. It was Jamie Slater's face she saw before her in the darkness, the dry amusement in his gray eyes. Then she remembered the feeling of wicked, surging heat as his gaze fell over the length of her. He had stayed away...

And he had been drawn back. Almost as if he was feeling the same thing.

She didn't need a lover, she told herself. She needed a hired gun. Maybe she would have to barter to gain what she wanted...

Barter! she charged herself.

And in the darkness she admitted that he could be as cold and hard and ruthless as stone, he could care for her not at all, or perhaps even want her with a curious interest.

It didn't matter. She hadn't thought about any man in over five years.

But she wanted this one. That he could deal well with a gun was all the better.

When she finally did sleep that night, it was with the stern reminder that she ought to be saying her prayers. That she ought to hope that Jamie Slater wanted nothing more to do with her, that the stoic colonel would take her to Wiltshire.

She could fight von Heusen, and she would. She just wasn't sure if she could fight von Heusen and all the decadent and shameful things she felt for Jamie Slater at the same time.

It was wicked.

It was true. If Joe had taught her anything, it was wisdom. She couldn't change what she was feeling, even if what she was feeling could only cause her pain.

Exhaustion overwhelmed her, and she slept. Slept, and dreamed. Of smoke-gray eyes, of a man with broad shoulders, taking her into his arms.

Naked, as she had been by the brook.

He was moving into a trap, Jamie thought the next night as he walked along to the Casey house, where Tess Stuart was. He was definitely moving into a trap, because he couldn't call Tess a liar. He did know the Indians well, and he couldn't let a huge war get started because everyone was unjustly blaming the Comanche. He was going to have to find out what had happened.

He paused at the door before knocking upon it, swallowing down a startling, near savage urge to thrust the door open and sweep the challenging and all too luscious Miss Stuart into his arms. No matter how he tried, he could not forget everything that he knew about her. No matter what gingham or frills or lace or velvet adorned her, he kept seeing beneath it.

He'd lied to her. She was very much alive. She spoke of passionate life and living with her every breath, her every word. Her spirit was ever at battle, never ceasing. She would stay on in Wiltshire, he was certain, no matter how stupid it would be for her to do so. She was determined to fight this von Heusen, and she would fight him even if they met on the plain and he was carrying a shotgun and she was completely unarmed.

If...if...Was the man really so dangerous?

He didn't want to believe her. He wanted to be a skeptic. But there was truth in her passion, in her determination. There was truth in the honesty of her beautiful, sea-shaded eyes, eyes that entered into his sleep and made him wonder what it would be like if she looked at him with her hair wound between them and around them in a web of passion.

Every time he was near her he felt it more. Something like a pounding beneath the earth, like a rattle of thunder across the sky. Every time...

And if he didn't watch out, the day would come when he would thrust wide a door and sweep her hard into his arms. He wouldn't give a damn then about Indians or white men or the time of day or even if the earth continued to turn. All that would matter would be the scent of her and the feel of her silken flesh beneath his fingers...

He was going to a dance, he reminded himself. And every officer in the post would be there, and the enlisted men, too. He gritted his teeth and willed his muscles and his body to cease tightening with the harsh and ragged desire that seemed to rule his every thought. He knocked on the door.

"Come in, Lieutenant."

He pushed open the door, irritated that he should want her so badly, determined that he would control himself. She was probably late, women always were. She was probably trying to pin up her hair, or fix her skirts or petticoats.

She wasn't. She was standing silently by the small fire that burned in the hearth. She didn't need to change a thing about her hair—it was tied back from her face with a blue ribbon, then exploded in a froth of sun-colored and honey ringlets. The tendrils curled over her shoulders and fell against the rise of her breasts.

Her gown was soft blue, with a darker colored velvet bodice over a skirt of swirling froth. The sleeves were puffed, baring much of her arms, and the velvet bodice was low, but just low enough to show the rise of her breasts, the beautiful texture of her flesh, the fascinating way the soft curls of her hair lay upon it. She was even more beautiful than he had seen her before, her eyes bright and fascinating with the light of challenge, her smile soft and untouched by tragedy this night.

"You're ready?"

"Yes, of course. You did say sunset, didn't you?"

He nodded. She reached for a blue silk stole and handed it to him. Woodenly he took it from her fingers and set it around her shoulders. The sweet scent of her hair rose against his nostrils, and the essence of it seemed to fill him. Damn. He'd tried so hard to gain control before entering the house. Now the scent of her was tearing through his senses, exciting his temper as well as his passions.

"Shall we go?"

"Yes, of course." Her smile, he decided, was a wanton's. Miss Stuart was not entirely innocent, but rather a woman completely aware of her power. She hadn't become a fluttering belle. Her intelligence was apparent, along with her rock-hard strength, in her steady gaze.

And still...her beauty, her femininity...they were breathtaking. Jon had seen it even when Jamie hadn't.

"Where is the dance?"

"In the alehouse," he said curtly. But then he determined that he knew the game himself; he would play it, too. He smiled graciously, capturing her hand and slipping it around his elbow. "The rest seems to have done you quite well. You're looking wonderfully—healthy."

"Why, thank you, Lieutenant. With such flowery compliments a girl could surely lose her head."

"What a little liar. You wouldn't lose your head if the entire Apache Nation was staring you down, would you, Miss Stuart?"

"There you go again, Lieutenant, what a dazzling compliment."

"Do you need compliments?"

"Maybe."

They had reached the open doors to the alehouse. Already music could be heard, the strains of a lively jig. The notes of the fiddle seemed to be loudest, and for a moment Jamie thought that Tess's smile wavered. He was suddenly displeased with the night, and with himself. She had gone through a harrowing experience, and she had come through it with tremendous spirit.

No more platitudes for this chit! he warned himself. But her eyes met his in the dim light spilling from the open doorway. So deep a blue they were mauve in the darkness, so wide and unwavering upon his. He wished suddenly that she hadn't been young, that she hadn't been beautiful. That she hadn't been different from any other woman he'd ever met in his life.

"Maybe you shouldn't have come tonight," he said softly.

She smiled. "I'm fine, Lieutenant, truly I am. Shall we go in?"

He nodded and escorted her on into the room. Dancers filled the floor, soldiers in uniform, officers with epaulets and brightly colored sashes, women in their sparkling finery. The floor seemed alive with the blue and gold of the uniforms, and with brilliant reds and greens and soft pastels, lovely silks and brocades, satins and velvets.

But none compared with the blue gown that Tess Stuart was wearing. No other garment seemed to so fit a woman, to cling to her shape, to conceal and enhance, to so artfully combine both purity and sweetly simmering sensuality. Like the touch of her fingers upon his arm. Like the scent of roses that seemed to fill him and make him mindless of what else went on.

Jamie saw Jon Red Feather coming toward them, and he swore softly beneath his breath. Normally the darned half-breed was as silent as the night. Suddenly these days he was expounding away with his Oxford eloquence.

"Miss Stuart! Jamie. Ah, you've made it at last. Miss Stuart, please don't think me too bold—Jamie! I dare demand the first dance!"

"Jon—" he began in protest.

"Jon! Good evening!"

The delight in Tess's voice was so obvious that Jamie wanted to spit. If the two of them were so damned all-fired eager to be together, Jon should have escorted her tonight. It wouldn't have made the least bit of difference to him.

The hell it wouldn't. She was his.

He'd found her, he'd touched her and he'd brought her back here. It might be a trap, but he was deep within it now, and there was no crawling out. Still, he had to be civil. Too bad they weren't out on the plain. He and Jon could go to it like savage kids. They'd done it before.

He smiled and bowed with the best of the Southern chivalry he could remember from the days before the war. "Jon—Miss Stuart, please. Just return her in one piece, Jon."

"He's trying to pretend that I take scalps. I don't, you know," Jon informed her gravely.

Tess smiled again—brilliantly. Everything about her lit up. Smiles for him, and taunts for me! And still, Miss Stuart, we are irrevocably bound, aren't we?

"Evenin', James," the colonel addressed him.

"Evenin', sir."

"I see that Miss Stuart has been whisked away." He nodded toward the dancers. "Well, she's lovely. A very welcome addition to our little soiree, eh?"

"Yes, sir."

"Ah! Well, you shan't be lonely long. There's Eliza coming to whisk you away, I dare say."

Eliza was on her way over. She had stopped to chat at the punch table, but now, with her fan fluttering against the heat of the night, she was hurrying around the dancers to greet him. He hadn't seen her since he'd come back with Tess.

But she knew. She knew that he'd come back with a woman, and she knew that he was with Tess tonight. He could see it in her velvet dark eyes. She was smiling, but it seemed that the curve of her lip hid a snarl.

She was still something to behold. Her neck was long and swan-like, her hair as dark as ebony, and though she was slender and graceful, a man could get lost for hours in her voluptuous breasts. Her skin was ivory and flawless, her lips red, her face lovely. Jamie knew she'd had her mind set on tormenting him for some time. He usually enjoyed her company because she was such a brazen piece of baggage. He'd seen her break half a dozen hearts before she'd determined to stomp on his, but he'd always managed to hold his distance from her. To take care that he never spoke a word that sounded like commitment.

He hadn't been able to refuse her constant seduction. He hadn't been her first lover, and he was sure that he wouldn't be her last.

She was especially seductive this evening; her ink-dark hair caught to one side of her head and plunging in a black cascade over one shoulder, her bodice so low-cut as to reveal the endless depths of the valley between her breasts, her kelly-green gown contrasting beautifully with the darkness of her hair and the perfect ivory of her complexion.

"Jamie, darlin'! Well, you have saved the first dance for me. I've missed you so!"

In full view of the company she slipped her arms around him, rose on tiptoe and kissed his lips.

He waited for something to stir inside him. He swore inwardly. It was Tess. He was obsessed, and any other touch would leave him cold until he had quenched that newfound fire...

"Eliza, nice to see you," he murmured, catching her arms and unwinding them from around him. She pouted prettily, but he barely noticed. He was looking past her, toward the dance floor where Tess smiled and laughed, swirled and dipped and whirled in his best friend's arms. They were striking together, the tall half-breed and the exquisite blond who looked so delicate but had a will of pure steel.

"Dance, yes!" he muttered, and he swept Eliza into his arms and onto the floor.

"I was afraid that you hadn't missed me!" she told him, her eyes growing dark.

"What? Of course I missed you," he said.

"You didn't come to see me last night."

"No, I had reports to fill out."

"I waited for you. Very late. Into the night."

"I'm sorry."

"I'll wait again."

It was promising. Maybe he could close his eyes and imagine that he held Tess's sun-honey blondness.

No. It wouldn't be fair.

He smiled. "Eliza, I brought Miss Stuart to the dance."

"Miss Stuart? Oh, yes! I heard about her! The zany woman who thinks white men are Comanche." She shuddered. "Honestly, Jamie, I understand how you might feel responsible, but just walk her home and then come on over."

"Can't, Eliza. Not tonight."

She looked furious for a moment, as if she was about to argue. But she fell silent, pressing closer to him. The musky scent she was wearing rose around him. He felt the pressure of her breasts, the flash of a thigh. She wanted to excite him.

"I'm glad to find you so understanding, Eliza," he said pleasantly.

"Of course. I'm always understanding," she told him gravely, sweetly.

Like hell, he thought. But he smiled. Jon was no longer dancing with Tess.

She'd already danced with half the men in the regiment, Jamie thought irritably. She was in the arms of a young sergeant now, a handsome towhead stripling! A kid who probably hadn't even shaved yet. And he was gushing all over her.

Just about to trip over his own darned tongue.

Jon reclaimed her. Jamie gritted his teeth, determined to watch his date for the evening no more.

He had no way of knowing that Tess Stuart was watching him every bit as covertly. Those strange stirrings rose inside her as she watched the ebony-haired enchantress laughing, pressing against him, heaving her bovine breasts beneath his nose. She was very anxious to be retrieved by Jon, and managed to dance her way over to the tall Sioux.

He promptly cut in and swept her around, smiling like the devil's own disciple.

"Mr. Red Feather?"

"Yes?"

"Who is the massive mount of mammary glands?"

He laughed and bent low to whisper against her ear. "That, Miss Stuart, is Eliza."

He lifted his head again and smiled benignly toward Jamie. "Keep an eye on that one," he warned Tess.

"I certainly intend to," she told him sweetly, then she tossed her hair and laughed, and the sound of her voice was like a melody on the air.

And every man in the place seemed to turn to her.

Including Jamie Slater.

Chapter Four

Tess didn't see how or when Jamie extricated himself from Miss Eliza, but within a few minutes, he was tapping on Jon's shoulder, claiming her for a dance.

She smiled serenely as they moved to the music. He must have attended many of these little balls. He was as accomplished at dancing as he was with riding and shooting. She felt suddenly as if she walked on air herself, as if the room and the people all around them faded, as if they shared more than a simple touch. Maybe they did. His eyes were boring into hers.

"Enjoying your conquests, Miss Stuart?"

She widened her eyes. "Whatever do you mean?"

"I mean every snot-nosed young trooper here is ready to lie down and die for you."

"Really?" she asked with a sweet note of astonishment. "Well, how very genteel of the lads, how kind! But tell me, Lieutenant, how am I doing with the others?"

His jaw twisted slightly, but there was still amusement to his smile.

"The graybeards, Miss Stuart, are quite willing to dig their own graves, if need be, for your cause."

"Oh, dear! Ah, well, let's hope that it need not be. But I'm curious, sir, how am I doing with the men between nineteen and ninety?"

"Would it please you to know that a number of them were probably quite ready to slit one another's throats for the mere bounty of your smile?"

She didn't know if he was teasing. Not anymore. The smoky quality was in his eyes again. She lowered her lashes, shivering slightly, wondering if he was really a man to play with so freely. Then she raised her eyes with a bold and sweeping challenge. "Thank goodness, sir, that you would not participate in such a skirmish! I mean, as one could see how heavily involved you are…"

"What?" he demanded, scowling.

"The bountiful brunette, Lieutenant. Miss Eliza."

"Oh, Eliza."

He said the name dismissively. Too dismissively. He knew Eliza well, maybe better than he wanted to at the moment.

"Yes, Eliza," she said pleasantly. "Are you engaged, Lieutenant?"

"Good heavens, no!"

"Ah, was the horror of that statement over the possibility of engagement, or over Eliza?"

"Miss Stuart, you are very presumptuous."

"Sir, no one is forcing you to dance with me."

His arms tightened around her. He was smiling, but there was a sizzle to the smile, and it sent little shock waves rippling all along her system. Maybe she was playing dangerously. It was delightful. Maybe she risked igniting his temper to extremes she had yet to know. She realized that she was willing to do so, that the storm taking place within her own heart and body was demanding that she do so.

"Miss Stuart, I am your escort to this dance, remember?" he said bluntly.

"Oh…yes, well, I suppose that I had forgotten. When I saw the way your lips became pasted together with Eliza's…"

"Jealous, Miss Stuart?"

"Well, how could I be? I have just entered into your life. I couldn't possibly mean to dissuade you from, er, liaisons you have been nurturing."

She heard the clenching of his teeth. The scowl that tightened his handsome features seemed to reach inside her and take her breath away. She felt his hand upon her waist, warm and powerful, and the fingers of his other hand so tightly entwined with hers that the pressure nearly caused pain. She inhaled a clean scent from him that also seemed to speak of the plain, of the rugged vistas, of the horseman, the marksman. Everything rugged, and everything striking.

He was a real son of a bitch, a small voice warned her.

It didn't matter...

"Do you always hop so recklessly into the fray, Miss Stuart?"

"Whatever do you mean? What fray, Lieutenant?"

"You've barbs on your tongue, ma'am."

"Why, Lieutenant! I'm only speaking frankly."

"Um. I still say there are barbs there. Perhaps I should discover if I am right..."

He was swift on his feet, agile and sure. In a moment he had danced her out the door and into the shadows on the porch. He swept her against a supporting pillar, then his mouth descended upon her, lips parted, parting hers. She had wanted this...this very thing. She had teased and goaded him, and now she had him. But the kiss was no casual dance-floor brush. It was a thing so searingly intimate that she lost all hope of breathing, all hope of standing upon her own two feet. His mouth encompassed hers, drawing from her all strength and will. The heat of his mouth filled and infused her, and his tongue swept by all barriers to ravage and invade.

And she did nothing to stop him, nothing to fight back, nothing to protest even the shocking intimacy of the invasion. He kissed her mouth as if he kissed all of her. His tongue touched every little crevice and nuance of her mouth and thrust with a rhythm that entered into her pulse, into her bloodstream. It was far different from anything she had ever experienced before. Anything. It brought tremors to her limbs and a swirling tempest within her belly; it singed her breasts and weakened her knees.

And worst of all, perhaps, she felt no remorse, no shame. She allowed herself to fall into his arms, to feel his strength support her, the rippling muscles of his chest and thighs...

Then his mouth pulled away from hers. She inhaled raggedly and lifted her eyes to meet his. It had been a game; she hadn't been expecting this, and she was suddenly very afraid that her eyes betrayed the depths of her innocence, of her shock, of the staggering sensations that had taken place within her. His eyes were heavily shadowed, and he didn't look at all like a man about to laugh with the pleasure of an easy conquest, but rather like one consumed with some blinding fury or emotion. But he didn't speak. She wanted to reach up and touch the sandy tendrils of his hair, fallen rakishly over his forehead, but she didn't dare move, she didn't dare touch him again, for there seemed to be something explosive about him.

"There she is!"

The accusing cry seemed to awaken them both. Jamie stepped back, surprised, frowning, looking around.

A plump woman was coming out on the porch. She was small and seemed exceedingly broad. Her hair was snow-white and swept up beneath a little cap, and her dress was old-fashioned, her petticoats as wide as they might have been during the war, her dark fringed stole from an earlier period.

She wasn't alone. People were spilling out behind her.

"Clara," Jamie said softly, still frowning. "Clara, what on earth is wrong?"

Clara seemed not to hear him. She pointed a finger at Tess. "You! You—you harlot! You hussy! You whore! Attacked by Indians, and crying out that white men fell upon you! How dare you! You should have been killed! God will smite you down with an arrow for lying! You trash, you white trash!"

"Clara!" Jamie shouted.

Tess, stunned by the violence of the attack, stared in silence.

"Clara, you're overwrought, but you owe this lady an apology, you can't know—"

"No!" Clara shrieked. "She's the devil's spawn!" Tess realized then that the porch was full of people.

The young soldiers who had been ready to die for her looked as if they'd gladly nail her to the wall.

"How many of us have lost our dear loved ones to the bloody savages? You, Lydia, the Pawnee took your only daughter! Charlie, the Comanche cost you your arm, and Jimmie, your boy Jim went down in that fight with the Apache. Heathens, bloody heathens, all of them! And now she's lying about what happened to her little wagon train. She won't let the men go after the real culprits, she wants a war with the white men! She wants us all at one another's throats so the bloody savages can move right in. She—"

"No!" Tess shouted furiously. "You don't understand, you weren't there, and don't you dare—"

"She ought to be tarred and feathered and thrown right out of here naked as a jay. Then she can run to her Indian buddies."

There was a startled moment of silence. Tess felt certain they were all about to step forward and tear her into little shreds.

"Yes, yes—" Clara began wildly. But she was interrupted.

The sound of a clinking spur struck loudly and discordantly upon the floor as Jamie stepped firmly between Tess and Clara. "That's enough!" Jamie stated flatly. "Clara, I don't know what got you going tonight, but you've no right to judge this girl, none at all. You owe her an apology, and I damned well mean it." He paused. Tess realized that he was looking across the crowd.

Looking straight at Eliza. And there was something about her eyes that told all, even if she tried to stare at Jamie with a look of pure innocence.

She had stirred up the people. Jamie had left her on the dance floor, and dear Miss Eliza had made the rounds, talking to those most vulnerable.

"But what if it is true, Lieutenant? What if Miss Stuart was seeing things? Then the Comanche or some other tribe is on the warpath, and if so, we've got to start fighting back!"

"I'll find out," Jamie said. "I promise you, I'll find out."

There was a gasp from the crowd. The sound had come from Eliza, Tess realized. Her plan had backfired.

Tess wasn't sure what victory she felt. Whatever move Jamie made, he made because he had been forced into it, a gentleman caught by circumstance into defending a lady's honor.

"I'm going to escort Miss Stuart to her home, and I'll look into things there. And I will find out the truth."

By then Jon Red Feather had come to stand next to his friend. It was a casual but defensive gesture. They were shoulder to shoulder. If any fighting had erupted, the handsome half-breed would have been ready. But maybe he had come for more than that. He edged forward, taking Clara's hands. "Give Jamie time," he told her.

The little woman looked up at Jon. "Oh, Jon! I didn't mean you."

"I know," he said, grinning. "I'm only half savage and heathen and barbarian."

She flushed brilliantly. "Jon..."

"It's all right, Clara. Heaven help us, if the Sioux Nation went to war now, I'm not at all sure where I would be at times." He raised his voice. "Every single one of you has, at one time or another, seen some savage injustice done to the Indians! You've been with commanders who think nothing of the murder of women and infants! How in hell can you possibly doubt this story!"

There were murmurs, then the crowd began to clear. Clara started to cry softly.

"I'll take her home," Jon told Jamie.

Jamie nodded. He and Tess watched as Jon escorted her through the alehouse.

"Well, damn it, it's just exactly what you wanted, isn't it?"

He was a far different man from the one who had kissed her with such staggering heat. She stiffened, wishing she could wash the taste of his lips from her own, trying to wipe the taste away with the back of her hand. "What I wanted! No! I never wanted to be called any of those things, Lieutenant, and I certainly never wanted to see an old woman in pain, nor did I ever particularly want to be threatened with being tarred and feathered!"

"You wanted me to go to war with your von Heusen."

"All right, yes! I wanted someone else to stand up against him."

She was backed against the pillar still. Her hands slipped behind her to reach for it for support. He turned on her, coming closer, leaning his hands upon the beam and bringing his face very close to hers. She was trapped by his arms, by the prison of his body. "And now," he said softly, "it's my battle."

"You're the damned cavalry, aren't you? You spent time enough telling me that the day that you dragged me into the dirt!"

"I dragged you into the dirt! Why, you little hellion! You're the one who came after me like a bat out of hell!"

It was there again, that feeling of something entirely combustible between them, of static charging the air, of lightning on a still night. She had to fight back, and quickly and hard, or she would lose everything.

"I was frightened out of my wits," she retorted, "not that you probably weren't worthy of everything I did!"

"Oh? Is that a fact? And have you taken to judging me, Miss Stuart?"

"Why the hell not? You're determined to judge me."

They were silent for a moment, and in that moment, they both heard a throat being cleared. Jamie swung around again. Sergeant Monahan was standing there, red-faced.

"Excuse me, Lieutenant."

"What is it, Monahan?"

"The, uh, the colonel wants to see you."

"Right after I escort Miss Stuart to her house."

"Er, pardon me, sir, but no, sir. The colonel says that I'm to escort her and that you're to see him immediately. About this business of your going to Wiltshire."

Jamie frowned, started to protest, then sighed. He cast Tess a warning glare, although she wasn't at all sure of what the warning was about. She was still trembling, she realized, still holding hard to the pillar.

Jamie bowed to her. "Good night, Miss Stuart. We'll leave as soon as possible."

He walked away with long, angry strides. Tess looked at Monahan. Monahan was watching Jamie go. "Well, that might be one heck of a confrontation," he muttered.

"Why?" Tess asked.

"What? Oh?" Monahan flushed, as if he had just realized she was there. "Why, nothing, miss..."

"Monahan!"

"Well, the colonel may try to stop him from going."

"What do you mean, might try? The colonel outranks him, doesn't he? Or am I missing something?"

"No, no, but Jamie is up for reenlistment. Technically, he could have walked away from the cavalry a month ago. Paperwork gets slow out here sometimes."

"But why would the colonel want to stop him from going?"

"Oh, the colonel probably wouldn't. Not by himself, that is."

"Monahan, you are near to frustrating me to tears! What are you talking about?"

Now Monahan was a brilliant red. He stuttered, then started again. "Miss Eliza is the one who might mind."

"So?"

"Eliza Worthingham."

"Monahan!"

"Oh, you don't know! Why, miss, Eliza is Colonel Worthingham's daughter.'

"Oh!" Tess cried, startled.

"Tarnation, I didn't mean to upset you none. Don't you worry. The lieutenant ain't nobody's fool, and he ain't about to have his life run by a skirt, even if Miss Eliza is a pretty piece of fluff. Ah, hell, not that you're not every bit as pretty—prettier!—but you see my point? He ain't ever gonna have his mind made up by a woman. Not any woman. Oh, dear, this ain't gettin' no better, not one wit! Come on, Miss Stuart, let me do one duty right and get you home for the night!"

"Ah, yes, thank you, I think that I am quite ready to retire," Tess told him.

He walked her through the now empty alehouse and she thought of how disastrously the evening had ended. Then she found that her fingers were fluttering to her lips and that she couldn't forget the way Jamie had kissed her.

She would never forget the way he had kissed her. Not if she never saw him again, not if she lived to be a hundred and two.

He wouldn't ever let himself be run by a woman...That was what Monahan had said. But if he came with her, he would feel he had been trapped into doing it. He had been forced to say he would come with her to calm down Clara.

But if he stayed...

Then it might be worse, because if he stayed after he had stated he would go, it would be because he had been ordered to stay—because of Eliza.

He's torn between the two of us, Tess thought. And which one of us will win?

They had come to the Casey house. Monahan opened her door and lit a lantern for her, then looked around the small building. "Seems clear," he said.

"Why, Lieutenant, this is a cavalry outpost! What would I be afraid of here?"

"Never can be too careful," Monahan said cheerfully. "We learn that out here, ma'am."

"Yes, I'm sure you do," she said softly. "Well, thank you. I do feel quite safe now."

He told her good-night and left. Tess sat down on the foot of the bed and slipped off her black leather dance slippers. Then she paused, feeling as if something in the place wasn't quite right. She stood up and looked around. She hadn't had much brought in from the wagon, but one trunk was shifted away from the wall when she was certain she had left it against the wall. Her brush, which she had set on the small vanity, had fallen to the floor.

She picked up the brush and set it on the vanity. Then she walked over to the trunk and opened it.

It wasn't in wild disarray, but she knew someone had been into it. She always folded her clothing meticulously and kept it in defined piles, her flatiron on the bottom of the chest, her heavy skirts next to it, her light blouses and lingerie on top. Things had been moved.

She sat again. Maybe Monahan was right. You never could be too careful. There was no one in the little house now, but there had been. Who?

Eliza. Tess was certain of it. She smiled. "Eliza," she whispered softly. "I've been dealing with the likes of von Heusen. Fighting you is going to be easy."

She finished undressing, slipped on the borrowed nightgown and crawled beneath the covers. Her eyes wouldn't close, though. She was ready to deal with Eliza...

But what if she had already lost the battle?

There was no way she could know until morning.

It was a horrible night. She kept feeling Jamie's kiss upon her lips again and again...

And no matter how she fought it, she kept imagining that kiss falling against her throat, her palm...and other places.

She slept very late. Despite the bugles and the commotion of a company heading out for a day's scouting, when Tess finally slept, she did so deeply and well.

It was nearly noon when she imagined she heard a sharp rapping on the door. She ignored it. Then she shot up as the door burst open and heavy footsteps fell within the house.

The covers fell away. Her hair was tousled and falling around her shoulders, her gown dislodged from one shoulder and draping precariously low over her breast. Startled and disoriented, she gasped when she saw Jamie Slater in full uniform, his plumed hat low over his eyes, his legs apart and his gloved hands on his hips as he stared at her.

"You," she muttered.

He swept his hat from his head, bowing very low. "Yes, do excuse me, Miss Stuart. I wanted to let you know that we would be leaving at the break of dawn tomorrow. I realize, of course, that dawn might be difficult for you, since you are still abed this midday, but I do intend to leave promptly. Are we understood?"

"Tomorrow! You're still—you're still taking me?"

His eyes narrowed sharply. "I said I was. Why wouldn't I be doing so?"

"No—uh, no reason." She allowed her lashes to fall, shading her eyes. "I was just worried that maybe…that maybe you hadn't meant what you said."

He was silent for a second. "Miss Stuart," he said softly, "I always mean what I say."

"I was just worried that you didn't really want to go—"

"Oh, for God's sake! I'm going. We're going. Tomorrow. That is, if you get up on time."

She smiled, then forgot her animosity toward him, and just about everything else for that matter. She threw back the covers and leaped from the bed and raced toward him, casting herself into his arms. His hands came around her as he held her uptight, his arms wrapping around her.

"Thank you!" she said earnestly. Then she realized what she had done and how she was standing. And that there wasn't much of anything between them. She could feel the pressure of her breasts against the hardness of his body, and she knew that the thin cotton gown wasn't hiding anything of herself.

She backed away, swallowing fiercely. "Thank you," she repeated. "I really do appreciate it. Very much. I don't suppose that you could ever understand, but I do." The gown was falling off her shoulder again. She tried to retrieve it. Then she realized that she was standing in the morning sunlight and that every curve and twist of her form, and even the shadows of her body, would be completely evident to him. And her body was warming, and she was certain that her breasts were swelling, and she was breathing far too quickly, and he could probably see the pounding of her heart.

"Sincerely, thank you." And she was still muttering. A broad grin stretched across his features. She plunged quickly into the bed beneath the covers.

"Miss Stuart?"

"Yes?"

"Do me a favor once we're under way, will you?"

"What's that?"

"Please don't chatter away endlessly like that, huh?"

"I never chatter!" she said indignantly.

"Never?" His brow arched.

She flushed. "Almost never. Lieutenant, do you realize how very rude you're being? You've disturbed my sleep, and now you haven't the decency to leave me alone to dress."

His eyes fell upon her. Lingered over her. He was still smiling. "Do excuse me then, Miss Stuart. But count on this—for the next few days, I'll disturb your sleep often."

He tipped his hat to her and strode from the room. Tess pulled the covers close around her, then she smiled and sank low into the bed.

It was a busy day for Jamie. Jon Red Feather was going to be accompanying him, but other than that, they would travel alone. Since he didn't know quite what he was going to come up against, he spent a fair amount of time determining what he wanted to pack on the supply horses and what he might bring in Tess Stuart's wagon.

Dealing with Colonel Worthingham hadn't been hard. Eliza had been behind the trouble, he had known that. Worthingham might be blind about his daughter, but he was a good officer. Not that Eliza wasn't careful. She had been with Worthingham when Jamie went to see him. She had spoken of the danger, of how Jamie was needed at the post, and she had been so sweet no one might ever have suspected her of having an evil thought.

Worthingham had suggested that another man might do the job; Jamie had politely reminded him that he wasn't officially in the cavalry anymore, and that had done the trick. He had three months now, three months on his own.

And Jon was his own man. He always had been. Jamie was glad Jon was coming along, even if he was being a thorn in Jamie's side over Tess. As if the minx needed any champions. The girl did know how to fight her own battles.

He didn't want to battle, he thought. He closed his eyes, then remembered the way she had looked that morning, half dressed and completely seductive, the outline of her delineated by the sunlight against the soft white cotton. And she had smiled and thrown herself into his arms. He remembered the taste and feel and texture of her and had known that he had to get out of the room before he took a running leap and fell upon her in the disarray of her gown and covers.

He was a fool. He should be steering as clear of her as he could. Instead, he had given his word to take her to Wiltshire. And he kept his word.

There was just so much he wanted from her in return. And she was desperate enough to give it.

That wasn't the way he wanted her, he told himself. But then he reflected that he wanted her in any way possible, and he wasn't quite sure ethics entered into the question.

And he had to stop thinking about her. He clenched his teeth and set to work.

It took most of the day to requisition the weapons and ammunition he wanted to take. It was dark by the time he was ready to return to his rooms. He wanted a good dinner and a long, hot bath before he started out on the trail.

His orderly would have arranged for his bath. When he opened the door to his office and saw that the lantern had been lit and a steaming hip bath set in the bedroom, he breathed a sigh of relief. He tossed his hat onto a chair, unbuckled his scabbard and holster and set his weapons on his desk. He pulled off his boots and left them where they fell. By the time he reached the doorway to the bedroom, his shirt was unbuttoned and he was flinging it on the floor. He was anxious for the bath.

But then he paused in his trousers, his eyes narrowing. He wasn't alone. Eliza was in the bedroom. And Eliza had been in his bath. She was curled up on his bed, her dark hair damp and forming tiny ringlets to frame her face. She wasn't exactly naked, but her appearance would have been less decadent if she had been. She was wearing a lace corset he could almost see through, and which lifted her cleavage to bold new heights. She wore some kind of silk and lace pantalets, and nothing else.

"I came to say goodbye," she told him huskily.

"Eliza, you're a fool," he told her irritably. "What the devil do you think you're doing in my room?"

"Aren't you glad to see me?"

"Frankly, no."

She curled up on the bed, watching him like a cat. "I'm not letting you go off with that little blond slut."

"Eliza, take a look at yourself and think about what you're saying."

"I'm in love with you!" She stood and walked toward him, swaying, her lips parted and damp. "I'm in love with you, Jamie, why do you think I've made love with you? Do you think a secret rendezvous is all right, but you're afraid of me being here because of my father?"

She had reached him. She started to slip her arms around his neck, but he caught her hands. "Eliza, I'm not afraid of your father. You should be. He'd send you back east in two seconds if he had the least idea about your trysts."

"He'd make you marry me!"

"No one will ever make me marry anyone."

"You owe me!" She pouted. "Jamie, I've lain with you—"

"Hm. And half of Companies C, D and E," he agreed.

She freed a hand, ready to slap him. He caught her hand, and for a moment they were very close. Then he saw her smile. Smile like a wanton, with tremendous pleasure. She was looking over his shoulder.

Tess was standing in the doorway. Chaste and beautiful with her golden ringlets piled atop her head, her pure white blouse buttoned to the throat, her full skirt navy and subdued, her only jewelry a brooch at her throat.

She stood there, very still.

"I was told by a young officer that you wanted to see me here, Lieutenant. I wouldn't have been so careless as to enter myself, but he pushed open the door, and so here I am, to my great embarrassment. Good evening, Miss Worthingham. Lieutenant, did you send for me?"

"I did not!"

"Then I must offer my apologies. Excuse me."

She turned.

"Wait a minute!" Jamie thundered.

Tess ignored him.

Eliza was laughing softly. He caught her and shook her hard. "You did this!"

"Mm. You'll never get beneath her skirts now, Jamie!" Eliza said happily.

Jamie didn't reply. He shoved her from him and walked away. He didn't give a damn that he was barefoot or bare-chested; he was just glad he still had his trousers on. He didn't know why it was so damned important that he catch Tess, he only knew that it was.

"Tess!"

She was walking away from him, ignoring him. He caught up with her and took hold of her shoulders, swinging her around. "Tess!"

"What?" She wrenched herself from his hold.

He circled her, determined to catch her if she moved. "I called you! Why the hell didn't you stop?"

Tess looked at him, wishing she could be half as calm or serene as she was pretending.

She hadn't suspected a thing. The young soldier had appeared at her door just minutes ago, and he had been very proper, and she had imagined his mission to be a true one. Lieutenant Slater had requested her presence at his office. She hadn't even known that his office and his bedroom were connected.

And she had thought that the summons sounded just like Jamie. He would give her some other trivial order about the next morning. Don't oversleep, don't be late, don't touch anything of mine that I set in your wagon.

And so she had come without a thought. Without a single thought.

She had never imagined what it would feel like to see him in another woman's arms. It had been awful seeing the brunette worse than naked, draped all over him. Her hair curling over his naked flesh. Her breasts cast against him, his arms locked upon her, the fever between them...

She inhaled and exhaled. She wondered if she had heard the words right between them. No one can make me marry anyone. That was what he had said to her. Wasn't it?

They had been lovers. He had all but admitted it. And maybe they would be again. Maybe he would take Tess to Wiltshire, and he would come back...

Maybe he shouldn't go to Wiltshire. Because if he did, if they were together, they would become lovers. And maybe he would be just as cool to her. Maybe making love meant nothing at all to him, when the desire within her was something that had never happened before. It was special, unique, precious.

But then again, she couldn't allow the brunette to win the game. Not this way. She didn't deserve to win anything this way.

"Damn you, Tess, will you listen to me?"

"I don't see what difference it makes, but go ahead."

He stared at her hard. "That was a setup."

She didn't reply. He caught her shoulders again, pulling her against him. "I'm telling you, it was a setup!"

She still didn't reply, and he looked into his eyes and swore suddenly. "Why the hell am I explaining this to you? Think what you want, Miss Stuart. To hell with you."

He left her standing in the street. She heard his angry stride as he started away.

"Lieutenant!" she called. She didn't turn around until she sensed that he had stopped. Then she turned to meet his eyes. "I'm very aware that what I just saw was a setup. I'm sorry for Miss Worthingham, that she felt it necessary to put on such a show. Perhaps you might want to provide her with a bit more tenderness or care."

He swore and walked away.

Tess smiled and started to her room. But then her smile faded. It had been a setup, but she had sent him right back to the enemy's arms.

When she went to bed that night she lay awake in torture, wondering what had happened next. She had advised him to offer tenderness.

Had he done so? Had he slept with the bewitching brunette in his arms, against his heart?

She tossed and turned in wretched anxiety and she very nearly overslept. If it wasn't for the timely arrival of Dolly Simmons, she would have done so.

"Up, up, now, Tess, dear! This is the cavalry, you know! Things are done by the dawn here. Lieutenant Slater will want to be on his way!"

Dolly had brought coffee. She slipped a tin mug into Tess's hands, then, chatting, picked up things in the room. "What are you wearing, dear, this nice brown cotton? Perfect choice for a hot day on the trail. And just one petticoat—no corset, of course. You'll be much more comfortable that way. Come on, now, Lieutenant Slater and Jon Red Feather are already out by the wagon."

Tess gulped down the coffee and was grateful when Dolly helped her slip into the brown traveling dress she had chosen. Then she frowned, realizing that Dolly was dressed for travel in a mauve suit with a huge, wide-brimmed hat on her head.

"Dolly?"

"I'm coming with you, my dear."

"You are?"

"Yes. You don't mind, do you?"

"No, no, I don't mind. It's just that..." She paused. In the outpost, it had almost been possible to forget that von Heusen offered death.

"Dolly, no one wants to believe me, but it could be very dangerous for you."

"Miss Stuart!" Dolly drew herself up and looked terribly dignified—and menacing. It would take a hearty soul to go to battle against Miss Simmons. "I have met danger all my life. I have lived in places that would make the ordinary woman's skin crawl. I have fought Apache, Comanche, Shoshone, Cheyenne and Sioux. I think that I will hold my own wherever I may go." She was quiet for a minute. "And besides," she added softly. "I've really nothing left here. I'd like to come with you. I'm a wicked good cook, and I can organize any type of household in a matter of hours."

Tess smiled. "Dolly, you're welcome," she assured her.

She finished dressing quickly and stuffed the last of her belongings in a portmanteau. She and Dolly gave the room a last look, then they departed together.

She almost didn't recognize Jamie when they came to the wagon. Instead of a uniform he wore a blue denim work shirt and pants and his knee-high boots. His sandy hair fell over his eyes as he cinched the girth on his huge horse, then cast her a quick stare. "It's about time."

"It's barely dawn."

He didn't reply, but nodded Dolly's way. He must have known that the older woman had determined on coming, because he didn't say a word about her appearance.

"Get up—I want to get started. Jon and I will take turns driving with you—there's no reason for you to completely destroy your hands again. And for God's sake, keep your gloves on."

"I can manage—"

He caught her arm as she was about to crawl up. "And don't tell me that anymore. I know you can manage. It's just that you can manage better if you listen to me. Got it?"

She saluted, gritting her teeth. "Got it, Lieutenant."

She climbed up and took the reins and Dolly got up beside her. The mules were harnessed, Jon was mounted and two packhorses were tethered to the rear of the wagon. All was ready for their departure.

Colonel Worthingham walked up as they were about to leave. "Goodbye, Miss Stuart, good luck."

"Thank you, sir."

"Lieutenant, Red Feather, take care. Remember, we're here if you need us."

"Thank you, sir!" Jamie wasn't in uniform, but he saluted smartly. The colonel stepped back.

"Jamie! Jamie, take care!" Eliza ran dramatically from the shadow of the command post. She raced to Jamie's horse and clutched his hands where they lay casually over the reins.

"Eliza, thank you, I'll be just fine," he said harshly.

"Eliza, come back, darlin'. Lieutenant Slater has ridden out again and again. You know he always makes it back." The colonel set his hands on his daughter's shoulders, drawing her back. Eliza didn't even glance at Tess, but Tess felt the hostility that rose from her.

She wondered again about what had happened after Jamie had left her last night, and she was infuriated that it should bother her so much, that it should hurt and dig into the very center of her being.

Maybe he would turn around now. Eliza was stunning this morning, her hair ebony against a yellow dress, her eyes huge with anguish. Tess held her breath. Then she realized that Jamie had picked up his reins, that he was shouting to her, telling her they were going.

She called out to the mules. The wagon rumbled forward.

She didn't look back. She followed Jamie and Jon Red Feather through the open gates of the compound, and she sighed with a soft sound of relief as she heard the gates closing behind her. They were really on their way. Jamie Slater was coming with her. Eliza hadn't been able to convince him to stay.

About last night...

She didn't know. She just didn't know. She needed a gun, she reminded herself. She needed a gunman.

It didn't matter that she wanted the man...

If rumor was right, he was one of the fastest guns in the west.

Maybe fortune was beginning to smile upon her just a little.

And maybe, just maybe, she was setting herself up for the heartbreak of a lifetime.

She couldn't think, and she couldn't worry. He was with her, and they were on their way, and for now, that just had to be enough.

Chapter Five

Jamie Slater didn't seem to do anything by half measures. When he set out to move, he moved.

They pushed hard throughout the morning, either Jamie or Jon riding ahead to scout out the road, the other riding with Dolly and Tess. Jamie was true to his word—somewhere around midmorning he called a halt, and Jon came up to take over the reins of the wagon. Dolly and Jon were comfortable together, old friends who knew one another well and respected what they knew. And both of them seemed genuinely fond of Tess, which was nice.

Dolly was full of stories. She didn't chatter, but she kept Tess amused with tales of Texas in times before Tess had been born. "Why, Will and I came out here long before Texas was a state. Before there was a Republic of Texas! And long, long before the Alamo. Why, I remember some of those boys, and it was a privilege to know them. Mountain men, they were good men. They were the stuff that Texans were made of. Will missed being at the Alamo by just a hairbreadth. He'd been sent out to deal with Cheyenne. By the time he came back, the boys were dead. They say that Davey Crockett was killed there, but that ain't true. The Mexicans took him prisoner, and they tortured him to death, that was what the boys said. He was a fiery old cuss. They never broke him. You can't break a mountain man. You can kill him, but you can't break him. Kind of like a Blackfoot, eh?"

"A Blackfoot—or an Englishwoman, eh, Dolly?" Jon agreed, grinning.

Dolly chuckled gleefully and agreed.

Tess found herself studying Jon's handsome features. There was no denying that the man had Indian blood, proud blood. His cheek-bones were wide and broad, his flesh was dark bronze. And his hair, too, was Indian, black as ink and straight as an arrow. But his eyes were a deep, startling green.

He caught her studying him, and she blushed. "I'm sorry. I didn't mean to be rude."

"It's all right. You're welcome to wonder about me. I'll tell you, because I like you. My father was a Blackfoot chief. My mother was the daughter of an English baronet."

"A baronet?"

"Um. Sir Roger Bennington. Actually, he's a very decent old fellow." He smiled.

"What does that make you?"

Jon laughed softly. "A half-breed Blackfoot. Sir Roger did not marry his daughter to an Indian. She was kidnapped, but she dis-covered that she was in love with my father. She stayed with the Blackfoot until my father was killed. Then she went back to England. She died there."

"I'm sorry."

"Don't be. They were both happy while they lived."

Tess hesitated. "Did you go to England with her? Is that where you acquired your accent?"

"My accent?" he repeated.

"Well, you don't sound like a Texan or an Indian."

"I'm not a Texan, except by choice for the moment. I was born in the Black Hills. And my father was still alive when I went to England. My mother convinced him that a half-breed needed every advantage. My mother knew that the Indian's day was dying. That the buffalo were being slaughtered. That the white men were going to push west, and push us west, until we were pushed right into the sea or given desert land as our reservations. Our prisons."

He spoke hard words, but he spoke them softly. "You don't seem very bitter," Tess commented.

"Bitter? I'm not. Bitterness is a wasted emotion. I ride with Jamie now because I choose to be with him. Some time this year, I'll go back to my father's people. And if the whim takes me, I'll go visit my grandfather in London. I enjoy the theater and opera there, and Grandfather is a hardy old cuss. I think he's actually damned pleased when people stare at his Indian grandson. Actually, I wear formal clothing rather well.'' He grinned ruefully, but then his grin faded as he studied her. ''I love the west, too. I love horses, and the feel of a good one racing beneath me. I love my tribe, and I love this harsh, dry land. And I've stayed with Jamie because he knows people. He's spent most of his life fighting, but he still knows people. He goes to war with men, but he never attacks children.''

He gazed at her curiously, looking her up and down, studying her. ''Jamie believes you. He's come into Indian villages and seen what certain white men are capable of leaving behind. There are many men in the cavalry who think that an infant Indian is still an Indian, and that it will grow to put an arrow in someone's back. There was a lieutenant who liked to order his soldiers to shoot the women, then bash the infants' heads together to save bullets.''

''God, how awful.''

''Jamie knows about things like that. God knows, he saw enough of it during the war.''

''There was nothing like that during the war—''

''Jamie came from the Kansas and Missouri border. There was all kinds of stuff like that.''

''Yes, but the war's over now,'' Dolly interrupted matter-of-factly. ''We need to put it behind us. Bless us and save us! It's been five years! And Mr. Grant is president now—''

''Mr. Grant could use some help out here in the west,'' Jon said dryly. He smiled again at Tess. ''Ever been to London?''

She shook her head. ''I've never been out of Texas.''

''Now that is a great loss. A girl like you ought to see the world.'' Jamie was heading toward them. ''Miss Stuart, you are welcome to travel with me at any time, in fact, I'd consider it quite an honor.''

Jamie was scowling. Tess lowered her lashes, knowing that Jon had said the words strictly for Jamie's benefit.

Jamie's great roan stallion was prancing around. ''We seem to be clear for quite a while ahead. Jon, want to ride again? I'll take over the reins for a while.''

''Sure thing.'' Jon pulled in on the reins. He started to hop down while Jamie dismounted from his horse. Tess looked at Jamie. ''I do appreciate your concern, but I've scarcely taken the reins myself—''

"Miss Stuart, I'll drive the wagon for a while now. After all, we wouldn't want to ruin the hands of a newspaper woman."

Dolly slapped her on the knee. "You let him drive!" she said, then she yawned. "I think I'll ride in back for a while." She smiled at Tess like a self-satisfied cat and crawled into the back of the wagon. Tess watched her stretch out on Uncle Joe's bunk. Jamie climbed up beside her and took the reins. Jon had untied his pinto from the back of the wagon. "I'll ride on ahead," he said.

Jamie nodded. Tess was left alone beside Jamie, very aware of the heat of his thigh despite the heat of the day.

They rode in silence, and the silence seemed to stretch on and on. Finally Jamie drawled out, "You made it on time this morning. Did you manage to have a good night's sleep?"

"Yes, I did," she lied pleasantly. She turned to him with her eyes innocently wide. "What about you, Lieutenant? Did you manage to have any sleep at all?"

He studied her eyes, then smiled slowly. "Yes, I slept." He didn't elaborate and Tess was infuriated. She wanted some kind of an answer on this subject, and he was determined not to give her one.

"You seem to have been having a darned nice morning," he commented.

"Have I?"

"I've known Jon Red Feather a long time now. I've never known him to talk so much."

"He's charming."

Jamie grunted. He flashed her a quick gaze and gave his attention to the road once again. "And I'm not?"

"No. You're impudent, insolent and a royal pain, Lieutenant Slater."

"Oh, is that so? Then why were you so anxious for my company?"

She inhaled sharply, staring at him. "Because you can shoot," she said flatly.

"Why, thank you, Miss Stuart! Thank you kindly. And you threw yourself right into my arms the other morning, half naked and all, just because I shoot."

"Right. Wrong! I was not half naked—"

"You felt as if you were."

"Lieutenant, you are a scurvy, low-down, no-good rodent—"

"But a no-good rodent who can shoot, right?"

"Precisely, Lieutenant," she said with a touch of silk. He nodded, looking ahead.

"You are awfully determined to stay in Wiltshire, Miss Stuart. Couldn't you run a newspaper somewhere else?"

"I could. But I wouldn't own the good cattle land that Joe—" She paused. "Well, it's all mine now."

"Is your life worth the land?"

"You don't understand. It's not just the land. Somebody needs to stand against this man."

"You do want it desperately."

He was watching her curiously, the hint of a curve to his lips. She frowned, wondering what he was up to.

"Yes. I do want it desperately. He killed Joe. He might not have ridden with the men, but he killed Joe. And I'm going to bring him down."

"With the help of a scurvy rodent who can shoot."

"With whatever help I can get. And you do believe me about the attack, I know you do."

He shrugged. "Maybe. I've still got my reservations, but I do intend to go into Wiltshire with you."

"And that's all?" she asked, horrified.

He smiled. "Just what, Miss Stuart, do you want out of me? Spell it out. We might need to come to a few terms here."

"But, but—" she sputtered. "But you said you'd find out the truth! You told Clara—"

"I told Clara I'd find out the truth. I didn't tell her that I'd go to war on your behalf."

"Bastard!" Tess spat out the epithet.

"Calm down, Miss Stuart! Such language from a very proper and genteel young Southern woman! I told you, say what you want, and we'll take it from there."

"What I want? Well, I...I want you to stay! Then when he sends his guns, I'll have my guns!"

"Jon Red Feather and I against a horde of hired gunmen. Mm. I should stand tall and let this man pump me full of bullets for the benefit of having you call me a scurvy rodent?"

Tess caught her breath and tried to control her temper. She lowered her lashes and counted to ten, then kept going to twenty, then started all over again because he was laughing at her. She moved suddenly, and he must have thought that she meant to strike him because he cast an imprisoning arm around her. She stiffened in his hold. "Lieutenant, this is completely unnecessary."

"Is it? I can't help but feel cautious around you, Miss Stuart."

She swore softly.

He laughed.

"Go ahead! Laugh!" she said angrily. "And just run like a cur with its tail between its legs when we get to Wiltshire."

"A cur? I thought I was a rodent."

"I can't find words for what you are, Lieutenant."

"Pity," he drawled. His eyes were on her, smoke and fire. His arm was warm and strong around her. The heat of the sun bore down on them, and she felt as if it touched her and brought a liquid rush throughout her. She could not draw her eyes from his, nor could she dispel the sudden, brilliant memory of his lips upon hers.

"We could bargain, Miss Stuart."

"Bargain?"

"Yes. If I'm going to die, I'd like it to be for a little more than a smile."

She stared at him. She felt a heat like that of the sun suffuse throughout her body, bringing a rampant beat to her heart, a flood of burning red to her cheeks and a tremor deep inside her. He could only mean one thing, she was certain. If he was going to stay, he wanted her.

She should have been outraged. She should have been able to say that he could be damned, that her honor was worth far more than her life.

Except that...

There was something that washed over the outrage like the deep, rich waves of the ocean. It was the same thing that caused the pulse to beat ever more fervently in the column of her throat, the thing that held her speechless. He watched her, that wry smile twisted so tauntingly into his features. He was horrid. He was awful.

He was exciting, sensual, masculine. The scent of him beguiled

her, just as his arms beckoned and just as his kiss evoked feelings
inside that she would never be able to forget.

She couldn't just stare at him. She moistened her lips and swallowed quickly, vowing that she would never let him know just how
deeply he did affect her.

"Did you bargain with Miss Eliza, Lieutenant?"

"Is she still on your mind?"

"Is she on yours?"

He cast back his head and laughed.

"The situation is not at all amusing, Lieutenant."

"Oh, but it is, Miss Stuart, it's very rich. As you might have
noticed, I didn't really need to bargain with Miss Worthingham. If
that's what you were inferring. And yet, I didn't happen to mention
yet what our bargain should be. Alas, I could see it in those huge,
innocent, violet eyes! He wants to sully my honor, this cavalry man.
For the price of a pair of spitting Colts! Her heart beats, and she
wonders—my cause! This is my cause! Shouldn't I lay down my
honor and my pride, and give all to this wretched rodent—all for
my cause?"

"Someone should shoot you," Tess warned him.

"Well, you're trying to make me into a target, aren't you? Ah,
but then maybe, just maybe, I could die with the exquisite Miss
Stuart's kiss still damp upon my lips…"

She squirmed. She did intend to slap him.

"Whoa, Miss Stuart!" He laughed, and his arm wound even
tighter against her. They were sitting like newlyweds, she thought
disgustedly. She was halfway atop his lap and she could barely
move.

"Lieutenant, you're squashing me!"

"I'm trying to save my jaw, Miss Stuart! Now calm down. You
are desperate, aren't you?" His eyes looked into hers, and a hard
note crept into his voice. "You would do anything—anything at all
that I asked. How very intriguing."

"Jamie Slater—"

"Jamie!"

A sharp call from Jon caught their attention. Jamie's arm fell from
around her shoulder, and he leaned forward, reining in. Jon was
riding hard toward them.

"What is it?"

"Company," Jon said.

"Comanche?"

"Yep."

"How many?"

"Fifty at least. They're covering the hill over the next dune."

"Is it a war party?"

"They're out in feathers and paint, but I think it's a show. I'm pretty sure it's Running River."

Tess watched as Jamie climbed from the wagon. She wondered if she should be frightened, and she wondered with greater exasperation if he should be walking away from her without a thought. He disappeared behind the wagon, then reappeared on his roan.

"Let's go see Running River," he told Jon.

"Wait a minute—" Tess began.

"You wanted to drive the wagon," Jamie called. "Pick up the reins. Drive."

Then he turned, and he and Jon raced forward. Swearing beneath her breath, Tess picked up the reins and called to the mules. They started plodding along.

Dolly crawled into the seat, puffing. "Comanche! Never did trust 'em."

The mules pulled the wagon over the dune. Tess felt as if her heart stopped, as if it caught in her throat.

The Comanche seemed to stretch as far as the eye could see. Bare-chested, in buckskin pants, with various types of feathers banded around their heads, they sat as still as ghosts. Many carried spears and shields, others wore quivers at their backs and held their bows proudly.

Not one moved.

They just sat on their horses, looking down at the small party that approached.

Tess wondered dismally if she was about to become the victim of a real Indian. Her heart thundered, and she dropped the reins. Jon and Jamie had pulled in before them, and they sat on their horses on the dune, watching the Comanche.

The sky seemed afire with the morning light. Earth and horizon seemed to stretch together in shades of dusty coral and crimson and gold. The quiet was eerie; not even the wind whispered in the sage-brush.

Then Jamie lifted his hand in some kind of greeting. A loud, shrieking cry sounded from atop the hill.

And then the Comanche were coming.

Tess screamed as the Indians started toward them in a blazing cloud of dust, their whoops and cries loud. No one could ride like a Comanche. The men lay braced against their ponies' necks, they swung beneath them, they righted themselves again. They came closer and closer. Their cries sounded ever louder.

Ever more deadly.

"My God, we're going to be butchered!" Tess breathed.

"No, no, I don't think so," Dolly told her calmly. Astonished, Tess stared at the woman. "Well, it's Running River. He and Jamie are blood brothers."

"Blood brothers," Tess repeated.

"Yes. The Comanche are warlike, of course. But not this tribe. Running River has been peaceful since Jamie came out here. He always deals with the lieutenant, and though there have been Comanche attacks, they've never been perpetrated by Gray Lake Comanche."

Tess was still unconvinced. There had never been a Comanche attack on Wiltshire—in fact some Comanche even came to town for work now and then—but she had heard about the things that could happen, and watching the extraordinary horsemen bear down upon them did nothing to ease her spirit.

"My God..." she breathed, sitting very still.

The riders were circling the wagon, shaking their spears and bows in the air. Now that they were closer, she could see that their faces and chests were painted in brilliant colors. She didn't move, although she didn't know if it was courage or pure terror that kept her still. She could see Jon and Jamie, still mounted, as they watched the thundering horses and their riders. Neither reached for a weapon.

It would be suicide, she thought. They were drastically outnumbered.

The Indians raced by them. The whoops and the cries were suddenly stilled, and there was silence. Only the dust remained to settle.

The Comanche were motionless again, surrounding the wagon and Jamie and Jon.

As Tess watched, Jamie lifted his hand again.

One of the Indians, his ink-black hair falling down the length of his naked back, wearing a band with a single dark feather, urged his mount closer. He walked his horse straight over to Jamie. Then he reached out his hand, and Jamie clasped it.

The Indian began to speak. Tess didn't recognize a word, but Jamie and Jon paid rapt attention.

Then Jamie responded in the Indian's own tongue, easily, effortlessly. Jon spoke, too, then the Comanche again.

"See," Dolly whispered. "It was a show. It was a performance. There never was any danger."

Tess exhaled silently. One question had been answered for her. She'd seen something like this before, but there had been differences. She'd seen the riders—but with saddled horses, in wigs and feathers and paint. They hadn't ridden like these Comanche. And they hadn't let out the terrible cries. They had been absolutely mute, carrying out their silent executions.

But she had a right to be afraid of this show.

"What's going on?" she asked Dolly.

"How should I know, dear? I don't speak that heathen gibberish!"

Tess stiffened, realizing that Jamie was gesturing to her.

The Indian he was talking to urged his pony toward her, followed closely by Jamie. Reining to a halt in front of her, the Comanche stared at her. He started to speak. Tess swallowed. He was lean, wiry, menacing in his paint, and yet when he spoke he smiled, and his teeth were good and strong, and the smile gave some strange appeal to his face.

Tess smiled in return. "What did he say?" she asked Jamie, between her teeth.

"He said that he did not kill your uncle."

"Tell him I know that."

Jamie spoke, then the chief broke into a barrage of words again. Lost, Tess kept nodding and smiling.

"What did he say now?"

"Oh. Well, I told him we were traveling to Wiltshire, and that I was going to try to prove that the white man had been guilty. If you made it worth my while, that is. The chief is suggesting that you make it worth my while. He thinks that you should bargain with me.''

"Oh!" Tess gasped furiously. As she frowned, the Comanche chief frowned, too.

"Oh, my, my!" Dolly murmured beneath her breath.

"Smile, Tess!" Jamie suggested casually.

She smiled. She locked her teeth, and she smiled. The chief spoke again, quietly.

"What did he say?" Tess demanded.

Jamie didn't answer her.

Jon did. "He said that you were very beautiful, and that Jamie should take good care of you."

The chief took Jamie's outstretched hand again, then lifted his spear high and cast back his head. A loud, startling cry rent the air. Then the riders were kicking up tremendous clouds of dust again, and racing across the plain. Moving like quicksilver, they touched the landscape and were gone. They disappeared over the hill from which they had come.

Then, slowly, the dust settled again.

Jamie turned to the wagon. "Come on, ladies. Let's make a little time here, shall we?"

Tess caught hold of the reins, called out to the mules and snapped the leather in a smart crack. The animals started off with a jolt.

A little while later, Jon rode by the wagon. He smiled to Tess and Dolly. "Ladies, are you both all right?"

"Just fine, Jon," Dolly told him.

"Tess?"

She nodded gravely. "Jon, was Jamie telling the truth?" She flushed slightly. "Did he tell me the truth about all the chief's words?"

Jon hedged slightly. "More or less. Running River went a little bit further than Jamie told you."

"Oh?"

Jon shrugged. "He said that it might have been Apache that attacked you. The Apache have refused any treaties, they are constantly warlike, and stray bands have been known to travel in this area frequently. The Comanche and the Apache have often been enemies.''

"Does Jamie know the Apache as well as he knows this Running River?''

"No. The Apache do not want to be known.''

Tess shivered, and Jon quickly amended his statement. "He does know a few of the warriors and chiefs. They will at least talk to him. He speaks the Apache language as well as he does the Comanche.''

"It's all heathen gibberish to me!'' Dolly announced.

Jon grinned at Tess, and Tess felt somewhat better. There was something very reassuring about Jamie's abilities. Maybe it could be proven that the Apache were no more guilty of the attack than the Comanche.

Jon waved and rode on ahead.

"I'll take the reins for a bit now,'' Dolly told her.

"You don't need to—''

"I'll be bored as tears if I don't put in my part, dear. Now hand them over.''

Tess grinned and complied.

They rode until sunset, then until the first cooling rays of the night touched them. Jamie and Jon knew the terrain. Again, they knew where to find water.

Tess climbed from the wagon the minute they stopped, stretching, trying to ease the discomfort in her back. Jamie pointed out the path through the trees to the little brook, and she started out in silence, aware that Dolly followed her.

The water moved over rock and along the earth, barely three inches of it, but she cupped her hands into it and drank thirstily, then splashed in huge handfuls over her face and throat, heedless that she soaked her gown. Beside her, Dolly dipped her handkerchief in the water and soaked her face and throat and arms with it. "Ah, the good lord doth deliver!'' she said cheerfully. "Jamie! Come on in, the water's fine, Lieutenant!''

Tess froze, aware only then that Jamie was standing silently behind her. Dolly hefted up her bulk. "Guess I'll head back and see if Jon's got a cooking fire started yet.''

She stepped by. Jamie knelt in Dolly's place. He doffed his hat and untied the kerchief from his throat, then soaked it as Dolly had. He leaned low and plunged in his whole head, then rubbed the kerchief over his throat and shoulders. Tess stared at him, unaware that she did so.

He smiled, watching her. She jumped slightly when he touched her cotton-clad shoulder.

"You're soaked," he told her.

"I suppose so."

He grinned, recalling memories of a different brook, a different time. "I rather like you wet."

"You—"

"Ah, now, please, Miss Stuart!"

She fell silent, but his smile faded and he sat on his haunches, folding his hands idly over his knees.

"We've got to talk, Tess."

She didn't intend to blush, but color rose swiftly to her cheeks. Damn him!

"What?" she said harshly.

"Well, I'm waiting to find out if you're going to bargain with me or not."

She was silent, feeling her body burn.

"Well?"

"You are a bastard."

"Come, come, now, Miss Stuart, will you bargain?"

She leaped to her feet. "Yes!" she spat at him. "Yes—and you were right, you knew damned well that I would do so. I am desperate. You can have anything. Anything that you want."

She swung around in what she hoped was indignant fury. She was suddenly blinded. She nearly tripped as she started forward. She reached for a branch to steady herself.

"Miss Stuart!" he called to her lightly.

"Oh, for God's sake! What now?" she demanded.

"Well, pardon me, but you didn't wait to hear just what it was that I wanted."

"What?" she gasped.

"I said—"

"But, but…"

She stared at him. He was still seated so comfortably on the ground, casual now, idly chewing upon a long blade of grass. "But, but, but, Miss Stuart! Where is your mind, dear lady, but deep, deep down in the gutter?"

He stood. Warily she backed away from him. "Listen, Lieutenant, I'm not sure that you do shoot well enough for all this! What do you want now?"

She backed straight into a tree. He was right in front of her, smiling. He stroked her cheek lightly with his knuckle and laughed softly as she indignantly twisted her face to the side.

"Still waters do run deep, eh, Miss Stuart? You ready to listen?"

"What—"

"Land."

"What?" she repeated, dazed.

"Land. I want some acreage. Some of your prime acreage, and maybe a few cattle. If I'm going to go out and die for this land, I'd like to have a bit of it in my own name."

"That's—that's what you want?"

"That's it."

"Land?"

"Land, Miss Stuart. I know you've heard the word."

She pressed against the tree, slipping her hands behind her to hold furtively to keep herself from falling. Then a crimson blush surged to her cheeks again, and she raged out in a tempest. "You! You made me think that—oh, God! You are the lowest, most horrid, most terrible—"

"Disappointed?" he interrupted pleasantly.

She shrieked something unintelligible and swung at him. He caught her hand before she could strike him, but she continued to pit herself against him. He pulled her against him, lacing his arms around her.

"Don't be angry—"

"Angry! I could gouge out your eyes—"

"Ouch! It would be hard as hell for me to aim at this von Heusen of yours if you did that."

"I could shoot off both your knee caps!"

"Then how could I get places to find out the truth?"

"All right! All right! You fight von Heusen, *then* I'll gouge out your eyes and shoot your knee caps. Now let go of me!"

"No, not yet, I'd be risking my eyesight, I'm afraid. Or my— ouch!'' he said as she stamped on his foot. Her feet were dangerous. And her knees.

"Don't even think about it!'' he warned her, pressing her so close against the tree trunk that she could barely breath. Nor could she kick him—his thigh was pressed close to hers. Her breasts heaved with agitation; her heart was thundering. His lips were close. So close to hers. He was going to kiss her again, she thought. And if he did, she'd probably let him get away with it, despite all he had done to her.

"Did you know that you have a really beautiful mouth, Miss Stuart?'' he asked, his own nearly touching it.

"Ah! Not nearly so beautiful as my cattle!'' she retorted.

He laughed softly again. "You are disappointed.''

"Don't deceive yourself, Lieutenant. I am vastly relieved.''

"Why don't I believe you?''

"Because you're an egotist and a scurvy rat.''

"Why is it that you just beguile me so, Tess Stuart? Is it that you taste like wine and smell of roses, even in the most god-awful heat of the day. Is it that fall of golden hair, or your eyes, like wild violets? No…it must be the tender words you're always whispering so gently to me. Words like…scurvy rat.''

"Lieutenant, will you please—''

"I do want you.''

"What?'' she cried.

"Very much. But I don't want to bargain about it. When you decide to be with me, you'll do so because you want to. You might have to think it through and weigh all the factors, or you might just wake up one night and come to realize that it's going to be, that there's just something there. I feel it when I touch you, when I'm near you.''

"You're a fool!''

"Am I?''

He leaned closer. He was going to kiss her again.

"Don't!'' she cried out.

He ignored the warning, taking her lips with his own, and though she mumbled a second protest, her mouth was already parting to his. And his tongue was deep, deep within her, and it touched her in places it could not possibly reach. She knew that he was right, and she hated him for it, but she needed him still, and she wanted him still. She trembled against the sweet savagery of his touch, and she felt the pressure of his body, of his thigh against hers, of more than his thigh. His hands were in her hair, stroking her face, rounding over the full rise of her breast, and she was still braced against him, unable to do anything other than feel.

Then he released her. She gasped raggedly and fell back. His lips lightly brushed first her forehead, then her cheeks. He smiled. "Egotist, eh?"

He was off guard. She slammed her knee against him. She didn't quite hit home, but she must have given him a good bruise in the thigh. He groaned at the pain, gritting his teeth, flashing her a lethal glare.

"Miss Stuart, if I didn't have some vague memory of being a gentleman—"

"If you have any memory at all, sir, it must be vague!"

"Miss Stuart, I should tan—"

"Do excuse me, Lieutenant," she said, attempting to step past him. "It's not that you haven't got decent lips, it's just that it's impossible to know where they've been before."

"Decent lips!"

"Decent, yes," she said sweetly, still walking.

He caught her arm and pulled her into his arms. "I could just—" he began, but then he laughed. "Impossible to know where they've been before! Why, honest to God! I do believe that you're jealous!"

"Not on your life, Lieutenant!" she protested.

But he touched his lips to hers again, sweeping her swiftly into realms she was just beginning to discover, then righting her just as quickly and dropping his arms. He cast his arm out, indicating the trail. "After you, Miss Stuart. I will always wait."

"You'll wait until you're old and gray!" she snapped. She was jealous, she thought. Anguished. It was painful to care like this, so deeply and so quickly.

He smiled serenely. "Will I?"

She managed to return the smile. "Not all women are like Miss Eliza, Lieutenant."

"No? I had rather thought that they were—at heart."

"You're mistaken."

"Maybe you're mistaken. Maybe most women are hypocrites."

"Oh, you are impossible!" Tess cried. She swung around and began to stride angrily toward the wagon.

But before she could reach the break in the bushes, he had pulled her back. She started to snap something to him, but the words caught in her throat when his smoky gaze fell upon her.

"Tess, you are different."

"Different from what?"

He smiled. "From any other woman I have met," he said softly.

Then he stepped past her and preceded her to the camp fire Jon had burning with a welcoming warmth and light.

Chapter Six

The delicious aroma of cooking was already filling the air as Tess stepped toward the fire. She inhaled deeply as she tried to dispel her immediate memories of Lieutenant Slater.

The fire had been set in the center of the clearing. A small animal roasted on a spit atop it. Jon, on his haunches, turned the spit. On a bed of hot rocks surrounding the fire sat a coffeepot.

Dolly was coming from the wagon with tin plates, and with mugs for the coffee. She smiled at Tess. "Rabbit! A nice, plump brown rabbit. Jon caught and skinned that thing in minutes flat. I do declare, he's a fine provider!"

"Yes, he is," Tess said, smiling at Jon. She strode past him and daintily swept her skirts beneath her to sink upon the ground. Jamie was coming across the clearing toward them, too. He sat beside her.

"You caught a big one," Jamie acknowledged. "Good."

"We need some water for this coffeepot," Dolly said.

"I'll get it," Jamie and Tess volunteered simultaneously.

"Fine, you get it," Tess said.

"No, you can go."

"But, Lieutenant—"

"Jon, give me the damned pot, will you?" Jamie said. He started toward the brook, then paused, looking back. "How's our supply in the barrels?"

"Good," Jon said. "Later we can fill the canteens."

Jamie nodded and started toward the water. Tess hesitated a minute, then started after him.

"Tess!" Dolly called.

"I'll be right back!"

"We'll never have coffee!" Dolly said dolefully.

Tess ignored her. She was panting and breathless, and wondering what in hell had made her rush into the den with the lion. She caught up with Jamie at the brook. When he wanted to, he could move quickly.

He stared at her as he filled the coffeepot, arching one brow.

"You want acreage," she said. "How much?"

"Well, now, I don't know. I haven't seen the property, have I?"

"Give me an idea."

He shrugged. His eyes were hard as he stared at her. "Half. Half of what you own."

She gasped, stunned. "You're insane!"

"I can ride back to the fort."

"But you don't even know what I own!"

"That's right. You're the one pushing the point here."

"A quarter."

"Half."

"Never!"

"Half. And that will be it. I won't ask another thing of you, Miss Stuart."

"Not on your life."

"We can ride right back." He stood and walked toward her. He didn't touch her, but he was smiling still. "Miss Stuart, normally I don't barter at all, not without seeing what it is I'm willing to risk my life for."

"You're in the cavalry. You risk your life daily."

"They pay me. And you—"

"I'll pay you wages."

He shook his head slowly. "You know what I want."

Tremors swept through her. She did know what he wanted—and he kept saying it was property. He kept smiling, and his eyes roamed up and down the length of her. "Like I said, I usually like to see what I'm buying with my time and my Colt. Since I trust you so, I'm willing to take a chance in this circumstance."

"A quarter," Tess said firmly.

"Half."

He walked by her quickly. She stumbled to keep up with him, but he moved too fast. She was still stumbling when he walked into the clearing. She slammed into him and he turned, lifting her chin.

"Half!" he whispered.

She pulled quickly away from him. "We'll discuss it later. I think you're insane. I think you're just as crooked as von Heusen. Just another Yankee carpetbagger."

He stiffened, dropped her chin and turned in harsh, military fashion, then took the coffeepot to the fire. He sank down across from Jon.

"Well, the coffee will taste much better once we've eaten that sizzlin' sweet rabbit all up!" Dolly said cheerfully.

"It's cooked enough for me," Jon said, leaning over and ripping off a leg. He winced as the meat burned his fingers, then he smiled. "Dig in!"

They all ate hungrily, and in silence. Jamie rose and brought a loaf of hard bread from the supply pack. It didn't matter that it was hard—it was delicious. And when they were finished eating, the coffee was done. It did taste wonderful after all the food, just as Dolly had so cheerfully suggested.

It grew dark as they sipped it. Velvet dark. The moon was a bare sliver in the sky, but there were hundreds of stars out, dotting the heavens.

"It's beautiful, isn't it?" Dolly said.

"Very nice," Tess agreed. She yawned. "We should take the dishes to the water and wash them now."

"Don't be absurd. It's dark as Hades," Jamie said harshly. His eyes were smoke when they touched her. He was furious, she realized. And it wasn't their arguing over the payment in acreage, it couldn't be. He liked to taunt her and anger her, the silver light of challenge was always in his eyes then.

But he wasn't feeling fondly toward her at all at the moment, she was certain. Her heart beat too hard as his eyes touched her, and she thought she saw something lethal in him, something that made her shiver, something that made her think she did not want him to be her enemy.

He was coming to fight her battle, she reminded herself. But then why did he look as if he wanted to strangle her?

"I—I can bring a lantern," she heard herself saying.

"Dammit, you can just wait until morning!" Jamie said irritably. He stood, tossing the last of his coffee into a bush. Then he strode away, disappearing into the darkness.

Tess cast a quick glance toward Jon. "What's the matter with him?"

Jon shrugged. "I don't know. You'll have to find out yourself." He stood and stretched. "Ladies, I suggest an early night."

"He's gone off on his own!" Tess said indignantly.

"He's taking first guard," Jon said softly.

"I'm going to bed," Dolly announced. "Tess, now you come, too."

Jon was dragging his saddle and blanket to the fire. He stretched out and closed his eyes, setting his hat over his face. Dolly headed for the wagon. Tess hesitated, then decided to go after Jamie.

She heard Jon rise as she moved into the bushes, and she swore softly, certain that he would follow her. He did. But before he could reach her, a hand snaked out for her, catching her arm, swinging her around. She tossed back her head and met Jamie's angry eyes. She wrenched free from his grasp. For safety's sake, she took a step backward.

"What are you doing?" he demanded.

"Looking for you."

"I told you not to run around in the dark!"

"But you—"

"Miss Stuart, from now on, you're taking orders from me. And from now on, you listen. And if I hear one more crack out of you about my being a Yank just like von Heusen, I'll tan your backside until it's the color of a Comanche. Are we understood?"

"No!" she snapped indignantly.

He took a single step toward her. In the near darkness, his eyes seemed to glitter with a menacing light.

She decided that she wasn't going to tempt fate any further that evening. She didn't think he made idle threats.

She turned and fled.

Jon was standing not far from the camp fire. He had seen her reach Jamie. She slowed her pace as she saw him. She smiled pleasantly and wished him good night.

"Good night, Tess," he told her.

She crawled into the wagon. Dolly was already softly snoring. Tess unhooked her shoes. Closing the cover of the wagon, she stripped down to her chemise and pantalets. She crawled into her bunk, closed her eyes and made every effort to sleep. Her heart was still pounding, and she didn't know if it was with vexation or excitement. He wanted her property, not her person, she reminded herself.

Then how could he seem to insinuate so much that seemed sensual when they talked about dry land? And then, of course, he could change so quickly. Lose his temper over simple words when he could tease so long himself...

She didn't understand, but he was occupying more and more of her mind. And more and more of her heart.

It was light when she awoke. Dolly was already up.

Tess quickly slipped into her dusty brown dress for the second day on the trail. She tied her shoes and slipped from the wagon. She could smell coffee brewing already, and something was cooking in a frying pan.

She could hear voices by the fire. Jon and Dolly, she determined. She started around the wagon then held still. Jamie, bare-chested, in only his boots and jeans, was shaving. His mirror was leaning against the steps at the front of the wagon, his shaving mug was on the second step, and he was wielding a straight razor against his cheeks. Apparently he caught sight of her in the mirror. He nicked himself and scowled deeply at her. She should have walked by. She could not. She smiled, enjoying the sight of him so. He had wonderful shoulders, broad and very bronze. He was nearly as dark as Jon, with powerfully bunched muscles in his arms and chest, and hard, unyielding ones at his lean waist. She swallowed suddenly. She'd seen lots of men bare-chested. The hands often stripped off their shirts after a long day and doused themselves with water at the troughs.

Jamie Slater's chest was different. She couldn't look at him and wonder if the herd was doing well. She looked at him and wondered what his flesh would feel like beneath her fingers.

Maybe he read her mind. Maybe her thoughts were obvious in her eyes. They were still locked with his in the mirror.

Her smile faded and she felt a crimson blush rising to her cheeks.

She prayed for motion then and she managed to move her feet and hurry past him to the fire.

"Fish!" she said delightedly.

"Freshwater fish, just wonderful," Dolly supplied happily.

"Jon, you're wonderful!" Tess claimed.

"Oh, I didn't catch these. Jamie did," he told her casually.

Dolly passed Tess a plate. "I'm taking a walk to the brook with a few of the utensils. I'll be right back."

"Thanks, Dolly," Tess said. Dolly winked. Jon smiled at Tess as she hungrily ate her fish.

"Coffee?" he asked her.

"Please."

He handed her a mug, then said something about finishing the harness. She was left alone with a beautiful, early morning sun and the delicious food and coffee.

She set down her plate and took a long swallow of coffee. She closed her eyes, inhaled the aroma and felt the heat. When she opened her eyes, Jamie was standing before her.

"Miss Stuart, you might want to hurry along a little. The rest of us have been up a while now, and I'm ready to ride. We can make Wiltshire by tomorrow if we keep moving."

She gazed up at his newly shaven face. All the planes and angles were handsome, smooth and rugged all at once—masculine...and still belligerent. It was war, she thought.

She sighed softly. "Why, Lieutenant, I, at least, am fully clothed. And I do promise that I can finish this coffee and the fish before you can be dressed and ready to ride."

"Then let's see it, huh?"

He started to walk by her. "Oh, Lieutenant," she called.

"What?"

"You're bleeding, sir. There seems to be a—a gash right at the tip of your chin. Have you been shaving long, sir?"

"Longer than you've been wearing a corset, Miss Stuart. A whole lot longer," he told her pleasantly. That time, when he stepped by, she quickly leaped to her feet, finished her coffee and, as quickly and delicately as possible, peeled the last of her fish from the bone. She glanced over her shoulder. He was buttoning the last button of his shirt.

She cast the last drop of coffee and bit of food into the ashes of the camp fire and raced for the steps to the driver's seat of the wagon.

She made it just as he rode up on his roan.

"I won," she told him.

"At best—and that's if I'm in the mood to be cavalier—it was a tie, Miss Stuart."

"At best for you, Lieutenant."

He smiled. "Half of your acreage, Tess."

"A quarter."

"That remains to be seen," he told her, riding close. "But then, a lot of things remain to be seen, don't they?" He nudged Lucifer and rode to the rear of the wagon. "Jon, you ready? Where's Dolly?"

"Here, here, I am coming, I do declare, the rush you boys get yourselves into! I was just down at the brook, cleaning up the pans, and there you are, riding off without me."

"Dolly! We'd never ride off without you!" Jamie promised her solemnly.

"Never," Jon echoed.

"But times awastin', Dolly," Jamie said. "And suddenly, I'm just darned eager to reach Wiltshire."

Dolly climbed onto the wagon. Tess lifted the reins against the mules, and they were under way again.

By late afternoon of the following day they had reached the outskirts of Wiltshire. Then Tess gave the directions to her home, a large ranch outside of town.

Tess held the reins. As the house came into view, she saw Jamie pull in on his big roan and stare. He glanced her way.

"That's it? That's your—ranch?"

"That's it."

He started to laugh suddenly, looking at Jon. Then he spurred the roan and raced toward the house. Tess flicked the reins and hurried after him with the rumbling wagon.

The house was magnificent. Joe had put years and years of work into the sprawling, two-story ranch house. There were two large barns to the left and a large red carriage house to the right. The vegetable garden, lush with summer, could be seen behind the house.

The paddocks, stretching before and behind, seemed to go on forever. Horses, her uncle's prize thoroughbreds, roamed in the paddocks, the year's foals seeming to dance alongside their mothers.

Tess knew about the weathered paint on the fine old house, however. Since the war, nothing much had been done. They had considered themselves lucky to hang on to the property once the battles had ended and the dust had died down. There were floorboards on the blue-gray porch that needed to be mended, and Tess thought that if Jamie Slater looked long and hard at the velvet drapes in the parlor, he would see the material was old and fraying.

In the past few years, all their efforts had gone into their battles with von Heusen.

She drove the wagon between the paddocks toward the house. Jamie and Jon were far ahead of her. They'd reached the clearing before the house, and Jamie was turning around on the huge roan, looking at everything around him. He was still amused—and pleased.

He must have thought I was a potato farmer and that he bartered himself for a few dusty acres! Tess decided. Well, he should be pleased.

The front door burst open as the wagon reached the clearing. Hank Riley, Joe's foreman, came hurrying down the steps, followed by Janey Holloway, who had worked for them since Tess had begun to work at the paper. Hank was as tall and skinny as a young oak sapling, with a weathered face so browned and crinkled that he sometimes looked like an Indian. Janey was young and plump and pretty, with sandy hair and soft gray eyes.

Jane stared from Jamie to the wagon, then screamed with joy, clutching her heart when she saw Tess. Hank didn't make a sound. He came hurrying down the steps of the porch and over to the wagon and reached right up, catching hold of Tess and swinging her down. He lifted her up and swung her around again, a smile crinkling his face to even greater depths. "Tess! The Lord be praised, but that man told us you were dead!"

"I'm not dead, Hank, I'm fine." Hank had set her down. Jane was crying softly. "Jane!" Tess took the young woman in her arms to comfort her. "It's all right! I'm here. I'm alive, I'm well!"

"Oh, Miss Tess! Miss Tess, it's just so wonderful to see you! He said he was coming back tonight, and at first we thought that you were him coming back a little early. He had the sheriff with him, you see, and he said as how everyone had heard that both you and your uncle had been killed in an Indian raid, and that the land would go up for public auction. Hank and me and the hands were to clear out. Well, the hands could stay on until the actual auction, but—'' She paused, gasping for breath.

Hank, casting a curious glance toward Jamie and Jon, continued the story indignantly. ''He said that since Jane and I might think ourselves too close to the family, we'd have to get out before we started stealing property from the deceased!''

''He—who the hell is he?'' Jamie demanded, dismounting.

Hank frowned, not about to answer the question until he had a signal from Tess. ''Well, Miss Tess, I'll answer him about who the hell he is—once this fellow tells me who the hell he is himself!''

Jamie's eyes narrowed, and his face started to look like thunder.

''Hank,'' Tess said quickly. ''This is Lieutenant Jamie Slater, he's with the cavalry. And Mr. Jon Red Feather. Hank, they've been gracious enough to see me home—''

''Then Joe really is dead,'' Hank said miserably.

She nodded.

He swallowed hard, looking into the distance. ''I'd kinda hoped, seeing you and all...Then he really did get it from the Indians.''

''No. From von Heusen.''

''Him again,'' Hank muttered.

''He—him,'' Jamie interjected. ''Are we, or are we not, talking about von Heusen all the way around here?''

''Of course!'' Tess stated firmly.

''You mean to tell me,'' Jamie said, striding toward Hank, ''that this von Heusen has already been here, telling you that the property is going to go up for public auction in lieu of being granted to legitimate heirs?''

''Yep, something like that.''

''Just like a vulture,'' Jon commented.

''Well, he'll be back,'' Hank promised. ''Soon enough. You'll get to meet him.''

Dolly, still on the wagon, cleared her throat. ''Oh, Dolly!'' Jamie exclaimed apologetically. He hurried around to help her down. Dolly smiled and took Hank's hand firmly.

"I'm Dolly Simmons, Hank. Nice to make your acquaintance. And you, too, young lady. Jane, isn't it?"

"Yes, ma'am."

"A fine name, a fine name. And I'm mighty parched. Perhaps we could go inside and have ourselves a sip of something."

"Yes, let's!" Tess said.

She started for the house. Jon dismounted and looped his pinto's reins around the hitching post in front of the house. Tess was halfway up the stairs before she realized that Jamie hadn't moved. He was still standing with the roan's reins in his hands.

"Jamie, come in, please," she said politely. A bit distantly perhaps—they were still involved in their fierce, personal battle. "We'll see to the wagon later. Hank and the boys will help."

He shook his head, looking at Hank, not her. "That the trail to follow into town?" he asked, pointing toward the road.

"Yep, that's it."

"Where's the action congregate around here?"

Hank was smiling but curious. "Why, the Bennington saloon. The best card games in town go on there, the best whiskey flows there, and the best girls—" He paused, glancing quickly toward the ladies. "Well, Lieutenant, the best entertainment in town can be found there, too."

Jamie nodded. Smiling at Tess, he told her, "I think that I'll take a ride in."

"Now?" she demanded. The best entertainment in town! Von Heusen was expected at the house, and he was about to ride off to enjoy himself with a dance-hall girl!

"No time like the present."

"But von Heusen is going to come here!"

"I don't want to meet Mr. von Heusen. Not just yet." He swung up on his horse and glanced at Jon. Tess tried hard to follow his gaze. Something passed between them, like eons of words, and yet it all happened in a few seconds.

Jon was staying with her. And still, she was furious. Jamie was demanding half her land and he wouldn't even stay around to meet his adversary.

"Lieutenant, if you head into town, perhaps you should stay there for the night,'' she snapped. They all stared at her. She had to control her temper. She had to quit caring.

He grinned. ''Why, Miss Stuart, do you think there'll be enough there to keep me occupied all night?''

''I imagine, Lieutenant, that that is entirely up to you. Do what you feel you must.''

She turned her back on him as quickly as she could. He was a free man, she thought furiously. He could do whatever he wanted to do, drink himself silly, consort with whores, gamble his life away. He sure as hell wasn't going to do it on her property, though!

He was going to do it, though. He didn't even enter the house, but turned and rode away. Tess tried very hard to look back, not to let anyone see that her eyes had misted with her ire and frustration.

Damned Yank. Damned Yank.

''It's a nice place you've got here,'' Jon complimented as they entered the house.

''Beautiful!'' Dolly exclaimed.

It wasn't exactly beautiful, Tess thought. But it was nice, and it was livable, too. The parlor into which they entered was vast, and it was combined with a big dining room that held a heavy carved Mexican table that could seat fourteen for dinner. To the left of the dining area, against the rear wall, was the broad staircase that led to the second floor. Nearer the door was Joe's desk, on a dais, perched on a cow skin. His large wing-chair was behind it, and two heavy leather chairs were situated before it. There was a spittoon in the corner for those who felt they absolutely must chew tobacco. In the center of the room, on a beautiful hooked rug, was a large, soft, brown leather sofa. It sat next to the fire, with matching chairs across from it and occasional tables beside it. There were bright Indian flower vases on the tables. There were flowers in the vases, and Tess smiled. Hank and Jane had kept up, no matter what.

''Well!'' Dolly said. ''Now this is nice! Tess, where would you like us to stay?''

''Oh!'' She had forgotten that even though Jamie Slater had ridden away the moment they arrived, she had other guests to attend to. ''I'm sorry. Upstairs, Dolly. Hank, we can wait a while on the other things, but let's bring up Dolly's trunks. Come up, please!'' She urged Dolly and Jon forward. When they reached the second-story landing, they looked down a long hallway with doors on either side and a big-paned window with velvet draperies at the end. "There are eight rooms up here," she murmured. "We shouldn't be wanting."

Jane, who had followed her up the stairs, cleared her throat softly. "Tess, your room is aired, and Joe's room is aired, and I just happened to air the back two, but I haven't touched the others yet. I was getting around to them, but then when we heard…When we heard that both you and Joe…Nothing seemed to make much sense anymore."

"That's all right," Tess said. "But we'll need linens and all for Mrs. Simmons and Mr. Red Feather. Can you see to that? We'll put them in those two rooms you aired."

"What about the lieutenant?"

"I believe he's staying in town. And should he wander back, well, he can wander into the barn."

Jon made a choking sound, then laughed. Dolly gave a little gasp. Tess didn't care. She walked grandly down the hall. "Dolly, this room here is more appropriate for a lady, I think. There's a big dressing table in here, and the light is wonderful in the morning."

"It is just wonderful!" Dolly said delightedly. "I love it!" She caught Tess's cheeks between her plump hands and gave her a kiss on the cheek. "I am so glad I came. And don't you dare wait on me. I'm here to help. Jane, you run along and get linens, and I'll get this bed made up, and then you show me around the house and tell me what I can do!"

"Dolly, you don't have to do anything but rest. It's been a long trip—"

"You hush, dear. I'm going to get to know my room!" She stepped inside, closing the door. Jane hurried down the hall to the little linen-storage room.

Tess smiled wryly at Jon. "She's wonderful, isn't she?"

"Dolly? Yes, she's a wonder."

"I didn't really give her the best room, Jon, both these rooms are big and have beautiful views. I think you'll be just as happy over here. The bed is large and firm, and it's very airy."

"I'll be quite comfortable wherever you put me," he assured her.

Smiling, he looked into the room, then backed out again. "I'll go help Hank with the trunks."

"If you're tired—"

"Tess, do I look tired? If von Heusen is coming back tonight, we want to look settled in, don't we?"

"It's interesting that you should feel that way. Apparently the lieutenant wasn't very worried."

"Don't underestimate him, Tess. He knows what he's doing."

"You would defend him no matter what, wouldn't you?"

"Because I know him," Jon said quietly, and he stepped past her, down the hall and down the stairs.

She'd best get moving herself, Tess decided. She turned and hurried down the hallway in Jon's wake. While the men unloaded the wagon, she could see to the horses and the mules.

Then she'd have to find out how many of the ranch hands had stayed around once they'd heard that von Heusen would be taking over.

And then she'd have to wait...for von Heusen himself.

The town of Wiltshire was not a little hole-in-the-wall, Jamie decided as he rode down the main street. It was really quite sophisticated, with rows and rows of Victorian houses with their cupolas and gingerbread lining the roads that ran off the main street. Along the main street were any number of businesses—two different mercantiles, a barbershop, a corset shop, a men's wear shop, a cooper, a photographer, a mortician, a pharmacy, a doctor, two lawyers, a boardinghouse for young ladies and an inn that boasted a sign, "Perry McCarthy's Shady Rest Hotel—Stop Here and Dine! We've a Restaurant for Any Respectable Traveler, Gentleman, Lady or Child."

He wondered how well Perry McCarthy was doing. The streets were very quiet.

In front of the barbershop a few men sat around and puffed on pipes. One was missing an arm, another was minus his left foot. A pair of crutches leaned against the wall behind him. The men looked at Jamie as he rode by. The war, Jamie thought. These men had fought in the war. Southerners, like he'd been. Even if Miss Stuart was insisting upon calling him a Yank. Well, he was a Yank. Hell, they were all Yanks now. Because the damn Yanks had won the war.

"Howdy," he called out to the group.

The fellow with the stump for an arm nodded. "Stranger in these parts, aren't you, mister?"

"Yes, sir, I am. But it seems to be a nice enough place."

"Used to be," the man minus the foot said, spitting on the ground. "Used to be. But then the varmints started coming in and taking over. You know how that is. You don't hail from these parts, but I don't think that's any Chicago accent you got on you, boy. Where you from?"

"Missouri," Jamie said.

"Missouri," the footless man repeated. He stroked his graying beard with a smile and settled back. "Well, now, I hope you stay a while."

"I was planning on it. I thought I'd buy some land."

"Don't think you're going to be able to, not good land. Oh, there's some land up to the north for sale, but it's pure desert. You don't want that, boy."

"Well, I'll look around. I heard that Joe Stuart was killed. Maybe I can get my hands on some of his land."

The man without the arm was up in a minute. "Don't you go looking around to be a vulture after Joe's place. You'll wind up dead yourself, young man."

"Maybe you'd better shut up, Carter," the other fellow muttered.

Jamie leaned down, smiling. "Fellows, Joe's niece is alive and well and kicking, I can tell you."

"Miss Tess!" The one named Carter gasped with pleasure. "Why, that's the best news I've heard since '61! You telling the truth there, boy?"

"Sir, I'm over thirty," Jamie politely told him. "And I think I count double time for the war, my friends, so that makes me pretty darned old, and nobody's boy."

"Sorry there, Carter and me, we didn't mean to offend."

"No offense taken. My name is Jamie Slater. I'm looking to buy land. You hear of anything, you let me know."

"We'll do that. But you aren't going to get the Stuart ranch. Von Heusen wants that. He wants it bad."

"But he doesn't want that other land. That's interesting," Jamie mused.

"Hope you stay a while," Carter said.

"Thanks. I intend to."

"My name's Jeremiah Miller, you need any more information, bo—young man, you look me up. Hell, anybody younger'n me is a boy, son!"

Jamie laughed and urged his mount on. He could see the saloon ahead. He reined in before it, tossed his reins over the tethering bar and entered through the swinging doors.

He paused for a minute, letting his eyes adjust to the dimness and the smoke. There was a piano player in the rear. A singer with a short mauve shirt that barely covered rich black petticoats and stockings perched on the piano. Her voice was as smoky as the atmosphere.

There was a bar to his right, running the length of the establishment. Two heavyset bartenders in white aprons leaned against the mahogany bar talking to customers. There were a number of patrons at the twenty or so tables in the place. Some were well-dressed small-town merchants, others were ranch men, wearing denim pants and spurs and tall, dusty hats. Their spurred boots were sometimes up on chairs or tables. It was a lazy crowd, it seemed, an interesting one.

The crowd went silent the minute Jamie entered the room. The singer forgot the lyrics to her song. The piano player swung around and stared, too.

"Howdy," Jamie said casually.

People stared. Then the brunette hopped off the piano and walked forward. "Hello, there," she said, frowning at the others, offering Jamie a broad smile. "What's the matter with you all! We've a stranger in town. Let's not make him think we haven't a single wit of manners between the lot of us!"

"Sure thing, Sherry, honey!" one of the cowboys called out. He let his feet fall to the floor. "Howdy, there, stranger. Welcome to Wiltshire. We ain't rude. We're just surprised. Strangers just don't come here very often very more."

"Why is that?" Jamie asked.

The cowboy shrugged, but not before looking around the room.

In one corner, a few men in suits were playing cards. "It ain't a good gamble, that's why," a tall, thin man with heavy iron-gray whiskers called out. "But you're here now, so come on in. Hardy!" He called to the bartender. "Give the stranger a whiskey, on me."

"Thank you kindly," Jamie said. He strode into the room. Sherry brought his whiskey. He sat across from the man who had invited him, next to a small, nervous man with wire-rimmed spectacles.

"My name's Edward Clancy," the bewhiskered man said, offering Jamie a hand. "I'm the editor of the *Wiltshire Sun*."

Jamie nearly betrayed his surprise. He kept a firm smile plastered to his face. "The *Sun*, huh? The newspaper?"

"The gossip rag," the man said flatly. "That's all I dare print, and I'm careful about that. Oh, well, I write up some articles about President Grant and about the Indians. But not much else."

"Why?"

"'Cause I like living," Edward Clancy said flatly. "We're playing poker. You in?"

Jamie pushed back his hair and reached into his pocket for money. "Sure, I'm in. I like to gamble."

"Then you're in the right town, mister. You're surely in the right town. What's your name?"

"Jamie. Jamie Slater."

Clancy smiled slowly. "I've heard of you. You're one of the Slater brothers. Why, I heard that you can hit a fly in the clouds with that—"

"Rumor," Jamie interrupted him. "Rumor, that's something I'd just as soon keep quiet for the time being."

"It's quiet. It's quiet." Clancy stared at him hard, then grinned again. "That's Doc Martin. He was one of Joe Stuart's best friends. We'll keep things quiet. Whatever you say."

"Thanks."

"We'll help you any way that we can," Doc volunteered.

"Information is what I need now," Jamie said, leaning closer. "Why does this von Heusen want the Stuart property so damn bad?"

"You know, we haven't figured that one out yet. We just haven't figured it out. But he does want it badly."

"Badly enough to kill?"

"Hell, yes, I think so. Why, if the Indians hadn't gotten old

Joe…'' His voice trailed away as he stared at Jamie. "It wasn't a tribe of Indians that came after him, was it?"

"Not according to Tess."

"Tess! She's alive!"

Jamie nodded. The look of pure, unadulterated joy on the man's face was somewhat irritating. The sun-honey blond seemed to be a golden angel around these parts.

Edward Clancy leaned so far across the table that he was nearly on top of it. His voice was soft; his features were knotted up and tense. "If Tess says it was von Heusen, it was von Heusen all right. Are you—are you going to stay around and fight him?"

"Yeah. Yeah, I guess so."

He didn't guess so. He was committed, and he knew it. He had been committed since he'd first seen Tess's face.

He just hadn't known it right away.

"Hell! Don't look now," Doc muttered suddenly.

"What?" Jamie demanded.

"Some of von Heusen's boys. The four fellows who just came in. The mean-looking ones."

They were a mean-looking group, Jamie decided. Lanky-haired, glitter-eyed. Two were light, two were dark-haired. One chewed tobacco incessantly.

The dark-haired man who chewed tobacco seemed to be the spokesman for the group. He slammed his fist on the bar, rattling all the glasses on it. He shouted to the bartender, who couldn't seem to move swiftly enough to the end of the bar.

"Hardy! What's the matter with you, ya gettin' old?" one of the men demanded. "Whiskey. And not the rotgut you serve the local swine. Give us the best in the house."

Hardy set a bottle on the bar. The man grasped him by the shirt collar and nearly pulled him over the bar. Hardy was starting to turn purple, and his attacker was laughing like a hyena.

"That's enough."

Jamie was on his feet. Once again, everyone went silent.

Von Heusen's men were silent, too. The four of them stared at him with astonishment. Then they began to smile.

"Who the hell are you?" asked the dark-haired brute.

"That doesn't matter. Let Hardy alone."

"Why, son, you don't know anything about this town at all, now, do you?"

"Let him go," Jamie repeated.

"He needs to be taught a lesson," one of the light-haired men said with a nasty snarl.

"Yeah. A fatal lesson."

In a flash, the man released the bartender. He drew his gun.

He was fast, but not fast enough. Before he could aim he had dropped the gun, howling in pain. His friends tried to draw.

Rapid shots sizzled from Jamie's Colts. The second man was on the floor, clutching his leg. The third grasped an arm. The fourth was on the floor. He might have been dead. Jamie didn't know or care.

He looked at Edward Clancy. "Thanks for the drink, friend," he said quietly.

Then he left the bar, walking over his fallen enemies.

Chapter Seven

By nightfall the wagon had been unloaded except for the printing press, which would be taken into town in the morning. Tess had even managed to fill the hip bath in the kitchen with steaming water and soak for a long time, washing away the dust and dirt from the trail. She kept reminding herself that von Heusen was coming back, but she felt strangely calm, despite the fact that Jamie had deserted them. Von Heusen wasn't going to come right up to the house and murder her. He hadn't the guts for that.

She dressed in a soft summer-green cotton and set about making dinner with Jane and Dolly to help her. She was accustomed to Jane, but it was really nice to have Dolly with her. Dolly kept up a steady stream of conversation, mostly about her husband, Will, and their days in the military. Her stories were spicy and fun, and Tess enjoyed them thoroughly.

They cooked a huge wild turkey on a spit and summer squash and green beans and apple turnovers. When the table was set and everything was ready, Tess went out to find Jon.

He was leaning against a pillar, a band tied around his dark hair and forehead, a repeating carbine held casually in his hand. He looked over the landscape.

"Dinner's on, Jon."

He glanced her way, smiling. "Thanks, Tess, but I think I'll wait out here a while longer, keep an eye on things."

"It's turkey and all kinds of good things. I'd like to repay you for the trip."

"I'll eat soon," he promised. She nodded and left him. Halfway inside the house she paused, wondering if he was looking for von Heusen or Jamie.

She hoped Jamie was eating stale, weevil-riddled bread somewhere. She had a feeling, though, that he was not.

She walked into the house and to the dining-room table. Hank had come in, and he was smiling. "The boys are out at the bunkhouse and they're pleased as peaches that you're home, Miss Tess. Well, them that's left. We've still got Roddy Morris, Sandy Harrison and Bill McDowell. They won't be going anywhere."

"Wonderful!" Tess told him. "Bring the boys in for dinner, will you, Hank?"

"They're already fixin' their suppers in the bunkhouse, Tess. We'll have a big Sunday dinner for them all, that's what we'll do."

"Fine. That sounds good, Hank. Now, let's all sit."

Dolly offered to say grace. She thanked God for His bounty, for their being alive and being together, then she asked God to take a good look at their enemies and see if He couldn't do something to put bad men in their proper place. "Amen," she finished.

"Amen," they all chorused.

Tess was about to take her first bite of dinner when she heard the sounds of horses' hooves. She set down her fork. How many of them had come with von Heusen? It sounded like five, no more.

"Excuse me," she said primly, setting her napkin carefully on the table and rising casually. It didn't matter. Dolly, Hank and Jane all catapulted to their feet, and they attached themselves to her like shadows as she walked to the door. She could hear voices before she reached it. Jon's first.

"That's close enough, fellows. Close enough."

"It's an Injun!"

"I said close enough."

Someone must have moved. A barrage of shots went off, followed by a startled silence.

Then von Heusen started to talk.

"Hold it, boys, hold your fire! I've just come to talk to Hank and Jane about removing themselves from the property—"

"There's no need for them to remove themselves from the property," Jon said. "This is private property, and the owner seems to want them here. One step nearer, boy," he warned someone, "and there'll be a hole in your chest where your heart used to be."

"Who in the blazes are you!" von Heusen thundered, losing his control.

"A friend."

"A friend! Well, listen here, you red-faced monkey. The Stuarts are dead. They were attacked by Comanche or Apache—"

"Apache?" Jon interrupted. She could hear something cold and dangerous in his voice. "Tell me, which Apache? Which Apache do you think did it? Or don't you know? I'll tell you, I'm damned sure it wasn't any Apache. Apache, any Apache, make war, or they go raiding. They make war to 'take death from their enemies.' They raid to fill their bellies. I haven't met an Apache yet who would leave dead cattle scattered with the corpses of men."

"Who the hell knows or cares what Apache!" von Heusen thundered. "It doesn't matter. Maybe it was Comanche—"

"Running River denies it."

"There are more tribes of Comanche!"

"Yes, there are," Jon said softly. "But the Comanche usually know what they're doing, too. When it comes to scalping a man.

"Of course, the whites have been scalping for a long time now. I read somewhere that they started scalping way back in the east in the sixteen hundreds. But still. White men in a hurry do a sloppy job. Neither a Comanche nor an Apache would do a sloppy job. No matter what his hurry."

"Takes an Injun to know!" someone muttered.

"Maybe we ought to string him up. Who knows? Maybe he's some renegade in charge of the party that did it himself!" von Heusen said.

"Let's hang him!"

"Let's see you try!" Jon said very softly.

"Hold it! Hold it!" von Heusen said. "Now listen, Joe Stuart and his family are dead. And this property is going to go up for public auction. Now I have—"

Tess had taken his statement as her cue. She threw open the door and stepped onto the porch behind Jon. "Correction, von Heusen. I am not dead."

Even in the dusky light that sifted down from the moon and the stars, Tess could see the startled look that flashed briefly across von Heusen's features.

He was a lean man, tall, spare. His features were almost cadaverous, his cheekbones sucked in, his chin very long and pointed. His eyes were coal black, and they seemed to burn from his skull. He sat atop his horse well, though. Jon had his repeating rifle aimed right at his heart, and von Heusen still sat casually, his hands draped over the pommel.

Around him were four of his men. He had about twenty hired guns on his place. Only four of them were with him. Tess didn't like it. He usually paid his visits with an escort of at least eight to ten.

It made her wonder where the rest of his men might be.

Von Heusen found his voice at last. "Why, Miss Stuart. I am delighted to see you alive and well."

"Like hell you are, von Heusen."

"That's uncalled for, ma'am."

"Be damned, you carpetbagging riffraff, but it is."

"Someone ought to wash your mouth out with a little soap, lady. I just came by—"

"You just came by to rob Joe of everything he ever had, now that you've murdered him!"

"You watch your accusation there, Miss Stuart."

"It's the truth. You know it, and I know it. And somehow, I'm going to prove it!"

Von Heusen was smiling. "I don't think so, little lady. No, I don't think so. You want to know what I do think?" He leaned toward her. It was just a fraction of an inch and he was still far away, but the gesture made her tremble inside. "I think that this ranch was meant to be mine, Miss Stuart. Now I've offered you good money for it. Real good money. And you still don't want to sell. Miss Stuart, I want you out of town."

"I'm not leaving."

"I wouldn't be so adamant, little lady. You may find that you leave in one way or another."

"You threatening her, von Heusen?" Jon asked.

"She seems to think that I'm guilty of something," von Heusen said. "The whole damned town can tell you that I was in the saloon playing cards the day the Indians attacked the Stuart train. The whole damned town can tell you that. But still, if the lady is so worried and so certain, well then, maybe she ought to plan on riding out of town. What do you think?''

''I think that you should give reasonable thought to the idea of riding out of town yourself, von Heusen,'' Jon warned quietly.

Von Heusen started to laugh. ''On the word of a half-breed Indian?''

He started to urge his mount closer to the porch. Jon fired a shot that must have sizzled a hairbreadth from the man's cheek. Von Heusen went as pale as the clouds.

''Hey, boss—'' one of his men began nervously.

Von Heusen lifted a hand. ''Calm down now, boys. Just because Miss Stuart's resorting to violence is no reason that we should. We'll be riding off now. But you remember what I said, Miss Stuart. I'd hate to see you leaving town other than all dressed up right pretty and in a comfortable stagecoach!'' He smiled at her. ''It is good to see you alive and well. Such a pretty, pretty woman. And all that blond hair. Blond hair alone is worth a pretty penny in certain places, did you know that?''

He stared at Tess. As he did so, she suddenly realized that she could smell smoke.

Suddenly she knew where the rest of von Heusen's men were. The smoke was coming from the direction of the carriage house. The printing press was in the wagon still, and the wagon was next to the buckboard and the chaise in the carriage house.

And so far, it had been a dry summer. If the carriage house went up in flames, the blaze could quickly spread to the house, to the barn, even to the stables.

Von Heusen was smiling.

''You bastard!'' she hissed at him. Jon hadn't moved; he didn't dare. If he moved the rifle a hair von Heusen just might decide to take advantage and shoot them all down.

They stood there, locked in the moment, von Heusen staring at Tess with a smile, Tess staring at him, hating him so fiercely that she should have been able to have willed him dead. It was lost now. All lost. The house, Joe's house. The press. It didn't even seem to bother von Heusen that he would slaughter all the horses.

Then suddenly, in the midst of von Heusen's triumph and her own despair, a commotion sounded from the direction of the carriage house. There was still smoke issuing from it—no sign of fire yet.

But men suddenly spilled out of it. Four of them, their hands held high above their heads. They nearly tripped as they walked, for someone had apparently ordered them to lower their breeches, and their pants were tight around their ankles. Three of them wore long johns; the fourth must have been buck naked. Tess only caught a glimpse of his bare legs, as he managed to stay behind the other three.

"Tarnation!" von Heusen swore. "You fools! What in bloody hell is going on—"

He broke off and never finished his question. From the smoke of the carriage house, another man appeared.

Tess felt her heart catch.

It was Jamie. He had a single gun trained on the men and he followed them out with the casual air von Heusen had had.

The men kept walking forward. The half-naked one paused, and Jamie nudged him forward.

"Ladies, do excuse me," Jamie apologized, "but they seemed to be a little more docile and trustworthy in this fashion."

"I'll kill you yet!" one of them muttered.

"Well, I don't doubt that you intend to try," Jamie assured him. Then he stared at the men still mounted upon their horses. "Which one of you is von Heusen?"

"I am Richard von Heusen. Who the hell are you?"

"Jamie Slater. But that doesn't matter. What does matter is that I own part of this spread now. And I'll thank you kindly to keep yourself and your half-sawed ruffians off my property, is that understood?"

"Your property—" von Heusen began.

"My property, yes. Now, take your arsonist friends here and move."

"You must be mistaken. Why would my men set fire to anything here?"

"Who knows why? But that was what they were doing. Ordinarily, of course, I'd want to get to know my new neighbors. But since you and the Stuarts don't seem to be very good friends, I really don't think you should stay. I bet dinner is on. Tess, is dinner on?''

''Yes!''

''Something good?''

His eyes touched hers across the dusky night. She nodded, fighting for speech. ''Turkey. Dressing. Squash. All sorts of things.''

''And getting cold. I do declare. Gentlemen, good night,'' Jamie said firmly. He prodded the men. ''Move 'em, now, von Heusen, or they'll start turning into corpses.''

''We're nine to one, you fool—''

''Nine to two. See my friend there? He could hit the hair in a man's nose at a thousand yards, and he's faster than greased lightning. You're outmanned, and outnumbered, you just don't know it yet.''

''We'll see about that,'' von Heusen said angrily. ''Get those half-naked idiots up on your horses!'' he ordered his mounted men. He jerked his mount around to face Tess and pointed a long finger at her. ''You'll pay for this, Miss Stuart. You'll pay dearly. I promise you.''

He swung around again, and his men followed. They raced off into the darkness, the horses' hooves pounding on the dry earth.

Silence and stillness fell over the small group on the porch. Jon Red Feather slowly lowered his rifle. He stared at Jamie. ''What the hell took you so long?''

''Well, there were four of them in the carriage house!'' Jamie announced indignantly. He strode up the stairs. Tess was still staring at him blankly when he tweaked her cheek and walked past her.

She managed to turn and follow him. He walked over to the table and sat, then pulled off a turkey leg and bit into it hungrily. Looking up, he saw Tess staring at him, Dolly and Jane on either side of her, and Jon and Hank on either side of the women. He paused in midbite.

''Do you all mind?''

Tess stood in front of him. ''Where did you go? How did you happen to come back right then?''

He chewed before answering her. ''I left the saloon as soon as I met a few friendly people—and a few not so friendly people. I knew he was coming out here. I didn't know he intended to burn you out.'' He paused, looking past Tess to Jon. ''Seems strange, doesn't it?

The man wants this property, but he doesn't seem to care if he destroys it. Makes you think, doesn't it?''

"Sure does.''

"Makes you think what?'' Tess asked irritably.

"Tess, think about it. It needs a little paint, a little shoring up here and there—but this is a darned nice house. Solid, sound, big. Then you've got the outbuildings, the carriages—and the horses. I haven't seen enough to really make an estimate on the value of the stock, but I imagine that we're talking hundreds and hundreds of dollars in horseflesh alone. And von Heusen doesn't care. He wants the property, but he doesn't care if he burns it to the ground.''

"He's a vile son of a bitch, that's why!'' Tess stated.

"Well, yes,'' Jamie acknowledged with a wry grin. "But there's more to it than that, I think.''

Dolly took a seat at the table again and spooned up a mouthful of squash. "Vile, certainly! Why, our dinner has gone quite cold!''

"That's the spirit, Dolly,'' Jamie told her. "Jon, sit. The turkey may be cold, but it's delicious.''

"That's it?'' Tess demanded heatedly.

"What do you mean, that's it?''

"Where did you go? What were you doing? You were supposed to be here!''

"Jon was here,'' Jamie said evenly.

"But—''

Jamie was buttering a roll. Jane and Hank and Jon sat and picked up their forks. Jamie's butter knife went still and his eyes were slightly narrowed as he stared at her. "Miss Stuart, I don't like the tone of this conversation. I came back in time to save your hide.''

"You wouldn't have had to rush back if you'd been here—where you should have been! You want to be paid so highly, and you can't even stick around!''

He stood suddenly. His knife clattered against a dish. "I don't argue like this in front of others, Miss Stuart.''

"There is no argument!'' she snapped.

"No, there isn't. I'll make it simple. Wherever I choose to go is my own business, Miss Stuart. You are not my keeper. And as to payment, hell, yes. Tomorrow we'll go into town and you'll turn over half interest in this place to me.''

She gasped aloud, stunned.

"Jamie, she doesn't understand what you're doing," Jon said, ignoring the rising tensions and reaching for a roll himself. "If you just explained—"

"Explained! Hell, I feel as if I'm up before the judge and jury!"

"Judge and jury! I really don't give a damn what you do with your time, but—"

"You begged me to come here, Tess."

"Begged!"

"Begged!"

"*Oh!*" she cried. Then she wound her fingers tightly together. "I don't argue in public either, Lieutenant!" she snapped. She was shaking, she realized. She'd been so damned amazed and grateful to see him, but she'd also been scared, and now she was furious and shaking and she wasn't even sure what she did want. She turned, having no taste left for dinner. Angrily she began to stride for the door.

"Tess!" He was on his feet, calling to her. He really expected her to stop because he had commanded her to.

She didn't stop, she didn't turn, she didn't even pause. She sailed straight for the front door. She would go to the carriage house to make sure the fire von Heusen's men had started had been stamped out.

"Jamie, give her a minute," Dolly suggested.

"The hell I will!" Jamie snapped.

Before Tess heard the door slam in her wake, she thought she heard Jamie's chair hit the floor as he pushed it over.

She started running toward the carriage house, anxious to reach it before he could see her. She was at the side door when she heard the front door to the house slam.

She slipped into the carriage house. She inhaled and exhaled, but couldn't smell any smoke. All she could smell was the fresh scent of the alfalfa hay that was being stored behind the chaise.

She fumbled in the darkness to light the gas lamp by the door. When the glow filled the carriage house, she went to check the wagon and the printing press. She crawled into the wagon and gave a soft sigh of relief as she saw that the printing press was fine. She sank down on one of the bunks.

"Tess! Where are you!"

Jamie was obviously angry. She clenched her teeth and tried to ignore him. She stepped from the wagon and went to the buckboard. No flames had lapped against it. The chaise, too, seemed untouched. Walking around, she discovered a half burned bale of hay. It had been dragged into the center of the room and lit. Von Heusen had meant it to be a slow fire. He had really meant to be long gone when the place burned.

She moved away from the hay and from the faint, acrid smell of fire that remained.

"Tess!"

He was still calling her, like a drill sergeant. With a sigh she determined that she would have to open the door, but she hesitated with her hand upon it. Where had he been? He'd been gone for hours. Had he really enjoyed the saloon so much? What part of the saloon?

And why was she torturing herself so thoroughly over him? She couldn't change the man.

The door slammed open before she could twist the knob. With a startled yelp she leaped back. Jamie was there, hatless, his shirt open at the neck, his hands on his hips, his sandy hair tousled casually over a brow, but his manner anything but casual.

"Why didn't you answer me?" he demanded.

"Because I didn't want to speak to you."

"It didn't occur to you that I might have been worried?"

"I could have been in and out of the carriage house all evening, and you wouldn't have known. What, I'm supposed to be on a ball and chain if you're around? But if you're not, it doesn't matter?"

She saw his jaw twist and a pulse tick hard against his throat. "That's about it, yes. Think you can live with the rules?"

"No!"

"Then I'm leaving."

"What?"

"You heard me."

"But—" In astonishment she stared at him. She inhaled sharply. She couldn't let him leave her. She couldn't!

But she thought he wouldn't go. He just wanted to see her beg.

"Leave," she told him. She'd call his bluff, she determined.

He turned and reached for the door. She thought quickly and desperately, then said, "I thought you liked the property. And the house, and the horses. And I thought you wanted half of everything. If you want it, you have to earn it."

He swung around. A smile curled his lip as he leaned against the door. "You just can't say please, can you?"

"It isn't that! My God, this isn't fair! You want thousands of dollars worth of property—"

"If von Heusen has his way, there won't be any property."

"But you're unfair!"

"Because I went to the saloon?"

"Because you weren't here!"

"But I was here. I was here exactly when you needed me." He walked toward her. She took a step back and tripped over the pile of half burned hay. He kept coming, and she reached out a hand, expecting he would help her up. He didn't.

He dropped down, half on top of her and half beside her, his arms braced over her chest so that she couldn't move. Gray eyes looked into hers. He'd had a shave in town, she thought. His cheeks were clean, and he smelled slightly of a cologne. He smelled good all over, like good clean soap and like a man. He'd had a bath, too, she realized, and her temper soared again. He had stayed at the saloon. He'd had a drink and a bath and maybe a meal and...

Maybe a woman.

"Get off of me, Yank!" she said angrily.

The smoke left his eyes. He stared at her with a gaze of cold steel. He leaned closer. So close that their faces nearly touched. The heat of his body was all around her, and she forgot everything, afraid, excited, wanting to escape him and run...

And wanting to know more of him.

"You're hurting me," she began.

"No, I'm not," he corrected her flatly. "And I'm not moving a hair, because I really want your attention. Now listen. I can go, or I can stay. The choice is yours. But if I stay, we do things my way. I'll try to explain. I'm not desperate for land, cattle, a house or money. I've done all right myself, thanks, despite the war, despite everything. But tomorrow, you're going to turn over half of this place to me on legal papers. That way you may have a chance of keeping it. Pay attention. You're a smart girl, Tess. Von Heusen thought that all he had to do was kill you and your uncle and he could have this place. You have no next of kin. But darlin', I've got plenty. I've got brothers, nieces and nephews. It would take von Heusen years to find them all if he did manage to kill both of us. That might give him some serious pause. Do you understand?''

Staring at him, Tess simply nodded. He was right, and every word he was saying made such perfect sense. And she wanted to be sensible. She wanted to be dignified, grateful, strong. She wanted to be able to fight her battles, but she could not fight alone.

If only she didn't want him as a man, if only she didn't grow jealous and angry so quickly. And yet...he still had that haunting aroma. His flesh would be slick and clean, and she wanted to know how the warmth would feel beneath her tongue.

The way he lay against her, she felt the thunder of his heart, and her own, and the beats seemed to rise together, and fall away, and rise together again, quick, wild, rampant. She felt his breath against her cheeks, and the iron lock of his thigh upon her own. She wanted to reach out and run her fingers through the sandy tendrils of hair that fell so hauntingly over his forehead, and so often shadowed and shaded his eyes, and hid his innermost thoughts.

''Yes? You do understand?''

''Yes!'' she cried out.

''And it all makes sense to you? You'll do what I'm asking you to do?''

''Yes. We'll go into town. As soon as I've stopped by the paper—''

''Before.''

''What difference does it make?''

''Maybe none. But the sooner von Heusen hears about this, the better things are going to be.''

''Fine!'' She was nearly screaming again. She was close to tears because she was desperate to escape him and the sensual blanketing of his body upon hers. ''Please, let me up!''

He rolled to his side, and she was free. ''You do sound more like him every day, though,'' she muttered heedlessly, rolling from him to rise and dust the hay from her gown. ''Carpetbagging Yanks, all of—''

"That's another thing we're going to get straight here once and for all!" he stated. Before she could flee as she had intended, his arm snaked around her, and she was tumbling into the hay again. He straddled her, and his hands pinned her down. "I'm not a Yank. I'm a U.S. Cavalry officer now, Miss Stuart, but I was born and bred in Missouri and I fought with Morgan for many long years in the war. As a *Reb*, Tess. Got that straight? Don't you ever go calling me a carpetbagging Yank again, and so help me God, I mean that! Understand?"

She stared at him blankly. She had called him a Yank a dozen times, and only now was he telling her the truth.

"Tess!"

"Yes!" she cried. She tore at her wrists and freed them from his grasp, then shoved him as hard as she could. He didn't move. "Either Jon or I should know where you are at all times. All right?"

"Yes!"

"No hiding in barns or carriage houses."

"I wasn't hiding! I was trying to make sure the fire was really out."

"I wouldn't have walked out of here without making sure the fire was out."

"Maybe I needed to see for myself. The printing press is in here."

"That damned press! It's everything to you."

"Yes! The paper does mean everything! It's the only means I have to tell the truth!"

He was silent for a moment. Then he moved slowly to his feet and reached down for her. She tried to ignore his helping hands, but they were quickly upon her. He stood her up, but he wasn't ready to release her yet.

"I know what I'm doing."

She inhaled the scent of him. "I do imagine that you do, Lieutenant."

"What does that mean?"

"You've had a nice bath, so it seems."

"And a shave."

"May I go now?"

He was smiling again. "Jealous little thing, aren't you?"

"Why should I be? I had a wonderfully pleasant afternoon with Mr. Red Feather. He's extremely well read and well traveled."

Jamie's eyes darkened and narrowed. For an instant she hated herself; she had no right to want to cause trouble between the friends. But she seemed driven to try and make Jamie angry.

And then it hit her like a bolt from the blue. She was falling in love with Jamie!

No! I am not in love with him, she thought in dismay.

But maybe she was. She wanted him. In ways she had never imagined a woman would ever want a man.

"It's important," Jamie repeated softly, "that Jon or I know where you are at all times. Did we get that one down yet?"

"Yes, thank you, I think we did. But since I do seem to get along much better with Jon, don't you think I should report to him, Lieutenant?" She twisted free and saluted stiffly.

He caught her shoulders and pulled her back. "You're a minx, Tess. A tart-mouthed little minx with siren's eyes and the longest claws this side of the Mississippi."

"Lieutenant, you're—"

"I'm not a Yank, or a carpetbagger, Tess, and so help me—"

"You're about to crush my shoulder blades, Lieutenant," she said as regally as she could manage.

"Oh." He released her. "Do excuse me."

"I try, Lieutenant. Daily. Hourly." She started for the door.

"Tess?"

She didn't turn.

"I could have made you beg, you know?"

She spun around. He was laughing. She raced forward in a sudden surge of energy and butted him in the stomach. Taken off guard, he fell into the singed hay.

She didn't stay to hear anything else he might have to say. She raced from the carriage house and back to the house, not pausing until she was inside. She leaned against the door, gasping for breath.

The dining table was clean. Jane came from the kitchen and paused when she saw Tess. "They've all gone to bed, Tess. Hank just went to the bunkhouse. Mr. Red Feather suggested that the hands take a few hours apiece on a kind of a guard duty. Roddy called in that big guard dog of his and he's going to have the dog on the porch, once he sees the lieutenant and tells the dog that the lieutenant is a friend. I was going to go to bed. It's been a big day for me, Miss Stuart. A real big day.''

Her eyes rolled and Tess laughed. Impulsively she gave Jane a big hug. It was a mistake. Jane looked as if she was going to start crying all over again. ''I'm just so happy that you're alive!'' she said.

''Thanks. And I'm happy to be home. Come on, let's go up.''

They walked up the stairs together. Jane hugged Tess quickly and fiercely again and headed toward her own room. Wearily Tess pushed open the door to her bedroom and walked in. Lighting the lamp at her bedside, she shed her clothing and dressed in a soft blue flannel nightgown. She sat in front of her dressing table and picked up the silver-embossed brush that had belonged to her mother. It was good to be home.

She pulled all the pins out of her hair—and then all the little pieces of hay that had stuck into it—and began to brush it. It fell down her shoulders, long and free. She brushed it mechanically for several minutes, staring at her reflection and not seeing a thing.

Jane had been right. It had been a big day.

But von Heusen had been beaten back. Between Jamie and Jon, he had been beaten back. She never had told Jamie that she was grateful. Truly grateful.

He never seemed to give her a chance to say thank you. He was on her side, but it seemed that she was always fighting him. At first, she had been fighting him to make him believe her. Now she was certain he believed her. He had met von Heusen. He couldn't have any doubt that von Heusen had been responsible for the attack on the wagon train.

And now...

Maybe she wasn't fighting him. Maybe she was fighting herself.

First it had been that darned Eliza. Tess had managed to walk away from Eliza with her dignity intact, but she had heard Jamie speaking to the woman. No one can make me marry anyone. No one can make me marry anyone...

So he wasn't the marrying kind.

She was. She wanted a man, a good man. She hadn't had much time to think about it, what with the war and then everything that had happened since. But when she thought for a moment, she knew. She didn't want to be a spinster. The paper was important to her, and she wasn't just copublisher and a reporter anymore, she was the only publisher. She had to keep it alive. But she wanted more, too. She wanted a husband, one she really loved, and one who loved her. And she wanted children, and she wanted to give them a world that wasn't forever tainted with the memories of conflict and death.

And she wanted Jamie Slater...

She wasn't at all sure how the two things intertwined—they didn't intertwine at all, she admitted. She sighed.

She had to get by the present for the moment. She had to survive von Heusen.

She shivered suddenly, violently, remembering the way von Heusen had threatened her. She would be getting out of town, he had told her. If not by stagecoach, then by some other means.

What could he do to her? She wasn't alone. She had help now.

But to pay for it she was about to turn over half her property—half of Uncle Joe's legacy to her—to Jamie Slater. If he chose, he could be her neighbor all her life. She could watch him, and torture herself day after day, wondering who he rode away to see, wondering what it was like when he took a woman into his arms.

She groaned and pushed away from the table. She couldn't solve a thing tonight. She needed some sleep. She needed some sleep very badly.

She doused the light and crawled beneath the covers. It felt so good to be in her own bed again. The sheets were cool and clean and fresh-smelling, and her mattress was soft and firm, and it seemed to caress her deliciously. A faint glow from the stars and the moon entered the room gently. It kept everything in dark shadows, and yet she could see the familiar shapes of her dressing table and her drawers and her little mahogany secretary desk.

The breeze wafted her curtains. She closed her eyes.

Perhaps she dozed for a moment. Not much time could have passed, and yet she suddenly became aware that something was different. Her door had been thrust open.

She wasn't alone.

Jamie was standing in the doorway, his hands on his hips, his body a silhouette in the soft hazy moonbeams. There was nothing soft or gentle about his stance, however. She could feel the anger that radiated from him.

"All right, Tess, where's my room?"

His room? "Oh!" she murmured. "Your room...well, I didn't think you were going to stay here."

Long strides brought him quickly across the room. She scrambled to a sitting position as he towered over her. "I just spent two days riding with you to get here. I spent two nights sleeping on the hard ground beneath the wagon."

"The hay in the barn is very soft."

"The hay in the barn is very soft," he repeated, staring at her. He leaned closer. "The hay in the barn is very soft? Is that what you said?" She felt his closeness in the shadows even as she inhaled his clean, fascinating, masculine scent. His eyes seemed silver in the darkness, satanic. She was riddled with trembling, so keenly aware of him that it was astonishing.

"You don't have a room for me?" he demanded.

"All right, I am sorry. But you were gone, and we were all exhausted. And you did have a bath somewhere...I just believed that you meant to sleep where you had bathed."

He was still for a moment—dead still. Then he smiled. "Miss Stuart, move over."

"What?"

"Move over. If there's no room for me, then I'll sleep here."

"Of all the nerve!"

"Hush! We share this bed, or we sleep in the hay together," he warned her.

He meant it! she thought, still incredulous. She started to rise, trying to escape from the bed. He caught her arm and pulled her gently back.

"Where are you going?" he whispered.

"Where else! You're bigger than I am—I can't throw you out! I'm going to the barn!"

"Wait."

"For what?" she demanded.

For what? Every pulse within her was alive and crying out. She felt him with the length of her body, with her heart, with her soul, with her womb. He did not hold her against him. He caressed her.

He was warm, and his smile and the white flash of his teeth in the night were compelling and hypnotic.

"I said that we'd go together," he told her. He swept her up, cocooned in a tangle of sheet and quilt. He held her tightly against his body and started for the door.

Her arms wound around his neck. She stared at the planes of his face and felt as if the soft magic of the moonbeams had wrapped around her. She should have been screaming, protesting, bringing down the house. But she was not. Her fingers grazed his nape, and she felt absurdly comfortable in his arms. He was dragging her out to the hay, she thought, and she did not care.

Nor was there anything secretive or furtive about his action. He moved with long strides and went down the stairway with little effort to be quiet. He opened the front door, bracing her weight with one arm, then let it close behind him. He stood on the porch and looked out into the night. Then he stared at her, and she knew that she was smiling.

"Where am I heading?"

"I don't know."

"Where do the hands sleep?"

"In the bunkhouse, by the far barn."

"Then I want the first barn?" he demanded softly.

She couldn't answer him. She wasn't sure what the question was. All she could think was that he meant her to sleep in the hay. She wasn't sure what else he meant for her to do there, but though she was in his arms now, and though he carried her with a certain force, she suddenly knew that what happened would be her choice. Still, he had caught hold of something deep within her, and she wasn't angry.

She smiled again as she looked at him and told him primly, "You, sir, are completely audacious."

"Maybe," he said, and smiled in return. Then it seemed they were locked there in the night, their eyes touching, and something else touching maybe, with the tenderness of the laughter they shared. Then the laughter faded.

He pulled her more tightly against him, higher within his arms. And as she watched him, fascinated, in the glow of the moonbeams, his lips parted upon hers, and the world seemed to explode as his kiss entered into her.

Darkness swirled around her, and sensation took flight.

She had to get away from him...and quickly.

No...she had to stay. She was where she wanted to be. Exactly where she wanted to be.

Chapter Eight

He carried her, in the moonlit night, to the barn. He entered it and laid her, in her cocoon of covers, in the rear of the building, where soft alfalfa lay freed from its bales, ready to be tossed to the horses. The smell of the hay was sweet, almost intoxicating.

He lay down beside her and brought the back of his hand against her cheek, touching the length of it, as if he studied just her cheek and found the form and texture both beautiful and fascinating. Then his finger roamed over the damp fullness of her lip. He watched the movement as he touched her, then his eyes met hers. She could still feel, in her memory, in the pulse that seemed to beat throughout her, the touch of his lips against hers. And yet when he kissed her again, though the feel was poignant, she knew that he would move away when he did.

He lay back against the hay, staring at the rafters and the ceiling. He groaned softly, then rolled suddenly, violently, to face her again. He didn't touch her, but leaned on an elbow to stare at her reproachfully.

"You couldn't have just arranged a room, for me, huh?"

"You couldn't have just stuck around for a while, huh?" she retorted. He was ruining it, dissolving the moonbeams, destroying the moment she had imagined and waited for.

He rolled on his back again. "Go to your room," he told her. "I had no right to drag you out here."

Tess leaped to her feet, her cheeks flaming, her body and soul in torment. She stared at him furiously. "You have no right to do what you're doing now! To ruin everything!"

"To ruin everything?" He scowled. "Tess! I'm trying damned

hard to do the decent thing!'' And she would never know what an effort it was taking. He felt on fire, as if he burned in a thousand hells. It had been all right before he touched her, before he felt her lips parting beneath his. Before he sensed her innocence and the sweet wildness beneath it, the passion, the sensuality that simmered and swept beneath it all, that promised heaven. She was different. He wasn't sure if he dared take her all the way, because he knew it would mean fragile ties that might bind him forever. He couldn't find a simple fascination in her beauty; it would be more, and though he couldn't begin to define it, it was there. He already slept with dreams of her haunting his mind; he never forgot for a moment the way she had looked upon the rock, as naked as Eve, as tempting as original sin.

"Tess, don't you see? I'm trying to let you go!"

She paused, and it seemed that she waited upon her toes, as if she would go or stay according to the way the breeze came. There was a curiously soft smile on her face, almost wistful, a look he had seldom seen. "What if I don't want to be let go?" she asked him very quietly, with a breathless, melodic whisper. He wasn't sure he had really heard the words. Real or not, they ignited embers within him. He came to his feet and looked at her across the small, shadowed distance that separated them. He could almost reach out and touch her. If he did, he would be lost. If he put his hands upon her now, he would never let her go.

"You have to make up your mind." He almost growled the words. "No strings, no promises, no guarantees. You should run. You should run from me just as fast as one of those thoroughbreds of yours."

"Why?"

She didn't move; she hadn't taken a step. There was a note of amusement and challenge in her voice. Her chin was raised high; her eyes were brilliant, nearly coal-black in the shadows. He forced himself to walk around her, but that was a mistake. The moon was filtering through the windows, and the light played havoc with the flannel gown she wore. Light touched fabric, molded it, saw through it. He felt again the softness of the woman he had held, and his hands itched to touch her again. A hunger took root inside him, one that made him long to caress and taste and know.

"Why?" He repeated her question.

The reasons were swiftly leaving his mind. If she was willing, he was more than anxious to drown in the sweet depths of her fascinating waters. He clenched his fingers and kept moving casually. "Because we're in a barn, because I've the distinct feeling you don't know what you're doing, because you're young and because you're probably the type of woman who ought to fall in love, deeply in love, with the right man, and have a band of gold, and all the rest. Because I'm the hardened refuse of an ill-fated war, and though I don't mind a fight, I wouldn't be looking for more than a lover."

She smiled. "Lieutenant, what makes you think I'd be looking for anything more than a lover?"

He almost groaned aloud. If she didn't leave soon...

"Tess, I don't think you know—"

"I'm twenty-four, Lieutenant. And just as much the refuse of an ill-fated war as you are. That war taught me a great deal. You can't always wait to seize what you want. Life is too short, too quickly severed."

She was smiling still, and there was something poignant about her words that caught hold of his heart. He had never seen her more beautiful, more feminine, more arresting. Her eyes were wide; her smile was gentle; her still form was compelling in the flannel that was draped over her shoulders, nearly falling from them, that conformed to the rise of her breasts, then fell to the floor. Her hair was a river of dazzling, honeyed light that caressed and embraced her, waving around her shoulders and falling almost to her waist. Her eyes... When he came close, he saw that they were not coal-black at all, but so deeply colored in the near darkness that they appeared to be a rich and hypnotic purple.

He held still. He watched her and tried to find the right words, the words that would get her to leave. She would hate him for humiliating and rejecting her, but maybe that would be better than what he wanted. To own her, to have all of her, to teach her everything she wanted to know so thoroughly that she would forget everything but the feel of him beside her...

"Come here then," he said hoarsely.

She still seemed to pause. Like a sprite, like a night witch or angel, he knew not which. A rueful curve came to her lips, and she said softly, "Jamie?"

"What?"

"Where did you take your bath?"

He smiled, too. "At the livery stables. Not at the saloon."

"Thank you," she murmured, then she took a step toward him, and another step, and she was in his arms.

His mouth closed upon hers, and he let his hands wander where they would. He had tried to do the decent thing. And it hadn't worked. So now...

She was fragrant, like a drug. He breathed in the scent of her hair and the scent of her flesh. He kissed her lips and her earlobe, and he pressed his tongue against the surge of her pulse at her throat, and he took her lips again, savoring the caress of her tongue, feeling the rise of heat and need and the rampant beat in his loins as the thrusts of their tongues became ever more erotic and telling. He stroked her body through the flannel, caressing her breast, finding the peak and massaging it to a hard pebble with his thumb and fingers. Then he cried out and lowered his mouth upon her, his teeth grazing the fullness of her breast and the hard peak through the fabric, the dampness of his mouth pervading it and bringing whispers and whimpers to her lips. She braced herself upon his shoulders, and cried out, falling against him. Trembling, he lifted her and set her on the cocoon of sheet and quilt in the hay. Then he stood over her, watching her. He ripped away the kerchief at his throat and slowly undid the buttons of his shirt. He watched her all the while, but her eyes did not close. He threw his shirt upon the hay, and pulled off his boots and socks, unbuckled his gun belt and then his pants belt and finally peeled away the last of his clothing. Her eyes closed at last, but not before her cheeks had taken on a dusky hue.

"You can still run," he told her harshly.

She shook her head. Her hair lay spread across the quilt and sheet and dangled into the hay around them. He knelt before her and set his hand upon the hem of her gown, pushing it up. She had beautiful feet. Small, the toenails neatly manicured. Her ankles were trim. Her calves were shapely.

He paused to press kisses against her kneecaps, then he continued, thrusting the gown up to her hips where he paused because his breath had caught. The entire length of her legs was fine and beautiful, and her hips were seductively flared. Her waist was very narrow, and she was endowed with the same touch of honey hair to add even greater purity and innocence to her beauty. That very touch of purity seemed to be driving him insane. A ragged pulse beat at his groin, and in his mind, and raged throughout his fingers and his limbs and all of his body. He buried his face against her belly, and a harsh sound escaped him, a cry of longing, of need, of desperate desire. Some soft sound escaped her, and she gasped when his lips moved upon her flesh, when he turned his head against her, his hair teasing the flesh of her abdomen, then his kiss and lips caressing it again.

As he kissed her he continued to push the gown up. The flannel raked over her breasts, over her hardened nipples. He rose and knelt over her again, taking each breast fully into his mouth. She was alabaster, as perfect as marble with the dusky, rose-tipped peaks, so hard, so compelling, drawing his body into a tighter, harder knot all the while, exciting him to an ungodly high with the mere whisper of her breath, the tiny gasps that escaped her, the sultry, sensual way her body moved against him. Such little movements, as if she was afraid, as if she discovered the haunting rhythms of making love.

He paused, meeting her eyes. Half-closed eyes—dazed, damp, luminous and honest—meeting his. Her gaze fell upon his naked and aroused body, and her eyes widened again. They met his again, and the beautiful flush of rose came to her cheeks. He reached for her gown and pulled it over her shoulders, and they knelt facing each other. She threw her arms shyly around him, but that served to press them together, all their nakedness, and he felt her breasts upon his chest as thoroughly as he knew that she felt the ripple of his muscle and the blinding heat that led him now.

He pressed her into the quilt, down, down, into the hay. He crawled over her again, seizing hold of her lips, kissing her until her breath came raggedly, until her breasts rose and fell heatedly in his hands, until she trembled wherever he touched her. Then he kissed her breasts again, fascinated by the shape and texture and by the perfect marble beauty. He lowered himself against her, near blinded by his own need yet driven to see that she felt no pain, that she savored this time between them as he did, that she remember the passion, the desperation, the aching, longing need.

He kissed her between her breasts, then strayed down the length of her breastbone. He touched her ribs with the tip of his tongue and delved deeply into her navel the same way. And then he dropped his head still lower. He felt her legs quiver and a quickening within her and heard the soft, shocked protest on her lips. But he ignored her and made love completely to her, delving into the very femininity of her. She cried out, this time not so softly. He laced his fingers with hers and touched and delved ever deeper. He brought the searing, damp heat of his kiss and caress to the very bud of her desire. Her fingers tightened painfully around his, but he wedged himself firmly between her thighs and tenderly caressed her. She whimpered, tossing her head so her hair spread out like a burst of sunrise. And still he drank ever more deeply of her sweet scent and taste, until he could feel the pulse of desire rising within her.

He crawled atop her then, discovering her eyes closed, her face ashen. And yet her fingers dug into his shoulders, and when he carefully lowered himself over her and pushed slowly within her, he found her damp and welcoming. He watched her face even as he thrust past the portals of her innocence, and she never cried out or murmured a single protest or whimper. He sheathed himself slowly inside her, then he held and caught hold of her chin.

Her eyes flew open, so large and dark, then they fluttered closed again as he took her lips and caressed her with long, slow, leisurely kisses—taking all of her mouth, exploring, tasting, savoring. And as he kissed her he began to move within her, strokes as soft as velvet, slow and evocative, coercive...

He felt something give within her when the pain had faded and the new pleasure began. There was an easing of her arms around him, and her long, enchanting legs wound tightly around him. Her fingertips grazed his shoulders, the nails lightly stroking. Soft sounds of passion began to escape her.

He thrust hard then, unleashing the passion that had grown and simmered and become explosive within him. He moved like the wind and like the earth, and he whispered to her, words that meant nothing, words that barely found syllables, and yet words that meant everything. Their lips met again and again, parted, fused and sealed together, as did their bodies. He felt himself grow slick with the heat they ignited in the night, and he knew that he could not hold on much longer. And still he fought the climax that clamored in his loins, in his heart, in his mind. He fought it, driving her ever upward, leaving her shivering in moonbeams, taking her ever higher. Then he felt it. A wild stiffening in her body, a stark moment in which she seemed to fight him, then she was trembling beneath him in great shudders.

He cast back his head. He felt a groan rumbling in his throat just as the heat and fever and excitement within him drew to a massive pitch. The sound escaped him, the life and energy and heat of his body shot from him, filling her. Again and again, shudders seized him, and he filled her again and again. Then he wrapped his arms around her and held her very tightly. He eased to her side, taking his weight from her but keeping his arms around her so that she fell atop him. She sighed softly. Damp tendrils of her hair curled over him. He touched it and remembered wondering how it would feel against him.

Like silk...it felt like silk. And it looked like the sun, so blond against the bronze of his skin. And she felt like silk, her body so slick with all that had been between then, covering him.

Her face lay against his chest. She didn't say a word, and she didn't seem to want to look at him.

"Are you all right?" he asked her, softly smoothing back a tendril of her hair.

She nodded against him.

"Did I—hurt you?"

She shook her head, but still she didn't say a word.

"You're not crying, are you?" he asked her.

"No!" she said in muffled, indignant protest.

"Women do, you know."

"Women do!" she repeated, speaking at last. She sat up, and her eyes met his. "How many women do you—did you...Oh, never mind!" She started to pull away. Her breasts swung heavy and fascinating before him, and he quickly laughed, pulling her back. His voice was husky when he spoke.

"I've never, never, been in a—er, circumstance like this one before."

"Like—"

"With a virgin," he said flatly.

She flushed crimson. He pulled her close to him. She was wiggling and squirming, ready to retreat now that it was all over, despite the way she had played the seductress so boldly. He didn't want to lose her.

"Tess!"

"What? Will you please—"

"I didn't go back to Eliza that night, either. The whole thing was a show—"

"Eliza is in love with you."

"Eliza is in love with a lot of people."

She paused, tossing her hair, studying him with her enormous eyes. "And what about you?"

"I'm not in love with anyone," he said. Again, he felt her pulling away. He tightened his hold around her. "But I am in love with your eyes. And I love the way you fight until the bitter end, though I could also strangle you for that same quality. I love the way you think, and I love the way you take care of the people around you, and I even love the way your eyes flash when you're jealous."

"I'm not jealous—"

"Then you're nosy. You were damned determined to know where I had taken my bath."

"Because—" She broke off, staring at him.

He grinned. "Because you weren't about to come near me if I had been near another woman, was that it?"

"Yes!"

He laughed again, hugged her close and rolled her over in the hay. "Never fear, my feisty little love. When I am near you, I will never find the need for another."

His lips closed over hers. He stroked his hand down the length of her, touching her openly and intimately. A sound rumbled in her throat against his kiss. He ignored her.

All the fires of hell were burning inside him again, and this time he need not be so slow, so careful. She had learned about tenderness. She was ready to learn about the tempest.

Later, when dawn neared, she slept. Jamie stared at the rafters as the first pale light of day appeared, impressed by the eagerness and complete abandon with which she had approached lovemaking. He had never known a feeling of such relaxation, of physical bliss as her sleeping body against his. She had learned many things this night...

She slept with her knee slightly curved upon him, her hair tangled around his shoulders and chest. He touched a strand lightly, and it was almost as if the gold and honey touched him back, as if it gave him warmth. He looked at her face, so beautiful, so perfect, her lips just slightly parted, cherry red in the first rays of light, tempting. He stroked her shoulder and her back. She moved against him, and he felt the warmth of her breath upon him as she sighed softly.

She had learned so much...

But he had learned a great deal that night, too. He had learned that he'd never really made love before. He'd had women, but he had never really, truly made love.

He'd never wanted anyone like he'd wanted her.

Wanted her still...

Who had taught whom? he wondered.

He kissed the soft skin of her back and wondered again at the ripple of longing that went through him. Then he sighed. He had to wake her up and let her go back to the house before the morning began, before the ranch came alive.

By nine that morning they arrived in town. Jamie drove the wagon with Tess sitting primly by his side.

Morning had changed things amazingly, he thought. Since he had awakened her, she had been distant. She had donned her flannel gown, and with it a peculiar silence. She hadn't seemed remorseful about anything; she had been cool and quiet. She hadn't sneaked back to the house; she had walked very calmly. She had promised him she would be ready in thirty minutes. When he had pressed his lips to hers on first awakening, she had responded with warmth, but already there had been that widening within her eyes, as if she thought that something very grave had gone on, something she hadn't quite realized at the time. He'd almost braced himself, waiting, but she hadn't anything to say to him at all. She had dressed quickly and walked to the house. Her chin was high, and she wasn't about to hide anything, but then again, Jamie thought, maybe she wasn't about to do anything again, either.

I never wanted to rush it! he reminded himself in silence. But he still hadn't found the right words to say to her, and she sat by him quietly as they rode into town. They didn't exchange five words.

It was early, and the streets were nearly still. Only a passerby or two walked the plank sidewalks in front of the bank and the barbershop and the offices of the *Wiltshire Sun*. Tess bit her lip and looked at the newspaper office, but she remained silent on that point. "Mr. Barrymore's office is right ahead. He was always Joe's solicitor."

"Well, then, fine, we're going to go see Mr. Barrymore."

He helped her from the wagon. She was dressed for spring, in light-blue-and-white checked muslin, with a matching wide-brimmed bonnet.

The touch of her fingers against his seemed electric. She met his eyes and flushed.

"We need to talk," he told her.

"I need to get to the newspaper," she retorted. "So hurry along now, will you?"

"Eager to turn it all over to me, eh?"

"I shall resent it to my dying day," she said sweetly, "but then, you *are* better than von Heusen."

"Such a compliment!" he teased, bowing low as he opened the door to the lawyer's office.

Tess started to reply, but instead smiled at the tall, lean man behind the desk. "Mr. Barrymore, how are you?" she inquired, walking forward, reaching out her hand.

The man rose instantly to his feet. He reached out for Tess's hand, but his eyes were on Jamie. Jamie winced inwardly, realizing this man had been in the saloon the other night when he had met von Heusen's boys.

Tess didn't see the recognition in his eyes. "Mr. Barrymore, this is Lieutenant Slater. Lieutenant, Mr. Barrymore, who has helped my family for years."

Mr. Barrymore was still staring at Jamie.

"Mr. Barrymore!" Tess said more sharply.

"Oh, my dear, my dear, I am so glad to see you! Of course, you know that Joe left everything in your name—"

"That's why I'm here," Tess said.

"Of course, of course—"

"No, you don't understand. I want to turn over half my holdings to Lieutenant Slater."

"Half your holdings?"

"Half."

At last, Mr. Barrymore looked at Tess. The pen he held in his hands nearly snapped as he stared at her. "Half?"

"Half."

He cleared his throat and stared at Jamie. "That will make you a very rich young man."

"I intend to pay the lady, but the money is going to be due to her in payments over the next few years. Can we draw up a schedule?" Jamie said.

Tess stared at him then. "You're going to pay me?"

"Of course. You didn't think I was just going to whisk away your property."

"Yes, but—"

"Tess," he said softly. "You're—I mean, the land is worth it."

He thought she was going to leap to her feet and scream. She managed not to. She leaned over the desk and smiled at Mr. Barrymore. "Make sure he pays the premium price then, will you?"

"Well, yes," Mr. Barrymore said nervously. He looked at Jamie, then he looked at Tess, then he cleared his throat. "You're sure this is what you want, Tess?"

"Yes."

"And Mister—er—Lieutenant Slater, would you, uh, like to explain how you want these payments to be made?"

"Certainly," Jamie said. He rattled off sums and amounts, and Mr. Barrymore began to write quickly. "And when we're done with this," Jamie said, "I need to make out a will, and Miss Stuart is going to do so, too. In the case of both our deaths, the property is to be equally divided in ownership between my two brothers, Cole Slater and Malachi Slater, and in case of *their* deaths, to their heirs."

He smiled at Tess reassuringly. "Oh, yeah, and Mr. Barrymore, I want you to make sure you talk about this. I want the whole town to know that there's just no way, no way at all, the Stuart spread is ever going to be up for sale. Do you understand me?"

Barrymore stayed silent for a long moment, then he began to

smile. "You've got it, Lieutenant Slater. Damn, but you've got it! Oh, excuse me, Tess. I plumb forgot you were sitting there!"

"How amusing," Tess said with a stiff smile.

"They'll know, all right, they'll know...." Mr. Barrymore was writing quickly. "I must hand it to you, Lieutenant, you do seem to know what you're doing with property and the law. Though it ain't surprising, not one bit. You sure do know what you're doing with those Colts of yours. Why, in all my life, I've never seen anything like the shootin' you did in the saloon the other night—"

"Shooting?" Tess interrupted, sitting straight.

"Oh, my, yes, you should have seen him! Some of those hooligans of Mr. von Heusen's come in and they were giving Hardy a bad time, but the Lieutenant here, he stood right up to them." Mr. Barrymore slapped his hand hard on his desk and hooted with laughter. "It was a joy to these weary eyes, Tess, it was! Didn't you tell Miss Stuart about it, Lieutenant? Hell—heck, boy, if it had been me, I'd have told the whole damned—darned—world about it!"

"I didn't seem to have the chance, Mr. Barrymore. When I got home, a few more of Mr. von Heusen's boys were at the ranch. And someone needed to tell those fellows that it wasn't a good thing to play with matches."

"You shot von Heusen's men in the saloon?" Tess asked, staring at him.

"Sure," Mr. Barrymore said cheerfully. "Why, you would have heard about it if you'd gone into the paper, Tess. The lieutenant was sitting with Ed Clancy and Doc."

Tess stood and stared at Jamie. "I think I'll take a little walk over to the *Wiltshire Sun* right now. I'm sure, Lieutenant Slater, that you know exactly how you want everything worded. Then Mr. Barrymore can draw up the papers and I will come back and sign them. Excuse me, will you?"

Jamie and Mr. Barrymore both stood quickly, but Tess was already at the door. She stormed out, feeling her face red, wondering if she should be furious with the man or if she should run back and kiss him. She wasn't going to do either—she was going to see Ed and find out exactly what had happened.

She walked into the *Wiltshire Sun* office as if she were a battleship. Harry, the printer, looked up from his plates. Edward, at work at his desk, also looked up. The naked joy in his eyes as he saw her made her first questions flee. He leaped up to hug her, nearly breaking every bone in her body. "I knew you were all right, Tess, because I saw Slater. But, girl, it does an old body good to see you!"

"Thank you, Edward, thank you!" she told him.

Harry, toothless and shy, was standing behind him. "And you, too, Harry, come here. Let me give you a big, sloppy kiss right on that jaw of yours!"

He flushed a bright red from his throat to his white, tufted hair, but he accepted a kiss and hugged her tightly in return. "We just kept doing the paper, Miss Tess. Even when they tried to tell us that you weren't coming back, we just kept the *Sun* going out on schedule. Every Tuesday, Thursday and Saturday, we had a *Wiltshire Sun* out on the street!"

"And I'm so grateful and so proud of both of you!" Tess assured him.

Edward cleared his throat. "Well, I didn't exactly have the news of the nation going out," he admitted. "Ah, hell, Tess! I didn't really have the balls to print too much. Von Heusen was breathing down my neck, and I—"

"You kept it going," Tess said. "And I'm grateful." She pulled off her gloves and headed for her desk. "Am I in time to get in a story for the Tuesday edition?"

"Yes, yes, Miss Stuart! I'll clean out the presses, I'll—"

"I've just got one story," Tess assured him. "But it's an important one. I want it on the front page."

She smiled at Edward and inserted paper into the newfangled typewriter she had insisted they buy. She closed her eyes, pausing for a moment, smelling the ink on Harry's plates. Then she smiled and started to type. She described the small wagon train, then she described the attack. She described the attackers, who had looked like white men painted up to look like Comanche. She wrote about being saved by the cavalry, then she wrote about Chief Running River and how he had sworn his people had not had anything to do with the attack. Then she wrote that she knew she was an eyewitness...and a survivor. She ended the piece with a bold accusation.

"Certain tyrants in this town will stoop to any means to bring about their chosen results. This town has been mercilessly seized upon. We've seen our friends and neighbors disappear. Some say it was the war, but the war has ended, and all good men are trying to repair broken fences and lend a helping hand. In this town, however, we have been met by evil. Yes, my friends, evil lives in man. The evil that killed a man like Joe Stuart. Joe Stuart's death must not be in vain. We must band together and fight the evil. It does not come from the war. It comes from a man, and no matter how he threatens, we can beat him—if we stand together.''

She left it at that. She hesitated for a moment, searching for better words, then shrugged. She had said what she wanted to say. She pulled the sheet of paper from the machine and handed it to Edward. ''Read this over for me, will you, Ed?''

His eyes were already racing over the piece. He was a swift proof-reader, and he quickly came to her final paragraph. His fingers trembled, and the paper wavered within them. ''Tess—''

''I want it out tomorrow,'' she said.

''Tess, he'll come after you lock, stock and barrel—''

''He already left me for dead once,'' she said.

''But, Tess—''

''Print it, please. And now tell me—what happened at the saloon the other night?''

Edward stared, trying to change his train of thought as quickly as she was changing the conversation. ''The other night? Why, Miss Tess, I was just in a little need of companionship—''

''Not that, Clancy, not that! I want to hear about the lieutenant.''

''The lieutenant?''

''Slater, Edward Clancy! Jamie Slater and the von Heusen men and the blazing guns.''

''Oh, it was something, Tess. Honest to God, but it was something!''

''Something? Fine. What? Tell me about it, please!''

''Why, he just come into the bar, and we all kind of greeted him—''

''Everyone in the place stared at him, wondering if he was dangerous or not?''

''Right, right. Doc and I were playing cards and we invited him over for a whiskey. He started asking questions right away, then von Heusen's guns came in. One of them had Hardy the bartender by the throat when Jamie Slater asked him to stop. The man laughed. Then they were all threatening to shoot up Slater, but that Slater, he had their number! Before you know it—one, two, three, four! All of them were lying on the floor and choking and crying and carrying on like babes. And Slater just stepped over them, cool as a cucumber, and walked over to the barber and got himself a shave and a bath.

"Well, of course, von Heusen's fellers, they were threatening him right and left, but those boys lit out of town as soon as Doc patched them up, lit straight out of town, they did. Don't know if they went back to von Heusen or if they rode away for good. I ain't seen a one of them since. Of course, one young feller, he ain't gonna be ridin' anywhere for a while, he kind of took his shot in the posterior section, if you know what I mean."

"I think I know what you mean," Tess said. She gave Ed another kiss on the cheek. "You take care now. I'll be in tomorrow morning. You make sure my piece goes on the front page."

"Yes, ma'am!"

Tess left the office and walked slowly down the street toward Mr. Barrymore's office.

What had she gotten?

She'd wanted a hired gun. And she'd gotten one. She railed against Jamie for leaving the ranch when he'd been finding out what he could—and shooting it out with some of von Heusen's toughs at the same time.

And gaining quite a reputation as he did so. She shivered suddenly. She'd seen him shoot the snake. She'd known that he was fast and good. She shouldn't have been surprised to hear that he had knocked down four of von Heusen's men in a matter of seconds. Then he'd humiliated von Heusen at the ranch...

Von Heusen was going to be mad, and he was going to be thirsting for blood. Her blood.

But she'd known she had to fight him. And she had Jamie. She'd wanted the gun.

And she'd wanted the man.

And now she had both.

She tightened her fingers around the drawstring of her little purse and stopped walking to lean against a wooden wall as a fierce trembling swelled within her. She swallowed hard and inhaled deeply as she remembered the previous night. She couldn't have been so brazen.

Or so wanton…or so decadent…or so searingly intimate. But she had been. He had warned her away. He had given her every opportunity. He had told her that she should be with a man who cared. He implied that he didn't care.

Surely that wasn't true. He liked her. There were things about her he loved.

But it didn't mean anything. That was the rub. It didn't mean anything at all. She was just a woman, a warm, willing body. Just like Eliza. She had thrown herself at him…

And one day he'd turn away from her, just as he had turned from Eliza.

She inhaled, exhaled, then forced herself to walk. She must not let it happen again. Even if it had been more than she had ever dreamed. She'd never imagined that making love could be so erotic, so wonderful. She'd never imagined that it was possible to feel so excited, so cherished, so explosive and so sated. She'd never imagined that a man's hands could do what his had done, or that a man's kiss could awaken everything in her body, or that a man could join with a woman so completely and bring about such splendor.

It could quickly become addictive…

But he didn't intend to stay. Even if he bought her land and settled down, he had made it clear that he didn't intend to stay with her.

She had taken care to sound independent, too. And now…

Now she wanted to lie down beside him again. She wanted to laugh and feel his touch and explore his shoulders and his chest and his long, muscled legs and…everything. Everything. Even the parts of the body that she couldn't quite bring herself to name aloud. She had wanted him. She'd never deny that. But now she was afraid of the longings that seemed to have escalated since she had known his touch. Having him hadn't quenched the desire at all.

It had set it all afire…

She was in front of the lawyer's office. She set her hand on the knob and twisted it and walked in. Mr. Barrymore was just finishing copying out a second set of papers. Jamie had obviously directed him as to what he should write.

"Good timing," Jamie said, applauding her. "We need your signature."

"Shouldn't I read the documents?"

"Be my guest."

Tess took the papers from Mr. Barrymore, but she couldn't quite manage to read. She pretended to, skimming the words. They all swam before her.

"We need a witness," Mr. Barrymore said.

"No problem," Jamie told him.

He stepped outside. A moment later, he was back with Doc. He signed one set of papers, then Mr. Barrymore and Doc signed as witnesses. Then Tess signed, not having the least idea of what was really on the papers, and her signature was witnessed, too.

"That's that, then!" Jamie said, pleased. He counted out gold coins to Mr. Barrymore, who seemed very pleased. So much was being done in paper currency lately.

"Let's go, Tess," Jamie said.

"Good day, Mr. Barrymore, Doc. Thank you," she told the lawyer. But Barrymore and Doc were hardly able to respond before Jamie had his hand on her elbow and was leading her out.

When they reached the wooden sidewalk, she wrenched her hand free. "Jamie, I just might not be ready to head home."

"We're not heading home," he told her.

"Then—"

"We're going to talk."

"What if I had something to do?" she demanded.

"It would have to wait."

"It wouldn't!"

"Today, Tess," he insisted, "it would."

The brim of his hat was pulled low over his eyes, and his hands were firmly on his hips.

"Now, listen—"

"You listen," he told her, wagging a finger beneath her nose. "I'm not going to live like this. We're going to straighten out the relationship."

"There is no—"

"The hell there isn't. Now get in the wagon, or I'll put you in it."

"You wouldn't—"

He took a step toward her. Before she knew it she was off her feet, then she was sitting in the wagon. She swung around, but he was beside her in an instant, and the reins were in his hands, and he was clucking to the thoroughbred that pulled the small conveyance.

Tess crossed her arms over her chest, staring straight ahead. "You are intolerable!" she told him.

"I just don't like a bunch of bull, that's all."

"Bull—"

"The way you're acting."

"I'm not acting—"

"I hope to hell you are."

"I don't know what you're talking about."

They were already out of town. He was silent for a moment. The horse picked up its gait and it seemed they were flying down the road. Then, suddenly, Jamie reined in. The horse slowed and Jamie hooked the reins around the brake. He jumped down and came around the wagon for Tess.

"What?" she demanded, staring down at him.

He reached up, placed his hands around her waist and lifted her down. When she was on the ground, his hands still stayed upon her. His eyes were like smoke, and his jaw was twisted. She knew that he did, indeed, intend to have things out.

She opened her mouth, wanting to protest again, wanting to deny and denounce him and run away. But she was trembling because that wasn't what she wanted at all. She wanted to trust him. She wanted to lean against him. And, most of all, she wanted to feel his lips upon hers again, as hot as the sun, as rich as the earth. But she didn't want to want him so badly...she didn't want to make a fool of herself, like Eliza.

Because, like Eliza, she was falling in love with him.

"Come on," he told her.

"Where?" she protested.

"Down by the water."

The road ran along the river. He held her hand and led her through the trees until they came to a little copse. They were alone with the sounds of the rippling waters, with the occasional call of a bird, the soft rustle of a tree. He drew her close, and when she stiffened, he drew her even closer.

"What is this?" he demanded.

She moistened her lips, staring at his eyes, then at his mouth. "What is—what?" she asked.

"Miss Stuart, I gave you a chance last night. Hell, I gave you several chances last night. You wanted to stay."

"I—"

"You wanted to make love."

"I...yes," she whispered.

"And now you're running. Why?"

"I'm not!" she protested. "It's just that—"

"I can't do it, Tess. I can't live with it if you think you can blow hot and cold in a matter of hours."

"I'm not!"

"Then what?"

"I'm just trying to give you...space!"

She lowered her head. She desperately wanted to put her shoulder against his shirt. She breathed in, smelling the clean male scent of him, and she felt a furious pulse take flight at her throat, in her heart, in her veins. He slid his fingers into her hair at the sides of her head and lifted her face. He stared, and she tried to return his gaze without faltering. But then his hand came to her breast. She murmured something softly, then she did lean against him. The sky seemed dazzling, but not so dazzling as the man.

"Tess, Tess!" he whispered to her, holding her close. "It's frightening, it's damned terrifying. You're coming to mean so much to me..."

His arms were around her. She parted her lips and moistened them with her tongue again. His parted and moved upon hers, and they melded and tasted until finally he drew his lips away. Then they sank down together upon a bed of leaves, with the river just beyond them. Their arms locked together and they kept kissing, tasting one another, and it seemed that the sound of the rushing water grew louder and louder.

Tess found that she was pressed into the leaves. His hands were upon her. She set her palms against his cheek, and desire took flight within her as she felt the planes and textures of his face. She thought confusedly that she loved the way he looked with his smoke-dark eyes and sandy, disheveled hair, with the rough touch and the rugged angles and lines of his face, the twist of his jaw. She wrapped her arms around him, sliding her fingers through the hair at his nape, drawing him to her for another kiss. The earth beneath her began to heat. She ran her fingers over the opening of his shirt. She felt the ripple of muscle with her fingertips. She teased at his buttons until his shirt opened, until she could reach her hands inside and slide her nails over his naked flesh and feel the trembling that she evoked.

She heard him groan and she felt his touch upon the tiny buttons of her dress, then she felt herself being freed from her gown. Her slip and her chemise remained, but they were no barrier to the feel of his searing kiss upon her body and breast. Soon her slip was wound beneath her, and she felt the earth with her bare flesh. His hard and driving manhood teased her for a split second, then drove within her with a startling, shattering thrust that swept her breath away.

The sun was above him. She heard curious cries, then realized that they came from her and that she was clinging to him, arching, writhing…meeting him, welcoming him, wanting him. She felt the slap of his body against hers, and it was earthy and real. She felt the sun upon his naked flesh, and that, too, was real. And she felt more…the certain heat, the glow of the sun, which heightened every swift pleasure, a touch of the blue, cloudy sky…

She was damp, and so aware of him within her, and aware of the rising ecstasy inside her body. Coiling tighter and tighter until she was crying out again, then gasping in a soft shriek as something came upon her so strong and sweet and volatile that it rent the whole of her with shivers, while something like hot nectar seemed to swamp her body. She couldn't move. She could scarcely breathe, and it seemed that the world went dark before the sun burst upon her again. And just as it did, he thrust hard within her and stayed and stared at her, the whole of his face tense and haunting and taut with passion. Then he exploded within her, and thrust and thrust again…and lay down beside her, wrapping her in his arms.

The sun was still above them.

''I'm afraid of you,'' Tess admitted.

He had been flat on the earth. He rose up on an elbow. ''What?''

"I'm afraid of caring too much."

He touched her cheek. "We're all afraid of caring too much."

"I don't believe you're afraid of anything."

He smiled, a crooked, rueful smile. "Yes, I am. I'm afraid of losing you right now."

"Right now," she repeated. "But what...what about tomorrow, Jamie? That's what frightens me."

"What do you mean?"

She shook her head. She rolled away from him, rising to her feet, straightening her slip and dusting bits of leaf and dirt and grass from it. She smiled at him, then hurried toward the water.

He must have stripped off the remnants of his clothing, for when he came up behind her, he was stark naked. He placed his hands around her waist and kissed her nape. Then he whispered in her ear, so softly that she wasn't sure she heard him. "Tomorrow? I'm not sure. But I think that I'm falling in love with you, Tess."

He left her, walking into the river, then ducking beneath the surface and swimming into the center of it. He rose, let out a cry and shivered. "It's damned cold for summer!" he called out to her.

Tess stooped and threw water over her face. She watched as Jamie dove beneath the surface again.

A twig snapped suddenly behind her. She leaped up, spinning around.

There were four of them. The so-called Indians. They were clothed in bronze paint and breechclouts. "Jamie!" she whispered.

But of course there was nothing he could do. The men were armed with bows and arrows, rifles, even a few tomahawks. They were going to kill her, she thought, and Jamie would never have time to reach the surface. And it would be her fault, because if she had talked to him this morning, he would never have brought her here, and he would never have become so involved with her that he forgot danger...

"Jamie!" she screamed as one of the men lunged toward her. She fought. She kicked, she scratched, she screamed and struggled, but a second man came up, grasping her legs, and between them, she was tossed over a shoulder. She still fought, clawing, screaming, pounding.

Bronze coloring came off in her hands...

"Tess!" Jamie was charging, naked and unarmed, out of the water. She saw his eyes. They met across the distance and locked with hers; the pain and the horror of the moment was mirrored between them.

"Tess!" He screamed her name again in a loud, long cry of anguish, and he was speeding furiously toward the embankment.

The man carrying Tess began to run with her. She craned her neck, straining to see Jamie. She saw him reaching the shallows, and she saw him running, running to the shore. He rammed one of the armed attackers with such violence and force that the man fell. He spun and kicked his next opponent, then thrust his fists against him in a fury.

But then Tess saw that another man was behind Jamie as he fought. She saw the second man raise a battle club and bring it down upon Jamie's head with all his strength.

She heard the cracking sound...

And she screamed as she saw Jamie crumple to the ground, and then she saw no more, for blackness descended over the sun.

Chapter Nine

Tess didn't know how much time passed before she regained consciousness. When she did, she was hanging facedown over the flanks of a sweating horse in front of the pseudo-Indian who had grabbed her. She was acutely uncomfortable. Although the sun was setting, it was still ferociously hot. The sticky, wet hair of the horse irritated her flesh, and the continual and monotonous thump-thump-thump of its gait was bringing a ferocious pain to her head. Her arms hurt, her back hurt, and her neck burned like blue blazes. She was a great mass of pain, and at first that was all she could think of.

After a while she remembered. She'd been kidnapped. The bronze paint worn by the "warrior" behind her was coming off on her flesh and chemise where the man's thighs and knees rubbed against her.

And Jamie Slater was by the river with his head bashed in. He couldn't be alive. He had fought for her, and he had been killed in the attempt.

Scalding tears stung her eyes. She fought back the urge to scream aloud. Jamie could perhaps have survived. Maybe he had just been knocked unconscious. They had left her for dead once, and she had survived. Jamie was tough. He had survived the war, he had…

She had seen the club come against his skull.

Still, she couldn't accept it. She had to believe that he was alive because if she didn't she wouldn't care if she lived or died.

Maybe there wasn't much chance of her surviving, anyway. Von Heusen didn't know yet that there was now no way he was going to get his hands on the Stuart holdings. She wondered briefly about the other Slater brothers and their wives. Would they come to Wiltshire to accept an inheritance? When they saw what had been happening, would they pick up her fight? Why should they?

Because they were probably close. Because Jamie wouldn't have taken the time and the care to see that things were done the way they were if his brothers weren't willing to fight. To fight for him. To avenge his death. No, no, he couldn't be dead. Please! God in heaven! she prayed silently. Don't let him be dead, don't let him be dead, don't let him be...

"Let's hold up here!" someone called out.

The horse she was thrown over ceased plodding. A second animal trotted up beside it. The man spoke again. "We've come far enough. Even if someone manages to find Slater's body, they won't be able to track us. Not across the river. And we left plenty of Comanche arrows behind. She still out, David?"

"Seems to be, Jeremiah."

"Well, that's good. Still, let's stop here for the night. By tomorrow afternoon we'll meet up with the Comancheros and turn the girl over to them."

Comancheros? Despite herself Tess felt a sizzle of terror sweep through her. They weren't exactly Mexicans, and they weren't exactly Indians; they were a wild grouping of both who savagely lived off the land. They raided, pillaged, murdered and raped without thought, and they made much of their income by selling arms illegally to the Apache.

Von Heusen meant to have his revenge this time. He hadn't planned a quick, easy death for her. He had consigned her to a living hell.

She couldn't let them give her to the Comancheros. Somehow, she was going to get the best of these men. And if they had killed Jamie, she had to see that they were brought to justice.

"Come on, let's get started setting up a camp for the night," the man David said. He started to dismount. "Boy, that did feel good, swinging that club against that bastard Slater. After everything he did to us out at the Stuart place the other night, I just wish I'd had time to gouge out his eyes."

"Or take a scalp?" Jeremiah suggested with laughter.

"Yeah—or take a scalp."

"Do you think Hubert and Smitty have made it back with the good word for von Heusen yet?"

"Probably. I told them to head straight back. Someone will find Slater's body soon enough. We want to make sure we can't be blamed for it. Come on, now, let's get her down and tied up before she comes to."

Jeremiah hopped off the horse. The one named David reached for her. The one whose hands would be forever stained with the blood of Jamie Slater.

Tess let out a wild scream when those hands touched her. She was ready. He wanted to gouge out eyes? Her fingers were flying madly for his. She caught him completely by surprise. He howled like an infant when her nails swiped his face, missing his eyes but digging deeply into the flesh of his cheek. He stumbled, and she tried to right herself upon the horse.

The animal, panicked by the screams, reared high, its forelegs kicking and flailing. Desperate as she was, Tess couldn't quite gain her balance. The horse came down on four legs, kicking up great clouds of dust, then rose, pawing the sunset-hued air once again. Tess went flying into the bushes.

She lost her breath and lay stunned for several seconds. David and Jeremiah were shouting at one another, David giving the orders. "Get the horse! Get the fool horse! I'm going for the girl."

Fear spurred her aching and bruised limbs into action. She managed to rise to her bare feet and race down a narrow trail between rows of dry bush. Her feet encountered rocks and stickers, and she gasped out and tried to pray. Despite the pain she kept running. She felt as if her lungs would burst, as if her calves would buckle, but she kept going, desperate to be free.

But arms suddenly swept around her legs, and she plunged forward into the dirt. Mouthfuls of it seemed to choke her and fill her nose. She gasped and choked and wheezed and finally managed to open her eyes.

David sat atop her, straddling her. He was still wearing a breech-clout and streaked theatrical paint, but he had discarded his black braided wig. His own reddish hair looked strange against the melted bronze paint, but matched the blood-red welts she had drawn across his face. He wasn't much past his early twenties, and might even have been halfway attractive if his way of life had not done things to his face and his eyes. Both were cold, and there was a permanent twist of dissatisfaction about his jaw. He smiled as he looked at her, enjoying her situation, reveling in his power and in her misery.

She swung out again and managed to connect her fist against his cheek. He swore and secured her wrists, then started laughing as he stared at her. "My, my, Miss Stuart, it is a pleasure to see you this way!"

She was barely clad, she realized. Her chemise was dusty and pulled high, leaving her midriff bare. And her cotton petticoat was rucked up against her knees; her legs were bare beneath it. As he stared at her she felt sick. She could see his intentions in his eyes, and she wanted to die.

Not long ago Jamie had whispered on the breeze that he thought he was falling in love with her. And not long ago, he had taught her what it was to feel feminine beyond belief, to know the beauty of a mutual yearning, a soaring passion, all the sweet and fascinating things that should be shared between a man and a woman. Not long ago.

And now this horrible man with blood on his hands was looking at her and laughing.

"I always did want to get to know you better, Tess!" he assured her.

He lowered himself against her. She twisted wildly, hating the feel of his greased flesh, despising him. He tried to find her lips. She twisted and thrashed and screamed, and still she felt him touching her.

"That's all right!" he hissed against her cheek. "It's all right. You'll come to like it soon enough. I'm real good. I'm real, real good. I'll have you screaming in a way you just ain't imagined yet, honey. And later on, you'll be grateful. 'Cause you're going to Nalte, one of the chiefs of the Mescalero Apache. He's wanted a blond woman like you for a long time. They say he tried a few raids to acquire one, but he kept coming up with brunettes. Our Comanchero friends promised him a beautiful young blond white woman. Nalte is tough, Miss Stuart. You'll be real glad that I initiated you into this…"

He tried to secure both her wrists with one hand while he spoke.

Tess fought him like a wildcat, delaying his purpose but losing her strength quickly. Nalte? An Apache?

Then the Comancheros were the delivery men. Von Heusen was dealing with the Comancheros, and the Comancheros were dealing with the Apache. She would be safe from the Comancheros...

Because she was meant for the Apache!

But she wasn't safe from David. She sobbed as she fought to free her wrists. She threw his weight from her hips, but he seemed to enjoy feeling her move against him. She twisted and sank her teeth into his fingers.

He shouted out in pain and sat hard on her, plunging his fingers into his mouth and staring at her murderously. Then his palm connected sharply with her cheek, and the world seemed to spin. His hands were upon her, upon her breasts, tugging at her petticoats.

"No!" she screamed in desperation and horror. But there was no one to help her out here. Jamie was by the river, dead. The vultures might well find his body before anyone else could. David's hands were upon her, and he was tugging on her clothes. He was about to violate the only beauty she had ever really dared to reach out and hold.

"Get off her!" someone suddenly roared. And David was plucked away from her.

Tess crawled quickly backward on her elbows. Her heart soared as she saw that David and Jeremiah were involved in a fistfight with one another. David was swinging and screaming at the same time.

"What the hell's the matter with you, Jeremiah? You can have your damned turn when I'm done—"

"No! Von Heusen said no! He promised the chief an innocent woman—"

"What do you think she was doing by the river with Slater?"

"I don't know anything! I saw the girl washing her face, and I saw Slater going for a swim. That's all I saw. Von Heusen promised the Comancheros an innocent. And he made us swear not to touch her. I'm not getting my balls shot off for your entertainment, and that's a damned fact."

"I give the orders here—"

"Von Heusen gives the orders here!"

Tess realized that she was just staring at them. They were fighting like madmen and not paying the least bit of attention to her, and she was just staring at them. She rolled over and stumbled to her feet. It was time to start running again, before David convinced Jeremiah that she was no innocent and that no one would ever know if the two of them used her, too.

She hadn't gone three steps before fingers laced into her hair, dragging her back. She gasped and sobbed, swinging and flailing out, but she was so exhausted, and in so much pain, that she knew that no matter what her will, she could not fight much longer.

"Stop it! Stop it! Come on, Miss Stuart, calm down, and make the night easier on all of us! I won't touch you, and he won't touch you, you understand? Just calm down."

It was Jeremiah who held her. He was as young as David, she decided. He had lanky blond hair and colorless blue eyes, but they didn't yet hold that absolute cold, cruel streak that touched David's. He almost smiled. "I'm going to get you something to wear. Then I'm going to tie you up. I have to. But I'll get you water, too, and something to eat. We're not going to touch you."

"Speak for yourself!" David snarled from a few steps away.

"We're not going to touch her!" Jeremiah snapped. "We're going to turn her over to the Comancheros, just like we promised von Heusen."

Tess didn't know who would win out. Jeremiah kept a firm grip upon her arm and pulled her along. She saw that there was a third horse on the trail, and that a number of rolled packs were tied on the animal's back. Jeremiah kept one hand and one eye on her as he tugged at the bundles to free them. When they fell to the ground, he pulled her down with him to dig into one.

"Here," he said roughly. "Take this. And get into it. But if you try anything funny, I'll turn my back and close my ears and David can do whatever the hell he wants. Understand?"

She understood. She hadn't the strength to fight them. She needed some sleep. She needed a little time to think and plan.

She snatched the clothing Jeremiah handed her. Apache, she thought. There were fine, soft trousers and a traditional blouse of buckskin with beadwork and tin cone pendants. She slipped into the bushes with the garments.

"You stay where I can hear you!" Jeremiah called.

"I'm here!" she replied.

The buckskin garments concealed much more than the tattered remnants of her clothes had. She couldn't believe she could be grateful to Jeremiah for anything, but she was glad of the clothing. If— not if, when!—she found her opportunity to escape, she would be much better able to weather the elements.

"You still there?" Jeremiah demanded.

Tess tossed her torn undergarments into the bushes and stepped out in the Apache attire.

"She should have had a skirt. No warrior trousers," David commented.

"She couldn't ride in a skirt," Jeremiah retorted.

Tess stood quietly. Jeremiah was the one to work on, she thought. He seemed to have a few human qualities left. She lowered her eyes and stood still.

"Miss Stuart, you come over here and let me tie your hands," he said.

She didn't move. "Please..." she murmured softly.

"Well..." Jeremiah began.

"Well, nothing! She's taking you strictly for a fool, that's what she's doing!" David strode over angrily and snatched the rope from Jeremiah's hands. He walked roughly toward Tess. Seeing his face, she almost panicked. She almost ran.

"Try it. I'd love it if you did!" he told her, his eyes narrowing. He meant it. He liked the chase, he liked the fight and he even liked the smell of blood.

She held out her hands mutely. David looped the rope around them tightly, tugging hard on the knot. Then he caught her arm and dragged her past the horses to the center of the little clearing where they had paused. He shoved her down to her knees and warned her, "Sit! Just sit!" He looked over to Jeremiah. "There's a creek down past the scrub bush over there. Nothing much. But you can go get rid of that paint. Then I'll decide if I trust you to keep an eye on her so I can do the same!"

Jeremiah hesitated. "Don't you go gettin' no ideas, now, David Birch."

"I ain't going to get any ideas! I want to get this blasted paint off, and that's all!"

Jeremiah walked to the bundles and picked up a satchel of clothing. He stared at David, then walked toward the brush.

Tess kept her eyes on David. He smiled as he watched her in turn. "You think you're going to get around Jeremiah, don't you? Well, you're not going to. I'm going to see to that. You're going to reach old Chief Nalte, and then you won't have to worry about writing those rabble-rousing pieces in that newspaper of yours anymore, ever again. You'll have lots of other things to think about." He cackled with laughter. "Lots and lots of other things. Like raising a whole little troop of papooses, yeah."

Tess edged around in the dirt, turning her back on him. He laughed all the harder, then he came forward and jerked her head back so her eyes watered as they met his. "I'm going to enjoy knowing where you are. Just like I enjoyed hearing Slater's skull crush this morning. I really got a kick out of that."

She forced herself to smile. "Maybe his skull didn't crush," she said very softly.

David gritted his teeth and yanked harder on her hair. "He's gone, lady. Dead and gone. And you don't need to worry about that no more, either."

He walked away, leaving her in peace at last. In time, Jeremiah returned, and he became her silent guard.

She hadn't the energy to say anything to him. They sat in silence while the darkness fell upon them. When David returned, the two men made a fire. There was cold chicken to eat and water from canteens, but they wouldn't untie Tess's hands, and the effort to eat suddenly seemed too great. She left the food, sipped some water and lay down in the dirt.

She tried to tell herself that Jamie was alive. Any minute now he would come rushing out from the bushes and kill the two men and take her away.

But he did not come. She closed her eyes in misery and tried to forget the nightmare visions of the day.

Jeremiah came over and tossed a blanket around her shoulders and shoved a pack beneath her head for a pillow. "Don't think about going nowhere," he warned her.

David obviously didn't think the warning was enough. He stood and walked to the piles by the packhorse and came back with a good length of rope. She tried to inch away from him, but he tied one end of the rope around her ankle. Pinching her cheek, he spoke directly into her face. "If you move, I'll feel it. If you run, I'll make you pay for it."

He walked away with the other end of the rope in his hand.

It didn't really matter. If she had been threatened by every demon in hell, she couldn't have run that night. She was too weary. Tears stung her eyes. When she closed them, she saw Jamie again, fighting, then falling. And she heard his whisper. *I think I'm falling in love with you...*

It hurt to close her eyes; it hurt to open them. She prayed for sleep against the nightmare images. She tried to tell herself that he was still alive. But he would have come for her if he was alive. He would have come.

And if he was not alive, well, then, she didn't want to live, either.

Jamie was alive, if only just barely.

Jon found him around midnight, when the moon was full and high. The wagon had come home without Jamie or Tess, but very late. Jon had to try and track them from town in the darkness, and even when he had found signs that the wagon had stopped and the two of them had walked toward the river, it still took him time to find Jamie's still, crumpled body.

He drew off his buckskin jacket and wrapped it around his friend. He touched the wound at Jamie's temple where the blood had dried. Carefully moving his fingers over the skull, he decided that it was not cracked or crushed. He took his kerchief to the river and soaked it and brought it back to Jamie, cleansing the blood away. Jamie's body was icy cold. He needed warmth, and quickly.

Jon rose carefully and lifted his friend's body into his arms. He called to his pinto and the animal obediently trotted over to him. Bracing Jamie's weight with his hand upon the pommel, he managed to somehow swing up with Jamie in his arms. Then he made a clucking sound and the animal took off at a smooth lope.

At the ranch, Dolly, Hank and Jane were waiting with anxious concern. When Jon burst in with Jamie's half-naked body, Jane gasped and turned white.

"Don't you dare faint on me, young lady!" Dolly ordered her.

"Bring him right to the sofa, Jon. Jane, you run upstairs and get blankets, lots of them. And you, Hank, I'm going to need a sewing kit for that wound. Some water and some alcohol to clean him up, and maybe a little for the lieutenant to sip. My, that's a mean and nasty bash!" Hank was on his way out. Jane was still staring in horror. "Move!" Dolly commanded her.

In a moment the young woman was back with blankets. Jon draped them around Jamie and rubbed his feet. Hank returned with water and a sewing kit, and Dolly began to clean the wound. A long gash ran into the left side of Jamie's temple.

"It's amazing he's still breathing!" Dolly murmured.

"He's Missouri tough," Jon told her. "He'll make it, you'll see."

"I intend to do my best to see that he does," Dolly assured Jon. She looked at him anxiously. "What about Tess?"

Jon shook his head. "I don't know. I had to get him back here before he died. I'm going back out to see what I can find." He lifted his hat to Dolly and left. At the door he paused and looked back. "Now, don't you let him die."

"I'm just going to sew him up. And I'm going to pray."

Jon hurried out.

But when he returned to the river, he discovered that whoever had attacked Jamie and Tess had made an escape through the water. He would need daylight to track them. There was nothing he could do that night.

But maybe there was. It was late, but saloons had a tendency to cater to the late crowd. Maybe he could find out more from casual conversation over a poker game than he could from a broken branch.

He turned the pinto toward town.

Jamie's dreams were occasionally dark and occasionally erotic, but always fevered.

He fought giants with buffalo headdresses. Then the battle would fade away, the powder would dissipate, the roar of the guns would cease. He wasn't fighting Yankees anymore, he tried to tell himself in his dream world. He was a Yankee, dressed in blue. He was a specialist in Indian affairs, a linguist...

And he knew Indians. He hadn't needed Jon Red Feather to tell him that the Apache didn't like scalping. It was a contaminating thing to them, and it had to be done with careful ritual. He should have known from the very beginning that the woman hadn't lied.

The woman. Tess...

And the Yankees were gone, and the Indians were gone, and he was lying by still, cool waters, and she was walking toward him. Her hair was like the sun, falling in soft, delicate tendrils over her breasts and down her back, and her smile was at once wistful and innocent and full of the most alluring promise. She knelt beside him and her fingers touched him, raking gently over his naked flesh. He couldn't take his eyes from her. Her eyes were so giving, velvet and deep, deep blue, and startling in their honesty. He had thought that she would run, but she had not. And now, no matter whether he woke or slept, she was with him, the sun-ray webs of honey-gold hair spinning around him and wrapping him in the sweetest splendor.

Her breath was soft against him. She leaned over him, and her breasts brushed against his chest, and he groaned aloud and waited. He wanted to pull her beneath him. He wanted to see her eyes widen and darken to mauve with the startling strength of passion. He wanted to feel her arms wrap around him.

But the smoke was coming again. The powder. And people were shouting; they were at war again. The war was over, but the fighting hadn't ended. It was the Indians.

It wasn't the Indians. That was it. They could dress up all they chose, but they were not Indians. They had Tess...he couldn't remember...yes! They had Tess, they had ridden away with her. By God! What they would do with her!

He awoke and jerked up. A staggering pain seized his temple, and he cried out hoarsely, grabbing his head. The pain slowly subsided to a dull thudding, and he opened his eyes.

Jon was sitting in front of him, watching him. Jamie groaned again. "What the hell happened? Where's Tess?"

"Von Heusen's pseudo-Comanche," Jon said calmly, still studying him.

Alarmed, beginning to remember much more clearly everything that had happened, Jamie sat up. He saw that his legs were bare, that he had only been covered with blankets, and he saw that Dolly and Jane and Hank were hovering anxiously behind Jon. He gritted his teeth against the new pain that had come with his movement, frowning. "Tess?"

"She was gone."

"Gone! And you didn't go for her?"

"Wait a minute, my friend," Jon warned him. "You were supposed to have been dead—that's the way they left you. You would have been dead, if I hadn't brought you here. I couldn't trail them in the dark—"

"You can trail anyone!" Jamie savagely reminded him.

"Not when they ran the river, not without some light," Jon said. "But I did find out where they're taking her."

"Where?" Jamie exploded. The sound of the word seemed to reverberate in his skull, and he grabbed it in an effort to ease the savage pain.

"They're taking her to the Comancheros. And the Comancheros are taking her to a renegade Apache chief down in Mexico named Nalte."

Jamie grabbed a blanket and staggered to his feet. Dolly cried out softly then scolded him, "Jamie Slater. What do you think you're doing? You can't go anywhere—"

Jon had risen, too. "Sit down, Jamie. I'll go."

"No! It's my fault they took her. I'm going after her."

"You're in no condition—"

"I'm in damn fine condition!" Jamie roared. The sound of his own voice ravaged his temple. He shook his head. "I need my pants. And if you don't want to be offended, Jane and Dolly, I need you two ladies to disappear. Now!"

"Jamie Slater—" Dolly began. But he was already rising. "Jamie—"

She turned around, pinkening. Jane let out a little gasp and went tearing up the stairs.

"Want to wait until I've got some clothes for you?" Jon asked dryly.

"I'll throw something down the stairs," Dolly said. She let out an indignant little snort. "Although what good you think you're going to do that girl when you can barely hold your head up, I don't know."

"I'll be with him," Jon said.

Dolly was heading up the stairs. "I'll go saddle up your horse," Hank told Jamie, heading out.

Jamie nodded his thanks, then confronted Jon. "You can't come with me. I need you here."

"You can't ride alone. You're in no shape to do so."

"Then I'll let you come as far as the border. Maybe we'll catch up with them before that. If not, you'll have to turn back. Jon, once I go after Tess, you'll be the only one who can stand against von Heusen here. You've got to do it." He shuddered and sat on the sofa. "Comancheros! She could already be dead! And after von Heusen's men—" He broke off, white, panicked. "I'll kill him," he swore. "I'll kill von Heusen with my bare hands, and every other man who came near her. Jesus, Jon, it was my own damned fault—"

"This was going on long before you came into it, Jamie. They meant to kill her on that wagon train. And it's not as bad as you think. Von Heusen's men won't touch her, and the Comancheros won't touch her, because Nalte wants his golden blond for himself, so I learned at the saloon."

"At the saloon?"

"There's a whore there named Rosy who knows von Heusen well—personally, that is. Every once in a while von Heusen sends for her, and she goes out to his ranch. Last time she was there, he was sending out messages and making plans. This Nalte has always wanted a blond woman for a bride. You know the Apache. They usually only take one wife, unless they consider themselves well able to afford more than one. Nalte does very well. He has an Indian bride, but he wants a white woman, too. A blond white woman. And his requirements go a little further. He wants an innocent white woman."

Jamie stared at Jon blankly, then his face began to pale again.

Jon frowned, then slowly sucked in his breath. "She isn't an innocent white woman any more, is that it?"

"Jamie Slater, here are your pants!" Dolly cried, dropping a pair of trousers down the staircase. Jamie wrapped the blanket around his waist and went to retrieve them. His hands were shaking as he stumbled into his pants. Dolly tossed down a shirt, and he shrugged it on also.

"Jamie!" Jon said.

Jamie paused, looking at his friend.

"Maybe they won't know. I doubt it's something that Tess is going to rush around telling them," Jon suggested.

"First, von Heusen's men are going to have to be damned afraid of him not to hurt her," Jamie said. "Then the Comancheros. Who the hell ever trusted a Comanchero?" He strode to the sofa and stared at Jon. "I've got to catch up with them before they get to this Nalte. Or I'll have to try to talk to Nalte himself."

"Yes, you'll very definitely have to talk to him," Jon said gravely. "And carefully, Jamie. Nalte will not be easy to deal with. He's watched wars and treaties go by for years, and he is a law entirely unto himself. He eschews everything white—except for the white men's guns, horses and women. He moved his people into the mountains when the white men took over the plains, rather than have to deal with them.

"He keeps to the old ways. His women do not buy cotton for their dresses, and his scouts do not wear cotton shirts. He moves about in a breechclout as do his braves in summer, in winter he warms himself with hides and furs. He is also intelligent, astute and very dangerous—an Apache to the core."

Hank had come in. "You need the cavalry," he said.

Jamie shook his head. "No, Hank. No. If I do that, they might kill her. If I don't catch up with them before they hand her over to Nalte, I'll have to speak with him personally and convince him to give her back. It's our only chance.

"Listen Hank, von Heusen is going to think that he has both Tess and me out of the picture. If anyone comes around, act as if you haven't seen either of us. That lawyer will let out the information about the will, and that will stall von Heusen for a little while."

He paused, then strode over to the big desk, sat and drew out a piece of paper. He wrote on it quickly. "Now Hank, you make sure that this telegraph gets out today, you understand? It's real important."

"Yes, Lieutenant Slater, I understand."

"Good. Jon will be back soon, and if I've any luck at all, I'll bring Tess home to you again." He paused. "If not, Hank, you hold tight. Help will come. Von Heusen isn't going to win this one." He stood again, gritting his teeth. "I'll be damned in hell a thousand times over before I let von Heusen win this one!'' He strode around the desk again in his bare feet. "Hank, I need a pair of boots that will fit me."

"Sure thing, Lieutenant. I'll find you something."

Jamie nodded. "Jon—I need new guns."

In silence, Jon left to fulfill the request. They'd come with plenty of guns, and he would know what Jamie wanted and what he needed.

Twenty minutes later the guns were assembled and Jon and Jamie were ready to ride out. Dolly had made some coffee, and Jamie drank some quickly, wincing as the hot liquid filled him. He felt a twitch at his temple and felt the stitches there for the first time. "You sewed me up, Dolly?"

"As pretty as a young girl's ball gown, Jamie."

"Thanks."

They moved outside. Jamie and Jon mounted with the others looking on.

"You bring Tess home now, you hear?" Hank said.

"Please, please, bring her home!" Jane added, her large doe eyes wide and damp.

Jamie smiled at Jane. "I'll bring her home. I promise, Jane. I'll bring her home, or I'll die trying."

He tugged on the reins, and he and Jon turned their mounts and started off.

The sun was rising already. It was falling in orange and gold splotches across the dry earth. Beyond them, it shimmered upon the mesas.

He'd been out a long time, Jamie reckoned. And von Heusen's men had already had Tess for a long time.

His muscles clenched tight, his jaw locked, he damned himself again and again for what had happened. He should have been more careful. They never should have had the opportunity to sneak up on him. Hell, if he'd been that careless during the war, he'd have been dead half a dozen times over. He'd always been so damned good: he could hear a twig drop in a forest, he could hear the rustle of trees when it wasn't just the wind, he could hear bare footsteps against the dry earth. But when it had mattered, he had failed.

He'd failed Tess...

He'd forgotten everything, staring into her violet-hued eyes, feeling her against him, hearing the whisper of her voice, the tremor of her words. He'd just had to prove something. She'd been so aloof, and he'd been so angry, and he hadn't known why…

Because she'd tried to draw away, and he hadn't been about to tolerate it. No, he hadn't been about to let it happen. He had just wanted her, and he hadn't wanted her to escape him.

He was falling in love with her.

So what? he mocked himself. He hadn't wanted to do so. He hadn't suggested that she marry him—he'd just wanted to touch her. To sleep with her. To feel her beneath him, her breath coming in a desperate rush, her hips and thighs moving, her eyes, those eyes, so wide and still, sultry upon his…

But he hadn't been able to let her walk away from him. He just hadn't been able to give her time.

And so she was gone.

He felt his jaw lock anew. She had infuriated him. No matter how he touched her, she could hold herself aloof. And his anger and determination had brought them both down.

Damn!

He didn't know that he had cast back his head and cried the word aloud with anguish until he saw that Jon was watching him. Until he saw the pity on his friend's bold features.

"It's too late for recriminations, my friend," Jon said quietly.

"Yeah. Too late."

"If you want her back, you'd better forget your feelings. You can't make any more mistakes."

"I won't," Jamie said.

"You should let me go alone."

"A half-breed Blackfoot? The Apache won't like you any better then they're going to like me."

"Nalte isn't going to be fond of either of us."

"I can deal with Nalte," Jamie said. He spurred his horse forward, calling to Jon to follow him.

He would deal with Nalte. One way or another, he would get Tess back.

One way or another.

Chapter Ten

Comancheros.

They lined the dry, dusty hilltop that overlooked the desert, seeming to go on forever, covering the horizon. A hundred of them, at least.

Her hands tied before her, Tess sat in her buckskins in front of Jeremiah on his big horse. She didn't know how long or how far they had ridden that day, but they had finally come to this desert that stretched to the mountains—a beautiful area, with myriad colors, a barren, forbidding area where the vultures sat upon the branches of the few scrawny trees, where cactus eked out an existence, where most life was lived in the cool that settled over the golden landscape by night. Soon, the terrain would change again, as they entered the mountains.

They were already in the land of the Apache. And Tess was realizing how little she knew of this feared tribe. She knew they were fierce, and that they did not go to reservations. She had read that President Grant had initiated a "peace policy" toward the Apache this year, but that meant one thing in Washington, quite another here. Apache...it took an Apache to track an Apache, so they said. Once Cochise had been a captive of the American Army, but the trap had infuriated him. He had drawn his knife, slit apart the tent—and disappeared. An entire cavalry company had been unable to find him.

She shivered. Perhaps more so than any other Indian on the Western frontier, the Apache could strike terror into the hearts of the people.

But nothing could be more fearsome than the Comancheros who

faced her now, staring down at their small group of three from the hillside and the horizon.

Tremors tore at her heart. She had ridden with Jeremiah and David for a day and a night and through much of this day as well, and she had done her very best with Jeremiah. She had looked for every possible opportunity to escape, but David had taken great care never to give her a chance. She was never alone. Even when she relieved herself, he was not more than a few steps away, and his promises of what he would do if she even tried to move made her weigh her circumstances very carefully. As long as she was with them, she was safe. Jeremiah wasn't going to let David touch her, and David was frightened enough of von Heusen to listen to Jeremiah.

Hour by hour she had dreamed. Jamie had to come for her. If he was alive, he would have to come for her. His sense of honor would let him do no less. But he had to come while she was still with David and Jeremiah. The odds would have been pretty even then, he could have ridden in with the sun and carried her away into the sunset. But he had not come, and although she could not allow herself to believe that he had been killed, she knew the odds were no longer even. Not even Jamie Slater could come riding into a throng of a hundred Comancheros, guns blazing, and carry her away. She was indeed here, and...

The Comancheros were all staring down at her.

Suddenly, wild screams and shrieks filled the air, and the army of Comancheros came galloping toward them. The cries made her heart flutter, and as they came nearer and nearer, Tess felt an even greater terror growing within her. She began to see their faces, and they were frightening. Most were Mexicans, dark, with long, scruffy beards and heavy, dipping mustaches. They wore hats and shirts and trousers and boots; many wore blankets over their shoulders. All were heavily armed, some with shell cases crisscrossed over their chests. They would not run out of bullets in a fight.

There were Indians, too. Renegades of many tribes, Tess thought, Apache, Comanche, Navaho, some in the Mexican regalia of their comrades, others in more traditional buckskin, at least two of them in simple breechclouts, riding nearly naked in the wind, hooting their triumph and their catcalls, racing around and around the three of them again and again.

They meant to terrify her! Tess thought angrily. Well, supposedly she wasn't in danger yet, even if she was so frightened that she wasn't sure if she could talk or move. David had been a nightmare, but this was far worse. Any dreams she had entertained of rescue fell crashing down into a horrible pit of despair. She had never felt more vulnerable in her life.

She swore, though, that she would not cower before these men who were so determined to unnerve her. They wanted to see tears, she thought. Panic and hysteria. She was close to giving them all that they desired, but she locked her jaw against its trembling and raised her chin. And as the Comancheros raced by her one by one, she kept her eyes levelly upon them, and she ignored the dirt that rose to choke her, bringing tears to her eyes. She sat very still, and she waited.

The horsemen rushed by, then doubled back, bringing their horses to a halt behind her. Jeremiah and David swung around to face them. Tess didn't know whether to find pleasure or new anxiety in the fact that her captors seemed as unnerved as she by the rugged Comancheros.

The Comancheros were all lined up again, and silent once more. The leader emerged, edging his horse forward. He was frightening indeed, with coal-dark hair and coal-dark eyes and a dark olive complexion. He had a great, drooping, handlebar mustache, and though he grew no beard, the rest of his face was not clean shaven. A western hat sat atop his head, the brim pulled low. His chest was crisscrossed with ammunition, and a long, lean cigarillo fell in a slash from the corner of his mouth.

He paused before them and reached into his pocket, then struck a match against his boot to light his cigarillo. He stared at Tess, a smile forming on his features.

"So, *amigos*, the goods are delivered, eh?" He smiled, staring at Tess. She returned his gaze. His smile deepened. "She stares at me hard. Maybe she will be just what Nalte desires. Untie her hands."

"Chavez, she is dangerous," Jeremiah warned him.

"Dangerous? One little blond girl is dangerous when there are a hundred men around her? I told you—untie her hands. Send her to me."

Tess felt the movement as Jeremiah reached for his knife. She heard the rasping sound as he severed the ties that bound her hands together. Instinctively she brought her hands before her, massaging her wrists where the rope had burned them.

"Come down here, *niña*," Chavez ordered.

She was ready to defy him; Jeremiah was not. He dismounted quickly from the horse and reached for Tess. He set her hastily on the ground, then moved away from her as if she were a rattler.

"There she is, good as new, just as we promised. Now, where is the gold, Chavez?"

Chavez motioned to one of the men behind him, a half-naked Indian wearing a headband of eagle feathers, a breechclout, twin leather strips of rifle bullets and nothing more. He carried a small leather satchel that he tossed to Jeremiah. Jeremiah instantly opened the bag. He let out a joyous whoop and looked to David.

"Gold. I mean gold!" He bit the coins, smiling wolfishly. "See, David, it was all worth it!"

"Wait, my friend," Chavez said. He took a step closer to Tess. "These rat piss, they did not touch you?"

Tess narrowed her eyes, then thought of her own safety. "No, they did not touch me."

Chavez nodded. "Nalte, he does not like to be betrayed." He raised his voice, shouting in Spanish. A Mexican rode up leading a small pinto pony. "You," he told Jeremiah and David. "You are done. You go. That is all. And you, woman, you will ride this horse."

She did not move. Jeremiah mounted his horse once again, but Tess made no move. Angry, Chavez urged his mount forward until his large buckskin was nearly stepping upon her. Still, she did not move. *"Niña—"*

"I'm not a girl, Chavez, and I have a name. It's Miss Stuart."

Chavez started to laugh. He laughed so hard that he crunched down on his cigarillo. He nearly swallowed part of it and started to choke.

When he caught his breath, he dismounted from his horse and thundered furiously over to her. He was a short man, she thought. One who looked much better on a horse than standing. She was almost as tall as he. She would be taller. She raised her chin and met his stare.

"Get on the horse," he said. Still, she refused to move. "Eh, *niña*, I am talking to you." He reached out a hard, callused palm and set it against her cheek. Tess slapped him with all the strength in her.

There was silence from every man there.

Then Chavez let loose with a spate of Spanish oaths. Tess thought he would strike her, but he did not. He lifted her, setting her upon the bare back of the pinto. She fought and clawed at him. His hat went flying into the dirt. Her nail imprinted a bright line upon his unshaven cheek.

He swore again, stooping to swoop up his hat.

"Hey, Chavez!" David snickered. "We warned you she was dangerous."

Chavez calmly pulled out his pistol and shot David through the heart.

Tess, who had despised David, nearly gasped aloud. She clenched her chattering teeth, managing to remain immobile and silent as she watched the red stain flare out on David's shirt. His eyes widened, and then glazed over, and he crashed down from his horse.

He had deserved it. He had savagely, heinously attacked Jamie. He had nearly raped her. And yet the cold brutality of his shooting sent waves of shock rippling within her.

"You—you shouldn't have done that," Jeremiah stuttered, shocked. "Mr. von Heusen, he—"

Jeremiah's words broke off in a scream as he saw Chavez lowering the still smoking pistol in his direction. Chavez was not a man of mercy. The pistol barked again.

That time Tess did scream. She catapulted from the pinto horse and threw herself against Chavez, clawing, raking, pummeling him. He swore, dropping the pistol, ducking her blows, trying desperately to seize her wrists. Finally he had her. His heavy arms locked around hers, and she was assailed with the scents of onion and sour breath and unwashed human flesh. A sickness nearly overwhelmed her, and she locked her jaw, standing very still as he stared into her eyes with his own coal-black ones.

"Don't be too dangerous—Miss Stuart. You see how I deal with people who can no longer serve me. You will behave until we have delivered you to Nalte. Do you understand?"

"No, I do not. I do not, because I do not give a damn!"

He swore again, savagely. His arms tightened around her as if he intended to break every rib in her body, but as suddenly he released her, thrusting her into the dirt. The dust rose high around her. Tess started to cough and choke. Chavez wrenched her up and helped her onto the pinto pony. The horse protested, letting out a shrill sound and prancing back and forth.

"You will ride!" Chavez yelled, his eyes black upon her.

Trying to maintain her balance, Tess reached for the reins. She wanted to protest; she wanted to fight.

But she said no more. She held the reins and leveled a glare at Chavez. She didn't want to be bound once again. At least she was not tied, and the pinto pony was sound and sturdy. Her dreams had escaped her, but now they were finding a rebirth. There were a hundred men surrounding her, but feeling the power of the horse beneath her, the determination reawakened within her that she would escape. She would survive.

"Ride!" Chavez roared again. She was going to obey him, and he knew it. He started to laugh. "Miss Stuart. Yes, Miss Stuart, you must ride! Nalte is waiting!"

The Comancheros shrieked again. Men lifted their rifles in the air; some chanted.

Horses pranced around, and their hooves hit the dust.

Then they were off. Tess found herself holding tight to the pinto lest she be thrown and trampled in the stampede.

"Damn!"

High atop a cliff where the mountain range began its craggy rise to the sky, Jamie threw himself against a rock near his perch overlooking the broad, dusty plain below. He closed his eyes in pain, then opened them to stare across at Jon, who was still squatting on the flats of his feet, staring down at the riders who were racing away in a cloud of dust. They had ridden hard and long, and they had nearly caught up with Tess before David and Jeremiah had come upon the Comancheros. Nearly. Not quite. They had come in time to watch the Comanchero kill von Heusen's men in cold blood, and in time to see Tess hit the mustachioed Mexican bandit.

And they had come in time to watch the men ride away with her.

"There was nothing to be done. Not now," Jon said unhappily.

Jamie nodded bitterly. "Tonight. We have to catch up with them tonight." He was silent for a moment, then he pulled off the low-brimmed hat he was wearing and slammed it against the dirt. "What the hell is the matter with that woman? Doesn't she realize that Chavez is a cold-blooded killer? He's going to rip her to shreds if she keeps that up! I could rip her to shreds myself right at this moment."

"She can hardly know that we're sitting up here watching her," Jon reminded him.

Jamie stood up, retrieved his hat and set his hands on his hips as he stared at the sun. Twilight was coming soon enough. He didn't want to follow so closely that they stood a chance of the Comancheros doubling back on them, but he didn't want to be very far behind. "She's getting closer and closer to Nalte's territory. I have to get her back before she winds up in Apache hands." He paused. "Before Nalte discovers that he hasn't been brought..."

"A virgin bride?" Jon suggested.

Jamie scowled. He was staring down where the dust still rose in the wake of the horses. "I met Cochise once," he murmured. "I admired the man. He was willing to meet with me under a flag of truce in spite of the number of times the cavalry betrayed his trust. He is our enemy, he is dangerous, but I would not hesitate to go to him. I wonder if this Nalte is a man like Cochise."

"Nalte is powerful," Jon said. "He is the head of his family, and the chief of many families. He usually makes war with the Mexicans because of the war they have made upon him, but he will deal with the Comancheros because they bring him the arms he needs to fight his battles. He is fiercely against the reservation life, and will battle for his land to the bitter end. But from what I have heard, he is still a man with ethics and honor."

Jamie inhaled and exhaled. "I just don't know. I'm going to try to get her back tonight," he said. "I daren't risk waiting to deal with Nalte."

He turned and started sliding down the cliff toward the small clearing in the rock where they had left the horses. "Coming?" he called to Jon.

"I'm right behind you," Jon assured him.

* * *

The Comancheros rode hard alongside the range until the daylight waned and night began to fall upon them. Then they moved into the mountains. The terrain became very rugged, and their pace slowed.

Chavez dropped back to ride beside Tess. "This is Nalte's territory. You will meet your bridegroom very soon." He sneered at her, very pleased with himself. Tess said nothing, but watched the man with as much disdain as possible. "Wait until you meet Nalte. He is tall and as strong as the rock. He crushes arrogant little girls between his fingers. He is fierce in his paint and breechclouts and he is merciless upon his enemies."

"Chavez, he cannot be anywhere near as repulsive as you," she said pleasantly. So pleasantly that it took several long moments for the smile to fade from his weathered features. He shook a fist in her face. "I have not given you to Nalte yet, little girl! You hold your tongue, or you will pay!"

He rode forward again. Tess shivered but kept her eyes straight ahead in the growing darkness. She could feel the horses and the men bunched around her, could feel their eyes upon her, could smell the sweat of their bodies. But she kept her eyes on the trail, looking neither left nor right, trying desperately not to acknowledge them— or her own fear.

The rocks stopped suddenly. They had come upon a small plateau studded with crude buildings barely discernible in the dusk. An open fire with a huge spit set above it burned in the center of the clearing, and there were women there and a number of armed men awaiting them. Tess figured it had to be a headquarters of sorts for Chavez in the mountains. Perhaps his last stronghold before it became Nalte's territory in full.

She remained on her horse as the men rushed into the clearing, yelling, screaming, calling to their women, cavorting as they dismounted.

Chavez rode over to her. "Welcome to my home, little girl." He laughed. " *Mi casa es su casa.* Always, my house is yours. Tomorrow, Nalte's tepee will be your home!" He roared with laughter, as if he had just said the most amusing thing in the world.

He dismounted from his horse and lifted her down from hers. He pulled her close against him, still roaring. "Maybe I will keep you myself. You have so much to learn about manners. Maybe you are like a very fine horse to be broken, eh? A magnificent mare to be ridden and tamed, eh?''

Tess struggled fiercely against him. He enjoyed her distress and continued to smile. She shouldn't fight him, she thought. He enjoyed it so very much.

But just as she went limp, a sharp female voice called out, ''Chavez!''

His features hardened. He did not release Tess, but turned around and stared at the dark-haired, buxom young woman coming toward him. She wore a white peasant blouse and a full, colorful skirt. Her brown feet were bare. She was young and pretty, but her features were wide and her hips showed signs of broadening with age and the birth of children. She scowled furiously at Tess and scolded Chavez in Spanish.

''Woman, shut your mouth!'' Chavez roared at her.

She did not stop talking until Chavez turned, his fist raised as if he would hit her. The woman fell silent, but her eyes were eloquent. Her look said that she hated Tess.

''I am Chavez, and I will do as I choose!'' he warned the dark-haired woman. He pushed Tess toward her. ''Take her. Take her to the house. I will come shortly.''

The woman put a hand on Tess's shoulder. Tess shook free from her hand. ''Don't touch me!'' she warned her sharply.

''What a woman!'' Chavez sighed, and Tess did not know if it was with mockery or pleasure. She gritted her teeth and stepped past the woman, striding toward a house she indicated.

The dark-haired woman hurried behind her.

The daylight was almost gone. By the glow of the fire, Tess tried to take measure of where she was. The rocks of the mountains rose all around them, but there were many trails that sprang from the clearing. She had no idea where they led, but if she could escape during the night, she could get some distance from Chavez.

''Stop! You stop, you *gringa* slut!'' the woman called out. Tess ignored her. She reached the house and threw open the door.

There were just two rooms there. One was a kitchen with dirty shelves and boxes. Old liquor bottles, chipped and broken, lay upon a dirty, rickety table. Beyond the kitchen was a bedroom.

Tess stared in horror. ''This is filthy. I cannot stay here.''

Behind them, Chavez laughed sourly.

"Anna, she is right. This is a sty. You will clean it up."

Anna turned and hit out at him. He grabbed her hands. She fought him wildly, then went limp. She pleaded with him in Spanish, her voice catching on a sob. Tess tried to ignore them. She looked around and saw there was a back door in the bedroom. She tried not to stare at it, wondering if it wasn't especially designed as an escape route for Chavez if a stronger force came after him.

She didn't want him to catch her staring at the door so she turned around and sat on one of the crude wooden chairs that surrounded the filthy table.

"Tell her to clean it up!" Anna suddenly said, stamping her foot hard on the floor.

"I will not," Tess said immediately. She crossed her arms over her chest. Chavez was convulsed with laughter once again. He unbuckled his gun belt and tossed it on the table on top of the debris. He sat in a chair opposite Tess and stared at her, still very amused, so it seemed. "She will not clean up your slop, Anna. She is Miss Stuart. She wears an Apache squaw's buckskins, but she is a lady. You don't know this, Anna, to be a lady. You must watch her. You musn't ask her to pick up swill." He stopped looking at Tess for a moment and slammed his fist against the table. "I am hungry, Anna. You will bring me something to eat. And you will bring something— for the lady."

Anna didn't like that at all. She began to argue again. This time Chavez rose and slapped her hard across the face. Anna stared at him, tears forming in her eyes. But she said no more, choosing to obey him. Chavez looked at Tess sternly. "That is how to handle a woman!" he told her firmly.

"That, Chavez, is not even the proper way to handle a dog," she told him.

But a second later it was all that she could do not to shrink away from him as he jumped to his feet and stood over her, his hand raised, ready to strike. She willed herself not to flinch. Slowly, his hand fell.

He smiled, then he laughed, and returned to his seat, still looking at her. "I would like to keep you here. I would like to see you change your tune. I would like to see you after your eyes had been blackened and your body used by every man here. Then you would not be so proud.''

''You could never really touch me, Chavez,'' she said softly. ''You can hurt Anna because she loves you. You cannot hurt a woman who despises you. That is something that you cannot even begin to understand.''

He looked at her, puzzled, then the door opened again. Anna was back with a plate of food for Chavez and one for Tess.

Tess didn't want to touch anything in the filthy hovel, but she thought again that she needed strength if she was going to escape, and she hadn't had anything but water all day. She accepted the plate Anna handed her, saying a soft, ''Thank you.'' Anna looked at her curiously, then went to sit in a chair facing Chavez, her head bowed.

Tess chewed the stringy beef she had been handed, and scooped up the beans with a spoon. She ate quickly but she still had not finished when Chavez let out a loud belch and wiped his face with the back of his sleeve. She glanced at him and felt ill. Knowing she could eat no more, she set her plate on the table.

''You see? She does not eat much, just little, little bites, like a lady,'' Chavez told Anna. He pushed himself back from the table and rose. Belching again, he growled at Anna to get out of his way. ''I will drink with my comrades!'' he said. He went to Tess and gripped her chin hard. ''I will come back when I have drunk my fill. And I will decide if you get to learn your lessons from me—or the Apache.''

Laughing, he released her, collected his guns from the table and strode out of the house. When he was gone, Tess stared at Anna, watching the woman's jealous face. Suddenly she leaped to her feet. ''Anna, listen to me. You want Chavez. I do not! Help me. Get me out of here.''

''No!'' Anna cried in alarm.

''You want him. I hate him! Please—''

''No! No, no, no! He will beat me! He might kill me.''

The woman wasn't going to help her, no matter how jealous she was. With a deep sigh of exasperation Tess wandered back to her chair. She closed her eyes for a moment. Lord, she was tired.

Seconds went by, then minutes. Anna stayed where she was, her head lowered. Tess looked longingly at the rear door. If she tried to escape, Anna would sound the alarm. She wouldn't have a chance.

She wondered how long Chavez had been gone. The Comancheros were all outside drinking. Drink might make Chavez think he wanted her more than he wanted the gold the Apache was paying for her. He was a brutally cruel man, she had to remember that. It wasn't difficult. She had only to close her eyes to remember how he had murdered Jeremiah and David in cold blood.

And then an idea came to her. She hurried over to Anna, falling to her knees before the woman in her excitement. "Anna! What if we fought? What if we pretend that I bested you and that I—"

"You could not beat me, *puta!*" Anna claimed.

"Anna! Chavez is your man! This is pretend. I tie you up. I gag you. Then I am gone, and you have Chavez, and he cannot hate you for letting me go. He must love you all the more for what I have done to you." Tess didn't know if that was true or not, but she was certain that Anna would survive Chavez, and equally certain that she might not do so herself. Anna's eyes had narrowed, as if she was giving the idea a great deal of speculation. Tess picked up a lock of her hair. "I am blond! That is what they want. If I stay, Chavez might throw you out."

That decided it. Anna stood and looked around the room. She rushed from the kitchen to the bedroom and found some scarves. "Is this good?"

"Yes, yes."

Anna moved to the hearth where she picked up a heavy cast-iron skillet. She thrust it toward Tess. "Hit me. You must hit me hard on the head. I must have a bruise."

"I—I don't think that I can—"

"You must! If Chavez should beat me, it would be much worse."

"All right," Tess agreed doubtfully. "Let's get in the bedroom. I want you to fall on the bed. I don't want to hurt you."

"You must hurt me some."

They walked into the bedroom. Like the kitchen, it was a mess— with the bed unmade and clothes strewn everywhere.

Anna stood before the bed. "Now hit me."

Tess closed her eyes and bit her lip. Then she raised the iron skillet high and brought it crashing down on Anna's head. The woman fell without a sound. Panicked, Tess checked to see if she had a pulse and if her lungs still rose and fell with her breath. Assured that the woman was alive, she set to tying her wrists and ankles and gagging her with the scarves.

She was just finishing the task when the front door slammed open. Chavez was back!

Tess ran to the rear door. She moved soundlessly and with tremendous speed, and yet it wasn't enough. The door stuck when she tugged upon it.

Chavez was behind her. He grappled her shoulders and spun her around, a rich growl thundering against his throat. Tess stared into his ebony eyes. His fingers closed around her throat. "You are dangerous! The *gringos* were right about you! You are trouble and you need to be taken care of, now!"

He was strangling her. She could barely breathe. In desperate self-defense she brought her knee slamming as hard as she could against his groin. It was a powerful and direct hit, and Chavez screamed out his pain, staggering back.

Tess did not want to stay to see if his condition improved. She grabbed the door again. Gasping, nearly crying, she strained against it.

Then, it opened. She nearly fell against Chavez, it opened so suddenly.

She was about to bolt through it when she gasped. Her heart seemed to stop in her chest, her knees grew weak, her mind went blank of anything other than the man standing in the doorway.

It was Jamie. He had come.

Hands on hips, he stood there, staring. The breadth of his shoulders filled the doorway. He seemed to tower over her and Chavez, and indeed, the entire room. He stared at Tess and at Chavez, swiftly summing up the situation.

He was alive! He had come for her. She had not allowed herself to believe he could be dead, but still he was a dream standing before her, the hero come to sweep her away. She was so stunned to see him she could not move, she could not utter a word, she couldn't even cry out her thrill at seeing him standing there alive, warm blood pulsing in his veins, his chest rising and falling with every breath he took.

She saw nothing but Jamie.

Chavez had not seemed to notice Jamie was there. Chavez was staring at Tess, and there was pure, cold murder in his coal-black eyes.

"Tess!" Jamie hissed to her. "Move!"

She found motion at last as Chavez charged after her. She pitched herself toward Jamie. He caught her shoulders, and his smoke-gray eyes stared sternly into hers.

"Go!" he commanded her. "Go, get out of here, run! Do you hear me? Get the hell out and run!"

Then he thrust her behind him and out the door, into the darkness of the night. Tess heard the sound of the impact as Chavez came thundering against Jamie.

She couldn't run. She paused and turned back.

Chavez had pulled his knife. The steel glistened in the pale moon-glow of the night.

"Jamie!" she cried.

But Jamie had seen the knife. She expected him to draw his Colt, but when he didn't she realized he couldn't draw down the entire camp upon them with the sounds of bullets.

He, too, drew a knife.

"Go!" he thundered to Tess.

Still she hesitated, tears forming on her eyes.

"Jamie—"

"Go! I'll deal with you later!"

His furious, high-handed tone finally sent her into motion. She had been kidnapped and abused, and now he was yelling at her.

Yelling at her...and facing Chavez with a knife.

She bit her lip, then turned and ran. The trail stretched out in the darkness before her, narrow, twisting, rising higher and higher into the mountains. Gasping for breath, half choking, half sobbing, Tess continued to run. She stumbled into a huge rock, glowing white in the moonlight. She caught hold of it, wincing against the pain in her feet, inhaling deeply and desperately. Then she started to run again, almost blind as the shrub grew thicker and rose higher, adding to the darkness of the night.

Staggering, she kept on running. She grabbed at shrubs, still running, heedless of discomfort or pain.

Then, in the darkness, she slammed against something with such impetus that she fell to the ground, barely catching herself to break the fall, scraping her palms with the rock and dirt beneath her hands. Stunned, she tossed the hair from her eyes and looked up, trying to discern what had happened.

She gasped yet made no noise, and her heart began to thunder with renewed terror.

He stood before her, naked except for a breechclout, his arms crossed over his chest. He was as tall as Jamie, as broad, and very, very dark. His hair was ebony and it streamed straight down his back. He was nearly copper in color, and his features were very strong and hard.

He reached down, grasped her wrists and drew her to her feet. Instinctively she tried to pull away from him. His grip upon her tightened. He smiled very slowly, and though she struggled, he held her tightly.

"Let me go," Tess said. "Jamie—er, Lieutenant Slater is right behind me, and he'll shoot you."

She was losing her mind. She was trying to explain things in English to an Apache savage.

"So you are the blond woman who costs so dearly," he responded in perfect English. "You have escaped the Comancheros. You will not escape me."

She shook her head wildly. "No! You do not understand me! Let me go. I've a friend. He's right behind me. He's killing that Comanchero and he's going to kill you. He—"

"Shut up, Sun-Colored Woman."

"My name is Tess. Or Miss Stuart. It's—"

"Sun-Colored Woman. That is to be your name. I am Nalte, and it will be so."

"Nalte!" she breathed. She had escaped the Comanchero to run into the arms of the very Apache who had ordered her as if she was dry goods for a mercantile store!

"You—you speak English," she said.

"Yes. Now you will come."

"No! Please, listen—"

He wasn't going to listen. He grasped her wrists and drew her over his shoulders. She slammed her fists furiously against him.

"Let me go, you savage! Let me go right now! You can't just buy a blond woman! Please…"

But he wasn't listening to her. He was moving fleetly up the trail. He didn't seem to be running, but the trail was disappearing beneath his feet, and they were moving higher and higher into the mountains. He was ignoring her pleas.

"Bastard!" she cried in furious panic. "Savage! Horrid, horrid savage!"

That brought him to a halt. He lifted her and slammed her down upon her knees. She tried to rise, and he pressed her down with such fury that she went still. He towered over her.

"Savage? You, a white woman, would call me savage? No one knows the meaning of brutality so well as your own kind. Let me tell you, Sun-Colored Woman, what the white man, the white soldier has done to us, to my people." The moon rose high, shimmering down upon him with sudden clarity. Nalte, his bronze shoulders slick and heavily muscled, walked around her.

"In 1862 your General James Carleton sent a dispatch unit through Apache Pass. Cochise and Mangas Coloradas lay in wait. There was a fierce battle, and Mangas Coloradas was seized from his horse. He was taken to Janos, but his followers told the doctors that he must be cured or their town would be destroyed. So he survived.

"Mangas Coloradas survived so that he could come a year later, under a flag of truce, to parlay with the soldiers and miners for peace. He was seized. Your general ordered that he have Mangas Coloradas the next morning, alive or dead. So do you know what your civilized white people did to him? They heated their bayonets in the fire, and they burned his legs, and when he protested, they shot him for trying to escape. It was not enough. They cut off his head, and they boiled it in a large pot. Do you understand? They boiled his head. But now you would sit there, and you would tell me that I am savage?"

She wasn't sitting, she was kneeling, in exactly the position in which he had pressed her. She was trembling, shaking like a leaf blown in winter, and she was praying that Jamie would arrive and rescue her.

But of course, she didn't know if Jamie was alive or dead. He had faced Chavez in a knife fight, and she couldn't know the outcome. And now she was facing an articulate Apache who seemed to have reason to want vengeance.

"You speak English exceptionally well," she said dryly.

He did not appreciate her sense of humor. He wrenched her to her feet and pulled her against him.

"You will find no mercy with me," he assured her. "Do not beg."

"I—I never beg," she said, but the words came out in a whisper. She wasn't certain if they were defiant or merely pathetic. It didn't matter. He pushed her forward, then tossed her over his shoulder again.

"No!" she protested wildly. She hit his back, but he did not notice her frantic effort. She braced against him and screamed, loudly... desperately.

Jamie...

Dear God, where was he now?

Perhaps it did not matter. Perhaps there was no help for either of them anymore.

Chapter Eleven

Nalte moved through the darkness so swiftly that Tess had little idea of how far they traveled. She felt as if they twisted and turned relentlessly, but slowly she realized that they were moving downhill. She tried at first to reason with him, but he ignored her, and it was painful to try to talk when she was held so tightly against him. She was exhausted, and the words she had said to Chavez were true at the very least. She wanted to be free from Nalte, but she did not feel the same loathing for the man that she had felt for Chavez.

And now she knew Jamie was alive. Or at least he had been alive. He had gone to battle Chavez, but now she had hope, if nothing else.

Hope...Could he come for her against Nalte? Could he slip out in the darkness and come furtively against the Apache? She didn't know what to think anymore. She hadn't thought that Nalte would speak English, but he did so, very well.

He halted suddenly, letting out the cry of a night bird, and was answered in kind. He started to walk again and they descended a final cliff to a clearing where tepees rose magically against the night sky, and where camp fires burned with soft glows, where only the movement of shadows could be seen.

Nalte set her down and let out the soft sound of a bird cry once again.

From the shadows a man emerged. He was dressed as Nalte was, in a breechclout. He wore high buckskin boots and numerous tight beaded necklaces, and carried what appeared to be a U.S. Army revolver. He began to speak with Nalte very quickly, and Nalte replied. Then the man turned and disappeared into the shadows. The Apache camp was sleeping, Tess thought.

"Come," Nalte told her, catching her arm and leading her across the camp. She saw more shadows. The camp might sleep, but men were on guard.

She started to shiver, realizing that now she had no defenses. She had enjoyed a certain safety with Jeremiah and David, so much so that she could even be sorry that Jeremiah had been killed so coldly. But now...

She had come here as Nalte's prize. That had been von Heusen's plan. The darkness lay all around them, and Nalte was leading her toward the largest tepee. It glowed in moonlight, and she could see the designs and colors upon it, the scenes of warfare, the furs attached to the flaps. Smoke rose from the hole where the structure poles met at the top indicating a fire within the tepee.

"Get in," Nalte said, thrusting her inside.

She nearly fell, but she regained her balance and stood quickly, ready to fight him whatever came. He let the flap fall over the entryway and crossed his arms over his chest and stared at her. She moved backward, noting the amusement that flickered in his dark eyes. She stumbled upon something, looked around and saw that blankets and packs of clothing were neatly rolled against the sides of the tepee and that there were several cooking utensils by the fire that burned in the center of the tepee. Its smoke escaped through the high hole.

There was a woman in the tepee already. A young, very pretty woman, who stared at Tess with wide eyes. Tess stared in return, coloring as dread filled her. Nalte had wanted a blond woman. He already had a wife. He intended to rape her here in front of his first wife.

He took a step toward her. She tightened her fingers into fists at her side. There was no escape here. This was not a place like the haphazard Comanchero dwelling. If she could escape Nalte she would only be caught by his warriors.

Jamie had been so close! Rescue had been within reach. But now she couldn't even hope that he would come against the Indians. Nalte would kill him.

Tess gazed from the young woman to the Indian. "You are a savage!" she shouted. Tossing her hair, she stared at him defiantly. "I don't want you. I don't want to be here! I was kidnapped for your entertainment! And now here sits your poor wife, and you think that you're going to...that you're going to...No!'' she shouted, for the flicker of amusement had deepened in his eyes, and he was striding toward her.

She lashed out wildly, her fists pummeling his chest. He seemed to barely notice her effort, and bent low to pick her up and throw her on a blanket roll. She opened her mouth to scream, but he did not come close to her.

He stepped back, watching her. "This is not my wife. This is my sister. And because of her, you will be safe from me this night. With the light we begin the ceremony that makes her a woman.'' He smiled at the woman, and there was deep affection in his gaze, but it faded when he looked at Tess again. "It is an important ceremony, a religious one.''

He turned and found another blanket roll. He had dismissed her entirely, Tess thought. She stared from the warrior to the young woman, longing to bolt for the opening. Nalte was already stretching out comfortably on his blanket.

The woman tried to smile at Tess. She patted the ground, indicating that Tess should sleep.

Tess swallowed, keeping a wary eye on Nalte. She pulled out a blanket and carefully lay down on it. Stretching out, she pretended to close her eyes. But she kept watching Nalte. When he slept, she would try to escape. If she could return to the trail in the mountains, she could possibly find Jamie.

Was he alone? she wondered. Or was Jon out there somewhere with him?

She was exhausted, and tears threatened her eyes. No matter how hard she tried, or how she fought, she never seemed to escape the fate that von Heusen had intended for her. Jeremiah and David were dead, and she could pray that Chavez was dead, yet it had done little for her. She was where von Heusen had intended she should be, and she was certain that men braver than she and far more knowledgeable of the rugged terrain could not escape the Apache.

Nalte was finally sleeping. She rose very carefully and tiptoed across the dry earth flooring of the tepee to the slit. She glanced at Nalte again. His eyes were closed, his features immobile. She started to slip beneath the flap.

A hand wound around her ankle, bringing her down hard upon the floor. In seconds the fierce warrior had crawled over her. His eyes were ebony in the night. "You have courage," he told her. "But you are stupid!"

"You speak of our savagery!" she charged him. "You deal with the despicable Comancheros, you buy rifles and women from them!"

"My sister is my only family," he told her in turn, "because the others were killed. Killed by white men. Beaten, skewered, broken and left to die. My mother died this way, my sisters. Babies, little babies. I have not brought you here to kill you. Not unless you force me to."

"You are holding me against my will."

He touched a long strand of her hair. He seemed reflective for a moment. "You will come to understand me," he told her. "You will learn our ways, and you will be happy here."

"I cannot be happy!" she told him desperately.

"We are not savages!"

She shook her head, moistening her lips. "No, no more so than we. But I am not what you wanted. I—"

"You are more than what I wanted," he interrupted, and he was smiling. "Now go back to sleep or I will forget that I keep a sacred vigil this night."

"Nalte, please—"

"Go back. Now."

She felt the tension in his arms and saw the fierce glitter in his eyes and she knew that his warning was not without good reason. Hastily she retreated. She curled into her blanket, pulling it around her ears. She shivered. She didn't hate the Indian, but he didn't understand that. She was not repulsed by him, but she had to be free, for she was not part of his society. She wanted revenge. She wanted von Heusen hurt as he had hurt her.

And she wanted Jamie. She was in love with him, and that hurt more than anything else. If it weren't for him, she could bear anything that happened...

But he was out there, somewhere. And she could never forget him.

Morning came, and the blanket was pulled away from Tess's shoulders. She gasped and opened her eyes, expecting to discover

Nalte, but it wasn't him. Several women stared at her. They spoke to her, but she didn't understand them.

They pulled her to her feet. She protested, but was ignored. Nalte's little sister smiled at her encouragingly. She had little choice, for the women set upon her arms and drew her along with them. They left the tepee to enter the family clearing. The sun was just beginning to shine down upon the camp. Men and women were busy, moving around. Some cleaned their weapons, others watched her with curiosity. The women moved around with buckets of water or with bowls of food.

A soft word was said to her, and she was moved forward. No one was cruel to her, but she couldn't have escaped the women who were determined to escort her.

She heard the stream before she saw it, as they walked a trail that brought them through trees and dense shrubs. From the trail she could hear the tinkling melody of the water, reminding her that she was very thirsty, and that there was a certain personal necessity she had to take care of. She was glad to be with the women, even though she flushed when they tugged at her buckskins, indicating that she was to strip and bathe.

Still, she felt better once the water was against her skin and once she had swallowed huge mouthfuls of it. She realized that the women were disappearing between a bank of trees, and she was certain the trees had to be the latrine. She followed them, and thought longingly once she was done of disappearing into the brush, but even as the thought came to her, she saw that two of her keepers had come for her. Again, they were not cruel, but the women with the ink-dark hair and the huge dark eyes placed firm hands upon her and took her to the stream.

There they ignored her. It was Nalte's sister who gained everyone's attention. Once she, too, had bathed, she was dressed in a soft, pale buckskin dress with shades of yellow coloring on it. A yellow paint was smeared over her face, and her hair was lovingly combed out and let loose to fall beneath her shoulders. Necklaces were placed upon her, beautiful pieces of beads and silver cones, and one rawhide strand with a claw upon it. She smiled during it all, flushed and lovely.

It was her ceremony day, Tess remembered. And then she realized

that she had not been forgotten after all. A woman called for her
from the bank of the stream. She had no choice but to crawl out and
let them stare at her. They whispered over her nakedness and she
flushed, backing away when they would have touched her. Her pale
skin was very different from their own, she knew. But it was her
hair that seemed to fascinate them most—both that upon her head
and that upon her body.

They didn't tease her long, but gave her a new outfit to wear. It
was a soft, pale buckskin much like Nalte's sister's dress, but with
no yellow on it. It fell just to her knees.

Her feet were still sore from her barefoot treks over the mountain
trails, and she had hoped that someone would give her soft doeskin
slippers to wear. But nothing was supplied for her feet, and when
she tried to ask one of the women, the Apache shook her head. They
were preparing to go back to the village, and Tess was to go with
them.

Tess wondered again about her chances of escaping, but she had
heard that the Apache women could be every bit as fierce as their
men. The women were excited about the young girl they had dressed
so carefully for her rite, but their eyes were still upon her. She
walked along, weary and desolate, trying to focus her thoughts on
her hatred of von Heusen so that she wouldn't be able to fear her
own future, and to wonder desperately about Jamie Slater.

Her eyes were lowered, her head was down when they came into
the village. She stumbled and looked up to see where she was going.

Looking across the compound she saw that four Indians were in
curious costumes with huge headdresses, obviously preparing for the
rites to come. But the Indians were staring across the compound at
a stranger who had come among them. For a moment he looked very
much like Nalte. Tess narrowed her eyes, watching the man, trying
to figure out why he looked so familiar. He was dressed in buckskins
from head to toe and he wore a cap adorned with eagle and owl
feathers. His hair was black and straight as Nalte's, but worn shorter.
Even as she stared at him, he turned slowly, pointing her way.

She gasped, stunned to see that the newcomer was Jon Red
Feather. He smiled at her briefly, a sign of encouragement, she
thought, then his expression quickly sobered again, and he continued
to talk to Nalte.

The tall Apache was dressed for the ceremony, too. He wore a fringed buckskin shirt, buckskin pants, high, laced boots and eagle feathers in his hair. He was also adorned with a turquoise amulet around his neck, and silver studs and beads upon his bonnet and shirt. He was listening to Jon Red Feather—and watching Tess gravely as he did.

Nalte nodded, and Jon let out a whistle.

Then Jamie rode into the clearing. He was in calico shirt, denim pants, knee-high boots and a Western hat. He didn't glance at Tess, but lifted a hand to Nalte. When he reached the chief, he slipped from the horse instantly and approached the man, speaking quickly.

She felt as if her heart slammed hard against her chest. He was a fool! she thought. He didn't know Nalte, he didn't know how the Apache chief hated the white man, nor did he seem to realize the things that had been done to the Apache by the cavalry. Fool! She wanted to scream to him, but she couldn't breathe, she could only pray that Nalte wouldn't slay him right on the spot.

Nalte shook his head violently.

Forty warriors suddenly drew their weapons, facing Jamie.

His Colts were around his waist, but he didn't make a move to touch them. He spoke calmly once again, and Nalte called out something sharply. Guns and war clubs were lowered.

Frightened still, Tess cried out, shaking off the hands of the women around her and racing toward Jamie. She pitched herself against him, but he caught her shoulders hard and thrust her away.

Thrust her away—straight into Nalte's arms. Her eyes widened with alarm and fury.

"What in God's name are you doing?" she gasped. She couldn't move. Nalte's dark fingers were a vise upon her.

Nor did Jamie seem to want her. His eyes flashed upon her with dark fury. "Stop it, Tess."

"But—"

"Stop it! Shut up!"

"Damn you, Jamie—"

He switched into the Apache language, addressing Nalte. At the last, he spoke English once again. "Nalte, may Jon Red Feather take the woman away so that we may speak without interruption?"

"Speak without interruption!" Tess flared.

But Nalte was nodding.

"Tess, come!" Jon called to her.

Apparently she didn't move quickly enough. Jamie reached for her arm and thrust her toward Jon. He pulled her away even as she protested. "Jon—"

"Tess, he's trying to negotiate for your return."

"They were going to shoot him! I had to do something." She tugged free of Jon and turned back to watch Jamie, still talking with Nalte. "What are they doing now?"

"Talking about prices."

"For what?"

"For you, of course," he told her with a crooked smile.

"How can Jamie pay Nalte?"

"Well, he can't pay him…not very much, that's why he's arguing that you aren't worth the price."

"I'm not worth the price!"

"Tess—"

Tears touched her eyes. "He shouldn't be here to begin with! He must not understand Nalte—"

"Nalte would have killed most men by now. He is seeing Jamie because he knows about him, he knows that Jamie has always been fair. Tess, keep your mouth shut, all right?"

She wanted to keep her mouth shut, but she was still in terror that the Apache would betray Jamie, as they had been betrayed so many times themselves. She was deliriously glad to see him and Jon, and she wanted to know about Chavez, but she was afraid to ask. Her temper was rising because she was so desperately scared of what was to come.

Before she could say more, Nalte came striding by with Jamie and his guard behind him. Jamie cast her a fiercely warning glare; Nalte barely glanced her way. They entered Nalte's dwelling.

"What are they doing now?" Tess demanded.

"Negotiating," Jon said briefly.

She started to shiver. Nalte didn't need to negotiate. He could kill Jamie and keep her. He had all the power. He could do anything he wanted to do.

"There's no hope!" she whispered.

Jon set his hands on her shoulders. "Courage, Tess. There is every hope. Nalte's little sister begins her puberty rite today. The rite goes on for four days. The woman over there will be her sponsor. She is of impeccable character, and she will stand for the sister. The man there with the buffalo horns upon his cap and the white eagle feathers, he is the shaman, the medicine man, and he will add the sacred religion to the ceremony. The girl is dressed for her role as White Painted Woman or White Shell Woman, a sacred maiden and one of the most important of the Apache supernaturals. She will pray to the sun. The dancers with the headdresses, they are the Gan, or Mountain Spring Dancers. It is an expensive ceremony, but Nalte is a great chief, and he has supplied much for his sister's rite. The Gan dancers symbolize the four directions. They are elaborate.''

Tess watched the dancers as they prepared for the day. They were painted black and white, and they carried huge fan racks and wore buckskin kilts. They carried wands. On their arms were trailers made of cloth and eagle feathers. Their huge masks had false eyes. The fan racks portrayed snakes and other creatures.

She shivered, grateful that Jon was there to assure her that the dancers were involved in a ceremonial rite and were not preparing for war. She looked into his green eyes and realized that he had kept talking to ease her mind from worry, and she was grateful to him.

"He must be furious to be disturbed today!" she whispered.

"He is not disturbed. He will make his decision quickly," Jon told her.

An Apache warrior emerged from Nalte's tent. He spoke briefly with Jon and took Tess by the arm.

"Jon!" she cried.

"Go with him," Jon ordered her. "He isn't going to hurt you. I'm wanted with Nalte. And you are not."

She didn't want to let Jon out of her sight, but he moved away resolutely, and she had no choice but to accompany the warrior who took her by the arm. Seconds later she was thrust into an empty tepee. The fire that had burned in the center was nearly out. On rocks beside it were corn cakes and dried meat. She hadn't been told she could, but she was alone and she was starving, so she helped herself.

She had barely bitten into the food when she became so nervous she couldn't chew. She set the food down and began to pace. After a while she sat again and looked sadly at her tender and torn feet. They would never be the same again.

Moments later, she heard a rush of air. She catapulted to her feet, staring toward the opening of the tepee. Jamie was coming in. She gasped softly, then raced toward him, flinging her arms around him.

He quickly untangled himself, staring fiercely into her eyes. "We're going to get out of this. If you can manage to behave."

"Behave!"

"Listen to me!" He shook her so hard that she felt her teeth rattle. Indignantly she tried to jerk away from him, but his grip on her was firm and he wasn't letting go.

"You're hurting me!"

"I'm hurting you! We're in the midst of a fiasco like this—"

"It wasn't my fault!"

His jaw twisted hard. "I know. It was mine. For being so damned determined to try to understand you.

She felt the color drain from her face. The planes of his face seemed very lean and hard. He was more bronze, tauter. There was a fresh scar upon his cheek. She wanted to touch it tenderly, but he was holding her with too great a vigor. And the smoky anger in his eyes told her he did not want her touch.

He had come for her. He had survived both von Heusen's guns and his fight with Chavez to come for her. But now she realized that he had come only because he considered himself responsible for what had happened to her. She paled, trying to pull from his grasp, but he wouldn't let her.

"The puberty rite for Nalte's sister will last four days. He will not attend to any other business during that time. Jon and I are to be his guests. You are to stay here, do you understand me?"

"Just stay here...for four days?" she whispered. "Can't I be with you?"

He swore, vehemently. "You were purchased, Tess! Damn it, don't you realize that? And not for your talents with a newspaper."

"Jamie, don't you start with me—"

"No, don't you start with me," he said heatedly. "You can manage yourself, and you can manage a lot, and you probably are a damned good rancher and newspaper woman. But if you try anything here, Tess, we'll both probably die. Do you understand? We're walking a very narrow line here. I've tried to explain von Heusen to Nalte. He has a sense of honor; there is a chance he will return you. But I can't do any of this if you interfere. Do you understand?"

She wrenched free of him at last. His hands fell upon his hips and his hat brim tipped over one eye, yet she could still see the silver glint in the other. She swung around and walked with her shoulders stiff and straight, then she sat Indian fashion upon a blanket roll. She mustn't let him see how hurt she was.

He didn't say anything else to her, but started to turn to leave. She couldn't stand that, and called out to him.

"Jamie!"

"What?" he demanded impatiently.

"What—" She paused, licking her lips. "What happened to Chavez?"

"He's dead," Jamie said flatly.

"And the Comancheros—"

"The Comancheros never saw me," he said. "But if we're going to get out of the mountains, we're going to need an Apache escort. So don't create problems."

"Me!"

"You," he said succinctly, and he was on his way out again.

"Jamie!"

"What now?"

She hesitated a second. "Thank you. Thank you for coming after me. Thank you for risking so much."

"You don't need to thank me. I owed you this."

This time he stayed, staring at her. But she couldn't speak anymore because sudden tears were welling behind her lashes and threatening to spill over on her cheeks. He owed her this. He had come for her because he owed her. She had dreamed that he was falling in love with her.

Maybe she was proving to be too much trouble. She had traded half her land for a hired gun. But she had never told her hired gun he was going to have to go after Comancheros and Apache as well as von Heusen's men.

"I'll remember to thank Jon," she said coolly. "He didn't owe me anything."

"You do that," Jamie told her. But still he didn't leave. He stood by the entrance, and she sat across from him, her knees crossed, her shoulders and back very straight, her hands resting upon her knees. The distance between them seemed immense, and yet she felt the touch of his eyes as if it was fire.

It was he who spoke this time, lightly, softly.

"Tess?"

"What?"

"Did—did any of them—hurt you?"

She knew what he meant. Her cheeks burned and her lashes fell over her cheeks. "David was a monster, and he probably would have killed me. Jeremiah wasn't so bad—he wouldn't let David touch me. I was sorry to see Jeremiah killed." Her voice faded slightly. "Especially the way he was killed. And Chavez…Well, you know about Chavez, because…because you were there."

"Yes, I know about Chavez. What about Nalte?"

She shook her head. "He let me be. Because of his sister."

She started, hearing the long, ragged exhalation of his breath. She thought, for a moment, that he would cross the distance between them and take her into his arms. He did not. She could scarcely breathe, longing to leap to her feet once again. But he had already set her from him. She wasn't going to touch him again.

"You're still Nalte's," he told her harshly.

She gazed at him, wondering what he meant. Then she realized that he would not touch her until he had completed his negotiations with the Apache chief.

He didn't say any more. He swung around and left, and she knew that even if she had called his name then, he would have left her.

The day wore on endlessly. Tess could hear the ceremonial drums beating and the chants of the puberty rite, but she could see nothing, and she was involved in nothing. She tried very hard to be patient, and to understand that everything rested upon negotiation.

Late in the afternoon, Jon came in. She almost leaped into his arms, but he was carrying a dish of food for her. He set it down, and she did hug him, fiercely.

"Eat," he told her. "You may need your strength."

She nodded and sat and looked suspiciously at her bowl. "What is it?" she asked.

"Something exotic and Apache," he told her, "beef. Probably from cattle taken in a raid. You should not worry. The Apache are very finicky about what they eat. They will not eat snake, for they believe that the creature is evil, and they will not eat evil meat. Here they are close enough to the plains to seek out the buffalo. They also hunt deer, antelope, elk and bighorn. Their food is quite safe, I assure you."

She flashed him a quick smile and ate the beef with her fingers. It was delicious.

"How does the ceremony progress?" she asked.

"The girl has been taken to the ceremonial tepee with her shaman. She has knelt down on the buckskin and lain prone to be massaged by her sponsor, and she has run in the four directions. Tonight she will dance in the ceremonial tepee, and others will dance in the center of the village."

He paused, looking at her. "I am leaving tonight. Nalte will not let you go until this ceremony is over, and we think it is important that I hurry to Wiltshire with the news that you have been found."

"Oh!" Tess said, setting down her bowl and staring at him. Then she moved across the tent and hugged him close. "I don't want you to leave. I'm so afraid for you."

"The Apache will see me past the Comancheros, as they will do for you if they choose to let you go."

"If—"

"When!" he assured her.

She pulled slightly away, staring into his deep green eyes and feeling as if she had found a friend she would cherish all her life. In his buckskins he appeared very much the Indian, but his words were those of the white man who knew her society and understood her fears.

"Oh, Jon, be careful!" she pleaded with him.

"I'm quite sure he will be."

Jamie's deep drawl startled them both. Tess stood quickly. Jon came to his feet more slowly, staring at Jamie.

"Sorry, I didn't mean to interrupt," Jamie said drily. He ducked beneath the flap and was gone.

Tess instinctively ran after him.

Jon caught her before she could leave. "You cannot go to him!"

he ordered her hoarsely. "He has explained to you. You are still Nalte's. You remain here, untouched, until a decision is made."

"But he—he misconstrued what he saw!" Tess wailed.

Jon offered her a dry smile. "Perhaps he deserved to, eh?" She didn't smile in return, and he hastened to reassure her. "He is my friend, and I am his. He knows we said goodbye and nothing more." He didn't let her answer, but gave her a quick squeeze. "I'll see you in Wiltshire," he whispered, then he was gone.

And she was left alone. Outside the light was fading. Darkness was coming, and despite the summer heat of the day, the night was coming with a chill. Tess shivered and wrapped her arms around herself, staring miserably at the center of the tent where the fire burned no longer.

Jamie walked almost blindly into the growing darkness of the night. Soon, the evening ceremonies for the young girl would begin, but at the moment, there was a lull as preparations were made. This puberty rite was one of the most important for the Apache. It was a structured society, a social one, and respect and honor were tremendously important.

The anger that seethed through him lightened for a moment as he thanked God that Nalte happened to be an exceptionally honorable man. Nalte had known when he first bargained with von Heusen that the man who intended to sell a blond woman to him had to be somewhat of an outcast in his own society. But he had not imagined the things Jamie told him. Jamie explained that von Heusen had made war on Tess and had tried to make the people around him believe it was the Comanche or the Apache who had carried out the raids. That had infuriated Nalte, and it had almost given him Tess.

Almost...

Nalte wasn't quite ready to let go.

Jamie clenched his teeth and his fists as he hurried past the circle of tepees and into the night. He wanted to reach the stream, to bathe his face in its coldness.

Yet even when he reached the stream, the water could do nothing to soothe him. He could not forget Tess's eyes—huge, violet and luminous upon his. She had been so straight and rigid, and yet she had seemed so very small and vulnerable when she had talked to him in the tent. She had explained the past few days with a simple dignity, and he had been so relieved to discover that she had received a minimum of abuse that his knees had gone weak. He had wanted to wrap her in his arms and promise her everything would be all right, that no one would ever hurt her again.

But he hadn't been able to do that. He couldn't make any promises. He didn't even dare touch her lest the emotion or the passion tear him apart and lead to Nalte's fury. But he had never hungered more deeply inside for her. She was always fighting; she was always strong. She had endured so much that she could be no less than strong. And yet now she had that air of vulnerability about her. She did need him. And he wanted to be all things to her.

He splashed more water on his face, and his temper cooled. He owed Jon so much—and not his anger. Yet he had been angry, seeing her trustingly in his friend's arms, seeing the tears in her eyes, the emotion within them. He wanted her. He wanted her in his arms.

He closed his eyes, and saw again the picture of the young woman with the luminous violet eyes and the soft storm of golden-red hair falling over her shoulders and down her back. So quiet and still, and somehow achingly soft in the bleached white buckskins. There'd been a strange serenity about her, a serenity she could not possibly be feeling. He'd felt impotent to be just standing there talking to her. He was her gun, her hired gun. He'd said that he'd protect her, but he hadn't been able to. Others had descended upon her, and she had endured fear and suffering at their hands. He'd been praying for a miracle. Praying that she hadn't been so abused that he'd never manage to live with himself again.

He'd never felt good about killing a man. Never. Not during the war, not after. But he'd wanted to kill von Heusen's men when they had taken her. He'd wanted to do more than kill them—he'd wanted to tear them limb from limb and watch them die in horrible agony. Chavez had taken that away from him. For the good of his soul, maybe it was just as well. It was hard for a man to live with that kind of hate. He knew. He'd watched it fester in his brother Cole, and it had nearly cost him his wife, Kristin.

Then there had been Chavez.

He'd never seen Chavez, except from the mountaintop. And watching the Comanchero shoot the men in cold blood had kept him from feeling the least remorse when Chavez had fallen beneath his blade. The fight between them had been cold, both men knowing that it was life or death. Jamie had been a little quicker, and Jon had managed to come around with the horses before the Comancheros knew that their leader had been visited, much less killed. The bound woman on the bed had never moved, and she hadn't seen anything. They were done with the Comancheros—for good, he hoped.

He smiled suddenly. He would have to ask Tess how the woman had come to be bound and tied on that bed. It would surely be an interesting story.

But when they had fled the Comancheros camp, Tess had been nowhere to be seen. They had tracked the trails up and down all night, calling softly to her. He hadn't been willing to admit that they had helped her elude the Comancheros only to send her into the arms of the Apache. But Jon knew the territory, and he knew something of Nalte. And in the end they had decided that the only way they could deal with the chief was to lay their cards on the table. Jamie was going to have to count on his reputation with the Indians.

Jon would change into his buckskin attire to approach Nalte first, then Jamie would ride in. It had been risky for them both. The Apache were a warlike people, and Nalte was known to hate the white man. But he had a reputation, too—one for upholding his own sense of honor and hospitality. Besides, it was obvious from the outskirts of the village that some big ceremony was going on, and a chief like Nalte didn't usually like blood on his hands during such an occasion.

And so they were here, and still waiting.

Darkness was falling upon the water. The moon glittered gently upon it, and the easy melody of the running water was gentle. It was a beautiful sight, this valley within the beginning of the fierce mountain ranges.

A beautiful place to die, Jamie thought.

Nalte had promised his decision about Tess as soon as the festivities for his sister had ended. Jon seemed to believe that the Apache chief had already determined he would return Tess, at some cost, of course, but he would return her.

But what if he did not?

Jamie knew he would never leave without her.

If Nalte decided against him, he would have to fight the chief. And if he won, the Apache would probably slay him in vengeance anyway. He might well die in this beautiful place, then there would be nothing more that he could do for Tess.

I'm sorry! he thought. I never should have become so involved. Falling in love with a beautiful angel has surely been the downfall of many a man. I couldn't let you go that morning. I had to make you see that the thing between us was right and that you couldn't turn away from it by the morning's light.

He hadn't had the edge he had needed, the edge that had kept him alive through so much.

So now they were here, and their fate rested on the decision of an Apache chief.

He liked Nalte. He had a keen intelligence, was well-versed in his own language and in English, well-aware of the world around him...And fighting to maintain the inheritance of a people despite an encroaching world. He was not so bad a man, Jamie thought. Rather he die and leave Tess to Nalte, than leave her to trash like David or Chavez. Nalte would never hurt her.

He clenched his fists and swore to the night sky. Then his thoughts raced as he sank on his haunches to stare at the rippling, moon-kissed water once again. I will not die here! Come heaven or hell, I will fight, and with every edge, and I will bring her home with me!

"Jamie!"

He thought he imagined the voice.

But then, as he stared into the water, her reflection was caught by the glow of the moon almost magically on the surface before him.

"Jamie..."

She was there. She was wearing the white buckskin dress he had seen before. Her hair was flowing, rich and waving, paler than usual in the water's reflection. Nor could the water catch the color of her eyes, that violet that was so extraordinary and so compelling, so quick to flash with anger, so deep when touched by her emotions. Nothing could catch that. No words, no mirrored image.

But the water did catch the softness he had glimpsed before, and he knew then why he had been falling in love with her so swiftly and so completely. She had great strength, she would never tire, and she would never cease to fight, for herself, for others, for the glory of all the great causes that caught her heart. She could not bear injustice, and she would never falter to overcome it.

But never could she be less than a woman, beautiful, giving, enwrapping all with the passion of her soul, and of her life. Once he had wanted only her smile to touch him. Once he had been enamored of the silk of her flesh, and the sweeping curves and slim angles of her form. Once...

But now he knew what it meant to love. It was desire, but more than desire. It was needing the smile as much as the passion. It was wanting to lie down by the still waters as much as to weather the tempestuous storm. It was wanting to share a lifetime together.

"Jamie..."

Once again, she whispered his name. He turned slowly, and saw that she did stand just behind him—no image, no dream, so much more than a reflection. In her bare feet with her bare calves, her dress falling just above her knees, she seemed exceptionally innocent.

The color of her eyes was true, deep as the night, dark as the desire that suddenly swept over him. He wanted her in his arms—but he dared not touch her. Not until Nalte made his decision.

He swallowed hard and came to his feet. He stared at her and hoped that his scowl was menacing. Yet he didn't even know if it remained upon his face, for he couldn't deny the moonlight or the strange, mystical sensation that seemed to touch her. She seemed to be of the supernatural, too beautiful to touch, an angel, a spirit, the spirit of life that pervaded the mountain.

"What are you doing out here?" he demanded harshly.

She smiled, a slow curl of her lips that touched her eyes to deep, shimmering radiance. She took a step toward him, shook her head slightly.

And reached for him.

Her arms came around him, giving, soft. She pressed against him. She was naked beneath the buckskin, and her breasts were full and flush against him, the hardened peaks seeming to rake his flesh despite the layers of clothes between them. Sparks tore into him, igniting great fires, ripping through his limbs, thundering down to his groin.

And then she kissed him. Her teeth grazed his lips, and the tip of her tongue encircled his lips, touched the roof of his mouth, swept into his mouth. There was a pounding so fierce he could not deny it.

He touched her. Touched her almost violently, his arms sweeping around her, his lips seizing hard upon hers, his tongue returning each sweet torment she had cast upon him.

He swept her from her feet and carried her to the soft embankment. He pressed her to the earth, his mouth still covering hers. He felt the soaring temptation of her nails raking lightly against his back, drawing new, shimmering sensations of deadly heat within him.

This was madness.

He drew his lips back from hers, and her eyes met his. Violet, beguiling, with a touch of fire, a touch of innocence. Sweetly wicked, she smiled again; she touched his cheek. Her lashes fell demurely, sultry, sensual against the pale marble beauty of her cheek.

She had come to seduce him.

He groaned aloud.

It was madness.

Nalte might well kill them both if he came upon him.

But the fire had spread throughout his limbs. Tension and desire pervaded his heart and his mind and knotted fiercely at his loin, driving him to madness. How could she smile so hauntingly, knowing that she invited him to doom...

He swore softly, and he touched her lower lip in the moon glow, meeting the wild violet beauty of her eyes.

"Lead me to death then, if you would, Miss Stuart. I cannot leave you now."

And he seized her lips once again with his own. The rich, verdant scent of the earth and stream surrounded them, and he was lost.

Chapter Twelve

"Die?" Tess whispered against his lips. Desperate to be near him that night, she had hardly believed the good fortune that had let her come to him, and now, in the magical splendor of the night, he was talking of dying in her arms.

He was so tense above her. His eyes raked over her with a hard edge, and his voice was harsh, but still she felt the depth of his longing. It was luxurious to be so coveted and so desired. And yet she wondered at his words, her eyes widening to his.

"Nalte," Jamie said, leaning high above her. "He would kill me in seconds if he found me with you. Is that your plan? To seduce me to my doom?"

She didn't reply right away. She smiled wickedly and smoothed his hair back from his face. "Would you really die for me?" she whispered softly.

He caught her hand where she touched him and drew her wrists together high over her head, staring down at her. She didn't know if he loved her or despised her in those seconds, but she did know that he wanted her. Tension constricted the length of his body, and muscles convulsed at his throat and within the tautness of his features.

"Is that what you want?" he demanded.

He wasn't smiling. She knew that she had probably tested him beyond endurance, so she whispered softly to him in the night. "No, I do not want you to die for me. Nalte knows that I am here."

"What?"

"He came to me and told me that I could go to you, that he had made his decision. We are to stay here until the ceremonies are complete for his sister, then the Apache will see that we are given an escort out of the mountains.''

''Nalte...knows?'' Jamie repeated.

She nodded solemnly. ''He said that you told him I was already your woman. He also said that you were either a fool or a very brave man to have come for me, and that a brave man deserves the respect of other brave men. And so he told me that you were here, and that I could come to you.''

He stared down at her, his grip hard upon her wrists as he tried to understand what she was telling him. Nalte had decided in their favor. There was no need to die here. He could leave with Tess.

He could leave with her.

And he could make love to her, here, tonight, in the shadow of the Apache's mountains, at the stream where life itself and the night seemed mystical.

He cried out harshly and lowered himself over her, his lips parting before they ever touched hers. He ravished her mouth, demanding that it open to his, and he seemed to taste and find all of her, his tongue delving ever deeper, his teeth teasing her lips, his breath mingling with hers, the whole of his kiss so deep and complete and sensual that it was raw and laid her bare. It touched her on a level so intimate that the very decadence aroused her to shattering heights. Then his lips left hers, and she was bereft. The night air touched her lips where they remained damp and moist from his touch.

His fingers were upon the rawhide laces of her buckskin dress. Her breasts spilled free to his touch, and his hand cupped and caressed them, his fingers stroking and arousing her nipples. Then his mouth formed hungrily around one nipple to suckle and tease the hardening bud, to send streams of excitement and desire sweeping through her limbs. She was glad of the darkness. Flushing, she wondered how it was the searing liquid fire of his kiss touched her breast, yet sent the molten longing to swirl to the base of her abdomen, and lower still to hover and deepen at the apex of her thighs.

It did not matter where he touched. He continued to kiss her as he slowly eased the buckskin from her body. He kissed the nape of her neck, and the tip of his tongue hovered at her earlobe, then ran a trail down her spine as he shifted her body to toss aside the dress. He kissed the inside of her upper arm, and she had never imagined that a touch could elicit such wild stirrings within her. Nor did he allow his kisses to stop there.

Soon she was lying prone upon the verdant earth again, so close to the water that it lapped at her ankles. And even the touch of the water added to the wonder and the magic. It caressed her as the breeze did, as his every touch did. She was whispering things to him, things she should never have said, things about the wonder and desire he created. She struggled to touch him in return, to know more and more of him. Her teeth sank gently upon his shoulders, and her tongue laved every tiny little wound. Her fingers stroked and massaged his shoulders and trembled over every ripple and bulge of his muscle beneath her touch. She shed his shirt, nearly ripping the buttons from it. She touched his chest with her tongue, and she moved lower and lower against him.

But then she found herself prone again, and his hands and lips were moving magic upon her. His kiss touched her, searingly hot. The cool water lapped over her feet and ankles, but the whole of her was achingly hot, a fire against the water. His lips touched her bare belly, and the arches of her feet, and her knees and her thighs. And then he kissed her warmly, intimately, at the very heart of her desire, kissed her body as he would kiss her lips, demanding all and giving her ecstasy in turn.

And still the cool stream washed against her. In the end she rose against him, and they knelt together in the shallows in the night, and her breasts moved against his chest as their lips fused once again, and then the fullness of their bodies. She led him down then to the rich earth, and crawled atop him, her hair a blaze of sunset kissed by the moon, her movements smooth and sultry as the touch of golden locks swung over his chest and belly.

In the magic of the night, to the rough and urgent murmurings of his husky voice, she rode the magic of the darkness, and of the man, until the beauty exploded within them and around them, until the sweet satiation and exhaustion seized them, until they were filled with one another. Only then did she fall against him. She didn't care about the future or the past; she only knew that she had come to him because she had wanted him. And because she loved him. Nothing else mattered, for she had learned that time and life and love were precious, and this night she had all three.

They were silent together as the moon cast its gentle glow on them. He stroked her hair softly and at long last he whispered, "It's true—Nalte sent you to me?"

She nodded happily against his chest. "It's true," she whispered.

"Thank God," he breathed.

"He's very upset."

"He is?"

"He doesn't like the idea that von Heusen has been causing so much trouble. He told me that the Apache raid, and that they make war, and that these are separate things. They raid for foodstuffs and other things they need, they do not raid to kill. When they make war, they do so to kill. But they do not kill children, and they do not slaughter animals needlessly. He says there is enough trouble between the whites and the Indians. He doesn't usually have much use for the Comanche himself, and the tribes have warred for generations, but he cannot see the Comanche blamed for a white man's sins."

"You had quite a long talk with him," Jamie commented.

"Jealous?" she asked sweetly.

He grunted.

She braced her hands upon his chest, staring deeply into his eyes. "I like him, Jamie."

Jamie laced his fingers behind his head as he watched her eyes. "Want to stay with him?" he asked.

Words, gentle words, self-betraying words, hovered on Tess's lips. I like Nalte, but I love you, she almost said. But she could not dispel the memory of Eliza hanging on to him, trying to force him to love her in return. She would never do that, she swore. It was dangerous to fall in love with Jamie Slater. If nothing else, Tess wanted her dignity left to her.

She forced a smile to her lips and asked lightly, "Trying to get rid of me?"

"You are a hell of a lot of trouble," he told her frankly.

"Yes, but you've already come this far."

"So I have."

"And I really am worth it."

"Are you?" His eyebrows shot up.

She nodded. Then she moved very low against him again. She let her hair float over his chest as she lowered her lips to his slick bronze flesh. She shimmied her body against him as she inched lower down the length of his body, her thighs locked around him, moving sinuously against him. She felt the quick rasp of his breath, and she let her lips linger upon the spot where she could hear the frantic beating of his heart.

Then she moved lower and lower, daring to touch him instinctively, exploring what was intensely male about him with little subtlety and tremendous fascination. Her body undulated upon his. She discovered her own prowess and power, and drove him nearly to madness. All that he had demanded of her she took in return. He shuddered violently beneath her touch, his fingers digging into the earth when she caressed him as boldly with her lips and tongue as he had done to her. He shouted out hoarsely, and she was soon pinned to the earth as he took her almost savagely, with a driving, explicit hunger that seemed to rend the very heavens.

And when the stars had exploded to dance within the night sky and go still again, he whispered tenderly against her ear, "My love, you are worth it indeed."

They stayed by the water a little while longer. Whatever came in the future, Tess knew that she would dream of this place as long as she lived.

She began to shiver, and he covered her in the doeskin dress once again, and then he suggested that they return to the tepee in the village.

They slept that night alone together in the tepee where she had been taken earlier that day. They slept, having shed their clothing once again, wound into one another's arms within the warm shelter of an Apache blanket.

When morning came, they were still together.

During the next few days, they were Nalte's honored guests. They attended the ceremonies for his sister, Little Flower, and Tess was amazed to find that she had discovered a strange peace here, living with the Apache. Nalte spent time with the two of them. Sometimes he ignored Tess and engaged in long conversations with Jamie in his Apache tongue. But sometimes he spoke in English, including Tess.

Once, when they were alone, Jamie having gone to join a hunting party, Nalte took it upon himself to teach her something about the Apache ways.

He explained to her about the Gan, or Mountain Spirit Dancers. In their masks, they impersonated the Mountains Spirits. They evoked the power of the supernaturals to cure illness, drive away evil and bring good fortune. They assembled in a cave, and under the guidance of a special Gan shaman, they donned their sacred costumes. They held great power, and therefore they were obliged to honor severe restrictions. They were not to recognize friends once they were in their attire, nor were they to dance incorrectly or to tamper with the sacred costume or clothing once it had been left within a secret cache. To disobey any of the restrictions could bring calamity down upon the dancer or his family or tribe. To disobey could bring about sickness, madness, even death.

"We are a people of ritual," he told her. "We celebrate the Holiness Rite and the Ceremonial Relay. For the Holiness Rite the shaman must go through arduous procedures, imitating the bear and the snake, and curing the people of the powerful bear and snake sicknesses. The Ceremonial Relay tells us of our food supply—game and the harvest of nature. Runners symbolize the sun and the animals, and the moon and the plants. If the sun runners win, game will be in plenty for us. If the moon runners win, then we will feast on the harvest of the plants."

"You live a good life here," Tess said.

"I live a good life, yes, but I fear the day when white men come to take it from me."

"But surely, here—"

"They will come, the white men will come. War will tear apart the mountains, and blood will stain the rivers. It is inevitable. But when the time comes, I will remember you, and Slater, and I will know that all whites are not the same. Yes, it is good here. Now. And you, I think that you are at peace."

She smiled at him. "I do not believe it, but yes, I am at peace here."

Nalte stared at the fire that burned in the center of the village. "You might have been happy had you stayed," he said quietly. "And maybe not. Our women are the gatherers. The first green vegetables are the yucca, and the women collect them. Then they must collect the mescal stalks and roast them and grind them into paste. We eat the mescal as paste, and as the cakes you have been given with your meals. It is a hard life.''

"A ranch is a hard life. And so is a newspaper," Tess said softly. She looked at him quickly. "A newspaper—"

"I know what a newspaper is. I lived in a town for many years when I was a child. I was captured with a war party and taken in by a minister's wife. I learned a lot about your society. A newspaper is a powerful weapon."

"It isn't a weapon at all," Tess protested.

"More powerful than a gun. Be careful with it," Nalte warned her. Then he asked her if she was Jamie's wife.

She flushed as she told him that she was not.

"But you are his woman," Nalte told her.

"It—it isn't the same thing," she said.

The Indian was lowering his head, smiling, and she remembered belatedly that he had chosen to let her go because of Jamie. "When an Apache marries, he goes to his wife's family. If she lives in a distant territory, then the man leaves and joins her family. Within it he may rise to be the leader, then he may become the leader of many families, and ultimately a great chief. But always, when it is possible, he joins his wife's family. He works for his wife's parents and elders, and he is known by them as 'he who carries burdens for me.' He speaks for her, and the man and the woman exchange gifts. A separate dwelling is made for the couple. She is his wife.

"But I tell you, Sun-Colored Woman, that it is the same among the Apache and the whites. When a man loves a woman, when he claims her for his own, when he is willing to give his life and his pride and his honor for her, that is when she is truly his wife, in his eyes and in the eyes of the great spirits, be they our gods or the one great God of the whites." He touched her cheek almost tenderly, then left her.

She thought about his words for a long time to come, and she wondered if Jamie did love her. Did he love her enough to stay with her, or would he tire of her, as he had tired of Eliza?

She had made love with him always of her own volition. She had wanted him as she had never known want before. But sometimes she wished that she had never given in to the temptation, for she felt that she had tasted forbidden fruit. She had found it very sweet, but she would perish when she could taste it no longer.

Nights were theirs. She never spoke, but came to him with her skin warmed by the fire, her body bathed by the stream, her hair soft and fragrant from the sun. She lay down beside him, and she loved him, and she tried not to think of the future.

On the fourth night of Little Flower's puberty rite, when the maiden had become a woman, Jamie was silent, holding her gently, staying motionless. Tess knew that he didn't sleep, and she shifted against him, asking him what was wrong.

"We're free to go home tomorrow," she whispered to him.

"Yes, or the next day," he said absently. "Nalte has been involved with his sister and us. He may be busy with tribal business tomorrow."

"What difference will a day make?"

He shook his head, still staring toward the top of the tepee and the poles that seemed to reach toward the stars. "A day will not make a difference. Nothing will a make a difference. That's the point. When we go home, Tess, von Heusen is still going to be there. And we still haven't any proof of what he is doing."

"But—but Jeremiah and David kidnapped me—and they left you for dead!" Tess protested.

"Jeremiah and David are dead. They can't be brought to trial, and they can't be forced to testify against von Heusen. We're right back where we started. And I know you. You'll head right back to that newspaper office of yours."

"Jamie, I have to!"

"You don't have to!" he told her savagely.

"Jamie—"

"We're going back, Tess, and we're going to fight von Heusen. But we have to do it by my rules."

"I don't—"

"That's right—you don't. You don't make a move without someone by your side, do you understand me? Things are going to get worse. Von Heusen may be thinking right now that you and I are gone. He may even have had a few moments of divine pleasure, thinking that he'd won at last. But Tess, by now he must have discovered that he can't get his hands on that property, even if we're both believed to be dead and gone. He's going to be furious when he finds it's willed to my family—and he's going to be ready for a full-scale war. We've got to pray that we're going to be ready for it.''

"Can we be?'' Tess whispered.

"Yes, we can,'' he said. But then he swung around on her, staring at her fiercely, clutching her chin with a grip so tight that it was painful. "But Tess, so help me God, you'll do it my way.''

"Jamie—''

"You'll do it my way!''

"Fine! All right!'' she snapped.

He dropped her jaw. Tears were stinging her eyes, and she quickly rolled away from him, furious that no matter how close it seemed they became, he still played the dictator.

And left her frightened that she was falling more and more deeply in love with a man who would wage war for her, who would risk his life for her...

And yet ride away in the end, when it mattered the most.

He did not reach for her, and she did not come back to touch him that night. Her back was cold, and she drew the blanket more fully around her.

She shivered in the night...

But the distance remained between them.

They spent one more day with the Apache, watching the sacred ritual when a young boy departed with his first hunting party. The boy's first four raids would be accompanied by ritual. This day he was instructed by the war shaman and accepted by the adult members of the party. He was given a drinking tube and a scratcher with lightning designs, and he was bestowed with a war cap.

Jamie spoke to her while they stood watching. He pointed to the war cap and told her, "It will not yet contain the spiritual power that belongs to the men. He must complete his passage before the spirits will enter into his cap.'' The men and women of the village were gathering around the boy to throw pollen upon him as he departed with the warriors. "It is a blessing,'' Jamie told her.

"And we are standing here, watching this, and these men and that boy will go off and raid some white settlement and perhaps kill our own kind," Tess murmured.

Jamie glared at her. "I'll thank you to keep your opinions to yourself. We're lucky to be leaving here alive. And, Miss Stuart, for your information, this party is moving against the Comancheros. I don't believe you can feel too much sympathy for that particular group."

She could not, but she didn't have a chance to tell him so. He turned her around and propelled her toward the tepee they were sharing. "Go in, be quiet. I'm going to ask Nalte if we might leave tomorrow."

She didn't hear, that afternoon, whether Nalte gave his permission. She waited endlessly for Jamie to return, but he did not. When it was dark one of the Apache women came to help her rekindle the fire and to give her a plate of beef and yams and mescal cakes. She ate halfheartedly and waited, but Jamie still didn't return. Finally her impatience brought her to the opening in the tent, and she looked out to see Jamie and Nalte and the victorious raiding party sitting around the central fire, laughing, talking, enjoying some newly arrived bottles of whiskey, and apparently enjoying one another as if they were long lost friends. In a fury she went to the fire and called Jamie's name sharply.

Every man there paused and stared at her, none of them more surprised or annoyed than Jamie. Nalte shot him a quick glance and said something in Apache. Jamie was quickly on his feet. He replied casually to the chief, but two rugged strides brought him to Tess. Before she could move or react he had butted her belly with his shoulder and lifted her precariously. Her head dangled dangerously down his back. She screamed out her protest, but Jamie ignored her and the Apache laughed, enjoying the show.

Within seconds they were back in the tepee. She landed hard on one of the blankets, desperately inhaling as he stared at her furiously. She might have thought at first that he was drunk, but the sharp fire in his eyes denied such a possibility. She accused him anyway before he could yell at her.

"You're totally inebriated!"

"Inebriated—you mean drunk, don't you? I wish I were. Drunk

enough to give you what you need! And what you need is a good switch taken to your hide.''

"Oh!" She shimmied up to her knees. "Don't you dare speak to me like that, Jamie Slater—"

"I don't think I'm just going to speak!" he warned her, his lashes falling over his eyes so that they were narrow and dangerous. "I think I'm going to act—"

She was on her feet instantly, running for the flap in the tent with a speed and agility as fleet as a doe's. But at the flap she paused, realizing that she would be running into a group of raucous Apaches.

She spun around, certain Jamie was almost upon her. But he was standing back, watching her with supreme arrogance and amusement. He had known she wouldn't run out of the tent.

She decided to take her chances with the Apache.

She didn't make it. Jamie had been still, but he came to motion in a flash. Just as she reached for the rawhide flap, his arms swept around her calves, and she came crashing down to the hard ground. She coughed and gagged and struggled against his weight to turn around and face him. He straddled her. Her simple doeskin dress was wound high around her hips, and she was naked beneath it. Jamie didn't seem to notice. He sat calmly upon her, crossing his arms over his chest, aware that she wouldn't be going anywhere at all.

He stared down at her. "Undisciplined—brat!"

"Brat! I'm twenty-four years old—"

"An old maid! Maybe that's half the problem."

She gasped, stunned by the remark, and started to struggle furiously beneath him. Her fingers wound into fists but he was ready, leaning forward to pin her wrists to the sides of her head. "I told you—it's done my way. You may be Miss Stuart, and you may be the publisher of the *Wiltshire Sun*, and you may own one of the finest ranches this side of the Mississippi, but you're with me now, and I warned you, it's going to be done my way! Especially among the Apache! You don't make a fool of a man in front of them!"

"But I just wanted to know what was going on!"

"I really should take a switch to you—but at some later date." The fury suddenly faded from his voice. He released her wrists, his hands massaging both tenderly and tempestuously through the splay of her hair. "Tess, Tess, what are we doing? We're going back to Wiltshire, and all hell will break loose when we get there. Let's not fight each other now."

She stared at his striking features, at the handsome and rugged angles and planes of his face, at the passion in his silver eyes. She trembled suddenly and wound her arms around him. "Hold me!" she whispered.

And he did.

They shed their clothing, and she thought that he made love to her more tenderly, more carefully, that night than he ever had before.

When the sun rose their naked bodies were entwined together in the soft shadows. She didn't want to leave, she thought. She could live among the Apache with Jamie forever.

But of course she couldn't. This was not her world, and she had vowed that she would fight von Heusen. Neither she nor Jamie could walk away now.

Jamie leaned over and kissed her lips, and she looked into his eyes.

"It's time," he told her.

He rose and dressed quickly, and she followed his example.

They did not leave with the dawn, for Nalte wanted another conference with Jamie. His sister, Little Flower, came to Tess to say goodbye. Tess had learned very little of the language, but she had been grateful for Little Flower's shy kindness. It seemed that Nalte was bestowing gifts on Tess—she was given a new outfit in which to ride, in pale buckskin, with fine tin cone pendants and beautiful beadwork. There was a long overdress that fell nearly to her knees, and beneath it, soft trousers so that she might ride easily. She was given boots at last, fine boots with rawhide bottoms and soft leggings to cover her calves. She thanked Little Flower as best as she could for the gifts, then kissed the young woman on the cheek.

Nalte came to her then. Little Flower fled, and Nalte watched Tess for several moments before speaking. "You will take the dress, too. Slater has told me that it will always be special to him."

She flushed. "Thank you. Thank you for the gifts. I've nothing to give you in return."

He shrugged. "I have gotten what I wanted from Slater. And I give you the gifts in his behalf. In our courting ritual, we exchange gifts, as I have told you.''

She smiled and lowered her head, wondering what Jamie had given him. ''Most of all, Nalte, I thank you for my freedom.''

He grunted and looked at her still. ''I understand that you are a warrior yourself.''

''A warrior?'' she said, startled.

''You take on men's battles.''

''I didn't really intend to. I just—I had to fight back.'' She paused. ''This man had my uncle murdered. Do you understand?''

''Yes, I understand. I will pray that the spirits will be with you.''

He left her then.

Jamie returned soon after. ''They are ready to ride,'' he told her. ''Let's go.''

She nodded and hurried after him. There was a small roan mare set aside for her use, and she silently accepted Jamie's help to mount the saddleless creature.

She was startled to see Jamie mounting a large paint gelding. She stared at him and said softly, ''Jamie, your own horse—''

''He's Nalte's now,'' Jamie said curtly.

''Your horse! But you loved that horse. Why on earth would you want to—''

She broke off. He hadn't wanted to give Nalte the horse. The horse had been the negotiation.

''I'm sorry, Jamie.''

''It doesn't matter,'' he said, and, turning his back, he rode ahead to talk to the half-naked warrior in a breechclout at the head of the party of a dozen or so, their escort through Comanchero territory. The Indian turned and she gasped, startled to see that it was Nalte.

She couldn't ponder the chief's participation in their ride then, for cries suddenly filled the air and they were leaving the village behind at a quick pace. Jouncing on her pony, Tess turned back.

Little Flower was waving to her. Tess smiled warmly and waved in turn.

They she turned again and hugged her knees to her pony. She had thought that she knew how to ride hard, but she had never ridden with the Apache before.

She realized she was learning about a hard ride all over again, from the very beginning.

By the time they stopped for the night, she could barely dismount, and when she did she nearly fell.

Jamie was there to catch her. She widened her eyes and stared at him and she wanted to straighten and show him that she could be strong. But her knees were buckling and she merely managed to whisper, "Oh, Jamie…"

He caught her before she fell. The Apache warriors were preparing a fire, and he carried her to it. One warrior stretched out a blanket for her, and a roll was stuffed beneath her head.

She never ate a meal that night for she fell asleep instantly.

Somewhere in the middle of the night she felt a new warmth. She opened her eyes and realized that Jamie had stretched next to her, and she was curled up in the shelter of his arms.

She stared up at the stars and was suddenly very afraid. She had wanted to go home, and they were going home. But Jamie was right, it would be open war now. She didn't want to die. She was just learning how to live.

She closed her eyes and curled her fingers around the strong male hand that curved beneath her breast. "Please God, please God, please God," she whispered. The rest of her prayer formed no words, but she knew it in her heart. She wanted to survive…and more.

She wanted to survive with Jamie. The life that was now so precious to her would be meaningless without him.

She closed her eyes again, and to her amazement, she slept once more.

The Apache stayed with them all the next day and the next night. Jamie seemed concerned for them, warning Nalte that they were moving into Comanche territory. But Nalte knew Running River, and he didn't seem concerned.

Tess tried to talk to Nalte, reminding him that many whites had believed von Heusen when he said that it had been Indians who caused all the trouble. Few of the new settlers knew there was a difference between Comanche and Apache.

Nalte, however, was resolute. He and the Apache rode with them to the outskirts of the town of Wiltshire. Then he lifted his spear high in the air and a shrill, blood-chilling cry escaped him. The Apache formed behind him.

"Goodbye, Slater, Sun-Colored Woman."

"Thank you. No matter what comes, Nalte, I will always be your friend," Jamie told him.

"I believe you." The chief moved forward, and he and Jamie clasped hands. Then Nalte swung his newly acquired mount around and his men raced off behind him.

Jamie watched them disappear in a cloud of Texas dust, then he looked at Tess. "This is it. We're almost home."

"Perhaps we should go into town—"

"No. We'll head to the ranch."

"But I need to put this in the paper—"

He swore, roughly, violently. "Tomorrow, Tess! We're going home. I tried to make a few arrangements for help. You can't go into town alone, and I have to get back to the ranch! Got it?"

"Got it!" she shouted back.

They weren't far. She swung her Apache mare around and nudged her to a fleeting gallop. She raced for a good ten minutes before she pulled up suddenly, a feeling of utter joy encompassing her heart as the ranch came into view. It was still standing. No one had burned it to the ground. Smoke was spewing from the chimney; Dolly or Jane must be cooking something inside. Life had gone on while she had been with the Apache. And the people who loved her had held on.

Jamie was behind her. She turned and shouted to him. "It's still standing!"

"Yes," he began.

She didn't let him say more. She nudged the mare hard again with her heels and thundered toward the ranch. She passed the paddocks and the beautiful mares with their foals and she felt joy cascade throughout her. Von Heusen hadn't beaten them—not yet.

She reined in the mare as she came to the house. Dust flew as the little horse pawed the ground. Tess leaped down and went racing for the front door. "Dolly, Jane, Hank!"

She stood in the entryway, looking at the large desk, at the stairway leading to the second floor, at the furniture in the parlor, at the dining table. She was home.

"They're here! Someone is here!" a voice shouted.

It was an unfamiliar voice. Tess stared in astonishment as a tall, slim blond woman came hurrying down the stairway. She was followed by a handsome little boy of about five, then a second blond woman with a serene and beautiful face.

"Miss Tess!"

Tess swung around as Jane hurried from the kitchen, throwing her arms around her. "I knew you'd come back, I just knew that you would!"

"Well." The first woman had reached the entryway. "I knew that Jamie wouldn't come back without you, of course," she said. "Where is he?"

Tess stared with astonishment at the two women and the little boy. Then the door burst open behind her. Jamie had arrived, but he wasn't alone. With him were two men, both as tall as he, with the handsome but rugged features of ranchers, of men who eked their existence from the land and the elements. They were talking, the three of them were talking, the darkest of them saying something about von Heusen.

Then Dolly emerged from the kitchen, wiping her hands on her apron. "Those twins!" she proclaimed. "The little darlings are going to eat us out of cookies and cakes, they are! Oh! Oh, Tess! Jamie, Lieutenant Slater, why you're home! You're home!" There were tears in her eyes, tears streaming down her cheeks. "I knew Tess wouldn't come home without her lieutenant. I knew you wouldn't!"

Dolly flung her arms around Jamie, and then Dolly and Jane were fighting to hug Tess, and she was trying to hug them back. But she still couldn't help staring at the strangers who were suddenly filling her house.

Twins? What twins?

The two blond women were kissing and hugging Jamie. Jamie was laughing in return and thanking both for coming. Tess wasn't sure if she would lose her temper or her mind first.

"Excuse me!" she said, but there was too much noise. "Excuse me!" she shouted. The room went still. She looked around, and then said frankly, "Excuse me, but—who are you?"

"Jamie!" the taller woman wailed. "You didn't tell her?"

Tess smiled sweetly. "No. No, he didn't tell me."

Jamie stepped forward. "These are my brothers, Cole and Malachi. And their wives, Kristin and Shannon. And that's my nephew, Gabe. And I take it that Shannon and Malachi's twins are in the kitchen—"

"The little darlings!" Dolly said rapturously.

"We've come because Jamie sent us a wire about von Heusen," Cole Slater told her.

Tess gasped. She stared at them all. So this was having a family. They were so close. They knew one another so well. They were happy and content, she could see it on their faces; they were serene with their world.

She shook her head. "Thank you, but—" She swung around on Jamie. "Jamie, you can't—they could get killed here!"

"Well, ma'am, I'm not planning on getting killed," Malachi told her, tipping back his hat. "I'm not planning on it at all. You see, we came to kill them if need be."

"You don't know von Heusen."

"Oh," Kristin said cheerfully, "we have known men a great deal like him." She smiled, stepping forward. "We're family, Tess. And that's what it's all about." She flashed Jamie a quick grin. "My brother-in-law was always there when I needed him," she said.

"Oh!" Shannon said suddenly. "Smell that! Oh, no, Jamie and Miss Stuart have come home at last, and it seems we've let dinner burn!"

She swung around, then looked back. "Well, isn't anyone hungry?"

And Tess realized she was starved.

She glanced at Jamie. She was still amazed, still in shock. But Kristin Slater set a hand upon her arm. "Come on! I promise you, things will start to look more reasonable after a good dinner and a full night's sleep!"

Jamie shrugged.

Tess felt herself gently pulled along.

Dinner...

The perfect end to the...perfect day?

Chapter Thirteen

They had just reached the table when Jon Red Feather came in with Hank. Tess let out a startled, joyful cry and raced to Jon, giving him a fierce hug. "You did come back! You made it out, and you came back!"

"Of course," he told her. "Someone had to be here to welcome the Slaters. I mean, this is practically a tribe. Have you realized that yet?"

"A tribe!" Kristin said indignantly. "Sit down, Jon, and watch your tongue, if you will. Jamie, by the way, you should marry this girl before you find out that you've got competition on your hands."

Jon laughed, and Tess flushed. She wasn't sure about Jamie's reaction. Kristin Slater started calmly doling out food into the numerous plates on the table.

It was a good thing it was a big house.

Uncle Joe, you would have loved to have seen this! she thought.

"If everyone would come sit down," Malachi said, pouring wine into the glasses around the table, "I think that Jon has something to tell Tess and Jamie."

"Yes, I do, as a matter of fact." Jon walked to the table and picked up a glass of wine. He smiled at Tess and Jamie. "Cheers," he said, raising his glass to his lips.

"Will you all please sit!" Cole said emphatically.

Tess sat at her own dining table—as she had been so politely ordered. Jamie sat beside her, and they stared at Jon, who looked at them.

"I have discovered why von Heusen is so particularly eager to seize hold of your land, Miss Stuart."

Tess gasped, and she and Jamie stood.

"Why?" Tess demanded.

Jon smiled, swirling his wine. "The railroad."

"Oh, my God!" Jamie said, sinking into his chair.

Tess stared at him. He obviously understood completely what was going on, but she didn't have the least idea.

"What?"

"Miss Stuart," Cole Slater told her, drawing out a chair and sitting back in it, "the railroad is coming through here. That means that this property is going to go sky-high in value. If you wanted to sell some land straight, it would be worth a small fortune."

"But there's more," Jon Red Feather told her softly. "If you do sell just the necessary land, the rest of your property will still go sky-rocketing in value—you'll be able to send your produce right out from your own doorstep. Tess, you're sitting on the best land this side of the Mississippi. And that's why von Heusen has been so desperate to get rid of you. With this property in his hands, he could really control a good percentage of western Texas."

Tess smiled slowly, looking at Jamie. "But—but he can't touch any of it now. He must know that! Half of it is in your name, and even if we hadn't returned—"

"Ownership would have come to Cole and me and our families," Malachi supplied for her.

"Well, he must know that."

"He does know that," Jon said. Gabe was sitting beside him, and he tousled the lad's brown hair to be rewarded with a fascinated smile. Jon smiled in turn, then gave Tess his attention again. "I let it be known that Jamie had found you and that he'd be bringing you home. I also went to see Edward Clancy and had him print up the arrival of Cole and Malachi—and I stressed the ability of the Slater brothers with their small arms."

"A couple of von Heusen's men rode out here the other day. But we uninvited them quickly," Kristin said, heaping mashed potatoes on a plate to pass to Jon.

"Cole or Malachi scared them away?" Tess asked.

"Oh, no, Shannon did," Kristin said. "She's an ace."

"I'm a decent shot," Shannon said demurely.

"She can hit a fly's eye at a hundred yards," Malachi said drily.

They all laughed, but Cole sobered quickly and spoke to Jamie in low, even tones. "The point is, this von Heusen knows that scare tactics aren't going to work with Miss Stuart anymore. No one can quite fathom what he'll pull next."

"Well, he'll have more to worry about after tomorrow," Tess said firmly. "I'm going to go to the paper and I'm going to give Clancy another front-page story. It's going to be all about David and Jeremiah and Mr. von Heusen's orders to see that I never returned."

"There might be a few problems with that," Jon advised her.

"Why?" Tess asked.

"Because Clancy and your printer gave in at last. Someone shot a few windows yesterday, and by last night, Clancy had thrown in the towel. He wanted you to know that he was sorry."

Tess inhaled and exhaled. "I can do it myself," she said.

"You won't have to do it yourself," Kristin corrected her, sitting at last with her own plate. "Dolly and Jane can keep the children here, and Shannon and I will come in and help you with the press. If you give us directions, we can surely follow them. The three of us will go into town first thing in the morning—"

"No!" Jamie said emphatically.

"I have to," Tess began, turning, ready to give battle. "Jamie, I've told you—"

"The three of you aren't going anywhere alone," he interrupted harshly. "It isn't safe. Dammit to hell, Tess! Don't you understand yet?"

"I understand that the newspaper has always been my major weapon."

"But right now it isn't enough. Okay, we'll go. You'll do your damned article, but we'll go together. Tess, what do I have to say to get through to you? When von Heusen attacks again, it's going to be all-out war."

She wanted to retort. She was furious. He was right, of course, but she still wanted to yell at him.

Fighting desperately to hold her tongue, she looked at Jon. "How did you find all this out?"

He shrugged. "I was still in buckskins when I came back, and I didn't change before I made a visit into town. Von Heusen had one of his guns follow me. I knew it, so I doubled back and got hold of

him. As it happened, Cole and Malachi had been riding in to meet
me.''

"And," Malachi said, grinning, "Jon just happened to be dressed
for the occasion."

Tess was still confused. Kristin sighed and explained. "Cole and
Malachi convinced von Heusen's hired goon that Jon was scarcely
more than a raw savage and that he actually delighted in human
flesh. Between the three of them they barely had to touch the fellow
before he was spilling everything he had ever known in his life."

Tess smiled and glanced at Jamie.

He was not smiling. She looked away quickly, pushing a piece of
roast around on her plate. They were a lot alike, the Slater brothers.
Cole was the darkest, with golden eyes—his little boy had those
eyes, even though he had his mother's soft blond hair. Malachi was
a golden blond with blue eyes, and Jamie was sandy-haired with his
smoke gray and silver eyes. But the planes of their faces were similar, strong and hard and weathered. She realized suddenly that she
would trust any of the brothers with anything she had.

And she didn't really mean to keep fighting Jamie. It just kept
coming out that way.

He stood up suddenly, his chair scraping back. "That was a fine
meal, Kristin, Shannon—Dolly?"

"We all contributed," Kristin told him.

"Well, thank you, but I think I need a little air. You got a good
cheroot on you anywhere, Cole?"

"Sure," said his brother, rising as well. He stopped by his wife's
chair and kissed her tenderly at the base of the neck before following
Jamie out.

"Seems like we're splitting up here," Malachi said.

"Well, don't stay on my account!" Shannon told him.

He laughed, shrugged at Jon, and the two of them left. Hank followed them and the women were left—Jane, who had barely said a
word, Dolly, who was unbelievably quiet, and Shannon and Kristin
and Tess.

"All this to make a meal, and then it's just wolfed down, and
then everyone runs—"

"Ma," Gabe suddenly interrupted from the end of the table. "I
cleaned my plate. Can I go join Pa?"

Kristin threw up her hands, and Tess felt some of the tension leave her as she laughed.

"Go!" Kristin told her son.

He smiled, excused himself politely to Tess and ran out of the house.

"We might as well pick up," Shannon said.

"Might as well."

Things went quickly with five of them to do the clearing, the scraping, the washing and the drying. Shannon asked Tess what it had been like with the Apache, and by the time she finished with her story about Jon and Jamie appearing at just the right time, they had finished the dishes. Jane and Dolly kissed Tess again and went to bed. Shannon and Kristin and Tess made tea and then sat around the kitchen table, staring at one another.

"And then this Nalte let you go—just because Jamie asked for you? He let you go to Jamie?" Kristin said.

Tess felt herself flush, wondering how to avoid saying the very thing the Indian chief had so clearly understood. "He, uh, he…"

"Oh, for God's sake, Kristin, they've been sleeping together and this Nalte man knew it!" Shannon exclaimed.

"Shannon!" Kristin protested.

"Well, all right, I'm terribly sorry, but Kristin and I both married Slater men. I know. They're so easy to want to shoot, but at the same time…" Her voice trailed away and she was really beautiful as she grinned. "Well, they are easy to sleep with. Seductive."

Tess knew she had to be a thousand shades of crimson.

Kristin sighed. "He's very much in love with you. I'm sure we'll see a wedding any day."

"I'm not terribly sure about that."

"He called us here. To protect your interests. He must love you."

"I've turned over half the property to him. It's his own property he's protecting."

"Um. Did he bargain for anything else?" Kristin asked her.

She didn't know why she was being so honest except that somehow she felt she had known the two women all her life.

Maybe it was because they had all become involved with Slater men.

"Maybe they just don't marry easily," Shannon suggested.

"But you're both married," Tess began.

"Cole had to marry me," Kristin said.

"Oh, the baby?"

"No!" Kristin laughed. "There was a horrible, horrible man after me. The war was going on and the only way he could count on some protection from some old acquaintances was to be able to say that I was his wife. He fell in love with me slowly; it took him a long time." She smiled sweetly at Shannon. "And Malachi had to marry Shannon."

"Well, he didn't have to," Shannon protested.

"The twins?" Tess asked.

"No, a shotgun," Shannon explained ruefully. They both laughed, and Shannon took a deep breath and tried to explain that Kristin was her sister, and that Kristin had been in trouble. She and Malachi had gone after her, and a kindly old couple had decided the two of them had to be married.

"But they'd been in love for years. They wouldn't admit it, of course, because they were too busy gouging one another's eyes out."

"Oh, it never was that bad!" Shannon protested.

"No, it was worse!" Kristin said. She stood up. "I think that we need a drop of brandy to go with this, too. Girls?"

Shannon and Tess both agreed. Then Tess yawned and complained that her buckskins were filthy and that she felt as if half of Texas was covering her. The sisters quickly had the hip tub out and filled, and Shannon was racing upstairs for French bath oil, and before she knew it Kristin was presenting her with a lilac nightgown that matched her eyes.

"I can't take these things!" Tess protested.

"But you can. It's all in the family," Shannon told her.

Tess shook her head. "I heard Jamie once. He said that no one would ever make him get married."

Kristin shrugged. "They can't force him—but he just might choose to do so on his own."

"Do you want him?" Shannon asked her.

Tess felt her heart beat hard and she closed her eyes. Yes! Yes, she wanted Jamie desperately. She had wanted him since his eyes had first fallen upon her, since he had killed the rattler, since he had told her in a soft voice that she was beautiful.

Since that day by the stream before the nightmare had begun and he had touched her and said, "I think I'm falling in love with you..."

But that had been before they had nearly been destroyed, before he had lost his beloved cavalry mount to retrieve her. She was trouble. He had told her that again and again. He had walked out at dinner because he had been so furious with her that he hadn't been able to stay at the table.

"Do you?" Shannon persisted.

"Yes," Tess admitted softly. "I want him. For keeps."

"Then forget the arguments. Even forget the fact that you'll probably never get along. I have," Shannon said cheerily. "Forget von Heusen, forget everything, and cherish what time you have together in peace."

"And get in the tub with the rose oil," Kristin suggested drily. "There's just nothing like a very sweet smell."

"And a see-through lilac gown to match your eyes! Aren't they beautiful eyes, Kristin?"

"And she's not jealous often," Kristin said, laughing.

Feeling loved and protected, Tess stepped into the water and felt the steam surround her. It was good to be home.

"I'm more worried now that I know just what this man is after," Jamie said.

He was sitting on the rocker on the porch. Jon was perched on the railing with Cole, and Malachi was seated across from him on the swing. It creaked slowly in the night air.

Jamie exhaled. He looked at his brothers. "Thanks for coming. I'm just wishing right now that I hadn't had you bring Kristin and Shannon."

"Jamie, you've known the McCahy girls a long time," Cole said drily. "And you should know at this point that they wouldn't have it any other way."

"I just don't know what this man might plan. I do know that he keeps twenty to thirty hired guns on his property at all times."

"We've met up with bad odds before," Malachi reminded him.

"God damn it, don't you understand what I'm trying to say? I don't want you, your wives or your children killed on my account."

Gabe came out then. He glanced at his father and it was obvious he had heard some of what had been said. He went straight up to his Uncle Jamie and took his trail-roughened face into his hands.

"There's right and wrong, Uncle Jamie, and you know that. And my pa and my ma, they say you have to fight what's wrong, because if you just give in, it'll bury you in the end. I don't mind fighting. Not if it's the right thing to do."

Jamie lifted his nephew and hugged him tightly.

Cole smiled. "I rest my case."

"Malachi, those twins of yours aren't quite three years old. You think they feel the same way?"

"Jamie, we're here, and that's it," Malachi said flatly. "Now, what about Tess?"

"What about her?" Jamie scowled. "She's the hardest creature to tangle with I have ever encountered, Yanks and Indians and rattlers included."

"Think you're going to marry her?" Malachi asked pleasantly.

"If he doesn't do so soon," Jon Red Feather supplied, "I will."

"Damn you, Jon—"

"I'll have to, to keep the poor woman honest."

Jamie groaned. "You know, the lot of you, you may be a man's kin and his best friend, but I'm telling you—"

"She's beautiful, very bright and has the will of a wildcat. Besides that, she's worth a damned fortune. He's already absconded with half her property," Malachi said.

"Wait a damned minute!" Jamie protested.

"The least you could do is marry her," Cole said.

Jamie threw up his hands. "Thank you, one and all, for coming. And now I'll thank you, one and all, to mind your own damned business. Good night."

He set Gabe on the rocker and headed into the house. He was halfway up the stairs before he realized he didn't know if he had a room in the house. His brothers and Kristin and Shannon and even the kids seemed very happily moved in.

But where the hell he was supposed to be, he didn't know.

He headed for Tess's room, wondering what her reaction was going to be. If she threatened to scream and bring the house down he thought he'd throttle her.

He tapped on her door, then pushed it open. "Tess?"

"Jamie?" She said his name softly, sweetly. Her voice touched the air like the fragrance of roses that seemed to be all around the room, light as stardust. Her whisper was sultry, as if he had awakened her.

He strode across the room then paused, seeing how the moon entered through the window and glowed upon her. Her hair was shining with greater splendor than any sunset, and it was spread out behind her as if each strand were a glorious ray of the sun.

She was dressed in violet, a shade that matched her eyes in the darkness of the night. A shade that was barely concealing, a shade that managed to enhance every beautiful line and curve of her body.

"Tess, where the hell—" He paused, clearing his throat, wondering why the hell he was getting so damned angry. "Tess, where am I supposed to—oh, the hell with it!" he growled.

He didn't see her smile as he dropped forcefully upon her, sweeping her into his arms. He didn't really see anything except the color of her hair, entwining and tangling around him. He breathed in the clean, sweet scent of her, and he could barely contain his longings. The Apache had kept them apart for the last two long nights. He hadn't realized how badly he could need her after such a short time, how much he could crave her. She was like a sweet a man thought he tasted once, and yet wanted more and more once he knew the exotic taste...

He kissed her fiercely, and he kissed her long, and he felt the frantic rise of her breasts against his hand as she lost her breath. Only when she trembled and gasped did he raise his head and stare at her. "I'm staying here. We're doing it my way, remember?"

She returned his stare. Her arms wound around him, and she pressed her lips to his, then she shoved him slightly away from her and started to open his shirt buttons. Slowly, achingly slowly, she opened them one by one, pressing her lips against his flesh. And when his shirt was cast aside she tenderly nipped and kissed his shoulders while she tugged at his belt buckle. She inched his pants slowly down his hips. Boldly, possessively she touched him, stroked him and trembled, her fingers shaking as he came hard as steel to her ministrations. Then he could stand no more of the sweet torture and she was on her back, with his lips savoring her body beneath the gauze of the lilac gown. He tasted her breasts and the valley between them and her navel and her upper thighs and teased her more intimately still until she was thrashing and calling his name to the moon-dusted night, begging that he come to her.

With the deepest pleasure, he obliged, and the feeling of being where he belonged within her was almost as great as the pure sexual excitement of being so tightly, so erotically sheathed. He shuddered with the force of his desire, and stroked deeper and deeper until they exploded as one. Then he took her tightly into his arms, glad of her lips pressed to his chest, her head burrowed against him.

You're mine, he longed to tell her. You were mine when I first found you, and mine when I came to Nalte to ask for you. You are mine this night...

And if we can only survive, you will be mine forever.

His thoughts gave pause, and he added silently: even if you are the most ornery and troublesome female in the western world.

In the morning his troublesome female was up and almost dressed by the time he had pulled on his trousers.

"Afraid of my family?" he asked her.

Tess looked his way curiously and shook her head. No man could be a finer lover, tender and tempestuous, but in the morning his temper always seemed to leave something to be desired. "I don't care what they know, if you're talking about our sleeping arrangements."

"I see. You think my older brother will insist that we marry."

"No one will ever force you to marry, Jamie. You said so yourself."

"So you're not planning on marriage."

"I try not to plan on anything."

She was at her dresser, brushing her hair. He slipped behind her, his chest still naked, and pulled her against him. He whispered against her ear. "What if you're already with child?"

She turned and faced him, looking him up and down. "You're nicely built, intelligent, I think, and your brothers don't seem to have too many flaws. If I have a child, it should be a darling one." She swung around to continue to brush her hair.

He laughed as he donned his shirt and socks and boots. "Tess, you are a hellion," he told her.

She smiled sweetly. "I just do the best I can with what I've got, Lieutenant. I'm going down for breakfast. I'm sure Dolly and Jane got things started very early with all those little children to feed. And I do want to be at the paper by eight. I've got to teach Kristin and Shannon how to work the press."

"I'm right with you," Jamie told her. But when she would have exited the room, he pulled her back. "We do things my way, remember."

"I remember," she said coolly.

"Everything."

"Meaning?"

"I'll tell you later," was all he said.

He stepped past her and hurried down the stairs. She followed him, convinced that he had only stopped her to prove to her that he could be down first.

Dolly and Jane were busy with the children, and they seemed like a couple of doting old aunts. Dolly beamed at Jamie. "I just can't wait until it's one of your little bundles I'm holding, Lieutenant!" she said. Of course she wasn't really holding Shannon's daughter—the child was squirming away, ready to chase a little string ball that was rolling across the floor.

"Yeah, soon enough, Dolly," Jamie said sweetly. To Tess's surprise he winked at her.

"Coffee!"

A cup was shoved into her hand by Malachi. "Jamie," he said, "I've told Hank to take Dolly and Jane and the children down to the storm cellar once we've gone. They're invisible there."

"Fine," Jamie said. "Dolly?"

"I understand, Lieutenant, I understand perfectly."

"I'll watch them," Hank promised. "Me and the hands, we'll stay in and down in the cellar with the children."

"Is everybody ready?" Jamie asked. He swallowed his coffee and set the cup on the table, then everyone was hurrying out. The children were taken to the cellar, and Dolly waved a cheerful hand to Tess. "You take care, missy, you hear?"

"Yes, Dolly, I promise! Thank you!"

Dolly disappeared into the storm cellar, and Hank followed, closing the door over them. Cole and Kristin stamped the dirt around so the opening was invisible.

By then Jon was coming around with the wagon, and Kristin and Shannon and Tess climbed up with him. The Slater brothers mounted their horses. Tess was aware that each was wearing a gun belt with two Colts. Each also had another gun attached to a saddle. They were well-armed, but managed to remain nonchalant.

Tess froze, praying that she wouldn't bring about one of these men's deaths. It was her fight. Her own. She had no right to get these men killed.

Maybe nothing would happen today. Maybe von Heusen would lie low. Maybe he would take his time to attack her again. She had written the truth once. After today, maybe more people would believe her. He couldn't kill everyone.

"Why don't you explain the press while we ride?" Jon suggested to her.

Tess gave him a grateful smile. If she talked, she would relax. "It's a small press, really, compared with many of the innovations they're coming up with today. But it's a small town, and we're a small paper. We set the type in a box called a chase. We tap our letters and words in with wooden mallets, ink the set type, then roll the papers through. It's very simple." She was just warming to the subject when Jon's voice interrupted her softly.

"The town is quiet today."

It was quiet. The streets were deserted. Not that it was usually busy at this time of the morning, but there was no one around. No one at all.

"Well," Tess murmured. "There's, uh, there's the paper over there. See, *Wiltshire Sun*. The place with all the windows broken out," she added drily.

"Well, you can set to typing your story while Kristin and I sweep up," Shannon said.

Tess nodded. There was a giant lump in her throat, though. Why was the town so damned deserted?

Jon stopped directly in front of the paper. Jamie had already dismounted, and he was watching the silent buildings for any sign of movement. Malachi came to the wagon and helped the women down.

"Get into the office," Jamie ordered curtly.

Tess didn't argue but did as he told her. Shannon and Kristin followed her.

"Will you look at this mess!" Kristin said, clicking her tongue.

"I should help you," Tess said.

"Will you please go type! We can handle this," Kristin said.

Tess nodded and walked to her desk and typewriter. She dusted fragments of glass from her chair and blew it from her papers and rolled a blank sheet into her typewriter.

She stared at it for just one second, then her fingers began to fly. She had a lot to say. A hell of a lot.

Time moved quickly. Kristin and Shannon moved around the room competently, and their presence didn't disturb Tess in the least. She was just getting to the part where Jeremiah and David had admitted their involvement with von Heusen when she heard a shout in the street.

The three of them froze. The shout came again.

"Tess! Tess Stuart! We know you're in there! And you're under arrest."

"Under arrest!" Tess gasped.

Then she heard Jamie respond from beyond the window, his voice harsh and firm as he met the threat.

"It's the sheriff, I think!" Shannon said, peeking around a broken window.

Tess joined her beside the window, and nodded.

"She's under arrest for what?" Jamie demanded.

"Slander and murder."

"Murder!"

"She killed two of Mr. von Heusen's men. She tricked them out into the open fields. I've witnesses to that effect. Then she shot them down cold."

Jamie let loose with a flaming oath. Then he was striding out to meet the sheriff face to face. Tess gripped the window frame.

"This is bull, and you know it. Von Heusen set you up to this. You're just a hired gun, like any other of his thugs."

"You shut your mouth, Slater. You're under arrest, too."

"For what?"

"Conspiracy to commit murder."

"Well, I'll tell you what, Sheriff, you just try to take me in."

Tess was never quite sure what propelled her, but before anyone could stop her, she was racing out to the street, streaking toward Jamie. She caught his arm and faced the sheriff, furious. "Don't you even think it! Don't you even try to drag him down into the mud and mire that you've created with von Heusen! Arrest me if you want to so damn badly—"

"Tess, damn you!" Jamie swore, swinging her around behind him. "What the hell are you doing out here? I told you—"

"Slater, shut up," came a new voice.

It was von Heusen. He came striding out from the saloon, his pale eyes shimmering with hatred, his white hair touched by the breeze. "Miss Stuart," he said, addressing Tess, "you are ever valiant. But I can't wait to hang this Reb. I just can't wait."

"You aren't ever going to hang me, von Heusen," Jamie said. "And you aren't ever going to have that property for the railroad."

Von Heusen's brows shot up. "So you know. You're quite a detective."

"I travel in good company," Jamie said with a shrug.

"It doesn't matter. The sheriff is my man. Aren't you, Harvey?"

"Von Heusen, don't say that," the sheriff began uneasily.

"Why? Who is going to stop us now?" von Heusen said. "I own the sheriff, and I own the magistrate, and I can damned well bet you I'm going to own the executioner. You're dead, Slater. As dead as a doornail."

"No. You may own the sheriff, but I've got a few guns around the place, too, von Heusen."

"Yeah, your brothers and that half-breed friend of yours. It's not enough. I've got guns all over this town."

As if to prove it, and obviously uncaring that he was about to commit murder in broad daylight, von Heusen raised his pistol and aimed straight at Jamie's heart.

But he didn't have a chance to fire. A gun cracked, and von Heusen grabbed his hand, screaming. And the streets came alive. There was a fearsome pounding of hooves, and war cries tore the air.

Jamie, astonished, bent low and whirled around. "Jesus!" he breathed.

The cavalry. The cavalry was coming, Sergeant Monahan in the lead. Nor were they alone. They were traveling, curiously enough, with a small band of Indians.

Apache.

"Jamie!"

Tess screamed his name and he swung around again even as the horses came tearing down the street.

Von Heusen had Tess. His right hand might be crippled and bleeding, but he held his pistol in his left hand, and the muzzle was pressed against her temple. He was backing toward the saloon.

"One more step and I blow her to kingdom come!" von Heusen warned Jamie.

Gunfire was spitting all around him. From behind a water barrel by the *Wiltshire Sun* office Cole was picking off von Heusen's men from the rooftops around them. Malachi and Jon were positioned behind the wagon, which they had overturned.

And the cavalry and the Apache were rushing in to the fantastic sound of a bugle call. It was quickly obvious that von Heusen's men would not be enough.

Except that von Heusen had Tess.

He disappeared through the swinging doors of the saloon. Jamie caught his breath, hearing Tess's screams as the man dragged her upstairs.

"The roof, Jamie! The roof!" Cole called to him.

He looked up. He made a leap toward the railing and swung himself up to the roof. A shot nearly made him trip and fall. He heard someone groan and saw a man fall to the ground. He looked across the street.

Cole smiled, blowing the smoke from his gun. "Dammit, Jamie, go get the girl!"

Jamie grinned and gave his brother a thumbs-up sign. Then he felt his blood run cold again. He was going to have to kill von Heusen if he wanted to live himself.

"You, Miss Stuart, have been a bloody thorn in my side since the beginning. You should have died in that raid on the wagon train, and if you'd had any damned sense, you would have stayed with that bleeding Apache."

Tess winced. Von Heusen's hold on her arm was vicious, and she could feel the cold steel pressed hard against her temple. She swallowed. If he killed her now, she was still the winner. She had to keep telling herself that, so she could keep fighting him.

"That bleeding Apache, as you call him, is here to kill you, von Heusen. The Apache and the cavalry are riding together. Just to kill you."

They had come to the top of the stairs. Von Heusen burst open the door to one of the rooms and threw her inside. Tess staggered across the room as von Heusen closed and bolted the door, putting a chair across it.

"What now, von Heusen?" Tess demanded.

He cast her an evil glare with his near colorless eyes, and she felt fear creep along her spine. He strode across the room to her, wrenching her by the hair. "You foolish, foolish little girl. You could have lived as that Indian's squaw, but now I promise you that you're going to pay dearly. One wrong move, and I'll scalp you myself. What a beautiful trophy that hair would be, eh, Miss Stuart?"

She spat at him. He pulled on her hair so hard that she was certain half of it left her head and, despite her efforts to choke back the sound, she cried out. She saw him smile at her pain, and it sickened her, and she realized that he liked hurting people, that killing gave him pleasure.

"What now? Now we wait. We wait for your ever gallant young cavalry hero to come running up those stairs. Then I shoot him dead. Then I use you to escape this town, and then maybe later I'll let you go, but more likely, I'll kill you. I'll kill you slow. I'll have you first, and I'll humiliate you every way I know how, and then I'll kill you bit by bit..."

She managed to jerk away from him, backing toward the window, staring at him. "You bastard! Why don't you just kill me now? I'll make your life a living hell. I'll never take a single step with you. Unless..."

"Unless?" He drew out his knife, a wickedly sharp and long bowie knife that glinted in the fraction of sunlight that entered the room.

"You leave Jamie alone. We'll go out by the roof right now and I'll come along without a protest—"

"How touching."

"If you kill him, I won't make a move."

"Oh, but I can make you," von Heusen told her softly. And maybe he could. He was walking toward her, his knife before him, twisting in his hands. "I'll just make you bleed a little now, but you'll feel it," he promised her.

She was going to scream or faint. She wanted desperately to fight, to be brave, but all she could see was the glinting steel. He was coming closer and closer, and she didn't know how brave she could be once that steel touched her.

"I'll make you bleed!" von Heusen promised again.

He was almost on top of her. She could see the razor sharpness of the blade, aimed toward her face.

The window shattered behind her, and a man came bursting through. Booted feet connected with von Heusen's chest and he was sent flying into the room. He landed hard and turned, ready to throw his knife straight at Tess's heart.

Jamie fired his Colt without hesitating, without a flicker of fear or remorse.

And von Heusen stared at him, startled. Then his colorless eyes closed for the last time, and he slumped to the floor.

Jamie strode over to Tess.

"Are you all right?" he demanded.

She nodded, her throat dry, her heart pounding.

"Dammit, Tess, I told you that this had to be my way."

"I—I was trying to do it your way!" she said. But then she looked at von Heusen again, and back to Jamie. And she passed out cold.

With a tender smile, Jamie lifted her into his arms and held her very close. He didn't look at von Heusen. He carried her into the light of day.

Chapter Fourteen

It was really amazing when one looked around, Tess thought.

She was having a barbecue. Well, the ranch was hosting a barbecue. Huge sides of beef were being roasted all around the property, the wine and beer and whiskey were flowing freely and all manner of entertainment was going on.

She was having a party—and the cavalry and the Apache and the townspeople and even the whores from the saloon were in attendance.

Nalte was her honored guest. She and Jamie had discovered that the Apache had never intended to leave the area, that he meant to find out about the man who would betray so many people. It was Nalte who had called in the cavalry, taking a tremendous chance when he had sent a messenger to the fort.

Tess was glad of the party, and she was grateful to feel a part of a huge family. She didn't have to be the only hostess. Kristin, always calm and capable and serene, was handling most of the social duties.

Still dazed from the events of the day, Tess wandered through the crowds rather aimlessly, welcoming the men who had been her friends after the wagon train had been raided, keeping the peace when it seemed that the rowdy Indians were getting too close to the rowdy whites. But she didn't need to take care of much of that. Cole and Malachi and Jon seemed to have a good eye on things, and Hank knew how to take care of the place.

She had just wandered into the kitchen when Jamie caught up with her.

As always, he didn't stand on ceremony, but caught her hand and told her bluntly that he wanted to talk to her.

"But Jamie, we've people—"

"Now, Tess."

She was alarmed when he started to drag her up the stairs, and she tugged on his hand. "Jamie—"

"Tess!" He groaned. She was too slow. He turned and swept her into his arms and ran the rest of the way up the stairs.

"Damn you, Jamie Slater—"

"I told you, Tess. Things were going to go my way today!"

They reached her room. Setting her down firmly upon her feet, he closed and locked the door and leaned against it. She backed away from him distrustfully. She moistened her lips. She still hadn't really talked to him. There had been so much commotion when she had first come to. Kristin and Shannon had insisted on taking care of her, and she hadn't realized until tonight that they had won not just a battle but the war.

"Thank you. Thank you for saving my life."

"You're welcome," he said briefly, striding across the room for her. "It seemed the least I could do."

"Yes, well, it's done now."

"Damn you, stand still."

"Jamie—"

He caught her. He caught her arms and he pulled her against him. He buried his face against her neck and he murmured softly. "Just think, you could be carrying a child. And it would be a fine child. Cute, beautiful, just like my brothers' kids."

"Jamie—"

He moved away from her, his eyes flittering silver as they met hers.

"I told you, we're doing things my way today. And we're going to get married."

She gasped, stunned. "Wh—what?"

"Married. Now."

"But why?"

"Well..." He touched her cheek, softly, gently, studying the movement of his fingers upon her face as if he were seeing it for the first time. "Well, for one, I'm damned afraid that if I don't, Nalte will determine to ride away with you again. He'd already warned me that I really better make you my woman in truth."

She stiffened. "Jamie, I heard you say yourself that no one could force you—"

"Then there's Kristin and Shannon. They'll never give me a moment's peace."

"Jamie—"

"Then I'll be damned if you'll be having any children of mine without me being present."

"But we don't even—"

"Then there's this," he said softly, and his lips touched hers more gently and tenderly than she had ever imagined possible, as if the moon itself touched her. She closed her eyes and she was back, back to a beautiful valley where they had made love beneath the moon, where their love had seemed so very right. Where magic had touched them despite all the odds.

"And this..."

He touched her forehead with his kiss. Then her cheeks, and her throat, and her lips again. "And most important, there is this. I love you, Tess. I love you. I want to marry you. I want to be beside you from this day forth, and I want to cherish you forever. Of course, I still want to throttle you. But most of all, I want to love you, and I want to be loved by you. I want to know your strength and even fight it sometimes, and I want to know your tenderness and your love and hold tight to them forever. How is that?"

"Oh, Jamie!" she whispered. Words failed her. She came up on her toes and kissed him. She teased his lower lip and his upper lip with her teeth and tongue, and she met his hunger with a fever of her own. A dizzying fire swept through her limbs, and she thought she could sleep beside him tonight, and every night, and she could feel his arms around her.

"Slater. Tess Slater." She sampled the name, but then tears touched her eyes and she threw her arms around him and kissed him again. "Oh, Jamie, I love you! I've loved you for so long now, and I thought that I didn't dare to believe in forever—"

"But you believed in yourself, Tess. Now you've got to learn to believe in me, too."

"I've always believed in you!"

"Then believe in this. I love you, and I will do so forever."

"Jamie..."

She would have lain down with him then. She would have tasted his flesh and savored his kiss and given him all and anything he wanted. She would always lie down with him anywhere, in any wilderness, and love him, and feel the sun or the moon upon them. It would not matter, as long as they were together.

But he was clutching her hand again. "Don't tempt me!" he warned her. "We've got to get downstairs and do this now. Before Nalte leaves."

"What?"

"We're getting married now, Tess. The chaplain is here, and Nalte is here, and my brothers are here, and I just can't think of a better time."

"Married? Now? Tonight?"

"Yes!"

They were out the door and he was pulling her down the stairs.

She tugged hard upon his hand. "Jamie!"

"What?"

"Today I promised to do things your way. I really can't promise to do that every day."

"Fine. I'll keep you in line," he said, and tugged her again. They reached the landing, and he shouted, "Cole! Tell the musicians and get the chaplain. She said yes!"

A rebel cry went up from the Slater brothers. The cavalry didn't seem to mind—in fact they joined right in. There was another sound, and Tess recognized Apache war whoops.

She tugged on Jamie's hand again, but he didn't notice. He kept walking. Kristin and Shannon and the children and Dolly and Jane and Jon and everyone were wishing her luck, and she was suddenly standing in front of a cavalry man wearing a chaplain's insignia.

"Jamie!" she whispered. "I'm really sorry about your horse."

"Don't be. Nalte gave him back to me as a wedding present."

"Oh! You're marrying me just to get your horse back!"

"Say, 'I do,' Tess."

She stared at the smiling chaplain and she heard the words but she didn't hear them. Oh, they would be cherished in her memory forever, but right now all she could think of was the feel of Jamie's hand upon her, and the promise of the security of it. It was time, and she said her vows. Then she was wearing a thin gold band, and everyone was wishing her luck once again. There were toasting and dancing, and she kissed Nalte, a huge sloppy kiss on his cheek.

But then she discovered herself in her new husband's arms again, and she was heading up the stairs again, and she didn't know if she was drunk with champagne or with happiness or with desire for this man who had come into her life and given her everything.

"Jamie!"

"What?"

"We've still got guests downstairs."

He groaned long and low and kicked open the door to their bedroom and walked determinedly over to the bed after kicking the door shut behind him.

Then he smiled wickedly. "My way, Tess. Everything is my way today."

Then he cast himself down upon her. He kissed her slowly and with seductive force, and she knew that there was nowhere she would rather be. When his silver eyes rose above her she smiled sweetly and breathlessly.

"Your way," she promised.

And he smiled, and he kissed her again.

And indeed, the night was delightfully passed...

His way.

* * * * *

INDULGE IN A QUIET MOMENT
WITH HARLEQUIN

Get a FREE
Quiet Moments Bath Spa

with just two proofs of purchase from
any of our four special collector's editions in May.

Harlequin® is sure to make your time special this Mother's Day
with four special collector's editions featuring a short story
PLUS a complete novel packaged together in one volume!

Collection #1 Intrigue abounds in a collection featuring *New York Times* bestselling author Barbara Delinsky and Kelsey Roberts.

Collection #2 Relationships? Weddings? Children? = *New York Times* bestselling author Debbie Macomber and Tara Taylor Quinn at their best!

Collection #3 Escape to the past with *New York Times* bestselling author Heather Graham and Gayle Wilson.

Collection #4 Go West! With *New York Times* bestselling author Joan Johnston and Vicki Lewis Thompson!

Plus Special Consumer Campaign!

Each of these four collector's editions will feature a
"FREE QUIET MOMENTS BATH SPA" offer.
See inside book in May for details.

Only from

HARLEQUIN®
Makes any time special®

Don't miss out! Look for this exciting promotion on sale in May 2001,
at your favorite retail outlet.

Visit us at www.eHarlequin.com   PHNCP01TR

USA Today bestselling author

STELLA CAMERON

and popular American Romance author

MURIEL JENSEN

come together in a special
Harlequin 2-in-1 collection.

Look for

Shadows and *Daddy in Demand*

On sale June 2001

HARLEQUIN®

Makes any time special ®

Three sizzling love stories
by today's hottest writers
can be found in...

Midnight Fantasies....

Feel the heat!

Available June 2001

MYSTERY LOVER—*Vicki Lewis Thompson*
When an unexpected storm hits, rancher Jonas Garfield takes cover in a nearby cave...and finds himself seduced senseless by an enigmatic temptress who refuses to tell him her name. All he knows is that this sexy woman wants him. And for Jonas, that's enough—for now....

AFTER HOURS—*Stephanie Bond*
Michael Pierce has always considered costume shop owner Rebecca Valentine no more than an associate—until he drops by her shop one night and witnesses the mousy wallflower's transformation into a seductive siren. Suddenly he's desperate to know her much better. But which woman is the real Rebecca?

SHOW AND TELL—*Kimberly Raye*
A naughty lingerie party. A forbidden fantasy. When Texas bad boy Dallas Jericho finds a slip of paper left over from the party, he is surprised—and aroused—to discover that he is good girl Laney Merriweather's wildest fantasy. So what can he do but show the lady what she's been missing....

MONTANA MAVERICKS

Bestselling author

SUSAN MALLERY

WILD WEST WIFE

THE ORIGINAL MONTANA MAVERICKS HISTORICAL NOVEL

**Jesse Kincaid had sworn off love forever.
But when the handsome rancher kidnaps
his enemy's mail-order bride to get revenge,
he ends up falling for his innocent captive!**

RETURN TO WHITEHORN, MONTANA, WITH

WILD WEST WIFE

Available July 2001

**And be sure to pick up
MONTANA MAVERICKS: BIG SKY GROOMS,
three brand-new historical stories about Montana's
most popular family, coming in August 2001.**

HARLEQUIN®

*M*akes any time special ®

Visit us at www.eHarlequin.com

PHWWWTR

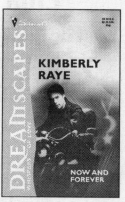